The Study Of Shakespeare's Poems

莎士比亚
诗歌研究 英汉对照

上

朱廷波 著

中国出版集团

世界图书出版公司

图书在版编目（CIP）数据

莎士比亚诗歌研究：英汉对照/朱廷波著. —广州：世界图书出版广东有限公司,2011.11

ISBN 978-7-5100-4087-0

Ⅰ.①莎…　Ⅱ.①朱…　Ⅲ.①莎士比亚,W.(1564～1616)—诗歌评论—英汉对照　Ⅳ.①I561.072

中国版本图书馆 CIP 数据核字（2011）第 228402 号

莎士比亚诗歌研究：英汉对照

责任编辑：	杨贵生　冯彦庄
责任技编：	刘上锦　余坤译
出版发行：	世界图书出版广东有限公司
	（广州市新港西路大江冲 25 号　邮编：510300）
电　　话：	020-84469182
http：	//www.gdst.com.cn
编辑邮箱：	edksy@qq.com
经　　销：	全国各地新华书店
印　　刷：	广东天鑫源印刷有限责任公司
印　　次：	2013 年 1 月第 1 版第 2 次印刷
规　　格：	710mm×1 000mm　1/16　66.75 印张　987 千字
书　　号：	ISBN 978-7-5100-4087-0/I·0247
定　　价：	130.00 元（共 2 册）

若因印装质量问题影响阅读，请与承印厂联系退换。

PREFACE

The creation of English poetry is the origin of Shakespeare's literary creation. Shakespeare's poems are the shining jewels in the treasure house of Shakespearean literature. In Shakespeare's poems readers can easily find the traces or shadows of the profound and shocking tragedies, the oft-quoted and widely loved comedies, the vigorous and forceful histories, and the wonderful and distant romances.

It is no doubt that there are too much thinking philosophy, and aesthetic theory in Shakespeare's famous sonnets. The long narrative *Venus and Adonis* is worth while reading by the romantic literary youth. Another long narrative *Lucrece* depicts the destroying of the extreme beauty which makes people keep sobbing and sighing. *A Lover's Complaint* tells how a lady unburdens herself of her grievances of her love tragedy. *The Passionate Pilgrim* is the incisive and vivid description of the romantic love affairs between the lad and the lass. *Sonnets to Sundry Notes of Music* plays the light music of the beautiful love and the tortuous life. *The Phoenix and Turtle* is very philosophical although it mainly eulogizes the holy and the noble. Poetry has its own significant form and its strict rule as well. Shakespeare strictly abides by the English versification and uses the beautiful and succinct poetic language to fully express all the above ideas and implications.

It has been dozens of years since I began to read and appreciate Shakespeare's poems, and have tried to write English poems. I admire Shakespeare's beautiful poems. I have been shocked by Shakespeare's beautiful poems. That's why I have a strong impulse to recommend the English original to the majority of Chinese readers. Since classical style of Chinese poetry is still the artistic form which the Chinese readers love to see and hear. I have also written over 1,000 poems in that genre or manner. To transplant or produce Shakespeare in China, the literary translation is no doubt a manner. My attempt to translate his poems in the classical style of Chinese poems is after my careful consideration of Chinese readers' reception, therefore, I focus my translation on succinctness and dexterity.

In the course of my translation, I read repeatedly the translations of many

1

前　言

　　英语诗歌创作是莎士比亚文学创作的起源。莎士比亚诗歌是莎士比亚文学宝库中璀璨的明珠。震撼心灵的悲剧、脍炙人口的喜剧、雄浑壮阔的历史剧、神妙悠远的传奇剧，都可以在莎士比亚的诗篇中看到影子。

　　著名的莎士比亚十四行诗涵盖了很多的思想哲理和艺术真谛。《维纳斯与阿童尼》很值得罗曼蒂克的文学青年研读，也可供深湛的学者进行学术探求。《露克丽丝》描绘的人间绝美却横遭摧残令人唏嘘不已。《情女怨》倾吐了千百年来女子对爱情悲剧的哀叹。《激情潮圣者》是男女青年浪漫爱情浓墨重彩的描绘。《情歌拾贝》奏响了美丽爱情和曲折人生的轻音乐。《凤凰与斑鸠》在赞美圣洁高贵时蕴含了太多的哲理。诗歌有诗歌的形式，诗歌有诗歌的规定。莎士比亚严格遵循英诗格律，用精美洗炼的诗歌语言，对上述种种意蕴都进行了淋漓尽致的表现。

　　笔者研读莎士比亚诗歌有年，也进行过一些英语诗歌创作，在惊羡莎士比亚诗歌精美的同时，也有向广大读者竭力推荐的强烈冲动。笔者同时有大量中文旧体诗的创作，因为中文旧体诗依然是中国广大读者喜闻乐见的艺术形式。在中国移植莎士比亚，翻译文学是一种手段。笔者尝试用旧体翻译他的诗歌应该说是慎重考虑了中国读者的接受问题，以精炼为重，以轻灵为要。

　　在翻译过程中，曾再三阅读

Chinese experts, such as Zhu Shenghao, Liang Shiqiu, Zhang Guruo, Yang Deyu, Tu An, Liang Zongdai, Huang Yushi, Fang Ping, Sun Dayu, Gu Zhengkun, Sun Fali, Cao Minglun, Ai Mei, Li Jie, Li Hongming, and Tian Weihua. Although they have variety of styles in their translation work, one phenomenon is obvious: too many Chinese characters are used which make the translation appear stagnant and sluggish. Readers can not taste the lively and nimble flavor of the original Shakespeare. This weakness is corrected with my attempt of the classical style of Chinese poetry, I wonder whether this manner would be teased or laughed at by my dear readers.

Shakespeare's Poems, as a display of my age long reading and study of the original Shakespeare, is composed bilingually both in English and Chinese in order to be checked out and internationalized. In the book, there is a larger space for the Chinese version of the English poems as a report of my real apprehension of Shakespeare's poems. All the suggestions and criticisms are highly valued and warmly welcome.

Shakespeare's Poems can be divided into 2 parts, the first part of which is the translation in the classical style of Chinese poems, arranged in a bilingual form in order for the readers to have a convenient contrast between English and Chinese with the necessarily detailed notes. Because of the great influence in Chinese for its rich and profound thinking, I frequently fall into deep pondering while translating Shakespeare's sonnets into Chinese, therefore, there is a comment in the prose form at the beginning of the notes of each sonnet, and there is also a further comment in the verse form at the end of each. There is no such format in each of the other poems. The second part of the book offers my comments on all the poems, although with the smaller space, concerning the serve for the Chinese readers and the foreign readers as well.

Shakespeare's Poems are also the crystal of my age long painstaking effort in the study of Shakespeare, which is totally my ingenious work with my profound move and emotion. It is my strong will to be dedicated to the cultural development and the ideal combination of the eastern culture and the western culture. Since it is my own arduous and tortuous exploration, it is hard to satisfy or meet every one's taste. All the comments and preaches from both home and abroad are sincerely acknowledged and appreciated.

Zhu Tingbo
June 8, 2011

朱生豪、梁实秋、张谷若、杨德豫、屠岸、梁宗岱、黄雨石、方平、孙大雨、辜正坤、孙法理、曹明伦、艾梅、李杰、李鸿鸣，以及田伟华等人的译文，尽管形式多样，但都有一个共同现象：用字过多，显得滞重，失去了莎士比亚原诗的活泼轻灵。试用中文旧体匡之，不知读者诸君如何哂笑。

《莎士比亚诗歌》一书是笔者多年研究莎士比亚的一个展示。全书英汉对照，以便查对，以便与国际接轨。书中英诗汉译部分占篇幅较大，因为是译者对莎士比亚诗歌的真实理解的汇报。纵有芹献之讥，视如醍醐灌顶。

《莎士比亚诗歌》分为译诗和评论两部分。第一部分为译诗，除英汉对照外，又有必要的注释，以方便读者理解。由于莎士比亚十四行诗在中国影响巨大，思想丰富，在翻译成旧体诗时感慨颇多，因而每首的注释前有评语，后有感言。其他诗篇没有这些格式。第二部分为评论，篇幅不大，纯英文，可供中外读者研读。

《莎士比亚诗歌》又是笔者多年研读莎士比亚的心血结晶，完全是缘事而著，有感而发，志在文化发展，心存中西合璧。艰辛探索之中，难免有不尽如人意之处，愿海内外高明不吝赐教。

朱廷波

2011 年 6 月 8 日

CONTENTS

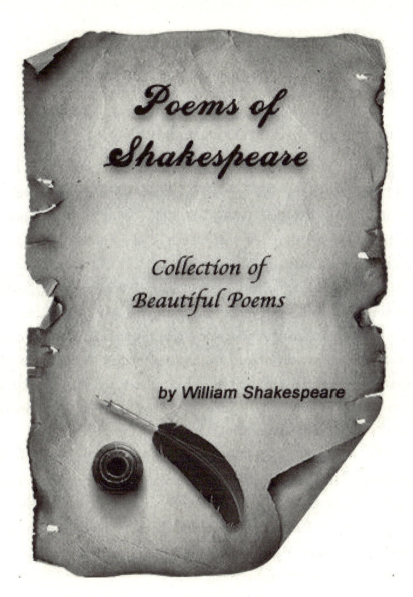

Poems of Shakespeare

Collection of
Beautiful Poems

by William Shakespeare

INTRODUCTION

It is well known that Shakespeare, as a playwright and poet as well, has created many beautiful poems, among which his sonnets are very popular in China. To have an overall review and research of all his poems is still a heavy task for the Chinese scholars.

At Shakespeare's age, and at all ages of human history, poem is regarded as the symbol of literature. Poem is regarded as the symbol of man of letters. The reason is that poem is beautiful for its own rhyme, rhythm, and its artistic images, and its beautiful, attractive and amusing descriptions. Poem is in close relationship with music and dancing which are the very beginning of the history of art creation. Poem can also be regarded as the very beginning of the history of literature for mankind all over the world.

(1) In 1593, William Shakespeare, at the age of 29, created his long narrative poem *Venus and Adonis*. The long poem was intended for the Earl of Southampton, because Shakespeare wanted to gain the Earl's sponsorship, i.e. financial support. The long poem got published during the period of plague when the theaters were closed. The long poem was printed many times because it was very popular, especially among the young readers.

The love story between Venus and Adonis is based on *Metamorphoses* written by Ovid. Venus, the goddess of beauty, courted unripe Adonis eagerly like an Amazon but in vain. Adonis was dead in his hunting of a wild boar. In his

引　言

　　莎士比亚不仅是一名家喻户晓的戏剧家，也是一名伟大的诗人，他的十四行诗在中国大受欢迎。对他的全部诗作进行全面分析研究，仍是学人的要务。

　　在莎士比亚时代，以及人类历史中的所有时代，诗歌都被认为是文学和文人的象征。原因在于诗歌很美，它有韵脚，有节奏；有艺术意象；有美妙的、富有魅力的、惬意的语言。诗歌与音乐舞蹈密切联系。音乐舞蹈则是艺术创造史的源头。诗歌可被看作是全世界人类文学史的源头。

　　（1）1593 年，29 岁的威廉·莎士比亚创作了长篇叙事诗《女神之恋》（即《维纳斯与阿童尼》）。该长诗是献给扫桑普顿伯爵的。因为莎士比亚想得到该贵族的赞助，以便在经济上得到接济。长诗出版时英国正闹鼠疫，剧场都停业了。但是长诗出版后立即大受欢迎，尤其是青年读者的最爱，因而一版再版。

　　维纳斯和阿童尼的爱情故事源于奥维德的《变形记》。爱情女神维纳斯好像亚马孙妇女，追求尚未成熟的阿童尼，结果却徒劳无功。阿童尼在打野猪时也不幸身亡。

long poem, Shakespeare depicts the nature and the animals in nature: Adonis' lustful horse, chasing a mare, and a timorous hare, a sensitive snail, and the wild boar, which symbolize the emotion, passion, love, lust of human being.

How to define this long narrative poem? Hallett Smith defines it as "a mythological-erotic poem" (*The Riverside Shakespeare*, Volume II, P.1704, 1972). John Jowell calls it a mythological poem (*The Oxford Shakespeare*, P.223, 2006). David Scott Kastan says it is "a current vogue of Ovidian erotic poetry" (*Shakespeare, The Poems*, P12, 1988). In my opinion, *Venus and Adonis* is a long love poem. Because of the love between man and woman, there is mankind. Because of the combination of heaven and earth, there is mankind, man and woman. Because of the combination of *Yin* and *Yang*, there is the existence of heaven and earth. To praise and describe this great combination and this great love is the holy task or mission of a great poet, because people need passion, love, even lust.

(2) In 1594, Shakespeare wrote *The Rape of Lucrece*. According to the original Ovid, the long narrative poem *The Rape Of Lucrece*, also dedicated to the young earl of Southampton, depicts a story taking place in ancient Rome. In the darkness of night, Tarquin ravished Lucrece, because Lucrece's husband Collatinus boasted the beauty and charily of his wife Lucrece. Collatinus avenged his wife Lucrece, who told him the event and committed suicide, on Tarquin, and overthrew the Roman tyranny.

If we say *Venus and Adonis* is a beauty's wooing of another beauty who is destroyed by savage, and it is also a healthy antidote to the asceticism of the Middle Ages, then Lucrece is the conflict between a devil and a beauty who is tragically ravished, and it is also a good antidote to the indulging in sensual pleasures, or evil lust. While Adonis is wooed by Venus in the bright daylight, Lucrece was ravished in the complete darkness of night. In the dark night, the devil, Tarquin, was even darker, and uglier while the beauty, Lucrece, was even

在长诗中，莎士比亚却描写了大自然和大自然中的动物：阿童尼发情的马，因追逐一匹母马而跑掉，以及敏感的蜗牛、胆小的野兔和粗暴的野猪。所有这些都象征着人类的情绪、激情、爱情和情欲。

怎么界定这首叙事长诗？哈莱特·史密斯称其为"一首神话色情诗"（河滨版《莎士比亚全集》第二卷，第 1704 页，1972 年版）。约翰·乔威尔称其为"一首神话诗"（牛津版《莎士比亚全集》，第 222 页，2006 年版）。大卫·司各特·凯斯坦称其为"当时奥维德色情诗的一种时尚"（班坦姆经典丛书《莎士比亚·诗歌卷》第 12 页，1988 年版）。在我看来，《维纳斯与阿童尼》是一首长篇爱情诗。由于男人与女人的爱情，才有人类。由于天和地的结合才有人类，才有男人和女人。由于阴阳相交才有天地存在。颂扬和描述这种伟大的结合，这种伟大的爱情，是伟大诗人的神圣义务和使命，因为人们需要激情，需要爱情，需要情欲。

（2）1594 年，莎士比亚创作了《露克丽丝》。这首叙事长诗取材于奥维德。该长诗也是献给年轻的扫桑普顿伯爵的。讲述的故事发生在古罗马。由于科拉廷纳斯夸耀他的妻子露克丽丝的美貌和贞洁，塔昆黑夜里强暴了露克丽丝。露克丽丝向科拉廷纳斯控诉塔昆的罪行后自杀。科拉廷纳斯向塔昆复仇，并推翻了罗马暴政。

如果说《维纳斯与阿童尼》讲的是一个美对另一个美的追求，而另一个美被残暴所毁灭，同时又是对中世纪禁欲主义的反叛，那么《露克丽丝》则是魔鬼与美女的冲突，美女悲惨地遭受了强暴，同时又是一个对于邪恶的纵欲主义的猛烈抨击。维纳斯追求阿童尼是在丽日蓝天之下，塔昆强暴露克丽丝则是发生在漆黑的夜晚。在漆黑的夜晚，魔鬼塔昆显得更阴暗，而美女露克丽丝则

brighter and fairer. The whole long narrative poem *The Rape of Lucrece* is the detailed artistic description of the process of the destruction of beauty, which is very moving and the readers feel sad and sighs for a very long time about the protagonist Lucrece. Therefore the moving long poem *The Rape of Lucrece* was published at least 6 times at that time.

(3) In the year 1609, the collection of Shakespeare's 154 sonnets was published.

Sonnet, meaning a "little sound" or "song", developed a Sicilian regional folk poem of varying rhymes. The first sonnets were written by the 13th century Italian poet Giacomo da Lentini (1200?—1250) of the Sicilian school between 1230 and 1266. Another Italian poet, Guittone d'Arezz (1235—1294) adopted the form and wrote at least 300 sonnets of his own.

Then came the genius of Dante Alighieri (1265—1321) whose sonnets are entitled *La vita nuova* to show his love to Beatrice and Francesco Petrarch (1304 —1374), whose sonnets are entitled *Il canzoniere*. Petrarchan sonnets are well-known both for the theme of his love to Laura and the rhyme scheme: mainly *abba abba cde cde* or *abba abba cdcdcd, abba abba cc edde,* and *abba abba cde cde,* Both Giovanni Bocaccio (1313—1375) and Michelangelo Buonarroti (1475—1564) wrote sonnets.

Based on the sonneteering tradition of Francesco Petrarch, there was a vogue of sennet writing in England in the 16th century. Both Sir Thomas Wyatt (1503—1542) and Henry Howard, Earl of Surrey (1517—1547), are regarded father of the English sonnet respectively. Sir Philip Sidney (1554—1586) an English poet, in 1591 published his collection of sonnets named *Astrophel and Stella*, which contained 108 sonnets in all to his lover Penelope. Edmund Spenser in 1595 published his own sonnet collection named *Amoretti* including 89 sonnets to Elizabeth Boyle whom he had wooed and married.

Shakespeare wrote 154 sonnets and had the collection published to earn his

更耀眼，更美丽动人。《露克丽丝》整个叙事长诗描写了美的毁灭的过程，详实细腻，极具艺术魅力，使读者十分惋惜，为美的毁灭唏嘘不已。在当时这部动人的长诗至少再版了 6 次。

　　（3）1609 年，莎士比亚的 154 首十四行诗出版。

　　十四行诗，原义为"小调"或"歌曲"。由西西里岛当地民歌发展而来，有各种不同的韵式。首先创作十四行诗的是 13 世纪的意大利诗人，1230—1266 年间的西西里诗派的吉亚柯莫·达·连蒂尼（1200？—1250）。其后是意大利诗人吉托尼·达·阿莱佐（1235—1294），他一生至少创作了 300 首十四行诗。

　　随之出现天才的但丁·阿里孟利（1265—1321），其十四行诗集名为《新生》，献给所爱的女子贝雅特丽齐。另一位天才为弗朗切斯柯·彼特拉克（1304—1374），其十四行诗集名为《歌集》，主要歌咏他对女友劳拉的爱情，形成著名的彼特拉克体十四行诗。其韵式主要为 *abba abba cde cde，abba abba cdcdcd，abba abba cc edde* 和 *abba abba cde cde*。乔万尼·薄伽丘（1313—1375）和米开兰基罗·博奥那洛第（1475—1564）也都创作十四行诗。

　　基于彼特拉克十四行诗传统，16 世纪的英国兴起了十四行诗热潮。托马斯·怀亚特爵士（1503—1542）和亨利·霍华德，萨里伯爵（1517—1547）各自分享着"英国十四行诗之父"的称号。英国诗人菲利普·锡德尼爵士（1554—1586）1591 年出版了十四行诗集《爱星者与星》，共收 108 首十四行诗，献给女子佩内洛普。埃德蒙·斯宾塞（1552—1599）于 1595 年出版他自己十四行诗集《小爱神》，共有 89 首，献给他苦苦追求最终喜结良缘的伊丽莎白·博伊尔小姐。

　　莎士比亚创作了 154 首十四行诗，

reputation as a lyric poet. Shakespeare's sonnet sequence can be divided into three parts: the first part, the longest one, contains 126 sonnets and the main theme of which is his friendship with a young noble man, although readers can find several other themes very easily; the second part is from 127—152, the theme of which is love, which is a unique one because Shakespeare falls in love with a dark lady whom he does not love so much; the third part is composed of only 2 sonnets, whose theme is art based on Greek or Roman mythology.

In contrast with the two patterns, one is the Italian pattern in metre, which contains 11 syllables each line; the other is the French pattern, which contains 12 syllables each line, the Shakespearean pattern is pentameter, i.e. 10 syllables each line. Based on the rhyme scheme invented by Earl of Surrey, Shakespeare used the rhyme scheme *abab cdcd efef gg* by Earl of Surrey almost in all of his sonnets. Shakespeare wrote his sonnets in a very strict way according to English versification, so nearly all of them are concise and beautiful. Therefore, when we Chinese translators intend to translate them in to Chinese, we'd better try to use only ten characters each line and employ the rhyme scheme *abab cdcd efef gg*, which is called the Shakespeare form or the English form.

(4) *A Lover's Complaint* was also published in 1609. There is a dispute that whether Shakespeare is the author or not. Reading through the poem, readers can easily feel the artistic genre is the same as that of his other works. Although it is uncertain whether Shakespeare wrote the poem, scholars can't find other poet who is certainty the author. The forsaken lady in the poem reminds readers of the lovers in classic Chinese literature such as *The Bride of Jiao Zhongqing* or *Peacocks Southeast Travelling* and *To the Tone Phoenix Hairping* by Tang Wan, and the heroine in Pushkin's (1799—1834) masterpiece *Eugenii Onegin*.

(5) There are several authors of *The Passionate Pilgrim* which is the the collection of the love poems. It is certain that Shakespeare wrote 5 poems in the book, or the collection, two of which are I and II and they are Shakespeare's

出版后赢得抒情诗人的声誉。莎士比亚的十四行诗序列可划分为三部分：第一部分最长，包括 126 首十四行诗，主题是和一位青年贵族的友谊，虽然读者在其中可以很容易地发现若干其他主题；第二部分为 127—152 首，主题为奇特的爱情，莎士比亚竟爱上了一个他并不怎么爱的黑夫人；第三部分只有两首十四行诗，主题是基于古希腊罗马神话的艺术问题。

十四行诗的"格"有意大利式的每行 11 个音节模式和法国式的每行 10 个音节模式。莎士比亚习惯用五步抑扬格，即每行 10 个音节。莎士比亚还继承了萨里伯爵的 abab cdcd efef gg 韵式。在十四行诗的创作中，莎士比亚基本上采用严格的英诗格律，因而语言优美，精辟。我们中国的翻译家们在翻译莎士比亚的十四行诗时，最好努力每行诗用 10 个汉字，并沿用莎士比亚十四行诗的韵式，也称英国韵式。

（4）《情女怨》也出版于 1609 年。该诗的作者是不是莎士比亚是个有争议的问题。阅读全诗，读者很容易就会发现其艺术风格、艺术手法和其他作品相似。虽然不能肯定就是莎士比亚写了这首诗，但是学者也找不出是哪个诗人写的。诗中被遗弃的女子使读者想起了中国古典文学《孔雀东南飞》中的焦仲卿妻，想起了宋词《钗头凤》及其词作者唐琬，也使得读者想起了普希金（1799—1837）的代表作《叶甫盖尼·奥涅金》中的女主人公达吉亚娜。

（5）爱情诗集《激情朝圣者》有若干个作者。确定无疑的有 5 首为莎士比亚的大作。其中第一首和第二首是莎士比亚的

sonnets; and three of which are 3, 5, and 16 from his comedy *Love's Labor's Lost*. Although scholars are not sure about the authority of the other poems, readers can still enjoy the true feeling and beauty of the poems. The line "sweet Cytherea, silting by a brook" and the whole poem will give young readers much more entertainment for its romance, its genuine love, and its natural or spontaneous passion.

(6) *Sonnets to Sundry Notes of Music*

Here the definition of sonnet should be "short poem", not the definition of "poem of fourteen 10-syllable (five-stress) lines with a particular rhyme-pattern variously arranged". The section *Sonnets to Sundry Notes of Music* which are composed of 6 short poems is included in the collection *The Passionate Pilgrim*. The meaning of "sonnets" is the same as the original meaning in the Italian language i.e. "little sound" or "song". Several nice, charming, and beautiful poems are collected in this section.

(7) Readers first read the poem *The Phoenix and Turtle* in 1607. In this poem Shakespeare expresses his philosophy of love: his transcendental ideal of a love existing eternally beyond death. The Chinese readers couldn't help thinking of the lines in classical Chinese literature "*We will be together, as birds flying in pairs in heaven; / On this earth we will be two trees joined in one, / Our branches intertwined*" written by the great poet Bai Juyi (772—846) in his famous long poem *Song of Immortal Love*.

Furthermore, the author also gives his pondering of the relationship between Shakespeare's poems and plays.

十四行诗；第三首、第五首和第十六首均来自莎士比亚的喜剧《爱的徒劳》。虽然专家学者不能肯定其他诗篇的作者，读者在阅读时仍然能感受到这些诗篇的真挚感情的艺术美。诗行"可爱的西塞利亚坐在一条河边"以及整个诗篇都会给年轻的读者很多很多艺术享受。由于诗篇很浪漫，爱情很真诚，其激情也是自然自发的流露。

（6）《情歌拾贝》

此处"十四行诗"界定为"短诗"，而不能界定为"十四行的每行 10 个音节，5 个重音的诗，有特定的韵式，又灵活多变"。《情歌拾贝》部分，由 6 首短诗组成一个集子，包含在诗集《激情朝圣者》里。"十四行诗"的含义与意大利原文的含义相同，即"小调"或"歌曲"。该部分收集了一些可爱的、迷人的、美丽的诗篇。

（7）读者在 1601 年读到《凤凰和斑鸠》。在这首诗里，莎士比亚写出了他的爱情哲学：他的超验理想是在死亡后爱情永恒存在。中国读者难免会想到中国古典文学中的名句："在天愿作比翼鸟，在地愿为连理枝。"该名句出自伟大诗人白居易（772—846）的名篇《长恨歌》。

此外，本书阐述了笔者对于莎士比亚诗歌和戏剧的关系的思考。

I SONNETS

TO THE ONLIE BEGETTER OF

THESE INSUING SONNETS

MR. W. H. ALL HAPPINESSE

AND THAT ETERNITIE

PROMISED

BY

OUR EVER-LIVING POET

WISHETH

THE WELL-WISHING

ADVENTURER IN

SETTING

FORTH

T.T.

　由 David Bevington 主编的 A BANTAM CLASSIC 的 Shakespeare, the Poems 的排列
方式为：

To the Only Begtter of These Ensuing
Sonnets

MR.W.H.

All Happiness and That Eternity Promised
by Our Ever-living Poet
Wisheth the Well-wishing Adventurer in
Setting Forth

　　　　　　　　　　　　　　　　　T.T.

I　十四行诗

赠唯一促成并刊行

十四行诗之

W. H. 先生幸福

并祝永生永恒

正好像

此

永生写诗人之

心底

由衷祝福

果断付梓之

出版

者

T. T.

梁实秋先生认为正常英语文法应该是："To the only begetter of these ensuing sonnets, Mr.W.H., the well-wishing adventurer in setting forth wisheth all happiness and that eternity promised by our ever-living poet, [signed] T.T."

献辞涉及三个人物，第一个为 begetter，即莎士比亚十四行诗出版的促成者，也就是 Mr.W.H.。第二个为 ever-living poet，即莎士比亚。第三个为 adventurer，即冒昧的出版者 Thomas Thorpe (T.T.)。

献辞中有出版商（者）对促成者的祝福以及莎士比亚的永恒祝愿。

译者感言：赞助永恒，诗人永恒。

出版巨制，益世丰功。

1

From fairest creatures we desire increase,

That thereby beauty's Rose might never die,

But as the riper should by time decease,

His tender heir might bear his memory;

But thou, contracted to thine own bright eyes,　　　　　*5*

Feed'st thy light's flame with self-substantial fuel,

Making a famine where abundance lies,

Thyself thy foe, to thy sweet self too cruel.

Thou that art now the world's fresh ornament,

And only herald to the gaudy spring,　　　　　*10*

Within thine own bud buriest thy content,

And, tender churl, makest waste in niggarding.

　　Pity the world, or else this glutton be,

　　To eat the world's due, by the grave and thee.

1—14 首、16—17 首为同一主题。这一首规劝年轻美貌的男朋友结婚生子，美貌常存。

5. thou: 第二人称代词，现代英语为 you；宾格为 thee，等于现代英语 you；所有格为 thy，现代英语为 your；物主代词为 thine，用于以元音或 h 开始的词前面，类似于 yours

6. feed'st: 与 thou 搭配，为第二人称单数动词 feedest，词尾形式有-est，-st 或-t 三种。正如第 9 行 art = are，第 11 行 buriest = bury，第 12 行 mak'st (makest) = make。

8. Thyself: yourself

10. herald: 传令官；使者
    gaudy: 华丽的，炫丽的

12. churl: 吝啬鬼
    niggarding: being mean, 吝啬

13. glutton: 贪食者，饕餮

1

艳羡最美者　　吾辈望多生
美丽玫瑰花　　永存勿凋零
奈何花开好　　终难逃飘零
后代可延续　　美好记忆中
勿自我欣赏　　一双亮眼睛　　　　　*5*
君身作燃料　　眼睛烈焰升
君以己为敌　　沃土变穷坑
君身本柔弱　　怎敌君无情
君生天地间　　鲜花伴君行
君为春使者　　独立锦绣情　　　　　*10*
为何自埋葬　　花蕾作坟茔
娇柔吝啬人　　浪费算计精
珍惜君今世　　勿学饕餮公
君口与坟墓　　苦果吞腹中

---

14. To eat the world's due: to devour what you owe the world
译者感言：丽质天生，多多益善。
　　　　　美艳延续，子女繁衍。

15

2

When forty winters shall besiege thy brow,

And dig deep trenches in thy beauty's field,

Thy youth's proud livery, so gazed on now,

Will be a totter'd weed, of small worth held;

Then being askt where all thy beauty lies,   5

Where all the treasure of thy lusty days;

To say, within thine own deep-sunken eyes,

Were an all-eating shame and thriftless praise.

How much more praise deserved thy beauty's use,

If thou couldst answer, 'This fair child of mine   10

Shall sum my count, and make my old excuse',

Proving his beauty by succession thine!

　　This were to be new made when thou art old,

　　And see thy blood warm when thou feel'st it cold.

　　该诗讲岁月无情，美貌易衰。比喻贴切，通俗易懂。

1. besiege: 包围；拥在周围
2. trench: v. 刻，挖；挖战壕 n.深沟，壕沟
3. livery: 仆从；衣服
4. totter: 蹒跚
8. thriftless: 不节俭的；无用的
11. sum my count: make up my account
　　add up my accounts: 结算我的账目
　　make my old excuse: justify me when I am old，使我老了有个交代
译者感言：光阴催人老，年龄不饶人。
　　　　　皱纹不可怕，后昆暖人心。

2

堂堂君相貌　　怎敌四十冬
美丽田野上　　沟壑刻深坑
青春着华服　　众人呆看中
一朝为衰草　　何人正眼睛
试问君知否　　美貌终凋零　　　　　5
韶华今何在　　瑰宝无影踪
君言在君目　　深陷皱纹丛
羞耻蛇吞象　　挥霍得颂声
君若善用美　　自然受赞同
君若答客问　　君将生美童　　　　　10
君美子总结　　勿怪老迈行
君证子美貌　　美貌子继承
若言君年迈　　垂老护新生
昔觉血冷却　　回暖阳气升

3

Look in thy glass, and tell the face thou viewest

Now is the time that face should form another;

Whose fresh repair if now thou not renewest,

Thou dost beguile the world, unbless some mother.

For where is she so fair whose unear'd womb   *5*

Disdains the tillage of thy husbandry?

Or who is he so fond will be the tomb

Of his self-love, to stop posterity?

Thou art thy mother's glass, and she in thee

Calls back the lovely April of her prime;   *10*

So thou through windows of thine age shalt see,

Despite of wrinkles, this thy golden time.

　　But if thou live, remember'd not to be,

　　Die single, and thine image dies with thee.

　　诗中 womb 和 tomb 的意象较为惊人。

4.　dost:　为动词 do 变体
　　beguile:　欺骗
　　unbless:　deny, 拒绝
5.　unear:　耕耘
6.　Disdains:　轻视
　　tillage:　耕耘
8.　self-love:　自恋
　　posterity:　子孙后代
译者感言:　面容正姣好，莫负淑女心。
　　　　　　沃土勤耕耘，福惠后来人。

3

手持菱花镜	开言示脸庞
时间不容缓	复制莫彷徨
面容正姣好	再多一个强
愿君勿欺世	辜负女红妆
享福做人母	女子喜心房
处子因娴静	春情漫无疆
子宫当育子	夫君开垦忙
愚男不容忍	无子继火香
君为令慈镜	身上溢芬芳
令慈青春貌	四月花飘香
皱纹布额头	开启暮年窗
探首试眺望	金色年华郎
君今活无欲	不为名传扬
孤独弃人世	形象也抛荒

右侧行号：5（第5行）、10（第10行）

4

Unthrifty loveliness, why dost thou spend

Upon thyself thy beauty's legacy?

Nature's bequest gives nothing, but doth lend;

And, being frank, she lends to those are free.

Then, beauteous niggard, why dost thou abuse   *5*

The bounteous largess given thee to give?

Profitless usurer, why dost thou use

So great a sum of sums, yet canst not live?

For having traffic with thy self alone,

Thou of thyself thy sweet self dost deceive.   *10*

Then how, when nature calls thee to be gone,

What acceptable audit canst thou leave?

   Thy unused beauty must be tomb'd with thee.

   Which, used, lives th' executor to be.

美貌青春应与责任同行，勿太矜持。
1. unthrifty: unprofitable, 无利润
2. legacy: 遗产
3. bequest: 遗产
4. frank: generous, 慷慨
6. beauteous: 慷慨的，丰裕的
   largess: gift, 赏赐物；慷慨
7. profitless usurer: 不善经营的放债人
8. live: make a living, 谋生
9. traffic: trade, 经营
10. Thou of thyself thy sweet self dost deceive: you trick yourself out of enjoying the best

4

试问俊男子　　缘何不珍惜

美貌好遗产　　岂容浪虚掷

自然设盛筵　　借君美貌资

面对慷慨者　　租出不问期

美貌吝啬子　　挥霍无度时　　　　5

自谓美如画　　出手不足惜

君放高利贷　　赔本又奢糜

万金一朝去　　生活苦叹息

好个胡涂人　　与己做生意

君身本娇嫩　　君将自身欺　　　　10

君念造物主　　一朝到归期

造物要账本　　君手有何资

不善用美貌　　坟墓抱芳姿

善用美者富　　遗嘱多商机

---

part of yourself, 你欺骗可爱的你自身

12. acceptable: 令人满意的

　　　audit: 查账

14. executor: 遗嘱执行人

译者感言：会用善算计，美貌为巨财。

　　　　　　美貌太私用，何人再往来？

5

Those hours, that with gentle work did frame

The lovely gaze where every eye doth dwell,

Will play the tyrants to the very same,

And that unfair which fairly doth excel:

For never-resting time leads summer on   *5*

To hideous winter and confounds him there;

Sap checkt with frost, and lusty leaves quite gone,

Beauty o'ersnow'd, and bareness everywhere;

Then, were not summer's distillation left,

A liquid pris'ner pent in walls of glass,   *10*

Beauty's effect with beauty were bereft,

Nor it, nor no remembrance what it was;

 But flowers distill'd, though they with winter meet,

 Leese but their show; their substance still lives sweet.

 1—8 行为一个句子，阅读时宜细心、耐心。该首诗讲与大自然抗争，善待青春美。
1. frame: 造就
2. gaze: 容貌
  dwell: 瞩目
3. the very same: 那同样可爱的容貌
4. And that unfair which fairly doth excel: And make ugly what now excels in beauty, 使得惊人美貌丑陋不堪
6. hideous: 丑陋的；可怕的
  confounds him there: destroys summer in winter, 在冬天里毁灭夏天
7. sap: 树液
  checkt: 停止
  lusty: 健壮的

5

自然出巧手	塑美有几时	
娇容惹怜爱	众目惊叹息	
自然暴君面	显露终有时	
绝代佳人老	毁美成败枝	
时光无休止	引出盛夏期	*5*
凄冷有冬日	毁之何足惜	
霜云生机苦	浓药落枯枝	
雪压美丽泣	荒寒似无极	
倘若夏末尽	幸躲浓缩期	
夏出玻璃瓶	香露散无迹	*10*
美貌芳香散	美貌自游离	
何人思芳香	何人美貌提	
鲜花经提纯	能闯严冬期	
艳色固消褪	尚留香甜资	

8　o'ersnow'd：冰雪覆盖的
9.　distillation：蒸馏
10. A liquid pris'ner：A liquid prisoner, rose water, 香水
　　Pent：pen 的过去式和过去分词，被关禁的
　　Walls of glass：玻璃器皿
11. bereft：lost, 失去
12. Nor it, nor no remembrance what it was: leaving neither itself nor any memory of what it had been, 美貌本身及其记忆均无存
13. distill'd：提炼过
14. leese：lose
译者感言：自然成人之美，自然毁人之美。
　　　　　美貌娇嫩鲜花，怎敌雪侮雪欺？

6

Then let not winter's ragged hand deface

In thee thy summer, ere thou be distill'd;

Make sweet some vial; treasure thou some place

With beauty's treasure, ere it be self-kill'd.

That use is not forbidden usury,   *5*

Which happies those that pay the willing loan;

That's for thyself to breed another thee,

Or ten times happier, be it ten for one;

Ten times thyself were happier than thou art,

If ten of thine ten times refigured thee;   *10*

Then what could death do, if thou shouldst depart.

Leaving thee living in posterity?

　　Be not self-willed, for thou art much too fair

　　To be death's conquest and make worms thine heir.

美需要自身复制。
1.　ragged:　rough, 粗糙的
　　deface:　损伤……外观
2.　ere:　before, 在……以前
　　distilled:　提取精华
3.　vial:　小瓶
5.　usury:　高利贷
6.　happies:　使幸福
10.　refigured:　duplicated, 复制
13.　self-willed:　固执的，顽固的

6

严冬粗野手	勿使毁君身	
君之盛夏日	尚未经提纯	
芳香装入瓶	勿使化烟云	
美貌宜珍藏	务必宝地寻	
借贷非违禁	取利心地纯	*5*
甘愿付利息	愿人得福津	
复制一个你	此说道理真	
一个生十个	十倍享福人	
十倍福何止	十个酷似君	
十倍翻几番	福渡有君亲	*10*
死神作何计	君若离凡尘	
千秋万代后	君活后人身	
君有真美貌	速速离迷津	
莫让蛆作后	莫控于死神	

译者感言：严冬酷暑任肆虐，贮存珍藏瓜瓞藤。
美貌延续后嗣盛，笑看人间美永恒。

7

Lo, in the orient when the gracious light

Lifts up his burning head, each under eye

Doth homage to his new-appearing sight,

Serving with looks his sacred majesty;

And having climb'd the steep-up heavenly hill,   *5*

Resembling strong youth in his middle age,

Yet mortal looks adore his beauty still,

Attending on his golden pilgrimage;

But when from highmost pitch, with weary car,

Like feeble age, he reeleth from the day,   *10*

The eyes, 'fore duteous, now converted are

From his low tract and look another way:

　So thou, thyself outgoing in thy noon,

　Unlooked on diest, unless thou get a son.

以太阳行程喻人生，应属常理。

1.　Lo:　看！瞧！

3.　homage:　效忠

4.　sacred:　上帝的，神圣的

　　majesty:　雄伟，庄严；君权；陛下

5.　steep-up:　陡峭的

7.　adore:　崇拜

8.　Attending:　跟随

9.　highmost pitch:　the highest point, 最高点

　　weary:　疲倦的，困乏的

7

东方何壮哉	慈祥光明天	
众生举头望	火红露笑颜	
向东而膜拜	太阳绽新颜	
威风慑众生	敢不献恭谦	
奋力向上爬	峻峭天中山	5
年富力强者	或云正中年	
众生皆崇拜	美貌好容颜	
众目齐关注	前程锦绣篇	
一旦车疲惫	顶点转下沿	
犹如衰年人	白昼步蹒跚	10
恭顺众目光	不知向谁边	
谁看下坡路	专注在云端	
君亦同红日	瞬间遇中天	
逝去无人理	除非儿膝前	

---

10. feeble: 虚弱 feeble age: 衰老的
    reeleth: reels, 蹒跚。第三人称单数动词词尾形式有-s 和-th 两种。-s 为北方音，-th
    为南方音
11. 'fore: before, 在……以前
    dutrous: dutiful, 恭顺的
    converted: 转变方向
14. Unlooked on diest: Will die without being looked up to, 死时无人照管
译者感言：红日艳阳中天好，亦有疲惫暗淡时。
　　　　　如日中天思繁衍，壮丽辉煌一周期。

8

Music to hear, why hear'st thou music sadly?

Sweets with sweets war not, joy delights in joy.

Why lovest thou that which thou receivest not gladly,

Or else receivest with pleasure thine annoy?

If the true concord of well-tuned sounds,   *5*

By unions married, do offend thine ear,

They do but sweetly chide thee, who confounds

In singleness the parts that thou shouldst bear.

Mark how one string, sweet husband to another,

Strikes each in each by mutual ordering;   *10*

Resembling sire and child and happy mother,

Who, all in one, one pleasing note do sing:

   Whose speechless song, being many, seeming one,

   Sings this to thee, 'Thou single wilt prove none'.

要建立一琴瑟和谐的家庭，全家其乐融融。

2.   war not: do not conflict, 不冲突
4.   annoy: 使烦恼
5.   concord: 和谐
7.   chide: 责骂
     confounds: 混淆；毁灭
8.   in singleness the parts that thou shouldst bear: 宁愿孤独；未尽到丈夫的责任
9.   Mark: 听
11.   sire: 父亲
14.   Thou single wilt prove none: by remaining unmarried, you will amount to nothing, 独身一人将一无所有

8

音乐供欣赏	君听何伤心	
甜蜜喜甜蜜	欢欣喜欢欣	
问君因何故	不喜却要亲	
自己寻烦恼	愁苦谁耳闻	
音乐贵和谐	音调动人心	5
飘入君耳中	音乐烦恼君	
婉言责怪君	怨君不随群	
孤独代和谐	生命无欢欣	
听上一根弦	再听另一根	
夫妻和谐弦	乐章为温馨	10
如见父与子	如见慈母亲	
三者同一体	共唱好乐音	
无音惟有乐	万乐归一音	
一言警示君	独身成孤魂	

译者感言：音乐悦耳多合弦，造化恩赐生精英。
　　　　　一朝春尽红颜老，钧天广乐歌承平。

9

Is it for fear to wet a widow's eye

That thou consumest thyself in single life?

Ah! If thou issueless shalt hap to die,

The world will wail thee, like a makeless wife;

The world will be thy widow, and still weep   5

That thou no form of thee hast left behind,

When every private widow well may keep

By children's eyes her husband's shape in mind.

Look, what an unthrift in the world doth spend

Shifts but his place, for still the world enjoys it;   10

But beauty's waste hath in the world an end,

And kept unused, the user so destroys it.

   No love toward others in that bosom sits

   That on himself such murd'rous shame commits.

寡妇心中的丈夫形象莫过于子女。财富别人可享用，美貌毁灭无踪影。

3. hap: happen, 发生
4. wail: 恸哭
    头韵 (alliteration) 使用：world, will, wail, wife
5. 头韵使用：   world, will, widow, weep
9. Look what: whatever, 无论什么，指财富
    unthrift: 浪子
10. his: whatever
    it: whatever
13. sits: exists, 存在
14. That on himself such murd'rous shame commits: who commits such shameful murder,

9

担忧寡妇泪	哭湿双眼睛
宁愿消耗掉	孤身过一生
叹君仙逝后	香火无继承
举世哀悼君	丧偶身飘零
举世为遗孀	齐为群伤情　　　5
君生为孤身	君去无音容
寡妇看儿女	专注在眼睛
心中想夫君	儿女影像清
试看浮浪子	万金掷水中
金去主人换	世间用无穷　　　10
美貌损耗画	一去无归程
有美却不用	毁于君手中
君今太冷酷	耻辱杀美容
君心如铁石	岂能爱众生

那位不知羞耻地自残
译者感言：寡妇舒心看儿女，儿女影像肖夫君。
　　　　　岂忍无情毁灭美，世人哀悼空伤心。

10

For shame deny that thou bear'st love to any,

Who for thyself art so unprovident.

Grant, if thou wilt, thou art beloved of many,

But that thou none lovest is most evident;

For thou art so possest with murd'rous hate,   *5*

That 'gainst thyself thou stick'st not to conspire,

Seeking that beauteous roof to ruinate,

Which to repair should be thy chief desire.

O, change thy thought, that I may change my mind!

Shall hate be fairer lodged than gentle love?   *10*

Be, as thy presence is, gracious and kind,

Or to thyself, at least, kind-hearted prove:

   Make thee another self, for love of me,

   That beauty still may live in thine or thee.

钟爱青春美丽的外表，视觉美是人类的最先需要。

1.   For shame deny: To avoid shame you should deny, 为避免耻辱，你应该否认

2.   unprovident: improvident, 无远见的
       who: thou, you

3.   Grant: 我承认

6.   stick'st not: 不惜
       conspire: 密谋策划

7.   ruinate: ruined, 毁灭

10.   lodged: 供给住宿

11.   Be, as thy presence is: 要像你的容貌一样
       presence: appearance, 外貌

10

否认爱他人	君言应羞惭	
君今正美貌	婚事不相干	
君心不愿改	众人慕君颜	
众人心如镜	君美无情缘	
君想谋害人	君心离恨天	*5*
不怜天然貌	毁己赴黄泉	
蓄意毁华屋	存心摧容颜	
君宜存欲念	修缮为主弦	
呼君快更张	我亦速改弦	
恨之居所陋	爱之殿堂鲜	*10*
一如君美貌	优雅温顺篇	
善待君自身	君过慈爱关	
君如真爱我	君结再生缘	
君美存君身	美貌后代传	

译者感言：人人皆爱青春美，莫使青春空芳菲。
　　　　　君看无情东逝水，韶华易逝无消息。

11

As fast as thou shalt wane, so fast thou grow'st

In one of thine, from that which thou departest;

And that fresh blood which youngly thou bestow'st

Thou mayst call thine when thou from youth convertest.

Herein lives wisdom, beauty, and increase;   *5*

Without this, folly, age, and cold decay:

If all were minded so, the times should cease,

And threescore year would make the world away.

Let those whom Nature hath not made for store,

Harsh, featureless, and rude, barrenly perish: *10*

Look, whom she best endow'd she gave the more;

Which bounteous gift thou shouldst in bounty cherish:

    She carved thee for her seal, and meant thereby

    Thou shouldst print more, not let that copy die.

人生短暂，全是大自然造化。华丽转身，福祉后代。

1.   wane: 衰落
3.   bestow'st: bestow, 把……赠与
4.   convertest: 转变
5.   Herein: 有孩子
7.   minded so: 像你的想法一样没有孩子
8.   threescore year: 60 年
9.   for store: 有孩子
10.   barrenly perish: 死而无后
11.   look whom: whomever, 不管是谁
12.   bounteous: 慷慨的

11

叹君衰也速　　正如君繁昌

君去子继承　　新生孩子强

青春血气盛　　青春得上苍

君若别青春　　子孙青春强

智慧美丽在　　兴盛更繁昌　　　　　*5*

倘若无子嗣　　愚钝老凄凉

人人思若此　　呜呼无时光

六十花甲止　　人归鸟有乡

造化不护佑　　何由告上苍

粗鲁凡庸死　　笨拙丑陋亡　　　　　*10*

试看得庞者　　恩赐如海洋

慷慨赐君美　　君宜常珍藏

造化雕刻君　　君美造化芳

君宜多盖印　　切勿毁印章

---

bounty: 慷慨
　　第 11 行中的两个 she，第 13 行中的 she，均指造物主。
译者感言：人生有青春，青春赋予人。
　　　　　　欢娱多朝气，美艳亘古存。

12

When I do count the clock that tells the time,

And see the brave day sunk in hideous night;

When I behold the violet past prime,

And sable curls all silver'd o'er with white;

When lofty trees I see barren of leaves,   *5*

Which erst from heat did canopy the herd,

And summer's green, all girded up in sheaves,

Borne on the bier with white and bristly beard;

Then of thy beauty do I question make,

That thou among the wastes of time must go,   *10*

Since sweets and beauties do themselves forsake,

And die as fast as they see others grow;

   And nothing 'gainst Time's scythe can make defence

   Save breed, to brave him when he takes thee hence.

   人如红日，人如鲜花，人如青草，人如庄稼。
2. brave: bright, 明亮的
   hideous: 丑陋的；可怕的
3. violet: 紫罗兰
4. sable: 黑的
   curls: 卷发
6. erst: erstwhile, 以前
   canopy: 华盖
7. girded: 束，缚
   sheaves: 捆
8. bier: 棺材架

12

钟表显时刻	吾亦数光阴	
明亮有白昼	狰狞黑夜沉	
吾望遇花期	紫罗兰味淳	
青丝卷纤蕊	苍白色如尘	
高高园中树	叶密落黄尘	*5*
前期挡酷热	遮阴护羊群	
夏日多青翠	今朝为束薪	
白发微微颤	有人来安魂	
见此吾有问	君美吾疑存	
一朝韶华逝	废墟化粉尘	*10*
美貌亲美貌	芳馨弃芳馨	
他者生长速	枯萎叹自身	
时光如镰刀	无物孰抗尊	
未遭时光护	及早生儿孙	

---

bristly: 毛发丛生的，短而硬的
beard: 胡须
11. forsake: 遗弃，抛弃
13. scythe: 长柄大镰刀
译者感言：岁月无情有时尽，人如草木盛而衰。
紫罗兰花枯萎日，青春麦苗变烧柴。

13

O that you were yourself! but, love, you are

No longer yours than you yourself here live:

Against this coming end you should prepare,

And your sweet semblance to some other give.

So should that beauty which you hold in lease   *5*

Find no determination; then you were

Yourself again, after yourself's decease,

When your sweet issue your sweet form should bear.

Who lets so fair a house fall to decay,

Which husbandry in honour might uphold   *10*

Against the stormy gusts of winter's day

And barren rage of death's eternal cold?

    O, none but unthrifts: dear my love, you know

    You had a father; let your son say so.

人生有租期，漂亮房子如何不倒？
1.　　love: my love, 我亲爱的
4.　　semblance: 外貌
6.　　determination: 满期
7.　　decease: 死亡，亡故
10.　　husbandry: 家政，节俭
　　　uphold: 支撑
11.　　gusts: gust 阵风
12.　　barren rage: ravaging which produces barrenness, 无情的破坏
13.　　untrifts: 浪子

13

想成真我乎	吾之可爱君	
寿命恒有数	人活于凡尘	
及早做准备	末日将来临	
美貌要延续	美貌传他人	
美貌有赁期	送人继芳馨	*5*
君若弃尘世	美貌得永存	
红消香断时	君能保自身	
优雅好儿女	存君优雅身	
华美大厦倾	何人不痛心	
真心诚意护	大厦承千钧	*10*
隆冬风肆虐	狂暴不能侵	
严寒太长久	死寂冷人心	
君为浪子乎	吾之至爱君	
要让子诉说	我有好父亲	

译者感言：生命有限，美貌有期。
　　　　　租赁青春，生子延期。

14

Not from the stars do I my judgement pluck;

And yet methinks I have astronomy,

But not to tell of good or evil luck,

Of plagues, of dearths, or seasons' quality;

Nor can I fortune to brief minutes tell。   *5*

Pointing to each his thunder, rain, and wind,

Or say with princes if it shall go well,

By oft predict that I in heaven find:

But from thine eyes my knowledge I derive,

And, constant stars, in them I read such art,   *10*

As truth and beauty shall together thrive,

If from thyself to store thou wouldst convert;

   Or else of thee this I prognosticate:

   Thy end is truth's and beauty's doom and date.

占星术说到如何使真与美并存。
4.　dearths:　饥馑
　　season's quality:　四季天气情况
5.　to brief minutes:　每时每刻
8.　oft predict:　经常的预言
10.　constant stars:　你的眼睛
　　art:　知识
11.　thrive:　繁盛
12.　from thyself to store:　你生育后人
　　convert:　回心转意
13.　prognosticate:　预言

14

吾自有判断　　非采自星辰
吾通占星术　　自思通古今
非为占吉凶　　非为赚金银
不推灾疫岁　　不算流年人
吾不推算时　　预卜吉和贞　　　5
何时飘泼雨　　何时雷电侵
不去算皇子　　不去算皇孙
只缘探天穹　　天机知几分
自君目光里　　术数吾自珍
君目如恒星　　吾原大道亲　　　10
真美共一体　　永传后世人
倘若君醒悟　　成家延子孙
倘若仍不悟　　预言奉告君
君身消亡日　　真无美无存

译者感言：我非占星看相人，时时为星忧青春。
　　　　　四季变化风霜雨，岂管王子与王孙。

41

15

When I consider every thing that grows

Holds in perfection but a little moment,

That this huge stage presenteth naught but shows

Whereon the stars in secret influence comment;

When I perceive that men as plants increase,   *5*

Cheered and checked even by the self-same sky,

Vaunt in their youthful sap, at height decrease,

And wear their brave state out of memory;

Then the conceit of this inconstant stay

Sets you most rich in youth before my sight,   *10*

Where wasteful Time debateth with decay,

To change your day of youth to sullied night;

　　And, all in war with Time, for love of you,

　　As he takes from you, I engraft you new.

　　　该诗不同于前十四首，谈时空与人生。
3.　　nought:　nothing
4.　　whereon:　在表演时
5.　　perceive:　观察
6.　　cheered and checked:　押头韵（alliteration）
　　　selfsame:　同一个
8.　　brave:　辉煌的
9.　　inconstant stay:　没有尽头的变化，人生无常
11.　　debateth with decay:　与腐朽共谋
12.　　sullied:　弄脏，玷污
14.　　engraft:　嫁接

15

吾常暗思忖	万物皆有生	
生命叹艰巨	全盛弹指中	
世界大剧场	人人在戏中	
上苍早有识	星宿安排成	
吾暇常静观	草木比人生	5
苍天阻拦衰	苍天鼓励成	
青春勃勃起	鼎盛转头空	
辉煌与靓丽	烟云记忆中	
人生思无常	世界叹浮生	
眼前君妙龄	青春自雍容	10
腐朽找时日	同谋皆无情	
将君青春日	化作夜无穷	
皆因吾爱君	吾与时光争	
吾为君嫁接	时光毁君容	

译者感言：生命有盛期，衰落一梦中。
　　　　　翩翩少年子，颓然病老翁。

43

16

But wherefore do not you a mightier way

Make war upon this bloody tyrant, Time?

And fortify yourself in your decay

With means more blessed than my barren rhyme?

Now stand you on the top of happy hours;   *5*

And many maiden gardens, yet unset,

With virtuous wish would bear your living flowers,

Much liker than your painted counterfeit;

So should the lines of that life repair,

Which this, Time's pencil, or my pupil pen,   *10*

Neither in inward worth nor outward fair,

Can make you live yourself in eyes of men.

　　To give away yourself keeps yourself still;

　　And you must live, drawn by your own sweet skill.

把时间比作暴君，不免偏执。辛勤耕耘处女地，责无旁贷。

1.　wherefore:　why, 为什么
3.　fortify:　使坚强
4.　blessed:　神圣的
　　barren:　useless, 无用的
6.　unset:　未种植
7.　virtuous:　有道德的
8.　counterfeit:　肖像
9.　repair:　再生
10.　pupil:　不熟练的

16

何不用心计	强力斗暴君
时间逞暴虐	血腥不忍闻
力量更强大	衰朽不属君
武器更神圣	远胜吾诗文
幸福好年华	巅峰多思忖	5
处子好花园	尚未逢耕耘
君子种鲜花	企盼君光临
鲜美人之最	画图怎及君
生命好线条	生命再延伸
时间如椽笔	笑吾笨墨痕	10
难绘君外貌	更难描君心
难使君美貌	再现于世人
君美欲恒久	君须献自身
君须用天赋	天地间永存

译者感言：时光如暴君，天赋葆青春。
　　　　　莫谓诗笔嫩，描尽天地新。

45

17

Who will believe my verse in time to come,

If it were filled with your most high deserts?

Though yet, heaven knows, it is but as a tomb

Which hides your life, and shows not half your parts.

If I could write the beauty of your eyes,   *5*

And in fresh numbers number all your graces,

The age to come would say, 'This poet lies,

Such heavenly touches ne'er toucht earthly faces.'

So should my papers, yellow'd with their age,

Be scorn'd, like old men of less truth than tongue;   *10*

And your true rights be term'd a poet's rage,

And stretchèd metre of an antique song:

　　But were some child of yours alive that time,

　　You should live twice, in it and in my rhyme.

　　诗歌是以写人的美好议态；诗歌言之有物。
4.　　parts:　优秀品质
6.　　fresh numbers:　生动的诗句
　　　number:　记述
7.　　The age to come:　后来人
8.　　touches:　笔触
10.　　less truth than tongue:　啰嗦
11.　　rage:　疯狂
12.　　stretchèd metre:　夸张的诗歌
　　　antique:　古时的

17

吾笔写诗篇	没人置信难	
满篇皆赞语	夸君也难堪	
固然遵天意	吾诗墓一般	
其中隐君体	五分也谓难	
吾愿写君目	美妙不可言	5
诗句求清丽	清丽写美颜	
后世或讥讽	谓吾扯谎言	
神笔天上有	天上岂人间	
凡人无福享	诗稿褐黄观	
吾遭世轻视	一如冬烘谈	10
君貌本绝纱	狂妄诗人言	
谓诗本古歌	勿夸夸其谈	
盼君有儿孙	儿孙好美颜	
君后与吾诗	同君万古传	

译者感言：诗人靠诗行，美貌诗颂扬。
　　　　　诗写青春永，诗真不夸张。
　　　　　好诗十七首，二百三八行。
　　　　　劝君快婚媾，剩男自闭乡。

18

Shall I compare thee to a summer's day?

Thou art more lovely and more temperate:

Rough winds do shake the darling buds of May,

And summer's lease hath all too short a date:

Sometime too hot the eye of heaven shines,   *5*

And often is his gold complexion dimm'd;

And every fair from fair sometime declines,

By chance, or nature's changing course, untrimm'd;

But thy eternal summer shall not fade,

Nor lose possession of that fair thou ow'st;   *10*

Nor shall Death brag thou wander'st in his shade,

When in eternal lines to time thou grow'st:

　　So long as men can breathe, or eyes can see,

　　So long lives this, and this gives life to thee.

　　写友人美貌将与诗人诗歌永存于世。简明易懂。
2.　temperate:　温和的
4.　lease:　租借期限
6.　complexion:　面部肤色
8.　untrimm'd:　美色不会消褪
11.　brag:　吹嘘
译者感言：夏日固美艳，何如君容颜。
　　　　　　吾诗与君貌，永留天地间。

18

君好有一比	能否比夏天
君比夏可爱	君比夏恭谦
五月狂风起	嫩蕊遭摧残
夏日匆匆过	时光瞬息间
有时苍穹目	太热太光鲜 *5*
金光固可爱	经常变容颜
美貌因可爱	不免凋朱颜
或因机会起	或因变自然
君之夏永恒	永不失光鲜
天生丽质永	不会弃路边 *10*
阴影君苟活	死神莫奢谈
倘若君永生	活于吾诗篇
倘若目能读	倘若人繁衍
倘若吾诗在	君寿如诗篇

19

Devouring Time, blunt thou the lion's paws,

And make the earth devour her own sweet brood;

Pluck the keen teeth from the fierce tiger's jaws,

And burn the long-lived phoenix in her blood;

Make glad and sorry seasons as thou fleet'st,   5

And do whate'er thou wilt, swift-footed Time,

To the wide world and all her fading sweets;

But I forbid thee one most heinous crime;

O, carve not with thy hours my love's fair brow,

Nor draw no lines there with thine antique pen;   10

Him in thy course untainted do allow

For beauty's pattern to succeeding men.

　　Yet, do thy worst, old Time; despite thy wrong,

　　My love shall in my verse ever live young.

仍写友人之美貌及诗人之诗歌。
1. Devouring: 吞食的，贪婪的
   blunt: 把……弄钝
2. brood: 孩子们
3. keen: 尖锐的
4. in her blood: 活生生地
5. fleet'st: 飞逝
7. sweets: 美好的一切
8. heinous: 极凶残的
10. antique pen: 老朽的画笔
11. untainted: 未污染的

19

时光贪无厌	狮爪钝不存
强迫黄土地	生命大口吞
时光欺猛虎	利牙拔无存
凤凰终涅槃	血尽何殷殷
时光飞逝去	季节有悲欣
驰聘大地上	时光如暴君
一切任汝意	灵秀化粉尘
禁汝滔天罪	吾意受天尊
呼汝勿乱刻	吾友好剑眉
线条莫胡画	老笔存自身
时光任飞逝	容友美貌存
后来多男子	模拟皆欢心
时光称古老	恶贯满盈身
吾友存吾诗	吾诗葆青春

5

10

12.　For beauty's pattern to succeeding men:　给后世男子留下美貌典范
译者感言：时光实凶残，万类毁一旦。
　　　　　时光莫肆虐，吾诗留美颜。

20

A woman's face, with Nature's own hand painted,

Hast thou, the master-mistress of my passion;

A woman's gentle heart, but not acquainted

With shifting change, as is false women's fashion;

An eye more bright than theirs, less false in rolling,   *5*

Gilding the object whereupon it gazeth;

A man in hue all hues in his controlling,

Which steals men's eyes, and women's souls amazeth.

And for a woman wert thou first created;

Till Nature, as she wrought thee, fell a-doting,   *10*

And by addition me of thee defeated,

By adding one thing to my purpose nothing.

   But since she pricked thee out for women's pleasure,

   Mine be thy love, and thy love's use their treasure.

第 20—25 首仍然赞颂友人美貌及诗人对友人之爱。

该首讲友人有美女之美，男女都为之销魂。

第 1 行到第 12 行为一个句子，主句为 A woman's face, with nature's hand painted, Hast thou，是诗中常见的倒装，用现代英语表达，正常语序为 You have a woman's face painted by nature's own hand.

7.　　hue:　风姿

10.　wrought:　wok 的过去式和过去分词，制造

　　　fell a –doting:　愚蠢之爱

12.　By adding one thing to my purpose nothing:　加上了一件对我无用的东西

13.　pricked:　prick, 选中

14.　thy love's use their treasure:　让妇女享用肉体

20

君有妇人面	造化亲绘成
情郎与情妇	全因吾多情
君心妇人弱	不染自纯清
反复无常习	荡妇无羞容
君目自明澈	无意弄风情	5
君目注视处	万物光辉生
君美云盖世	众美无影踪
男子神迷乱	女子魂销镕
造物起初意	君身元女英
孰知塑造时	身困眼朦胧	10
吾本爱君身	造化不容情
误添一物上	吾意一场空
造物塑造君	留与妇人争
吾爱留与吾	情欲送多情

译者感言：造物赐君美妇容，貌美心美笑春风。
　　　　　但愿造物留君美，吾诗盛赞女多情。

21

So is it not with me as with that Muse

Stirr'd by a painted beauty to his verse,

Who heaven itself for ornament doth use,

And every fair with his fair doth rehearse;

Making a couplement of proud compare,   *5*

With sun and moon, with earth and sea's rich gems,

With April's first-born flowers, and all things rare

That heaven's air in this huge rondure hems.

O, let me, true in love, but truly write,

And then believe me, my love is as fair   *10*

As any mother's child, though not so bright

As those gold candles fixt in heaven's air:

  Let them say more that like of hearsay well;

  1 will not praise that purpose not to sell.

真心夸赞美人勿需华丽辞藻，朴素的语言更有魅力。
2. a painted beauty: 脂粉美人，画上美人
3. Who heaven itself for ornament doth use: 用天价来形容
5. couplement: 配对
8. rondure: 宇宙
    hems: hem，边缘
9. but: 只能
12. gold candles: 星辰
13. hearsay: 传闻
14. I will not praise that purpose not to sell: 我不想卖货，所以不想夸赞

21

吾与彼缪斯　　毕竟大不同
彼诗画美貌　　震颜撼心灵
天堂饰娇娃　　诗艺却平平
藻丽装美女　　繁化堆美容
骄傲写佳丽　　浮华夸女英　　　　　*5*
日月共大海　　珍珠出沧溟
四月花初放　　奇珍异宝同
乾坤称渺远　　浩叹望苍穹
嗟乎吾诗真　　真诗写真情
吾诗君可信　　吾美诗句中　　　　　*10*
固然非明亮　　吾爱母亲生
蜡烛亮金色　　霞光自天宫
他人多狂言　　吹嘘不由衷
吾产非兜售　　过誉非真情

译者感言：吾诗虽质朴，远胜华丽辞。
　　　　　脂粉不足贵，平中以求奇。

22

My glass shall not persuade me I am old,

So long as youth and thou are of one date;

But when in thee tin-le's furrows I behold,

Then look I death my days should expiate.

For all that beauty that doth cover thee   5

Is but the seemly raiment of my heart,

Which in my breast doth live, as thine in me.

How can I, then, be elder than thou art?

O, therefore, love, be of thyself so wary

As I, not for myself, but for thee will;   10

Bearing thy heart, which l will keep so chary

As tender nurse her babe from faring ill.

  Presume not on thy heart when mine is slain;

  Thou gavest me thine not to give back again.

胸中永远装着朋友，心里永远年轻。
2.　of one date: 同驻
3.　furrows: 沟；犁沟。诗中指皱纹
4.　expiate: 赎罪，诗中为结束
6.　raiment: 衣饰
9.　wary: 珍重
11.　chary: 谨慎小心的
12.　faring: 结果是
13.　Presume: 指望
译者感言：菱花镜中红颜老，春秋大梦盼长生。
　　　　　朋友呵护心相印，诗人爱友山海情。

22

吾有菱花镜　　　不让吾龙钟
青春相伴随　　　君今正年轻
君面刻满痕　　　时光叹无情
吾愿死神至　　　补偿无常生
君有无限美　　　装点君仪容　　　　5
吾心有君美　　　华衣衬雍容
君胸吾心驻　　　吾心驻君胸
言吾比君老　　　此理太不通
呼君吾至爱　　　珍重慰平生
正如吾自爱　　　思君不了情　　　　10
君心吾呵护　　　吾心处吾胸
防儿患疾病　　　乳娘护幼婴
倘若吾心死　　　君心酆都城
君心已赐吾　　　收回万不能

23

As an unperfect actor on the stage,

Who, with his fear is put besides his part,

Or some fierce thing replete with too much rage,

Whose strength's abundance weakens his own heart;

So I, for fear of trust, forget to say   5

The perfect ceremony of love's rite,

And in mine own love's strength seem to decay,

O'ercharged with burthen of mine own love's might.

O, let my books be, then, the eloquence

And dumb presagers of my speaking breast;   10

Who plead for love, and look for recompense,

More than that tongue that more hath more expressed.

    O, learn to read what silent love hath writ:

    To hear with eyes belongs to love's fine wit.

用不太熟悉演技的演员的忘台词来表示真爱者的真情。

2.　　put besides his part: 忘了台词

3.　　replete: 充满的

6.　　rite: 仪式，典礼

9.　　eloquence: 雄辩

11.　plead: 恳求

　　　recompense: 酬报

12.　More than that tongue that more hath more expressed: 三个 more 用于同一个诗行，颇具匠心，颇有真意。白话译为：比那些絮絮叨叨的话语更强

译者感言：用力过猛则出格，过于在意事不成。

　　　　　　缠绵多情无限爱，尽在默默无语中。

58

23

若不谙演技　　笨拙当演员
台上偏慌乱　　角色忘一边
猛兽固凶猛　　狂吼也枉然
威力忌太猛　　雄心受伤残
吾亦因恐惧　　自信去悄然　　　　　　　　*5*
记忆情场上　　表爱需宏篇
爱情太用力　　吾气息奄奄
爱情太沉重　　吾无力承担
呼君读吾诗　　吾诗全无言
默默无言诗　　倾诉吾心田　　　　　　　*10*
替吾去求爱　　为讨人喜欢
多读见多情　　多情似无言
请君耐心读　　沉默爱情篇
君用眼睛听　　美妙爱情言

24

Mine eye hath play'd the painter, and hath stell'd

Thy beauty's form in table of my heart;

My body is the frame wherein 'tis held,

And pèrspective it is best painter's art.

For through the painter must you see his skill,　　　　*5*

To find where your true image pictured lies;

Which in my bosom's shop is hanging still,

That hath his windows glazed with thine eyes.

Now see what good turns eyes for eyes have done:

Mine eyes have drawn thy shape, and thine for me　　*10*

Are windows to my breast, where-through the sun

　Delights to peep, to gaze therein on thee;

　　Yet eyes this cunning want to grace their art,

　　They draw but what they see, know not the heart.

绘画技巧再高，也不能不刻画心灵。
1. stell'd:　steel，刻画，一版本为 steeld
4. pèrspective:　透视法
7. bosom:　胸
8. glazed:　装玻璃于
9. Now see what good turns eyes for eyes have done:　眼睛对眼睛有多大的好处
11. where-through:　Through which, 通过
12. peep:　偷看
13. this cunning want:　欠缺这个技巧
　　grace:　使增光，使优美

24

吾目为画家　　诚为君写真
君貌上画板　　美貌居吾心
吾身作画框　　倩影存吾身
吾有透视法　　画家珍宝存
君见画家面　　可知画艺真　　　　　　5
君有压众貌　　画里真容新
君居吾胸臆　　内室挂写真
君心为窗牖　　俊目玻璃纯
美目帮美目　　相助又相亲
吾目绘君影　　君目爱吾身　　　　　　10
为吾畅心扉　　日光万点金
阿波罗瞥见　　俏然凝视君
吾凭目画像　　艺业欠芳馨
单绘目中美　　何如画内心

译者感言：愿乞画家画美貌，由表及里画心灵。
　　　　　透视岂为纯技法，透视心灵大功成。

25

Let those who are in favour with their stars

Of public honour and proud titles boast,

Whilst I, whom fortune of such triumph bars,

Unlooked for joy in that I honour most.

Great princes' favourites their fair leaves spread   *5*

But as the marigold at the sun's eye;

And in themselves their pride lies burièd,

For at a frown they in their glory die.

The painful warrior famousèd for fight,

After a thousand victories once foiled,   *10*

Is from the book of honour razed quite,

And all the rest forgot for which he toiled:

    Then happy I, that love and am belovèd

    Where I may not remove nor be removèd.

荣耀可供一时夸耀，而心中之爱永恒。

3.　Whilst I, whom fortune of such triumph bars:　While I whom is excluded from such
　　triumph, 这样的荣耀于我无缘

4.　Unlooked for:　预料之外

5.　Great princes' favourites:　帝王宠幸的人们

6.　marigold:　万寿菊

7.　burièd:　buried, 埋葬，死去

9.　famousèd:　famous, 有名的

10.　foiled:　挫败的

11.　razed:　erased, 注销

12.　And all the rest forget for which he toiled:　别人忘记了往日的功勋

25

吉星高照者	官运亨通人	
逢人便夸耀	高官厚禄身	
吾与此无缘	煊赫属他人	
吾有吾最爱	心中多欢欣	
花瓣舒展者	帝王有宠臣	5
金盏花怒放	日光万点金	
骄横瞬间逝	荣耀葬荒坟	
豪华烟云散	帝王一皱眉	
名将沙场苦	百战百胜身	
胜利复胜利	一败何人闻	10
光荣史册上	注销名不存	
世人皆忘记	名将多苦辛	
感吾多幸运	爱吾吾爱人	
不遭君抛弃	岂能抛弃君	

13. belovèd: beloved, 被人爱
14. removèd: removed, 移情，抛弃
译者感言：功勋卓著，沙场点兵。
　　　　　小有失误，全无功名。
　　　　　吾有真情，吾得真情。
　　　　　不弃不离，吾爱常青。

26

Lord of my love, to whom in vassalage

Thy merit hath my duty strongly knit,

To thee I send this written ambassage,

To witness duty, not to show my wit;

Duty so great, which wit so poor as mine   5

May make seem bare, in wanting words to show it,

But that I hope some good conceit of thine

In thy soul's thought, all naked, will bestow it;

Till whatsoever star that guides my moving,

Points on me graciously with fair aspèct,   10

And puts apparel on my tottered loving,

To show me worthy of thy sweet respect:

　　Then may I dare to boast how I do love thee;

　　Till then not show my head where thou mayst prove me.

该首为前 25 首的献诗，或叫做前 25 首的概述。

1.　vassalage:　臣属

3.　ambassage:　formal message, 书面作品

8.　bestow:　把……赠与

10.　aspèct:　aspect, 显象

11.　apparel:　衣服，服饰

　　　tottered:　tattered, 撕碎的；褴褛的

译者感言：至爱为神圣，至爱受尊崇。

　　　　　　至爱诗裸露，至爱诗深情。

26

君为爱主宰	为君献忠诚	
主宰多功德	效劳吾尽忠	
向君献诗句	信使为言明	
言吾尽本份	非为卖才能	
本份应为首	吾愧乏才能	5
空洞无物句	吾意写不清	
愿君拨冗阅	阅过喜心中	
愿君赏拙句	感君赐慧明	
直至某星宿	指吾向前行	
优雅指引吾	和悦带笑容	10
吾爱因寒微	君赐锦衣明	
君宠在锦衣	锦衣显吾容	
吾乃敢放言	爱君多深情	
此刻吾垂首	待君察分明	

27

Weary with toil, I haste me to my bed,

The dear repose for limbs with travel tired;

But then begins a journey in my head,

To work my mind, when body's work's expired:

For then my thoughts, from far where I abide,   5

Intend a zealous pilgrimage to thee,

And keep my drooping eyelids open wide,

Looking on darkness which the blind do see:

Save that my soul's imaginary sight

Presents thy shadow to my sightless view,   10

Which, like a jewel hung in ghastly night,

Makes black night beauteous, and her old face new.

　Lo, thus, by day my limbs, by night my mind,

　For thee and for myself no quiet find.

第 27—31 首，写与友人分手后诗人的牵挂。
该首讲对友人的昼思夜想。
2.　repose:　休息
4.　expired:　满期
5.　abide:　居住
6.　zealous:　热情的
7.　drooping:　下垂
11.　ghastly:　恐怖的
译者感言：疲惫身心，梦里也思君。
　　　　　黑暗无光，君美在心房。

27

辛劳身疲惫　　匆忙躺上床
旅途四肢累　　休息喜心房
此刻心不闲　　旅行向远方
身卧心旅途　　脑海白帆扬
远方在召唤　　吾思在翱翔　　　　　*5*
热情去朝圣　　为君向远方
眼睑太沉重　　睁大不思量
吾目向暗处　　盲人正凄惶
目盲心非暗　　想象发亮光
想象携君影　　不嫌吾目盲　　　　　*10*
苍天黝黑处　　宝石悬放光
黑色变美丽　　旧貌新脸宠
嗟吾身心累　　日夜苦奔忙
为君跑断腿　　为君想断肠

28

How can I, then, return in happy plight,

That am debarred the benefit of rest?

When day's oppression is not eased by night,

But day by night, and night by day, opprest?

And each, though enemies to either's reign,   *5*

Do in consent shake hands to torture me;

The one by toil, the other to complain

How far I toil, still farther off from thee.

I tell the day, to please him thou art bright,

And dost him grace when clouds do blot the heaven: *10*

So flatter I the swart-complexioned night,

When sparkling stars twire not thou gild'st the even.

　　But day doth daily draw my sorrows longer,

　　And night doth nightly make grief's strength seem stronger.

对朋友昼思夜想。白天饱受煎熬，晚上更甚。

1.　plight:　境况
2.　debarred:　排除
5.　reign:　君主统治
6.　consent:　同意
11.　swart-complexioned:　swart, 黝黑的
12.　twire:　twinkle, 眨眼
　　gild'st:　gild, 使有光彩
译者感言：日夜思君君不见，君容艳美艳阳天。
　　　　　君美远胜自然美，靓丽华丽君光鲜。

28

应归则须归　　如何心怡然
身子不能歇　　脑子不得闲
白昼负荷重　　黑夜受熬煎
日夜受威逼　　重负不可堪
白昼与黑夜　　为敌斗不闲　　　　　　　　*5*
企图压迫吾　　携手为权奸
劳苦与抱怨　　两样武器全
日夜奔波苦　　君远在天边
为取悦白昼　　言君最光鲜
天上乌云布　　君雅开天颜　　　　　　　　*10*
为讨好黑夜　　旧计谋开篇
群星不眨眼　　君亮银河边
白昼日日过　　使吾愁苦延
黑夜夜夜逝　　无尽悲伤添

29

When, in disgrace with fortune and men's eyes,

I all alone beweep my outcast state,

And trouble deaf heaven with my bootless cries,

And look upon myself, and curse my fate,

Wishing me like to one more rich in hope,   *5*

Featured like him, like him with friends possest,

Desiring this man's art, and that man's scope,

With what I most enjoy contented least;

Yet in these thoughts myself almost despising,

Haply I think on thee, and then my state,   *10*

Like to the lark at break of day arising

From sullen earth, sings hymns at heaven's gate;

   For thy sweet love remember'd such wealth brings,

   That then I scorn to change my state with kings.

写诗人在文学上的不自信。

1. disgrace: 丢脸
2. beweep: 悲欢
   outcast: 无家可归的
3. bootless: 无用的
5. more rich in hope: 前程远大；财运亨通
7. scope: 广博的才能
8. With what I most enjoy contented least: least contented with what I most enjoy, 最不满意我最喜欢的
9. despising: 看不起
10. Haply: 偶然地

29

叹时运不济	世人白眼狼	
飘零身世安	独处自哀伤	
呼天天不应	耳聋怨上苍	
低头顾自身	命运吾谤伤	
愿吾似富人	前程多辉煌	*5*
他人多朋友	仪表又堂堂	
羡才华横溢	慕文采飞扬	
吾有至乐事	不满弃路旁	
自卑情结人	轻己近荒唐	
猛然想到君	吾思云飞扬	*10*
阴沉大地远	破晓云雀翔	
天国大门近	高唱仙乐章	
思君有至爱	携来百宝箱	
吾缘吾自重	不屑换帝王	

---

12. sullen:　阴沉的
13. thy sweet love remember'd:　thinking of your love, 想到你甜美的爱

译者感言：艺人自视，文人相轻。
　　　　　写出自我，笑逐哀鸿。

30

When to the sessions of sweet silent thought

I summon up remembrance of things past,

I sigh the lack of many a thing I sought,

And with old woes new wail my dear time's waste:

Then can I drown an eye, unused to flow,   5

For precious friends hid in death's dateless night,

And weep afresh love's long-since-cancell'd woe,

And moan the expense of many a vanisht sight:

Then can I grieve at grievances foregone,

And heavily from woe to woe tell o'er   10

The sad account of fore-bemoanèd moan,

Which I new pay as if not paid before.

    But if the while I think on thee, dear friend,

    All losses are restored, and sorrows end.

    诗人沉湎于回忆不遂人愿的往事。

1—2. When to the sessions of sweet silent thought / I summon up remembrance of things past:
When I summon up remembrance of past things to the sessions of sweet silent thought,
当我仔细回忆已往的事情，沉醉于甜蜜的静静的思想的殿堂

4.   wail: 恸哭

5.   drown: 把……淹死

7.   cancelled: 抵销

8.   moan: 呻吟

9.   foregone: forego 的过去分词，以前的

10.   tell o'er: 细数

11.   fore-bemoanèd: 以前痛心的事情

30

一朝被传唤　　往事吾品尝
温和静穆思　　对簿在公堂
吾辈多少事　　苦寻愿未偿
旧恨犹未已　　新哭岁月荒
眼泪干已久　　再次泪汪汪　　　　　5
冥夜无情阻　　好友在望乡
苦痛早勾销　　痛哭爱心伤
往事如烟散　　哀叹多凄惶
悲叹悲苦事　　悲苦堵心房
惨痛思惨痛　　悲凉复悲凉　　　　　10
伤心多账目　　细数愁断肠
似未还旧债　　又还新饥荒
喜呼吾好友　　想君喜洋洋
失去皆复得　　扫尽穷哀伤

译者感言：回忆过去无可非，不能自拔则可悲。
　　　　　伤心流泪随风去，青山流水映晴晖。

73

31

Thy bosom is endeared with all hearts,

Which I by lacking have supposed dead;

And there reigns love, and all love's loving parts,

And all those friends which I thought buried.

How many a holy and obsequious tear   5

Hath dear religious love stolen from mine eye,

As interest of the dead, which now appear

But things removed that hidden in thee lie!

Thou art the grave where buried love doth live,

Hung with the trophies of my lovers gone,   10

Who all their parts of me to thee did give;

That due of many now is thine alone;

  Their images I loved I view in thee,

  And thou, all they, hast all the all of me.

在与友人长期分别的日子里，不知流了多少哀伤的眼泪。

5.　　obsequious:　虔诚哀悼的

7.　　As interest of the dead:　死者应得的权益

8.　　But things removed that hidden in thee lie:　权益移居，却藏在你的心里

10.　lovers gone:　死去的朋友们

12.　That due of many:　众人应得的一切

14.　all the all of me:　all there is, and all there ever was, of me, 我现在和过去的一切

译者感言：与友分离珠泪流，深情厚意藏心头。

　　　　　生离死别同中外，笑口常开春意稠。

31

君心愈可爱	众心聚胸中
吾谓众心灭	早已无影踪
君心爱统治	爱岂分重轻
一切亡故友	埋葬君心中
多少圣洁泪	多少哀悼情
偷偷出吾目	皆因爱虔诚
逝者早逝去	今现君目中
逝者辞别吾	驻入君心灵
君心作坟墓	埋葬旧爱情
情人纪念物	满挂墓不空
吾情交君手	逝者全算清
逝者多情爱	君独享爱情
吾爱逝者影	君身显分明
君身爱总和	永占吾心灵

5

10

32

If thou survive my well-contented day,

When that churl Death my bones with dust shall cover,

And shalt by fortune once more re-survey

These poor rude lines of thy deceasèd lover:

Compare them with the bett'ring of the time,   *5*

And though they be outstripped by every pen,

Reserve them for my love, not for their rhyme,

Exceeded by the height of happier men.

O, then vouchsafe me but this loving thought:

'Had my friend's Muse grown with this growing age,   *10*

A dearer birth than this his love had brought,

To march in ranks of better equipage:

　　But since he died, and poets better prove,

　　Theirs for their style I'll read, his for his love'.

该首为第 27—31 首的献诗。
诗人不怕别人的诗篇比自己强，诗歌进步是必然的。
2.　churl: 粗暴的
3.　re-survey: 再读
4.　deceasèd: dead, 死去的
5.　bett'ring: bettering, 改进的
6.　outstripped: 超过
9.　vouchsafe: 赐予
12.　equipage: 装备，此处指诗歌
14.　his: 我朋友的诗歌

32

倘若君健在	吾已入荒坟
死神忒粗鲁	葬吾叛天恩
偶尔翻遗物	君见吾诗存
吾诗虽云劣	真心献情人
诗非时尚句	诗无飘逸魂
笔笔羞惭至	句句冷汗淋
祈君念真爱	谬赏吾诗存
时下众诗友	飘逸诗不群
呼喊缪斯女	赐吾思爱神
吾友诗才富	时光助诗魂
真爱出好句	灵感更清纯
独步诗坛友	诗篇曰超人
吾友身已去	他人诗无邻
他诗赏文采	友诗赏真心

5

10

译者感言：诗歌多敌手，至要在真情。
　　　　　真金埋沙漠，瓦缶赛雷鸣。

33

Full many a glorious morning have I seen

Flatter the mountain-tops with sovereign eye,

Kissing with golden face the meadows green,

Gilding pale streams with heavenly alchemy;

Anon permit the basest clouds to ride   *5*

With ugly rack on his celestial face,

And from the fòrlorn world his visage hide,

Stealing unseen to west with this disgrace;

Even so my sun one early morn did shine

With all-triumphant splendour on my brow;   *10*

But, out, alack, he was but one hour mine,

The region cloud hath masked him from me now.

    Yet him for this my love no whit disdaineth;

    Suns of the world may stain when heaven's sun staineth.

    第 33—35 首写与朋友友谊的沉默期。第 33 首的起首四行是景物描绘佳作。整首写友谊被乌云遮挡。

2.   sovereign: 君主

3.   meadows: medow, 草地

4.   alchemy: 炼金术

5.   Anon: 立刻

        permit: 允许

6.   rack: 流云

7.   fòrlorn: forlorn, 孤独凄凉的

8.   disgrace: 失去美；羞耻

11.   alack: 啊呀

33

吾生有眼福　　多欢好清晨

清晨升光彩　　山顶璀璨寻

亲吻草坪绿　　脸庞色纯金

天穹炼金术　　暗溪黄色纯

倏忽乌云到　　卑贱偏降临　　*5*

阿波罗丰姿　　竟然罩丑云

天颜遭遮蔽　　孤凄寂寞人

满面蒙羞辱　　俏然日西沉

命乖遭厄运　　也曾亮清晨

万丈光芒照　　抚吾额与鬓　　*10*

呜呼此刻短　　一个钟点亲

空中乌云厚　　美貌却无存

吾心无抱怨　　吾爱寄日神

太阳神蒙垢　　更莫问凡尘

---

12. region: 天上的
13. whit: 丝毫
    disdaineth: disdain, 鄙视
译者感言：君爱自然美，美妙贵永恒。
　　　　　天上风云变，不可变友情。

34

Why didst thou promise such a beauteous day,

And make me travel forth without my cloak,

To let base clouds o'ertake me in my way,

Hiding thy bravery in their rotten smoke?

'Tis not enough that through the cloud thou break,   5

To dry the rain on my storm-beaten face,

For no man well of such a salve can speak

That heals the wound, and cures not the disgrace:

Nor can thy shame give physic to my grief;

Though thou repent, yet I have still the loss: 10

The offender's sorrow lends but weak relief

To him that bears the strong offence's cross.

    Ah, but those tears are pearl which thy love sheeds,

    And they are rich, and ransom all ill deeds.

朋友的言语是好是坏，似乎难以判断。第 8 行要耐心寻味。

2.　　cloak:　大氅
3.　　base:　卑鄙的
7.　　salve:　药膏
10.　repent:　忏悔
11.　weak:　菲薄的
12.　strong offence's cross:　沉重的耻辱十字架
13.　sheeds:　流出
14.　ransom:　赎罪
译者感言：人言利益为永恒，莫信莫逆之友情。
　　　　　　风云变幻似难测，良心不亏积善行。

34

为何君问口	预言好天光
不带外衣游	轻信将吾诳
卑贱乌云起	旅途怎躲藏
腐败毒雾至	君美面无光
纵然君尽力	衡破乌云墙
君勉力除雨	擦干吾脸宠
无人问尊口	美言君颂扬
虽能医伤处	疗羞难祛恙
君言君愧疚	亦难治心伤
纵然君忏悔	吾失难补偿
害人者愁苦	受害者断肠
吾负十字架	蒙羞苦难当
呜呼洒珠泪	君爱一何强
君泪价连城	全是赎罪方

5

10

35

No more be grieved at that which thou hast done:

Roses have thorns, and silver fountains mud;

Clouds and eclipses stain both moon and sun,

And loathsome canker lives in sweetest bud.

All men make faults, and even I in this,   *5*

Authorizing thy trespass with compare,

Myself corrupting, salving thy amiss,

Excusing 'their sins more than thy sins are';

For to thy sensual fault I bring in sense,—

Thy adverse party is thy advocate, —   *10*

And 'gainst myself a lawful plea commence:

Such civil war is in my love and hate,

    That I an accessary needs must be

    To that sweet thief which sourly robs from me.

以天象比情感，以清泉比友谊，诗人意在宽恕。

4.   loathsome: 可厌的
       canker: 害虫
5.   Authorizing: Justifying, 开脱
       trespass: 违规
7.   salving: 掩饰
       amiss： 罪过
9.   in sense: 用香气遮盖
10.   adverse party: 原告
       advocate: 辩护士
11.   plea: 抗辩

35

固然君有过　　不必太忧伤

玫瑰也有刺　　清泉有泥汤

乌云与亏蚀　　日月少辉光

娇嫩花蕾内　　可恶毛虫藏

人人皆有错　　吾岂免荒唐　　　　　*5*

为君掩过失　　设法用比方

替君开罪责　　先把吾弄脏

君本有大错　　宽恕不应当

君有风流债　　吾替君付账

君罪有原告　　如今律师当　　　　　*10*

合法吾抗辩　　按律遵宪章

内心起征战　　爱憎敌双方

吾心有需求　　忍把同谋当

风流作强盗　　劫吾难躲藏

---

13. accessary: accessory, 同谋
14. sourly: 残酷地
译者感言：鲜花尚且有刺，清泉也有污泥。
　　　　　交友宽仁为贵，坦坦荡荡求奇。

36

Let me confess that we two must be twain,

Although our undivided loves are one:

So shall those blots that do with me remain,

Without thy help, by me be borne alone.

In our two loves there is but one respect,   *5*

Though in our lives a separable spite,

Which though it alter not love's sole effect,

Yet doth it steal sweet hours from love's delight.

I may not evermore acknowledge thee,

Lest my bewailèd guilt should do thee shame;   *10*

Nor thou with public kindness honour me,

Unless thou take that honour from thy name;

　　But do not so; I love thee in such sort,

　　As, thou being mine, mine is thy good report.

　　第 36，37，39 首，均表达 "相爱者合一" 的思考。该首承认命运摆布不得不分离，有耻辱也由诗人承担。

1.　confess: 承认

　　twain: 二；一对

3.　blots: 不雅观的事物

4.　borne: bear 的过去分词，忍受

6.　separable: 可分离的

　　spite: 恶意

7.　alter: 改变

10.　bewailèd: 悲伤的

14.　report: 声誉

36

吾许吾坦言　　吾与君必分
君爱与吾爱　　一体称纯真
吾身有瑕玼　　虽多不劳君
君请勿多虑　　吾自担在身
君爱与吾爱　　至诚一颗心　　　　　5
恶魔偏挑衅　　命运隔二心
用意固险恶　　怎变爱纯真
欢聚多佳日　　偷去随谁人
吾戒高声语　　知己送与君
羞愧君不语　　吾罪恐累君　　　　　10
君勿夸吾好　　尤当避众人
如此君誉损　　君岂能甘心
君切莫夸吾　　吾爱君情深
君身即吾身　　替吾名誉存

译者感言：世间珍宝存友情，命运多舛异路程。
　　　　　忍悲含辱表大爱，慷慨为人保名声。

37

As a decrepit father takes delight

To see his active child do deeds of youth,

So I, made lame by Fortune's dearest spite,

Take all my comfort of thy worth and truth;

For whether beauty, birth, or wealth, or wit,   *5*

Or any of these all, or all, or more,

Entitled in their parts do crowned sit,

I make my love engrafted to this store:

So then I air not lame, poor, nor despised,

Whilst that this shadow doth such substance give   *10*

That I in thy abundance am sufficed,

And by a part of all thy glory live.

    Look what is best, that best I wish in thee:

    This wish I have; then ten times happy me !

朋友至善至美，高贵高雅，诗人受益匪浅。

1. decrepit: 老弱的
3. spite: 伤害
4. worth and truth: 善良与忠诚
7. Entitled in their parts do crowned sit: 像国王和王后一样，与其他优秀质量一道存在于你一身
8. engrafted: 嫁接
9. despised: 鄙视，藐视
11. sufficed: 满足……需要
13. look what: whatever, 不管什么

37

如同年迈父　　欣赏自内心
子女多活泼　　巧妙演青春
吾身同此理　　摧残受艰辛
吾寻欢洽事　　君善君真淳
智慧与家产　　美貌与出身　　　　*5*
言多或言寡　　再多也属君
多寡皆无憾　　完美君身存
吾将爱枝条　　嫁接君须根
不再被抛弃　　不受残与贫
仅此一幻影　　恩赐受于君　　　　*10*
君富吾充实　　满足又欢欣
分享君盛誉　　安然度光阴
至善与至美　　归君世无存
但凭此心愿　　厚福养身心

译者感言：无情命运折磨人，友谊安慰得宽心。
　　　　　世间珍宝全归友，善行得报长精神。

38

How can my Muse want subject to invent,

While thou dost breathe, that pour'st into my verse

Thine own sweet argument, too excellent

For every vulgar paper to rehearse?

O, give thyself the thanks, if aught in me   5

Worthy perusal stand against thy sight;

For who's so dumb that cannot write to thee,

When thou thyself dost give invention light?

Be thou the tenth Muse, ten times more in worth

Than those old nine which rhymers invocate;   10

And he that calls on thee, let him bring forth

Eternal numbers to outlive long date.

　　If my slight Muse do please these curious days,

　　The pain be mine, but thine shall be the praise.

赞誉朋友的诗作超过文艺女神。
1.　　want subject to invent:　缺乏创作主题
4.　　vulgar:　粗俗的，庸俗的
　　　rehearse:　重复
5.　　aught in me:　我诗作中的任何东西
6.　　perusal:　细读
10.　rhymers:　作打油诗的蹩脚诗人
　　　invocate:　invoke, 祈求
12.　numbers:　诗歌
　　　outlive:　比……活得长

38

吾诗无主题	缪斯渺难寻	
君有生命在	注入吾诗存	
吾言乃妙论	妙论存至真	
纸劣留诗句	诗句颂诗魂	
呼君应谢己	读吾真诗文	*5*
吾诗有真意	真意须珍存	
哑巴得灵感	赋诗献与君	
缪斯亲哑巴	诗中颂扬君	
第十缪斯职	君任勿让人	
十倍胜前九	古老缪斯神	*10*
有人求助君	令其作诗文	
珠圆玉润字	丽句千古存	
吾叹灵感少	诗与挑剔人	
痛苦留与君	赞誉应归君	

译者感言：九大缪斯世所稀，灵感赋予辛勤诗。
　　　　　第十缪斯美十倍，骇我握笔山海驰。

39

O, how thy worth with manners may I sing,

When thou art all the better part of me?

What can mine own praise to mine own self bring?

And what is't but mine own when I praise thee?

Even for this let us divided live,   5

And our dear love lose name of single one,

That by this separation I may give

That due to thee which thou deservest alone.

O absence, what a torment wouldst thou prove,

Were it not thy sour leisure gave sweet leave   10

To entertain the time with thoughts of love,

Which time and thoughts so sweetly doth deceive,

   And that thou teachest how to make one twain,

   By praising him here who doth hence remain!

　　友情把两个人合而一。分离是一人分为两部分。友情不分远近。该诗明白畅晓，写别离而文笔轻快自如。
1.　manners: 恰如其分，体面
4.　is't: is it
9.　absence: 别离
10.　sour: 残酷的
11.　entertain: 打
13.　make one twain: 使一个人成为两份
14.　hence: 别的地方
译者感言：何物能比友情深，两友恰似一个人。
　　　　　　别离思念多夸赞，团聚之日抖精神。

39

嗟乎君多美	吾赞君由衷	
君身全占有	吾身之精英	
君若自夸耀	人疑用何能	
吾若颂扬君	赞吾一般同	
吾与君必分	出自吾心胸	*5*
全由甜蜜爱	君无独身名	
分离吾有思	归还吾有情	
全部之赞美	君独享其成	
呜呼伤离别	折磨多苦衷	
君若有闲暇	苦甜允同行	*10*
吾有爱之想	愉悦时光中	
时光与情思	皆被蜜语蒙	
君教一分二	吾意领君情	
君虽离别去	吾诗颂君明	

40

Take all my loves, my love, yea, take them all;

What hast thou then more than thou hadst before?

No love, my love, that thou mayst true love call;

All mine was thine before thou hadst this more.

Then, if for my love thou my love receivest,   *5*

I cannot blame thee for my love thou usest;

But yet be blamed, if thou this self deceivest

By wilful taste of what thyself refusest.

I do forgive thy robbery, gentle thief,

Although thou steal thee all my poverty;   *10*

And yet, love knows, it is a greater grief

To bear love's wrong than hate's known injury.

    Lascivious grace, in whom all ill well shows,

    Kill me with spites; yet we must not be foes.

第 40—42 首写朋友与一女子有私。

第 40 首写发现朋友与并不爱的女子胡缠，并表示宽容。第 1、3、5、6、11、12 行中 love 一词共出现 9 次，阅读时应细细琢磨，品味诗人用词用心之甘苦。

1.　yea:　是，是的

8.　wilful:　贪欲的

10.　steal thee:　take for yourself, 你已偷去

12.　known:　open, 公开的

13.　lascivious:　好色的

　　all ill well shows: all that is bad seems good, 一切坏事表面上看起来漂亮

译者感言：全心爱朋友，朋友竟有私。

　　　　　　朋友移情爱，莎氏真情痴。

40

吾爱携吾爱　　全携吾爱情
新爱比旧爱　　不知孰重轻
吾言告吾爱　　乱呼无爱情
吾爱为君爱　　君携吾爱行
君因有吾爱　　吾爱拥怀中　　　　　　*5*
吾拥吾之爱　　不责不心疼
吾将指责君　　自欺不由衷
纠缠非所爱　　君竟滥用情
无奈原谅君　　窃贼且温情
君盗吾财宝　　囊中已空空　　　　　　*10*
堕入爱河里　　忍辱不欲生
天下难堪事　　受痛几分轻
君风流性感　　劣迹成正宗
创伤痛杀吾　　敌视君心疼

41

Those pretty wrongs that liberty commits,

When I am sometime absent from thy heart,

Thy beauty and thy years full well befits,

For still temptation follows where thou art.

Gentle thou art, and therefore to be won,   *5*

Beauteous thou art, therefore to be assailed;

And when a woman woos, what woman's son

Will sourly leave her till she have prevailed?

Ay me! but yet thou mightst my seat forbear,

And chide thy beauty and thy straying youth,   *10*

Who lead thee in their riot even there

Where thou art forced to break a twofold truth,—

　Hers, by thy beauty tempting her to thee,

　Thine, by thy beauty being false to me.

写朋友因年轻美貌而受到诱惑。
1.　pretty wrongs:　美丽的好事
3.　befits:　适合
4.　still:　always, 总是
6.　assailed:　进攻
8.　sourly:　rudely, 粗鲁地
　　prevailed:　胜
9.　forbear:　避免
10.　chide:　责骂
11.　riot:　放荡
　　a two fold truth:　双重的誓约

41

君犯风流罪　　君成放荡人
一旦有时日　　吾不居君心
君有潘安貌　　君正值青春
无论君何往　　总遇诱惑人
君风流儒雅　　怎敌众钗裙　　　　5
君美艳英俊　　败于女追寻
女人来求欢　　女人生君身
岂能断然拒　　不享一家春
呜呼吾告君　　吾位勿常侵
申申吾詈君　　惹祸如西门　　　　10
难敌春情涌　　意乱情迷人
逼君竟毁约　　双重誓不存
女与吾有誓　　君美诱女身
君对吾有誓　　君美誓烟云

译者感言：男人一半是女人，女人一半是男人。
　　　　　男人女人皆爱美，风流倜傥逗风神。

42

That thou hast her, it is not all my grief,

And yet it may be said I loved her dearly;

That she hath thee, is of my wailing chief',

A loss in love that touches me more nearly.

Loving offenders, thus I will excuse ye:—　　　　　　　　*5*

Thou dost love her, because thou know'st I love her;

And for my sake even so doth she abuse me,

Suff'ring my friend for my sake to approve her.

If I lose thee, my loss is my love's gain,

And losing her, my friend hath found that loss;　　　*10*

Both find each other, and I lose both twain,

And both for my sake lay on me this cross:

　　But here's the joy; my friend and I are one;

　　Sweet flattery! then she loves but me alone.

朋友夺走情侣，诗人试图自我解嘲。

3.　　wailing:　悲痛的

5.　　Loving offenders:　爱之冒犯者
　　　ye:　第二人称复数形式，你们两人。

7.　　abuse:　欺骗

8.　　suff'ring:　allowing, 允许
　　　apporove her: 试用她

11.　both twain:　both, the two of them, 他们二人

12.　lay on me this cross:　让我背十字架

14.　flattery:　甜美的逢迎

42

友竟占有她	非吾全心疼	
坦言对君语	吾有深爱情	
她竟占有友	吾痛不欲生	
吾竟失去爱	触动更深层	
爱之冒犯者	吾为二人评	5
君爱吾之爱	吾爱君洞明	
她竟欺骗吾	她晓吾爱情	
无奈竟允友	爱她因吾行	
倘若吾失君	吾失君爱成	
倘若吾弃她	吾弃友获丰	10
二人皆有获	吾今两手空	
二人皆为吾	折磨吾苦行	
谓此为快事	吾友一体成	
甜蜜奉承语	她爱吾由衷	

译者感言：朋友无耻夺人妻，难以饶恕恨不依。
情爱专一岂能忍，诗中无奈自嘘唏。

43

When most I wink, then do mine eyes best see,

For all the day they view things unrespected;

But when I sleep, in dreams they look on thee,

And, darkly bright, are bright in dark directed.

Then thou, whose shadow shadows doth make bright,　　5

How would thy shadow's form form happy show

To the clear day with thy much clearer light,

When to unseeing eyes thy shade shines so!

How would, I say, mine eyes be blessed made

By looking on thee in the living day,　　　　　　10

When in dead night thy fair imperfect shade

Through heavy sleep on sightless eyes doth stay!

　　All days are nights to see till I see thee,

　　And nights bright days when dreams do show thee me.

　　第 43—55 首,连同第 27—31 首,共计 13+5=18 首,均写与朋友天各一方难别之情。
该首写朋友在胸,一片光明。
1.　wink: 睡眠
2.　unrespected: 不关注
3.　they: 我的眼睛
4.　are bright in dark directed: 黑暗中指明道路
5.　shadow: 影像
　　shadows: 黑暗
8.　unseeing eyes: 闭着的眼睛
9.　my eyes be blessed made: 我的眼睛何等幸福
10.　the living: 充满生气的白天

43

待吾闭目睡　　反而看最清
白昼纷纷事　　平凡入眼睛
待吾过梦乡　　梦中睹君容
光明中黑暗　　黑暗中光明
君有暗形象　　暗中亮明灯　　　　　5
君相有真形　　真形美景成
清明白昼光　　白昼光清明
吾虽双目闭　　君相辉煌行
吾言言吾愿　　白昼睹君容
吾目天赐福　　幸福漾吾胸　　　　　10
吾相残缺美　　沉寂长夜灯
照吾酣睡目　　通体透光明
白昼尽黑夜　　若不睹君容
梦中若见君　　黑夜白昼中

译者感言：忠诚朋友一片天，义气中外皆美谈。
　　　　　心中豁亮多明目，他人天使伊甸园。

44

If the dull substance of my flesh were thought,

Injurious distance should not stop my way;

For then, despite of space, I would be brought,

From limits far remote, where thou dost stay.

No matter then although my foot did stand　　　　　　*5*

Upon the farthest earth removed from thee;

For nimble thought can jump both sea and land,

As soon as think the place where he would be.

But, ah, thought kills me, that I am not thought,

To leap large lengths of miles when thou art gone,　　*10*

But that, so much of earth and water wrought,

I must attend time's leisure with my moan;

　　Receiving naught by elements so slow

　　But heavy tears, badges of either's woe.

尽管肉体沉重，天各一方，心灵相通无碍。
1.　dull substance:　沉重无灵气的物质，即构成万物四大元素之土与水。
2.　injurious:　有害的
7.　nimble:　灵活的
11.　wrought:　made, 制成
12.　moan:　呻吟
14.　badges:　sign, 标志
译者感言：土水气火四元素，万物构成本其宗。
　　　　　　陋质沉重土与水，千里万里心相通。

44

吾身重元素　　思想身体存
距离云残酷　　不能挡肉身
迢迢烟云路　　奈何阻重深
带吾至芳居　　立住吾脚跟
天涯海角阻　　吾仍追随君　　　　　*5*
路远人情厚　　于吾见真心
敏捷夸思想　　跨海越山林
迅疾超光速　　港站皆随心
吾身非思想　　思想愧煞人
无力越万里　　君去难见君　　　　　*10*
太多滞重物　　水土育吾身
心与君团聚　　悲伤求光阴
元素忒滞重　　吾愿如流云
惟留重浊泪　　悲苦两酸辛

45

The other two, slight air and purging fire,

Are both with thee, wherever I abide;

The first my thought, the other my desire,

These present-absent with swift motion slide.

For when these quicker elements are gone   5

In tender embassy of love to thee,

My life, being made of four, with two alone

Sinks down to death, opprest with melancholy;

Until life's composition be recured

By those swift messengers return'd from thee,   10

Who even but now come back again, assured

Of thy fair health, recounting it to me;

    This told, I joy; but then no longer glad,

    I send them back again, and straight grow sad.

另外两种元素气与火在友谊中的神奇功能。
1. purging: 净化
2. abide: 居住
3. The first: 气
   the other: 火
4. slide: 来往
6. embassy: 重任
9. recured: 恢复
11. assured: 使确信，保证
12. recounting: 描述
13. This told, I joy: 听到这个，我很高兴

45

另有两元素	纯火与柔风	
无论吾何往	都伴君行踪	
前者为思想	后者欲望行	
忽缓又忽现	轻盈小精灵	
如此快元素	迅速向君行	5
携吾去见君	温柔爱河清	
吾身四元素	十成减五成	
水土濒死亡	夏梦云压城	
命本不该绝	肌体得平衡	
快捷归使者	气火元素轻	10
此刻二者归	向吾报君情	
齐向吾保证	君身得康宁	
闻此初喜悦	喜悦不久停	
吾遣二使归	受伤深几重	

14.　straight:　立即

译者感言：四体液说欧风行，多血胆汁阳气生。
　　　　　　忧郁黏液多沉重，四种元素源可轻。

46

Mine eye and heart are at a mortal war,

How to divide the conquest of thy sight;

Mine eye my heart thy picture's sight would bar,

My heart mine eye the freedom of that right.

My heart doth plead that thou in him dost lie—   *5*

A closet never pierced with crystal eyes—

But the defendant doth that plea deny,

And says in him thy fair appearance lies.

To 'cide this title is impannellèd

A quest of thoughts, all tenants to the heart;   *10*

And by their verdict is determined

The clear eye's moiety and the dear heart's part:

    As thus; mine eye's due is thy outward part,

    And my heart's right thy inward love of heart.

观察认知上心和眼的不协和。

1.   mortal war: 生死冲突
2.   conquest: 征服；掠取物
3.   Mine eye my heart thy picture's sight would bar: My eye would forbid my heart to see your image, 我的眼睛禁止我的心观看你的形象
4.   My heart mine eye the freedom of that right: 我的心不准我的眼睛有观看的自由
5.   closet: 密室；私室
7.   defendant: 被告
9.   'cide: decide
     impannellèd: empanel, 选任陪审
10.   tenants: 租户；佃户

46

吾目与吾心	正作殊死拼
试问其缘由	君美难均分
吾目已有意	君相隔吾心
吾心不让目	不甘权限侵
吾心已都明	君潜意何深　　5
水晶般明目	难穿宝箱心
吾目作辩护	否认申辩人
言说君倩影	俏丽目中存
决定该权限	交与仲裁人
思想陪审团	租房心内存　　10
共同作宣判	如此为判文
明眸分一半	真心一半分
吾目有份额	享君貌惊人
吾心有权限	享君爱情真

11. verdict: 陪审团的裁决
12. moiety: 法律上的一半
13. due: 应得物
译者感言：观看美艳者，心眼自不同。
　　　　　外貌与思想，何人能分清。

47

Betwixt mine eye and heart a league is took,

And each doth good turns now unto the other;

When that mine eye is famished for a look,

Or heart in love with sighs himself doth smother,

With my love's picture then my eye doth feast,   5

And to the painted banquet bids my heart;

Another time mine eye is my heart's guest,

And in his thoughts of love doth share a part;

So, either by thy picture or my love,

Thyself away art present still with me;   10

For thou not farther than my thoughts canst move,

And I am still with them, and they with thee;

  Or, if they sleep, thy picture in my sight

  Awakes my heart to heart's and eye's delight.

心和眼都能用时观赏美，享受美。

1.   league: 盟约
3.   famished: 使挨饿
4.   smother: 使窒息
5.   feast: 盛宴
6.   the painted banquet: （画里）的宴席
     bids: 邀请
12. them, they: thoughts, 思念
14. Awakes my heart to heart's and eye's delight: 唤醒我的心，去享受心和眼的欢愉
译者感言：秀色可餐美宴席，心眼同盟赴佳期。
          有美何妨尽情赏，红颜褪去化春泥。

47

业已签协议	吾目与吾心	
轮流让便利	轮流利益分	
一旦目饥饿	缘由未见君	
或云心窒息	叹息痴情人	
吾目设盛筵	君之画像陈	*5*
吾心受邀请	赴宴赏写真	
有时心请客	吾目座上宾	
缱绻甜蜜意	目心得均分	
或凭君画像	或凭吾爱深	
君因远离别	犹亲胜比邻	*10*
君居天涯远	怎抵吾思君	
吾永随思想	想君吾难寝	
思想倘入眠	吾目君容亲	
将吾心唤醒	心目同欢欣	

48

How careful was I, when I took my way,

Each trifle under truest bars to thrust,

That to my use it might unusèd stay

From hands of falsehood, in sure wards of trust!

But thou, to whom my jewels trifles are,   *5*

Most worthy comfort, now my greatest grief,

Thou, best of dearest, and mine only care,

Art left the prey of every vulgar thief.

Thee have I not locked up in any chest,

Save where thou art not, though I feel thou art,   *10*

Within the gentle closure of my breast,

From whence at pleasure thou mayst come and part;

　　And even thence thou wilt be stol'n, I fear.

　　For truth proves thievish for a prize so dear.

第 48 首写朋友远胜一切珍宝，朋友珍藏在诗人胸中。

1.　took my way:　我走上旅途
2.　trifle:　小东西
　　thrust:　塞
3.　to my use it might unusèd stay:　在我使用之前，先把它好好保藏
4.　wards:　安全的地方
8.　vulgar thief:　凡庸的窃贼
9.　Thee have I not locked up in any chest:　我没有把你锁在任何箱子里
10.　Save where thou art not:　除了你不在的地方
12.　whence:　where
13.　thence:　there

48

吾未上路时	处处都小心
物件虽琐碎	保险柜中存
聊供回家用	用时不费心
不让遭亵渎	心术不正人
面对君直言	珠宝值几文　　*5*
往日吾风光	今朝吾伤神
惟一之挂念	互爱又互亲
君自有珍宝	市井掠夺心
吾未能设法	保险柜锁君
君不在吾胸	吾想把君存　　*10*
吾胸保险柜	温柔又温馨
自来任君意	自去随君心
即使藏吾胸	犹恐盗君身
面对此珍宝	圣贤把手伸

14.　truth:　诚实
　　　proves thievish:　变成窃贼
译者感言：朋友重于世间珍，友情无价千古存。
　　　　　生命友情泰山价，义字当先四海闻。

49

Against that time, if ever that time come,

When I shall see thee frown on my defects,

Whenas thy love hath cast his utmost sum,

Called to that audit by advised respects;

Against that time when thou shalt strangely pass;　　*5*

And scarcely greet me with that sun, thine eye,

When love, converted from the thing it was,

Shall reasons find of settled gravity;

Against that time do I ensconce me here

Within the knowledge of mine own desert.　　*10*

And this my hand against myself uprear,

To guard the lawful reasons on thy part:

To leave poor me thou hast the strength of laws,

Since why to love I can allege no cause.

　　该诗由一个句子构成，主句在第 9 行，Against that time 出现三次。曲写人情冷暖，提防有一天人走茶凉，读时应沉静细品。
2.　defects:　缺点
3.　whenas:　when
　　cast his utmost sum:　结清他最后的账目
4.　called:　要求价还
　　audit:　清账
　　advised respects:　careful consideration, 仔细考虑
6.　greet:　迎接；察觉
8.　shall reasons find of settled gravity:　理由产生出冷静的自重
9.　ensconce:　隐蔽

49

提防那一日	或许真来临	
因吾地位贱	皱眉竟有君	
挥金君爱吾	手中无分文	
决心清账目	顾虑逼迫君	
提防那一日	君视吾路人	*5*
君目赛丽日	见吾目无神	
一旦爱情忘	不复往日纯	
堂皇找借口	严肃又认真	
提防那一日	堡垒藏吾身	
自知有短处	先为反省人	*10*
而后吾举手	当众誓言真	
合理又合法	辩护吾为君	
君今抛弃吾	法律有条文	
为何吾爱君	吾乏理由申	

---

10. desert: 值得
11. uprear: 举手宣誓作证
14. allege: 提出
译者感言：语言思维缠不清，复杂心情离别声。
　　　　　阳光美目一朝去，朋友抛弃莫心惊。

50

How heavy do I journey on the way,

When what I seek—my weary travel's end—

Doth teach that ease and that repose to say,

'Thus far the miles are measured from thy friend!'

The beast that bears me, tired with my woe,   *5*

Plods dully on, to bear that weight in me,

As if by some instinct the wretch did know

His rider loved not speed, being made from thee;

The bloody spur cannot provoke him on

That sometimes anger thrusts into his hide;   *10*

Which heavily he answers with a groan,

More sharp to me than spurring to his side;

   For that same groan doth put this in my mind;

   My grief lies onward, and my joy behind.

   第 50，51 首为同一主题。写诗人与朋友分手的心情。诗人骑马离友远行，心情不好，马也遭了罪！

3.   repose:　安歇

6.   plods:　沉重缓慢地走

7.   wretch:　可怜的马

9.   spur:　踢马刺

     provoke:　刺激

10. thrusts:　刺

     hide:　兽皮

11. groan:　呻吟

14. onward:　在我面前

50

骑马吾上路	忧愁在旅程	
路上常思索	寻计不苦行	
安静对吾语	憩息言由衷	
路途因迢递	友人有权衡	
坐骑驮吾走	厌倦吾伤情	5
慢走又慢走	吾愁压畜牲	
坐骑晓人意	或许出本能	
主人不情愿	别君火速行	
马刺已带血	催马赶路程	
马刺踢马肚	马也不前冲	10
坐骑作答复	沉痛化哀鸣	
马使吾心伤	踢马益无情	
哀鸣勾心事	心智失平衡	
欢乐成往事	悲哀满旅程	

behind: 已经过去

译者感言：离友而去如丢魂，马刺带血脸阴沉。
　　　　　哑巴牲口遭了罪，如何使君免苦辛。

51

Thus can my love excuse the slow offence

Of my dull bearer when from thee I speed:

From where thou art 'why should I haste me thence?

Till I return, of posting is no need.

O, what excuse will my poor beast then find,   *5*

When swift extremity can seem but slow?

Then should I spur, though mounted on the wind,

In winged speed no motion shall I know:

Then can no horse with my desire keep pace;

Therefore desire, of perfect'st love being made,   *10*

Shall neigh, no dull flesh in his fiery race;

But love, for love, thus shall excuse my jade, ——

   Since from thee going he went wilful-slow,

   Towards thee I'll run, and give him leave to go.

马的快慢完全决定于一个人的心情。
1.   excuse: 原谅
4.   posting: 骑马快行
7.   mounted on the wind: 骑着风
8.   winged speed: 风速
     motion: 运动
10. of perfect'st love being made: being made of the most perfect love, 由最纯粹的爱做成
11. neigh: 马嘶
     no dull flesh: 摆脱肉体
     fiery race: 飞驰
12. jade: 马

51

如此吾之爱	不怨冒犯侵
吾不嫌马快	吾马如离君
若要离君去	匆匆为何因
如若赶回程	如箭之归心
呜呼吾坐骑	不遇宽恕人
纵然最高速	也显慢吞吞
骑马似乘风	马刺也加身
追风马蹄疾	嫌慢怨风神
可怜凡间马	难遂欲望人
吾有无瑕爱	情欲为起因
狂奔岂凡马	嘶鸣缘归心
马累得宽恕	慈悲有爱神
若离君而去	慢走是成心
归途不骑马	吾自奔向君

5

10

13. from thee going he went wilful-slow: 马因与你别离而故意慢行
14. give him leave to go: 让马慢走

译者感言：衡量标准全在心，宇宙之大不足论。
　　　　　速度至快电光速，不及造化之毫分。

52

So am I as the rich, whose blessèd key

Can bring him to his sweet up-locked treasure,

The which he will not every hour survey,

For blunting the fine point of seldom pleasure.

Therefore are feasts so solemn and so rare,   *5*

Since seldom coming, in the long year set,

Like stones of worth they thinly placed are,

Or captain jewels in the carcanet.

So is the time that keeps you, as my chest,

Or as the wardrobe which the robe doth hide,   *10*

To make some special instant special blest,

By new unfolding his imprison'd pride.

　　Blessed are you, Whose worthiness gives scope,

　　Being had to triumph, being lacked to hope.

感情如珍宝，诗人如感情富翁。
1.　blessèd:　幸运的
3.　The which:　which
　　survey:　检查欣赏
4.　blunting:　弄钝
6.　Since seldom coming in the long year set:　在漫长的一年之中难得有几次
8.　carcanet:　珠宝项圈
11.　special instant special blest:　在特殊时间的特殊光彩
12.　new:　newly
13.　scope:　许可证

52

吾像彼富翁	钥匙拿手中
彼有可爱宝	库门吾可通
彼非随时检	验看库房情
惊喜彼所爱	常看变稀松
盛大节日少	总在企盼中
漫长一年里	难得几回逢
犹如希世宝	偶见人心惊
又如大宝石	项琏见晶莹
时光吾宝库	吾身收藏中
时光吾衣柜	华服耀眼明
特殊佳节到	偶而一展容
辉煌得重现	藏久更见精
君福上天赐	优点谁数清
有君欢乐在	不见憧憬生

5

10

14. Being had to triumph, being lacked to hope: 有你在时感到十分欢喜,你离去了仍抱着希望

译者感言：财宝比感情，几多人共鸣。

　　　　　隐形之财富，情商正时兴。

117

53

What is your substance, where of are you made,

That millions of strange shadows on you tend?

Since every one hath, every one, one shade,

And you, but one, can every shadow lend.

Describe Adonis, and the counterfeit   5

Is poorly imitated after you;

On Helen's cheek all art of beauty set,

And you in Grecian tires are painted new;

Speak of the spring, and foison of the year;

The one doth shadow of your beauty show,   10

The other as your bounty doth appear;

And you in every blessed shape we know.

　　In all external grace you have some part,

　　But you like none, none you, for constant heart.

　　朋友貌美，天下美男子大美女都无法相比。

2.　　tend: attend, 跟随

5.　　Adonis: 阿童尼，美少年
　　counterfeit: 肖像

7.　　Helen: 海伦，西方美人

8.　　tires: 装饰

9.　　foison: 丰收；丰饶

11.　　bounty: 慷慨，恩惠

12.　　every blessed shape: every fair form, 各种优美的身形

14.　　you like none, none you, for constant heart: 你不像任何人，任何人也不像你，在不变心方面

53

君系何物质　　何物塑造君

百万奇形象　　均归君一身

既然一影像　　只归于一人

为何百万象　　均归君一身

描写阿童尼　　肖像有写真　　　　*5*

人称之赝品　　拙劣模仿君

勾画海伦面　　一切技巧新

希腊美公主　　君为着装人

明媚说春景　　丰饶写秋深

前者君形影　　形影君美淳　　　　*10*

后者君丰饶　　丰饶君示人

一切美形象　　侪辈看在心

一切外在美　　都与君平分

君心非常人　　君心自坚贞

译者感言：朋友美胜维纳斯，朋友美优阿童尼。

如此美貌心灵造，诗人诗笔出语奇。

54

O, how much more doth beauty beauteous seem

By that sweet ornament which truth doth give!

The rose looks fair, but fairer we it deem

For that sweet odour which doth in it live.

The canker-blooms have full as deep a dye   5

As the perfumed tincture of the roses,

Hang on such thorns, and play as wantonly

When summer's breath their maskèd buds discloses:

But, for their virtue only is their show,

They live unwoo'd, and unrespected fade;   10

Die to themselves. Sweet roses do not so;

Of their sweet deaths are sweetest odours made;

   And so of you, beauteous and lovely youth,

   When that shall vade, my verse distils your truth.

用芳香的玫瑰比喻美貌，远胜野蔷薇。

3.　　deem: 认为

5.　　canker: 溃疡；害虫

　　　blooms: 花

6.　　tincture: 色泽；颜料

7.　　wantonly: 任性地；放荡地

8.　　maskèd: 隐藏的

10.　unrespected: 不注意地

14.　that: your beauty, 你的美貌

　　　vade: fade, 枯萎

　　　distils: 蒸馏；提取……精华

54

美之为美者	真诚益温馨
美须真点缀	美妙称绝伦
玫瑰花因美	吾等思香淳
倾倒赏花者	一缕清香魂
无香野玫瑰	丰肥颜色深
秾丽好颜色	芳香玫瑰邻
挂于刺枝上	花开招蜂亲
一朝夏风至	蕾藏也销魂
野玫瑰花好	好处在形真
花开无人爱	花落寂无闻
死去自灭迹	怎比玫瑰馨
玫瑰甜蜜死	甜蜜最可人
君亦如玫瑰	美丽可爱春
韶华易逝去	吾诗提精纯

5

10

译者感言：妖艳动人红玫瑰，芬芳香甜沁人心。
　　　　　精华提取留春色，少年可人惜光阴。

55

Not marble, nor the gilded monuments

Of princes, shall outlive this powerful rhyme;

But you shall shine more bright in these contents

Than unswept stone, besmear'd with sluttish time.

When wasteful war shall statues overturn,   5

And broils root out the work of masonry,

Nor Mars his sword nor war's quick fire shall burn

The living record of your memory.

'Gainst death and all-oblivious enmity

Shall you pace forth; your praise shall still find room   10

Even in the eyes of all posterity

That wears this world out to the ending doom.

   So, till the judgement that yourself arise,

   You live in this, and dwell in lovers' eyes.

诗歌寿命长于磐石。

1. marble:　大理石
   gilded monuments:　镀金的纪念碑
4. unswept stone:　没打扫过的石碑
   besmeared:　弄脏
   sluttish:　邋遢的
6. broils:　争吵；骚乱
   masonry:　石建筑
9. oblivious:　忘却的
   enmity:　敌意
11. posterity:　后裔

55

亦非大理石	亦非碑镀金
王公思永久	强力吾诗存
凭吾写诗句	永葆君青春
君辉胜脏石	无情岁月侵
战争绝人性	雕像毁无存　　5
暴乱摧文明	建筑成粉尘
任凭战神剑	任凭兵火焚
记忆永不灭	鲜活记载君
不怕灭记忆	敢于斗死神
阔步向前迈	君有美名存　　10
后世子孙敬	举目仰至尊
后世延万代	除非末日临
接受审判前	君有美艳身
爱者眼中宝	诗里君恒存

译者感言：一切事务皆相对，无极大道近天机。

　　　　　诗歌磐石竞永远，聚讼万年徒嘘唏。

56

Sweet love, renew thy force; be it not said

Thy edge should blunter be than appetite,

Which but to-day by feeding is allay'd,

To-morrow sharpen'd in his former might;

So, love, be thou; although to-day thou fill   *5*

Thy hungry eyes even till they wink with fullness,

To-morrow see again, and do not kill

The spirit of love with a perpetual dullness.

Let this sad int'rim like the ocean be

Which parts the shore, where two contracted new   *10*

Come daily to the banks, that, when they see

Return of love, more blest may be the view;

    Or call it winter, which, being full of care,

    Makes summer's welcome thrice more wisht, more rare.

与"爱"讲话。爱起来似乎没个够。

1.　be it not said:　不要让人说
2.　blunter:　钝的
3.　allayed:　减轻
6.　wink:　眨眼
8.　perpetual:　永远的
9.　int'rim:　interim, 间歇
12.　blest:　赐福
译者感言：爱情甜蜜润心房，爱情餐饮生活长。
　　　　　　爱情饥饿不可忍，爱情初夏清风凉。

56

甜蜜之爱情	今可振雄风	
勿让人言钝	食欲胜爱情	
尽管今有食	满足肚丰盈	
明朝不果腹	饥饿更无情	
爱情亦如此	纵然饱眼睛	*5*
缘由眼饥饿	闭眼因太撑	
明日还想看	不会杀爱情	
漫长枯燥事	爱神难经营	
疏远期凄苦	浩瀚类沧溟	
拆散二情侣	热恋两岸情	*10*
隔海遥相望	朝朝暮暮情	
直至爱还日	相见情更浓	
因为忧充满	或可称为冬	
殷盼因稀有	夏来吾欢迎	

57

Being your slave, what should I do but tend

Upon the hours and times of your desire?

I have no precious time at all to spend,

Nor services to do, till you require.

Nor dare I chide the world-without-end hour   5

Whilst I, my sovereign, watch the clock for you,

Nor think the bitterness of absence sour

When you have bid your servant once adieu;

Nor dare I question with my jealous thought

Where you may be, or your affairs suppose,   10

But, like a sad slave, stay and think of nought

Save, where you are how happy you make those.

    So true a fool is love, that in your Will,

    Though you do any thing, he thinks no ill.

表现对友人的忠诚，如中国的高山流水恩义。

5.   chide: 责骂

6.   whilst: while
       sovereign: 君主

7.   sour: 心酸

8.   bid: 表示
       adieu: 再见

12.   Save, where you are how happy you make those: Except how happy you make those who are with you. 除了和你相处的人是多幸福

13.   So true a fool is love: 爱真是个傻瓜

57

甘为君奴仆	甘愿听传呼	
无论何时刻	为君欲望卒	
吾无宝贵时	不言有他图	
不敢自安排	只应君需求	
不敢怨时日	太长没理由	*5*
呼君吾主人	守时吾心留	
离别不敢想	酸痛苦心头	
仆人君解雇	那时君记否	
岂敢怀嫉妒	问君听情由	
何方君欲往	何事君欲谋	*10*
悲伤如奴仆	岂敢有他图	
惟想君约会	相聚乐悠悠	
爱乃真傻仆	随时听君呼	
君做任何事	赞美又伺候	

译者感言：高山流水诚高义，友人背弃伤别离。
　　　　　赤心守望归旧好，为奴静候再会期。

58

That god forbid that made me first your slave,

I should in thought control your times of pleasure,

Or at your hand the account of hours to crave,

Being your vassal, bound to stay your leisure!

O, let me suffer, being at your beck,   *5*

The imprison'd absence of your liberty;

And patience, tame to sufferance, bide each check,

Without accusing you of injury.

Be where you list, your charter is so strong,

That you yourself may privilege your time   *10*

To what you will; to you it doth belong

Yourself to pardon of self-doing crime.

    I am to wait, though waiting so be hell;

    Not blame your pleasure, be it ill or well.

同第 57 首，写诗人为友人奴仆，忍耐着责难和孤苦。

3. crave: 恳求；热望

    at your hand the account of hours to crave: 希望看到你的时间账本

4. vassal: 陪臣；奴仆

5. beck: 召唤

6. The imprison'd absence of your liberty: 你的自由离去让我像坐牢一样寂寞孤苦

7. tame to sufferance: 对苦难的驯服

    bide: 忍耐

    check: 指责，非难

8. injury: 不公正

58

神意本如此	吾为奴事君	
不容控制君	享乐之光阴	
不许干涉君	恳求之光阴	
作为君奴仆	听从放任君	
呜呼吾隐忍	摆弄任凭君	*5*
君可监禁吾	自由之外人	
逆来顺受者	默默含苦辛	
君已伤害吾	吾无怨恨心	
地方随意往	君为特权人	
君随心所欲	君有罪在身	*10*
君可自赦免	随心所欲人	
吾自耐心等	等候地火焚	
不责君放荡	好坏也不分	

9.　list:　喜欢
　　charter:　特权
译者感言：忠心为友为奴仆，甘愿寂寞无自由。
　　　　　　逆来顺受遭苦厄，苦海有涯君好逑。

59

If there be nothing new, but that which is

Hath been before, how are our brains beguiled,

Which, labouring for invention, bear amiss

The second burthen of a former child!

O, that record could with a backward look,   5

Even of five hundred courses of the sun,

Show me your image in some antique book,

Since mind at first in character was done!

That I might see what the old world could say

To this composed wonder of your frame;   10

Whether we are mended, or whe'r better they.

Or whether revolution be the same.

    O, sure I am, the wits of former days

    To subjects worse have given admiring praise.

第 59—75 首的主题为时间。该首讲朋友是多少世纪才出现的翩翩形体。

1.   is: exists, 存在
2.   Hath: Has
       beguiled: 欺骗
3.   bear amiss: brear amiss, 徒劳
4.   burthen: burden, 负担
5.   record: memory, 记忆
6.   five hundred courses of the sun: 五百年
8.   Since mind at first in character was done: 自从思想首先形成文字
11.   mended: 改进
12.   revolution: 循环

59

世上无新事	希腊古贤言
倘若为至理	吾辈心智偏
苦心勤创造	到头成枉然
前世之稚子	今生来人间
呜呼负担重	但愿倒流年 *5*
太阳天上转	已达五百圈
示吾君形象	古书寻某篇
从来靠文字	思想能讲全
如此吾能悟	旧世有何言
造就君玉体	风度自翩翩 *10*
吾辈正进步	还是胜从前
变来又变去	皆作如是观
吾敢直言兮	古时之圣贤
所赞之对象	远逊君容颜

译者感言：大象衍化生奇才，五百年后俊友来。
　　　　　赞颂多务多层次，何人聆听笑颜开。

60

Like as the waves make towards the pebbled shore,

So do our minutes hasten to their end;

Each changing place with that which goes before,

In sequent toil all forwards do contend.

Nativity, once in the main of light,   *5*

Crawls to maturity, wherewith being crown'd,

Crookèd eclipses 'gainst his glory fight,

And Time that gave doth now his gift confound.

Time doth transfix the flourish set on youth,

And delves the parallels in beauty's brow;   *10*

Feeds on the rarities of nature's truth,

And nothing stands but for his scythe to mow:

   And yet, to times in hope my verse shall stand,

   Praising thy worth, despite his cruel hand.

时间像大镰刀一样无情，在摧残着美妙的青春。

1. pebbled: 卵石的
3. changing place with: 代替
4. sequent: 连续的
   contend: 竞争，斗争
5. Nativity: 新生的婴儿
   main: 沧海，海洋
7. Crookèd: crooked, 邪恶的
   eclipses: [天]食
8. confound: 把···毁减掉
9. transfix: 移动

60

犹如波涛滚	卵石堤岩冲	
吾辈人生路	匆匆每分钟	
每分钟变化	变化每分钟	
连续见戮力	争先赶前程	
本来为雅童	跃入光海中	*5*
爬着壮年到	冠冕一时荣	
邪恶来侵蚀	遮没君光明	
时光前赠物	今撕物无形	
时光赠娇艳	青春美无踪	
刻君额折皱	夺君潘安容	*10*
自然有杰作	珍品吞腹中	
时光镰刀过	何物能逃生	
时光敢面对	吾诗超时空	
时光任残酷	诗颂君美名	

---

10. delves: 挖，掘
    parallels: 皱纹
12. mow: 刈，割
译者感言：事业有成靠时间，容颜摧残怨时间。
　　　　　时间并非无情物，善待时间好少年。

61

Is it thy will, thy image should keep open
My heavy eyelids to the weary night?
Dost thou desire my slumbers should be broken,
While shadows like to thee do mock my sight?
Is it thy spirit that thou send'st from thee   5
So far from home into my deeds to pry,
To find out shames and idle hours in me.
The scope and tenour of thy jealousy?
O, no! thy love, though much, is not so great;
It is my love that keeps mine eye awake;   10
Mine own true love that doth my rest defeat,
To play the watchman ever for thy sake:
    For thee watch I whilst thou dost wake elsewhere,
    From me far off, with others all too near.

友人的形象干扰了诗人的睡眠。
1.   Is it thy will, thy image should keep open:
     你是否想让你的影像使我总睁开
3.   slumbers: slmber, 睡眠
6.   pry: 窥探
8.   tenour: tenor, 意图
14. From me far off, with others all too near: 离我远远的，却和别人那么亲近
译者感言：朋友放荡远离去，不知为何难成眠。
          不见恨别图谋面，相逢或许更无言。

61

君是否有意　　试图用君形

撑开吾眼睑　　沉重对夜空

试图用欲望　　使吾睡不成

貌似君影子　　戏弄吾眼睛

是否君差遣　　一位小精灵　　　　　*5*

远道来替吾　　察看君行踪

是否吾越轨　　是否吾无行

成为君借口　　嫉妒已构成

呜呼吾言否　　爱广非沉雄

正因吾有爱　　难以闭眼睛　　　　　*10*

吾夜不能寐　　吾爱出真情

吾为君守夜　　直到红日升

吾在此守候　　别处逍遥宫

远远离开君　　他人享君情

62

Sin of self-love possesseth all mine eye,

And all my soul, and all my every part;

And for this sin there is no remedy,

It is so grounded inward in my heart.

Methinks no face so gracious is as mine,   5

No shape so true, no truth of such account;

And for myself mine own worth do define,

As I all other in all worths surmount.

But when my glass shows me myself indeed,

Beated and chopt with tanned antiquity,   10

Mine own self-love quite contrary I read;

Self so self-loving were iniquity.

 'Tis thee, myself, that for myself I praise,

 Painting my age with beauty of thy days.

自爱是一种罪过，较容易进入，读下去复杂。

4. grounded: 生根

7. for myself mine own worth do define: 我的优点在于界定我自己

8. As I all others in all worth surmount: 我超过了所有人的长处

10. tanned: 把……晒黑

  antiquity: 老年

12. Self so self-loving were iniquity: 自己这样自爱是一种罪

13. 'Tis thee, myself, that for myself I praise: 你就是我自己，我歌颂我就是为了你

译者感言：自感自爱自超尘，一切赞美为友人。

    镜中自知老年至，岂能顿悟去凡心。

62

全因吾自爱　　双眼雾朦胧
蒙住身全部　　蒙住吾魂灵
如此之罪孽　　医方潜无踪
它已缠住吾　　扎根在心灵
吾信无人比　　眉目美传情　　　　5
端正又英俊　　坦率又雍容
莫谓吾自信　　优点自己评
一身聚众美　　吾美居巅峰
一朝见真吾　　镜中见真容
面皱色憔悴　　苍老枯槁形　　　　*10*
始悟自爱苦　　方晓自怜疼
顾影自怜者　　太甚罪非轻
颂君犹颂君　　歌曲表心声
掩饰吾年岁　　用君美颜容

63

Against my love shall be as I am now,

With Time's injurious hand crushed and o'erworn;

When hours have drain'd his blood, and fill'd his brow

With lines and wrinkles; when his youthful morn

Hath travell'd on to age's steepy night;   5

And all those beauties whereof now he's king

Are vanishing or vanished out of sight,

Stealing away the treasure of his spring;

For such a time do I now fortify

Against confounding age's cruel knife,   10

That he shall never cut from memory

My sweet love's beauty, though my lover's life:

　　His beauty shall in these black lines be seen,

　　And they shall live, and he in them still green.

第 63—68 首，6 首诗全写诗人与所爱之人的对话。

该首写无情的时光会夺去爱人的青春美貌，诗人想在其诗歌里使其所爱之人永葆青春。

1.　Against my love shall be as I am now:　预防我之所爱将来会和我一样
2.　injurious:　有害的；致伤的
　　crushd:　粉碎
　　o'erworn:　消耗
3.　drain'd:　吸干
4.　morn:　morning，清晨
5.　steepy:　崎岖，陡峭
10.　confounding:　把……毁灭

63

吾爱犹如吾	对吾实无情	
任凭光阴虐	毒手损磨平	
光阴吮干血	滔威眉头逞	
沟壑皱纹满	青春痛无声	
青春入迟暮	生命路难平	*5*
风流青春貌	倜傥又多情	
或云正逝去	或曰逝无踪	
青春被偷去	宝藏被盗清	
为防此时刻	秣马又厉兵	
暮年如利剑	残酷又无情	*10*
光阴无此能	割断记忆情	
吾爱留甜美	吾爱无生命	
吾爱将永在	黝黑诗行中	
黝黑诗存世	吾爱万年青	

12.　though my lover's life:　虽然能砍断我爱人的生命
译者感言：青春本是时光恩，美貌缘由时光亲。·
　　　　　赐与收回时光意，天道轮回时光珍。

64

When I have seen by Time's fell hand defaced

The rich proud cost of outworn buried age;

When sometime lofty towers I see down-razed.

And brass eternal slave to mortal rage;

When I have seen the hungry ocean-gain   *5*

Advantage on the kingdom of the shore,

And the firm soil win of the watery main,

Increasing store with loss, and loss with store;

When I have seen such interchange of state,

Or state itself confounded to decay;   *10*

Ruin hath taught me thus to ruminate,—

That Time will come and take my love away.

  This thought is as a death, which cannot choose

  But weep to have that which it fears to lose.

　　得失无常，盈亏自然。第 1 行到第 12 行为一个句子，四个由 when 引导的时间状语从句，主句为第 11 行和第 12 行。脉络较为清晰。
1.　　fell: 残暴的
　　　defaced: 损伤外观
3.　　razed: 抹去
4.　　brass: 黄铜；高级官员
　　　mortal rage: 人类的暴力与愤怒
8.　　Increasing store with loss, and loss with store: 自己贮存的增加是由于别人的损失，弥补自己的损失是拿走别人的贮存
10.　confounded: 减少的
11.　ruminate: 沉思默想

64

时光之毒手	眼见来摧残	
无情毁富丽	前世豪华篇	
巍巍高塔倒	眼见化云烟	
永久之雕像	遭劫难保全	
吾见大海饿	吞噬忒贪婪	5
陆地之王国	大海三尺涎	
坚实岸上土	大海霸地盘	
得为彼所失	失为彼增添	
吾见吾变幻	情景多变迁	
盛况自有数	注定会凋残	10
废墟教会吾	沉思情爱缘	
时光无情至	吾爱携天边	
此念犹如死	难过选择关	
掩泣抓吾爱	恐失韶华年	

14.　weep to have that which it fears to lose:　哭泣着去占有害怕失去的东西

译者感言：河东河西三十年，山静水转得失间。

　　　　　无上正觉人间少，生存下去精进观。

65

Since brass, nor stone, nor earth, nor boundless sea,

But sad mortality o'ersways their power,

How with this rage shall beauty hold a plea,

Whose action is no stronger than a flower?

O, how shall summer's honey breath hold out   5

Against the wrackful siege of battering days,

When rocks impregnable are not so stout,

Nor gates of steel so strong, but Time decays?

O fearful meditation, where alack,

Shall Time's best jewel from Time's chest lie hid?   10

Or what strong hand can hold his swift foot back?

Or who his spoil of beauty can forbid?

   O, none, unless this miracle have might,

   That in black ink my love may still shine bright.

  人生无常，荣华富贵与美貌红颜如云烟。
2. mortality: 死亡
    o'ersways: 使倾覆
3. plea: 抗辩
4. Whose action is no stronger than a flower: 美的生命力不比一朵鲜花强
6. wreckful: ruinous, 毁灭的
    siege: 围攻
    battering: batter, 连续猛击
7. impregnable: 攻不破的
8. but time decays: 都不可避免地毁于时间
9. meditation: 思想

65

铜石与陆地　　大海莽苍苍
活力遭毒手　　阴惨曰死亡
美貌变娇弱　　如何对衰亡
衰亡性暴虐　　花比美貌强
呜呼夏气息　　如蜜之甘芳　　　　*5*
日日对暴虐　　围追堵截狂
君见磐石坚　　无奈也衰亡
君见铁门固　　锈蚀因时光
呜呼思可怖　　嗟夫处何乡
时光之至宝　　如何躲时光　　　　*10*
何处有巨手　　扯腿挡时光
何人能禁止　　美貌不抛荒
嗟手实无奈　　奇迹力量强
黝黑墨迹里　　吾爱放光芒

---

12. spoil: 劫掠
译者感言：瞬间享受即永恒，痛苦本自贪欲生。
　　　　　得失不计常安乐，清风明月诗无穷。

66

Tired with all these, for restful death I cry, —

As to behold desert a beggar born,

And needy Nothing trimm'd in jollity,

And purest Faith unhappily forsworn,

And gilded Honour shamefully misplaced,   5

And maiden Virtue rudely strumpeted.

And fight Perfection wrongfully disgraced,

And Strength by limping Sway disabled,

And Art made tongue-tied by Authority,

And Folly, doctor-like, controlling skill,   10

And simple Truth miscall'd Simplicity,

And captive Good attending captain Ill;

    Tired with all these, from these would I be gone,

    Save that, to die, I leave my love alone.

前 12 行为一个句子，有 10 行以连词 and 开头，可谓排比手法一典范。该诗揭示了许多社会上黑白颠倒，善恶不分，真假不辨等丑恶行径。

2.　As to behold desert a beggar born:　比如看到一个天才注定要生下来就是乞丐
3.　trimm'd:　打扮起来
　　jollity:　欢乐
4.　forsworn:　放弃
6.　strumpeted:　沦落为妓女
8.　limping sway:　跛子弄歪
10. folly, doctor-like, controlling skill:　愚蠢像博士控制着才华
译者感言：善恶并存天地生，三十六计思虑精。
　　　　　　抱怨痛斥不足贵，斗战能胜非恩荣。

66

厌倦一切事	吾求入黄泉	
恰如吾眼见	英才乞路边	
庸才草包兮	华衣最光鲜	
最终誓约兮	毁弃称无端	
滥送胡赏兮	高官名头衔	*5*
贞洁少女兮	狂暴遭摧残	
完美正义兮	蒙受不白冤	
健全民众兮	不抵瘸子权	
文化艺术兮	缄口对权奸	
伪博士帽兮	控制吾大贤	*10*
朴素真理兮	下士笑简单	
善伺候恶兮	恶行当长官	
厌倦一切事	吾想离人间	
只恐吾离去	吾爱形影单	

67

Ah, wherefore with infection should he live,

And with his presence grace impiety,

That sin by him advantage should achieve,

And lace itself with his society?

Why should false painting imitate his cheek,   *5*

And steal dead seeing of his living hue?

Why should poor beauty indirectly seek

Roses of shadow, since his rose is true?

Why should he live, now Nature bankrout is,

Beggar'd of blood to blush through lively veins?   *10*

For she hath no exchequer now but his,

And, proud of many, lives upon his gains.

    O, him she stores, to show what wealth she had

    In days long since, before these last so bad.

    诗人不愿同流合污。第 5—8 行写得很是优美，易读。大自然赐人以美，还要收回来保存。

1.   infection: 腐败
2.   impiety: 不虔诚
    with his presence grace impiety: 让人亵渎他的风雅
4.   lace: 用带子车紧
6.   hue: 颜色
9.   bankrout: bankrupt, 倒闭
11. exchequer: 国库；资金
12. lives upon his gains: 靠他的财源生活
14. In days long since: 在从前的日子

67

悲夫叹伊人	腐朽伴生活	
绰约有丰姿	亵渎受折磨	
亦有罪孽伴	伊人叹苦多	
装扮掩耳目	伊人竟为何	
美艳面颊上	骗人脂粉多	*5*
窃取死容颜	取代神鲜活	
伊人本玫瑰	寻美悲为何	
伊人美本真	玫瑰影描摹	
造化已破产	伊人仍苟活	
缺血滋朱颜	独自叹蹉跎	*10*
她有伊人美	此外空张罗	
往昔俊彦泉	今靠伊人活	
叹她藏伊人	以显财宝多	
藏宝过去时	今朝苦生活	

these last so bad: 最近这些日子如此糟糕
译者感言：道德高尚美容光，艳如玫瑰放清香。
　　　　　鲜活生动红尘世，难得开口笑群芳。

68

Thus is his cheek the map of days outworn,

When beauty lived and died as flowers do now,

Before these bastard signs of fair were born,

Or durst inhabit on a living brow;

Before the golden tresses of the dead,   5

The right of sepulchres, were shorn away,

To live a second life on second head;

Ere beauty's dead fleece made another gay;

In him those holy antique hours are seen,

Without all ornament, it self and true,   10

Making no summer of another's green,

Robbing no old to dress his beauty new;

   And him as for a map doth Nature store,

   To show false Art what beauty was of yore.

揭露用死人头发作假发，以及涂脂涂粉等恶俗之陋习。

1.　days outworn:　过去
3.　bastard:　伪装；卑劣
4.　durst:　胆大的
6.　sepulchres:　坟墓
7.　second head:　另一个人的头脑里
8.　fleece:　羊毛，头发
9.　antique hours:　往昔
10.　it self and true:　原来面目
12.　Robbing no old to dress his beauty new:　不掠夺故人来打扮新人
13.　him as for a map doth nature store:　大自然把他像图册一样保存

68

伊人面颊上	往昔岁月稠
美貌有衰盛	花开花落图
今朝假造美	往日此艺无
纵有假玩艺	胆敢上人头
亡者有金发	埋葬入坟丘
谁人曾动剪	无人斗胆偷
今朝得重视	戴上他人头
金发为他者	添美又遮羞
圣洁时刻在	峥嵘岁月稠
素面朝天者	铅美暗粉污
他者青翠色	勿作夏天图
不能盗死者	臭美制新服
伊人造化藏	恰如藏宝图
涂脂抹粉者	应叹古人优

5

10

14. of yore: 往昔，年华。整行意为"给假艺术展示过去的真美"

译者感言：素面朝天美淳真，善待故人最善心。

天生地造时运至，切莫轻抛贵精勤。

69

Those parts of thee that the world's eye doth view

Want nothing that the thought of hearts can mend;

All tongues, the voice of souls, give thee that due,

Uttering bare truth, even so as foes commend.

Thy outward thus with outward praise is crowned;　　　*5*

But those same tongues, that give thee so thine own,

In other accents do this praise confound

By seeing farther than the eye hath shown.

They look into the beauty of thy mind,

And that, in guess, they measure by thy deeds;　　　*10*

Then, churls, their thoughts, although their eyes were kind,

To thy fair flower add the rank smell of weeds:

　　But why thy odour matcheth not thy show,

　　The soil is this, that thou dost common grow.

外貌美、内心美以及生存环境对人的影响。

2.　Want nothing that the thought of hearts can mend:　什么也不欠缺，谁也想不出修改的主意

3.　give thee that due:　对待你很公正

4.　even so as foes commend:　这样即使敌人也无法否认

5.　outward praise:　公开的赞扬
　　crowned:　酬劳

7.　confound:　挫败

11.　churls:　性情粗暴

12.　rank smell of weeds:　野草的极难闻的气味

14.　soil:　生存环境

69

世人目共睹　　君之真容颜

无处不美丽　　无由去增删

君有好口碑　　由衷赞君颜

真心话出口　　敌手无案翻

君有外在美　　外美赢赞言　　　　5

同样为喉舌　　对君言另篇

深处估量君　　眼睛撂一边

另篇另腔调　　君之美摧残

窥探灵魂处　　内心美另言

或曰凭猜度　　君行衡量言　　　　10

纵然众粗鄙　　众目良善观

莠草之腐臭　　君之鲜花添

为何君声誉　　不符君美颜

土壤原如此　　污浊已不堪

译者感言：天生貌美众口夸，心灵之美称上佳。
　　　　　生活环境适愚昧，伟人圣者遭倾轧。

70

That thou art blamed shall not be thy defect,

For slander's mark was ever yet the fair;

The ornament of beauty is suspect,

A crow that flies in heaven's sweetest air.

So thou be good, slander doth but approve   5

Thy worth the greater, being wooed of time;

For canker vice the sweetest buds doth love,

And thou present'st a pure unstained prime.

Thou hast past by the ambush of young days,

Either not assailed, or victor being charged;   10

Yet this thy praise cannot be so thy praise,

To tie up envy evermore enlarged:

    If some suspect of ill masked not thy show,

    Then thou alone kingdoms of hearts shouldst owe.

青春美貌肯定会受到攻击责难，木秀于林，风必摧之。

1. defect: 错误
2. slander: 流言
   mark: 靶子
3. suspect: 猜忌
4. crow: 乌鸦
6. being wooed of time: 受到时光的追求，即青春韶华
7. vice: 恶，罪恶
8. unstained: 洁白无瑕
9. ambush: 埋伏
10. assailed: 攻击

70

君遭人诽谤	君错何人详
美丽为靶子	流言故谤伤
美丽遇猜忌	人谓美丽妆
长空碧如洗	一只乌鸦翔
若君有美德	毁谤假文章　　5
反证君高价	追恋有时光
甜蜜花蕾里	毒虫最爱藏
君年正纯洁	盛期多芳香
危险期度过	青春岁月长
君未遭埋伏	或曰敌不强　　10
如此赞美君	赞词长缨长
难缚嫉妒口	嫉妒愈猖狂
恶意之猜忌	未能仪容伤
君已众口得	君天下无双

12.　To tie up envy evermore enlarged:　拴住已经十分扩张的嫉妒
译者感言：年轻貌美乐逍遥，长舌流言脑后抛。
　　　　　　鲜花何惧毒虫害，遍吐芳香胜琼瑶。

71

No longer mourn for me when I am dead

Than you shall hear the surly sullen bell

Give warning to the world that I am fled

From this vile world, with vilest worms to dwell:

Nay, if you read this line, remember not   5

The hand that writ it; for I love you so,

That I in your sweet thoughts would be forgot,

If thinking on me then should make you woe.

O, if, I say, you look upon this verse

When I perhaps compounded am with clay,   10

Do not so much as my poor name rehearse;

But let your love even with my life decay;

    Lest the wise world should look into your moan,

    And mock you with me after I am gone.

丧钟为人送葬，蛆虫吞噬，人化为泥土，对朋友的爱却没有改变。

2.　surly:　阴郁的
　　　sullen:　愁眉不展的
3.　fled:　flee 的过去时，表示状态，意为我离开
4.　vile:　邪恶的
　　　vilest:　vilest, 最邪恶的
10.　compounded:　和……混在一起
11.　rehearse:　重复
13.　look into your moan:　追问你受的伤
14.　mock you with me after I am gone:　你我死后同样受到嘲弄

71

一朝吾去世	沉滞凄凉钟	
务必君节哀	不可放悲声	
通告世人知	今世吾无踪	
告别恶浊世	去会最毒虫	
君若读此诗	不必太动容	5
勿念谁手笔	爱君吾深情	
君思太甜蜜	记忆得永生	
倘若想到吾	君感胸口疼	
呜呼吾有言	吾诗更有情	
倘若那时刻	吾化泥土中	10
吾去固可怜	不必念吾名	
吾爱如吾命	化土无影踪	
唯恐光明界	闻君悲恸声	
吾已离尘世	人笑君多情	

译者感言：忽有一日闻丧钟，有人送行也从容。
　　　　　飘忽而来飘忽去，不染污秽朝天宫。

155

72

O, lest the world should task you to recite

What merit lived in me, that you should love,

After my death, dear love, forget me quite,

For you in me can nothing worthy prove;

Unless you would devise some virtuous lie,   *5*

To do more for me than mine own desert,

And hang more praise upon deceasèd I

Than niggard truth would willingly impart:

O, lest your true love may seem false in this,

That you for love speak well of me untrue,   *10*

My name be buried where my body is,

And live no more to shame nor me nor you.

　For I am shamed by that which I bring forth,

　And so should you, to love things nothing worth.

爱会产生善意的谎言。本来稀松平常的东西会受到不应该的称赞。此诗讲述简单。
1.　recite:　告辞
2.　merit:　长处
4.　For you in me can nothing worthy prove:　你在我身上找不到值得夸口的东西
5.　virtuous:　善良的
7.　deceasèd I:　长眠的我
8.　niggard:　吝啬的
　　impart:　昭示
10.　you for love speak well of me untrue:　你为了爱我而说假话称赞我
12.　live no more to shame nor me nor you:　不再活着而使我们二人都遭到羞辱

72

吾恐世人兮	问君何德行	
在世何功劳	君赐钟爱情	
吾离尘世后	悄然忘音容	
吾无些许事	劳君去动情	
善意之谎言	说出或许行	*5*
吾若有价值	过奖未必通	
吾身已长眠	过誉无用功	
勿浮夸过度	忌荒诞不经	
君宜明察兮	真爱成假情	
人恐君之爱	假经变真经	*10*
吾身已辞世	陪葬有吾名	
勿让名留世	君与吾羞蒙	
为吾携之物	满面带羞容	
君爱无须爱	君亦感脸红	

译者感言：审美之事任人评，黑白颠倒假大空。
　　　　　丑说成美美变丑，呼唤圣贤念包公。

73

That time of year thou mayst in me behold

When yellow leaves, or none, or few, do hang

Upon those boughs which shake against the cold,

Bare ruin'd choirs, where late the sweet birds sang.

In me thou see'st the twilight of such day   5

As after sunset fadeth in the west;

Which by and by black night doth take away,

Death's second self, that seals up all in rest.

In me thou see'st the glowing of such fire,

That on the ashes of his youth doth lie,   10

As the death-bed whereon it must expire.

Consumed with that which it was nourisht by.

   This thou perceivest, which makes thy love more strong,

   To love that well which thou must leave ere long.

   以 45 岁的年龄写老年的感觉，难为莎士比亚了，却也写出真情实感。诗的开头和中间都是一般道理。

2.   or none, or few: 或者树叶尽落，或者挂着几片叶子

3.   boughs: 大树枝

4.   choirs: 唱诗班，唱诗坛

8.   Death's second half: 死亡的化身，即黑夜

    that seals up all in rest: 封盖住一切，使其安息

11.   expire: 断气

12.   Consumed with that which it was nourished by: 用滋养生命的东西把生命耗尽

13.   perceivest: perceive, 察觉

14.   ere long: 不久

73

或许君见吾	生命入秋天
枝头黄叶落	或留几叶悬
瑟瑟对秋风	身寒心亦寒
舞台已荒废	往昔鸟声欢
君于吾身上	残光见苍然
正如夕阳落	西天暮衰残
黑夜已降临	死亡彼代言
携带死亡去	密封离恨天
君见吾身上	火热青春年
躺在灰烬里	曾风度翩翩
恰似躺灵床	气息已奄奄
火焰滋养吾	又与吾颓颜
君见此一切	君爱大无边
为爱君速去	归期是何年

5

10

译者感言：孤寂凄凉了此生，残叶寒塘叹冷清。
　　　　　善行善念慰忠骨，一点爱心伴晚钟。

74

But be contented: when that fell arrest

Without all bail shall carry me away,

My life hath in this line some interest,

Which for memorial still with thee shall stay.

When thou reviewest this, thou dost review   *5*

The very part was consecrate to thee:

The earth can have but earth, which is his due;

My spirit is thine, the better part of me:

So, then, thou hast but lost the dregs of life,

The prey of worms, my body being dead;   *10*

The coward conquest of a wretch's knife,

Too base of thee to be remembered.

    The worth of that is that which it contains,

    And that is this, and this with thee remains.

该首仍写死亡，用了一些法律术语。
1.　　fell: 致命的
2.　　bail: 保释
6.　　The very part was consecrate to thee:　奉献。此行意为，最好的部分献给了你
7.　　The earth can have but earth:　尘土只能收回尘土
　　　　due:　应得物
8.　　the better part of me:　精神
9.　　dregs:　残渣
11.　wretch's:　可耻的人，这里指时间
12.　base:　低级的

74

吾请君勿虑	拘捕固凶残	
亦无人保释	带吾上南监	
吾命有利息	利存吾诗篇	
作为纪念品	长伴君身边	
该诗请君读	再读吾诗篇	5
拙诗有主旨	精萃为君言	
尘土归尘土	本原为本原	
神思吾精髓	神思为君贤	
君因有所失	生命渣滓篇	
吾去留躯壳	蛆虫得饱餐	10
时光如镰刀	怯懦遭凶残	
躯壳何足贵	君勿凋朱颜	
所贵归何处	躯壳最里边	
吾诗即所贵	与君永世传	

---

13. The worth of that is that which it contains: 躯体的价值大于其包含的精神
14. that is this: 精神就是我的诗
译者感言：只把躯体留死神，何人来交保释金。
　　　　　　自觉精神更宝贵，不悟无物难染尘。

75

So are you to my thoughts as food to life,

Or as sweet-season'd showers are to the ground;

And for the peace of you I hold such strife

As 'twixt a miser and his wealth is found;

Now proud as an enjoyer, and anon   5

Doubting the filching age will steal his treasure;

Now counting best to be with you alone,

Then better'd that the world may see my pleasure:

Sometime all full with feasting on your sight,

And by and by clean starved for a look;   10

Possessing or pursumg no delight,

Save what is had or must from you be took.

   Thus do I pine and surfeit day by day,

   Or gluttoning on all, or all away.

把朋友看成是精神食粮，想饱餐朋友的美色、秀色，也没有什么节制。

3.   strife: 精神斗争，精神挣扎

4.   'twixt: between, 在……之间

5.   anon: 不久以后

6.   filching: 偷

7.   counting: 考虑，认为

9.   Sometime all full with feasting on your sight: 有时候我已饱餐了你的秀色

10. by and by: 很快

     clean: 完全地

12. Save: 除了

13. pine: 饥饿；渴望；憔悴

75

吾与吾思想	食物与民生
甘霖及时降	大地享太平
为君之和顺	吾心不安宁
犹如守财奴	总为财富争
或为财富喜	或为财伤情
身处惯偷世	梁上君子行
有时想见君	独与君谈情
自觉最幸运	世人皆知情
有时吾拼命	饱餐君芳容
忽而又喊饿	惟觉腹空空
吾不图安乐	亦缺世恩荣
除非君欲赐	君已赐吾生
如此天天饱	如此腹空空
暴食或暴饮	西风与西风

5

10

---

surfeit: 饮食过度

14. gluttoning: 大吃

译者感言：动人美色如美景，见到艰难离时空。
　　　　　深度旅游固可敬，仙桃一口牡丹红。

76

Why is my verse so barren of new pride,

So far from variation or quick change?

Why, with the time, do I not glance aside

To new-found methods and to compounds strange?

Why write I still all one, ever the same,　　　　　　　　5

And keep invention in a noted weed,

That every word doth almost tell my name,

Showing their birth, and where they did proceed?

O, know, sweet love, I always write of you,

And you and love are still my argument;　　　　　　　10

So all my best is dressing old words new,

Spending again what is already spent:

　For as the sun is daily new and old,

　So is my love still telling what is told.

　　第 76—79 首，写诗人自愧诗作比不上另一诗人。本首写诗人诗才欠缺，风格千篇一律。诗句流畅易读。

1.　barren: 贫乏的

4.　compounds strange:　诡异的复合名词

6.　noted weed:　陈旧的风格体裁

8.　proceed:　发出

10.　argument:　主题

11.　all my best is dressing old words new:　我的最妙处在于写诗时旧瓶装新酒

译者感言：写作贵在多诗才，变化万千意象来。

　　　　　　花样翻新缪斯顾，真情二字窍门开。

76

人言吾诗句	缺乏颜色新	
不善时尚礼	多样变化勤	
为何不追风	诗法效他人	
笔调好创意	复合词求新	
为何同一体	为何特单纯	*5*
为何曰创作	华服曰超群	
几乎每一字	吾名已示人	
表明其身世	显示其家门	
吾爱应知兮	吾诗惟写君	
吾身无情爱	入诗入吾心	*10*
吾诗最长处	旧瓶装酒新	
旧词已用过	再用亦温馨	
太阳每日落	太阳每日新	
吾爱已讲述	愈讲愈情深	

77

Thy glass will show thee how thy beauties wear,

Thy dial how thy precious minutes waste;

The vacant leaves thy mind's imprint will bear,

And of this book this learning mayst thou taste.

The wrinkles which thy glass will truly show,   5

Of mouthed graves will give thee memory;

Thou by thy dial's shady stealth mayst know

Time's thievish progress to eternity.

Look, what thy memory cannot contain,

Commit to these waste blanks, and thou shalt find   10

Those children nursed, deliver'd from thy brain,

To take a new acquaintance of thy mind.

    These offices, so oft as thou wilt look,

    Shall profit thee, and much enrich thy book.

    日月如梭，韶华易逝。诗歌写在本子上，可以留住些许记忆。

2.   dial: 日晷

3.   The vacant leaves: 空白页

        imprint: 印

6.   mouthed: open-mouthed，张着大口的

8.   eternity: 永恒

10.   Commit to these waste blanks: 记在这些白纸上

12.   take a new acquaintance of thy mind: 在你脑海里留下新的印象

13.   offices: 镜子

译者感言：日晷提醒流年逝，菱花显示美有期。

            空白纸本留诗句，人类存在见情痴。

77

菱花告诉君　　美颜正衰残
日晷提醒君　　宝镜光阴完
时光空白页　　君思留诗篇
请君细品味　　书中有箴言
菱花告实情　　皱纹在里边　　　　　　5
坟墓大张口　　君应虑残年
勤君早醒悟　　日晷阴影言
光阴正溜走　　永恒步蹒跚
凡事难保留　　均交此荒滩
不被记忆累　　君另有新篇　　　　　　10
君有群儿女　　皆与念结缘
催君再审视　　新友非一般
君身有要务　　勤政无清闲
君得益非浅　　书多济世言

78

So oft have I invoked thee for my Muse,

And found such fair assistance in my verse,

As every alien pen hath got my use,

And under thee their poesy disperse.

Thine eyes, that taught the dumb on high to sing,   *5*

And heavy ignorance aloft to fly,

Have added feathers to the learned's wing,

And given grace double majesty.

Yet be most proud of that which I compile,

Whose influence is thine, and born of thee: *10*

In others'works thou dost but mend the style,

And arts with thy sweet graces graced be;

But thou art all my art, and dost advance

As high as learning my rude ignorance.

把朋友当作灵感的缪斯。此缪斯无比神奇，点石成金。

1.   invoked: 乞求，恳求
3.   alien: 异己的
     hath got my use: 学了我的窍门
4.   poesy: 诗歌
     disperse: 出版发行
5.   on high: 大声
6.   aloft to fly: 翱翔高空
8.   double majesty: 双重的尊严
9.   compile: 创作
11. mend: 改进

78

君为吾缪斯	吾常求诗神	
念吾诗篇里	获取灵感真	
每位作诗人	皆学吾窍门	
全由君惠顾	他者教诗文	
君目催哑巴	唱诗响入云	*5*
愚顽也获利	高飞夸不群	
恰如驯鹰术	博学添羽新	
温文尔雅者	双重威严人	
而今吾有诗	自豪自属君	
诗来君影响	诗生自君身	*10*
格调多润饰	他者教诗文	
他者发诗文	优雅助清新	
对于吾创作	君投全身心	
君送愚钝吾	扶摇上青云	

13.　advance：提高

译者感言：写诗感谢众女神，朋友真情得诗心。
　　　　　诗艺才学皆有长，他人摹仿渡要津。

79

Whilst I alone did call upon thy aid,

My verse alone had all thy gentle grace;

But now my gracious numbers are decay'd,

And my sick Muse doth give another place.

I grant, sweet love, thy lovely argument   *5*

Deserves the travail of a worthier pen;

Yet what of thee thy poet doth invent

He robs thee of, and pays it thee again.

He lends thee virtue, and he stole that word

From thy behaviour; beauty doth he give,   *10*

And found it in thy cheek; he can afford

No praise to thee but what in thee doth live.

　　Then thank him not for that which he doth say,

　　Since what he owes thee thou thyself dost pay.

诗歌创作的艰辛。诗作得到人们的喜爱更需要时日。

3. gracious numbers: 优雅的诗歌
4. give another place: 让位于别人
6. travail: 苦功
12. No praise to thee but what in thee doth live: 称赞的话没有一句是你自身不具备的
14. he owes thee thou thyself dost pay: 他所欠你的正是你的确已付出的。诗中的 he 同第 8 行的 He，均指另一个诗人

译者感言：文人相轻实可悲，艺人自视他人非。
　　　　　　众口难调追虚誉，智商情商感颜回。

79

吾曾只身去	真心求助君	
吾诗独有韵	优雅而温馨	
今朝吾诗变	诗句失清新	
吾有病缪斯	宝座让他人	
吾爱容吾言	吾认吾爱亲	*5*
君爱题材美	椽笔赋诗新	
他者诗篇献	着力赞颂君	
诗篇去自君	抢来又献人	
他者赐美德	偷儿造语新	
新语本君行	君容如美神	*10*
他者颂君美	用意非本心	
赞美词种种	早该归于君	
他者多好语	不劳君谢忱	
他者还君债	君收自安心	

80

O, how I faint when I of you do write,

Knowing a better spirit doth use your name,

And in the praise thereof spends all his might,

To make me tongue-tied, speaking of your fame!

But since your worth, wide as the ocean is,   *5*

The humble as the proudest sail doth bear,

My saucy bark, inferior far to his,

On your broad main doth wilfully appear.

Your shallowest help will hold me up afloat,

While he upon your soundless deep doth ride;   *10*

Or, being wracked, I am worthless boat,

He of tall building and of goodly pride:

    Then if he thrive, and I be cast away,

    The worst was this; my love was my decay.

诗人对自己的诗歌有太多的不自信。把自己的创作比作大海中微不足道的一叶扁舟。

1.   faint: 心灰意懒

3.   in the praise thereof spends all his might: 他用尽全力对你加以称赞

4.   tongue-tied: 箝口结舌

7.   saucy bark: 莽撞的树皮，即诗人的诗歌

8.   broad main: 浩淼的海面

9.   shallowest: 最浅的

       help: 海水

       afloat: 浮泛

10.   soundless deep: 无底的深海

80

<table>
<tr><td>吾觉气馁兮</td><td>握笔写到君</td><td></td></tr>
<tr><td>用君之大名</td><td>杰出有他人</td><td></td></tr>
<tr><td>他人尽全力</td><td>诗篇歌颂君</td><td></td></tr>
<tr><td>为使吾缄口</td><td>君之大名尊</td><td></td></tr>
<tr><td>君有大恩德</td><td>天高海洋深</td><td>5</td></tr>
<tr><td>大海载大船</td><td>小船也施仁</td><td></td></tr>
<tr><td>吾有小舢板</td><td>自卑不敢拼</td><td></td></tr>
<tr><td>浩瀚沧溟里</td><td>不做撑船人</td><td></td></tr>
<tr><td>浅浅一汪水</td><td>足容舴艋身</td><td></td></tr>
<tr><td>他人之艨艟</td><td>悄航大洋深</td><td>10</td></tr>
<tr><td>一叶舟覆吾</td><td>叹不名一文</td><td></td></tr>
<tr><td>他船称富丽</td><td>高耸自骄矜</td><td></td></tr>
<tr><td>倘若他船返</td><td>吾舟翻不闻</td><td></td></tr>
<tr><td>最糟莫过此</td><td>吾爱毁吾身</td><td></td></tr>
</table>

---

11. wracked: 沉没
12. goodly pride: 壮丽
13. cast away: 抛弃；沉船
14. my love was my decay: 我的爱就是我的毁灭

译者感言：诗国驰骋喜骏马，大海扬帆驾艨艟。
　　　　　一叶扁舟富诗意，诗人悲音触心灵。

81

Or I shall live your epitaph to make,

Or you survive when I in earth am rotten;

From hence your memory death cannot take,

Although in me each part will be forgotten.

Your name from hence immortal life shall have,   *5*

Though I, once gone, to all the world must die;

The earth can yield me but a common grave,

When you entombed in men's eyes shall lie.

Your monument shall be my gentle verse,

Which eyes not yet created shall o'er-read;   *10*

And tongues to be your being shall rehearse,

When all the breathers of this world are dead;

　You still shall live-such virtue hath my pen—

　Where breath most breathes, even in the mouths of men.

即使朋友离开人世，其大名将永垂万古，因为有诗人不朽的诗句。

1.　epitaph: 墓志铭
3.　From hence: 离开这个世界
4.　in me each part: 我的一切
6.　to all the world must die: 死后默默无闻
7.　yield: 给与
10.　eyes not yet created shall o'er-read: 未来的眼睛将会反复阅读
11.　tongues to be your being shall rehearse: 未来的舌头将反复吟诵你的生平
13.　virtue: 力量，魅力
译者感言：死后人身化泥土，功名利禄如云浮。
　　　　　　不朽名声人思念，善良愿望神仙图。

81

<table>
<tr><td>或曰吾存世</td><td>撰君墓志铭</td><td></td></tr>
<tr><td>或曰吾化土</td><td>君寿曰长生</td><td></td></tr>
<tr><td>死神曰无计</td><td>君名记忆中</td><td></td></tr>
<tr><td>尽管吾一切</td><td>人们忘无踪</td><td></td></tr>
<tr><td>长生不老者</td><td>吾君享尊荣</td><td>5</td></tr>
<tr><td>尽管吾逝去</td><td>尘世涉无踪</td><td></td></tr>
<tr><td>一抔黄土掩</td><td>坟丘忒普通</td><td></td></tr>
<tr><td>君将埋心底</td><td>万人心目中</td><td></td></tr>
<tr><td>吾有诗优美</td><td>写君墓碑丰</td><td></td></tr>
<tr><td>后世有众目</td><td>细读感心胸</td><td>10</td></tr>
<tr><td>后世有众口</td><td>吟咏胜诵经</td><td></td></tr>
<tr><td>今朝之尘世</td><td>众生逝无踪</td><td></td></tr>
<tr><td>吾笔挽狂澜</td><td>吾君得永生</td><td></td></tr>
<tr><td>鲜活生命里</td><td>万众口碑中</td><td></td></tr>
</table>

82

I grant thou wert not married to my Muse,

And therefore mayst without attaint o'erlook

The dedicated words which writers use

Of their fair subject, blessing every book.

Thou art as fair in knowledge as in hue,   5

Finding thy worth a limit past my praise;

And therefore art enforced to seek anew

Some fresher stamp of the time-bettering days.

And do so, love; yet when they have devised

What strainèd touches rhetoric can lend,   10

Thou truly fair wert truly sympathized

In true plain words by thy true-telling friend;

And their gross painting might be better used

Where cheeks need blood; in thee it is abused.

尽管别的许多诗人辞藻华丽，花样翻新，却比不上笃实质朴的真话。

1. wert: were
2. attaint: 污点
3. dedicated: 忠诚的；奉献的
4. blessing every book: 奖赏每本诗集的作者
5. hue: 容貌
6. a limit past: 超过界限
7. enforced: 强迫
8. the time-bettering days: 风格更新的时代
9. they: 同第三行的 writers，即别的诗人
10. strainèd touches: 浮夸的辞藻

82

君与吾缪斯　　未结好姻缘
承认君自由　　随意君浏览
他者有诗作　　诗多高雅言
颂扬美君子　　庇佑好诗篇
君才美出众　　君美貌非凡　　　　　　5
君行有成德　　吾颂难成篇
无奈君另谋　　寻求新结缘
文风追时尚　　诗章图新鲜
吾爱尽随意　　他者多赞言
旨在描绘君　　夸饰以成篇　　　　　　10
君身有真美　　真美得自天
真美用真语　　真语挚友言
脂粉因秾丽　　岂增君玉颜
面颊缺血色　　涂抹或红鲜

---

13. gross painting: 浓施脂粉
14. abused: 滥用；误用
译者感言：作诗不外写做人，阅历思维出语新。
　　　　　大朴大华各自爱，千姿百态始到真。

83

I never saw that you did painting need,

And therefore to your fair no painting get;

I found, or thought I found, you did exceed

The barren tender of a poet's debt:

And therefore have I slept in your report,   5

That you yourself, being extant, well might show

How far a modern quill doth come too short,

Speaking of worth, what worth in you doth grow.

This silence for my sin you did impute,

Which shall be most my glory, being dumb;   10

For I impair not beauty, being mute,

When others would give life, and bring a tomb.

　　There lives more life in one of your fair eyes

　　Than both your poets can in praise devise.

对朋友的美保持沉默。无言的赞美有更强大的生命力。

4.　The barren tender of a poet's debt:　barren, 无价值的；tender, 应付的债。该行诗意为
　　"一个诗人必须偿还的无价值的债务"

5.　have I slept in your report:　我休息了一下，没有再赞颂你

6.　extant:　现尚存的

7.　quill:　翎笔，即鹅毛笔

8.　speaking of worth:　讲到美德

9.　This silence for my sin you did impute:　You did impute this silence for my sin.
　　impute:　归咎于。你把我的沉默看作是罪行

11.　impair:　损伤

83

从来无此意	君须涂脂粉	
君有潘安貌	素面方见真	
吾意吾有悟	君美胜斯文	
他人有诗句	无聊献与君	
因此吾嗜睡	无诗赞美君	*5*
君生于今世	可以告世人	
庸俗鹅毛笔	无力来写真	
若言君才德	无以复加身	
沉默违君意	误认吾罪人	
无言为吾誉	沉默是黄金	*10*
吾无言哑口	何提君美真	
他言赐永生	实则为荒坟	
君自有明目	明目善察心	
诔词岂长寿	君胜两诗人	

译者感言：美貌也靠诗赞颂，美丽辞藻叹贫穷。
　　　　　容颜鲜活姿态妙，常看常新花园行。

84

Who is it that says most? which can say more

Than this rich praise, that you alone are you?

In whose confine immured is the store

Which should example where your equal grew.

Lean penury within that pen doth dwell   *5*

That to his subject lends not some small glory;

But he that writes of you, if he can tell

That you are you, so dignifies his story;

Let him but copy what in you is writ,

Not making worse what nature made so clear,   *10*

And such a counterpart shall fame his wit,

Making his style admired everywhere.

　　You to your beauteous blessings add a curse,

　　Being fond on praise, which makes your praises worse.

"唯你是你" 是对美的最高赞美。第 1—4 行要细细咀嚼，回环往复，方可得其真义。
3.　confine: 范围
　　immured: 监禁
4.　example: 说明
　　where your equal grew: 来和你匹敌
5.　Lean: 瘦的；贫瘠的
　　penury: 赤贫
　　pen: 诗人
6.　to his subject lends not some small glory: 不能给他所写的物件增一点光
8.　dignifies: 加以荣誉
11.　counterpart: 照抄

84

谁人能超越	谁人能说清	
谁人享盛誉	非君谁尊荣	
君藏君之美	全为美颜容	
富源自身蕴	吾与君争宠	
寒酸有秃笔	岂能来争锋	*5*
难添花上锦	寸辉不能增	
写者若言语	君有真我容	
堂皇誉其句	仿君文名隆	
造物有奇迹	损伤人心疼	
他者事模仿	遂有大名声	*10*
随处有赞誉	文采胜但丁	
海内作诗者	追捧其文风	
君有君美貌	增添喝彩声	
不因贪赞誉	赞誉鸿毛轻	

13.　　You to your beauteous blessings add a curse:　你对于你的美好祝福加以诅咒
译者感言：郊寒岛瘦好诗好，清水芙蓉我醉心。
　　　　　瘦硬通神少陵句，苦读漫游诗法新。

85

My tongue-tied Muse in manners holds her still,

While comments of your praise, richly compiled,

Reserve their character with golden quill,

And precious phrase by all the Muses filed.

I think good thoughts, whilst other write good words,   *5*

And, like unlettered clerk, still cry Amen

To every hymn that able spirit affords

In polisht form of well-refinèd pen.

Hearing you praised, I say 'Tis so,' tis true,

And to the most of praise add something more;   *10*

But that is in my thought, whose love to you,

Though words come hindmost, holds his rank before.

    Then others for the breath of words respect,

    Me for my dumb thoughts, speaking in effect.

这首诗仍在写诗人喜欢朴实的文风，仍在赞扬哑口无言之珍贵。
1. in manners: 为礼貌起见
3. their character with golden quill: 他们的鹅毛笔写下的辉煌文字
4. filed: 锉光
6. unlettered clerk: 不识字的牧师
7. hymn: 赞美诗，圣歌
   able spirit: 有天赋的诗人
   affords: 提供
8. well-refinèd pen: 精炼的笔调
9. Hearing you praised: 听到有人赞美你
11. whose love to you: 我对你的爱

85

吾有哑缪斯	礼貌默无言	
他人赞美君	巨制加鸿篇	
辉煌有诗句	下笔成千言	
缪斯全上阵	赞词谋珠联	
吾思新创意	他者写好言	5
牧师欠文墨	阿门叫声连	
名家名颂词	妙文曰连篇	
精美曰文笔	锤炼高人言	
连声曰诺诺	颂君响耳边	
若遇最佳颂	吾将字句添	10
深心出字句	心灵爱之源	
最迟出字句	爱意最居先	
他人诗华丽	可敬有长编	
吾思喜静默	可敬无虚言	

---

12. hindmost: 最落后
    rank: 高位，显贵
13. others for the breath of words respect: respect others for their words, 尊敬他们，为他们的言辞

译者感言：有人喜雄辩滔滔，有人爱风格高标。
　　　　　莫责怪文风质朴，道不远人真情剖。

86

Was it the proud full sail of his great verse,

Bound for the prize of all-too-precious you,

That did my ripe thoughts in my brain inhearse,

Making their tomb the womb wherein they grew?

Was it his spirit, by spirits taught to write   *5*

Above a mortal pitch, that struck me dead?

No, neither he, nor his compeers by night

Giving him aid, my verse astonished.

He, nor that affable familiar ghost

Which nightly gulls him with intelligence,   *10*

As victors, of my silence cannot boast;

I was not sick of any fear from thence:

    But when your countenance fill'd up his lime.

    Then lackt I matter; that enfeebled mine.

另一个诗人的雄浑诗句给了诗人太大的刺激，几乎把作者吓晕。

1. his: 另一个诗人的
2. Bound for the prize of all too precious you: 前去劫掠太宝贵的你
3. inhearse: 葬送；暂不写诗
4. the womb: 诗人的思想
5. spirit: 想象力
   spirits: 追随个人的精灵
6. mortal pitch: 道德高度
   struck me dead: 使我哑口无言
7. compeers: 朋友，同志
8. astonished: 因惊诧而沉默

86

他者雄诗句	大海扬风帆
见君就劫掠	君价称顶尖
君思固成熟	禁锢无诗篇
脑中已窒息	子官坟墓观
他者有灵魂	幽灵任教官　　　　*5*
诗作惊俗眼	致使吾伤残
岂能让他者	伙伴子夜天
助他成诗赋	吾诗却软瘫
他者难得逞	幽灵助无干
幽灵称友善	欺他智不全　　　　*10*
自夸控制吾	噤吾若寒蝉
宁可被打死	吾不会吓瘫
惟有君激励	助他壮诗篇
吾将失灵感	作品尽空言

9.　affable:　和蔼可亲的，殷勤的
10.　gulls:　欺骗
11.　victors:　胜利者
12.　from thence:　他和他的精灵
13.　countenance:　嘉许，鼓励
14.　enfeebled:　削弱
译者感言：诗应得气气须壮，气壮山河人气强。
　　　　　　阴阳互补勿偏废，众口夸赞个性扬。

87

Farewell! thou art too dear for my possessing,

And like enough thou know'st thy estimate:

The charter of thy worth gives thee releasing;

My bonds in thee are all determinate.

For how do I hold thee but by thy granting?   *5*

And for that riches where is my deserving?

The cause of this fair gift in me is wanting,

And so my patent back again is swerving.

Thyself thou gavest, thy own worth then not knowing,

Or me, to whom thou gavest it, else mistaking;   *10*

So thy great gift, upon misprision growing,

Comes home again, on better judgement making.

    Thus have I had thee, as a dream doth flatter,

    In sleep a king, but waking no such matter.

诗人认为高攀不上他的好友。诗中用了一些法律词语。

2.   like enough: 显然
    estimate: 价值
3.   releasing: 退出
    bonds: 根据誓约应得的权利
5.   how do I hold thee but by thy granting: 不经您准许，我怎样占有你
6.   for that riches where is my deserving: 我怎能配上享受那份财富
7.   The cause of this fair gift: 这种美惠的理由
8.   patent: 专利
    swerving: 转向
9.   thy own worth then not knowing: 你未清楚自身的价值

87

吾与君离别	君贵攀难成	
君知君身价	显然不可轻	
君有权取舍	身份感天公	
吾与君契约	至此皆有终	
未经君允诺	岂能霸君情	5
君财称巨富	享有吾无功	
无由伸吾手	厚礼收难成	
无奈交专利	呜呼吾心疼	
二人有情爱	君价君不清	
君钟情于吾	错爱吾心惊	10
大礼君错赠	吾心知肚明	
经过细思忖	又回君门庭	
吾曾占有君	春秋大梦中	
梦中吾称帝	梦醒万事空	

---

10. Or me, to whom thou gavest it, else mistaking:　Or else mistaking me, to whom you gave it. 诗中"it"指厚礼，意为：也许你看错了我，看成了受惠者

11. misprision: 错误
　　growing: 产生

13. flatter: 得意

译者感言：朋友相交靠感情，不必自卑不骄横。
　　　　　　切莫奢望图占有，相帮度难灵犀通。

88

When thou shalt be disposed to set me light,

And place my merit in the eye of scorn,

Upon thy side against myself I'll fight,

And prove thee virtuous, though thou art forsworn.

With mine own weakness being best acquainted,   *5*

Upon thy part I can set down a story

Of faults conceal'd, wherein I am attainted;

That thou, in losing me, shalt win much glory:

And I by this will be a gainer too;

For bending all my loving thoughts on thee,   *10*

The injuries that to myself I do,

Doing thee vantage, double-vantage me.

    Such is my love, to thee I so belong,

    That for thy right myself will bear all wrong.

朋友可以看不起诗人，诗人可以忍受一切。如果真如此，则难能可贵。

1.   disposed: 决定
     light: 看轻
4.   forsworn: 发誓抛弃
6.   Upon thy part: 以你的名义
     set down a story: 捏造谎言
7.   concealed: 隐藏，隐瞒
     attainted: 感染
10.   bending: 倾注
12.   vantage: 优势

88

倘若有一日	君将吾看轻
使吾受轻蔑	处广众大厅
吾亦跟随君	申斥已无能
证实非君错	固然少交情
弱点吾自知	缺憾吾自明　　5
吾不避隐私	自责黑包公
吾错无人指	吾伤无人疼
吾言为君助	吾离因吾行
君行亦助吾	吾赢好名声
吾倾一腔爱	同君山海情　　10
吾自诋毁吾	吾自有苦衷
于君大有利	于吾倍收成
如此表吾爱	于君一股绳
为君有美誉	苦恼吾担承

译者感言：交友二字贵宽容，彼此大度增感情。
　　　　　平等亲爱危难助，大爱无疆慕飞鸿。

89

Say that thou didst forsake me for some fault,

And I will comment upon that offence:

Speak of my lameness, and I straight will halt,

Against thy reasons making no defence.

Thou canst not, love, disgrace me half so ill,   5

To set a form upon desired change,

As I'll myself disgrace: knowing thy will,

I will acquaintance strangle, and look strange;

Be absent from thy walks; and in my tongue

Thy sweet beloved name no more shall dwell,   10

Lest I, too much profane, should do it wrong,

And haply of our old acquaintance tell.

 For thee, against myself I'll vow debate,

 For I must ne'er love him whom thou dost hate.

友人抛弃诗人或许是因为诗人有什么过错。诗中表现对友人的理解。
1. forsake: 遗弃
2. offence: 冒犯
3. lameness: 瘸子
 halt: 跛行
5. disgrace me half so ill: 我难堪的一半
6. To set a form upon: 借给一个好容貌
7. thy will: 你想要的
8. strangle: 使窒息
 look strange: 作为陌路人
9. Be absent from thy walks: 避免在你的路上走

89

若言君抛弃	吾错为原因	
吾对君冒犯	缘故诉与君	
呼吾为瘸拐	立即现吾身	
君有君理由	吾岂冤屈伸	
君爱使小性	辱吾事纷纷	*5*
难堪吾自悟	惟吾知君心	
不及一半罪	自贬自认真	
与君绝来日	同为陌路人	
远离君常往	舌端不提君	
君姓固甜蜜	君名固可亲	*10*
惟恐太亵渎	惟恐错毫分	
往昔一旦忆	交往情景新	
发誓自我战	缘由只为君	
吾生不钟爱	君之陌路人	

11.　profane:　亵渎
12.　tell:　谈起
13.　vow debate:　发誓要打一仗
14.　him:　Shakespeare，莎士比亚
译者感言：爱情盲目爱粗鲁，为了爱情装胡涂。
　　　　　襟怀坦白言可敬，爱人无情无缘由。

90

Then hate me when thou wilt; if ever, now;

Now, while the world is bent my deeds to cross,

Join with the spite of fortune, make me bow,

And do not drop in for an after-loss:

Ah, do not, when my heart hath 'scaped this sorrow,   *5*

Come in the rearward of a conquered woe;

Give not a windy night a rainy morrow,

To linger out a purposed overthrow.

If thou wilt leave me, do not leave me last,

When other petty griefs have done their spite,   *10*

But in the onset come: so shall I taste

At first the very worst of fortune's might;

　　And other strains of woe, which now seem woe,

　　Compared with loss of thee will not seem so.

　　恨的发泄要及时，朋友的痛恨可以容忍。长痛不如短痛，不要在未来落井下石。

1.　if ever: 要恨
2.　bent: 决定
　　my deeds to cross: 反对我
3.　the spite of fortune: 命运的恶意，即恶运
4.　drop in for an after-loss: 落井下石
5.　'scaped: escaped, recovered from, 恢复，摆脱
6.　rearward: rearguard, 后卫，殿后
　　conquered woe: 克服的悲哀
7.　Give not a windy night a rainy morrow: 今晚是狂风，明天别来暴雨
8.　linger out: 拖延

90

要恨君就恨	要报现如今	
如今世人谋	攻吾遭光阴	
命运神连手	讨吾逼屈身	
命运多舛过	意外厄运临	
万伤方痊愈	又添创伤新	*5*
呼君鸿门宴	又添创伤新	
勿在暴雨后	再降雨淋淋	
勿拖延劫难	注定该降临	
君欲离开吾	勿作最后人	
莫让琐碎事	折磨伤吾心	*10*
浩劫早些来	试吾遭难身	
最坏之命运	吾先尝苦辛	
千种伤心事	而今伤吾心	
比之失去君	伤心何足论	

9.　last:　at the end, 等到最后
10.　have done their spite:　肆尽暴虐
11.　in the onset:　在开始
12.　might:　手段
13.　straints:　种类
译者感言：快人快语对亲朋，要恨早点恨分明。
　　　　　　受得煎熬是铁汉，八十一难正果成。

91

Some glory in their birth, some in their skill,

Some in their wealth, some in their bodies' force;

Some in their garments, though new-fangled ill;

Some in their hawks and hounds, some in their horse;

And every humour hath his adjunct pleasure,   *5*

Wherein it finds a joy above the rest:

But these particulars are not my measure;

All these I better in one general best.

Thy love is better than high birth to me,

Richer than wealth, prouder than garments' cost,   *10*

Of more delight than hawks or horses be;

And having thee, of all men's pride I boast:

    Wretched in this alone, that thou mayst take

    All this away, and me most wretched make.

人人都有值得夸耀的资本。诗人认为最值得夸耀的是所爱的人。

3. new-fangled ill: 式样新奇难看
4. hawks and hounds: 猎鹰与猎犬
5. adjunct: 附属
8. All these I better in one general best: 在所有这些里边，我有一项最大的快乐
9. high birth: 你的高贵门第
12. of all men's pride I boast: 我可以笑傲全世界
13. Wretched in this alone: 唯一可怜的是
14. me most wretched make: 使我极度可怜
译者感言：各种夸耀出人本，生活目标苦追寻。
　　　　　得一知音无价宝，一道闪光亘古存。

91

有人夸门第　　有人夸学高
有人夸体壮　　有人夸富豪
有人夸华衣　　病态称时髦
有人夸鹰犬　　有人夸马膘
世上嗜好异　　趣味莫承包　　　　　　　*5*
酷爱某一个　　其余皆可抛
尽管众夸口　　兴趣总不高
吾自有最爱　　最爱乐陶陶
吾爱胜豪宅　　胜过门第高
比财更富有　　华衣傲气消　　　　　　　*10*
雄鹰或骏马　　岂追马逍遥
吾幸拥有君　　荣耀夸天高
君将事掠抢　　不幸吾心焦
一切皆无影　　惟余泪滔滔

92

But do thy worst to steal thyself away,

For term of life thou art assurèd mine;

And life no longer than thy love will stay,

For it depends upon that love of thine.

Then need I not to fear the worst of wrongs,   *5*

When in the least of them my life hath end.

I see a better state to me belongs

Than that which on thy humour doth depend:

Thou canst not vex me with inconstant mind,

Since that my life on thy revolt doth lie.   *10*

O, what a happy title do I find,

Happy to have thy love, happy to die!

    But what's so blessed-fair that fears no blot?

    Thou mayst be false, and yet I know it not.

朋友想方设法离开诗人，朋友可能会变心，诗人认为只要得到过爱，死而无憾。

1.   do thy worst: 你不顾一切，不择手段
      steal thyself away: 你悄悄溜走
2.   For term of life: 只要我活着
      thou art assurè mine: 你肯定是我的
3.   life no longer than thy love will stay: 我的生命不比你的爱更长久
4.   it: 我的生命
6.   them: 冷淡和三心二意
7.   better state: 天堂
8.   on thy humour doth depend: 依靠看你的脸色生活
9.   vex: 使烦恼

92

君机关算尽	自己偷自身	
只要吾存世	君总属吾人	
生命因长久	怎及君爱深	
吾欲活下去	君爱不离分	
纵被无情弃	不怀恐惧心	5
君略有此意	今世吾不存	
另有好境界	吾悟属吾身	
胜看君脸色	苟活无灵魂	
君无常反复	吾无烦恼心	
君若一翻脸	吾命即归阴	10
呜呼吾荣幸	权利归一身	
荣幸得君爱	荣幸他世人	
世上多美事	何惧瑕疵侵	
君子纵有错	永不入吾心	

inconstant mind: 三心二意
10. on thy revolt: 在你变心时
13. blessed-fair: 美满
    blot: 污损
译者感言：人间真爱存人间，无情抛弃无情缘。
　　　　　知足常乐笑万事，淡化处理自在天。

93

So shall I live, supposing thou art true,

Like a deceived husband; so love's face

May still seem love to me, though altered new;

Thy looks with me, thy heart in other place:

For there can live no hatred in thine eye,   5

Therefore in that I cannot know thy change.

In many's looks the false heart's history

Is writ in moods and frowns and wrinkles strange;

But heaven in thy creation did decree

That in thy face sweet love should ever dwell;   10

Whate'er thy thoughts or thy heart's workings be,

Thy looks should nothing thence but sweetness tell.

　　How like Eve's apple doth thy beauty grow.

　　If thy sweet virtue answer not thy show!

　　恋人变心，却没有常人常有的发脾气、皱眉头，而是满腹温柔的爱。
3.　　though altered new: 虽然你变心
7.　　In many's looks: 许多人的气色上
8.　　wrinkles strange: 冷漠的皱纹
9.　　decree: 法令，政令
11.　　workings: 变幻，精神活动
12.　　thence: 因此
14.　　If thy sweet virtue answer not thy show: 如果你的美德，配不上你的容貌
译者感言：人言貌美不忠诚，忠诚或许貌不行。
　　　　　如此怪圈何时了，难解难猜入迷宫。

93

吾可活下去	误认君忠贞
丈夫受蒙骗	妻子已变心
诚然朱颜改	于吾仍可亲
眼睛似望吾	心儿何处寻
君之眼睛里	敌意不能存

5

吾观君美目	岂知君变心
朝三暮四者	流露不由人
性燥眉头扭	冷漠超皱纹
此事早已定	上帝创造君
柔情与蜜意	君面永留存

10

无论起何念	无论生何心
如视吾君面	欢喜又温馨
夏娃之苹果	美貌秀色真
美德不光顾	美貌皮相存

94

They that have power to hurt and will do none,

That do not do the thing they most do show,

Who, moving others, are themselves as stone,

Unmoved, cold, and to temptation slow;

They rightly do inherit heaven's graces,   5

And husband nature's riches from expense;

They are the lords and owners of their faces,

Others but stewards of their excellence.

The summer's flower is to the summer sweet,

Though to itself it only live and die;   10

But if that flower with base infection meet,

The basest weed outbraves his dignity;

   For sweetest things turn sourest by their deeds;

   Lilies that fester smell far worse than weeds.

洁身自好，保持天然美。美丽的花儿一旦腐烂，远不如莠草。

2.   do not do the thing they most do show: do show, 好像要做。不做人们以为他们要做的事

5.   heaven's graces: 上苍的恩宠

6.   husband: 贮藏和保管

    expense: 浪费

8.   stewards: 看门人

11. base infection: 恶疾感染

12. outbraves: 压倒，战胜

14. fester: 溃烂

94

有力伤人者	却不把人伤	
欲作一件事	未做又何妨	
感动人他者	坚如磐石刚	
稳固而峻冷	诱惑无主张	
继承上苍爱	顺理而成章	*5*
上苍赐财产	节约善储藏	
他者好面貌	自主又自强	
有人替跑腿	才貌享辉煌	
夏天鲜花艳	夏天人观光	
鲜花从自然	自谢自吐芳	*10*
鲜花染恶疾	何处找仙方	
最贱之莠草	自贵欺花王	
化为最腐朽	本原为最香	
百合若云败	不比腐草强	

译者感言：永存善念多善行，美貌惠人美心灵。
　　　　　善恶有报神目电，真善美积侍苍生。

95

How sweet and lovely dost thou make the shame

Which, like a canker in the fragrant rose,

Doth spot the beauty of thy budding name!

O, in what sweets dost thou thy sins enclose!

That tongue that tells the story of thy days,   *5*

Making lascivious comments on thy sport,

Cannot dispraise but in a kind of praise;

Naming thy name blesses an ill report.

O, what a mansion have those vices got

Which for their habitation chose out thee,   *10*

Where beauty's veil doth cover every blot,

And all things turn to fair that eyes can see!

   Take heed, dear heart, of this large privilege;

   The hardest knife ill-used doth lose his edge.

朋友在掩饰所犯的错误。诗人批评朋友沾花惹草，行为不检点。

3.   thy budding name: 你含苞待放的美名
4.   in what sweets dost thou thy sins enclose: 用什么香料遮蒙你的罪行
6.   lascivious: 好色的；挑动情欲的
7.   dispraise: 谴责
8.   Naming thy name blesses an ill report: 提到你的名字就把诬蔑说成是好事
9.   mansion: 大厦；官邸
     vices: 罪恶
11.   veil: 面纱
     blot: 污渍

95

耻辱君点缀	可爱又温馨	
玫瑰正馥郁	毛虫卧花心	
花苞亦美妙	不堪污浊侵	
呜呼君掩饰	罪愆香料闻	
如簧之巧舌	日常生活人	*5*
君行为失检	沾花惹草闻	
君论非申斥	君论夸奖人	
提及君名姓	坏事好新闻	
呜呼一豪宅	罪恶宅内寝	
他者挑选君	安乐窝里人	*10*
美丽纱面罩	污点全藏身	
凡目之所见	一切美善真	
吾爱宜谨慎	权大宜当心	
宝剑世少有	误用锋不存	

13.　Take heed:　要谨慎

　　　privilege:　自由

译者感言：富贵不淫君子行，诱惑面前何人清。

　　　　　　更甚知错不认错，廉耻苦涩圣贤成。

96

Some say, thy fault is youth, some wantonness;

Some say, thy grace is youth and gentle sport;

Both grace and faults are loved of more and less;

Thou makest faults graces that to thee resort.

As on the finger of a throned queen   *5*

The basest jewel will be well esteemed,

So are those errors that in thee are seen

To truths translated, and for true things deemed.

How many lambs might the stern wolf betray,

It like a lamb he could his looks translate!   *10*

How many gazers mightst thou lead away,

If thou wouldst use the strength of all thy state!

    But do not so; I love thee in such sort,

    As thou being mine, mine is thy good report.

　　这一首似为第 76—95 首的献诗，却和诗歌创作艺术不相干。第 13—14 行与第 36 首的完全重复。

1. wantonness: 淫荡
2. sport: 风流
4. to thee resort: 在你身上
8. To truths translated, and for true things deemed: 变成真理，并被认为是真理
9. stern: 恶毒的
   betray: 引诱
10. translate: 改变
11. gazers: 羡慕者
12. state: 人格，地位

96

有人言君错	放荡年轻人
有人言君雅	青春浪漫心
错处与魅力	人们都欢欣
错处化优秀	只因存君身
譬如宝石贵	女王指上神
倘若属最劣	膜拜不乏人
于君亦如此	瑕疵亦属君
瑕疵德行变	推崇为至真
群羊受欺侮	恶狼藏祸心
恶狼披羊皮	难识面目真
众人君引诱	慕君却误身
君使风流性	花样曰翻新
君切莫夸吾	君爱君情深
君身即吾身	替吾名誉存

第5行对应"5"，第10行对应"10"。

13. in such sort: 这样的
14. report: 光荣
译者感言：爱情盲目无是非，正道邪门区别微。
　　　　　凛然正气尚可贵，介山敬仰介子推。

97

How like a winter hath my absence been

From thee, the pleasure of the fleeting year!

What freezings have I felt, what dark days seen!

What old December's bareness every where!

And yet this time removed was summer's time;   5

The teeming autumn, big with rich increase,

Bearing the wanton burthen of the prime,

Like widow'd wombs after their lords' decease:

Yet this abundant issue seem'd to me

But hope of orphans and unfather'd fruit;   10

For summer and his pleasures wait on thee,

And, thou away, the very birds are mute;

    Or, if they sing, 'tis with so dull a cheer,

    That leaves look pale, dreading the winter's near.

第 97—108 首，主要写诗人与朋友关系的冷冷热热。该首写别离犹如荒寒的冬季。
2.   fleeting year: 时光流转
5.   this time removed: 离别的时间
6.   teeming: 充满
      big: 怀孕
7.   burthen: burden, 负担
8.   decease: 死亡
10. hope of orphans: 无父孤儿的希望
12. the very birds: 那些鸟儿
13. with so dull a cheer: 如此情绪低落
14. dreading: 生怕

97

与君离别苦　　俨然严冬情

似水流年去　　欢乐何时逢

严寒似无尽　　黑暗似无穷

岁尾十二月　　萧瑟西北风

正值夏末日　　君别泪涕零　　　　　*5*

秋天望收获　　蕴藏硕果丰

春天狂欢日　　春天称丰盈

恰似一寡妇　　失夫子宫隆

如此之秋实　　全寓吾目中

哀哉遗腹子　　好果缺人疼　　　　　*10*

夏日有欢乐　　候君来忘情

君今离别去　　鸟儿默无声

即使鸟鸣啭　　凄楚不堪听

树叶残淡色　　畏惧临寒冬

译者感言：生离死别中外同，分手凄凉度寒冬。
山寒水瘦孤鹤影，仰首苍天叹飘零。

98

From you have I been absent in the spring,

When proud-pied April, drest in all his trim,

Hath put a spirit of youth in every thing,

That heavy Saturn laught and leapt with him.

Yet nor the lays of birds, nor the sweet smell   *5*

Of different flowers in odour and in hue,

Could make me any summer's story tell,

Or from their proud lap pluck them where they grew:

Nor did I wonder at the lily's white,

Nor praise the deep vermilion in the rose;   *10*

They were but sweet, but figures of delight,

Drawn after you,—you pattern of all those.

   Yet seem'd it winter still, and, you away,

   As with your shadow I with these did play.

   即使在烂漫的春天，离别也是寒冬。
2.   proud-pied: 斑驳的，颜色的。五彩缤纷的
     trim: 好衣服
4.   Saturn: 土星；农神
5.   lays: 歌儿
8.   lap: 花圃
10. vermilion: 朱红色的
12. Drawn: 描绘
     you pattern of all those: 你是那一切的模型
14. play: 玩

98

与君分别日　　恰恰在阳春
四月呈五彩　　盛装悦人心
万物阳气盛　　青春浪漫人
农神本忧郁　　雀跃欢呼闻
百鸟鸣啭美　　气息送温馨　　　　*5*
百花缤纷色　　芳香千里闻
均难改变吾　　夏天故事真
百花采无力　　山谷溢芳馨
百合洁白笑　　不能惊吾心
玫瑰深红喜　　难以醒吾神　　　　*10*
二者形悦目　　二者色迷人
二者皆师恩　　君为二者魂
只因君别去　　寒冬比阳春
吾赏花娱乐　　花影随君身

译者感言：春花春天离别情，万紫千红众心惊。
　　　　　芳香酷似黄连苦，鸟鸣哀怨万里程。

99

The forward violet thus did I chide:

Sweet thief, whence didst thou steal thy sweet that smells,

If not from my love's breath? The purple pride

Which on thy soft cheek for complexion dwells

In my love's veins thou hast too grossly dyed.   5

The lily I condemned for thy hand;

And buds of marjoram had stolen thy hair;

The roses fearfully on thorns did stand,

One blushing shame, another white despair;

A third, nor red nor white, had stolen of both.   10

And to his robbery had annexed thy breath;

But, for his theft, in pride of all his growth

A vengeful canker eat him up to death.

More flowers I noted, yet I none could see

But sweet or colour it had stolen from thee.   15

　　该首 15 行，第 1 行为引子，与第 3，5 行押韵。诗中写各种艳丽的花都比喻诗人所爱的人。

1. chide: 责骂
4. complexion: 肤色
　　dwells: 住，寓于
5. too grossly dyed: 大胆地染
6. condemned: 谴责
7. marjoram: 薄荷花
9. One blushing shame, another white despair: 一朵因害羞而通红，一朵因绝望而煞白。
　　原诗高妙简练，试依原音节译作：一朵羞红，另一朵绝望白

99

吾今要指责	紫罗兰早芳
温柔之贼盗	何处盗其香
吾爱之气息	紫色之辉煌
君有嫩面目	吾爱染脸庞
吾爱之血管	君染事张扬	5
吾言君之手	百合花偷香
茉莉已盗走	秀发之飘扬
玫瑰心颤栗	刺上立惊惶
红者言羞涩	白者曰慌张
非红非白者	有羞亦有慌	10
于其赃物上	有君气芬芳
全由其盗窃	乘机花辉煌
毛虫寻报复	花儿食精光
吾见花无数	未见一花良
或曰窃其色	或曰盗其香	15

11. annexed:　附加
13. vengeful:　报复的
译者感言：鲜花娇艳五彩霞，鲜花芬芳香万家。
　　　　　花美人美清香醉，养眼养心烹清茶。

100

Where art thou, Muse, that thou forget'st so long

To speak of that which gives thee all thy might?

Spend'st thou thy fury on some worthless song,

Dark'ning thy power to lend base subjects light?

Return, forgetful Muse, and straight redeem   *5*

In gentle numbers time so idly spent;

Sing to the ear that doth thy lays esteem,

And gives thy pen both skill and argument.

Rise, resty Muse, my love's sweet face survey,

If Time have any wrinkle graven there;   *10*

If any, be a satire to decay,

And make time's spoils despised everywhere.

    Give my love fame faster than Time wastes life;

    So thou prevent'st his scythe and crooked knife.

该诗写文艺女神不要偷懒，要歌唱爱人的青春美貌。

2.   might: 力量
3.   fury: 暴怒；猛烈；诗的热情
5.   redeem: 赎回
6.   In gentle numbers time so idly spent: 用优美的诗歌赎回虚度的光阴
7.   esteem: 尊重，尊敬
8.   skill and argument: 才情和故事
9.   survey: 审视
10.   graven: 刻下的
11.   be a satire to decay: 作为对衰老的嘲讽
12.   time's spoils: 时间的消耗

100

缪斯知何处	遗忘时日长	
君威有源头	为何不歌唱	
激情君浪费	无味写诗章	
消耗君精力	俗物得其光	
缪斯正健忘	归来莫倘徉	5
光阴已虚度	旋律唤回乡	
为君有旋律	知音必赏光	
知音赠伟力	知音赠华章	
缪斯勿慵懒	起身观脸庞	
美容刻皱纹	吾爱怨时光	10
倘若皱纹起	嘲讽老鞋帮	
唤众齐痛斥	劫掠之时光	
抢在时光前	吾爱美名扬	
时间弯镰刀	抵御免受伤	

---

14. crooked: 弯的

译者感言:灵感源于好年华,诗意来自貌如花。

　　　　　喜庆欢乐苍生爱,生存质量牵万家。

101

O truant Muse, what shall be thy amends

For thy neglect of truth in beauty dyed?

Both truth and beauty on my love depends;

So dost thou too, and therein dignified.

Make answer, Muse; wilt thou not haply say,   *5*

Truth needs no colour, with his colour fixt;

Beauty no pencil, beauty's truth to lay;

But best is best, if never intermixed?

Because he needs no praise, wilt thou be dumb?

Excuse not silence so: for't lies in thee   *10*

To make him much outlive a gilded tomb,

And to be praised of ages yet to be.

 Then do thy office, Muse; I teach thee how

 To make him seem long hence as he shows now.

 真正的美是不需要装饰的。
1. truant: 玩忽职守者；旷课者
 amends: 改正，改进
2. truth in beauty dyed: 被美渲染的真
4. therein: 在那里；在其中
5. haply: perhaps, 或许
6. Truth needs no colour, with his colour fixed: 真有固定色彩，不需要再加颜色
7. pencil: 画笔
 lay: 画在画布上
8. best is best: 最佳永远是最佳
 intermixed: 使混杂

101

玩忽职守者	缪斯要补偿	
为何怠慢美	真诚也遭殃	
吾爱依仗美	真诚岂可伤	
于君亦如此	缘此君辉煌	
或许君有语	缪斯答其详	5
真纯勿须色	本色自生光	
美艳勿须笔	涂抹真美伤	
最美即最美	多语太牵强	
岂唯不须赞	缪斯无诗章	
勿为沉默护	诗神有灵光	10
较彼造金坟	使其名更扬	
世世代代赞	享誉万年长	
吾诲公干人	缪斯听其详	
吾爱如今日	经久美弥彰	

---

10. Excuse not silence so: 不要为这样的沉默辩护

12. yet to be: 未来的

13. do thy office: 当仁不让

14. hence: 从此以后

译者感言：道不远人美本真，朴素无华触人心。
　　　　　炉火纯青随个性，沸腾张扬贵有神。

102

My love is strengthen'd, though more weak in seeming;

I love not less, though less the show appear:

Than love is merchandized whose rich esteeming

The owner's tongue doth publish everywhere.

Our love was new, and then but in the spring,   *5*

When I was wont to greet it with my lays;

As Philomel in summer's front doth sing,

And stops her pipe in growth of riper days:

Not that the summer is less pleasant now

Than when her mournful hymns did hush the night,   *10*

But that wild music burthens every bough,

And sweets grown common lose their dear delight.

    Therefore, like her, I sometime hold my tongue,

    Because I would not dull you with my song.

爱心的增强不能单靠诗歌。
3.　merchandized: 通商；推销
　　esteeming: 崇拜
5.　then but in the spring: 当时正当春天
6.　wont: 惯于
　　greet: 向…致意
7.　Philomel: [希神]菲罗墨拉，夜莺
8.　riper days: 盛夏的日子
10.　hymns: 赞歌
　　hush the night: 使得长夜屏息
11.　burthens: 成为负担

102

恍若更柔弱	吾爱实大增	
吾爱无寸减	表面缩几成	
爱情作商品	囤积居奇经	
若将爱情责	吹嘘四海听	
两心相倾慕	相恋沐春风	*5*
表爱有诗赋	诗赋颂爱情	
菲罗墨拉女	奇辱化夜莺	
希腊神话事	夏初啼连声	
夏去歌声歇	今夏非昔情	
欢欣不如昨	静夜闻夜莺	*10*
喧嚣歌聒噪	树枝难支撑	
欢乐成常事	珍爱云无踪	
缄口共无言	吾意师夜莺	
不忍讨君嫌	吾今停歌声	

12.　sweets grown common:　美好的变成太普通
14.　I would not dull you with my song:　我不想用我的歌烦你
译者感言：阳春美景心欢畅，夜莺啼鸣痛断肠。
　　　　　爱恨交织不能理，情感深时大文章。

103

Alack, what poverty my Muse brings forth,

That having such a scope to show her pride,

The argument, all bare, is of more worth

Than when it hath my added praise beside!

O, blame me not, if I no more can write!   *5*

Look in your glass, and there appears a face

That overgoes my blunt invention quite,

Dulling my lines, and doing me disgrace.

Were it not sinful, then, striving to mend,

To mar the subject that before was well?   *10*

For to no other pass my verses tend

Than of your graces and your gifts to tell;

  And more, much more, than in my verse can sit,

  Your own glass shows you when you look in it.

赞美朴素的诗神。美的东西勿须添描。

2. scope: 机遇；天地
3. The argument all bare: 赤裸的题材
4. beside: 加上
7. overgoes: 超过
    blunt: 钝的；生硬的
8. Dulling my lines: 使我的诗句枯燥乏味
9. mend: 改进
10. mar: 毁坏
11. to no other pass my verses tend: 我的诗没有其他目标
13. more, much more than in my verse can sit: 比我诗中所写的要多得多

103

嗟夫吾缪斯	所携实寒伧	
尽管尽其力	随心展华章	
题材去铅华	价值更无双	
远胜吾诗法	颂扬忒夸张	
呜呼莫怪吾	才尽赛江郎	*5*
手持菱花镜	觑见脸一张	
吾诗句粗劣	创意不敢当	
远胜吾诗作	可餐秀色香	
慎勿事雕琢	愈描画愈脏	
原本好题材	获罪雕饰忙	*10*
不求出奇彩	不图放异香	
吾诗写君雅	君才亦表彰	
君揽镜自照	君仪态万方	
吾诗图尽力	岂敢不自量	

译者感言：莎翁之诗见纯真，朴实无华寓意深。
　　　　　　不抢眼球摄魂魄，天生地造美妙人。

104

To me, fair friend, you never can be old,

For as you were when first your eye I eyed,

Such seems your beauty still. Three winters' cold

Have from the forests shook three summers' pride;

Three beauteous springs to yellow autumn turned   *5*

In process of the seasons have I seen,

Three April perfumes in three hot Junes burned,

Since first I saw you fresh, which yet are green.

Ah, yet doth beauty, like a dial hand,

Steal from his figure, and no pace perceived;   *10*

So your sweet hue, which methinks still doth stand,

Hath motion, and mine eye may be deceived:

   For fear of which, hear this, thou age unbred, —

   Ere you were born was beauty's summer dead.

借季节喻人生，春天和秋天的描述简洁优美抒情。

2.   your eye I eyed:　我的眼睛看见你的眼睛。句中用了三个相同元音[ai]，英语修辞学上叫做 epizeuxis（紧接反复）。试据其音节译为：吾睹君目

4.   pride:　盛容

5.   Three beauteous springs to yellow autumn turned:　三度阳春翠绿化作三次秋天枯黄

7.   burned:　燃烧；消失

9.   a dial hand:　日晷上的时针

10.   his figure:　他的踪影

11.   stand:　常驻

12.   motion:　移动

13.   unbred:　未来的

104

美貌吾好友	永远祛衰颜
首次观君目	吾睹君当年
仍葆君美貌	三度三九天
风采之盛夏	林中三凋残
三春经三度	黄叶秋斑斓	5
时序岁更替	吾睹其变迁
四月之香气	三度六月烟
初见君鲜靓	今见君嫩鲜
美貌兮日晷	钟面针一般
悄悄兮溜走	步态孰曾观	10
君思君美貌	静止不动弹
实则正移动	吾目受欺瞒
人人有此虑	后世听吾言
尔等未出世	美貌过盛年

---

14. Ere you were born was beauty's summer dead: 你尚未出生，美好的夏天已经过去
译者感言：人美可经三度春，眼波秋水洗纤尘。
时光飞逝轻松过，安享天年爱后昆。

105

Let not my love be call'd idolatry,

Nor my beloved as an idol show,

Since all alike my songs and praises be

To one, of one, still such, and ever so.

Kind is my love to-day, to-morrow kind,   *5*

Still constant in a wondrous excellence;

Therefore my verse to constancy confined,

One thing expressing, leaves out difference.

Fair, kind, and true, is all my argument, ——

Fair, kind, and true, varying to other words;   *10*

And in this change is my invention spent,

Three themes in one, which wondrous scope affords.

   Fair, kind, and true, have often lived alone,

   Which three till now never kept seat in one,

    诗人对爱情和爱人的赞美是真诚的。"美貌"、"温柔"、"忠实"三个词在第 9 行、10 行和第 13 行三次重复出现。

1.   idolatry: 偶像崇拜
2.   idol: 偶像
3.   all alike my songs and praises be: 我所有的诗歌的赞美
4.   To one, of one, still such, and ever so: 献给一个,赞扬一个,始终如此,永不变样
5.   kind…kind: 该行首尾用同一个单词,英语修辞学称之为 epanalepsis,即首尾同词
6.   wondrous: wonderful,奇妙的
7.   confined: 保持
8.   One thing expressing, leaves out difference: 只一种事情,全省掉差异
10. varying to others words: 用不同的词表达

105

偶像之崇拜	莫称吾爱情	
偶像之表演	吾爱岂相同	
所有吾诗颂	献与一人听	
千诗与万颂	同调一个声	
吾爱今日好	吾爱明日红	*5*
惊人之美艳	美艳到永恒	
吾诗同君艳	永不改诗风	
惟言一心事	只表一盛情	
惟颂真善美	主题显诗中	
惟歌真善美	变化本其宗	*10*
惟寓此变化	想象力无穷	
三题合而一	地广任驰聘	
真善美三者	素常慎独行	
如今成一体	三圣坐春风	

.12.　scope:　境界
　　　afford:　担负得起；给予
14.　kept seat in one:　集于一身
译者感言：有血有肉有情感，爱人青春鲜活观。
　　　　　善良亲切人性化，道德才华留凡间。

106

When in the chronicle of wasted time

I see descriptions of the fairest wights,

And beauty making beautiful old rhyme

In praise of ladies dead and lovely knights,

Then, in the blazon of sweet beauty's best,   *5*

Of hand, of foot, of lip, of eye, of brow,

I see their antique pen would have expressed

Even such a beauty as you master now.

So all their praises are but prophecies

Of this our time, all you prefiguring;   *10*

And, for they looked but with divining eyes,

They had not skill enough your worth to sing:

   For we, which now behold these present days,

   Have eyes to wonder, but lack tongues to praise.

风流人物仅限于外貌描写的表面化。
1. chronicle: 史纪，纪年
2. wights: 人物
3. beauty making beautiful old rhyme: 美人为古诗添美感
5. blazon: 纹章的确切说明
    sweet beauty's best: 甜美的美人最佳的部位
8. Even such a beauty as you master now: 确实是你现在所有的美貌
9. prophecies: 预言
10. prefiguring: 预示
11. divining eyes: 想象的眼

106

悠悠岁月去	万年并千秋	
代有好诗篇	歌唱最风流	
美人古韵里	古美不胜收	
赞颂古美女	骑士风当优	
美女有最美	甜美君好述	*5*
唇眼眉毛媚	纤手加玉足	
吾见古老笔	描绘美人图	
图绘君美貌	大卫雕像俦	
赞颂即预言	预言美不休	
写美之现状	现代美更优	*10*
人用预测眼	观物察症候	
他人乏技巧	颂君价堪愁	
吾辈观当下	吾辈赏风流	
惟有目光羡	赞美口才无	

译者感言：美人手足目眉唇，美妙无处不动人。
　　　　　可怜可爱可吟诵，心灵写出始通神。

107

Not mine own fears, nor the prophetic soul

Of the wide world dreaming on things to come,

Can yet the lease of my true love control,

Supposed as forfeit to a confined doom.

The mortal moon hath her eclipse endured,   *5*

And the sad augurs mock their own presage;

Incertainties now crown themselves assured,

And peace proclaims olives of endless age.

Now with the drops of this most balmy time

My love looks fresh, and Death to me subscribes,   *10*

Since, spite of him, I'll live in this poor rhyme,

While he insults o'er dull and speechless tribes:

　　And thou in this shalt find thy monument,

　　When tyrants' crests and tombs of brass are spent.

诗人自信其诗作不朽。象征和平的橄榄枝远胜秘密武器。

3.　lease:　租约
4.　forfeit:　罚款
　　confined doom:　注定的命运
6.　augurs:　占卜官
　　presage:　预示
8.　olives:　橄榄树
9.　balmy:　芬芳的，香脂的
10.　subscribes:　投降
11.　spite:　恶意
12.　tribes:　种族，部落

107

吾常怀忧虑	世人有预言	
乾坤无边际	梦想事无缘	
吾爱真难控	期限虚幻间	
注定有末日	此爱遭怪圈	
凡尘之明月	月蚀缺半边	5
不祥预言客	自嘲自家言	
多少不确定	彼此不相安	
和平已宣告	青翠绿橄榄	
太平盛世雨	沾溉尧舜天	
吾爱愈鲜靓	死神败祈怜	10
吾视而不见	吾活拙诗篇	
愚钝之聚落	受辱受欺瞒	
君留纪念碑	吾诗为君颜	
暴君失勋饰	暴君毁铜棺	

---

14. crests：盔，勋饰

译者感言：平和简静艺术魂，橄榄枝赠从艺人。

　　　　　　修到全无火气处，自品自赏自访真。

108

What's in the brain, that ink may character,

Which hath not figured to thee my true spirit?

What's new to speak, what new to register,

That may express my love, or thy dear merit?

Nothing, sweet boy; but yet, like prayers divine,   5

I must each day say o'er the very same;

Counting no old thing old, thou mine, I thine,

Even as when first I hallowed thy fair name.

So that eternal love in love's fresh case

Weighs not the dust and injury of age,   10

Nor gives to necessary wrinkles place,

But makes antiquity for aye his page;

   Finding the first conceit of love there bred,

   Where time and outward form would show it dead.

诗人作诗唯求其真，不一味追求新奇。

1. character: 描写
2. figured: 描述
3. register: 纪录
4. merit: 价值，身份
5. prayers divine: 虔诚的祷词
6. o'er: 重复
7. counting: 认为
8. hallowed: 崇敬
9. case: 容貌
10. weighs not: 忽视

108

何事脑海里	笔墨已形容	
难以对君语	难叙吾深情	
何事话语里	何事记录中	
难表君之美	难言吾爱情	
告君曰无有	牧师每日功	*5*
每日祈祷语	吾言每日同	
老调不嫌老	献诗有初衷	
君为吾所有	吾为君仆从	
爱情新万古	爱情享永恒	
岁月任伤害	身躯任尘蒙	*10*
皱纹难避免	屈服吾不能	
永远轻衰老	爱情之侍童	
吾见爱繁育	重燃新热情	
何虑时光毁	何虑颓然形	

---

12. antiquity: 古代
    for aye: for ever, 永远
    page: 童仆
13. conceit: 热情，自负
译者感言：不必苦求新信息，真言一句总称奇。
　　　　　　终生受用用不尽，传薪后世点痴迷。

109

O, never say that I was false of heart,

Though absence seem'd my flame to qualify.

As easy might I from myself depart

As from my soul, which in thy breast doth lie;

That is my home of love: if I have ranged,   *5*

Like him that travels I return again,

Just to the time, not with the time exchanged,

So that myself bring water for my stain.

Never believe, though in my nature reigned

All frailties that besiege all kinds of blood,   *10*

That it could so preposterously be stain'd,

To leave for nothing all thy sum of good;

   For nothing this wide universe I call,

   Save thou, my Rose; in it thou art my all.

第 109—126 首感慨命运多舛，但对朋友是丹心赤诚。该首写朋友就是一切。
2.　my flame to qualify: 冷却我的热情
3.　As easy: 反语，意为如此困难
4.　in thy breast doth lie: 存在于你胸中。此句英语甚优美含蓄
5.　ranged: 游荡
7.　to the time: 准时
8.　stain: 污点
9.　reigned: 盛行
10.　frailties: 弱点
　　besiege: 围困
11.　preposterously: 反常地，荒谬地

109

求君慎言兮	莫谓吾移情	
固然有别离	吾情火焰生	
告别灵魂难	离间本性同	
吾有吾灵魂	灵魂驻君胸	
吾爱得其居	吾有吾游踪	*5*
游子家门返	归家叙别情	
准时回乡土	时变心本同	
吾去打清水	污点吾洗清	
劝君勿轻信	采花吾行踪	
各类情欲狂	污染吾心灵	*10*
荒唐无气质	脆弱又凡庸	
岂能君捐弃	为一文不名	
若言三千界	吾亦不动情	
吾有大财富	君身玫瑰红	

12. To leave for nothing all thy sum of good: 为不值一文的东西而把你弃捐
13. For nothing this wide universe I call: 这浩淼的宇宙对我来说只是一个虚空
译者感言：尽管生平多舛误，思考环宇望太清。
　　　　　万事万物皆乌有，挚友诗歌梦魂中。

110

Alas,'tis true I have gone here and there,

And made myself a motley to the view,

Gored mine own thoughts, sold cheap what is most dear,

Made old offences of affections new;

Most true it is that I have lookt on truth   *5*

Askance and strangely; but, by all above,

These blenches gave my heart another youth,

And worse essays proved thee my best of love.

Now all is done, have what shall have no end;

Mine appetite I never more will grind   *10*

On newer proof, to try an older friend,

A god in love, to whom I am confined.

　　Then give me welcome, next my heaven the best,

　　Even to thy pure and most most loving breast.

　　诗人曾为戏子，交了新朋友，忘掉了老朋友。又重新极其看重老朋友。
2.　motley:　斑衣小丑
3.　Gored:　伤害
4.　Made old offences of affections new:　结新交而忘旧友
6.　Askance:　斜眼看
7.　blenches:　不贞行为
9.　have what shall have no end:　接受没有穷尽的友谊
10.　grind:　磨
11.　try an older friend:　考验我的一位老朋友
12.　to whom I am confined:　拘禁我的（神祇）

110

嗟呼叹属实	四海吾行踪
斑衣演小丑	呜呼扮优伶
吾心有刺痛	廉价售倾城
新交忘旧友	冒犯代友情
千真万确事	吾观忠贞情	5
侧目而陌生	对天吾誓盟
不贞之行为	反证新热情
尝试云失败	吾对君最忠
一切成过去	惟留爱永恒
吾固有爱欲	不再乱用情	10
用新考验旧	荒诞吾胡行
吾爱君惟有	奉君为神明
求君迎迓吾	仅次天国行
君怀诚可贵	君胸洁胜冰

14. Even to thy pure and most most loving breast: 进入你那纯洁和极其可爱的胸怀里
译者感言：人生如戏戏人生，戏中有戏寓真诚。
　　　　　喜新厌旧看稚幼，喜旧厌新多老翁。

111

O, for my sake do you with Fortune chide,

The goddess of my harmful deeds,

That did not better for my life provide

Than public means which public manners breeds.

Thence comes it that my name receives a brand;   *5*

And almost thence my nature is subdued

To what it works in, like the dyer's hand:

Pity me, then, and wish I were renew'd;

Whilst, like a willing patient, I will drink

Potions of eisel 'gainst my strong infection;   *10*

No bitterness that I will bitter think,

Nor double penance, to correct correction.

   Pity me, then, dear friend, and I assure ye

   Even that your pity is enough to cure me.

诗人对其舞台生涯颇有微辞，要求朋友怜悯他。

1.   chide: 责备；骂
3.   did not better for my life provide: provided nothing better, 没有为我的生活提供较佳的条件
4.   public means: 舞台生涯
     public manners: 见面熟，卖弄
5.   Thence: 于是
6.   subdued: 征服；抑制
7.   To what it works in: 感染了工作环境的色彩
10. potions: 饮剂
     eisel: vinegar, 醋

111

呼君责命运	仅为吾之身	
使吾学坏者	命运之女神	
女神不佑吾	好运不来临	
吾从娱乐业	娱乐取悦人	
吾名打烙印	烙印辱吾心	*5*
本性亦感染	风俗谈何淳	
恰似染工手	各样颜色侵	
祈求怜悯吾	洁身不染尘	
此时吾处境	温顺一病人	
遵嘱饮酸醋	意在送瘟神	*10*
苦药不嫌苦	茹苦又含辛	
苦行为赎罪	苦行赎吾身	
好友怜悯吾	吾为担保人	
君之怜悯术	足以正吾身	

---

11. No bitterness that I will bitter think: 多苦的药我也不嫌苦
12. penance: 补赎；苦行
　　　correct correction: 双倍的惩罚
译者感言：娱乐业万古千秋，优伶戏子低名头。
　　　　　艺术家理当自贵，十年一戏闯九州。

112

Your love and pity doth the impression fill

Which vulgar scandal stampt upon my brow;

For what care I who calls me well or ill,

So you o'er-green my bad, my good allow?

You are my all-the-world, and I must strive   *5*

To know my shames and praises from your tongue;

None else to me, nor I to none alive,

That my steeled sense or changes right or wrong.

In so profound abysm I throw all care

Of others' voices, that my adder's sense   *10*

To critic and to flatterer stopped are.

Mark how with my neglect I do dispense:

　You are so strongly in my purpose bred,

　That all the world besides methinks are dead.

不管他人如何品评，全当耳旁风。普天之下，只有这位朋友为知音。
1.　fill:　抹平
2.　vulgar scandal:　世俗的戏
3.　what care I:　我何必管它
4.　o'er-green:　以绿藤或青草遮盖
　　allow:　承认
7.　None else to me, nor I to none alive:　别人对我，我对任何人，都不能够
8.　changes: 改变，其宾语为 steeled sense
9.　abysm:　abyss, 深渊
10.　adder's:　蝰蛇
11.　flatterer:　奉承者

112

助吾疗伤痛	君之爱怜心	
众人滥诽谤	额头烙疤痕	
别人言好赖	西天之流云	
吾错君遮盖	吾功君扬芬	
君为大千界	君言吾灵魂	*5*
吾力图知晓	褒贬口照心	
人与吾皆死	吾与世埃尘	
重吾善恶者	不变唯有君	
他人之言语	抛入沟壑深	
毁誉随它去	学做淡泊人	*10*
蛇类遇逗弄	充耳尚不闻	
看吾自解嘲	冷傲视红尘	
君于吾心底	扎根万丈深	
天地惟留君	浊世不复存	

12. Mark: 看
    dispense: 豁免
13. in my purpose bred: 生在我心里
译者感言：朋友赐与爱和怜，珍存珍惜度长年。
　　　　　飞短流长任他去，苍松绝壁吞霞烟。

113

Since I left you, mine eye is in my mind;

And that which governs me to go about

Doth part his function, and is partly blind,

Seems seeing, but effectually is out;

For it no form delivers to the heart   5

Of bird, of flower, or shape, which it doth latch:

Of his quick objects hath the mind no part,

Nor his own vision holds what it doth catch;

For if it see the rudest or gentlest sight,

The most sweet favour or deformed'st creature,   *10*

The mountain or the sea, the day or night,

The crow or dove, it shapes them to your feature:

    Incapable of more, replete with you,

    My most true mind thus maketh mine untrue.

   与朋友分别后，因思念过去，世间万事万物皆不在眼中。

4.   effectually: 有效地

5.   no form delivers to the heart: 不能把形状传入心中

6.   latch: 逮住

7.   Of his quick objects hath the mind no part: 心中没有瞬间的物象

8.   Nor his own vision holds what it doth catch: 眼里留不住眼睛所看见的东西

10.   sweet: 吸引人的

13.   replete: 充满的

译者感言：山海情怀花鸟情，美人昼夜万花丛。
           一叶障目失大计，天地生我烟霞中。

113

自从离开君　　吾目居吾心
目为一器官　　指引行路人
部分功能去　　部分入迷津
表面在凝视　　实际不经心
心房无形态　　心房无温馨　　　　　5
鲜花无踪影　　俊鸟无妙言
万物因生动　　心房无法亲
瞬间过幻影　　目光难留真
大俗目所见　　大雅目留神
或见最美女　　或睹最丑人　　　　　10
高山与大海　　白昼与黄昏
白鸽与乌鸦　　幻化成君身
皆为君占据　　无力再分心
吾心最忠诚　　吾目入迷津

114

Or whether doth my mind, being crown'd with you,

Drink up the monarch's plague, this flattery?

Or whether shall I say, mine eye saith true,

And that your love taught it this alchemy,

To make of monsters and things indigest   *5*

Such cherubins as your sweet self resemble,

Creating every bad a perfect best,

As fast as objects to his beams assemble?

O,'tis the first; 'tis flatt'ry in my seeing,

And my great mind most kingly drinks it up: *10*

Mine eye well knows what with his gust is greeing,

And to his palate doth prepare the cup:

    If it be poison'd, 'tis the lesser sin

    That mine eye loves it, and doth first begin.

诗人偏爱朋友，情人眼里出西施。
2.   monarch's:　君主，帝王
      plague:　瘟疫
4.   alchemy:　炼金术
6.   cherubins:　小天使
7.   Creating every bad a perfect best:　每个坏东西都造成完美
8.   As fast as:　立刻
      beams:　眼睛放光
      assemble:　容貌
11.   gust:　味；欣赏
      greeing:　同意；高兴

114

或曰吾之心	有君自称王	
帝王赐鸩酒	谄媚称强梁	
吾应评吾目	吾目未说诳	
君爱诲吾目	炼金神术强	
思过有妖怪	向善有魔王	5
智慧小天使	美貌似君翔	
丑怪变完美	畸形鲜花香	
变化之神速	皆由目之光	
呜呼叹前者	吾目谄媚诳	
吾心曰伟岸	吞咽入肚肠	10
吾目知其味	其味深而长	
迎合其口味	饮料为君尝	
倘若杯有毒	罪小莫心慌	
吾目曰钟爱	独自先喝光	

12. palate: 腭；味觉；鉴赏力
译者感言：审美天生带感情，心爱之物胜水晶。
　　　　　音容笑貌慈祥意，赏心悦目睡梦中。

115

Those lines that I before have writ do lie,

Even those that said I could not love you dearer.

Yet then my judgement knew no reason why

My most full flame should afterwards burn clearer.

But reckoning Time, whose millioned accidents   5

Creep in 'twixt vows, and change decrees of kings,

Tan sacred beauty, blunt the sharp'st intents,

Divert strong minds to the course of alt'ring things;

Alas, why, fearing of Time's tyranny,

Might I not then say, 'Now I love you best,   10

When I was certain o'er incertainty,

Crowning the present, doubting of the rest?

  Love is a babe; then might I not say so,

  To give full growth to that which still doth grow.

诗歌里的言辞不可全信，时间是最好的试金石。
2.   I could not love you dearer: 我爱你到极点
4.   full flame: 炽热的火焰
5.   reckoning time: 考虑到时间
      millioned accidents: 无数次事故
6.   Creep in 'twixt vows: 爬进誓言之间
      decrees: 法令，政令
7.   Tan: 晒黑
      blunt: 弄钝
8.   Divert: 牵制
11.   I was certain o'er incertainty: 我去掉疑虑，充满信心

115

昔日吾诗句	皆为吾谎言	
无诗不为谎	即使信誓篇	
吾固能判断	探由不着边	
吾情赤烈焰	烧亮半边天	
时光百万次	吾想无情年	*5*
毁山盟海誓	抗君命圣言	
摧花容月貌	折壮志云天	
天道万物变	如尘意志坚	
呜呼惧岁月	时光暴君般	
悔吾不知时	吾爱未坦言	*10*
吾知永恒变	爱君在心田	
吾疑未来事	关注惟眼前	
爱为婴幼儿	吾爱难明言	
吾忧爱成长	成熟露光鲜	

译者感言：表像之美有诗歌，时光荏苒莫蹉跎。
　　　　　真情实感真呵护，爱之婴儿福惠多。

116

Let me not to the marriage of true minds

Admit impediments. Love is not love

Which alters when it alteration finds,

Or bends with the remover to remove:

O, no! it is an ever-fixed mark.   5

That looks on tempests, and is never shaken,

It is the star to every wandering bark,

Whose worth's unknown, although his height be taken.

Love's not Time's fool, though rosy lips and cheeks

Within his bending sickle's compass come;   10

Love alters not with his brief hours and weeks,

But bears it out even to the edge of doom.

    If this be error, and upon me proved,

    I never writ, nor no man ever loved.

两个真心相爱的人的精神支柱：爱情。在 154 首里被称作第一名篇。

2.   impediments: 障碍物

5.   mark: beacon or lighthouse, 灯塔

7.   star: 北极星

      bark: 船

10. bending sickle's compass: 弯弯镰刀的割断

      come: 主语为 rosy lips and cheeks

11. brief hours and weeks: 不是确指小时和星期，而是描述时光的短暂

12. the edge of doom: 世界末日

14. writ: wrote, 写诗

      nor no man ever loved: 没有人爱过

116

恕吾不承认	妨碍真婚姻	
两情若相爱	两颗真诚心	
见变情亦变	山盟岂是真	
随风转舵者	海誓非清纯	
呜呼人之爱	灯塔照眼新	*5*
永恒对风暴	巍然立脚跟	
明星闪闪亮	指点船迷津	
其高或可测	其奥似难寻	
真爱非尤物	时光莫近身	
樱唇朱颜女	时光镰刀侵	*10*
时光叹流转	爱岂浮萍心	
爱抗光阴走	地老天荒新	
人证吾说伪	异端去害人	
吾从未写诗	吾爱何曾存	

译者感言：真爱犹如北极星，真爱犹如航标灯。
　　　　　时光无情难侵害，樱唇桃腮笑春风。

117

Accuse me thus: that I have scanted all

Wherein I should your great deserts repay;

Forgot upon your dearest love to call,

Whereto all bonds do tie me day by day;

That I have frequent been with unknown minds,   *5*

And given to time your own dear-purchased right;

That I have hoisted rail to all the winds

Which should transport me farthest from your sight.

Book both my wilfulness and errors down,

And on just proof surmise accumulate;   *10*

Bring me within the level of your frown,

But shoot not at me in your wakened hate;

    Since my appeal says I did strive to prove

    The constancy and virtue of your love.

疏远朋友而结交了另外一些人，请求朋友宽恕。
1.   scanted: 减少
2.   Wherein: 在哪方面
      deserts: 美德
3.   to call: 慰问
4.   Where to: To which, 向那里
      bonds: 羁绊
6.   given to time: 付诸流光
7.   hoisted sail to all the winds: 见风使舵
10.   surmise: 猜测
      accumulate: 增加

117

如此控告吾	告吾不作声	
君恩应酬谢	春晖雨露情	
君施深厚爱	吾欠致谢声	
一日复一日	友谊羁绊绳	
结交新朋友	放荡吾无行	*5*
君权付流水	高价购不赢	
扬帆随吾意	岂管何处风	
离君最远处	不见不心疼	
记下吾任性	吾错莫宽容	
真凭实据处	揣测亦跟风	*10*
对吾眉头皱	默默受苦刑	
切莫射杀吾	怨毒应缓行	
吾言为抗辩	急语为抗争	
证明吾之爱	坚定加忠诚	

12.　wakened:　唤醒

译者感言：交友莫忌朋友多，老友老酒真快活。
　　　　　　吮血卖友世所恨，友谊长久义字托。

118

Like as, to make our appetites more keen,

With eager compounds we our palate urge;

As, to prevent our maladies unseen,

We sicken to shun sickness when we purge;

Even so, being full of your ne'er-cloying sweetness,   *5*

To bitter sauces did I frame my feeding;

And, sick of welfare, found a kind of meetness

To be diseased, ere that there was true needing.

Thus policy in love, t'anticipate

The ills that were not, grew to faults assured,   *10*

And brought to medicine a healthful state,

Which, rank of goodness, would by ill be cured:

But thence I learn, and find the lesson true,

Drugs poison him that so fell sick of you.

用药不当，反成病痛。爱是生活的调味品，使用不当，就会成毒药。

1. Like as: Just as, 正好像
2. palate: 腭；爱好，味觉，鉴赏力
4. sicken: 使生病
    shun: 避免
    purge: 服用泻药
5. Even: Just, 正是
6. feeding: diet, 食谱
7. welfare: 健康，康乐
    meetness: 健康
9. t'anticipate: to anticipate, 预防

118

恰如增食欲	恰如胃口开
辛辣加佐料	送上舌端来
有时服泻药	健康巧安排
为防患重疾	小病患应该
甜蜜食不厌	饱尝已开怀	5
苦汁反为美	佐餐勿疑猜
只因太健康	不需亦安排
小病来一场	正中吾下怀
情场有手段	预言有病灾
生病不必要	反而招祸来	10
健康乱用药	药物三分灾
痛苦医康健	此方太不该
由此吾醒悟	教训训蠢材
相思病无药	用药毒成灾

10. faults assured: 真正病
12. rank of: 充满
    by ill be cured: 求疾病来治病
译者感言：饮食不当成毒药，用药粗心病难逃。
　　　　　真爱真金讲分寸，需求理智乐春宵。

119

What potions have I drunk of Siren tears,

Distilled from limbecks foul as hell within;

Applying fears to hopes, and hopes to fears,

Still losing when I saw myself to win!

What wretched errors hath my heart committed,   *5*

Whilst it bath thought itself so blessèd never!

How have mine eyes out of their spheres been fitted

In the distraction of this madding fever!

O benefit of ill! now I find true

That better is by evil still made better;   *10*

And ruined love, when it is built anew,

Grows fairer than at first, more strong, far greater.

So I return rebuked to my content,

And gain by ill thrice more than I have spent.

受到诱惑，误入岐途，在错误中吸取教训，收获更大些。

1.　Siren:　〔希神〕塞壬，海妖；迷人的美女
2.　Distilled:　蒸馏
　　limbecks:　alembic，蒸馏器
　　foul:　邪恶的
3.　Applying:　把……用于
5.　wretched:　可怜的
6.　so blessèd never:　never so blessed，从未有过的幸福
8.　distraction:　发狂
10.　better is by evil still made better:　由于堕落善的确变得更善
11.　ruined love when it is built anew:　被毁坏的爱一旦重新建好

119

希腊神话里	海妖最迷人	
吾饮其泪水	地狱阴森森	
吾心似蒸锅	污汁是非浑	
希望与恐惧	得失不能分	
似得实失去	不幸罪孽心	5
自认最快乐	却有不幸临	
吾目不能已	夺眶求爱真	
爱恋成狂热	吾乱方寸心	
祸福相倚兮	此刻出迷津	
只因有罪恶	高尚入青云	10
爱情已破碎	修好求出新	
更美更强大	辉煌胜原身	
虽然吾受罚	却归满意心	
罹祸反获益	三倍胜世人	

13.　rebuked:　指责，谴责
14.　gain by ills thrice more than I have spent:　由于堕落我的收获比损失多三倍
译者感言：感性支配人发狂，放荡纵欲知荒唐。
　　　　　千金不换顿悟者，失败毁灭功昭彰。

120

That you were once unkind befriends me now.

And for that sorrow which I then did feel

Needs must I under my transgression bow,

Unless my nerves were brass or hammered steel.

For if you were by my unkindness shaken,   *5*

As I by yours, y' have past a hell of time;

And I, a tyrant, have no leisure taken

To weigh how once I suffered in your crime.

O, that our night of woe might have remember'd

My deepest sense, how hard true sorrow hits,   *10*

And soon to you, as you to me then, tender'd

The humble salve which wounded bosoms fits!

　　But that, your trespass, now becomes a fee;

　　Mine ransoms yours, and yours must ransom me.

因负心而悔过。诗人与朋友都有过错，都给对方感情上造成伤害。

1.　befriends: 亲近
3.　transgression: 过错；违规
4.　brass or hammered steel: 铜或精铜
8.　To weigh how once I suffered in your crime: 来掂量我曾经怎样经受你的罪行对我的打击
11.　tender'd: 提供
12.　humble: 谦卑的，恭顺的
　　salve: 药膏
13.　trespass: 冒犯
　　fee: 赎罪费

120

过去君真心	益吾于现今	
想起其哀痛	忆及其苦辛	
因为要悔过	重负伤吾心	
铜钢硬意志	无心无肺人	
倘若君惊愕	怨吾太负心	5
正如君负吾	地火煎熬君	
无暇细思忖	怨吾为暴君	
无暇去考虑	君罪吾伤身	
吾辈悲痛兮	耿耿存吾心	
莫忘吾最痛	苦痛伤最深	10
正如君负吾	迅疾送与君	
赶快敷膏药	疗伤慰君心	
往昔君负吾	如今成赎金	
吾赎君之罪	君赎吾自身	

14.　ransoms:　赎金
译者感言：人生对错趋平衡，你错我错相携行。
　　　　　　圣贤圣徒皆有过，静坐思过慰平生。

121

'Tis better to be vile than vile esteemed,

When not to be receives reproach of being;

And the just pleasure lost, which is so deemed

Not by our feeling, but by others' seeing;

For why should others' false adulterate eyes   5

Give salutation to my sportive blood?

Or on my frailtiès why are frailer spies,

Which in their wills count bad what I think good?

No, I am that I am; and they that level

At my abuses reckon up their own: 10

I may be straight, though they themselves be bevel;

By their rank thoughts my deeds must not be shown;

   Unless this general evil they maintain—

   All men are bad, and in their badness reign.

诗人遭受到别人攻击漫骂。别人以小人之心度君子之腹。
1.   vile: 卑鄙的；邪恶的
     vile esteemed; 尊重，这个表达法意为徒负恶名
2.   When not to be receives reproach of being: 当没有作恶而受到谴责
3.   so deemed: 认为，表达法意为妄加恶声
5.   adulterate: 虚伪淫秽的
6.   salutation: 致意
     sportive: 情欲
7.   frailtiès: 弱点
8.   count: 认为
10. abuses: 弱点

121

宁可真卑劣　　聊胜卑劣名

本来吾无罪　　却背罪名行

娱乐本合法　　至今无影踪

判断靠偏见　　不虑人盛情

他人虚伪眼　　淫欲卖风情　　　　　*5*

岂能秋波送　　辱吾爱真诚

为何有弱者　　窥探吾弱行

吾意为好者　　诬为坏事情

吾行自端正　　人言耳边风

诬吾卑劣者　　卑劣其本能　　　　　*10*

吾乃耿介士　　他人弯弯行

小人度君子　　小肚鸡肠声

除非他人语　　邪教刮歪风

人类性本恶　　世间恶人横

---

　　reckon up:　宣扬

11.　bevel:　不轨

12.　rank:　极坏的

13.　general evil:　所有的人都是恶

14.　in their badness reign:　以他的恶德统治别人

译者感言：说三道四是小人，襟怀坦荡君子心。

　　　　　　浩然正气须静养，异端邪说道边尘。

122

Thy gift, thy tables, are within my brain

Full character'd with lasting memory,

Which shall above that idle rank remain,

Beyond all date, even to eternity:

Or, at the least, so long as brain and heart   *5*

Have faculty by nature to subsist;

Till each to razed oblivion yield his part

Of thee, thy record never can be mist.

That poor retention could not so much hold,

Nor need I tallies thy dear love to score;   *10*

Therefore to give them from me was I bold,

To trust those tables that receive thee more:

   To keep an adjunct to remember thee

   Were to import forgetfulness in me.

笔记本上记得再多，诗写得再多，也不如把朋友牢牢记在心里。

1. tables: 笔记本
3. idle rank: 无聊的名位
6. faculty by nature: 自然能量
    subsist: 生存
7. razed oblivion: 抹掉一切的遗忘
9. retention: 保持，记忆力；笔记本
10. tallies: 符签
    score: 列举
13. adjunct: 助手；辅助
14. import: 意指

122

君赠吾锦册	吾已铭记心	
锦册字写满	记忆曰长新	
远非闲呻吟	真情实感亲	
时日全超越	永恒记情真	
或曰长期有	长期葆清纯	*5*
头脑能占据	心胸能保存	
除非二者损	遗忘成狂人	
君之记录在	丢失则失魂	
锦册可怜物	恒久谁人闻	
吾意不必要	符木刻君心	*10*
爱君吾冒昧	锦册掷黄尘	
吾君多记载	记载吾心存	
若靠备忘录	才能铭记君	
无疑吾默认	遗忘君是真	

译者感言：心学亘古一谜团，哲学心理苦不堪。
散文诗歌情发泄，他者共鸣始心宽。

123

No, Time, thou shalt not boast that I do change:

Thy pyramids built up with newer might

To me are nothing novel, nothing strange;

They are but dressings of a former sight.

Our dates are brief, and therefore we admire   *5*

What thou dost foist upon us that is old;

And rather make them born to our desire

Than think that we before have heard them told.

Thy registers and thee I both defy,

Not wondering at the present, nor the past;   *10*

For thy records and what we see doth lie,

Made more or less by thy continual haste.

   This I do vow, and this shall ever be,

   I will be true, despite thy scythe and thee.

表现诗人对时间的轻蔑，诗人认为忠贞不渝是超越时空的。

2.　　pyramids:　金字塔

　　　　might:　技术

3.　　novel:　新奇

6.　　foist:　蒙混

9.　　defy:　对抗；蔑视

10.　Not wondering at the present, nor the past:　既不惊诧现在，也不惊羡以往

12.　thy continual haste:　你的匆忙之中

译者感言：狠哉时间大镰刀，一切在劫运难逃。

　　　　　　成功毁败均由时，不堕轮回荷香飘。

123

时光莫夸口　　道吾已变心
新造金字塔　　自谓技巧新
吾方不奇异　　吾意不崭新
其实旧景致　　新装迷惑人
言人生苦短　　叹无情光阴　　　　5
赞旧货有赠　　混骗手段真
吾辈适心愿　　此言出内心
不愿多思想　　先前早耳闻
吾轻其记录　　时光莫蒙人
不惊诧既往　　不惊诧现今　　　　10
吾辈视记录　　说谎岂有真
多少皆是谎　　匆匆造留痕
因此吾发誓　　永远铭记君
吾君与镰刀　　岂碍吾忠贞

124

If my dear love were but the child of state,

It might for Fortune's bastard be unfather'd,

As subject to Time's love or to Time's hate,

Weeds among weeds, or flowers with flowers

    gathered.

No, it was builded far from accident;   *5*

It suffers not in smiling pomp, nor falls

Under the blow of thralled discontent,

Whereto the inviting time our fashion calls:

It fears not policy, that heretic,

Which works on leases of short-number'd hours,   *10*

But all alone stands hugely politic,

That it nor grows with heat nor drowns with showers.

    To this I witness call the fools of time,

    Which die for goodness, who have lived for crime.

歌颂凛然正气。如香草，如鲜花，遗世独立，举世皆混我独清。

1. the child of state: 势利的孩子
2. bastard: 私生子
   unfathered: 无父的
4. Weeds among weeds, or flow'rs with flowers gathered: 不管是香草还是野草，不管是香花还是野花，都一样被人们采摘刈割
6. pomp: 华丽；壮观
7. thralled: 奴隶，奴役
8. whereto: 向该处
   the inviting time: 目前的吸引人的时代

124

倘或吾深爱	宠儿出高门	
命运私生子	不知亲父亲	
任由时光恶	任由时光亲	
莠草莠草鄙	鲜花鲜花新	
命运任摆布	偶建绝非真	*5*
快乐得意至	不甘随俗尘	
失意打击下	屹立冲霄云	
盛世有时尚	盛世有浮沉	
异端不轻信	邪说莫认真	
何惧权谋狠	权谋实利亲	*10*
于爱卓然立	巍巍独超群	
不随温暖长	不被大雨侵	
玩世不恭者	吾传为证人	
生时多造孽	想善死神临	

our fasion calls: 我们的时代风尚
9.　It fears not policy: 它不怕阴谋
　　heretic: 异端邪说
11.　hugely: 巨大地
　　politic: 贤明；巍然
13.　witness call: 要求作证
　　the fools of time: 被时光愚弄的人们
14.　Which: fools, 小人；被时光愚弄的人们
译者感言：艰苦卓绝学苍松，风狂雨骤想雄鹰。
　　　　　人间当得清气在，真金砂埋藏光明。

125

Were't aught to me I bore the canopy,

With my extern the outward honouring,

Or laid great bases for eternity,

Which proves more short than waste or ruining?

Have I not seen dwellers on form and favour   *5*

Lose all, and more, by paying too much rent,

For compound sweet foregoing simple savour,

Pitiful thrivers, in their gazing spent?

No, let me be obsequious in thy heart,

And take thou my oblation, poor but free,   *10*

Which is not mixt with seconds, knows no art,

But mutual render, only me for thee.

 Hence, thou suborned informer! a true soul

 When most impeached stands least in thy control.

歌颂由衷的爱，反对哗众取宠的追捧。
1. bore: bear, 负担；擎举
  canopy: 华盖
2. extern: 表面行为
  the outward honouring: 受人爱戴的公众人物
5. dwellers on form and favour: 住户；拘泥于仪表的人
7. For compound sweet forgoing simple savour: 追求奢华而放弃简朴
8. thrivers: 赢利者
  in their gazing spent: 贪图观赏而凋谢
9. obsequious: 逢迎的；忠诚的
10. oblation: 祭品；献礼

125

于吾有何益	吾将华盖擎
表面多恭维	公开赞颂声
奠定大基础	旨在获永恒
时比荒凉短	逝去毁灭惊
吾岂未领教	他人重虚荣 5
租金不堪付	造成大亏空
贪奢华糜费	失淡定真经
辉煌在表面	破产有富翁
吾非重皮相	拜君于心中
请受吾献礼	礼薄吾忠诚 10
其中无次货	其中无私情
彼此送情意	彼此心相通
假誓进谗者	岂污真正经
胡言乱道耻	君子自从容

11. seconds: 次品
 knows no art: 没有什么心机
12. render: 报答
13. suborned: 收买；教唆
14. impeached: 诬告
译者感言：君看轻表面文章，真英雄不事张扬。
　　　　　　君小视声色犬马，大豪杰保国开疆。

126

O thou, my lovely boy, who in thy power

Dost hold Time's fickle glass, his sickle-hour;

Who hast by waning grown, and therein show'st

Thy lovers withering, as thy sweet self grow'st;

If Nature, sovereign mistress over wrack,　　　　　　　5

As thou goest onwards, still win pluck thee back,

She keeps thee to this purpose, that her skill

May Time disgrace, and wretched minutes kill.

Yet fear her, O thou minion of her pleasure!

She may detain, but not still keep, her treasure:　　　10

Her audit, though delay'd, answer'd must be,

And her quietus is to render thee.

　　该首为致男友诗的最后一首，只有 12 行。韵式为 *aa bb cc dd ee ff*。本诗讲自然、时间和青春的关系，告诫青年不要被自然的表象所迷惑。

2.　fickle: 易变的
　　sickle: 镰刀
3.　waning: 月亏
5.　sovereign: 君王
　　wrack: 破灭
8.　May time disgrace, and wretched minutes kill: 使时间蒙羞，把可怜的分秒杀掉
9.　minion: 宠儿
10.　detain: 留住
11.　audit: 审计；总账

126

可爱小伙子	可以来控制
时光小镰刀	变幻沙漏时
日月盈亏人	展示向大众
爱人在枯萎	君竟在兴隆
执掌人亏盈	造化大主宰 5
君要大步跨	后腿她扯拽
只要想卖弄	她有大力量
不让分秒走	羞辱好时光
君要畏惧她	君乃小乖乖
暂时服从她	永远不再来 10
最终要清算	暂时宽限论
债务要偿还	她还君青春

12. quietus: 去世；消灭
译者感言：为人贵乎有精神，山海情怀日月心。
　　　　　勇猛精进留文字，美妙青春美妙人。

127

In the old age black was not counted fair,

Or if it were, it bore not beauty's name;

But now is black beauty's successive heir,

And beauty slander'd with a bastard shame:

For since each hand hath put on nature's power,   *5*

Fairing the foul with art's false borrowed face,

Sweet beauty hath no name, no holy bower,

But is profaned, if not lives in disgrace.

Therefore my mistress' eyes are raven black,

Her eyes so suited, and they mourners seem   *10*

At such who, not born fair, no beauty lack,

Slandering creation with a false esteem:

　　Yet so they mourn, becoming of their woe,

　　That every tongue says beauty should look so.

第 127—152 首，写的是一位黑夫人。本诗叙述黑夫人美的理由。

1.　counted: 认为
3.　successive: 连续的
4.　slandered: 诽谤
　　bastard shame: 私生子的恶名
6.　Fairing the foul with art's false borrowed face: 用艺术的假面来美化丑
7.　bower: 闺房
8.　profaned: 亵渎
9.　raven: 乌鸦
10.　so suited: 相亲；以同样的颜色打扮

127

古代称黑色	与美不相干	
即使称作美	也与美无缘	
而今黑得势	继美合法权	
美为私生子	蒙羞不开颜	
人人用手段	倚靠大自然	*5*
制造一假面	美化丑容颜	
美貌不尊重	美貌失神龛	
纵不言蒙垢	难过亵渎关	
吾爱眉毛色	天上乌鸦般	
眼珠亦黑色	哀悼似不堪	*10*
天生不美者	并非缺美颜	
倚靠伪造美	只毁大自然	
人们之哀伤	化为痛苦观	
美即如此状	吾听众人言	

---

mourners: 悲痛的人

11. not born fair, no beauty lack: 生来不美，但并不缺乏美貌

12. esteem: 尊重；判断

译者感言：白色漂亮黑迷人，含蓄凝重也销魂。
　　　　　沉醉感情融洽处，柳浪莺声天外音。

128

How oft, when thou, my music, music play'st,

Upon that blessed wood whose motion sounds

With thy sweet fingers, when thou gently sway'st

The wiry concord that mine ear confounds,

Do I envy those jacks that nimble leap   *5*

To kiss the tender inward of thy hand,

Whilst my poor lips, which should that harvest reap,

At the wood's boldness by thee blushing stand!

To be so tickled, they would change their state

And situation with those dancing chips,   *10*

O'er whom thy fingers walk with gentle gait,

Making dead wood more blest than living lips.

　　Since saucy jacks so happy are in this,

　　Give them thy fingers, me thy lips to kiss.

对黑夫人弹奏音乐的玉指的感受。
1.　thou, my music, music play'st:　你是我的音乐，你演奏音乐
4.　concord:　和谐
　　confounds:　混淆；令惊惶
5.　jacks:　古铜琴声弦槌下的枕木
　　nimble leap:　轻快地跳
8.　blushing stand:　红着脸站着
9.　tickled:　挑逗
　　chips:　木键
11.　gait:　步态，步法
12.　blest:　福分，快乐

128

不知多少次	见君玉指弹
君为吾音乐	木键有福缘
木键发音响	玉指轻拨弦
乐音迷吾耳	闻弦想联翩
敏捷键盘动	吾妒也妄然	5
木键吻柔指	手掌嫩而纤
可怜吾有口	嘴唇无福缘
只能含羞看	键狂戏婵娟
吾唇欲收获	温柔乡里天
感触思交换	舞姿美翩翩	10
玉指轻轻摸	吾多不平言
木键无生态	怎比嘴唇鲜
木键狂无礼	竟有艳福缘
手指赐木键	樱唇吾尝鲜

13. saucy: 冒失的，荒唐的
译者感言：演奏音乐有情人，玉指纤纤女怀春。
爱君苦不遂心愿，此身化作古钢琴。

129

The expense of spirit in a waste of shame

Is lust in action; and till action lust

Is perjured, murd'rous, bloody, full of blame,

Savage, extreme, rude, cruel, not to trust;

Enjoyed no sooner but despised straight;　　　　5

Past reason hunted; and no sooner had,

Past reason hated, as a swallowed bait,

On purpose laid to make the taker mad;

Mad in pursuit, and in possession so;

Had, having, and in quest to have, extreme;　　　10

A bliss in proof, and proved, a very woe;

Before, a joy proposed; behind a dream.

　　All this the world well knows; yet none knows well

　　To shun the heaven that leads men to this hell.

写色欲之诱惑及其灾祸，振聋发聩。
1.　a waste of shame:　可耻的浪费
2.　lust in action:　色欲在行动
　　action:　色欲行为
3.　perjured:　发假誓
　　full of blame:　充满了罪
5.　Enjoyed no sooner but despised straight:　刚一满足，立刻感到乏味
6.　Past reason hunted:　毫不理智地追求
7.　Past reason hated:　毫不理智地厌恶
　　a swallowed bait:　吞下的钓饵
11.　A bliss in proof:　享受快乐

129

可耻之浪费	消耗之精神	
肉欲满足后	之前更害人	
狡诈去犯罪	凶残血淋淋	
极端又粗野	鲁莽阴森森	
无信尝欢乐	浅尝弃与人	*5*
求欢无理智	到手就变心	
憎恶无理智	误将鱼饵吞	
鱼饵故意设	疯狂吞掉魂	
求欢时疯狂	占有疯无邻	
已有与现有	未有皆诱人	*10*
幸福谓体验	体验后祸临	
事前图欢乐	事后春梦寻	
人人知陷阱	谁人悟金针	
天堂如地狱	纵欲误青春	

a very woe: 完全的苦恼

12. a joy proposed: 巴望的快乐

14. shun: 躲避

译者感言：自古色欲一把刀，诱杀痴人命千条。
　　　　　玩物丧志贪色毁，天堂地狱一步遥。

130

My mistress'eyes are nothing like the sun;

Coral is far more red than her lips'red:

If snow be white, why then her breasts are dun;

If hairs be wires, black wires grow on her head.

I have seen roses damasked, red and white,   *5*

But no such roses see I in her cheeks;

And in some perfumes is there more delight

Than in the breath that from my mistress reeks.

I love to hear her speak, yet well I know

That music hath a far more pleasing sound;   *10*

I grant I never saw a goddess go;

My mistress, when she walks, treads on the ground.

　　And yet, by heaven, l think my love as rare

　　As any she belied with false compare.

冷静地描写黑肤情人的外貌，最后两行写情人眼里出西施。

2.　　Coral：珊瑚

3.　　dun：暗褐色

5.　　damasked：大马士革绸

7.　　in some perfumes is there more delight：有些香水更浓

8.　　reeks：冒气

11.　　I grant I never saw a goddess go：我承认没见过女神走路

14.　　belied：被追捧的

13—14. as rare / As any she belied with false compare：美丽胜过任何被人捧作天仙的美女

译者感言：橱窗美女谁有神，无血无肉可怜人。

　　　　　　情感道德比尤物，喜怒哀乐牵动心。

130

吾爱之眼睛　　　全不像太阳

吾爱樱唇红　　　珊瑚更有光

白雪算雪白　　　吾爱胸褐黄

吾爱钢铁丝　　　吾爱黑发长

粉红当玫瑰　　　白里透红香　　　　　*5*

吾爱双颊俏　　　玫瑰乌有乡

醉人多香水　　　心喜面吉祥

呼吸吾爱口　　　不闻此芬芳

吾爱吾爱语　　　心里却亮堂

吾爱嗓子好　　　音乐美感强　　　　　*10*

吾认吾浅见　　　未见仙女翔

吾爱有步态　　　大地上倘佯

呜呼对天誓　　　吾爱美貌强

天下多美女　　　吾爱美相当

131

Thou art as tyrannous, so as thou art,

As those whose beauties proudly make them cruel;

For well thou know'st to my dear doting heart

Thou art the fairest and most precious jewel.

Yet, in good faith, some say that thee behold,   5

Thy face hath not the power to make love groan,

To say they err I dare not be so bold,

Although I swear it to myself alone.

And, to be sure that is not false I swear,

A thousand groans, but thinking on thy face,   10

One on another's neck do witness bear

Thy black is fairest in my judgement's place.

    In nothing art thou black save in thy deeds,

    And thence this slander as I think proceeds.

诗人注意到了人们对黑夫人的看法。
1.　tyrannous: 残暴的
3.　doting: 痴情的
5.　behold: 看见
　　some say that thee behold: 见过你的一些人说
6.　groan: 呻吟
11.　bear: 提供
11—12.　One on another's neck do witness bear
　　　Thy black is fairest in my judgement's place:
　　　此两行意为：一个接一个的证据证明，你的黑在我心中是最美的
13.　save in thy deeds: 除了你的行为

131

君模样如此	骄横如暴君	
酷似姝丽女	残忍之美人	
缘由君知晓	爱君吾痴心	
君美称绝色	世上最奇珍	
知君者坦言	吾言实告君	*5*
君有美容貌	无人叹倾心	
明说他人错	吾非放胆人	
纵然心断定	明哲保自身	
对君吾赌咒	吾语非失真	
呻吟千百次	想君面容亲	*10*
呻吟不断线	证实吾爱君	
君于吾目中	黑美极芳芬	
一点也不黑	君黑在良心	
吾想皆为此	诬蔑乱纷纷	

14.　thence:　因此；往那里

　　　this slander as I think proceeds:　我想生出这样的诽谤

译者感言：情人眼里黑珍珠，岂管他者意见殊。

　　　　　力排众议留笑柄，爱情盲目入迷途。

132

Thine eyes I love, and they, as pitying me,

Knowing thy heart torments me with disdain,

Have put on black, and loving mourners be,

Looking with pretty ruth upon my pain.

And truly not the morning sun of heaven   *5*

Better becomes the gray cheeks of the east,

Nor that full star that ushers in the even

Doth half that glory to the sober west,

As those two mourning eyes become thy face:

O, let it, then, as well beseem thy heart   *10*

To mourn for me, since mourning doth thee grace,

And suit thy pity like in every part.

　　Then will I swear Beauty herself is black,

　　And all they foul that thy complexion lack.

黑夫人对诗人看不起，诗人仍然喜欢黑夫人。
2.　　torment:　苦痛
　　　disdain:　藐视
3.　　loving mourners be:　亲近的悲痛者
4.　　ruth:　同情
7.　　ushers:　做先导
　　　even:　evening, 晚上
8.　　sober:　冷静，稳重；朴素
9.　　those two mourning eyes:　那双泪眼
10.　beseem:　适合
12.　suit thy pity like in every part:　给你各部分哀怜都穿同样的服装
14.　all they foul that thy complexion lack:　缺少你的肤色的那些人就都是丑

132

吾爱君眼睛	眼睛在同情	
知君轻蔑吾	折磨吾心疼	
眼睛披黑色	爱寓悲伤中	
怜悯吾痛苦	姣好目光明	
坦然对君言	朝阳升天空	5
难以去美化	东方灰面容	
夜晚叹先导	无奈启明星	
西方天清冷	对半赐光明	
难比君双目	朦胧泪眼睛	
呜呼告伤痛	能与君美容	10
请来光顾吾	伤痛风韵生	
怜悯君全身	全身和弦鸣	
吾誓黑即美	美因黑更精	
他人皆丑陋	缺君黑面容	

译者感言：西人喜欢黑眼睛，此事特例在莎翁。
　　　　　眼中好恶知多少，冷静头脑观言行。

133

Beshrew that heart that makes my heart to groan

For that deep wound it gives my friend and me!

Is't not enough to torture me alone,

But slave to slavery my sweet'st friend must be?

Me from myseif thy cruel eye hath taken,   *5*

And my next self thou harder hast engrossed:

Of him, myself, and thee, I am forsaken;

A torment thrice threefold thus to be crossed.

Prison my heart in thy steel bosom's ward,

But then my friend's heart let my poor heart bail;   *10*

Whoe'er keeps me, let my heart be his guard;

Thou canst not then use rigour in my jail:

   And yet thou wilt; for I, being pent in thee,

   Perforce am thine, and all that is in me.

黑夫人的眼睛又夺走了诗人的朋友。

1.   Beshrew: 诅咒
5.   taken: 勾走
6.   harder: 更有把握
    engrossed: 独占
7.   forsaken: 被遗弃
8.   A torment thrice threefold: 三三九倍的苦痛
    crossed: 使受挫折
9.   ward: 牢房
10. bail: 保释
12. rigour: 严厉

133

诅咒那颗心　　那心伤吾心

伤吾伤吾友　　伤痛如比深

那心不满足　　岂伤吾一人

吾友亦遭殃　　奴下奴之身

君目忒冷酷　　掳吾下狠心　　　　　　　*5*

又有一个吾　　被掳现如今

君友以及吾　　弃吾似路人

三三九重难　　煎熬含苦辛

君有铁心肠　　囚吾囚吾心

吾心属不幸　　保友心似金　　　　　　　*10*

岂管谁囚吾　　吾心守护神

狱中各有吾　　不容伤友身

君会如此做　　因吾囚君心

吾心之全部　　属君非他人

---

13. pent: 被关起来的
14. Perforce: 必然地
　　 am thine: 属于你
译者感言：狐媚勾人两眼睛，多少男儿动痴情。
　　　　　风月宝鉴勤拂拭，距离生美到手空。

134

So, now I have confest that he is thine,

And I myself am mortgaged to thy will,

Myself I'll forfeit, so that other mine

Thou wilt restore, to be my comfort still:

But thou wilt not, nor he will not be free,   *5*

For thou art covetous, and he is kind;

He learn'd but, surety-like, to write for me,

Under that bond that him as fast doth bind.

The statute of thy beauty thou wilt take,

Thou usurer, that putt'st forth all to use,   *10*

And sue a friend came debtor for my sake;

So him I lose through my unkind abuse.

 Him have I lost; thou hast both him and me:

 He pays the whole, and yet am I not free.

 诗人的情人放美貌高利贷，其中有较多的法律用语。

2. mortgaged: 抵押

3. forfeit: 被没收

3—4.so that other mine / Thou wilt restore: 好教你释放另一个给我

6. covetous: 贪心的

7. surety-like: 像保证人

9. statute: 特权；法规

10. usurer: 高利贷者

11. sue: 控告

  came debtor: who became a debtor, 成为负债者

14. He pays the whole, and yet am I not free: 他的债已还清，我还欠着债

134

吾已承认兮	他应属于君	
任由君吩咐	吾有抵押身	
吾愿献自己	吾身已两分	
请君释放吾	全我享温馨	
君意不释放	一半仍恋君	5
因君贪婪甚	因他大善心	
于吾效忠券	他做保证人	
有人设羁绊	紧缚他自身	
君持美卖据	索取担保金	
君放高利贷	财迷兼利昏	10
为吾负债友	君告吾寒心	
吾女欺负吾	吾失友何寻	
吾友已失去	友吾君皆擒	
友已全还债	吾债有千金	

译者感言：美貌财富暴利赢，玩弄权利图兴隆。
几人红尘称窥破，逍遥淡泊度平生。

135

Whoever hath her wish, thou hast thy *Will*,

And *Will* to boot, and *Will* in overplus;

More than enough and I that vex thee still,

To thy sweet will making addition thus.

Wilt thou, whose will is large and spacious,   5

Not once vouchsafe to hide my will in thine?

Shall will in others seem right gracious,

And in my will no fair acceptance shine?

The sea, all water, yet receives rain still.

And in abundance addeth to his store;   10

So thou, being rich in *Will*, add to thy *Will*

One will of mine, to make thy large *Will* more.

    Let no unkind, no fair beseechers kill;

    Think all but one, and me in that one *Will*.

    本诗写诗人与情人的缱绻。诗中 will 一词有 13 个之多，有愿望、情欲、性器、莎翁及朋友等多重含义。

2.   to boot: 除此以外，再者
        overplus: 剩余；过多
3.   that: who
        vex: 使烦恼
6.   vouchsafe: 赐予
8.   shine: 光线
10.   in abundance addeth to his store: 大大增加他的贮藏量
11.   So thou being rich in *Will* add to thy *Will*:   您心愿多，应加在你的威廉身上
13.   beseechers: 求爱者

135

女有女满意　　君有君威尔

已加一威尔　　再加一威尔

太多吾生厌　　烦恼君何时

如此性挑逗　　君情甜滋滋

君生欲壑广　　欲壑深千尺　　　　　5

可否容吾进　　销魂华清池

人有情欲对　　优雅风情迷

君拒吾情欲　　吾欲禁如斯

沧溟皆为水　　云雨乐滋滋

雨水增容量　　量大乐难支　　　　　10

君有威尔兮　　吾亦一威尔

吾爱君加上　　君爱近无极

无情用否字　　好客竟远离

一视同仁待　　吾做一威尔

14.　Think all but one, and me in that one *Will*:　让众愿同一愿，我也在这一愿里

译者感言：放胆写情有莎翁，曲折反复不了情。

　　　　　如此折磨孰堪忍，抛却红尘望虚空。

136

If thy soul check thee that I come so near,

Swear to thy blind soul that I was thy *Will*,

And will, thy soul knows, is admitted there;

Thus far for love my love-suit sweet fulfil.

Will will fulfil the treasure of thy love,   5

Ay, fill it full with wills, and my will one.

In things of great receipt with ease we prove

Among a number one is reckoned none:

Then in the number let me pass untold,

I hough in thy store's account I one must be;   10

For nothing hold me, so it please thee hold

That nothing me, a something, sweet, to thee:

   Make but my name thy love, and love that still,

   And then thou lovest me, for my name is *Will*.

期望黑夫人永远爱威廉·莎士比亚。同样的单词 will 出现 7 次之多。

1. check: 责备
3. will, thy soul knows, is admitted there: "心愿"，你的灵魂明白，你对情人一律欢迎
4. my love-suit sweet fulfil: 我对爱的追求如了愿
5. *Will* fulfill the treasure of thy love: 威廉会充实你爱情的宝库
6. my will one: 我也有一份
7. receipt: 能力
8. Among a number one is reckoned none: 一个不算什么
9. in the number let me pass untold: 算也就算一个数
11. it please thee hold: 你可以认为
12. nothing me: 微不足道的我

136

君心莫嗔怪	怨君之热情	
吾本一威尔	告君盲心灵	
情爱皆不拒	君自心里明	
总算心如愿	追君吾由衷	
吾爱有宝库	威尔填充盈	*5*
爱已填满兮	吾爱计其中	
账目数额巨	吾辈有真经	
再加一个进	账目不做声	
容吾混进账	莫让他人听	
于君总账内	容吾势必行	*10*
吾本不足道	君心宜轻松	
对此草木体	君知其至诚	
仅爱吾名姓	愿君爱永恒	
爱名即爱吾	威尔乃吾名	

13.　Make but my name thy love, and love that still:　只爱我的名字，爱到永远
译者感言：可叹身处热恋期，感情细腻却痴迷。
　　　　　　纠缠纷扰如何理，一朝过去梦依稀。

137

Thou blind fool, Love, what dost thou to mine eyes,

That they behold, and see not what they see?

They know what beauty is, see where it lies,

Yet what the best is take the worst to be.

If eyes, corrupt by over-partial looks,   *5*

Be anchored in the bay where all men ride,

Why of eyes' falsehood hast thou forged hooks,

Whereto the judgement of my heart is tied?

Why should my heart think that a several plot

Which my heart knows the wide world's common place?   *10*

Or mine eyes seeing this, say this is not,

To put fair truth upon so foul a face?

   In things right true my heart and eyes have erred,

   And to this false plague are they now transferred.

诗人恼恨自己眼睛的错觉，不知道什么是真正的美。

4.   what the best is take the worst to be: 我的眼睛把最丑的看成最美的

5.   over-partial: 爱的偏见

6.   Be anchored in the bay where all men ride: 在人人都停泊的港湾抛锚

7.   forged: 锻造

      hooks: 钩子；爱的偏见

9.   a several plot: 一块私有的土地

12.   put fair truth upon so foul a face: 把真美送给如此丑的一张脸

13.   In things right true my heart and eyes have erred: 我的心和眼错过了真美人

137

爱神盲而愚　　面对吾眼睛

汝用何手段　　瞪眼看不清

眼知何为美　　美为何方灵

然则知何故　　最恶当最精

倘若受诱惑　　偏爱误用情　　　　5

抛锚港湾里　　大众鼓帆行

为何眼虚幻　　汝用做钩绳

吾心被拴紧　　理智困胸中

认作私地产　　吾心非不明

大众应共享　　为何不分清　　　　10

为何吾眼睛　　看见说无踪

乃至辱美貌　　硬配丑脸形

错过真美女　　吾心吾眼睛

该吾活受罪　　见丑动风情

14.　false plague:　丑妇人
　　　transferred:　给出

译者感言：有了感情有美人，没有感情美失真。
　　　　　　差异距离皆为美，一朝到手又图新。

138

When my love swears that she is made of truth,

I do believe her, though I know she lies,

That she might think me some untutored youth,

Unlearned in the world's false subtleties.

Thus vainly thinking that she thinks me young,   *5*

Although she knows my days are past the best,

Simply I credit her false-speaking tongue:

On both sides thus is simple truth suppressed.

But wherefore says she not she is unjust?

And wherefore say not I that I am old?   *10*

O, love's best habit is in seeming trust,

And age in love loves not to have years told:

    Therefore I lie with her and she with me,

    And in our faults by lies we flattered be.

情人之间互相欺骗，诗人年纪比黑夫人要大，但不致于衰老。

3. untutored: 无知的
4. subtleties: 狡诈
7. I credit her false-speaking tongue: 我信任她的花言巧语
8. suppressed: 隐瞒
9. wherefore: why, 为什么
11. love's best habit is in seeming trust: 爱的最佳外表便是貌似忠心
12. age in love loves not to have years told: 恋爱中的老人不爱提到年纪
14. in our faults by lies we flattered be: 在互相欺骗中我们得到满足

译者感言：所谓爱情多谎言，嫣然一笑意缠绵。

        时光苦难见真性，贪图恩爱一时间。

138

吾爱有海誓	言她情真纯	
吾笃信吾爱	知谎不认真	
好使她认为	无知青年人	
不知虚伪世	不知奸谋深	
妄想她认为	吾年正青春	5
她心如明镜	盛年吾无存	
明知她撒谎	吾信非真心	
双方打交道	不以诚为邻	
为何吾不言	她心非忠贞	
为何她不语	吾乃衰年人	10
呜呼最佳爱	外表忠诚寻	
老者谈恋爱	不喜该青春	
吾对她撒谎	她言亦非真	
双方皆有短	假话保自身	

139

O, call not me to justify the wrong

That thy unkindness lays upon my heart;

Wound me not with thine eye, but with thy tongue;

Use power with power, and slay me not by art.

Tell me thou lovest elsewhere; but in my sight,   *5*

Dear heart, forbear to glance thine eye aside;

What need'st thou wound with cunning, when thy might

Is more than my o'erpressed defence can bide?

Let me excuse thee: ah, my love well knows

Her pretty looks have been mine enemies;   *10*

And therefore from my face she turns my foes,

That they elsewhere might dart their injuries;

    Yet do not so; but since I am near slain,

    Km me outright with looks, and rid my pain.

描述黑夫人对诗人冷漠，却对别人眉来眼去。

4. Use power with power:　狠狠地使用力量
6. forbear:　抑制
   glance thine eye aside:　向旁边张望
7—8. What need'st thou wound with cunning when thy might
   Is more than my o'erpressed defence can bide:
   你何必耍手段害人，在你的强硬压迫之下我岂能有所抗拒
9. my love well knows:　我的爱人明白
11. she turns my foes:　她把我的敌人移开
12. dart their injuries:　投掷。他们放射害人的毒镞

139

莫让吾恕兮	吾乃冷漠人	
君之不友好	耿耿于吾心	
勿用眼伤吾	可用言伤身	
力量加力量	莫施计谋深	
言君另有爱	吾之亲爱人	5
君在君身旁	目光莫乱寻	
吾有大力量	狡计不可亲	
处君重压下	岂容反抗身	
呜呼吾恕君	吾爱知其因	
她有海伦貌	美目敌入侵	10
她引敌人去	别处去勾魂	
面上敌人去	他地灾祸临	
切莫如斯为	杀吾太狠心	
用眼睛杀吾	解脱痛苦身	

14. outright: 直率地
    rid: 使除去
译者感言：意中人水性杨花，热度降咫尺天涯。
         牛皮看破美看破，竹篱茅舍老农家。

140

Be wise as thou art cruel; do not press

My tongue-tied patience with too much disdain;

Lest sorrow lend me words, and words express

The manner of my pity-wanting pain.

If I might teach thee wit, better it were,   *5*

Though not to love, yet, love, to tell me so;

As testy sick men, when their deaths be near,

No news but health from their physicians know;

For, if I should despair, I should grow mad,

And in my madness might speak ill of thee: *10*

Now this ill-wresting world is grown so bad,

Mad slanderers by mad ears believed be.

   That I may not be so, nor thou belied.

   Bear thine eyes straight, though thy proud heart go wide.

变心的情人逼人太甚。诗人祈求情人违心地说爱诗人本人。

1.　press:　压迫
2.　tongue-tied:　张口结舌
3.　Lest:　免得
4.　pity-wanting pain:　失去怜悯的痛苦
6.　Though not to love, yet, love, to tell me so:　你虽不爱我，爱人，也说你爱我
9.　if I should despair, I should grow mad:　如果我绝望，我就会疯狂
11.　ill-wresting:　把一切迫使成邪恶的
12.　Mad slanderers by mad ears believed be:　疯狂的诽谤被疯狂的耳朵相信
13.　belied:　给人以假相

140

如君之残忍	明智奉告君	
无言去忍受	莫做凌辱人	
悲伤赐吾语	吾语表情真	
缘何失宠幸	缘何苦在心	
倘若吾教君	最佳请爱神	5
吾爱非爱吾	言爱赐吾身	
急躁悲痛者	死期已降临	
医者言出口	惟听康复音	
倘或吾绝望	吾狂乃万分	
疯狂乱言语	恶语伤害君	10
邪恶有今世	颇多小人心	
人耳变疯狂	疯狂咒骂人	
吾不受其累	众口莫伤君	
君目直视吾	君心上青云	

14.　Bear thine eyes straight:　你眼睛正视
　　　thy proud heart go wide:　你心傲放荡
译者感言：不死心者好可怜，不懈努力想青天。
　　　　　几句好话得宽慰，心迷一人不思迁。

141

In faith, I do not love thee with mine eyes,

For they in thee a thousand errors note;

But 'tis my heart that loves what they despise,

Who, in despite of view, is pleased to dote;

Nor are mine ears with thy tongue's tune delighted;　　　*5*

Nor tender feeling to base touches prone,

Nor taste, nor smell, desire to be invited

To any sensual feast with thee alone:

But my five wits nor my five senses can

Dissuade one foolish heart from serving thee,　　　*10*

Who leaves unswayed the likeness of a man,

Thy proud heart's slave and vassal wretch to be:

　　Only my plague thus far I count my gain,

　　That she that makes me sin awards me pain.

诗人与情人有节制的情爱，以及诗人的负罪感。

2.　　note:　注意到

4.　　dote:　溺爱，过分喜爱。全句意思为：我的心一味溺爱，不管眼睛

6.　　prone:　易于的

9.　　five wits:　五智，即智慧，想象力，幻想，评估能力和记忆力

　　　　five senses:　五感觉，即听，看，尝，触和闻

11.　　unswayed:　不受影响的，不为所动的

12.　　vassal:　奴隶

　　　　wretch:　无耻之徒；卑鄙的人

13.　　Only my **plague** thus far I count my gain:　我受苦难至今，只有一项好处

141

君恕吾直言　　吾目非爱君

吾目已注视　　千种毛病身

吾心有钟爱　　吾目小看人

外貌不压众　　疯狂热恋君

不愿聆君语　　于耳厌君音　　　　　　5

不愿君抚摸　　触觉自有心

不愿君招待　　二者不欢欣

君有肉欲筵　　决意不陪君

心智曰五种　　五种器官分

未能断吾爱　　凝情海样深　　　　　　10

吾身无主宰　　有感无灵魂

君心谓高傲　　为奴侍奉勤

吾得一益处　　受苦熬到今

她使吾犯罪　　她赐吾苦辛

14.　she that makes me sin awards me pain:　她引诱我犯罪，也教会我受苦

译者感言：冷汗欲出观诗文，恨海情天勾冤魂。

世人参悟廉洁理，放任妄想罪惊心。

142

Love is my sin, and thy dear virtue hate,

Hate of my sin, grounded on sinful loving:

O, but with mine compare thou thine own state,

And thou shalt find it merits not reproving;

Or, if it do, not from those lips of thine,   5

That have profaned their scarlet ornaments

And sealed false bonds of love as oft as mine,

Robbed others' beds' revenues of their rents.

Be it lawful I love thee, as thou lovest those

Whom thine eyes woo as mine importune thee: 10

Root pity in thy heart, that, when it grows,

Thy pity may deserve to pitied be.

　If thou dost seek to have what thou dost hide,

　By self-example mayst thou be denied!

诗人情妇移情别爱，读者读到此诗难免心生不快。

1.　thy dear virtue hate:　恨是你的美德

2.　Hate of my sin:　恨我的罪过
　　Grounded on sinful loving:　由于罪过的爱

3.　with mine compare thou thine own state:　compare your own state with mine. 把你的处境与我的相比较

4.　merits not:　不该
　　reproving:　责骂；谴责

6.　profaned: profane　亵渎

7.　sealed false bonds of love:　屡次偷订爱的假盟

8.　Robbed others' beds' revenues of their rents:　抢夺别人床第上应得的租金

142

爱乃吾罪过	恨乃君德行
君恨吾之罪	带罪之爱情
君之处境兮	比之吾轻松
君意不该怪	吾情出忠诚
倘或君欲怪	嘴唇莫作声
皆因君嘴唇	玷污其艳红
君唇如吾唇	惯于一夜情
他人床有租	掠夺称利赢
君别爱合法	吾合法钟情
君惹吾追求	君目惹蝶蜂
君心怜悯植	怜悯长于胸
培植终有果	怜悯怜悯逢
倘若君藏宝	伸手去讨封
君有先例在	他人岂逢迎

右侧行号: 5 (第5行)、10 (第10行)

10. importune: 纠缠，追求
14. self-example: 自己的榜样
译者感言：莫谓人生是狂欢，游戏人生苦不堪。
　　　　　　天理昭彰莫轻率，精诚所至正果观。

143

Lo, as a careful housewife runs to catch

One of her feathered creatures broke away,

Sets down her babe, and makes all swift dispatch

In pursuit of the thing she would have stay;

Whilst her neglected child holds her in chase,   *5*

Cries to catch her whose busy care is bent

To follow that which flies before her face,

Not prizing her poor infant's discontent:

So runn'st thou after that which flies from thee,

Whilst I thy babe chase thee afar behind;   *10*

But if thou catch thy hope, turn back to me,

And play the mother's part, kiss me, be kind:

So will I pray that thou mayst have thy *Will*,

If thou turn back, and my loud crying still.

用母亲追家禽，孩子追母亲的故事，来表达诗人对情妇的追求。

1.　Lo:　看哪

2.　feathered creatures:　母鸡

3.　dispatch:　迅速办理，敏捷

4.　In pursuit of the thing she would have stay:　她急着追逐想要追回的东西

5.　holds her in chase:　想要追上她

6.　whose busy care is bent:　她只管一心追母鸡

8.　Not prizing her poor infant's discontent:　不把她孩子的哭喊放在心上

10.　chase thee afar behind:　在你身后追你

13.　thy *Will*:　你的愿望（欲望，威廉）

14.　If thou turn back, and my loud crying still:　如果你回过头来止住我的哭喊

143

请看一主妇	辛苦追家禽
养鸡知几何	一只逃出门
婴孩不能管	急忙去追寻
主妇疾步走	东西更揪心
婴孩被抛下	又来追妇人 *5*
婴孩在哭喊	哭喊追母亲
一心在追鸡	鸡飞牵妇心
孩儿哭可怜	主妇不怜悯
君追登徒子	劳力徒伤神
婴孩即是吾	苦苦追求君 *10*
君若遂心愿	还望回转身
柔肠亲吻吾	不愧好母亲
愿君生威尔	吾之祈祷真
倘若君回顾	止吾啼喊人

译者感言：世间只有感情真，深厚永恒得人心。
　　　　　　一味追求终有报，孩子不舍慈母亲。

144

Two loves l have of comfort and despair,

Which like two spirits do suggest me still:

The better angel is a man right fair,

The worser spirit a woman coloured ill.

To win me soon to hell, my female evil   *5*

Tempteth my better angel from my side,

And would corrupt my saint to be a devil,

Wooing his purity with her foul pride.

And whether that my angel be turn'd fiend

Suspect I may, yet not directly tell;   *10*

But being both from me, both to each friend,

I guess one angel in another's hell:

　　Yet this shall I ne'er know, but live in doubt,

　　Till my bad angel fire my good one out.

诗人对黑夫人强烈不满，指责黑夫人的肤色，谴责黑夫人引诱他的朋友。

2. do suggest me still: 老纠缠着我
3. The better angel is a man right fair: 善天使是个相貌堂堂的男子
4. The worser spirit a woman coloured ill: 恶精灵是个黑脸妇人
8. Wooing his purity with her foul pride: 用她邪恶的骄傲追求他的纯洁
9. fiend: 恶魔
11. being both from me, both to each friend: 两者都扔下我，而结成朋友
14. my bad angel fire my good one out: 我的恶天使把我的善天使赶走

译者感言：路子难走常彷徨，甜蜜诱惑鲜花香。
　　　　　矢志不渝世人敬，哭倒长城羡孟姜。

144

舒心与绝望	充吾二爱人	
总在驱使吾	两个守护神	
善者为天使	貌徒大卫寻	
恶者似精怪	黑面一妇人	
那位母夜叉	骗吾地狱寻	5
善良美天使	被诱离吾身	
蛊惑善天使	恶魔堕其心	
邪恶加纵欲	破坏其纯真	
是否变魔鬼	天使已沉沦	
仅管有疑窦	结论何处寻	10
二者均离吾	结成朋友亲	
吾猜一天使	堕入地狱门	
真情吾难探	永远疑心存	
真至那恶魔	释放天使身	

145

Those lips that Love's own hand did make

Breathed forth the sound that said 'I hate'

To me that languished for her sake:

But when she saw my woeful state.

Straight in her heart did mercy come,   *5*

Chiding that tongue that ever sweet

Was used in giving gentle doom;

And taught it thus anew to greet;

'I hate' she altered with an end,

That follow'd it as gentle day   *10*

Doth follow night, who like a fiend

From heaven to hell is flown away;

    'I hate' from hate away she threw.

    And saved my life, saying—'Not you.'

对恋人的深情使诗人憔悴，恋人的只言片语却极有份量。诗为四音步，通俗易读。

3.   languished: 憔悴，焦思
4.   woeful: 悲哀的
6.   Chiding: 责骂
7.   gentle doom: 甜蜜的判词
8.   taught it thus anew to greet: 教它重新说起
9.   altered: 改变
12.   Frow heav'n to hell is flown away: 把它从天堂甩进地狱
13.   'I hate' from hate away she throw: 她把"我恨"抛弃
14.   saved my life, saying 'not you': 她的一句话救了我的命："不是你"

145

爱神亲塑　　两颗樱唇

两字轻吐　　怒恨冲心

日夜苦念　　憔悴病身

她若会吾　　伤痛悲辛

立涌心头　　慈悲怜悯　　　　　　5

责怪舌头　　甜言惑人

蜜语欺众　　拒言温存

改口添字　　字眼气人

怒恨出口　　其后语辛

如此变化　　犹如昼临　　　　　　10

白昼继夜　　恶魔阴森

离伊甸园　　入地狱门

吾恨出口　　她抛狠心

非君出口　　拯救吾身

译者感言：充满诗意初恋人，心情飞扬敬花神。

感情世界众生相，探幽控寂不染尘。

146

Poor soul, the centre of my sinful earth—

My sinful earth these rebel powers array—

Why dost thou pine within and suffer dearth,

Painting thy outward walls so costly gay?

Why so large cost, having so short a lease,   *5*

Dost thou upon thy fading mansion spend?

Shall worms, inheritors of this excess,

Eat up thy charge? is this thy body's end?

Then, soul, live thou upon thy servant's loss,

And let that pine to aggravate thy store;   *10*

Buy terms divine in selling hours of dross;

Within be fed, without be rich no more:

So shalt thou feed on Death, that feeds on men,

And Death once dead, there's no more dying then.

描写灵与肉的关系，诗人认为内心的丰富胜过豪华的物质享受。

1. my sinful earth: 我的有罪的身躯
2. array: 包围
3. pine: 憔悴
    dearth: 饥馑
6. Dost thou upon thy fading masion spend?: 对你的倾颓中的大厦，你还要花费？
7. inheritors of this excess: 这个奢华的继承者
8. thy charge: 你的肉体
9. live thou upon thy servant's loss: 你靠你的肉体的消瘦度日
10. aggravate: 恶化

146

可怜吾灵魂	罪躯之中心
围攻遭叛逆	汝超叛逆军
暗中憔悴甚	为何饥饿侵
装潢于外壁	辉煌掷万金
花钱淌海水	租期犹寸阴
房屋颓欲坠	花钱白费心
铺张喂蛆虫	继承代世人
吃掉汝躯体	肉体归泉林
呜呼汝灵魂	折磨汝自身
憔悴日复日	意在积金银
永恒租期买	卖掉俗光阴
内心勤滋养	外富莫再亲
死神食世人	汝今食死神
一朝死神死	死亡不降临

5

10

11. dross: 废物；浪费的时光。全句意思为：拿无用的时间来买永恒
12. Within be fed, without be rich no more: 内心需要营养，外表勿需太堂皇
译者感言：内心平衡即天堂，心物二字费评章。
　　　　　心物皆空大彻悟，山水依旧拜慈航。

147

My love is as a fever, longing still

For that which longer nurseth the disease;

Feeding on that which doth preserve the ill,

The uncertain sickly appetite to please.

My reason, the physician to my love,　　　　　　　　　*5*

Angry that his prescriptions are not kept,

Hath left me, and I desp'rate now approve

Desire is death, which physic did except.

Past cure I am, now reason is past care,

And frantic mad with evermore unrest;　　　　　　　　*10*

My thoughts and my discourse as madmen's are,

At random from the truth vainly exprest;

　　For I have sworn thee fair, and thought thee bright,

　　Who art as black as hell, as dark as night.

诗人一时狂热，眼里的情妇美丽皎洁。如今心绪骤变，情妇像地狱一样黑暗可怜。

1.　longing still:　老在盼望
2.　longer:　副词，长期地
3.　Feeding on:　以……当食粮
6.　prescriptions:　处方
7.　desp'rate:　desperate, 绝望的
8.　physic did except　医家禁忌
9.　Past cure I am:　我无可救药
　　reason is past care:　失去了理智
10.　frantic mad:　狂癫
　　evermore unrest:　惶惑不安

147

吾爱似热病	渴望有食粮
维持病长久	更加不健康
胃口不控制	胃口不正常
渴望不能久	渴望非药方
爱情有医生	理智为良方
因为不遵嘱	理智怒满腔
挥手别吾去	绝望复彷徨
医界有禁忌	肉欲即死亡
吾已无药救	理智不思量
心神愈不安	神智愈癫狂
吾已成疯子	思维愚人乡
言语也荒诞	混乱无篇章
发誓君美艳	思想君辉煌
君真黑地狱	君黑冬夜长

5

10

14.　Who art as black as hell, as dark as night:　你像地狱一样黑，像夜一样暗
译者感言：千古之谜为爱情，理智欲念理难清。
　　　　　　磨合宽容入佳境，珍惜打造水晶宫。

148

O me, what eyes hath Love put in my head,

Which have no correspondence with true sight!

Or, if they have, where is my judgement fled,

That censures falsely what they see aright?

If that be fair whereon my false eyes dote,   *5*

What means the world to say it is not so?

If it be not, then love doth well denote

Love's eye is not so true as all men's; no.

How can it? O, how can Love's eye be true,

That is so vexed with watching and with tears?   *10*

No marvel, then, though I mistake my view;

The sun itself sees not till heaven clears.

   O cunning Love! with tears thou keep'st me blind,

   Lest eyes well seeing thy foul faults should find.

爱情力量惊人，能令多少痴男痴女彻夜失眼，眼泪不干。

2. Which have no correspondence with true sight: 竟没有与实物相符合的目光
3. fled: flee, 逃跑
4. censures: 非难，指责；判断
5. whereon: 在什么上面
    dote: 溺爱
6. What means the world to say it is not so: 为什么世人都说不承认
7. denote: 指示，表示
10. vexed: 苦恼的
11. marvel: 奇迹
12. The sun itself sees not till heaven clears: 要到天晴，太阳才照得明亮

148

苍天兮爱神	赐吾何眼光	
吾脑不知真	真假吾彷徨	
倘或能分辨	判断怎荒唐	
判断知何去	真切而无章	
吾目若昏花	所迷真辉煌	*5*
世人有异议	理由寻何方	
如若真不美	爱情意义详	
情人眼非众	不如众眼强	
如何强似众	爱眼兮精详	
望眼兮欲穿	为何泪汪汪	*10*
即使吾看错	何由忒惊慌	
太阳于晴日	明察亲万方	
狡黠之爱兮	泪水使吾盲	
憔恐明双目	罪恶自昭彰	

14.　Lest eyes well seeing thy foul faults should find:　否则明察的眼睛会发现你的邪恶的
　　　缺点

译者感言：感情心学探难清，如醉如狂如癫疯。
　　　　　以泪洗面无人晓，凄风苦雨伴孤灯。

149

Canst thou, O cruel! say I love thee not,

When I against myself with thee partake?

Do I not think on thee, when I forgot

Am of myself, all tyrant for thy sake?

Who hateth thee that I do call my friend? 5

On whom frown'st thou that I do fawn upon?

Nay, if thou lour'st on me, do I not spend

Revenge upon myself with present moan?

That merit do I in myself respect,

That is so proud thy service to despise, 10

When all my best doth worship thy defect,

Commanded by the motion of thine eyes?

But, love, hate on, for now I know thy mind;

Those that can see thou lovest, and I am blind.

诗人为自己因情妇秋波一转而忘情感到懊恼。

1. cruel: 狠心的
2. I against myself with thee partake: partake, 参与。我站在你一边，来反对我自己
3-4. I forgot / Am of myself, all tyrant for thy sake: 我忘了我自己，为了你，一个十足的暴君
6. On whom frown'st thou that I do fawn upon: fawn upon, 奉承，讨好。有哪个对你皱眉的人我却向他讨好
7. lour'st: 皱眉
9. merit: 优点
10. That is so proud thy service to despise: 如此骄傲而小视
11. all my best doth worship thy defect: 我全力崇拜的是你的缺陷

149

吾君兮残忍	何言吾憎君	
吾与君一道	反吾有决心	
吾岂不想君	遗忘吾因君	
全忘吾自己	暴君冤死人	
何人吾称友	君恨吾知音	5
君若皱眉头	吾岂讨欢欣	
君若迁怒吾	吾亦恼自身	
痛恨吾惹祸	悲叹复酸辛	
有时吾有悟	优点可自尊	
自尊亦自傲	不屑自称臣	10
吾之最佳者	膜拜缺陷君	
流转秋波送	指挥痴心人	
然而君须恨	吾已知君心	
爱彼有眼者	吾盲君莫亲	

12.　Commanded by the motion of thine eyes:　受你的眼睛的转动的指挥
14.　Those that can see thou lov'st, and I am blind:　你爱的那些人眼光明亮，而我是个瞎子
译者感言：放电触电在秋波，情男痴女浪漫多。
　　　　　　酒色财气无情剑，苍生含泪斩情魔。

150

O, from what power hast thou this powerful might

With insufficiency my heart to sway?

To make me give the lie to my true sight,

And swear that brightness doth not grace the day?

Whence hast thou this becoming of things ill,　　　　　5

That in the very refuse of thy deeds

There is such strength and warrantise of skill,

That, in my mind, thy worst all best exceeds?

Who taught thee how to make me love thee more,

The more I hear and see just cause of hate?　　　　　10

O, though I love what others do abhor,

With others thou shouldst not abhor my state;

　　If thy unworthiness raised love in me,

　　More worthy I to be beloved of thee.

　　感叹丑恶竟然化为美艳。
2.　insufficiency: 不充分
　　sway: 支配，统治
5.　Whence: 从何处
　　becoming of things ill: 化邪恶为神奇
6.　in the very refuse of thy deeds: 在你的所有的人所不齿的表现里
7.　warranties: 保证
8.　thy worst all best exceeds: 你的极恶超过一切至善
11.　abhor: 憎恶
译者感言: 所谓感情一瞬间，欲望冲动乱心田。
　　　　　欲壑难填成拖累，醒悟远观山水缘。

150

呜呼君魅力	何为魅力源	
无德无才貌	支配吾心田	
忠实吾有视	诬为说谎言	
白昼非明媚	优雅非白天	
变丑以为美	何为计谋源	*5*
君行极无聊	竟让吾开颜	
其中有力量	其中智慧篇	
君有极恶处	吾心里大观	
吾爱君愈甚	何人赐奇缘	
见闻日益广	教吾恨君言	*10*
呜呼吾所爱	人憎成长编	
君勿乱仿效	憎恨吾心田	
君本无价值	爱君想联翩	
君应更爱吾	吾心与君连	

151

Love is too young to know what conscience is;

Yet who knows not conscience is born of love?

Then, gentle cheater, urge not my amiss,

Lest guilty of my faults thy sweet self prove:

For, thou betraying me, I do betray   5

My nobler part to my gross body's treason;

My soul doth tell my body that he may

Triumph in love; flesh stays no farther reason;

But, rising at thy name, doth point out thee

As his triumphant prize. Proud of this pride,   10

He is contented thy poor drudge to be,

To stand in thy affairs, fan by thy side.

    No want of conscience hold it that I call

    Her 'love' for whose dear love I rise and fall.

诗人与情妇做爱。情欲、无奈和忏悔交织在一起。
1. conscience: 良心
2. who knows not conscience is born of love: 谁不知道良心产生于爱情
3. urge not my amiss: 别专找我的错
4. Lest guilty of my faults thy sweet self prove: 否则我的罪也牵连到温婉的你
6. nobler part: 灵魂
    my gross body's treason: 我叛逆的粗鄙的肉体
8. flesh stays no farther reason: 那块肉不耐烦听道理
9. rising at thy name: 一听到你的名字就振作起来
    point out thee: 指着你
10. Proud of this pride: 骄傲得喜开颜

151

爱神尚年幼	不知其良心	
无人不知晓	良心源爱神	
温柔欺诈者	请勿刁难人	
以免吾罪孽	牵连甜蜜君	
皆因君骗吾	吾骗吾灵魂	5
灵魂本高贵	责与叛变身	
灵魂告笨体	笨体听认真	
情场护全胜	肉体成静音	
一听君芳名	挺身指向君	
胜利护奖赏	傲慢自豪心	10
他竟心情愿	为奴伺候人	
站立君左右	操劳倒下身	
吾呼其良心	为此多辛勤	
吾称她至爱	时倒时挺身	

---

11. He is contented thy poor drudge to be: 做苦工的。他情愿做你的可怜的苦工
13. No want of conscience hold it that I call: 不要认为这是没有良心，我喊
14. Her 'love' for whose dear love I rise and fall: 我把她称作"爱"，为她的爱我起来又
    倒下
译者感言：哀人生之脆弱，叹理智之无能。
        可怜兮肉欲， 难达兮清明。

152

In loving thee thou know'st I am forsworn,
But thou art twice forsworn to me love swearing;
In act thy bed-vow broke, and new faith torn
In vowing new hate after new love bearing.
But why of two oaths' breach do I accuse thee,   *5*
When I break twenty? I am perjured most;
For all my vows are oaths but to misuse thee,
And all my honest faith in thee is lost:
For I have sworn deep oaths of thy deep kindness,
Oaths of thy love, thy truth, thy constancy;   *10*
And to enlighten thee gave eyes to blindness,
Or made them swear against the thing they see;
　For I have sworn thee fair; more perjured I,
　To swear against the truth so foul a lie!

该首为写黑夫人的最后一首。诗中描述双方都屡次违背爱的誓言。
1.　forsworn: forswear, 发誓抛弃
2.　thou art twice forsworn to me love swearing: 你发誓爱我，却两次背誓
3.　torn: tear, 撕毁
4.　new love bearing: 结下新欢
5.　breach: 违犯；破坏
6.　I break twenty: 我背誓二十次
　　perjured: 发假誓
9.　I have sworn deep oaths of thy deep kindness: 我曾经发过重誓说你情爱深深
11.　enlighten thee gave eyes to blindness: 为了照亮你，我宁愿瞎眼
13.　I have sworn thee fair: 我曾经发誓说你美

152

君知吾爱君	失信又背盟
君亦发誓言	爱吾两毁盟
床头交欢时	盟誓毁灭中
新欢兼新恨	新盟难逃生
君有两毁盟	责君不容情 *5*
毁盟二十次	吾惯于背盟
发尽天下誓	对君非真情
吾与君之交	早已失忠诚
吾发过重誓	言君深厚情
虚夸君之爱	忠贞与忠诚 *10*
为增君光辉	让吾目失明
吾目发假誓	黑白不分清
吾言君美丽	假誓更无情
卑劣虚伪谎	真情痛失声

14. To swear against the truth so foul a lie: 我发的誓不符真相，是邪恶的谎话
译者感言：两人本来为偷情，爱之誓言荒唐经。
　　　　　爱欲过程惊人世，纯洁忠诚万里行。

153

Cupid laid by his brand, and fell asleep:

A maid of Dian's this advantage found,

And his love-kindling fire did quickly steep

In a cold valley-fountain of that ground;

Which borrow'd from this holy fire of Love   5

A dateless lively heat, still to endure,

And grew a seething bath, which yet men prove

Against strange maladies a sovereign cure.

But at my mistress' eye Love's brand new-fired,

The boy for trial needs would touch my breast;   10

I, sick withal, the help of bath desired,

And thither hied, a sad distempered guest,

    But found no cure; the bath for my help lies

    Where Cupid got new fire,—my mistress' eyes.

    第 153—154 首借希腊罗马神话咏叹爱情。该首讲小爱神丘比特的火炬浸入山泉可治病，又能点燃爱情之火。

1.   Cupid: 罗马神话中的爱神丘比特
     brand: 火把
2.   Dian: 罗马神话中的月亮和狩猎女神
     found: 看见
3.   love-kindling: 点燃爱情的
     steep: 浸泡
5.   this holy fire of love: 这圣洁的爱情之火
6.   dateless lively heat: 永无尽期的不灭的热
     endure: 燃烧

153

爱神丘比特	放下火炬眠	
月神狄安娜	侍女伴月仙	
乘机盗爱火	火把�降情缘	
泉水借爱火	爱火神圣篇	
永久得热量	温暖亿万年	5
热气腾腾起	冷泉变温泉	
人们皆有证	疗疾解疑难	
爱神点火炬	吾爱目中燃	
爱神须试探	先触吾胸间	
自此吾罹病	渴望浴温泉	10
全身病难忍	焦燥苦难言	
医治全无效	吾爱目变泉	
爱神燃火炬	令吾再爱怜	

---

7. seething: 沸腾的
8. strange maladies: 疑难杂症
   sovereign cure: 神奇功效
10. The boy for trial needs would touch my breast: 为了试验那孩子要碰一下我的胸口
11. withal: with it, 由于那一碰
12. thither: 那里
    hied: 赶往
    distempered: 生病的；坏脾气的
13. the bath for my help: 能救治我的温泉
译者感言：活泼可爱小爱神，火炬神力服众心。
　　　　　七情六欲天造就，虎色图成惊世人。

154

The little Love-god lying once asleep

Laid by his side his heart-inflaming brand,

Whilst many nymphs that vowed chaste life to keep

Came tripping by; but in her maiden hand

The fairest votary took up that fire   5

Which many legions of true hearts had warm'd;

And so the general of hot desire

Was sleeping by a virgin hand disarmed.

This brand she quenchèd in a cool well by,

Which from Love's fire took heat perpetual,   10

Growing a bath and healthful remedy

For men diseased; but I, my mistress' thrall,

    Came there for cure, and this by that I prove,

    Love's fire heats water, water cools not love.

该首与前一首大意相同。诗人坚信清冷的泉水浇不灭爱情的火焰。

2. heart-inflaming: 点燃内心火焰
3. whilst: while
    nymphs: 宁芙，希腊罗马神话中居于山林水泽的仙女
    vowed chaste life to keep: 誓守贞操
4. tripping: 轻快地
5. votary: 信徒
6. legions: 众多
7. the general of hot desire: 热烈欲望的主宰
8. a virgin hand disarmed: 一位贞女的素手解除武装
9. quenchèd: 熄灭

154

躺下即入睡	可爱小爱神	
身旁放火炬	点燃情人心	
宁芙众仙女	圣洁守自身	
轻轻舞步起	翩翩美降临	
其中有绝艳	嫩手火炬亲	*5*
真心燃无数	温暖又温馨	
胸中欲火烈	霸主乃将军	
蒙头正酣睡	卸甲缘女贞	
贞女盗火炬	沉泉水深深	
泉水得爱火	热量恒古今	*10*
妙哉变温泉	沐浴可健身	
人患疾得治	吾爱奴吾身	
奔泉为医治	吾得证据真	
爱火烧热水	爱火水难吞	

---

12. thrall: 奴隶
14. Love's fire heats water, water cools not love: 爱情之火可烧热泉水，冷泉水不能冷却爱情

译者感言：贞洁仙女守贞操，偷盗火炬爱火烧。
　　　　　爱情之火蕴奥义，神秘诱人春花娇。

II VENUS AND ADONIS

Vilia miretur vulgus: mihi flauus Apollo
Pocula Castalia plena ministret aqua.

—— Ovid

　　此两句诗源于奥维德（Ovid 公元前 43—18）的《爱情诗》（*Amore* 第一卷第十五首第 35—36 行）。

　　有两种英语译文，一种出自 Bate, Jonathan 的 *William Shakespeare Complete Works*: *Let the rabble admire worthless things, / May golden Apollo supply me with cups full of water*

II　女神之恋

平凡人只爱好毫无价值之物
金色之阿波罗赐我缪斯灵泉

　　　　　　——奥维德

TO THE RIGHT HONORABLE HENRIE WRIOTHESLEY[1],

EARLE[2] OF SOUTHAMPTON, AND BARON[3] OF TITCHFIELD

Right Honourable,

I know not how I shall offend in dedicating[4] my unpolished lines to your Lordship, nor how the worlde will censure[5] mee for choosing so strong a proppe[6] to support so weake a burthen, only if your Honour seem but pleased, I account[7] myself highly praised, and vow to take advantage of all idle houres, till I have honoured you with some graver labour[8]. But if the first heire of my invention prove deformed, I shall be sorie it had so noble a god-father[9]: and never after eare[10] so barren a land, for feare[11] it yeeld[12] me still so bad a harvest, I leaue[13] it to your Honourable suruey[14], and your Honor to your hearts content, which I wish may alwaies[15] answere your owne wish, and the worlds hopefull expectation.

Your Honors in all dutie,

William Shakespeare.

1. Henry Wriotheley: 亨利·瑞奥塞斯利（1573—1624）
2. Earle: 伯爵
3. Baron: 男爵；贵族
4. dedicating: 奉献
5. censure: 判断
6. proppe: 靠山
7. account: 认为
8. graver labor: 更严肃的创作，即《露克丽丝》

敬献

扫桑普顿伯爵、梯契菲尔德男爵

亨利·瑞奥塞斯利阁下

阁下台鉴：

　　仆难料拙诗献上后会有何罪过。若寻如此强大之赞助于如此菲薄之负荷，世人如何指责，仆亦未可知。承蒙阁下赞助，不胜荣幸之至。仆焚膏继晷，费尽艰辛，以不负阁下抬爱。如证实拙诗之首要继承者为畸形，仆实遗憾传承者竟有如此高贵之教父。仆将不在此贫瘠土地耕耘，意恐再次歉收。敬请阁下甄别，但愿阁下合意。阁下为世人之厚望，仆随时听从驱策。

阁下之仆从

威廉·莎士比亚

---

9. god-father: 教父
10. eare: 耕耘
11. feare: fear, 担心
12. yeeld: yield, 产生
13. leaue: leave, 离开
14. suruey: survey, 俯瞰；检查
15. alwaies: always, 总是

1

Even as the sun with purple-color'd face

Had ta'en his last leave of the weeping morn,

Rose-cheek'd Adonis hied him to the chase;

Hunting he lov'd, but love he laugh'd to scorn.

 Sick-thoughted Venus makes amain unto him,   *5*

 And like a bold-fac'd suitor 'gins to woo him.

2

"Thrice fairer than myself," thus she began,

"The field's chief flower, sweet above compare,

Stain to all nymphs, more lovely than a man,

More white and red than doves or roses are,   *10*

 Nature, that made thee with herself at strife,

 Saith that the world hath ending with thy life.

(1—12)

1

3. hied:　赶往

5. amain:　急速

6. suitor:　追逐者

　'gins:　begins，开始

2

7. Thrice:　三倍

9. Stain:　染色

　nymphs:　宁芙, 希腊罗马神话中的山林水泽仙女

11. with herself at strife:　大自然的努力

12. Saith:　(大自然)说

1

鲜红面庞太阳神

依依惜别洒泪晨

玫瑰面容阿童尼

喜猎嘲讽恋爱人

女神相思追求苦　　　　　5

厚颜求美求爱勤

2

女神盛赞阿童尼

田野鲜花敢斗奇

宁芙倾心俊男走

玫瑰平庸白鸽离　　　　　10

大象衍化夸造化

你若仙去天道微

（1—12）

3

"Vouchsafe, thou wonder, to alight thy steed,

And rein his proud head to the saddle-bow;

If thou wilt deign this favor, for thy meed   *15*

A thousand honey secrets shalt thou know.

 Here come and sit, where never serpent hisses,

 And being set, I'll smother thee with kisses;

4

"And yet not cloy thy lips with loath'd satiety,

But rather famish them amid their plenty,   *20*

Making them red, and pale, with fresh variety—

Ten kisses short as one, one long as twenty.

 A summer's day will seem an hour but short,

 Being wasted in such time-beguiling sport."

(13—24)

3
13. Vouchsafe: 赐予
 alight: 从马背上下来
14. rein: 拴紧
 saddle bow: 马鞍的前穹
15. deign: 俯准
 meed: 应得的一份
18. smother: 使透不过气来

4
19. cloy: 使吃腻
 loath'd satiety: 厌恶的过饱
24. time-beguiling sport: 消遣时光的游戏

3

请快下马美少年
骄傲头颅勒前鞍
你要报答知好意　　　　　15
体味心灵百倍甜
这儿没有蛇吐信
坐下我吻须尽欢

4

勿使饱食腻嘴唇
美食流涎受煞人　　　　　20
鲜红白皙嘴唇饱
一吻长过二十吻
夏日一刻嫌更短
消磨时光逍遥神

（13—24）

5

With this she seizeth on his sweating palm,   25

The president of pith and livelihood,

And trembling in her passion, calls it balm,

Earth's sovereign salve, to do a goddess good.

   Being so enrag'd, desire doth lend her force

   Courageously to pluck him from his horse.   30

6

Over one arm the lusty courser's rein,

Under her other was the tender boy,

Who blush'd, and pouted in a dull disdain,

With leaden appetite, unapt to toy;

   She red and hot as coals of glowing fire,   35

   He red for shame, but frosty in desire.

(25—36)

5
26. precedent: 标志
   pith: 性欲力量
27. balm: 香脂
28. sovereign: 无上（良方）
   salve: 药方

6
31. courser: 马
   rein: 缰绳
33. pouted: 撅嘴
   disdain: 蔑视
34. unapt: 不愿意；不能
   toy: 爱之游戏

5

女神抓手汗淋淋　　　　　25
少年精力称过人
她言香脂热恋抖
慷慨草地助女神
欲火中烧力量猛
马上拉下少年人　　　　　30

6

女神手牵马缰绳
手挽俊男脸通红
轻视撅嘴无兴趣
不愿游戏赏女容
炭火灼烧她脸红　　　　　35
少年羞辱情霜冰

（25—36）

7

The studded bridle on a ragged bough

Nimply she fastens (O how quick is love!);

The steed is stalled up, and even now

To tie the rider she begins to prove.   *40*

  Backward she push'd him, as she would be thrust,

  And govern'd him in strength, though not in lust.

8

So soon was she along as he was down,

Each leaning on their elbows and their hips.

Now doth she stroke his cheek, now doth he frown,   *45*

And 'gins to chide, but soon she stops his lips,

  And kissing speaks, with lustful language broken,

  "If thou wilt chide, thy lips shall never open."

(37—48)

7

37. studded:　布满饰钉的
 bridle:　缰绳，马勒
 ragged bough:　树枝
39. steed:　马
 stall:　拴；系
40. prove:　尝试
41. thrust:　撞

8

43. along:　在地上边
44. Each:　两个人（维纳斯与阿童尼）
46. chide:　责骂

7

树枝灵巧系缰绳
女神性急缘爱情
彩缰拴好一骏马
骑马之人绳索中   *40*
猛撞少年向后转
控制男身难控情

8

少年躺下陪女神
胳膊支地有双臀
女摸男脸眉头皱   *45*
男要指责女堵唇
边吻少年边说爱
你要骂我甭启唇

（37—48）

9

He burns with bashful shame, she with her tears

Doth quench the maiden burning of his cheeks;   *50*

Then with her windy sighs and golden hairs

To fan and blow them dry again she seeks.

    He saith she is immodest, blames her miss;

    What follows more, she murders with a kiss.

10

Even as an empty eagle, sharp by fast,   *55*

Tires with her beak on feathers, flesh, and bone,

Shaking her wings, devouring all in haste,

Till either gorge be stuff 'd, or prey be gone;

    Even so she kiss'd his brow, his cheek, his chin,

    And where she ends, she doth anew begin.   *60*

(*39—60*)

9

49. bashful: 害羞的
50. quench: 熄灭
51. windy sighs: 风一样的叹息
53. miss: 放肆
54. murders: 打断

10

55. empty eagle: 饥饿的鹰
    fast: 长久无食而饥饿
56. Tires: 撕裂
57. devouring: 吞
58. gorge: 鹰的喉咙
59. chin: 下巴

9

女流眼泪男脸红
浇灭男脸火升腾　　　　50
风样叹息金色发
扇干吹干忙乱中
男斥女神失仪范
女用亲吻不想听

10

女馋活像一饿鹰　　　　55
利喙撕羽骨肉红
狼吞虎咽扇双翅
吃饱吃净方尽兴
吻他下巴又颊额
一遍一遍有激情　　　　60

（39—60）

11

Forc'd to content, but never to obey,

Panting he lies, and breatheth in her face.

She feedeth on the steam, as on a prey,

And calls it heavenly moisture, air of grace,

    Wishing her cheeks were gardens full of flowers,　　*65*

    So they were dewed with such distilling showers.

12

Look how a bird lies tangled in a net,

So fast'ned in her arms Adonis lies;

Pure shame and awed resistance made him fret,

Which bred more beauty in his angry eyes.　　*70*

    Rain added to a river that is rank

    Perforce will force it overflow the bank.

(61—72)

11

62. Panting:　气喘
    breatheth in her face:　喘气喷到她脸上
63. as on a prey:　像吃美味（捕获物）
64. heavenly moisture:　天堂的润气
66. dewed:　被雨露滋润
    distilling:　滴下

12

67. tangled:　纠缠；纠结
69. awed resistance:　由于害怕而不敢抵抗
    fret:　恼怒
70. bred:　滋生
71. rank:　充满
72. Perforce:　势必

11

少年被迫从女神
躺地气喘脸上喷
女神吸气尝美味
上天赐福降甘霖
双颊花园花争艳　　　　　　65
好雨润泽女承恩

12

鸟儿被缠困网罗
少年被搂无奈何
无法抗拒羞成怒
恼羞之人姿态多　　　　　　70
急湍河水遇暴雨
泛滥冲堤动干戈

（61—72）

13

Still she entreats, and prettily entreats,

For to a pretty car she tunes her tale.

Still is he sullen, still he low'rs and frets,   75

'Twixt crimson shame and anger ashy-pale.

   Being red, she loves him best, and being white,

   Her best is bettered with a more delight.

14

Look how he can, she cannot choose but love,

And by her fair immortal hand she swears   80

From his soft bosom never to remove

Till he take truce with her contending tears,

   Which long have rain'd , making her cheeks all wet,

   And one sweet kiss shall pay this comptless debt.

(73—84)

13

73. entreats: 恳求
    prettily: 漂亮地
75. sullen: 绷着脸不高兴的
    low'rs: frawns, 皱眉
    frets: 恼怒
76. crimson: 深红；绯红
    ashy-pale: 灰白
78. Her best is bettered with a more delight:
    她愈高兴地显出美妙的姿态

14

80. her fair immortal hand: 她的美妙的仙
    女玉手
81. his soft bosom: 他的柔嫩的胸
82. take truce: 制造和平
    contending tears: 攻击的眼泪
84. comptless: 数不清的

338

13

女神恳求莺燕声
面对少年诉真情
他仍嗔怒眉头皱 　　　　　75
脸色煞白又通红
满面通红女神爱
面色煞白女动容

14

不管面色女衷情
举手发誓美姿容 　　　　　80
愿手永存柔怀上
少年求和泪眼睛
满面难止女神泪
一个甜吻债务清

（73—84）

15

Upon this promise did he raise his chin,   *85*

Like a divedapper peering through a wave,

Who being look'd on, ducks as quickly in;

So offers he to give what she did crave,

But when her lips were ready for his pay,

He winks, and turns his lips another way.   *90*

16

Never did passenger in summer's heat

More thirst for drink than she for this good turn

Her help she sees, but help she cannot get,

She bathes in water, yet her fire must burn.

"O, pity", 'gan she cry, "flint-hearted boy,   *95*

'Tis but a kiss I beg, why art thou coy?

(85—96)

15

86. divedapper: 鹏鹏

87. ducks as quickly in: 急忙钻入水里

88. So offers he to give what she did crave:
他（阿童尼）打算给她恳求的

90. winks: 眨眼；故意忽视

16

93. Her help: 她的救星

94. She bathes in water, yet her fire must
burn: 她泡在清水里，她的火仍在燃
烧；泡身清泉火焰临

95. flint-hearted boy: 铁石心肠的少年

96. coy: 怕羞的；忸怩的

15

听她此言男抬头　　　　85
鹧鸪浪中窥根由
发现有人水里洇
献上双唇女神求
女神芳唇愿接受
闭目扭唇男害羞　　　　90

16

炎炎盛夏有旅人
焦渴难比该女神
恍若清泉难靠近
泡身清泉火焰临
她呼少年好心狠　　　　95
为何羞涩不亲吻

（85—96）

341

17

"I have been wooed, as I entreat thee now,

Even by the stern and direful god of war,

Whose sinowy neck in battle ne'er did bow,

Who conquers where he comes in every jar,   *100*

 Yet hath he been my captive, and my slave,

 And begg'd for that which thou unask'd shalt have.

18

"Over my altars hath he hung his lance,

His batt'red shield, his unconttolled crest,

And for my sake hath learn'd to sport and dance,   *105*

To toy, to wanton, dally, smile, and jest,

 Scorning his churlish drum, and ensign red,

 Making my arms his field, his tent my bed.

(97—108)

17
98. direful: 可怕的
99. sinowy: 强壮的；肌肉发达的
100. jar: 战斗

18
103. altars: 祭坛
 lance: 长矛

104. crest: 盔
106. toy: 游戏
 wanton: 淫荡
 dally: 调戏
 jest: 打趣
107. churlish drum: 粗暴的鼓
 ensign: 军旗

17

我也苦苦被追求
猛厉战神也低头
挺着脖子上战场
攻无不克鬼神愁　　　　　　　*100*
如今见我成奴隶
他求不用你动手

18

盾矛挂在我神坛
盔缨无敌战盾斑
学我嬉戏又舞蹈　　　　　　　*105*
放浪调情想求欢
红旗战鼓皆不顾
我怀战场床营盘

（97—108）

19

"Thus he that overrul'd I overswayed,

Leading him prisoner in a red-rose chain;   *110*

Strong-temper'd steel his stronger strength obeyed,

Yet was he servile to my coy disdain.

  O, be not proud, nor brag not of thy might,

  For mast'ring her that foiled the god of fight.

20

"Touch but my lips with those fair lips of thine—   *115*

Though mine be not so fair, yet are they red—

The kiss shall be thine own as well as mine.

What seest thou in the ground? hold up thy head,

  Look in mine eyeballs, there thy beauty lies;

  Then why not lips on lips, since eyes in eyes?   *120*

(109—120)

19

109. he that overrul'd I overswayed:　君临一切的他被我征服

110. a red-rose chain:　红玫瑰链子

111. Strong-temper'd steel his stronger strength obeyed:　百炼钢也屈从于他的强力

102. servile:　奴隶的
　　my coy disdain:　我的含羞的诱惑的

不屑

113. nor brag not of thy might:　不要夸耀你的力量大

114. foiled:　打败

20

118. What seest thou in the ground:　你在地上看见了什么

120. eyes in eyes:　眼睛中有眼睛

19

不可一世服女神
粉红锁链套他身　　　　　　110
精钢难敌他膂力
娇羞摆布他甘心
叫声少年甭傲慢
能服战神有女人

20

用你美唇触我唇　　　　　　115
我唇不美红可人
你唇亲我还归你
抬起头来看女神
我眼存有你美貌
对视为何不对唇　　　　　　120

（109—120）

21

"Art thou asham'd to kiss? then wink again,

And I will wink, so shall the day seem night.

Love keeps his revels where there are but twain;

Be bold to play, our sport is not in sight;

　　These blue-veined violets whereon we lean　　　*125*

　　Never can blab, nor know not what we mean.

22

"The tender spring upon thy tempting lip

Shows thee unripe; yet mayst thou well be tasted.

Make use of time, let not advantage slip,

Beauty within itself should not be wasted.　　　*130*

　　Fair, flowers that are not gath'red in their prime

　　Rot, and consume themselves in little time.

　　　　　　　　　　　　　　　　　　　　　　　　(121—132)

21

121. wink:　闭眼

123. revels:　狂欢

　　　twain:　两个人

124. sport:　娱乐；游戏

125. blue-veined violets:　蓝色筋脉的紫罗兰

126. blad:　泄密

22

127. tender spring:　男孩唇上的茸茸的胡子

　　　tempting lip:　诱人的嘴唇

130. Beauty within itself should not be wasted:　自身的美不可浪费

21

不要闭眼羞接吻
白昼闭目夜降临
幽会畅怀两情侣
放胆亲热无外人
紫罗兰花压身下　　125
不懂亲爱语不闻

22

唇上茸毛真诱人
尚未成熟秀色新
抓住机遇莫错过
美貌轻抛何处寻　　130
鲜花盛开及时采
不采瞬间碾作尘

（121—132）

23

"Were I hard-favor'd, foul, or wrinkled old,

Ill-nurtur'd, crooked, churlish, harsh in voice:

O'erworn, despised, rheumatic, and cold,   *135*

Thick-sighted, barren, lean, and lacking juice,

    Then mightst thou pause, for then I were not for thee,

    But having no defects, why dost abhor me?

24

"Thou canst not see one wrinkle in my brow,

Mine eyes are grey, and bright, and quick in turning;   *140*

My beauty as the spring doth yearly grow,

My flesh is soft and plump, my marrow burning,

    My smooth moist hand, were it with thy hand felt,

    Would in thy palm dissolve, or seem to melt.

(133—144)

23
133. hard-favor'd: 长得丑
    foul: 邪恶
134. crooked: 扭曲的
    churlish: 粗暴；吝啬
    harsh: 刺耳
135. O'erworn: 衰老
    despised: 被人看不起
    rheumatic: 眼睛流泪的
136. lean: 干瘦

lacking juice: 缺乏汁液的
138. defects: 缺点
    abhor: 厌恶
24
141. grow: 更新
142. soft and plump: 柔软而丰满
    marrow: 精华
    burning: 性热情的
144. dissolve: 溶解
    melt: 融化；酥融

23

我若面丑布皱纹
声哑性乖行粗蠢
衰老风湿冷毒恶
视茫枯干缺教人　　　　　135
你该犹豫我不配
为何抛弃女美神

24

君难见我额上纹
蓝眼明亮动招人　　　　　140
我美甘泉年年涨
柔肌白腴有风神
玉手润滑轻抚摸
化于君手何处寻

　　　　　　　　　　　　　　　　（133—144）

349

25

"Bid me discourse, I will enchant thine ear,   *145*

Or like a fairy trip upon the green,

Or like a nymph, with long dishevelled hair,

Dance on the sands, and yet no footing seen.

   Love is a spirit all compact of fire,

   Not gross to sink, but light, and will aspire.   *150*

26

"Witness this primrose bank whereon I lie,

These forceless flowers like sturdy trees support me;

Two strengthless doves will draw me through the sky,

From morn till night, even where I list to sport me.

   Is love so light, sweet boy, and may it be   *155*

   That thou should think it heavy unto thee?

(145—156)

25

145. Bid: 吩咐

    discourse: 话语

    enchant: 使喜悦

146. a fairy trip upon the green: 绿草地上仙女的步子

147. disheveled hair: 松散的头发

149. all compact of fire: 全由情火凝聚成

150. Not gross to sink: 不因重浊而下沉

    aspire: 飘举

26

151. primrose: 报春花

152. sturdy: 强健，茁壮

154. list: 欲望

    sport: 使愉快

25

听我讲话像妖精　　　　　*145*

仙女草地舞娉婷

宁芙长发披散美

沙地起舞足迹轻

爱情精灵烈火做

永坠偏要冉冉升　　　　　*150*

26

我躺河岸樱草丛

娇花像枝将我撑

双鸽托我重霄九

早晚由我定行踪

爱情轻盈问小伙　　　　　*155*

为何怕重不担承

（145—156）

27

"Is thine own heart to thine own face affected?

Can thy right hand seize love upon thy left?

Then woo thyself, be of thyself rejected;

Steal thine own freedom, and complain on theft.   *160*

　　Narcissus so himself himself forsook,

　　And died to kiss his shadow in the brook.

28

"Torches are made to light, jewels to wear,

Dainties to taste, fresh beauty for the use,

Herbs for their smell, and sappy plants to bear: *165*

Things growing to themselves are growth's abuse.

　　Seeds spring from seeds, and beauty breedeth beauty;

　　Thou wast begot, to get it is thy duty.

(157—168)

27

157. affected:　爱怜

159. woo thyself, be of thyself rejected:
　　追求自己，遭自己拒绝

161. Narcissus:　希腊神话中的那喀索斯，
　　自己恋上自己水中的影子，死后化成
　　水仙花；水仙花；净化
　　forsook:　forsake, 放弃，抛弃

162. brook:　溪流

28

164. Dainties:　美味的食物

165. Herbs:　草本植物
　　sappy:　树液多的
　　bear:　结果实

166. abuse:　滥用

27

是否自爱自娇容
左右手握抱爱情
自我爱恋遭自拒
自由自偷怨贼横　　　　　　160
那喀索斯自遗弃
自吻自影死河中

28

珠宝佩戴火炬燃
美味品尝享美鲜
花草为香树为果　　　　　　165
单为自生常理偏
种子生种美生美
你生要把后代传

（157—168）

353

29

"Upon the earth's increase why shouldst thou feed,

Unless the earth with thy increase be fed?   *170*

By law of nature thou art bound to breed,

That thine may live, when thou thyself art dead;

   And so in spite of death thou dost survive,

   In that thy likeness still is left alive."

30

By this the love-sick queen began to sweat,   *175*

For where they lay the shadow had forsook them,

And Titan, tired in the midday heat,

With burning eye did hotly overlook them,

   Wishing Adonis had his team to guide,

   So he were like him, and by Venus side.   *180*

(169—180)

29

169-170. Upon the earth's increase why should thou feed
         Unless the earth with thy increase be fed?
         在地球上万物繁衍，你得到享用
         你为什么不去生育，来给地球以回报？

172. thine: 你的后代

174. likeness: 形象
     still: 永远

29

享用造化之厚恩

感恩之情后代存　　　　　　170

繁衍子孙自然法

你虽身死存子孙

尽管死去你长有

你有后裔代代新

30

相思女神热汗流　　　　　　175

所卧草地树荫无

炎炎正午日神倦

眼瞪二人怒火出

想让少年飞车管

他亲女神乐绸缪　　　　　　180

（169—180）

30

175. love-sick:　相思病

177. Titan:　希腊神话中的巨人，一说为太阳神，相当于罗马神话中的 Apollo（阿波罗）

178. overlook:　俯视

179. Wishing Adonis had his team to guide:　希望阿童尼去驾驭他的马匹

180. So he were like him, and by Venus side:　这样他可以取代阿童尼，随在维纳斯身边

31

And now Adonis, with a lazy sprite,

And with a heavy, dark, disliking eye,

His low'ring brows o'erwhelming his fair sight,

Like misty vapors when they blot the sky,

  Souring his cheeks, cries, "Fie, no more of love! *185*

  The sun doth bum my face, I must remove."

32

"Ay me," quoth Venus, "young, and so unkind,

What bare excuses mak'st thou to be gone!

I'll sigh celestial breath, whose gentle wind

Shall cool the heat of this descending sun;   *190*

  I'll make a shadow for thee of my hairs;

  If they burn too, I'll quench them with my tears.

(181—192)

31
181. sprite:　精神
183. o'erwhelming:　压住，挡住
184. misty vapors:　云雾般的蒸气
  blot:　遮暗
185. Souring:　使变得讨厌无趣
  Fie:　呸！

32
187. quoth:　说
188. bare:　没有价值的
189. celestial breath:　吐一口仙气
190. descending:　落下
192. quench:　熄灭

31

少年厌恶无精神

双眼怒气露阴沉

英俊面庞眉头锁

雾气遮蔽天庭阴

板起面孔斥责爱   *185*

躲日我得快离身

32

女神叹他太薄情

离开理由不能听

我招凉风吐仙气

夕阳炎热潜无踪   *190*

我用秀发把你遮

秀发燃烧泪水倾

(181—192)

357

33

"The sun that shines from heaven shines but warm,

And lo I lie between that sun and thee;

The heat I have from thence doth little harm,　　　　*195*

Thine eye darts forth the fire that burneth me,

　And were I not immortal, life were done,

　Between this heavenly and earthly sun.

34

"Art thou obdurate, flinty, hard as steel?

Nay, more than flint, for stone at rain relenteth.　　　*200*

Art thou a woman's son and canst not feel

What 'tis to love, how want of love tormenteth?

　O, had thy mother borne so hard a mind,

　She had not brought forth thee, but died unkind.

(193—204)

33

195. thence:　天上的太阳

196. darts:　飞快的一瞥

197. were done:　结束

34

199. obdurate:　冷酷无情，顽固不化

200. Nay:　不

flint:　燧石

relenteth:　减弱

202. how want of love tormenteth:　缺少爱
如何受折磨

204. She had not brought forth thee, but died
unkind:　她不会生下你，她会不仁慈
地死去

33

温暖照耀好太阳
我为少年遮阳光
炽热于我无大害　　　　195
你眼冒火把我伤
我若非神处天地
两阳照我命不长

34

愚顽石头硬似钢
雨水穿石莫太强　　　　200
女人生你领悟爱
没有爱情苦难当
你母像你心肠狠
不会生你找无常

(193—204)

35

"What am I that thou shouldst contemn me this?   *205*

Or what great danger dwells upon my suit?

What were thy lips the worse, for one poor kiss?

Speak, fair, but speak fair words, or else be mute.

   Give me one kiss, I'll give it thee again,

   And one for int'rest, if thou wilt have twain.   *210*

36

"Fie, liveless picture, cold and senseless stone,

Well-painted idol, image dull and dead,

Statue contenting but the eye alone,

Thing like a man, but of no woman bred!

   Thou art no man, though of a man's complexion,   *215*

   For men will kiss even by their own direction."

(205—216)

35

205. contemn: 蔑视
206. suit: 求爱

36

212. idol: 偶像
213. Statue contenting: 使眼睛得到满足

的雕像，罗马传说中塞浦路斯国王皮
格马利翁（Pygmalion），热恋他自己
创作的少女雕像

215. complexion: 面部，面容
216. direction: 本质，本性

35

奚落不知我女神　　　　　*205*

我追求你何祸临

吻我一下有何苦

不讲情话莫启唇

吻我一下我有报

我付利息吻两吻　　　　　*210*

36

呸呸石头冷无情

涂彩偶像愚不灵

眼睛仅看一雕像

像人却非女人生

不是男人空仪表　　　　　*215*

男人接吻主动行

（205—216）

361

37

This said, impatience chokes her pleading tongue,

And swelling passion doth provoke a pause.

Red cheeks and fiery eyes blaze forth her wrong;

Being judge in love, she cannot right her cause.   *220*

 And now she weeps, and now she fain would speak,

 And now her sobs do her intendments break.

38

Sometimes she shakes her head, and then his hand,

Now gazeth she on him, now on the ground;

Sometime her arms infold him like a band: *225*

She would, he will not in her arms be bound;

 And when from thence he struggles to be gone,

 She locks her lily fingers one in one.

(217—228)

37
217. pleading tongue:　善辩护的舌头
218. swelling passion:　高涨的激情
219. blaze forth:　熊熊燃烧
 wrong:　受到委屈的感情
220. judge:　法官
 right:　赢得
221. fain:　高兴地

222. intendments:　意图

38
225. band:　箍带
226. would:　愿意
228. lily fingers:　百合花般的玉指

37

能言会道她躁烦
情绪亢奋神不安
哀愁脸红眼喷火
主宰爱情难伸冤　　　　　220
又是诉怨又哭泣
呜咽打断女神言

38

又是摆手又摇头
又看少年又低头
女神臂中少年搂　　　　　225
少年不愿女神愁
多次怀中想逃走
玉指锁住百合箍

（217—228）

39

"Fondling," she saith, "since I have hemm'd thee here

Within the circuit of this ivory pale,   *230*

I'll be a park, and thou shalt be my deer:

Feed where thou wilt, on mountain, or in dale;

   Graze on my lips, and if those hills be dry,

   Stray lower, where the pleasant fountains lie.

40

"Within this limit is relief enough,   *235*

Sweet bottom grass and high delightful plain,

Round rising hillocks, brakes obscure and rough,

To shelter thee from tempest and from rain;

   Then be my deer, since I am such a park,

   No dog shall rouse thee, though a thousand bark." *240*

(229—240)

39

229. Fondling:　被宠爱的人
　　　hemm'd:　包围
230. circuit:　圈子
　　　ivory pale:　象牙栅栏
232. dale:　溪谷
233. Graze:　吃草
234. Stray lower:　信步走下去
　　（译者按：该诗节洋溢着田园牧歌的情

调，含蓄的语言里蕴含着火热的爱情。不瘟不火，不蔓不枝，中和之美，诗情画意，大自然母亲的温柔美跃然纸上）

40

237. hillocks:　小丘
　　　brakes:　灌木丛
　　　obscure and rough:　遮掩而蓬乱粗陋

39

叫声冤家搂怀中
象牙栅栏走不成　　　　230
我为花园你小鹿
觅食幽谷或高峰
先在我唇吃嫩草
下有欢乐泉水声

40

随意漫游我花园　　　　235
幽谷芳草乐高山
圆丘突起小树乱
躲风避雨你随缘
我为园圃你为鹿
千狗狂吠只等闲　　　　240

（229—240）

365

41

At this Adonis smiles as in disdain,

That in each cheek appears a pretty dimple;

Love made those hollows, if himself were slain,

He might be buried in a tomb so simple,

    Foreknowing well, if there he came to lie,   *245*

    Why, there Love liv'd, and there he could not die.

42

These lovely caves, these round enchanting pits,

Open'd their mouths to swallow Venus' liking.

Being mad before, how doth she now for wits?

Struck dead at first, what needs a second striking?   *250*

   Poor queen of love, in thine own law forlorn,

   To love a cheek that smiles at thee in scorn!

(241—252)

41
242. dimple: 酒窝
243. hollows: 洼地，山谷；酒窝
245. Foreknowing: 预知

42
247. enchanting pits: 使人心醉的坑儿
249. for wits: out of wits, 意乱情迷
251. in thine own law forlorn: 被你的法则困住

41

少年微笑仍气生
两个酒窝好梨形
爱为少年酒窝造
被杀纯洁葬坟茔
他知葬身酒窝里 　　　　　245
爱神居住他永恒

42

可爱酒窝诱人坑
张口欲吞女神情
她已迷狂失理性
死去活来去围城 　　　　　250
可怜爱神被爱困
少年嘲笑女爱疯

（241—252）

367

43

Now which way shall she turn? what shall she say?

Her words are done, her woes the more increasing;

The time is-spent, her object will away,   *255*

And from her twining arms doth urge releasing.

　"Pity," she cries, "some favor, some remorse!"

　A way he springs, and hasteth to his horse.

44

But lo from forth a copse that neighbors by,

A breeding jennet, lusty, young, and proud,   *260*

Adonis' trampling courser doth espy;

And forth she rushes, snorts, and neighs aloud.

　The strong-neck'd steed, being tied unto a tree,

　Breaketh his rein, and to her straight goes he.

(253—264)

43
256. twining arms: 缠绕环抱的双臂
257. some favor, some remorse: 给些恩
　义，给些同情

44
259. copse: 灌木林
260. breeding jennet: 生育繁殖期的西班

牙母马
261. trampling: 跳动
　courser: 骏马
　espy: 窥见
262. snorts: 喷鼻
　neighs: 嘶鸣
263. steed: 骏马
264. rein: 缰绳

43

女神何去又何从
话已说完忧怨增
时光过完爱要走　　　　　255
在她怀中求放松
女神求男多爱怜
少年寻马跃起行

44

但看附近有树丛
发情母马正年轻　　　　　260
看见少年之骏马
冲向前去伴嘶鸣
强项骏马拴在树
挣断缰绳奔多情

（253—264）

45

Imperiously he leaps, he neighs, he bounds,   *265*

And now his woven girths he breaks asunder;

The bearing earth with his hard hoof he wounds,

Whose hollow womb resounds like heaven's thunder;

　The iron bit he crusheth 'tween his teeth,

　Controlling what he was controlled with.   *270*

46

His cars up-prick'd, his braided hanging mane

Upon his compass'd crest now stand on end,

His nostrils drink the air, and forth again

As from a furnace, vapors doth he send;

　His eye, which scornfully glisters like fire,   *275*

　Shows his hot courage and his high desire.

(265—276)

45

265. Imperiously:　雄伟地，傲慢地

266. girths:　肚带，马鞍绑带
　　asunder:　分开

269. iron bit:　马铁，马勒

270. Controlling what he was controlled
　with:　控制了控制他的东西

46

271. up-prick'd:　竖起
　　braided hanging mane:　编成辫子的
　　马鬃

272. compass'd crest:　弓形的马的项脊

45

跳动吼叫向前冲   *265*

线织肚带断无形

硬蹄蹋坏承载地

天雷轰鸣空子宫

愤怒咬断口中铁

谁控制谁颠倒行   *270*

46

耳朵竖起垂马鬃

直立马颈不倒倾

鼻孔吸气喷白雾

熔炉燃烧蒸气腾

眼中闪光露轻蔑   *275*

情欲猛烈胆气增

（265—276）

47

Sometimes he trots, as if he told the steps,

With gentle majesty and modest pride;

Anon he rears upright, curvets, and leaps,

As who should say, "Lo thus my strength is tried;   *280*

    And this I do to captivate the eye

    Of the fair breeder that is standing by."

48

What recketh he his rider's angry stir,

His flattering "Holla," or his "Stand, I say"?

What cares he now for curb, or pricking spur,   *285*

For rich caparisons, or trappings gay?

    He sees his love, and nothing else he sees,

    For nothing else with his proud sight agrees.

(277—288)

47
277. trots: 小跑
279. Anon: 不久
    rears: 直立
    curvets: 腾跃
281. captivate: 迷住
282. fair breeder: 漂亮的生育期的母马

48
283. recketh: 顾虑；注意
    stir: 愤怒
285. curb: 勒马的链条或皮带；笼头
    pricking spur: 马刺
286. caparisons: 华丽的鞍辔
    trappings gay: 美好的马饰

47

有时小跑数步伐
威雅谦傲皆可夸
有时直立大纵跳
向人高喊称行家　　　　　280
母马看我露一手
她站那里美如花

48

不理主人发雷霆
讨好呼喊叫停声
不怕笼头与马刺　　　　　285
马衣饰物富丽空
此刻惟有目中爱
骄傲万物相不中

（277—288）

49

Look when a painter would surpass the life

In limning out a well-proportioned steed,   *290*

His art with nature's workmanship at strife,

As if the dead the living should exceed;

　　So did this horse excel a common one,

　　In shape, in courage, color, pace, and bone.

50

Round-hoof'd, short-jointed, fetlocks shag and long,   *295*

Broad breast, full eye, small head, and nostril wide,

High crest, short ears, straight legs and passing strong,

Thin mane, thick tail, broad buttock, tender hide:

　　Look what a horse should have he did not lack,

　　Save a proud rider on so proud a back.   *300*

(289—300)

49

289. surpass:　超越

290. limning:　绘制

291. workmanship:　手艺

　　　 at strife:　竞赛

293. excel:　优于

50

295. fetlocks:　马蹄后的丛毛

　　　 shag:　粗浓蓬松的

297. crest:　马的项脊

298. mane:　马鬃

　　　 tender hide:　柔软的马皮

300. Save:　除了

49

画家作画超时空
笔下骏马骨匀称 290
艺术自然争优越
仿佛死者胜于生
这匹骏马非凡响
毛骨神气好外形

50

蹄圆跗短毛粗长 295
胸阔目美鼻孔扬
颈高耳短四腿健
鬃细尾粗臀圆光
头小皮柔好骏马
高手未骑奔四方 300

（289—300）

51

Sometimes he scuds far of, and there he stares,

Anon he starts at stirring of a feather;

To bid the wind a base he now prepares,

And whe'er he run, or fly, they know not whether;

    For through his mane and tail the high wind sings,   *305*

    Fanning the hairs, who wave like feath'red wings.

52

He looks upon his love, and neighs unto her,

She answers him, as if she knew his mind;

Being proud as females are, to see him woo her,

She puts on outward strangeness, seems unkind,   *310*

    Spurns at his love, and scorns the heat he feels,

    Beating his kind embracements with her heels.

(301—312)

51
301. scuds: 飞奔
302. feather: 羽毛
303. base: 游戏，竞赛
304. whether: 是否

52
310. outward strangeness: 外表冷漠
311. Spurns: 践踏；踢开
312. embracements: 拥抱

51

时而冲刺时回观
羽毛颤动惊动颜
打算与风玩游戏
或追或逃弄清难
鬃尾之间风呼啸　　　　305
体毛吹动羽翼般

52

看着母马它嘶鸣
母马回答像知情
雌者被追真骄傲
故作姿态冷冰冰　　　　310
踢她所爱笑情热
亲昵拥抱可不成

（301—312）

53

Then like a melancholy malcontent,

He vails his tail that like a falling plume

Cool shadow to his melting buttock lent; *315*

He stamps, and bites the poor flies in his fume.

　　His love, perceiving how he was enrag'd,

　　Grew kinder, and his fury was assuag'd.

54

His testy master goeth about to take him,

When lo the unback'd breeder, full of fear, *320*

Jealous of catching, swiftly doth forsake him,

With her the horse, and left Adonis there.

　　As they were mad unto the wood they hie them,

　　Outstripping crows that strive to overfly them.

(313—324)

53

313. malcontent:　不满者；失意之人

314. vails:　垂下

315. lent:　借出

316. stamps:　踩踏
　　fume:　激动

317. perceiving:　看见，察觉
　　enraged:　激怒

318. assuag'd:　缓和的；安静的

54

319. testy:　坏脾气的

320. unbacked breeder:　没有骑手的母马

323. hie them:　两匹马匆匆跑

324. Outstripping:　超过；胜过

53

失恋垂头太伤心
垂下尾巴羽状纹
冷却将融之臀部   *315*
愤怒踩踏蝇飞临
母马见它太暴躁
怜它减它怒火侵

54

主人恼怒牵马匹
未鞍母马远离急   *320*
心怀恐惧怕捉住
马跑单留阿童尼
两马疯狂树林跑
惊鸦难追空叹息

（313—324）

379

55

All swoll'n with chafing, down Adonis sits,   *325*

Banning his boist'rous and unruly beast;

And now the happy season once more fits

That love-sick love by pleading may be blest;

   For lovers say, the heart hath treble wrong

   When it is barr'd the aidance of the tongue.   *330*

56

An oven that is stopp'd, or river stay'd,

Burneth more hotly, swelleth with more rage;

So of concealed sorrow may be said,

Free vent of words love's fire doth assuage,

   But when the heart's attorney once is mute,   *335*

   The client breaks, as desperate in his suit.

(253—336)

55
325. swol'n: swollen, 臌胀的
    chafing: 发怒
326. Banning: 咒骂，诅咒
    boist'rous: boisterous, 狂暴的
327. the happy season once more fits: 幸福的时刻正好到来
328. love-sick love by pleading may be blest: 害相思的维纳斯有福气再去求情
329. hath treble wrong: 三倍折磨
330. aidance: 帮忙

55

少年坐地心愁烦

咒骂牲畜管束难

美好机会又来到

相思女神求爱怜

情侣内心伤三倍

舌不帮忙增凄惨　　　　　　　　　*330*

56

封住炉灶淤塞河

燃烧更猛洪涝多

悲哀窝心亦如此

倾诉爱火可消磨

内心辩护不言语　　　　　　　　　*335*

官司事主成蹉跎

（*253—336*）

56

333. concealed:　压抑的

334. vent:　发泄

assuage:　减轻

335. attorney:　律师

336. as desperate in his suit:　官司打输心破碎

57

He sees her coming, and begins to glow,

Even as a dying coal revives with wind,

And with his bonnet hides his angry brow,

Looks on the dull earth with disturbed mind,   *340*

　　Taking no notice that she is so nigh,

　　For all askance he holds her in his eye.

58

O what a sight it was wistly to view,

How she came stealing to the wayward boy,

To note the fighting conflict of her hue,   *345*

How white and red each other did destroy!

　　But now her cheek was pale, and by and by

　　It flash'd forth fire, as lightning from the sky.

(337—348)

57
337. glow:　燃烧
339. bonnet:　帽
340. disturbed mind:　烦恼的心
341. nigh:　靠近他
342. askance:　斜眼看

58
343. wistly:　想望地
344. wayward:　任性的
345. hue:　脸色
347. by and by:　不久以后
348. flash'd:　使闪烁

57

见她走来他脸红
渐灭炭火红腾腾
帽压前额愤怒遮
心乱看地地无情　　　　　　340
女神靠近不理会
眼望别处察其行

58

观此场景人动心
任性少年女悄临
面上色彩正交战　　　　　　345
细白羞红争惹人
两颊细白只一瞬
满面羞红电火云

（337—348）

59

Now was she just before him as he sat,

And like a lowly lover down she kneels;   *350*

With one fair hand she heaveth up his hat,

Her other tender hand his fair cheek feels:

   His tend'rer cheek receives her soft hand's print,

   As apt as new-fall'n snow takes any dint.

60

O what a war of looks was then between them!   *355*

Her eyes petitioners to his eyes suing,

His eyes saw her eyes as they had not seen them,

Her eyes wooed still, his eyes disdain'd the wooing;

   And all this dumb play had his acts made plain

   With tears which chorus-like her eyes did rain.   *360*

(349—360)

59
350. lowly lover:　低下的情人
351. heaveth:　举起
354. apt:　灵巧的
   dint:　陷痕

60
356. petitioners:　请求者
   suing:　请求
359. dumb play:　哑剧
360. chorus-like:　像合唱队一样

59

少年坐地女近前
跪下屈辱情人观   *350*
玉手为他掀软帽
再用柔指抚俊颜
嫩面呈露纤手印
新雪留痕温柔篇

60

火热交战有两情   *355*
女目求情男眼睛
少年看女如不见
女求男厌难通融
幕幕交待演哑剧
女神泪雨遮眼睛   *360*

(349—360)

61

Full gently now she takes him by the hand,

A lily prison'd in a jail of snow,

Or ivory in an alablaster band,

So white a friend engirts so white a foe:

    This beauteous combat, willful and unwilling,   *365*

    Showed like two silver doves that sit a-billing.

62

Once more the engine of her thoughts began:

"O fairest mover on this mortal round,

Would thou wert as I am, and I a man,

My heart all whole as thine, thy heart my wound!   *370*

    For one sweet look thy help I would assure thee,

    Though nothing but my body's bane would cure thee."

(361—372)

61

363. alablaster: alabaster，雪花石膏
364. engirts: 关押
366. a-billing: 鸟亲嘴

62

368. fairest mover: 最美的生灵
371. For one sweet look thy help I would assure thee: 我愿向你保证，我需要你温柔的眼神
372. bane: 毁灭

61

紧拉少年手温柔
百合雪花牢里囚
白玉圈里象牙套
白友落入白敌箍
一攻一守美争斗　　　　　365
银鸽亲嘴双美图

62

思维启动女开言
最俊少年尘世间
我变作你你变我
两心完好你凄惨　　　　　370
和颜对我你得解
毁我身躯你保全

（361—372）

63

"Give me my hand," saith he, "why dost thou feel it?"

"Give me my heart," saith she, "and thou shalt have it.

O, give it me, lest thy hard heart do steel it,   *375*

And being steel'd soft sighs can never grave it.

    Then love's deep groans I never shall regard,

    Because Adonis' heart hath made mine hard."

64

"For shame," he cries, "let go, and let me go,

My day's delight is past, my horse is gone,   *380*

And 'tis your fault I am bereft him so.

I pray you hence, and leave me here alone,

    For all my mind, my thought, my busy care,

    Is how to get my palfrey from the mare."

(373—384)

63

375. lest:　唯恐

376. grave:　铭刻

377. deep groans:　沉痛呻吟

64

381. bereft:　抢夺

382. hence:　走开

384. palfrey:　有鞍的马

63

男求放手抚摸停

女要还心手才松

铁石心肠硬化女　　　　　　375

女心硬化情潜踪

女神不解情侣苦

少年使我心无情

64

羞啊放手求女神

骏马跑失怎欢欣　　　　　　380

今因你错我失马

求你离开甬再亲

找回骏马我盘算

离开母马收花心

(373—384)

389

65

Thus she replies: "Thy palfrey, as he should,   *385*

Welcomes the warm approach of sweet desire;

Affection is a coal that must be cool'd,

Else suffer'd it will set the heart on fire.

   The sea hath bounds, but deep desire hath none,

   Therefore no marvel though thy horse be gone.   *390*

66

"How like a jade he stood, tied to the tree,

Servilely master'd with a leathern rein!

But when he saw his love, his youth's fair fee,

He held such petty bondage in disdain,

   Throwing the base thong from his bending crest,   *395*

   Enfranchising his mouth, his back, his breast.

(385—396)

65
387. Affection: 情欲，爱欲
390. no marvel: 毫不稀奇

66
391. jade: 没用的没有价值的老马
392. Servilely: 奴隶般地

393. his youth's fair fee: 他的青春美的报
   偿
395. base thong: 卑贱的皮带
   bending crest: 驯服的项脊
396. Enfranchising: 使自由

65

女答骏马路正当　　　385
春情萌动喜洋洋
爱如炭火须冷静
不加控制心烧光
大海有边欲无岸
马跑无奇莫惊慌　　　390

66

活像劣马树上拴
皮革缰绳绝欢颜
青春艳福遇所爱
小小束缚不足观
颈上缰绳轻甩去　　　395
口背胸身赛神仙

（385—396）

67

"Who sees his true-love in her naked bed,

Teaching the sheets a whiter hue than white,

But when his glutton eye so full hath fed,

His other agents aim at like delight?   *400*

  Who is so faint that dares not be so bold

  To touch the fire, the weather being cold?

68

"Let me excuse thy courser, gentle boy,

And learn of him, I heartily beseech thee,

To take advantage on presented joy;   *405*

Though I were dumb, yet his proceedings teach thee.

  O, learn to love, the lesson is but plain,

  And once made perfect, never lost again."

(397—408)

67
398. Teaching: 展示
399. glutton: 贪食者
400. agents: 感官
401. faint: 胆小

68
403. courser: 骏马
404. beseech: 恳求
405. presented joy: 恩赐的欢乐
406. proceedings: 先前做的事

67

真爱情人裸在床

被单更白发柔光

饕餮眼睛艳福饱

诸多感官饿得慌　　　　　　　　　*400*

数九寒天偏怯懦

不敢近火远躲藏

68

叫声小哥骏马夸

求你学马学到家

快乐来临要享受　　　　　　　　　*405*

向马学习乐无涯

学习欢爱课容易

一旦入门成最佳

（*397—408*）

69

"I know not love," quoth he, "nor will not know it,

Unless it be a boar, and then I chase it;   *410*

'Tis much to borrow, and I will not owe it;

My love to love is love but to disgrace it,

　　For I have heard it is a life in death,

　　That laughs and weeps, and all but with a breath.

70

"Who wears a garment shapeless and unfinish'd?   *415*

Who plucks the bud before one leaf put forth?"

If springing things be any jot diminish'd,

They wither in their prime, prove nothing worth;

　　The colt that's back'd and burthen'd being young,

　　Loseth his pride, and never waxeth strong.   *420*

(409—420)

69
412. My love to love is love but to disgrace
　　it:　我对爱的爱是爱蔑视它

70
417. jot:　一点儿
418. wither:　枯萎
419. colt:　小马
420. waxeth:　成长

69

不懂不想学爱情
追猎野猪少年功　　　　410
情债苦恼我不欠
我爱之爱垃圾扔
我闻爱为活人死
呼吸化为哭笑声

70

谁愿穿衣不成形　　　　415
未叶采蕾理不通
万物成长微受创
未盛先枯价值空
马驹幼小先负重
锐气磨消难健雄　　　　420

（409—420）

71

"You hurt my hand with wringing, let us part,

And leave this idle theme, this bootless chat;

Remove your siege from my unyielding heart,

To love's alarms it will not open the gate;

　　Dismiss your vows, your feigned tears, your flatt'ry, *425*

　　For where a heart is hard they make no batt'ry."

72

"What, canst thou talk?" quoth she, "hast thou a tongue?

O would thou hadst not, or I had no hearing!

Thy mermaid's voice hath done me double wrong;

I had my load before, now press'd with bearing:　　*430*

　　Melodious discord, heavenly tune harsh sounding,

　　Ears' deep sweet music, and heart's deep sore wounding.

(421—432)

71

421. wringing: 拧，扭，捏
422. bootless: 无用的
423. siege: 围攻
424. alarms: 警觉
425. feigned: 假装的
426. batt'ry: battery，冲击

72

429. mermaid's: 美人鱼的
431. Melodious discord: 动听的噪声，和
　　谐的嘈杂
　　harsh: 刺耳的
432. deep sweet music: 超甜蜜的音乐
　　deep sore wounding: 超痛的创伤

71

你握我手我手疼
分手无聊万事空
你攻猛烈我不退
爱情大门难打通
誓赞假泪不济事　　　　　425
我心如铁不怕攻

72

女神问男竟开言
无舌无耳痴少年
语言伤女更难受
满怀忧伤又翻番　　　　　430
和谐嘈杂天仙调
刺耳甜歌痛万重

（421—432）

73

"Had I no eyes but ears, my ears would love
That inward beauty and invisible,
Or were I deaf, thy outward parts would move   435
Each part in me that were but sensible;
  Though neither eyes nor ears to hear nor see,
  Yet should I be in love by touching thee.

74

"Say that the sense of feeling were bereft me,
And that I could not see, nor hear, nor touch,   *440*
And nothing but the very smell were left me,
Yet would my love to thee be still as much,
  For from the stillitory of thy face excelling
  Comes breath perfum'd, that breedeth love by smelling.

(*433—444*)

73
434. That inward beauty and invisible:
  那种内在的眼睛看不见的美
437. Though: 虽然具有

74
442. Yet would my love to thee be still as
  much: 对你的爱还会一如既往
443. stillitory: 蒸馏器
  thy face excelling: 美妙的面庞

73

我若有耳无眼睛
内在之爱看不清
我聋可感女风度　　　　　　435
身上感官解风情
无耳去闻无眼瞅
触摸到你爱意生

74

纵然触觉去无踪
视听抚摸都不行　　　　　　440
还有嗅觉留给我
对你深爱不减轻
俊美面庞蒸馏器
喷出香气育爱情

（433—444）

75

"But O, what banquet wert thou to the taste,   *445*

Being nurse and feeder of the other four!

Would they not wish the feast might ever last,

And bid Suspicion double-lock the door,

   Lest Jealousy, that sour unwelcome guest,

   Should by his stealing in disturb the feast?"   *450*

76

Once more the ruby-color'd portal open'd,

Which to his speech did honey passage yield,

Like a red morn, that ever yet betoken'd

Wrack to the seaman, tempest to the field,

   Sorrow to shepherds, woe unto the birds,   *455*

   Gusts and foul flaws to herdmen and to herds.

(445—456)

75
448. Suspicion: 警觉
449. Jealousy: 忧虑
   sour: 酸的；敌对的

76
451. ruby-color'd portal: 红宝石色的门
453. red morn: 满天红霞的清晨
   betoken'd: 预示的
454. Wrack: 失事船只
456. foul flaws: 恶劣的狂风

75

盛筵味道靠品评　　　　445
四种感觉味先行
全望盛筵能持久
猜疑大门关双重
以免嫉妒不速客
偷搅筵席理不通　　　　450

76

少年朱唇再开张
语言出唇胜蜜糖
满天朝霞永预示
海难地上暴雨强
禽鸟哀愁牧人苦　　　　455
狂风阴霾袭牛羊

（445—456）

77

This ill presage advisedly she marketh:

Even as the wind is hush'd before it raineth,

Or as the wolf doth grin before he barketh,

Or as the berry breaks before it staineth,　　　　　*460*

　　Or like the deadly bullet of a gun,

　　His meaning struck her ere his words begun.

78

And at his look she flatly falleth down,

For looks kill love, and love by looks reviveth:

A smile recures the wounding of a frown.　　　　　465

But blessed bankrupt that by love so thriveth!

　　The silly boy, believing she is dead,

　　Claps her pale cheek, till clapping makes it red;

(457—468)

77

457. presage:　预兆

458. hush'd:　静下来的

459. grin:　露齿而笑

460. as the berry breaks before it staineth:
在沾染之前浆果先破裂

78

464. reviveth:　苏醒，复活

465. recures:　疗治

466. bankrupt:　破产；晕倒

77

女神留意有不祥
不等雨来风安祥
狼嗥之前先狞笑
浆果未腐皮破光　　　460
致命子弹枪膛射
少年未言女神伤

78

看见脸色倒女神
爱之死活靠此人
微笑可医皱眉痛　　　465
晕倒为福少年临
冤家以为女神死
轻拍粉颊泛红晕

（457—468）

79

And all amaz'd, brake off his late intent,

For sharply he did think to reprehend her,   *470*

Which cunning love did wittily prevent:

Fair fall the wit that can so well defend her!

    For on the grass she lies as she were slain,

    Till his breath breatheth life in her again.

80

He wrings her nose, he strikes her on the cheeks,   *475*

He bends her fingers, holds her pulses hard,

He chafes her lips, a thousand ways he seeks

To mend the hurt that his unkindness marr'd,

    He kisses her, and she by her good will

    Will never rise, so he will kiss her still.   *480*

(469—480)

79

469. brake: broke，打破

470. reprehend: 痛骂

471. cunning love did wittily prevent:
聪明的维纳斯女神机智地防卫

472. Fair fall the wit that can so well defend
her: 聪明地及时地倒地保护了她

80

476. holds her pulses hard: 紧按她的脉搏

477. chafes: 擦热

478. marr'd: 损坏，弄糟

79

改变主张因慌神

痛骂教训那美人　　　　　470

狡猾之爱设计巧

自卫生智装迷昏

躺在草地她装死

等他呼吸赛甘霖

80

拍面捏鼻少年忙　　　　　475

弯指号脉神紧张

揉她嘴唇千条计

补救粗暴招祸殃

他亲吻她她自愿

永不起身亲吻香　　　　　480

（469—480）

81

The night of sorrow now is turn'd to day:

Her two blue windows faintly she upheaveth,

Like the fair sun, when in his fresh array

He cheers the morn, and all the earth relieveth;

 And as the bright sun glorifies the sky,   *485*

 So is her face illumin'd with her eye,

82

Whose beams upon his hairless face are fix'd,

As if from thence they borrowed all their shine.

Were never four such lamps together mix'd,

Had not his clouded with his brow's repine;   *490*

 But hers, which through the crystal tears gave light,

 Shone like the moon in water seen by night.

（481—492）

81
482. upheaveth: 升起
483. array: 装扮
485. glorifies: 使辉煌

82
487. hairless: 光滑的
490. repine: 不满，埋怨

81

哀愁黑夜变白天
娇柔开启蓝窗鲜
美丽太阳衣华丽
大地无阴晨光篇
天上明日庄严照　　485
眼睛照亮面容鲜

82

盯住无须俊少年
眼光借自何神仙
不能相混灯四盏
眉毛遮眼真新鲜　　490
她眼晶莹淌珠泪
夜月闪亮水里边

（481—492）

83

"O, where am I?" quoth she, "in earth or heaven,

Or in the ocean drench'd, or in the fire?

What hour is this? or morn or weary even?   *495*

Do I delight to die, or life desire?

   But now I liv'd, and life was death's annoy,

   But now I died, and death was lively joy.

84

"O, thou, didst kill me, kill me once again.

Thy eyes' shrowd tutor, that hard heart of thine,   *500*

Hath taught them scornful tricks, and such disdain

That they have murd'red this poor heart of mine,

   And these mine eyes, true leaders to their queen,

   But for thy piteous lips no more had seen."

(493—504)

83

494. drench'd: 浸透

495. weary: 困乏的

496. delight to die, or life desire: 快乐地死去还是追求生活

497. death's annoy: 死亡的烦恼

500. shrewd tutor: 精明厉害的导师

503. leaders to their queen: 引向女王的忠实的领路

504. piteous lips: 怜悯的嘴唇

83

女问尘世或天堂
火烧还是没海洋
清晨还是慵懒夜 495
想死想活费思量
活着如死多烦恼
死了享受爱无疆

84

少年杀我可翻番
眼为恶师狠心肝 500
鄙视戏弄太傲慢
我心被害谁人怜
双眼忠实为领路
可视亏你嘴唇怜

（493—504）

85

"Long may they kiss each other for this cure!   *505*

O, never let their crimson liveries wear!

And as they last, their verdour still endure,

To drive infection from the dangerous year!

   That the star-gazers, having writ on death,

   May say, the plague is banish'd by thy breath   *510*

86

"Pure lips, sweet seals in my soft lips imprinted,

What bargains may I make, still to be sealing?

To sell myself I can be well contented,

So thou wilt buy, and pay, and use good dealing,

   Which purchase if thou make, for fear of slips,   *515*

   Set thy seal manual on my wax-red lips.

（*505—516*）

85

506. crimson liveries:　红袍

507. verdure:　青葱；

509. star-gazers:　占星家

   writ on:　预言

86

512. bargains:　交易，讨价还价

513. To sell myself I can be well contented:
　　就是卖我自己，我也心甘情愿

515. for fear of slips:　为防出错，担心有闪
　　失

516. seal manual:　标记；吻
　　wax-red lips:　蜡一样透明的红嘴唇

85

既有此功长久吻　　　　　505

华服鲜红火样新

深长之吻味隽永

祛病消灾害不侵

占卜之人观星斗

瘟疫赶走气息新　　　　　510

86

我有柔唇印纯唇

甜印没完立据人

单凭亲吻自身卖

愿买付钱要真心

愿立字据负责任　　　　　515

印章盖上我红唇

（505—516）

87

"A thousand kisses buys my heart from me,

And pay them at thy leisure, one by one.

What is ten hundred touches unto thee?

Are they not quickly told and quickly gone?   *520*

   Say for non-payment that the debt should double,

   Is twenty hundred kisses such a trouble?"

88

"Fair queen," quoth he, "if any love you owe me,

Measure my strangeness with my unripe years;

Before I know myself, seek not to know me,   *525*

No fisher but the ungrown fry forbears;

   The mellow plum doth fall, the green sticks fast,

   Or being early pluck'd, is sour to taste.

(517—528)

87

520. Are they not quickly told and quickly gone: 岂不是很快清账，不再拖欠；付完点清账目真

521. non-payment: 拖欠债务

88

524. Measure my strangeness with my unripe years: 用我的未成年来衡量我的冷漠

525. seek not to know me: 不用想知道我

526. fisher: 渔夫

   fry: 鱼苗

   forbears: 避免

527. mellow plum: 早熟的梅子

528. pluck'd: 采摘

87

千吻可买我真心
逐一还我闲暇临
千次接触特容易
付完点清账目真　　　　　　520
拖延付款债加倍
还要付你两千吻

88

叫声美神你有情
我未成年不会疯
我不省事莫攀我　　　　　　525
看见小鱼渔夫疼
梅熟自落青梅挂
早摘酸涩不精明

（517—528）

413

89

"Look the world's comforter with weary gait

His day's hot task hath ended in the west;   *530*

The owl (night's herald) shrieks, 'tis very late;

The sheep are gone to fold, birds to their nest,

   And coal-black clouds that shadow heaven's light

   Do summon us to part, and bid good night.

90

"Now let me say 'Good night,' and so say you;   *535*

If you will say, so, you shall have a kiss."

"Good night," quoth she, and ere he says "Adieu,"

The honey fee of parting tend'red is;

   Her arms do lend his neck a sweet embrace;

   Incorporate then they seem, face grows to face.   *540*

(529—540)

89

529. comforter: 安慰者，即太阳
   weary gait: 疲劳的步态
531. herald: 传令官
   shrieks: 尖叫
532. fold: 羊栏
534. summon: 召唤
   bid good night: 道晚安

90

538. tend'red: 甜蜜回报
540. incorporate: 结合，合并

89

安慰世界步蹒跚
炎热任务整一天　　　　　*530*
黑夜先驱枭鸟叫
鸟儿回巢羊归栏
煤黑乌云天遮暗
呼唤分手道晚安

90

我说再见你晚安　　　　　*535*
愿赠一吻我心宽
女说再见少年慢
送上亲吻比蜜甜
甜蜜玉臂少年搂
脸贴着脸一体观　　　　　*540*

（529—540）

415

91

Till breathless he disjoin'd and backward drew
The heavenly moisture, that sweet coral mouth,
Whose precious taste her thirsty lips well knew,
Whereon they surfeit, yet complain on drouth;
 He with her plenty press'd, she faint with dearth,   *545*
 Their lips together glued, fall to the earth.

92

Now quick desire hath caught the yielding prey,
And glutton-like she feeds, yet never filleth;
Her lips are conquerors, his lips obey,
Paying what ransom the insulter willeth;   *550*
 Whose vulture thought doth pitch the price so high
 That she will draw his lips' rich treasure dry.

(541—552)

91
542. coral: 珊瑚
544. surfeit: 过量
  drouth: 干旱
545. dearth: 不足，饥馑
546. glued: 胶合

92
550. ransom: 赎金
  insulter: 自吹自擂的征服者
551. vulture thought: 贪欲
  pitch: 竭力推销，叫卖
552. lips' rich treasure: 唾液

91

少年气喘后退身
挪开琼浆珊瑚唇
焦唇已知美滋味
饱尝痛饮还贪心
丰腴身子紧倚靠　　　　545
一同倒地唇对唇

92

猎物投降欲望强
狼吞虎咽乐无疆
女唇征服男唇退
攻者掠夺退者降　　　　550
贪欲鹰鹞要天价
红唇珍宝吮吸光

（541—552）

93

And having felt the sweetness of the spoil,

With blindfold fury she begins to forage;

Her face doth reek and smoke, her blood doth boil,   *555*

And careless lust stirs up a desperate courage,

　　Planting oblivion, beating reason back,

　　Forgetting shame's pure blush and honor's wrack.

94

Hot, faint, and weary, with her hard embracing,

Like a wild bird being tam'd with too much handling, *560*

Or as the fleet-foot roe that's tir'd with chasing,

Or like the froward infant still'd with dandling,

　　He now obeys, and now no more resisteth,

　　While she takes all she can, not all she listeth.

（553—564）

93

553. spoil:　阿童尼的嘴
554. blindfold:　盲目的
　　forage:　抢劫
555. reek:　蒸气
556. careless lust:　不顾一切的欲望
　　desperate courage:　放肆的勇气
557. Planting oblivion:　忘掉一切
558. honor's wrack:　名誉毁坏

94

560. handling:　摆弄
561. fleet-foot roe:　善跑的雄獐
562. still'd:　让安静
　　dandling:　播弄
564. not all she listeth:　不是她的全部欲
　　望

93

猎物美味已品尝
狂乱盲目塞肚肠
淫汗蒸腾血鼎沸　　　　555
色胆如天勇气扬
忘掉一切失理性
不怕脸红名泡汤

94

紧搂顿感倦热晕
野鸟倚人经久驯　　　　560
獐鹿善跑筋累断
婴儿淘气逗听人
少年顺从不再犟
女尽如愿生贪心

（553—564）

95

What wax so frozen but dissolves with temp'ring,   *565*

And yields at last to every light impression?

Things out of hope are compass'd oft with vent'ring,

Chiefly in love, whose leave exceeds commission;

    Affection faints not like a pale-fac'd coward,

    But then woos best when most his choice is forward.   *570*

96

When he did frown, O had she then gave over,

Such nectar from his lips she had not suck'd.

Foul words and frowns must not repel a lover;

What though the rose have prickles, yet 'tis pluck'd!

    Were beauty under twenty locks kept fast,   *575*

    Yet love breaks through, and picks them all at last.

(565—576)

95

565. but dissolves:　不能融化

    temp'ring:　捏

566. impression:　轻轻一按

567. compass'd:　取得

    vent'ring:　冒险

568. whose leave exceeds commission:　其放纵超过了范围

569. Affection faints not like a pale-fac'd coward:　爱欲不像脸色苍白的懦夫晕倒

95

硬蜡揉捏热速溶　　　　　*565*

露出印痕手按轻

无望之事靠冒险

分外温存得爱情

白脸懦夫怕情爱

对象倔强加劲攻　　　　　*570*

96

不因皱眉女手停

红唇玉液吸不成

恶言皱眉难驱爱

多刺敢采玫瑰红

锁爱大门二十道　　　　　*575*

破门救美勇爱情

（565—576）

96

572. nectar:　众神饮的酒，玉液琼浆

573. repel:　击退

574. prickles:　刺

575. kept fast:　禁锢

576. picks them all at last:　最终把锁一一打开

421

97

For pity now she can no more detain him;

The poor fool prays her that he may depart.

She is resolv'd no longer to restrain him,

Bids him farewell, and look well to her heart,   *580*

   The which, by Cupid's bow she doth protest,

   He carries thence incaged in his breast.

98

"Sweet boy," she says, "this night I'll waste in sorrow,

For my sick heart commands mine eyes to watch.

Tell me, Love's master, shall we meet to-morrow?   *585*

Say, shall we, shall we? wilt thou make the match?"

   He tells her no, to-morrow he intends

   To hunt the boar with certain of his friends.

(577—588)

97

577. detain: 扣留

580. look well to her heart: 好好看护她的心

581. The which: which

582. thence: 从那里

98

583. sweet boy: 甜蜜的好孩子

586. wilt thou make the match: 你会不会与我约会

97

可惜无法再留人
少年欲走求女神
不留少年女决定
道别爱护女神心　　　　580
爱神弓前女发誓
心随他去锁何深

98

女言男去忧心烦
苦苦相思安睡难
问声少年爱之主　　　　585
明朝愿聚请开言
他言不愿约朋友
去打野猪供消遣

（577—588）

423

99

"The boar!" quoth she, whereat a sudden pale,

Like lawn being spread upon the blushing rose,   *590*

Usurps her cheek; she trembles at his tale,

And on his neck her yoking arms she throws.

　　She sinketh down, still hanging by his neck,

　　He on her belly falls, she on her back.

100

Now is she in the very lists of love,   *595*

Her champion mounted or the hot encounter;

All is imaginary she doth prove,

He will not manage her, although he mount her,

　　That worse than Tantalus' is her annoy,

　　To clip Elysium and to lack her joy.   *600*

(589—600)

99
589. whereat: 对那个
591. Usurps: 袭击

100
595. lists: 决斗场
596. champion: 战士，武士
598. manage: 运用；驾驭

599. Tantalus: 希腊神话中宙斯与宁芙之子坦塔罗斯，因偷神食与琼浆给凡人而受罚。坦塔罗斯被拘留在冥界神湖里，渴时见水不能饮，饿时见果不得食
600. clip: 拥抱
　　Elysium: 希腊神话中的天堂乐土

99

闻言野猪脸惨白
红玫瑰上薄纱来   590
他话吓她浑身抖
忙把少年搂进怀
女身仰卧仍在搂
少年跌上肚皮来

100

决斗场上女爱情   595
她有勇士拼命争
事实证明皆幻想
男骑女身欲不兴
望梅止渴女烦恼
拥抱天堂一场空   600

(589—600)

101

Even so poor birds, deceiv'd with painted grapes,

Do surfeit by the eye and pine the maw;

Even so she languisheth in her mishaps,

As those poor birds that helpless berries saw.

　The warm effects which she in him finds missing　*605*

　She seeks to kindle with continual kissing.

102

But all in vain, good queen, it will not be;

She hath assay'd as much as may be prov'd.

Her pleading hath deserv'd a greater fee;

She's love, she loves, and yet she is not lov'd.　　*610*

　"Fie, fie," he says, "you crush me, let me go,

　You have no reason to withhold me so."

(601—612)

101

601. painted grapes:　公元前 5 世纪古希腊
　　画家 Zeuxis 所画之葡萄，鸟儿以为是
　　真葡萄，故飞来啄食
602. surfeit:　使饮食过度
　　pine:　为……悲哀
　　maw:　胃
603. languisheth:　变得衰弱无力
　　mishaps:　不幸

606. kindle:　点燃

102

608. assay'd:　尝试
609. pleading:　请求
610. She's love, she loves, and yet she is not
　　lov'd:　她有爱，她爱，却得不到爱
611. crush:　搂坏
612. withhold:　搂住不放

426

101

呆鸟受骗图画中

葡萄美味腹中空

难堪时运偏不济

画中葡萄呆鸟情

女情如火男不动　　　　605

女神求爱吻不停

102

终为泡影爱不成

机关算尽成虚空

乞求愿得大酬报

爱神求爱不领情　　　　610

他言窒息甭再搂

紧搂不放理不通

（601—612）

103

"Thou hadst been gone," quoth she, "sweet boy, ere this,

But that thou toldst me thou wouldst hunt the boar.

O, be advis'd, thou know'st not what it is   *615*

With javelin's point a churlish swine to gore,

    Whose tushes never sheath'd he whetteth still,

    Like to a mortal butcher bent to kill.

104

"On his bow-back he hath a battle set

Of bristly pikes that ever threat his foes,   *620*

His eyes like glow-worms shine when he doth fret,

His snout digs sepulchres where e'er he goes;

    Being mov'd, he strikes, what e'er is in his way,

    And whom he strikes his crooked tushes slay.

(613—624)

103

616. javelin's: 标枪的
    churlish: 难驾驭的；粗暴的
    swine: 猪
    gore: 血；伤口
617. tushes: 獠牙
    whetteth: 磨快
618. mortal butcher: 残忍的屠夫

104

619. bow-back: 弓形的背
    battle set: 士兵的盔甲
620. bristly: 短而硬的
    pikes: 锐利的武器
621. glow-worms: 萤火虫
    fret: 使烦恼
622. snout: 拱嘴
    sepulchers: 坟墓
623. mov'd: 惹恼

103

女言我该放你行
要打野猪可不成
当心要知太危险　　　615
镖枪难扎野猪凶
獠牙不收不停戳
好杀屠夫心已横

104

弓形背上耸鬃毛
威慑敌胆利剑刀　　　620
两眼发怒萤火闪
鼻拱好像把坟刨
发起怒来胡乱撞
弯曲獠牙冤魂招

（613—624）

105

"His brawny sides, with hairy bristles armed,   *625*

Are better proof than thy spear's point can enter;

His short thick neck cannot be easily harmed;

Being ireful, on the lion he will venter.

　The thorny brambles and embracing bushes,

　As fearful of him, part, through whom he rushes.   *630*

106

"Alas, he nought esteems that face of thine,

To which Love's eyes pays tributary gazes,

Nor thy soft hands, sweet lips, and crystal eyne,

Whose full perfection all the world amazes,

　But having thee at vantage (wondrous dread!)   *635*

　Would root these beauties as he roots the mead.

(625—636)

105
625. brawny: 强壮的
　　 bristles: 鬃毛
628. ireful: 发怒的
　　 venter: 冒险
629. brambles: 荆棘
　　 embracing bushes: 缠结的灌木丛

106
631. nought: 无；使成泡影
　　 esteems: 尊敬
632. tributary: 含情脉脉的
635. at vantage: 利用
　　 wondrous dread: 极其可怕
636. mead: 草地

105

强壮两肋竖钢鬃　　　　625
枪尖扎透不可能
脖子粗短难伤害
怒时敢与狮争雄
深密灌木长荆棘
见它躲开怕骄横　　　　630

106

呜呼俊面它不观
情人眼里看不完
明眸香唇手何物
柔美世人惊眼缘
它拦住你真恐怖　　　　635
拱杀俊美泥土般

（625—636）

431

107

"O, let him keep his loathsome cabin still!

Beauty hath nought to do with such foul fiends.

Come not within his danger by thy will,

They that thrive well take counsel of their friends.   *640*

　　When thou didst name the boar, not to dissemble,

　　I fear'd thy fortune, and my joints did tremble.

108

"Didst thou not mark my face? was it not white?

Sawest thou not signs of fear lurk in mine eye?

Grew I not faint, and fell I not downright?   *645*

Within my bosom, whereon thou dost lie,

　　My boding heart pants, beats, and takes no rest,

　　But like an earthquake, shakes thee on my breast.

(637—648)

107

637. loathsome: 讨厌的

638. foul fiends: 丑恶的魔鬼

640. thrive well: 很成功

　　　take counsel: 听劝告

641. dissemble: 掩饰

108

643. mark: 注意

644. lurk: 埋伏；潜藏

645. downright: 直截了当地

646. whereon: 在什么上面

647. boding heart: 有凶兆的心

　　　pants: 气喘，心跳

107

永远让它呆脏窝

俊美不可碰恶魔

不可故意去冒险

得志不听友劝多　　　　　*640*

你提野猪我胆颤

四肢为你打哆嗦

108

不察脸白我心惊

不观眼藏恐怖情

身子摇晃要摔倒　　　　　*645*

你倒我怀倚我胸

听我喘息心急跳

胸口有你摇不停

（637—648）

109

"For where Love reigns, disturbing Jealousy

Doth call himself Affection's sentinel,   *650*

Gives false alarms, suggesteth mutiny,

And in a peaceful hour doth cry, 'Kill, kill!'

   Distemp'ring gentle Love in his desire,

   As air and water do abate the fire.

110

"This sour informer, this bate-breeding spy,   *655*

This canker that eats up Love's tender spring,

This carry-tale, dissentious Jealousy,

That sometime true news, sometime false doth bring,

   Knocks at my heart, and whispers in mine ear,

   That if I love thee, I thy death should fear;   *660*

(649—660)

109
650. sentinel: 哨兵
651. mutiny: 兵变
653. Distemp'ring: 担心；造成动乱
654. abate: 减轻

110
655. sour informer: 邪恶的告密者
     bate-breeding spy: 制造骚乱的间谍
656. canker: 蛀虫
657. carry-tale: 流言蜚语的
     dissentious: 不同意见的

109

爱情统治疑虑生
自称情盛有哨兵   *650*
警报不实藏危险
平安无事喊杀声
有意搅乱缠绵爱
风雨熄灭烈火熊

110

奸刁间谍阴谋家   *655*
蛀虫吃掉爱嫩芽
长舌离间生疑虑
真假难辨莫信它
它敲我心对我语
我防你死情爱加   *660*

（649—660）

435

111

"And more than so, presenteth to mine eye

The picture of an angry-chafing boar,

Under whose sharp fangs, on his back doth lie

An image like thyself, all stain'd with gore,

 Whose blood upon the fresh flowers being shed, *665*

 Doth make them droop with griefand hang the head.

112

"What should I do, seeing thee so indeed,

That tremble at th' imagination?

The thought of it doth make my faint heart bleed,

And fear doth teach it divination: *670*

 I prophesy thy death, my living sorrow,

 If thou encounter with the boar tomorrow.

(661—672)

111
662. angry-chafing:　狂怒
663. fangs:　尖牙
666. droop:　垂下

112
669. faint heart:　脆弱的心
670. fear doth teach it divination:　恐惧的
　　　确给了我预感
671. prophesy:　预言
　　　living sorrow:　永久的悲痛

111

它还描图我眼前
狂怒野猪露凶残
利牙之下一人躺
血肉模糊像少年
鲜花之上热血洒　　　　　*665*
花儿悲伤垂眼帘

112

想象此景怕此图
浑身发抖真无谋
想到此事心流血
恐惧事发你命休　　　　　*670*
预言你死我活苦
假如天明会野猪

（661—672）

437

113

"But if thou needs wilt hunt, be rul'd by me,

Uncouple at the timorous flying hare,

Or at the fox which lives by subtilty,   *675*

Or at the roe which no encounter dare;

   Pursue these fearful creatures o'er the downs,

   And on thy well-breath'd horse deep with thy hounds.

114

"And when thou hast on foot the purblind hare,

Mark the poor wretch, to overshoot his troubles,   *680*

How he outruns the wind, and with what care

He cranks and crosses with a thousand doubles:

   The many musits through the which he goes

   Are like a labyrinth to amaze his foes.

(673—684)

113
674. Uncouple: 松开猎犬皮带使其追逐
    timorous: 胆小的
675. subtlity: 狡猾
676. roe: 獐
677. downs: 丘陵草原
678. well-breath'd: 壮健的
    hounds: 猎犬

114
679. hast on foot: 追逐
    purblind: 半瞎的
680. poor wretch: 可怜的东西
    overshoot: 逃避
682. cranks: 曲折行进
683. musits: 篱笆的漏洞
684. labyrinth: 迷宫

113

你要打猎听我言
胆小野兔放猎犬
或追狐狸太狡猾　　　　675
或追麋鹿一溜烟
胆小动物靠骏马
群犬齐追轻围歼

114

你追野兔眼模糊
看见即跑它前头　　　　680
惊慌逃窜超风速
千百转变八阵图
树篱洞穴全穿过
迷宫惑敌有计谋

（673—684）

115

"Sometimes he runs among a flock of sheep,   *685*

To make the cunning hounds mistake their smell,

And sometimes where earth-delving conies keep,

To stop the loud pursuers in their yell,

    And sometimes sorteth with a herd of deer:

    Danger deviseth shifts, wit waits on fear,   *690*

116

"For there his smell with others being mingled,

The hot scent-snuffing hounds are driven to doubt,

Ceasing their clamorous cry till they have singled

With much ado the cold fault cleanly out;

    Then do they spend their mouths: echo replies,   *695*

    As if another chase were in the skies.

(685—696)

115
687. earth-delving:　在地上挖洞
　　　conies:　兔；蹄兔
689. sorteth:　混合到一起
690. shifts:　诡计

116
692. hot scent-snuffing:　嗅着热气追踪的
693. clamorous:　喧闹的
694. the cold fault cleanly out:　辨出已变
　　　冷的气味
695. echo replies:　回声在回答

115

时而混入绵羊群　　　　685
机灵猎犬嗅失真
时而钻进兔子洞
猎犬狂吠变哑音
时而群鹿以为伍
智伴恐怖急计临　　　　690

116

气味混杂猎犬迷
紧追不舍生迟疑
吠声暂停细分辨
寻到气味费心机
小鸣谷应犬狂吠　　　　695
仿佛天宫也狩围

（685—696）

441

117

"By this, poor wat, far off upon a hill,

Stands on his hinder-legs with list'ning ear.

To hearken if his foes pursue him still.

Anon their loud alarums he doth hear,   *700*

   And now his grief may be compared well

   To one sore sick that hears the passing bell.

118

"Then shalt thou see the dew-bedabbled wretch

Turn, and return, indenting with the way;

Each envious brier his weary legs do scratch,   *705*

Each shadow makes him stop, each murmur stay,

   For misery is trodden on by many,

   And being low, never reliev'd by any.

(697—708)

117
697. wat：兔子
699. hearken：听
700. Anon：不久以后
    alarums：警报
702. sore sick：病入膏肓

118
703. dew-bedabbled：露水溅湿的

704. indenting：弯弯曲曲
705. envious brier：恶意的荆棘
    scratch：抓破
707. For misery is trodden on by many：悲惨被许多人践踏；落难之时众人踩
708. And, being low, never reliev'd by any：由于低微任何人都不会解救；踩倒在地无救援

117

可怜野兔上远山
后腿站立听天边
不知敌方仍追赶
很快听到喊声喧　　　　700
它之苦恼有一比
痛入膏肓丧钟传

118

满身露水真可怜
转跑弯路没个完
恶意荆棘刺累腿　　　　705
见影闻声不敢前
落难总遭众人踩
踩倒在地无救援

（697—708）

119

"Lie quietly, and hear a little more,

Nay, do not struggle, for thou shalt not rise.   *710*

To make thee hate the hunting of the boar,

Unlike myself thou hear'st me moralize,

    Applying this to that, and so to so,

    For love can comment upon every woe.

120

"Where did I leave?" "No matter where," quoth he,   *715*

"Leave me, and then the story aptly ends;

The night is spent." "Why, what of that?" quoth she.

"I am," quoth he, "expected of my friends,

    And now'tis dark, and going I shall fall."

    "In night," quoth she, "desire sees best of all."   *720*

(709—720)

119
712. moralize: 说教
713. Applying this to that, and so to so:
    例举事实打比方；举例比方立论苦
714. For love can comment upon every woe:
    爱能解释各种苦痛；爱对折磨讲一番

120
715. leave: 停止
716. aptly: 易于
717. what of that: 那又怎么啦
719. going I shall fall: 走路我会摔跤

119

好好躺着听我言
挣扎逃去难上难　　　　　　710
痛恨追猎野猪猛
正色训你理由全
举例比方立论苦
爱对折磨讲一番

120

女讲何处男不言　　　　　　715
男求女停故事完
女言天黑没关系
男说朋友约在先
天黑走路怕摔倒
女言情欲夜里观　　　　　　720

（709—720）

121

"But if thou fall, O then imagine this,

The earth, in love with thee, thy footing trips,

And all is but to rob thee of a kiss.

Rich preys make true men thieves; so do thy lips

　　Make modest Dian cloudy and forlorn,　　　　　*725*

　　Lest she should steal a kiss and die forsworn.

122

"Now of this dark night I perceive the reason:

Cynthia for shame obscures her silver shine,

Till forging Nature be condemn'd of treason,

For stealing moulds from heaven that were divine,　　*730*

　　Wherein she fram'd thee, in high heaven's despite,

　　To shame the sun by day, and her by night.

(721—732)

121

723. rob thee of a kiss: 抢劫你一个吻

724. preys: 毁坏

725. Dian: Diana, 月亮女神

　　forlorn: 可怜；孤独凄凉

726. steal a kiss: 偷吻

　　forsworn: 悔恨；发伪誓的

122

728. Cynthia: 辛西娅，即月亮女神黛安娜
　　（Diana）

　　obscures: 遮掩

729. forging: 欺骗的；伪造的

730. moulds: 模式；模子

731. Wherein: 在那里

　　in⋯despite: 违背

121

你若摔倒有原因
大地爱你把你亲
巧借机会亲吻你
好人强盗见宝珍
谦和月神愁眉锁　　　　　725
生怕偷吻坏节贞

122

夜黑我今悟原因
月亮收光羞见人
判处自然伪造罪
窃取模型仿天神　　　　　730
上天铸造你蔑视
日羞太阳夜月神

（721—732）

447

123

"And therefore hath she brib'd the Destinies

To cross the curious workmanship of Nature,

To mingle beauty with infirmities,   *735*

And pure perfection with impure defeature,

  Making it subject to the tyranny

  Of mad mischances and much misery:

124

"As burning fevers, agues pale and faint,

Life-poisoning pestilence, and frenzies wood,   *740*

The marrow-eating sickness, whose attaint

Disorder breeds by heating of the blood;

  Surfeits, imposthumes, grief, and damn'd despair

  Swear Nature's death for framing thee so fair.

(733—744)

123
733. the Destinies: 命运三女神
734. cross: 挫败
     curious: 奇妙的
     workmanship: 手艺
735. infirmities: 缺点
736. pure perfection: 纯洁的完美
     impure defeature: 不纯的缺陷
738. mischances: 不幸

124
739. agues: 疟疾
740. pestilence: 瘟疫
     frenzies wood: 狂乱疯癫
741. marrow-eating sickness: 吞食精髓的
     疾病
     attaint: 感染
742. Disorder breeds: 产生紊乱
743. Surfeits: 饮食过度
     imposthumes: 脓肿

123

因此她买命运神
阻挠造化奇妙新
美妙之中搀缺陷　　　　735
完美加丑有几分
凡人难逃此粗暴
意外变故惨祸临

124

热病疟疾摧残人
瘟疫疯癫毒害侵　　　　740
恶疾吸髓病患起
血液沸腾不安临
饕餮脓忧生绝望
诅咒自然造美神

（733—744）

125

"And not the least of all these maladies   745

But in one minute's fight brings beauty under;

Both favor, savor, hue, and qualities,

Whereat th' impartial gazer late did wonder,

    Are on the sudden wasted, thaw'd and done,

    As mountain snow melts with the midday sun.   750

126

"Therefore despite of fruitless chastity,

Love-lacking vestals, and self-loving nuns,

That on the earth would breed a scarcity

And barren dearth of daughters and of sons,

    Be prodigal: the lamp that burns by night   755

    Dries up his oil to lend the world his light.

(745—756)

125
745. maladies: 疾病
747. savor: 风味
748. th' impartial gazer: 公正的观察
749. thaw'd: 融化

126
752. vestals: 女祭司
753. scarcity: 缺乏
754. dearth: 饥馑
755. prodigal: 挥霍的
756. Dries up his oil to lend the world his light: 耗尽自己的油为世界带来光明

125

所有疾病取最轻　　　　　745

毁美只需一分钟

美姿色泽知何去

正人方才赞誉中

憔悴消毁顷刻事

心雪融化日当空　　　　　750

126

无有果实讲贞操

修女尼姑爱欲抛

贫瘠干枯地球上

无儿无女少根苗

放纵黑夜灯点燃　　　　　755

耗油发光时代潮

（745—756）

127

"What is thy body but a swallowing grave,

Seeming to bury that posterity

Which by the rights of time thou needs must have,

If thou destroy them not in dark obscurity?   *760*

　　If so, the world will hold thee in disdain,

　　Sith in thy pride so fair a hope is slain.

128

"So in thyself thyself art made away,

A mischief worse than civil home-bred strife,

Or theirs whose desperate hands themselves do slay,   *765*

Or butcher sire that reaves his son of life.

　　Foul cank'ring rust the hidden treasure frets,

　　But gold that's put to use more gold begets."

(757—768)

127
758. posterity:　子孙，后裔
760. obscurity:　暗淡
762. Sith:　因为

128
763. art made away:　毁灭
764. civil home-bred strife: 同室操戈, 祸起萧墙
765. desperate hands:　绝望的手
766. sire:　父亲
　　　reaves:　劫掠
767. Foul cank'ring rust:　邪恶的侵蚀的铁锈
　　　frets:　吃掉
768. begets:　父亲生子女

127

身体张口像墓坑
后代仿佛葬其中
自然赋权该生子
为何灭根黑暗中　　　　　　760
如此行为世人贬
傲慢毁美希望空

128

自我毁灭天不容
甚于萧墙祸乱生
自残轻生因绝望　　　　　　765
凶残父亲杀亲生
烂锈侵吞久藏宝
黄金多用黄金赢

（757—768）

453

129

"Nay then," quoth Adon, "you will fall again

Into your idle over-handled theme.   *770*

The kiss I gave you is bestow'd in vain,

And all in vain you strive against the stream,

   For by this black-fac'd night, desire's foul nurse,

   Your treatise makes me like you worse and worse.

130

"If love have lent you twenty thousand tongues,   *775*

And every tongue more moving than your own,

Bewitching like the wanton mermaid's songs,

Yet from mine ear the tempting tune is blown;

   For know my heart stands armed in mine ear,

   And will not let a false sound enter there."   *780*

(769—780)

129

770. idle over-handled theme:　无聊的陈旧
　　的话题

771. bestow'd:　赠与

772. stream:　潮流

774. treatise:　论文

130

777. Bewitching:　着迷
　　wanton mermaid's songs:　销魂的美
　　人鱼的歌声

778. tempting tune:　诱人的曲调

129

男让住口太絮叨
老套岂能格调高 *770*
我亲吻你归白送
逆流挣扎你徒劳
黑夜生欲可作证
话语烦我你更糟

130

千万巧舌缘爱情 *775*
每条都比你中听
淫荡鲛人歌迷客
勾魂淫词耳边风
须知我心设防御
岂容放进虚伪声 *780*

（769—780）

131

"Lest the deceiving harmony should run

Into the quiet closure of my breast,

And then my little heart were quite undone,

In his bedchamber to be barr'd of rest.

   No, lady, no, my heart longs not to groan,   *785*

   But soundly sleeps, while now it sleeps alone

132

"What have you urg'd that I cannot reprove?

The path is smooth that leadeth on to danger.

I hate not love, but your device in love,

That lends embracements unto every stranger.   *790*

   You do it for increase: O strange excuse!

   When reason is the bawd to lust's abuse.

(781—792)

131

781. Lest: 否则

782. closure: 关闭

783. undone: 破坏

784. bedchamber: 卧室

    be barr'd of rest: 不能休息

132

787. reprove: 指责

790. lends: 提供

    embracement: 拥抱

791. strange excuse: 奇怪的理由

792. bawd: 鸨母

    lust's abuse: 淫欲的理由

131

不让闯入骗人声

侵蚀纯洁平静胸

尚幼心灵被毁掉

床上辗转睡不宁

夫人莫让我心痛　　　　　　785

心愿独睡灵台清

132

你说哪条难反驳

道路平坦危险多

我不恨爱恨算计

拥抱生人为结果　　　　　　790

理由竟然为生育

理性老鸨淫快活

(781—792)

133

"Call it not love, for Love to heaven is fled,

Since sweating Lust on earth usurp'd his name,

Under whose simple semblance he hath fed   *795*

Upon fresh beauty, blotting it with blame;

   Which the hot tyrant stains, and soon bereaves,

   As caterpillars do the tender leaves.

134

"Love comforteth like sunshine after rain,

But Lust's effect is tempest after sun;   *800*

Love's gentle spring doth always fresh remain,

Lust's winter comes ere summer half be done;

   Love surfeits not, Lust like a glutton dies;

   Love is all truth, Lust full of forged lies.

(793—804)

133

793. fled:　飞

794. usurp'd:　篡夺

795. semblance:　外貌

796. blotting it with blame:　污损抵毁美

797. hot tyrant:　淫欲的暴君

    stains: 玷污

    bereaves:　毁坏；使丧失

798. caterpillars:　毛虫

134

799. comforteth:　安慰

804. forged lies:　谎言

133

非爱爱已回天庭
流汗淫欲盗其声
淫欲天真外形借 795
鲜活之美成秽形
暴君辱美糟踏美
虫咬嫩芽祸害生

134

爱情舒适雨后阳
淫欲好天风雨狂 800
爱情新春清爽暖
淫欲以冬代夏忙
爱情宜人淫欲死
爱情理正淫欲诳

459

135

"More I could tell, but more I dare not say,   *805*

The text is old, the orator too green,

Therefore in sadness, now I will away;

My face is full of shame, my heart of teen,

    Mine ears, that to your wanton talk attended,

    Do burn themselves for having so offended."   *810*

136

With this he breaketh from the sweet embrace

Of those fair arms which bound him to her breast

And homeward through the dark laund runs apace

Leaves Love upon her back, deeply distress'd.

    Look how a bright star shooteth from the sky,   *815*

    So glides he in the night from Venus' eye.

(805—816)

135

808. my heart of teen: 我的忧伤的心

809. to your wanton talk attended: 听了你
    放荡的语言

810. having so offended: 如此刺耳

136

813. laund: 林中空地

    apace: 飞快地

814. distress'd: 悲痛地

816. glides: 滑行

135

我有话讲不敢贫　　　　　805
重弹老调少年人
颇感伤心我离去
满面羞惭凄苦心
我耳听你放荡语
发烧全因秽语侵　　　　　810

136

挣脱拥抱少年人
一直紧搂痴女神
穿过黑地向家跑
女神仰卧悲哀深
流星如何过天际　　　　　815
少年如何离女神

（805—816）

461

137

Which after him she darts, as one on shore

Gazing upon a late-embarked friend,

Till the wild waves will have him seen no more,

Whose ridges with the meeting clouds contend;   *820*

   So did the merciless and pitchy night

   Fold in the object that did feed her sight.

138

Whereat amaz'd as one that unaware

Hath dropp'd a precious jewel in the flood,

Or 'stonish'd as night-wand'rers often are,   *825*

Their light blown out in some mistrustful wood,

   Even so confounded in the dark she lay,

   Having lost the fair discovery of her way.

(817—828)

137

817. darts: 急冲
818. late-embarked: 刚登上船
820. ridges: 脊
   with the meeting clouds contend: 与白云抗争
821. pitchy: 漆黑
822. Fold in the object: 把物体遮掩

138

826. mistrustful wood: 可怕的树林
827. confounded: 迷惑
828. the fair discovery of her way: 她路上美妙的发现

137

女神岸边送离人
望友扬帆离海滨
狂浪翻滚友不见
大水滔天斗白云　　　　　　820
无情漆黑在今夜
遮蔽伊人难女神

138

茫然女神无意中
洪流坠宝杳无声
惊愕旅人行夜路　　　　　　825
树林险恶灭灯笼
茫然身卧黑暗里
路迷俊男无影踪

（817—828）

139

And now she beats her heart, whereat it groans,

That all the neighbor caves, as seeming troubled,   *830*

Make verbal repetition of her moans;

Passion on passion deeply is redoubled:

   "Ay me!" she cries, and twenty times, "Woe, woe!"

   And twenty echoes twenty times cry so.

140

She marking them begins a wailing note,   *835*

And sings extemporally a woeful ditty,

How love makes young men thrall, and old men dote,

How love is wise in folly, foolish-witty.

   Her heavy anthem still concludes in woe,

   And still the choir of echoes answer so.   *840*

(829—840)

139

830. neighbor caves: 附近的山洞
831. verbal repetition: 口头重复
      moans: 呜咽声
832. Passion on passion: 激情回报激情
833. woe: 哀哉

140

835. marking: 注意到

wailing note: 悲苦的歌
836. extemporally: 即兴
      woeful ditty: 哀愁的小曲
837. thrall: 迷惑
      dote: 溺爱
838. wise in folly: 愚中有智
      foolish-witty: 智中有愚
839. heavy anthem: 沉重的颂歌
840. choir: 合唱，合奏

139

声声哀哭女捶胸

邻近山洞痛伤情　　　　　830

重复女神之哀吟

激情深沉会激情

苦叫苍天二十次

同样答复有回声

140

唱起悲歌闻回音　　　　　835

短歌哀怨流出唇

受迷青年昏老朽

聪明变笨智者蠢

沉重悲歌苦结尾

回声合唱也酸辛　　　　　840

（829—840）

141

Her song was tedious, and outwore the night,

For lovers' hours are long, though seeming short;

If pleas'd themselves, others they think delight

In such-like circumstance, with such-like sport.

   Their copious stories, oftentimes begun,   *845*

   End without audience, and are never done.

142

For who hath she to spend the night withal,

But idle sounds resembling parasits,

Like shrill-tongu'd tapsters answering every call,

Soothing the humor of fantastic wits?   *850*

   She says, "'Tis so," they answer all, "'Tis so,"

   And would say after her, if she said "No".

                                                    (841—852)

141
841. outwore: 消磨；长过
844. such-like sport: 这样的消遣
845. copious stories: 冗长的故事
    oftentimes: 经常
846. are never done: 永远没有结束

142
847. withal: with
848. idle sounds: 回声
    resembling: 类似
    parasites: 应声虫
849. shrill-tongu'd: 尖嗓门的
    tapsters: 侍者，酒保，跑堂
850. Soothing the humor of fantastic wits:
    抚慰无法捉摸的顾客的情绪

141

漫漫长夜女悲歌
情侣时长似无多
梦想众人同欢乐
此情此景感情合
冗长故事有板眼　　　　845
没人聆听仍啰嗦

142

谁度良宵陪女神
应声虫般有回音
尖嗓酒保答应客
抚慰酒客人微醺　　　　850
女言如此答如此
不字出唇有回音

（841—852）

143

Lo here the gentle lark, weary of rest,

From his moist cabinet mounts up on high,

And wakes the morning, from whose silver breast   *855*

The sun ariseth in his majesty,

    Who doth the world so gloriously behold

    That cedar tops and hills seem burnish'd gold.

144

Venus salutes him with this fair good morrow:

"O thou clear god, and patron of all light,   *860*

From whom each lamp and shining star doth borrow

The beauteous influence that makes him bright,

    There lives a son that suck'd an earthly mother,

    May lend thee light, as thou dost lend to other."

(853—864)

143
853. the gentle lark: 驯雅的云雀
858. cedar tops: 雪松顶

144
859. salutes: 问好
    with this fair good morrow: 日安
860. patron: 恩赐
862. beauteous influence: 美的影响
863. a son: 阿童尼

143

宿后云雀体轻盈
露湿楼处飞高空
惊醒清晨银胸露 855
太阳威仪冉冉升
光芒万丈照尘世
山巅松顶金光明

144

女道早安饮佩情
辉煌天神放光明 860
不吝借光与星灯
美丽璀灿光源兴
少年吮吸地母奶
仿学太阳赐光明

(853—864)

145

This said, she hasteth to a myrtle grove,   865

Musing the morning is so much o'erworn,

And yet she hears no tidings of her love.

She hearkens for his hounds and for his horn;

   Anon she hears them chant it lustily,

   And all in haste she coasteth to the cry.   870

146

And as she runs, the bushes in the way,

Some catch her by the neck, some kiss her face,

Some twine about her thigh to make her stay.

She wildly breaketh from their strict embrace,

   Like a milch doe, whose swelling dugs do ache,   875

   Hasting to feed her fawn hid in some brake.

(865—876)

145

865. myrtle grove: 桃金娘树丛

866. Musing: 纳闷

    o'erworn: 过去

867. tidings: 消息

869. chant it lustily: 高声喧哗

870. coasteth: 长途追赶

146

873. twine: 缠绕

875. milch doe: 哺乳期的母鹿

    swelling dugs: 胀痛的乳房

876. fawn: 小鹿

    brake: 矮树林

145

说完走向桃金娘　　　　　865
纳闷快完之晨光
所爱少年今何在
猎犬号角细听详
不久共响喧哗起
赶向那边女匆忙　　　　　870

146

女神奔跑灌木丛
抓她脖子吻面容
想让她停缠大腿
野蛮拥抱逃难成
好像乳胀一母鹿　　　　　875
幼畜待哺灌木中

（865—876）

147

By this she hears the hounds are at a bay,

Whereat she starts like one that spies an adder

Wreath'd up in fatal folds just in his way,

The fear whereof doth make him shake and shudder; *880*

  Even so the timorous yelping of the hounds

  Appalls her senses, and her spirit confounds.

148

For now she knows it is no gentle chase,

But the blunt boar, rough bear, or lion proud,

Because the cry remaineth in one place,   *885*

Where fearfully the dogs exclaim aloud;

  Finding their enemy to be so curst,

  They all strain court'sy who shall cope him first.

(877—888)

147
877. at a bay:　陷入困境
878. spies:　发现
　　adder:　毒蛇
879. Wreath'd:　盘绕
　　fatal folds:　要命的一盘
880. whereof:　关于那个
　　shudder:　战栗
881. yelping:　犬吠
882. Appals:　使丧胆

confounds:　使惊惶失措

148
883. no gentle chase:　凶险的追猎
884. blunt:　生硬的
　　rough bear:　莽撞的熊
887. curst:　恶意的
888. strain:　使紧张
　　court'sy:　谦让
　　cope:　对付

147

听到猎物扑猎犬
如见毒蛇惊恐间
凶险成盘挡去路
惊慌发抖女神癫　　　　　880
猎犬虽叫声怯懦
意乱神迷何以堪

148

女神已知猎物凶
狮傲熊莽野猪横
喧嚣之声来一处　　　　　885
猎犬恐惧更高声
发现敌手真残暴
谁也不敢抢先攻

（877—888）

149

This dismal cry rings sadly in her ear,

Through which it enters to surprise her heart,   *890*

Who overcome by doubt, and bloodless fear,

With cold-pale weakness numbs cach feeling part:

  Like soldiers when their captain once doth yield,

  They basely fly, and dare not stay the field.

150

Thus stands she in a trembling ecstasy,   *895*

Till cheering up her senses all dismay'd,

She tells them 'tis a causeless fantasy,

And childish error that they are afraid;

  Bids them leave quaking, bids them fear nomore —

  And with that word, she spied the hunted boar,   *900*

(889—900)

149
889. dismal: 凄凉，阴沉
892. cold-pale: 虚冷苍白
894. basely fly: 可耻地逃窜

150
895. ecstasy: 痉挛
897. causeless fantasy: 全然的想象
899. quaking: 颤抖

149

耳边犬吠声阴惨

穿过耳鼓心胆寒　　　　890

女神难受心疑惧

苍白虚麻冷感官

主帅投降士卒见

溃散逃命一溜烟

150

停步战栗神紧张　　　　895

沮丧感官兴奋帮

女神安慰皆虚幻

幼稚错觉成恐慌

不要害怕别发抖

正说野猪跑身旁　　　　900

（889—900）

151

Whose frothy mouth bepainted all with red,

Like milk and blood being mingled both together,

A second fear through all her sinews spread,

Which madly hurries her she knows not whither;

　　This way she runs, and now she will no further,　*905*

　　But back retires to rate the boar for murther.

152

A thousand spleens bear her a thousand ways,

She treads the path that she untreads again;

Her more than haste is mated with delays,

Like the proceedings of a drunken brain,　　　　*910*

　　Full of respects, yet nought at all respecting,

　　In hand with all things, nought at all effecting.

(901—912)

151
901. frothy: 起泡沫的
　　bepainted: 涂抹
903. sinews: 肌腱
906. to rate the boar for murther: 咒骂那
　　伤人的野猪

152
907. spleens: 恐惧
909. Her more than haste is mated with
　　delays: 她的过于匆忙陪随着迟疑
910. proceedings: 举动
911. yet nought at all respecting: 什么也
　　没考虑
912. nought at all effecting: 什么效果也
　　没有

151

野猪吐沫血染红
鲜奶鲜血相交融
二次恐惧射筋肉
催她疯跑她不明
跑向此地停脚步　　　　　905
咒骂野猪杀人精

152

千种恐惧千道通
刚踏上路又回程
时而火急时犹豫
醉鬼头脑羊痫疯　　　　　910
太多顾虑欠决断
想做一切无一成

（901—912）

153

Here kennel'd in a brake she finds a hound,

And asks the weary caitiff for his master,

And there another licking of his wound,   *915*

'Gainst venom'd sores the only sovereign plaster,

 And here she meets another sadly scowling,

 To whom she speaks, and he replies with howling.

154

When he hath ceas'd his ill-resounding noise,

Another flap-mouth'd mourner, black and grim,   *920*

Against the welkin volleys out his voice;

Another, and another, answer him,

 Clapping their proud tails to the ground below,

 Shaking their scratch'd ears, bleeding as they go.

（913—924）

153
913. kennel'd: 窝藏
914. caitiff: 卑鄙的
915. licking: 舔
916. venom'd: 恶毒的
 sovereign: 最高的，无上的
 plaster: 膏药
917. scowling: 皱眉
918. howling: 嚎叫

154
919. ill-resounding: 凄厉的回响
920. flap-mouth'd: 嘴唇下垂的
 grim: 冷酷无情的
921. welkin: 天空，苍穹
 volleys: 连声发出咒骂
923. Clapping: 拍，拖
924. scratch'd: 抓破的

153

发现猎犬藏林中
探问此犬主人踪
猎犬再向伤口舔　　　　　915
止痛妙药有奇功
又见一犬貌愁苦
回答女问嚎几声

154

凄厉叫声他方停
忧伤嘴垂有畜生　　　　　920
向天狂吠排炮射
群狗乱叫齐应声
骄傲尾巴敲大地
伤耳摇晃鲜血红

（913—924）

155

Look how the world's poor people are amazed   *925*

At apparitions, signs, and prodigies,

Whereon with fearful eyes they long have gazed,

Infusing them with dreadful prophecies;

    So she at these sad signs draws up her breath,

    And sighing it again, exclaims on Death.   *930*

156

"Hard-favor'd tyrant, ugly, meager, lean,

Hateful divorce of love"—thus chides she Death—

"Grim-grinning ghost, earth's worm, what dost thou mean

To stifle beauty, and to steal his breath?

    Who when he liv'd, his breath and beauty set   *935*

    Gloss on the rose, smell to the violet.

(925—936)

155

926. appartions: 幻象
    prodigies: 怪象
928. Infusing: 灌输
    prophecies: 预言
929. draws up her breath: 她倒吸了一口气
930. exclaims on Death: 斥责死神

156

931. Hard-favor'd tyrant: 丑恶的暴君
    meager: 瘦的
    lean: 精瘦的
932. Hateful divorce of love: 可恨的爱情杀手
    chides: 责骂
933. Grim-grinning ghost: 狞笑的鬼
934. stifle: 使窒息
935. Gloss on the rose: 给玫瑰以光泽

155

多惶惑兮有世人　　　925
见异见凶见鬼魂
惊恐目光长凝望
可怕景象出内心
目睹惨象倒吸气
再叹口气责死神　　　930

156

丑陋瘦枯恶暴君
女骂毁婚拆情人
狞笑恶鬼蛆钻土
扼杀美貌何居心
美有呼吸增光艳　　　935
紫罗兰香玫瑰馨

(925—936)

157

"If he be dead—O no, it cannot be,

Seeing his beauty, thou shouldst strike at it:

O yes, it may, thou hast no eyes to see,

But hatefully at random dost thou hit.   *940*

    Thy mark is feeble age, but thy false dart

    Mistakes that aim, and cleaves an infant's heart.

158

"Hadst thou but bid beware, then he had spoke,

And hearing him, thy power had lost his power.

The Destinies will curse thee for this stroke: *945*

They bid thee crop a weed, thou pluck'st flower.

    Love's golden arrow at him should have fled,

    And not Death's ebon dart to strike him dead.

(937—948)

157
938. strike: 勾销
940. random: 盲目
941. Thy mark is feeble age: 你的目标是哀年
    false dart: 投错标枪
942. cleaves: 劈开

158
944. thy power had lost his power: 你的威力失去了其威力
948. ebon: 黑的

157

少年死去不可能
看见美男不心疼
你做恶事没有眼
任意掠杀你横行　　　　　940
目标衰年箭不准
错靶穿心正年轻

158

你若提醒他应声
听他说话你劲松
命运女神诅咒你　　　　　945
除草鲜花一命倾
飞向少年为金箭
死神黑箭太无情

（937—948）

159

"Dost thou drink tears, that thou provok'st such weeping?

What may a heavy groan advantage thee?　　　　*950*

Why hast thou cast into eternal sleeping

Those eyes that taught all other eyes to see?

　Now Nature cares not for thy mortal vigor,

　Since her best work is ruin'd with thy rigor."

160

Here overcome, as one full of despair,　　　　*955*

She vail'd her eyelids, who like sluices stopp'd

The crystal tide that from her two cheeks fair

In the sweet channel of her bosom dropp'd;

　But through the flood-gates breaks the silver rain,

　And with his strong course opens them again.　　*960*

(949—960)

159
949. provok'st:　惹起
950. advantage:　益处
951. cast:　使陷于
953. mortal vigor:　生杀大权
954. rigor:　冷酷，铁石心肠

160
956. vail'd:　垂下
　　　sluices:　闸门
959. floodgates:　洪水闸门
960. strong course:　汹涌的激流

159

你喝眼泪我伤情
何图偏听号啕声 950
为何让他眠千古
少年眼睛万物明
自杀不怕你杀害
她之杰作付秋风

160

苦痛极度绝望人 955
眼睑水闸关情真
桃腮水晶洪流挡
未落酥胸甜渠存
防洪闸门银雨淋
秀目重睁缘女神 960

（949—960）

161

O how her eyes and tears did lend and borrow!

Her eye seen in the tears, tears in her eye,

Both crystals, where they view'd each other's sorrow,

Sorrow that friendly sighs sought still to dry;

    But like a stormy day, now wind, now rain,   *965*

    Sighs dry her cheeks, tears make them wet again.

162

Variable passions throng her constant woe,

As striving who should best become her grief;

All entertain'd, each passion labors so,

That every present sorrow seemeth chief,   *970*

    But none is best; then join they all together,

    Like many clouds consulting for foul weather.

(961—972)

161
961. lend and borrow:　互为镜子
964. still:　持续不断地

162
967. throng:　拥挤
972. consulting for foul weather:　商量酿成坏天气

161

眼泪租赁秀目勤

秀目眼泪掩映深

皆为水晶双方苦

朋友哀叹减酸辛

天变风狂暴雨淋　　　　965

叹气吹颊雨水侵

162

无尽悲伤涌激情

争为第一哀恸声

都被接受齐努力

每个哀怨主悲鸣　　　　970

难分高下须齐聚

乌云层层起雨风

（961—972）

163

By this, far off, she hears some huntsman hallow;

A nurse's song ne'er pleas'd her babe so well.

The dire imagination she did follow   *975*

This sound of hope doth labor to expel,

   For now reviving joy bids her rejoice,

   And flatters her it is Adonis' voice.

164

Whereat her tears began to turn their tide,

Being prison'd in her eye, like pearls in glass,   *980*

Yet sometimes falls an orient drop beside,

Which her cheek melts, as scorning it should pass

   To wash the foul face of the sluttish ground,

   Who is but drunken when she seemeth drown'd.

(973—984)

163

973. hallow:　喊叫

974. babe:　婴儿

975. dire:　灾难的

976. doth labor to expel:　为她驱除干净

164

981. orient drop:　光辉夺目的下落的泪珠

    beside:　附近

982. scorning:　不屑做

983. sluttish:　淫荡的

984. Who is but drunken when she seemeth drown'd:　大地好像因她的眼泪而醉，她却被眼泪淹没

163

远听猎人呼喊声
摇篮曲逊彼动听
恐怖想象她困扰　　　　　　975
希望之声驱除清
欢乐复活女神乐
少年声音女领情

164

泪水倒流好女神
眼中玻璃罩奇珍　　　　　　980
偶有一珠掉落下
面颊融化不染尘
永洗大地脏面目
大地微醺醉美人

（973—984）

165

O hard-believing love, how strange it seems!   *985*

Not to believe, and yet too credulous:

Thy weal and woe are both of them extremes;

Despair and hope makes thee ridiculous:

    The one doth flatter thee in thoughts unlikely,

    In likely thoughts the other kills thee quickly.   *990*

166

Now she unweaves the web that she hath wrought,

Adonis lives, and Death is not to blame;

It was not she that call'd him all to naught;

Now she adds honors to his hateful name:

    She clepes him king of graves, and grave for kings, *995*

    Imperious supreme of all mortal things.

(985—996)

165

985. hard-believing love: 难以置信的爱情

986. credulous: 轻信的

987. weal: 幸福

989. unlikely: 怀疑的

990. In likely thoughts the other kills thee quickly: 以可信的想法立刻杀死你

166

991. unweave: 解开
    web: 网；恐怖想象

994. his hateful name: 他（死神）的可恨的名字

995. clepes: 称呼

996. Imperious: 帝王一般的

165

匪夷所思疑爱情　　　　985
不信轻信难分清
大喜大悲极端事
绝望希望荒谬生
荒诞不经奉承你
危言耸听命凋零　　　　990

166

自编之网自解绳
死神无罪少年生
方才所讲信口吐
可恶名上加尊称
众墓之王众王墓　　　　995
独尊神管众生灵

（985—996）

167

"No, no," quoth she, "sweet Death, I did but jest,

Yet pardon me, I felt a kind of fear

When as I met the boar, that bloody beast,

Which knows no pity, but is still severe;   *1000*

　　Then, gentle shadow(truth I must confess),

　　I rail'd on thee, fearing my love's decesse.

168

"'Tis not my fault, the boar provok'd my tongue,

Be wreak'd on him, invisible commander;

'Tis he, foul creature, that hath done thee wrong,   *1005*

I did but act, he's author of thy slander.

　　Grief hath two tongues, and never woman yet

　　Could rule them both without ten women's wit."

(997—1008)

167

997. sweet Death:　好死神

　　jest:　玩笑

1000. still:　总是

　　severe:　杀气腾腾

1001. gentle shadow:　温柔的阴影

　　truth I must confess:　我必须讲真话

1002. rail'd on:　咒骂

decesse:　decease，死亡

168

1004. wreak'd:　报仇

　　invisible commander:　冥冥中的主宰

1006. I did but act:　我说了出来

167

女言取笑污死神
恕我当时恐惧心
碰到嗜血野猪狠
永远残暴无慈根　　　　　1000
幽灵容我说真相
骂你为救心上人

168

野猪惹起我多言
冥王找它报仇冤
肮脏畜生冒犯你　　　　　1005
诽谤它造我谣传
悲哀两舌女无奈
十女智慧抚舌安

（997—1008）

169

Thus hoping that Adonis is alive,

Her rash suspect she doth extenuate,   *1010*

And that his beauty may the better thrive,

With Death she humbly doth insinuate;

   Tells him of trophies, statues, tombs, and stories

   His victories, his triumphs, and his glories.

170

"O Jove," quoth she, "how much a fool was I,   *1015*

To be of such a weak and silly mind,

To wail his death who lives, and must not die

Till mutual overthrow of mortal kind!

   For he being dead, with him is beauty slain,

   And beauty dead, black chaos comes again.   *1020*

(1009—1020)

169

1010. rash:　过于匆忙

    extenuate:　减轻

1012. insinuate:　巴结，讨好

1013. trophies:　战利品

170

1015. Jove:　Jupite, 罗马神话中的主神朱庇特

1017. wail:　恸哭

1018. mutual overthrow of motal kind:　互相推翻毁灭人生

1020. black chaos:　太初混沌；黑暗的混乱

169

希望生还好少年
鲁莽疑心已放宽　　　　　　　1010
想让少年美更健
讨好死神低声言
墓像碑碣全赞颂
胜利荣誉奏凯旋

170

叫声天帝我真蠢　　　　　　　1015
心情虚弱头脑昏
少年活着竟哀悼
不到末日他永存
他若死去美毁灭
美容死去黑暗临　　　　　　　1020

（1009—1020）

495

171

"Fie, fie, fond love, thou art as full of fear

As one with treasure laden, hemm'd with thieves;

Trifles, unwitnessed with eye or ear,

Thy coward heart with false bethinking grieves."

    Even at this word she hears a merry horn   *1025*

    Whereat she leaps, that was but late forlorn.

172

As falcons to the lure, away she flies,

The grass stoops not, she treads on it so light,

And in her haste unfortunately spies

The foul boar's conquest on her fair delight,   *1030*

    Which seen, her eyes as murd'red with the view,

    Like stars asham'd of day, themselves withdrew;

(1021—1032)

171

1021. fond love: 愚蠢的爱，痴情的爱

1022. with treasure laden: 装满财宝
    hemm'd with thieves: 被贼包围

1023—1024. Trifles, unwitnessed with eye
    or ear, / Thy coward heart with false
    bethinking grieves: mere trifles, not
    actually seen by eye or heard by ear,
grieve your cowardly heart with false
imaginings (*A Bantam Classic
Shakespeare The Poems p58*)，不是
亲眼看见、亲耳听见的皮毛小事，其
虚假的想象使得怯懦的心瞎悲哀；小
事眼耳无法证，可怕幻想害女神

1026. forlorn: 阴郁

496

171

充满恐惧爱痴心

身携珠宝遇强人

小事眼耳无法证

可怕幻想害女神

言罢闻听号角远   1025

方才沉闷今欢欣

172

猎鹰应唤奔女神

草叶不弯步轻云

匆忙碰见坏场面

野猪征服心爱人   1030

目睹惨象瞎双眼

星隐羞见白昼临

(1021—1032)

172

1027. falcons: 猎鹰
　　　lure: 用以诱回猎鹰的一束羽毛
1028. stoops: 躬下身
1030. conquest: 掠取物
1031. as murd'red with the view: 被眼前的景象杀死

173

Or as the snail, whose tender horns being hit,

Shrinks backward in his shelly cave with pain,

And there, all smoth'red up, in shade doth sit,   *1035*

Long after fearing to creep forth again;

　　So at his bloody view her eyes are fled

　　Into the deep-dark cabins of her head,

174

Where they resign their office, and their light,

To the disposing of her troubled brain,   *1040*

Who bids them still consort with ugly night,

And never wound the heart with looks again,

　　Who like a king perplexed in his throne,

　　By their suggestion, gives a deadly groan.

(1033—1044)

173

1035. all smoth'red up:　憋着气
1037. her eyes are fled:　她的眼睛逃避
1038. deep-dark cabins:　漆黑的小房，喻
　　　眼眶

174

1039. resign:　交出
1040. disposing:　控制
1041. consort:　伴随
1043. perplexed:　困惑
　　　throne:　宝座
1044. suggestion:　诱惑

173

好像蜗牛触角伤
忍痛退缩壳中藏
掩盖一切无动静　　　　1035
长久不爬太恐慌
血肉模糊冲入眼
逃进脑中小黑房

174

交出职务交日光
交出困惑脑筋伤　　　　1040
奉命永远陪丑夜
美观外界心已伤
心如国王宝座愣
爱到感染悲叹长

（1033—1044）

175

Whereat each tributary subject quakes,   *1045*

As when the wind imprison'd in the ground,

Struggling for passage, earth's foundation shakes,

Which with cold terror doth men's minds confound.

   This mutiny each part doth so surprise

   That from their dark beds once more leap her eyes.   *1050*

176

An being open'd, threw unwilling light

Upon the wide wound that the boar had trench'd

In his soft flank, whose wonted lily white

With purple tears, that his wound wept, was drench'd

   No flow'r was nigh, no grass, herb, leaf, or weed,   *1055*

   But stole his blood, and seem'd with him to bleed.

(1045—1056)

175

1045. tributary: 属下

1049. This munity each part doth so surprise:
   这个暴乱使她身上各个器官震惊

1050. dark beds: 眼眶

176

1052. trench'd: 戳

1053. soft flank: 嫩腰；软胁
   wonted lily white: 通常百合花般的
   细白

1054. his wound wept was drench'd: 他的
   伤口在哭泣，被（紫色的眼泪）染红

1055. nigh: 附近
   stole: 侵占

175

开始发抖有属臣　　　　　　*1045*
怜似狂风困地心
挣扎欲出大地动
战栗恐怖吓敌人
浑身器官像暴乱
黑夜跳出露眼神　　　　　　*1050*

176

眼睛睁开不忍观
野猪戳腰大伤惨
软肋白肉红血染
殷殷血流泪斑斑
附近花卉野草叶　　　　　　*1055*
浸透鲜血流不完

（1045—1056）

177

This solemn sympathy poor Venus noteth,

Over one shoulder doth she hang her head;

Dumbly she passions, franticly she doteth,

She thinks he could not, die, he is not dead;   *1060*

    Her voice is stopp'd, her joints forget to bow,

    Her eyes are mad that they have wept till now.

178

Upon his hurt she looks so steadfastly,

That her sight dazzling makes the wound seem three,

And then she reprehends her mangling eye,   *1065*

That makes more gashes where no breach should be.

    His face seems twain, each several limb is doubled,

    For oft the eye mistakes, the brain being troubled.

(1057—1068)

177

1056. solemn sympathy: 庄严的同情

1059. Dumbly she passions: 哑然无声的悲痛

    franticly she doteth: 发疯恋爱

1061. her joints forget to bow: 她膝关节忘了弯曲

177

庄严同情感女神
头垂肩上痛伤心
默默悲痛癫狂爱
想着鲜活少年人　　　　　　1060
声音堵塞忘下跪
眼睛发病哭到今

178

细察伤口费眼神
伤口变三女眼晕
眼睛模糊女神骂　　　　　　1065
没有伤处血淋淋
两套肢体两张脸
心慌意乱眼发昏

(1057—1068)

178
1063. steadfastly: 固定地，不变地
1064. dazzling: 眩晕
1065. reprehends: 严责，申斥
      mangling eye: 模糊的眼
1066. gashes: 深长的伤口
      breach: 裂口
1067. each several limb is doubled: several，单个的；四肢中的每一个都成双
1068. For oft the eye mistakes, the brain being troubled: 经常眼睛看错，是因为脑子困惑；
      心慌意乱眼发昏

179

"My tongue cannot express my grief for one,

And yet," quoth she, "behold two Adonis dead!"   *1070*

My sighs are blown away, my salt tears gone,

Mine eyes are turn'd to fire, my heart to lead:

　Heavy heart's lead, melt at mine eyes' red fire,

　So shall I die by drops of hot desire.

180

"Alas, poor world, what treasure hast thou lost!   *1075*

What face remains alive that's worth the viewing?

Whose tongue is music now? What canst thou boast

Of things long since, or any thing ensuing?

　The flowers are sweet, their colors fresh and trim,

　But true sweet beauty liv'd and died with him.   *1080*

(1069—1080)

179

1069. My tongue cannot express my grief
　　for one: 为一个阿童尼我的舌头不
　　能表达我的悲伤

180

1077. What canst thou boast: 你有什么可
　　吹嘘

1078. Of things long since, or any thing
　　ensuing: 古代的事情，或者未来的
　　一切

1079. trim: 整洁漂亮

179

一舌难表两悲伤

两个少年死神忙　　　　　　1070

叹息耗尽无咸泪

我心如铅眼冒光

心铅沉重融眼火

热爱滴水见无常

180

可怜尘世失奇珍　　　　　　1075

何人脸面引女神

何种语言似音乐

何事可夸观古今

看花鲜艳亭亭立

真美曾存随逝人

（1069—1080）

181

"Bonnet nor veil henceforth no creature wear!

Nor sun nor wind will ever strive to kiss you:

Having no fair to lose, you need not fear,

The sun doth scorn you, and the wind doth hiss you.

　　But when Adonis liv'd, sun and sharp air　　　　*1085*

　　Lurk'd like two thieves, to rob him of his fair.

182

"And therefore would he put his bonnet on,

Under whose brim the gaudy sun would peep;

The wind would blow it off, and being gone,

Play with his locks; then would Adonis weep;　　　*1090*

　　And straight, in pity of his tender years,

　　They both would strive who first should dry his tears.

(1081—1092)

181
1081. Bonnet: 女帽
　　　veil: 面纱
　　　henceforth: 从今以后
1084. hiss: 发出嘶嘶声
1086. Lurk'd: 潜伏

182
1088. brim: 边缘
　　　gaudy sun: 炫丽的太阳
1090. locks: 头发
1092. They: 风与太阳

181

今后不必戴帽纱
风日不抢吻面颊
无美可失无所惧
太阳不看风不刮
少年活时惹风日　　　　　1085
强盗来抢美回家

182

快快戴帽美少年
阳光偷瞧帽下沿
一旦风起吹落帽
玩弄头发泪涟涟　　　　　1090
全为伶悯他年少
抢先助他泪始干

　　　　　　　　　　　　　　　（1081—1092）

183

"To see his face the lion walk'd along

Behind some hedge, because he would not fear him;

To recreate himself when he hath song,   *1095*

The tiger would be tame, and gently hear him;

   If he had spoke, the wolf would leave his prey,

   And never fright the silly lamb that day.

184

"When he beheld his shadow in the brook,

The fishes spread on it their golden gills;   *1100*

When he was by, the birds such pleasure took,

That some would sing, some other in their bills

   Would bring him mulberries and ripe-red cherries:

   He fed them with his sight, they him with berries.

（1093—1104）

183

1093. walk'd along: 走开

1904. hedge: 篱笆

   he would not fear him: 他（它）不
会惊吓他（阿童尼）

1098. fright: 使惊恐

184

1100. spread on it: 在水面上暴露

   golden gills: 金鳃

1102. in their bills: 用它们的喙

1103. mulberries: 桑椹

   ripe-red cherries: 成熟的红樱桃

183

狮子想把俊男观
怕扰足轻篱后边
全为消遣小曲唱　　　　　1095
老虎谛听学圣贤
他言野狼丢猎物
无辜羔羊放一边

184

跪着溪边照面容
游鱼金鲤水上情　　　　　1100
飞鸟喜他身靠近
或用其啄或用鸣
樱桃红熟有桑椹
用美用果交换情

（1093—1104）

185

"But this foul, grim, and urchin-snouted boar,   *1105*

Whose downward eye still looketh for a grave,

Ne'er saw the beauteous livery that he wore —

Witness the entertainment that he gave.

　　If he did see his face, why then I know

　　He thought to kiss him, and hath kill'd him so.   *1110*

186

"'Tis true, 'tis true, thus was Adonis slain:

He ran upon the boar with his sharp spear,

Who did not whet his teeth at him again,

But by a kiss thought to persuade him there;

　　And nuzzling in his flank, the loving swine   *1115*

　　Sheath'd unaware the tusk in his soft groin.

(*1105—1116*)

185

1105. grim:　残忍的

　　　urchin-snouted:　刺猬般拱嘴的

1107. beauteous livery:　美丽的侍从；吸引

　　人的容貌

186

1113. whet:　磨快

1115. nuzzling:　用鼻子伸入

1116. Sheath'd unaware:　无意中刺入皮

　　肉

　　soft groin:　柔软的腹股沟

185

残忍拱嘴一野猪　　　　　　1105
恶眼寻坟贼溜溜
美丽装束看不见
却能证明他应酬
我知看见少年脸
本想亲吻男命休　　　　　　1110

186

的确如此男命休
他挺尖矛刺野猪
不再磨牙撅拱嘴
只想亲吻不耍粗
在他腰上胡乱拱　　　　　　1115
牙穿鼠蹊血模糊

（1105—1116）

511

187

"Had I been tooth'd like him, I must confess,

With kissing him I should have kill'd him first,

But he is dead, and never did he bless

My youth with his, the more am I accurst."   *1120*

With this she falleth in the place she stood,

And stains her face with his congealed blood.

188

She looks upon his lips, and they are pale,

She takes him by the hand, and that is cold,

She whispers in his ears a heavy tale,   *1125*

As if they heard the woeful words she told;

She lifts the coffer-lids that close his eyes,

Where lo, two lamps burnt out in darkness lies,

（1117—1128）

187

1117. tooth'd: 在……装牙齿

     confess: 承认

1119. never did he bless: 他从来没有祝福

1120. accurst: 不幸

1122. congealed: 凝结的

188

1125. a heavy tale: 悲伤的故事

1126. woeful words: 凄苦的倾诉

1127. coffer-lids: 保险箱盖；眼皮

187

我像野猪獠牙长
也要吻他一命亡
少年人死青春去
我亦梦断温柔乡　　　　　　　*1120*
边说女神倒原地
少年血污染脸庞

188

望唇唇白无血红
拉手手凉如冷冰
耳边低诉凄惨语　　　　　　　*1125*
好像少年还能听
女神掀开两眼皮
一片黑暗熄两灯

　　　　　　　　　　　　　　　　　　(1117—1128)

189

Two glasses, where herself herself beheld

A thousand times, and now no more reflect,   *1130*

Their virtue lost, wherein they late excell'd,

And every beauty robb'd of his effect.

"Wonder of time," quoth she, "this is my spite,

That thou being dead, the day should yet be light."

190

"Since thou art dead, lo here I prophesy,   *1135*

Sorrow on love hereafter shall attend;

It shall be waited on with jealousy,

Find sweet beginning, but unsavory end;

Ne'er settled equally, but high or low,

That all love's pleasure shall not match his woe.   *1140*

(*1129—1140*)

189

1131. Their virtue lost: 它们的能力（光华）失去
      late excell'd: 新近晶莹绝伦
1132. every beauty robb'd of his effect:
      每种美都失去功效
1133. spite: 不幸

190

1136. Sorrow on love hereafter shall attend:
      痛苦将陪伴着爱情；悲痛永伴爱身边
1137. jealousy: 警觉
1138. unsavory end: 不幸的结局

189

千次自照两镜明
现在照镜镜无踪　　　　　*1130*
原有光彩成昏暗
各种美妙失功能
她言奇迹真可恼
人死白昼还光明

190

你人已死预言听　　　　　*1135*
悲痛永伴爱同行
嫉妒也在旁边等
开局甜蜜结局疼
或高或低难如意
悲喜相比后者轻　　　　　*1140*

(1129—1140)

191

"It shall be fickle, false, and full of fraud,

Bud, and be blasted, in a breathing while,

The bottom poison, and the top o'erstraw'd

With sweets that shall the truest sight beguile;

 The strongest body shall it make most weak,   *1145*

 Strike the wise dumb, and teach the fool to speak.

192

"It shall be sparing, and too full of riot,

Teaching decrepit age to tread the measures;

The staring ruffian shall it keep in quiet,

Pluck down the rich, enrich the poor with treasures;   *1150*

 It shall be raging mad, and silly mild,

 Make the young old, the old become a child.

(1141—1152)

191
1141. fickle: 感情易变的
  full of fraud: 充满虚情假意
1142. Bud: 含苞
  be blasted: 被摧毁
  in a breathing while: 瞬息之间
1143. bottom poison: 底部毒药
  top o'erstraw'd: 上面香草

1144. beguile: 受骗
1146. Strike: 使得

191

虚假善变是爱情
含苞枯萎呼吸同
根部藏毒梢甜蜜
最明眼光难看清
最壮身体变虚弱　　　　　　*1145*
愚蠢能言智无声

192

爱情小气特荒唐
老者跳舞学娇娘
粗野无赖装安静
杀富济贫有主张　　　　　　*1150*
又是狂暴又温柔
老幼颠倒魅力强

（1141—1152）

192

1147. sparing: 小气，吝啬
　　　too full of riot: 形骸放荡
1148. decrepit age: 老朽
　　　tread the measures: 翩翩起舞
1149. staring ruffian: 无耻的流氓
1150. Pluck down the rich: 使富人败家
1151. raging mad: 咆哮疯狂

silly mild: 虚弱温柔
　（译者按：该段与第 66 首十四行
诗相似，更像《雅典的泰门》第四
幕第三场第 26—45 行泰门的独
白）

193

"It shall suspect where is no cause of fear,

It shall not fear where it should most mistrust,

It shall be merciful, and too severe,   *1155*

And most deceiving when it seems most just;

   Perverse it shall be, where it shows most toward,

   Put fear to valor, courage to the coward.

194

"It shall be cause of war and dire events,

And set dissension 'twixt the son and sire,   *1160*

Subject and servile to all discontents,

As dry combustious matter is to fire.

   Sith in his prime, Death doth my love destroy,

   They that love best, their loves shall not enjoy."

(1153—1164)

193
1155. severe: 严厉
1157. Perverse: 堕落的；固执的
1158. valor: 勇敢, 勇猛

194
1159. dire: 灾难的，悲剧的
1160. dissension: 不和，纠纷
1161. servile: 奴隶的
     all discontents: 一切不满
1162. dry combustions matter: 干燥的可
     燃物

193

不该怀疑偏恐慌
最该恐惧又不防
好像慈善太严厉　　　　1155
公道欺诈巧伪装
乖僻偏爱装雅驯
勇士变怯懦夫强

194

引起灾祸与战争
父子之间事不平　　　　1160
陷入烦恼受摆布
干柴烈火烧不停
死神夺我少年美
意浓难享真爱情

（1153—1164）

195

By this the boy that by her side lay kill'd   *1165*

Was melted like a vapor from her sight,

And in his blood that on the ground lay spill'd,

A purple flow'r sprung up, check'red with white,

    Resembling well his pale cheeks and the blood

    Which in round drops upon their whiteness stood. *1170*

196

She bows her head, the new-sprung flow'r to smell,

Comparing it to her Adonis' breath,

And says within her bosom it shall dwell,

Since he himself is reft from her by death.

    She crops the stalk, and in the breach appears   *1175*

    Green-dropping sap, which she compares to tears.

(1165—1176)

195
1165. that: who
1167. spill'd: 洒，溅出
1168. check'red: 交替变换
1170. in round drops upon their whiteness stood: 圆点滴站立在白色的花瓣上

196
1171. bows: 弯下，垂下
1173. within her bosom: 在她的香怀
1175. crops the stalk: 掐断花茎
1176. Green-dropping sap: 滴滴绿汁

195

此刻身边美少年　　　　　　*1165*

清烟轻飏上九天

一滩鲜血地面洒

紫花生处镶白边

苍白面孔鲜红血　　　　　　*1170*

滴入白中如珠圆

196

低头闻花女神情

花如少年又新生

她言花儿酥胸住

少年已入死神宫

手掐花茎折断处　　　　　　*1175*

绿汁滴滴眼泪同

（1165—1176）

197

"Poor flow'r", quoth she, "this was thy father's guise—"

Sweet issue of a more sweet-smelling sire—

For every little grief to wet his eyes;

To grow unto himself was his desire,   *1180*

And so 'tis thine, but know it is as good

To wither in my breast as in his blood.

198

"Here was thy father's bed, here in my breast;

Thou art the next of blood, and 'tis thy right.

Lo in this hollow cradle take thy rest,   *1185*

My throbbing heart shall rock thee day and night;

　　There shall not be one minute in an hour

　　Wherein I will not kiss my sweet love's flow'r."

(1177—1188)

197

1177. guise: 形象；外观

1178. Sweet issue of a more sweet-smelling sire: 更美更香的父亲生下的甜美的后代；尔父更美更芬芳

1180. To grow unto himself was his desire: 长大成人是他的愿望；酷似自己长成人

198

1185. hollow cradle: 空谷似的软摇篮

1186. throbbing heart: 悸动的心

1187. not be one minute in an hour: 每时每刻不停息

197

可怜风花像父亲

尔父更美更芳芬

小小苦恼湿双眼

酷似自己长成人　　　　　　1180

你也一样须知晓

如血枯萎我胸襟

198

尔父床设我酥胸

嫡亲有权来继承

空空摇篮你未躺　　　　　　1185

我心跳荡日夜情

摇晃鲜花争分秒

亲吻芳菲慰魂灵

（1177—1188）

199

Thus weary of the world, away she hies,

And yokes her silver doves, by whose swift aid   *1190*

Their mistress mounted through the empty skies,

In her light chariot, quickly is convey'd,

    Holding their course to Paphos, where their queen

    Means to immure herself, and not be seen.

(1189—1194)

199
1189. away she hies: 她匆匆离去
1190. yokes: 驾驭；给……上轭
1191. mistress: 女主人
1192. chariot: 漂亮的车，凯旋车
    convey'd: 运送
1193. Paphos: 帕福斯，地中海东部塞浦路斯（Cyprus）岛的古城，为女神维纳斯（Venus）和美少年阿童尼（Adonis）的崇拜地
1144. immure: 禁闭；与世隔绝

199

厌倦人世走女神

银鸽驾驭上青云　　　　1190

长空万里她静坐

轻车迅飞圣岛临

帕福斯乃崇拜地

从此隐居藏真身

（1189—1194）

POSTSCRIPT

Shakespeare, a man of letters known to every household, was first a poet. The long narrative *Venus and Adonis* written by him with great passion was read and appreciated far and wide after 15 printings. More than 20 years ago when I read it I felt extremely excited and decided to put it into Chinese version as the 7 character one line poem, rhymed *aa ba ca*. The translation is going to be published with detailed notes based on *The Temple Shakespeare* and *The Riverside Shakespeare*. My hearty thanks are given to Professor Li Funing for his earnest instruction and to Professor Gu Zhengkun for his kind effort. I will feel very grateful to the valuable criticism from my dear readers.

(Zhu Tingbo)

小　记

家喻户晓的莎士比亚首先是一个诗人，他以火热的激情所写的长诗《维纳斯与阿童尼》一发表就广为流传。二十年前译者初读此诗作就激动不已，遂潜心将其译成中文七言诗，押 *aa ba ca* 韵，力求通顺畅晓。"冷却"时间可谓久矣。所据版本为河滨版《莎士比亚》。今拟付梓，英汉对照，加了注释，依据殿堂版和河滨版，中文为主。翻译此诗时李赋宁先生的谆谆教诲言犹在耳，辜正坤先生的鼎力相助没齿不忘。海内同道，知我罪我，不胜感佩。

（朱廷波）

The Study Of Shakespeare's Poems

莎士比亚诗歌研究

英汉对照

下

朱廷波 著

中国出版集团

世界图书出版公司

图书在版编目（CIP）数据

莎士比亚诗歌研究：英汉对照/朱廷波著. —广州：世界
图书出版广东有限公司,2011.11

ISBN 978-7-5100-4087-0

Ⅰ.①莎…　Ⅱ.①朱…　Ⅲ.①莎士比亚,W.(1564～
1616)—诗歌评论—英汉对照 Ⅳ.①I561.072

中国版本图书馆 CIP 数据核字（2011）第 228402 号

莎士比亚诗歌研究：英汉对照

责任编辑： 杨贵生　冯彦庄

责任技编： 刘上锦　余坤译

出版发行： 世界图书出版广东有限公司

　　　　　（广州市新港西路大江冲 25 号　邮编：510300）

电　　话：020-84469182

http：//www.gdst.com.cn

编辑邮箱：edksy@qq.com

经　　销：全国各地新华书店

印　　刷：广东天鑫源印刷有限责任公司

印　　次：2013 年 1 月第 1 版第 2 次印刷

规　　格：710mm×1 000mm　1/16　66.75 印张　987 千字

书　　号：ISBN 978-7-5100-4087-0/I·0247

定　　价：130.00 元（共 2 册）

若因印装质量问题影响阅读，请与承印厂联系退换。

CONTENTS

Poems of Shakespeare

Collection of Beautiful Poems

by William Shakespeare

III LUCRECE

TO THE RIGHT HONOURABLE HENRY WRIOTHESLEY,
EARL OF SOUTHAMPTON, AND BARON OF TITCHFIELD.

The love I dedicate to your Lordship is without end; whereof this pamphlet[1], without beginning, is but a superfluous moiety[2]. The warrant[3] I have of your honourable disposition, not the worth of my untutor'd lines, makes it assured of acceptance. What I have done is yours; what I have to do is yours; being part in all I have, devoted yours. Were my worth greater, my duty would show greater; meantime, as it is, it is bound to your Lordship, to whom I wish long Life, still lengthen'd with all happiness.

Your Lordship's in all duty,

William Shakespeare.

---

1. pamphlet: short publication, 短篇作品
2. moiety: small part, 小部分
3. warrant: assurance, possibly suggesting that Shakespeare had been rewarded for *Venus and Adonis*, 担保，可能指莎士比亚因《维纳斯与阿童尼》而得到的奖赏

Ⅲ　露克丽丝

扫桑普顿伯爵，提切菲尔德男爵，
亨利·雷奥蒂斯利阁下：

　　仆对阁下之爱无尽头。拙作虽然无端，亦自知谫陋，承蒙阁下重金恩赐，实感诗句拙野，切望阁下能受。仆之所为为阁下，仆之将为为阁下。仆之部分及全体，均当属于阁下。倘仆之能力有进，其责任当更重。于此同时，拙作谨奉献阁下，恭祝阁下福寿绵长。

阁下之忠仆
威廉·莎士比亚

THE ARGUMENT[1]

Lucius Tarquinius[2] (for his excessive pride surnamed Superbus[3]), after he had caused his own father-in-law Servius Tullius[4] to be cruelly murder'd, and, contrary to the Roman laws and customs, not requiring or staying for the people's suffrages[5], had possest himself of the kingdom, went, accompanied with his sons and other noblemen of Rome, to besiege Ardea[6]. During which siege the principal men of the army meeting one evening at the tent of Sextus Tarquinius[7], the king's son, in their discourses after supper every one commended the virtues of his own wife; among whom Collatinus[8] extoll'd the incomparable chastity of his wife Lucretia[9]. In that pleasant humour they all posted[10] to Rome; and intending, by their secret and sudden arrival, to make trial of that which every one had before avouched[11], only Collatinus finds his wife, though it were late in the night, spinning amongst her maids: the other ladies were all found dancing and revelling[12], or in several disports[13]. Whereupon the noblemen yielded Collatinus the victory, and his wife the fame. At that time Sextus Tarquinius being inflamed with Lucrece' beauty, yet smothering[14] his passions for the present, departed with the rest back to the camp; from whence[15] he shortly after privily[16] withdrew

---

1. argument: summary, plot outline, 故事梗概
2. Lucius Tarquinius: last king of Rome (reigned 535—510 B.C.) 路西乌斯·塔昆尼乌斯（公元前 535—510 在位），古罗马第七代（末代）皇帝
3. Superbus: (L.)proud, 骄傲的，自大狂
4. Servius Tullius: sixth king of Rome (reigned 578—535 B.C.), killed when his daughter drove her chariot over him, 赛夫乌斯·图里乌斯（公元前 578—535 在位），古罗马第六代皇帝，其女用战车将其轧死
5. suffrages: vote，投票
6. Ardea: 阿迪丝，a city about 25 miles south of Rome，古罗马重镇，离古罗马城南大约 25 英里

概　要

　　路西乌斯·塔昆尼乌斯，因过于骄傲人称休帕勃斯。他使其岳父塞夫乌斯·图里乌斯惨遭杀害。他还违反罗马法律和习俗，也未听候民众同意，擅自篡夺王位。后由儿子们及其他罗马贵族跟随，围攻阿迪亚。围攻期间，国王儿子塔昆，在其帐内晚餐后与众将官闲话，众人皆赞己妻之贞淑。有一名叫科拉廷之将官自诩夫人露克丽丝之出众贞洁。众将官饶有兴致，回到罗马，欲秘验妻房是否贞淑。惟有科拉廷发现，夤夜之际，其妻仍与侍女一起纺织。他人之妻均在跳舞赴宴，寻欢作乐。众人承认科拉廷为胜利者。此时，塔昆因露克丽丝之美而欲火中烧，勉强克制住自己，与众将官返回营帐。又私自出营，

---

7. Sextus Tarquinius: Tarquin in this poem, 诗中的塔昆
8. Collatinus: Collatine in this poem, 诗中的科拉廷
9. Lucretia: Lucrece in this poem, 诗中的露克丽丝
10. posted: rode with speed, 骑马疾驶
11. avouched: assert, 断言
12. reveling: make merry, 尽情欢乐
13. disports: amusements, 嬉戏
14. smothering: die from lack of air, 使窒息，把……闷死
15. whence: from where, 从那个地方，从那里
16. privily: secretly, 私下地，秘密地

himself, and was (according to his estate[17]) royally entertan'd and lodged by Lucrece at Collatium[18]. The same night he treacherously[19] stealeth into her chamber, violently ravisht her, and early in the morning speedeth away. Lucrece, in this lamentable plight[20], hastily dispatcheth messengers, one to Rome for her father, another to the camp for Collatine. They came, the one accompanied with Junius Brutus, the other with Publius Valerius; and finding Lucrece attired[21] in mourning habit, demanded the cause of her sorrow. She, first taking an oath of them for her revenge, reveal'd the actor, and whole manner of his dealing, and withal[22] suddenly stabb'd herself. Which done, with one consent they all vow'd to root out the whole hated family of the Tarquins; and bearing the dead body to Rome, Brutus acquainted the people with the doer and manner of the vile[23] deed, with a bitter invective[24] against the tyranny of the king: wherewith[25] the people were so moved, that with one consent and a general acclamation[26] the Tarquins were all exiled[27], and the state government changed from kings to consuls[28].

---

17. estate: status, 地位
18. Collatium: a town 10 miles north-east of Rome, 科拉廷乌姆，位于罗马城东北 10 英里处
19. treacherously: behaving vith or showing treachery, 叛逆地, 不忠地
20. plight: serious and difficult situation or condition, 困境
21. attired: dress, 穿衣
22. withal: with this told, 说过之后
23. vile: extremely disgusting, 非常令人厌恶的
24. invective: violent attack in words, 猛烈抨击
25. wherewith: at which, 由于那缘故
26. acclamation: loud and enthusiastic approval, 高声而热烈的赞同

潜到科拉廷乌姆，以此身份，受到盛大欢迎，并留宿。其夜，塔昆偷偷进入露克丽丝卧室，强暴了她，黎明又匆忙离去。露克丽丝悲恸欲绝，急忙派遣使者，一往罗马见其父，一往军营见其夫科拉廷。二人都到，一由裘利乌斯·布鲁特斯协同，一由普伯利乌斯·华莱利乌斯协同。只见露克丽斯身穿丧服，急问其故。露卿首先要求二人发誓为她报仇，随后说出罪犯名姓及犯罪事实，之后用匕首自杀身亡。如此烈举，使得二人一齐发誓要推翻众叛亲离之塔昆王朝。遂抬尸体到罗马，布鲁特斯向民众宣布了罪人及其罪行，猛烈抨击国王暴政。民众深为所动，异口同声，要求把塔昆家族全部放逐。国家政体由君主制变为执政官制。

27. exiled: send sb. into exile, 放逐
28. consuls: either of the two magistrates who ruled in ancient Rome before it became an Empire, 古罗马成为帝国之前的两个执政官之一

1

From the besieged Ardea all in post,

Borne by the trustless wings of false desire,

Lust-breathed Tarquin leaves the Roman host,

And to Collatium bears the lightless fire

Which, in pale embers hid, lurks to aspire   *5*

    And girdle with embracing flames the waist

    Of Collatine's fair love, Lucrece the chaste.

2

Haply that name of 'chaste' unhap'ly set

This bateless edge on his keen appetite;

When Collatine unwisely did not let   *10*

To praise the clear unmatched red and white

Which triumpht in that sky of his delight,

    Where mortal stars, as bright as heaven's beauties,

    With pure aspects did him peculiar duties.

(1—14)

1
1. besieged: 围攻
   post: haste, 匆忙
2. Borne: bear, 承受
3. Lust-breathed: inspired by or
   well-exercised in lust, 充满淫邪的欲念
   host: army, 军队
5. embers: 燃眉

lurks: 潜伏, 埋伏; 潜藏
aspire: rise, 升起
6. girdle: encircle, embrace, 环抱

2
8. Haply: perhaps, 或许
9. bateless: impossible to blunt, 强烈的
   keen: sharp, 尖锐的

1

守卫阿狄亚围城
叵测欲火燃心胸
塔昆溜号出军营
潜赴城堡科拉廷
灰藏无光之火星　　　　　　　　*5*
露克丽丝贞洁容
烈焰燃起搂怀中

2

不幸贞洁之美名
塔昆情欲胜刀锋
贞女有夫科拉廷　　　　　　　　*10*
不智盛赞白透红
仰视佳丽上天宫
佳丽美目超群星
纯情柔光献柔情

（*1—14*）

13. mortal stars: Lucrece's eyes, 露克丽丝的眼睛
14. pure aspects: 冰清玉洁的目光
　　peculiar duties: 向他效忠

3

For he the night before, in Tarquin's tent,   *15*

Unlock't the treasure of his happy state;

What priceless wealth the heavens had him tent

In the possession of his beauteous mate;

Reckoning his fortune at such high-proud rate,

    That kings might be espoused to more fame,   *20*

    But king nor peer to such a peerless dame:

4

O happiness enjoy'd but of a few!

And, if possest, as soon decay'd and done

As is the morning's silver-melting dew

Against the golden splendour of the sun!   *25*

An expired date, cancell'd ere well begun:

    Honour and beauty, in the owner's arms,

    Are weakly fortressed from a world of harms.

(15—28)

3
15. Tarquin: 塔昆
18. beauteous: beautiful, 美丽的
19. Reckoning: 以为
20. espoused: married, 结婚
21. peerless: unequalled, 无与伦比

4
23. done: destroyed, 毁灭
24. silver-melting dew: 消融的银白的露水
25. splendour: 金辉
26. expired: 终止
     cancell'd: 取消
28. fortressed: 堡垒

3

前日塔昆帐逢中   *15*

宣示幸福科拉廷

上天赐福自天官

贤妻侍奉女花容

志得意满乐融融

帝王威望遍寰中   *20*

如此艳福怅望空

4

少数人享福寿荣

一旦到手变西风

好似白露清晨融

太阳金色光环中   *25*

刚要开场便告终

怀拥贞节与美容

难抵罪孽邪恶情

（15—28）

5

Beauty itself doth of itself persuade

The eyes of men without an orator;   *30*

What needeth, then, apologies be made,

To set forth that which is so singular?

Or why is Collatine the publisher

   Of that rich jewel he should keep unknown

   From thievish ears, because it is his own?   *35*

6

Perchance his boast of Lucrece' sovereignty

Suggested this proud issue of a king;

For by our ears our hearts oft tainted be:

Perchance that envy of so rich a thing,

Braving compare, disdainfully did sting   *40*

   His high-pitcht thoughts, that meaner men should vaunt

   That golden hap which their superiors want.

（29—42）

5
30. orator:　演说家
31. apologies:　defense, 申述
32. singular:　unique, 奇特的
35. thievish:　贼似的

6
36. Perchance:　或许
   sovereignty:　绝色美貌
37. Suggested:　诱惑
38. tainted:　影响
40. Braving compare:　举世无比
   disdainfully:　轻蔑地，倨傲地
41. vaunt:　吹嘘

5

美貌何须言辩雄

征服男人双眼睛　　　　　　　　30

为何饶舌科拉廷

大庭广众赞露卿

人间奇珍貌倾城

珍宝应处秘藏中

谨访被盗祸乱生　　　　　　　　35

6

因夸露卿美娇容

狂傲王子邪念生

常人耳闻邪念萌

也许艳羡美事情

无情反差刺狂生　　　　　　　　40

臣下竟然夸己能

他享艳福君不成

（29—42）

7

But some untimely thought did instigate

His all-too-timeless speed, if none of those:

His honour, his affairs, his friends, his state,   *45*

Neglected all, with swift intent he goes

To quench the coal which in his liver glows.

　　O rash-false heat, wrapt in repentant cold,

　　Thy hasty spring still blasts, and ne'er grows old!

8

When at Collatium this false lord arrived,   *50*

Well was he welcomed by the Roman dame,

Within whose face Beauty and Virtue strived

Which of them both should underprop her fame:

When Virtue bragg'd, Beauty would blush for shame;

　　When Beauty boasted blushes, in despite   *55*

　　Virtue would stain that o'er with silver white.

(43—56)

7
43. instigate: 教唆；怂恿
46. swift intent: 匆匆忙忙
47. quench: 扑灭
48. rash-false heat: 轻狂的欲火
　　repentant: 后悔的
49. hasty spring: 过早的萌芽
　　blasts: 枯萎

8
51. dame: 贵妇人
53. underprop: 支撑
55. beauty boasted blushes: 美貌炫耀其
　　绯红
　　in despite: 防卫
56. stain: 染

7

非份之想偏纵容
催促塔昆胡乱行
不顾名份与友情 　　　　　　45
军务轻抛急匆匆
肝中欲火不让生
呜呼内烧表面冷
青春速衰成老翁

8

科拉廷阿姆行踪 　　　　　　50
罗马女郎诚欢迎
狂徒窥见美善争
何人支撑贞操名
贞操吹嘘美脸红
美貌红晕骄傲情 　　　　　　55
贞操银白笼真容

（43—56）

541

9

But Beauty, in that white intituled,

From Venus' doves doth challenge that fair field:

Then Virtue claims from Beauty Beauty's red,

Which Virtue gave the golden age to gild   *60*

Their silver cheeks, and call'd it then their shield;

 Teaching them thus to use it in the fight,—

 When shame assail'd, the red should fence the white.

10

This heraldry in Lucrece' face was seen,

Argued by Beauty's red and Virtue's white: *65*

Of either's colour was the other queen,

Proving from world's minority their right:

Yet their ambition makes them still to fight;

 The sovereignty of either being so great,

 That oft they interchange each other's seat.   *70*

（57—70）

9
57. intituled: 命名
61. shield: 盾
63. assail'd: 攻击
64. fence: 保护

10
65. heraldry: 纹章
67. minority: 黄金时代，蒙昧时期
69. sovereignty: 君权

9

美貌染白妙趣生
美神白鸽仙鸟称
贞操也提美貌红
黄金时代饰娇容　　　　　　　　60
白颊镀金金盾称
羞辱袭来自卫成
保卫洁白靠色红

10

纹章现于女面容
贞操为白美貌红　　　　　　　　65
自视女王对方卿
威权赫赫自古成
野心促使苦斗争
双方权力欲升腾
争夺主位起刀兵　　　　　　　　70

　　　　　　　　　　　　　　（57—70）

11

This silent war of lilies and of roses,

Which Tarquin view'd in her fair face's field,

In their pure ranks his traitor eye encloses;

Where, lest between them both it should be kill'd,

The coward captive vanquished doth yield   *75*

  To those two armies that would let him go,

  Rather than triumph in so false a foe.

12

Now thinks he that her husband's shallow tongue,—

The niggard prodigal that praised her so,—

In that high task hath done her beauty wrong,   *80*

Which far exceeds his barren skill to show:

Therefore that praise which Collatine doth owe

  Enchanted Tarquin answers with surmise,

  In silent wonder of still-gazing eyes.

(71—84)

11
73. ranks:大军
74. lest:恐怕
75. The coward captive: 怯懦的俘虏
    vanquished: 征服

12
79. niggard: 吝啬鬼
    prodigal: 浪费者
83. Enchanted: 用魔法迷惑
    surmise: 推测，想象

11

百合蔷薇静中争
塔昆偷觑美面容
两军捕捉贼眼睛
惟恐阵前送小命
怯懦俘虏喊连声　　　　　　75
投降示爱放他行
胜之不伍无耻兵

12

此刻想起科拉廷
吝啬赞妻浅薄空
不配绝色丈夫轻　　　　　　80
才薄不堪誉娇容
所欠赞语须补充
色迷塔昆想象中
静呆痴看大眼睛

（71—84）

13

This earthly saint, adored by this devil,   85

Little suspecteth the false worshipper;

For unstain'd thoughts do seldom dream on evil;

Birds never limed no secret bushes fear:

So guiltless she securely gives good cheer

　　And reverend welcome to her princely guest,   90

　　Whose inward ill no outward harm exprest:

14

For that he colour'd with his high estate,

Hiding base sin in plaits of majesty;

That nothing in him seem'd inordinate,

Save sometime too much wonder of his eye,   95

Which, having all, all could not satisfy;

　　But, poorly rich, so wanteth in his store,

　　That, coly'd with much, he pineth still for more.

(85—98)

13
85. adored: 崇拜
86. worshipper: 礼拜者，崇拜者
88. limed: 用粘鸟胶捕捉
90. reverend: 可尊敬的，敬畏的

14
92. estate: 等级
93. plaits: 褶
94. inordinate: 放纵的
97. so wanteth in his store: 如此贪心不足
98. cloy'd: 使过饱
　　pineth: 渴望

13

人间圣女恶魔情　　　　　　　　85
圣女不疑虚伪行
客伪心纯不防兵
飞鸟黑树林不惊
未被胶粘好心情
无愧坦然待客情　　　　　　　　90
王子奸诈不言声

14

奸恶被掩身高层
威仪皱褶恶隐形
居心叵测无影踪
有时马脚露眼睛　　　　　　　　95
一切在目心未平
可怜富者贪尊荣
腰缠万贯仍嫌穷

（85—98）

15

But she, that never coped with stranger eyes,

Could pick no meaning from their parling looks,   *100*

Nor read the subtle-shining secrecies

Writ in the glassy margents of such books:

She toucht no unknown baits, nor fear'd no hooks;

  Nor could she moralize his wanton sight,

  More than his eyes were open'd to the light.   *105*

16

He stories to her ears her husband's fame,

Won in the fields of fruitful Italy;

And decks with praises Collatine's high name,

Made glorious by his manly chivalry

With bruised arms and wreaths of victory: *110*

  Her joy with heaved-up hand she doth express,

  And, wordless, so greets heaven for his success.

(99—112)

15
100. parling: 会说话的
102. glassy margents: 书页边的注释
103. baits: 诱饵
104. moralize: 解释
    wanton: 淫乱的

16
107. fields of fruitful Italy: 意大利的肥沃
    原野
108. decks: 装饰，打扮
109. chivalry: 骑士气概
110. bruised: 使青肿

15

未见生人之眼睛
美人不解眉目情　　　　　　　　　*100*
脸上表情也不懂
奇书注释看不明
未吞钓饵不机警
未解一双贼眼睛
只道睁开对光明　　　　　　　　　*105*

16

对女讲述夫英名
意大利野战兵赢
推崇家声科拉廷
勇武侠义得美名
戎装受创花冠红　　　　　　　　　*110*
女举双手贺夫情
感激上苍默无声

（99—112）

17

Far from the purpose of his coming thither,

He makes excuses for his being there:

No cloudy show of stormy blustering weather   *115*

Doth yet in his fair welkin once appear;

Till sable Night, mother of dread and fear,

   Upon the world dim darkness doth display,

   And in her vaulty prison stows the Day.

18

For then is Tarquin brought unto his bed,   *120*

Intending weariness with heavy sprite;

For, after supper, long he questioned

With modest Lucrece, and wore out the night:

Now leaden slumber with life's strength doth fight;

   And every one to rest themselves betakes,   *125*

   Save thieves, and cares, and troubled minds, that wakes.

(113—126)

17
115. blustering: 呼啸狂吹的
116. welkin: 天空，苍穹
117. sable: 黑色
119. vaulty: 穹隆

stows: 贮藏
18
121. sprite: spirit, 精神
124. slumber: 沉睡状态
125. betake: 去，往

17

塔昆不言为何行
信口胡诌隐真情
风暴险霾无影踪   *115*
只见碧空万里晴
恐怖惊惧黑夜空
妖母黑暗展穹窿
白昼囚禁监牢中

18

塔昆现被床边送   *120*
装作疲备不堪形
晚饭之后长话丛
多礼露卿多宽容
睡意生命相抗争
人想睡眠之安宁   *125*
淫贼烦躁胡乱行

（113—126）

19

As one of which doth Tarquin lie revolving

The sundry dangers of his will's obtaining;

Yet ever to obtain his will resolving,

Though weak-built hopes persuade him to abstaining:　　*130*

Despair to gain doth traffic oft for gaining;

　　And when great treasure is the meed proposed,

　　Though death be adjunct, there's no death supposed.

20

Those that much covet are with gain so fond,

That what they have not, that which they possess,　　*135*

They scatter and unloose it from their bond,

And so, by hoping more, they have but less;

Or, gaining more, the profit of excess

　　Is but to surfeit, and such griefs sustain,

　　That they prove bankrout in this poor-rich gain.　　*140*

(127—140)

19

128. sundry: 各种各样的

130. abstaining: 放弃

131. Despair to gain doth traffic oft for gaining: traffic, 交易。越是绝望越想成

132. meed: 奖赏

133. adjunct: 在手边的

20

134. covet: 妄想别人的东西

136. unloose: 放松

　　bond: 占有

138. excess: 超过量

139. surfeit: 过量

　　sustain: 蒙受，遭受

19

塔昆睡眠难安宁

盘算乘机鬼魅行

决心阴谋早得逞

无望之事应飘零　　　　　　　130

越是绝望越想成

为图大利不顾命

纵然一死也从容

20

贪心大者惟想赢

已有资本全抛空　　　　　　　135

未得之利也经营

只因贪大两手空

努力多赚利也成

过多利润累身形

金玉其外破产中　　　　　　　140

（127—140）

21

The aim of all is but to nurse the life

With honour, wealth, and ease, in waning age;

And in this aim there is such thwarting strife,

That one for all, or all for one we gage;

As life for honour in fell battle's rage;   *145*

   Honour for wealth; and oft that wealth doth cost

   The death of all, and all together lost.

22

So that in vent'ring ill we leave to be

The things we are for that which we expect;

And this ambitious foul infirmity,   *150*

In having much, torments us with defect

Of that we have: so then we do neglect

   The thing we have; and, all for want of wit,

   Make something nothing by augmenting it.

(141—154)

21
142. waning: 迟暮
143. thwarting: 对抗
144. gage: 冒险
145. fell: 凶猛的

22
148. vent'ring ill: 莽撞冒险
     leave to be: 放任
150. ambitious foul infirmity: 丑恶的病
     态的野心
151. defect: 无效
153. want of wit: 没有智慧
154. argumenting: 夸大

21

人人都愿享富荣
舒适安闲过一生
面面俱到苦难行
一无所获一生空
甘冒战火为尊荣　　　　　　　145
为成富翁损尊荣
死亡毁灭缘富荣

22

侪辈冒险不改容
本有财富仍追踪
贪心不足苦经营　　　　　　　150
图谋贪多迷真情
智慧缺乏忘尊荣
费尽心机成虚空
一文不值夸连城

　　　　　　　　　　　（141—154）

23

Such hazard now must doting Tarquin make,   155

Pawning his honour to obtain his lust;

And for himself himself he must forsake:

Then where is truth, if there be no self-trust?

When shall he think to find a stranger just,

When he himself himself confounds, betrays   160

To slanderous tongues and wretched hateful days?

24

Now stole upon the time the dead of night,

When heavy sleep had closed up mortal eyes:

No comfortable star did lend his light,

No noise but owls' and wolves' death-boding cries;   165

Now serves the season that they may surprise

The silly lambs: pure thoughts are dead and still,

While lust and murder wakes to stain and kill.

(155—168)

23
155. doting: 淫昏的
156. Pawning: 抵押
157. forsake: 抛弃
160. confounds: 打败，推翻
161. slanderous tongues: 世人的唾弃
    wretched hateful days: 悲惨的遭人
    痛恨的日子

24
164. comfortable star: 安静的星儿
165. death-boding cries: 预告死亡凶信的
    叫声
    boding, 预兆的，凶兆的
166. serves the season: 正是时候
168. stain: 污辱

23

淫昏塔昆冒险行　　　　　　　　*155*

为达淫欲抛尊荣

全为私己失本容

失去自尊真无踪

岂望他人表真诚

遭人唾骂毁己行　　　　　　　　*160*

人人痛恨不聊生

24

夜幕沉沉已三更

睡眠闭住人眼睛

星星也不放光明

静中枭叫与狼鸣　　　　　　　　*165*

纯洁羔羊遭进攻

良心善念死灭中

淫欲凶杀逞威风

（*155—168*）

557

25

And now this lustful lord leapt from his bed,

Throwing his mantle rudely o'er his arm;   *170*

Is madly tossed between desire and dread;

Th'one sweetly flatters, th'other feareth harm;

But honest fear, bewitched with lust's foul charm,

   Doth too-too oft betake him to retire,

     Beaten away by brain-sick rude desire.   *175*

26

His falchion on a flint he softly smiteth,

That from the cold stone sparks of fire do fly;

Whereat a waxen torch forthwith he lighteth,

Which must be lode-star to his lustful eye;

And to the flame thus speaks advisedly,   *180*

   'As from this cold flint I enforced this fire,

   So Lucrece must I force to my desire'.

(169—182)

25
170. mantle: 披风
171. tossed: 摇摆的
173. bewitched: 着迷
     foul charm: 邪恶的魅力
174. too-too: 非常
     betake him: 使得他
175. brain-sick: 发疯

26
176. falchion: 弯形大刀
     flint: 燧石
     smiteth: 重击
178. Whereat: At which, 在那里
179. lodestar: 北极星
180. advisedly: 考虑过
     地, 蓄意地
181. enforced: 实施

25

淫欲王子邪火升
床上跃起袍一扔　　　　　　　　　　*170*
袍搭臂上躁惧生
一为开心一担惊
恐惧难敌欲火升
欲火魔法逼回营
塔昆昏头仗不赢　　　　　　　　　　*175*

26

弯刀轻敲石冷冰
塔昆见石冒火星
点蜡为炬闪光明
引他淫眼北斗星
面对火焰讲其凶　　　　　　　　　　*180*
我逼冷石冒火星
露克丽丝从我行

（*169—182*）

27

Here pale with fear he cloth premeditate

The dangers of his loathsome enterprise,

And in his inward mind he doth debate   *185*

What following sorrow may on this arise:

Then looking scornfully, he doth despise

   His naked armour of still-slaughter'd lust,

   And justly thus controls his thoughts unjust:

28

'Fair torch, burn out thy light, and lend it not   *190*

To darken her whose light excelleth thine:

And die, unhallow'd thoughts, before you blot

With your uncleanness that which is divine;

Offer pure incense to so pure a shrine:

   Let fair humanity abhor the deed   195

   That spots and stains love's modest snow-white weed.

(183—196)

27

183. premeditate: 预告，思考，预谋

184. loathsome: 讨厌的

185—186. in his inward mind he doth debate/ what following sorrow may on this arise: 铤而走险心翻腾，难卜引起何苦痛

188. armour: 盔甲

28

191. excelleth: 胜过；优于

192. unhallow'd thoughts: 邪念

194. incense: 香

195. abhor: 憎恶，厌恶

27

脸色苍白神情惊
暗中思忖己丑行
铤而走险心翻腾　　　　　　　　　185
难卜引起何苦痛
塔昆满面鄙夷情
肉欲武器会消停
自责邪念自无情

28

蜡烛亮光应烧馨　　　　　　　　　190
女胜汝亮勿遮卿
空想该死勿逞凶
肮脏玷污她圣容
清梦焚于神龛中
公正人性弃丑行　　　　　　　　　195
纯爱雪白衣鲜明

（183—196）

29

'O shame to knighthood and to shining arms!

O foul dishonour to my household's grave!

O impious act, including all foul harms!

A martial man to be soft fancy's slave!　　　　　*200*

True valour still a true respect should have;

　　Then my digression is so vile, so base,

　　That it will live engraven in my face.

30

'Yea, though I die, the scandal will survive,

And be an eye-sore in my golden coat;　　　　　*205*

Some loathsome dash the herald will contrive;

To cipher me how fondly I did dote;

That my posterity, shamed with the note,

　　Shall curse my bones, and hold it for no sin

　　To wish that I their father had not been.　　　　*210*

（197—210）

29
198. grave: 坟墓
199. impious: 邪恶的；不敬的
200. martial: 军事的；尚武的
201. valour: 勇猛
202. digression: 堕落
　　 vile: 卑鄙的
203. engraven: 铭刻

30
205. Eye-sore: 丑的东西
206. herald: 英国司宗谱纹章的官
　　　 contrive: 设法做到
207. cipher: 用密码书写；用文字表达
　　　 fondly: 愚蠢地
　　　 dote: 淫昏

29

武士羞兮武器痛
辱我祖上之门庭
此为毁损之恶行
军人被虏为爱情　　　　　　　　　*200*
一切不顾非真勇
卑鄙放荡为我行
若此刻面永难馨

30

然而我死留恶名
勋章之上有丑形　　　　　　　　　*205*
污色损我勋章荣
荒谬痴恋我有征
后人因我失面容
骸骨受诅因罪行
心愿无此恶祖宗　　　　　　　　　*210*

　　　　　　　　　　　　　　（*197—210*）

31

'What win I, if I gain the thing I seek?

A dream, a breath, a froth of fleeting joy.

Who buys a minute's mirth to wail a week?

Or sells eternity to get a toy?

For one sweet grape who will the vine destroy?   *215*

    Or what fond begger, but to touch the crown,

    Would with the ceptre straight be stricken down?

32

'If Collatinus dream of my intent,

Will he not wake, and in a desperate rage

Post hither, this vile purpose to prevent?   *220*

This siege that hath engirt his marriage,

This blur to youth, this sorrow to the sage,

    This dying virtue, this surviving shame,

    Whose crime will bear an ever-during blame?

(211—224)

31
212. a froth of fleeting joy:　像泡沫一样飞
　　逝的欢情
213. mirth:　欢笑，高兴
　　wail:　恸哭
216. fond:　愚蠢的
　　crown:　王冠
217. sceptre:　王杖

32
219. desperate rage:　怒气冲冲
221. siege:　包围
　　engirt:　包围
222. blur:　涂污
　　sage:　年高望重的人

31

即使如愿有何赢
梦幻暂欢泡影空
孰肯暂欢付长痛
为得玩艺卖永恒
摘一葡萄毁全藤　　　　　　　　215
何处乞丐令牌惩
欲摸王冠愚蠢行

32

科拉廷倘若梦醒
或许他怒气冲冲
速赶来阻我劣行　　　　　　　　220
此乃对婚姻进攻
青年羞耻老年痛
性命攸关耻难平
耻辱柱上钉罪行

(211—224)

33

'O, what excuse can my invention make,   225

When thou shalt charge me with so black a deed?

Will not my tongue be mute, my frail joints shake,

Mine eyes forego their light, my false heart bleed?

The guilt being great, the fear cloth still exceed;

    And extreme fear can neither fight nor fly,   230

    But coward-like with trembling terror die.

34

'Had Collatinus kill'd my son or sire,

Or lain in ambush to betray my life,

Or were he not my dear friend, this desire

Might have excuse to work upon his wife,   235

As in revenge or quittal of such strife:

    But as he is my kinsman, my dear friend,

    The shame and fault finds no excuse nor end.

(225—238)

33
227. frail: 脆弱的，虚弱的
    joints: 四肢
228. forego: 失去

34
232. sire: 父亲
233. lain: lie 的过去分词
    ambush: 埋伏
235. work upon: 攻击，虐待
236. quittal: （偿）还；报复
237. kinsman: 族人；亲属

33

呜呼我有此罪行　　　　　　　　　*225*
君若指控怎说清
张口结舌痛神经
目盲虚伪心血红
恐惧大过我恶行
不能逃避不敢争　　　　　　　　　*230*
等死懦夫战兢兢

34

如果弑父科拉廷
杀子埋伏取我命
并非我想之亲朋
也许有由辱露卿　　　　　　　　　*235*
复仇举动敢斗争
柯为我友找亲朋
耻错无解憾终生

（225—238）

35

'Shameful it is; —ay, if the fact be known:

Hateful it is; —there is no hate in loving: 240

I'll beg her love;—but she is not her own:

The worst is but denial and reproving:

My will is strong, past reason's weak removing.

   Who fears a sentence or an old man's saw

   Shall by a painted cloth be kept in awe.'   245

36

Thus, graceless, holds he disputation

'Tween frozen conscience and hot burning will,

And with good thoughts makes dispensation,

Urging the worser sense for vantage still;

Which in a moment doth confound and kill   250

   Ail pure effects, and doth so far proceed,

   That what is vile shows like a virtuous deed.

（239—252）

35

239. ay: 是，当然

242. reproving: 责骂，谴责

243. past reason's weak removing:
超过了虚弱的理性

244. sentence: 说教
saw: 说教

245. kept in awe: 受威胁的

36

248. good thoughts: 善念
dispensation: 通权达变

249. vantage: 利益

250. confound: 把…毁灭掉

251. effects: 意念；影响

35

事情败露耻羞容
可恨不存爱情中   *240*
我若求爱她难定
最糟她拒斥连声
我欲难倒我理性
笃信老者箴言铭
看见油画敬意生   *245*

36

邪恶之人在权衡
欲火燃烧良心冰
利用善念搞变通
曲解正道妙处赢
一念之差恶意生   *250*
毁灭一切善良情
卑鄙事当好事成

          （239—252）

37

Quoth he, 'she took me kindly by the hand,

And gazed for tidings in my eager eyes,

Fearing some hard news from the warlike band,   *255*

Where her beloved Collatinus lies.

O, how her fear did make her colour rise!

    First red as roses that on lawn we lay,

    Then white as lawn, the roses took away.

38

'And bow her hand, in my hand being lockt,   260

Forced it to tremble with her loyal fear!

Which struck her sad, and then it faster rockt,

Until her husband's welfare she did hear;

Whereat she smiled with so sweet a cheer,

    That had Narcissus seen her as she stood,   *265*

    Self-love had never drown'd him in the flood.

(253—266)

37
253. Quoth: 说
254. tidings: 消息
255. warlike band: 战友

38
265. Narcissus: in Greek mythology, a beautiful young man who fell in love with his own reflection in a pool, [希神]那喀索斯，一个爱上自己水塘中影子的美少年

37

塔昆言说好露卿
握住我手问夫情
我眼色迷怎言明　　　　　　　255
她受亲友探吉凶
惊见担忧面晕红
先为玫瑰开草坪
后变雪白花无踪

38

现牵她手我手中　　　　　　　260
她手颤抖她忠诚
恐惧最绊急匆匆
夫君战事闻渐平
欣然嫣笑艳倾城
那西赛斯若见卿　　　　　　　265
不会自恋跳水中

（253—266）

39

'Why hunt I, then, for colour or excuses?

All orators are dumb when beauty pleadeth;

Poor wretches have remorse in poor abuses;

Love thrives not in the heart that shadows dreadeth: *270*

Affection is my captain, and he leadeth;

   And when his gaudy banner is display'd,

   The coward fights, and will not be dismay'd.

40

'Then, childish fear avaunt! debating die!

Respect and reason wait on wrinkled age!   *275*

My heart shall never countermand mine eye:

Sad pause and deep regard beseems the sage;

My part is youth, and beats these from the stage:

   Desire my pilot is, beauty my prize;

   Then who fears sinking where such treasure lies?   *280*

(267—280)

39
268. pleadeth: 辩护
269. wretches: 不幸的人
    remorse: 悔恨
271. leadeth: 领导
272. gaudy: 炫丽的
273. dismayed: 灰心

40
274. avaunt: begone, 去，滚
276. countermand: 取消
277. beseems: 适合
278. beats these from the stage: 不管这一切
279. pilot: 向导
    beauty my prize: 我的目标是红颜

39

为何找理来讲情
美人开言辩者惊
小人小错无面容
顾忌太多爱不生　　　　　　　　　270
情欲主宰我听从
主宰彩旗一挥动
懦夫生胆去斗争

40

恐惧速去疑无生
老年皱纹伴理性　　　　　　　　　275
我心永不叛眼睛
圣者谦谨三思行
一切不顾我年轻
欲望为导美动情
面对二宝孰惶恐　　　　　　　　　280

（267—280）

41

As corn o'ergrown by weeds, so heedful fear

Is almost choked by uuresisted lust.

Away he steals with open listening ear,

Full of foul hope and full of fond mistrust;

Both which, as servitors to the unjust,   285

　　So cross him with their opposite persuasion,

　　That now he vows a league, and now invasion.

42

Within his thought her heavenly image sits,

And in the self-same seat sits Collatine;

That eye which looks on her confounds his wits;   290

That eye which him beholds, as more divine,

Unto a view so false will not incline;

　　But with a pure appeal seeks to the heart,

　　Which once corrupted takes the worser part;

(281—294)

41
281. heedful: 注意的，留心的
283. open listening ear: 竖起耳朵倾听
284. fond mistrust: 愚蠢的谨慎
285. servitors: 侍从
286. their opposite persuasion: 相反的主张
287. league: 和平条约

42
289. self-same: 完全一样的
290. confounds: 挫败
292. incline: 屈身
293. a pure appeal: 纯真的呼吁
294. once corrupted takes the worser part:
　　　一经腐蚀，竟投向恶的一方

41

如同稼禾野草封
放纵欲望惧不生
竖起耳朵他潜踪
邪念疑惧正抗行
恶人怪圈铁律中 285
理由相左他心惊
不知是退还是攻

42

美女仙姿驻心中
同时闯进科拉廷
一见美女便乱情 290
一见将军欲念空
眼花缭乱势转轻
求助内心有眼睛
心若堕落恶念生

(281—294)

43

And therein heartens up his servile powers,   *295*

Who, flatter'd by their leader's jocund show,

Stuff up his lust, as minutes fall up hours;

And as their captain, so their pride doth grow,

Paying more slavish tribute than they owe.

   By reprobate desire thus madly led,   *300*

   The Roman lord marcheth to Luerece' bed.

44

The locks between her chamber and his will,

Each one by him enforced, retires his ward;

But, as they open, they all rate his ill,

Which drives the creeping thief to some regard: *305*

The threshold grates the door to have him heard;

   Night-wandering weasels shriek to see him there;

   They fright him, yet he still pursues his fear.

（295—308）

43

295. servile: 奴隶的

296. jocund: 欢乐的，快活的

299. slavish: 奴隶的

300. reprobate: 堕落的

44

303. ward: 锁孔

304. they all rate his ill: 都对他斥责

305. to some regard: 小心翼翼

306. threshold: 门坎，门

    grates: 擦响

307. weasels: 鼬鼠，黄鼠狼

    shriek: 尖叫

308. fright: 恐怖，惊吓

43

邪念驻使愚勇生　　　　　　　　295
内心竟然满赞成
欲望膨胀分秒增
心为统帅身快轻
毕恭毕敬表忠诚
邪念导引王子疯　　　　　　　　300
大步欲跨女帐中

44

欲望女房锁数重
塔昆开启手无情
开锁岂顾斥责声
逼迫潜贼益潜踪　　　　　　　　305
门坎门响泄密情
夜行鼬鼠叫声惊
不顾惊示恐怖行

（295—308）

45

As each unwilling portal yields him way,

Through little vents and crannies of the place   *310*

The wind wars with his torch to make him stay,

And blows the smoke of it into his face,

Extinguishing his conduct in this case;

    But his hot heart, which fond desire doth scorch,

    Puffs forth another wind that fires the torch: *315*

46

And being lighted, by the light he spies

Lucretia's glove, wherein her needle sticks:

He takes it from the rushes where it lies,

And griping it, the needle his finger pricks;

As who should say, 'This glove to wanton tricks   *320*

    Is not inured; return again in haste;

    Thou see'st our mistress' ornaments are chaste.'

（*309—322*）

45

309. portal: 门
310. vents: 通风孔
    crannies: 缝隙
313. Extinguishing: 熄灭
314. fond desire: 淫欲
    scorch: 烧焦

46

316. spies: 察见
318. rushes: 古罗马以苇草铺地的风尚
319. griping: 紧握
    pricks: 刺
320. wanton tricks: 调戏
321. inured: 使习惯不利条件

45

门道勉强允通行
缝隙丝丝过小风　　　　　　　310
风吹烛光阻其行
烛烟吹面直劝中
有意迷他阻行踪
淫心邪火正升腾
又吹欲火蜡烛明　　　　　　　315

46

蜡炬重燃见详情
露卿手套锈针清
灯心草上拣起惊
只因手握指刺疼
似言调戏事不成　　　　　　　320
知趣速速回军营
夫人饰物勿慢轻

(309—322)

47

But all these poor forbiddings could not stay him;

He in the worst sense consters their denial:

The doors, the wind, the glove, that did delay him,　　　325

He takes for accidental things of trial;

Or as those bars which stop the hourly dial,

　　Who with a lingering stay his course doth let,

　　Till every minute pays the hour his debt.

48

'So, so,' quoth he, 'these lets attend the time,　　　330

Like little frosts that sometime threat the spring,

To add a more rejoicing to the prime,

And give the sneaped birds more cause to sing.

Pain pays the income of each precious thing;

　　Huge rocks, high winds, strong pirates, shelves and sands, 335

　　The merchant fears, ere rich at home he lands.'

(323—336)

47

324. consters: 解释
326. He takes for accidental things of trial:
　　他认为都是偶然遇到的事情
327. bars: 分秒指针
　　dial: 钟面
328. with a lingering stay his course doth let:
　　缓慢移动妨碍他的进展

48

330. these lets attend the time: 这些障碍
　　是时间的一部分
332. add a more rejoicing to the prime:
　　使阳光显得格外可爱
333. sneaped birds: 冻僵的鸟儿

47

可怜阻力行不通
塔昆恶言解释轻
拦阻手套与门风　　　　　　　325
他意偶然小事情
分针秒针迟报钟
缓慢微动阻他行
分秒凑成一点钟

48

因此分秒阻我行　　　　　　　330
正像春日有霜情
更显阳春欢乐声
鸟儿冻僵鸣啭清
有苦幸福不显平
浅滩大盗巨礁风　　　　　　　335
先于荣归商贾惊

　　　　　　　　　　　　（323—336）

---

334. Pain pays the income of each precious thing:
经过痛苦，宝贵的东西才有价值
335. pirates: 海盗
shelves: 沙丘

49

Now is he come unto the chamber-door

That shuts him from the heaven of his thought,

Which with a yielding latch, and with no more,

Hath barr'd him from the blessed thing he sought.   *340*

So from himself impiety hath wrought,

   That for his prey to pray he doth begin,

   As if the heavens should countenance his sin.

50

But in the midst of his unfruitful prayer,

Having solicited th' eternal power   *345*

That his foul thoughts might compass his fair fair,

And they would stand auspicious to the hour,

Even there he starts: —quoth he, 'I must deflower:

   The powers to whom I pray abhor this fact,

   How can they, then, assist me in the act?   *350*

(337—350)

49

338. shuts him from the heaven of his
    thought: 阻他天堂至乐情

339. a yielding latch: 一道脆弱的门闩

340. the blessed thing: 艳福

341. impiety: 不虔诚
    wrought: work 的过去分词，使得

342. his prey to pray: 使攫捕那猎物

343. countenance: 支持

50

345. solicited: 恳求

346. compass his fair fair: 获取他的佳人

347. auspicious: 吉利的；顺利的

348. deflower: 强暴

349. abhor: 厌恶

49

房门近前塔昆行

阻他天堂至乐情

一道门闩似可轻

春秋大梦一场空　　　　　　340

邪念驱使总心惊

为获猎物求三清

恍若上天助罪行

50

无效祈祷过程中

恳求永恒之神灵　　　　　　345

助他邪念猎美容

护他到时顺心情

突变主意言心静

蹂躏女性天不容

岂能帮我犯罪行　　　　　　350

（337—350）

51

'Then Love and Fortune be my gods, my guide!

My will is backt with resolution:

Thoughts are but dreams till their effects be tried;

The blackest sin is elear'd with absolution;

Against love's fire fear's frost hath dissolution.   355

   The eye of heaven is out, and misty night

   Covers the shame that follows sweet delight.'

52

This said, his guilty hand phick'd up the latch,

And with his knee the door he opens wide.

The dove sleeps fast that this night-owl will catch: 360

Thus treason works ere traitors be espied.

Who sees the lurking serpent steps aside;

   But she, sound sleeping, fearing no such thing,

   Lies at the mercy of his mortal sting.

(351—364)

51

354. absolution: 赦免；忏悔

356. The eye of heaven is out: 太阳已经隐起

     misty night: 雾夜

52

358. pluck'd up: 拉起

361. espied: 发现

362. lurking serpent: 潜藏的毒蛇

364. Lies at the mercy of his mortal sting: 躺着任由他的毒手摆布

51

爱神运神路指明
主意决心未支撑
不付实施念头空
十恶不赦免议中
若遇爱火寒霜融　　　　　　*355*
太阳隐去昏夜中
欢乐之后掩羞容

52

言罢罪手门闩中
膝盖顶门求畅通
鸽子偏遭猫头鹰　　　　　　*360*
未防叛者阴谋成
发现毒蛇躲无踪
美女熟睡未防凶
卧床残受狠毒刑

　　　　　　　　　　　　　　（*351—364*）

53

Into the chamber wickedly he stalks,   *365*

And gazeth on her yet-unstained bed.

The curtains being close, about he walks,

Roiling his greedy eyeballs in his head:

By their high treason is his heart misled;

   Which gives the watch-word to his hand full soon   *370*

   To draw the cloud that hides the silver moon.

54

Look, as the fair and fiery-pointed sun,

Rushing from forth a cloud, bereaves our sight;

Even so, the curtain drawn, his eyes begun

To wink, being blinded with a greater light: *375*

Whether it is that she reflects so bright,

   That dazzleth them, or else some shame supposed;

   But blind they are, and keep themselves enclosed.

(365—378)

53

365. wickedly: 阴险地
     stalks: 蹑手蹑脚地走
367. about he walks: 走来走去
370. watch-word: 暗语，暗号；口令
     full: very, 非常
371. cloud: bed curtain, 床幔

54

372. fiery-pointed: 燃烧的光芒四射的
373. bereaves: 剥夺
377. dazzleth: 使目眩
     some shame supposed: 也许有一些
     羞耻之心

53

阴险潜入卧室中　　　　　　　　　*365*
卧榻未污色眼横
床幔紧闭来回行
头上转动淫眼睛
心中邪念随眼生
心对其手发号令　　　　　　　　　*370*
扯开乌云见月明

54

光芒四射骄阳明
冲破云儿耀眼睛
床幔一开刺目明
光强眼闭盲人行　　　　　　　　　*375*
或因美人光艳升
或因有愧想胡行
目盲紧闭双眼睛

（*365—378*）

55

O, had they in that darksome prison died!

Then had they seen the period of their ill;   *380*

Then Collatine again, by Luerece' side,

In his dear bed might have reposed still:

But they must ope, this blessed league to kill;

   And holy-thoughted Lucrece to their sight

    Must sell her joy, her life, her world's delight.   *385*

56

Her lily hand her rosy cheek lies under,

Cozening the pillow of a lawful kiss;

Who, therefore angry, seems to part in sunder,

Swelling on either side to want his bliss;

Between whose hills her head entombed is: *390*

   Where, like a virtuous monument, she lies,

    To be admired of lewd unhallow'd eyes.

(379—392)

55
379. darksome: 黑暗的
382. reposed: 睡觉
383. ope: 睁开
    blessed league: 幸福的一对
384. holy-thoughted: 圣洁的
385. sell: 牺牲

56
387. Cozening: 夺取
388. sunder: 裂开
389. Swelling: 肿胀
    bliss: 狂喜；福
391. a virtuous monument: 一尊圣像
392. lewd: 淫荡的
    unhallow'd: 亵渎的

55

呜呼双目死牢中
滔天大罪怎得逞　　　　　　380
科拉廷护妻露卿
纯洁卧榻睡安宁
眼睛得睁害娇容
圣洁露卿要牺牲
抛弃欢乐丧今生　　　　　　385

56

手托香腮熟睡中
枕头欲吻却不成
勃然大怒塌陷空
两头翘起亲露卿
头埋夹心有两峰　　　　　　390
善良雕像女花容
淫秽眼睛羡慕生

（379—392）

589

57

Without the bed her other fair hand was,

On the green coverlet; whose perfect white

Show'd like an April daisy on the grass,   *395*

With pearly sweat, resembling dew of night.

Her eyes, like marigolds, had sheathed their light,

   And canopied in darkness sweetly lay,

   Till they might open to adorn the day.

58

Her hair, like golden threads, play'd with her breath;   *400*

O modest wantons! wanton modesty!

Showing life's triumph in the map of death,

And death's dim look in life's mortality:

Each in her deep themselves so beautify,

   As if between them twain there were no strife,   *405*

   But that life lived in death, and death in life.

(393—406)

57

394. coverlet: 床罩

395. daisy: 雏菊

397. marigolds: 金兰花
     sheathed: 包

398. canopied: 用天篷遮盖

399. adorn: 装饰

58

401. modest wantons! wanton modesty:
     文雅纵乐两相生

402. the map of death: 死的图像

403. death's dim look in life's mortality:
     有限的生命中有死亡的阴影

405. twain: 二，一对

57
一只玉手眼帘中
绿色罩单衬白明
四月雏菊绿草中　　　　　　395
汗水如珠像夜空
眼如芳草收光明
金盏草睡黑暗中
且等白昼点缀生

58
发如金线呼吸轻　　　　　　400
文雅纵乐两相生
沉睡如死观生命
睡眠生命后者生
生死相交睡眠中
两者之间无斗争　　　　　　405
生在死里死中生

（393—406）

59

Her breasts, like ivory globes circled with blue,

A pair of maiden worlds unconquered,

Save of their lord no bearing yoke they knew,

And him by oath they truly honoured,   *410*

These worlds in Tarquin new ambition bred;

   Who, like a foul usurper, went about

   From this fair throne to heave the owner out.

60

What could he see but mightily he noted?

What did he note but strongly he desired?   *415*

What he beheld, on that he firmly doted,

And in his will his wilful eye he tired.

With more than admiration he admired

   Her azure veins, her alablaster skin,

   Her coral lips, her snow-white dimpled chin.   *420*

(*407—420*)

59

409. Save of their lord no bearing yoke they knew: 除了主人之外不受任何人的奴役

410. And him by oath they truly honored: 只对他忠贞敬奉，将誓约始终恪守

412. foul usurper: 邪恶的篡位者

413. heave: 扔

60

414. mightily he noted: 他全神贯注

416. firmly doted: 欲火中烧，想据为已有

417. tired: 精疲力竭的；满足的

419. azure: 蔚蓝色的

59
双乳象牙映蓝空
纯洁贞淑未遭凶
主人尽享恩爱情
信誓旦旦心海盟　　　　　　　　　*410*
塔昆对女一计生
篡位夺权不放松
赶走主人宝座空

60
何处看到不心惊
何处注意欲不生　　　　　　　　　*415*
何处关注不生情
百看不够馋眼睛
羡慕之外加钦敬
皮肤白皙血管青
酒窝嘴唇珊瑚红　　　　　　　　　*420*

　　　　　　　　　　　　（*407—420*）

593

61

As the grim lion fawneth o'er his prey,

Sharp hunger by the conquest satisfied,

So o'er this sleeping soul doth Tarquin stay,

His rage of lust by gazing qualified;

Slacked, not suppressed; for standing by her side,   *425*

 His eye, which late this mutiny restrains,

 Unto a greater uproar tempts his veins:

62

And they, like straggling slaves for pillage fighting,

Obdurate vassals fell exploits effecting,

In bloody death and ravishment delighting,   *430*

Nor children's tears nor mothers' groans respecting,

Swell in their pride, the onset still expecting:

 Anon his beating heart, alarum striking,

 Gives the hot charge, and bids them do their liking.

(421—434)

61

421. grim: 残忍的
　　 fawneth: 讨好

424. qualified: 减少

425. Slacked: 缓和的
　　 suppressed: 抑制的

426. mutiny: 叛乱，暴动

62

428. straggling: 最下层的叛兵；散兵游勇

　　 pillage: 破坏

429. Obdurate: 冷酷无情的
　　 vassals: 奴隶
　　 fell exploits effecting: 做野蛮的事情

61

雄狮温存猎物生
饥饿初疗人安宁
塔昆容女睡梦中
亲看或许欲火平
虽平未熄站帐中　　　　　425
眼睛骚动刚刚平
又引脉管血沸腾

62

眼睛劫掠如散兵
狠心奴才抢夺疯
残杀奸淫乐趣生　　　　　430
母亲孩儿恸哭声
眼睛瞪大盼进攻
心跳怦怦响号声
眼睛任转下令攻

（421—434）

432. onset: 进攻
433. Anon: 立刻
　　alarum: alarm, 号声
434. bids: 命令，吩咐

63

His drumming heart cheers up his burning eye,   *435*

His eye commends the leading to his hand;

His hand, as proud of such a dignity,

Smoking with pride, marcht on to make his stand

On her bare breast, the heart of all her land;

 Whose ranks of blue veins, as his hand did scale,   *440*

 Left their round turrets destitute and pale.

64

They, mustering to the quiet cabinet

Where their dear governess and lady lies,

Do tell her she is dreadfully beset,

And fright her with confusion of their cries: *445*

She, much amazed, breaks ope her lockt-up eyes,

 Who, peeping forth this tumult to behold,

 Are by his flaming torch dimm'd and controll'd.

(435—448)

63

435. drumming heart: 咚咚如鼓响的心
438. Smoking with pride: 骄气凌人
439. the heart of all her land: 她全部领土
  的中心
440. ranks of blue veins: 蓝色脉管
  scale: 触及
441. turrets: 圆塔
  destitute: 赤贫的；被抛弃的

64

442. mustering: 聚集
443. governess: 女主人
444. dreadfully: 可怕地
  beset: 困扰
445. fright: frighten, 使惊恐
447. tumult: 吵闹，骚动

63

心跳如鼓眼睛红　　　　　　　435

眼命黑手施暴行

黑手骄傲掌尊荣

骄气凌人大步行

侵女枢纽摸酥胸

血管微蓝抚摸中　　　　　　　440

圆塔两座黯伤情

64

血液急奔心房中

露卿为主本和平

急告被困万千重

乱喊狂叫女受惊　　　　　　　445

惊慌失措睁眼睛

偷看欲知何事情

火炬耀眼眼难睁

（435—448）

597

65

Imagine her as one in dead of night

From forth dull sleep by dreadful fancy waking,   *450*

That thinks she hath beheld soma ghastly sprite,

Whose grim aspect sets every joint a-shaking;

What terror 'tis! but she, in worser taking,

 From sleep disturbed, heedfully doth view

 The sight which makes supposed terror true.   *455*

66

Wrapt and confounded in a thousand fears,

Like to a new-kill'd bird she trembling lies;

She dares not look; yet, winking, there appears

Quick-shifting antics, ugly in her eyes:

Such shadows ate the weak brain's forgeries;   *460*

 Who, angry that the eyes fly from their lights,

 In darkness daunts them with more dreadful sights.

(449—462)

65
451. ghastly: 鬼一样的
  sprite: 鬼怪
452. grim: 可憎的，可怜的
454. heedfully: 谨慎地

66
456. confounded: 惊惶的，惶惑的
458. winking: 眨眼的
459. antics: 怪物
460. forgeries: 伪造品，赝品
462. daunts: 威吓；惊愕

65

试想一女深夜中

噩梦惊醒睡难成　　　　　　　　　*450*

以为方才见妖精

魂不附体欲逃生

噩梦可怖事更惊

睡中醒来眼看清

心中恐怖成真情　　　　　　　　　*455*

66

千万恐怖困露卿

小鸟被杀腿乱蹬

不敢观看眼又睁

怪物闪动丑妖精

虚弱头脑虚幻情　　　　　　　　　*460*

愤恨之极眼不明

更恶景象更恶形

　　　　　　　　　　　　　　（449—462）

67

His hand, that yet remains upon her breast,—

Rude ram, to hatter such an ivory wall! —

May feel her heart—poor citizen! —distressed,   *465*

Wounding itself to death, rise up and fall,

Beating her bulk, that his hand shakes withal.

   This moves in him more rage, and lesser pity,

   To make the breach, and enter this sweet city.

68

First, like a trumpet, doth his tongue begin   *470*

To sound a parley to his heartless foe;

Who o'er the white sheet peers her whiter chin,

The reason of this rash alarm to know,

Which he by dumb demeanour seeks to show;

   But she with vehement prayers urgeth still   *475*

   Under what colour he commits this ill

                                             (463—476)

67

464. ram: 撞墙槌
     batter: 连续猛击，炮击
465. distressed: 悲伤的，苦恼的，
     忧伤的
467. bulk: 躯体
     withal: 以此，于此
469. breach: 缺口，裂口

68

471. parley: 谈判
472. chin: 颏，下巴
473. rash alarm: 悍然进攻
474. demeanour: 行为
475. vehement: 强烈的
     urgeth still: 仍然追求
476. colour: 理由

67

那一只手摸酥胸

粗鲁撞击象牙城

可感女心痛不生　　　　　　　　　　465

上下跳动毁灭中

撞击女身手颤动

塔昆更凶寡怜情

撞出窟窿进甜城

68

像只喇叭嘴吹声　　　　　　　　　　470

怯懦之鼓闻军情

白颊伸出被单明

悍然进攻有何名

他借手势不由衷

义正辞严有露卿　　　　　　　　　　475

凭甚做出坏事情

（463—476）

69

Thus he replies: 'The colour in thy face—

That even for anger makes the lily pale,

And the red rose blush at her own disgrace—

Shall plead for me and tell my loving tale: *480*

Under that colour am I come to scale

 Thy never-conquer'd fort: the fault is thine,

 For those thine eyes betray thee unto mine.

70

'Thus I forestall thee, if thou mean to chide:

Thy beauty hath ensnared thee to this night,   *485*

Where thou with patience must my will abide;

My will that marks thee for my earth's delight,

Which I to conquer sought with all my might;

 But as reproof and reason beat it dead,

 By thy bright beauty was it newly bred.   *490*

(477—490)

69

479. at her own disgrace: 蔷薇自觉羞愧
480. plead: 恳求
481. colour: 理由
  scale: 攀登
482. fort: 堡垒
483. betray thee unto mine: 把你出卖给我

69

塔昆答言因君容

百合变白怒气冲

羞惭面则蔷薇红

两者能诉我衷情　　　　　　　480

尔有堡垒我攀登

一切怪你理由明

出卖你身两眼睛

70

你要怪我我怪卿

卿美酿成今夜情　　　　　　　485

服服帖帖卿要从

向卿求欢卿肚明

我尽全力欲成功

理性良知扑淫念

美貌煽灰火焰生　　　　　　　490

（477—490）

70

484．forestall：　责怪
485．ensnared：　使入圈套
486．abide：　服从
487．My will that marks thee for my earth's delight：
　　　我要从你身上享受人间的欢情
488．Which I to conquer sought with all my might：
　　　这是我竭尽全力要征服的
489．reproof：　谴责

71

'I see what crosses my attempt will bring;

I know what thorns the growing rose defends;

I think the honey guarded with a sting;

All this beforehand counsel comprehends:

But will is deaf, and hears no heedful friends;　　　　495

　　Only he hath an eye to gaze on beauty,

　　And dotes on what he looks, 'gainst law or duty.

72

'I have debated, even in my soul,

What wrong, what shame, what sorrow I shall breed;

But nothing can affection's course control,　　　　500

Or stop the headlong fury of his speed.

I know repentant tears ensue the deed,

　　Reproach, disdain, and deadly enmity;

　　Yet strive I to embrace mine infamy.'

(491—504)

71

491. crosses: 麻烦
492. what thorns the growing rose defends:
　　生长的攻瑰用什么样的尖刺防卫
493. the honey: 蜂蜜
494. counsel: 商议
　　comprehends: 了解；包含

72

498. debated: 盘算

500. nothing can affection's course control:
　　什么也控制不住奔突的激情
501. headlong: 轻率地
502. repentant: 忏悔的
　　ensue: 保证
503. Reproach: 责备
　　disdain: 蔑视
　　enmity: 敌意

71

我知我图何报应
我知刺护蔷薇红
我知蜇针护蜜蜂
一切事前我皆通
朋友难劝吾热情   495
兴致勃勃赏美容
为爱岂顾法和情

72

我自盘算我心中
何悲何辱何罪行
欲火中烧谁能阻   500
火急状态疯狂形
事后泪洒悔恨生
自怪自贬多敌意
虽为狂举我不松

（491—504）

73

This said, he shakes aloft his Roman blade,   505

Which, like a falcon towering in the skies,

Coucheth the fowl below with his wings' shade,

Whose crooked beak threats if he mount he dies:

So under his insulting falchion lies

    Harmless Lucretia, marking what he tells   510

      With trembling fear, as fowl hear falcon's bells.

74

'Lucrece,' quoth he, 'this night I must enjoy thee:

If thou deny, then force must work my way,

For in thy bed I purpose to destroy thee:

That done, some worthless slave of thine I'll slay,   515

To kill thine honour with thy life's decay;

    And in thy dead arms do I mean to place him,

      Swearing I slew him, seeing thee embrace him.

(505—518)

73

505. aloft: 高高地

506. falcon: 鹰

507. Coucheth: 让蹲伏收敛

508. Whose crooked beak threats if he mount he dies: 它的弯弯的钩嘴威胁着，哪个家禽敢动弹就立即送命

509. falchion: 刀，剑

510. marking: 听

74

513. force must work my way: 我只好用暴力进行

515. slay: 杀

516. life's decay: 死亡

518. Swearing: 赌咒说

73

言罢宝剑高高擎   *505*
盘旋长空如雄鹰
家禽收敛畏翅影
钩嘴威慑动无生
横逼胁迫有露卿
无奈听命战兢兢   *510*
家禽闻铃惧苍鹰

74

今夜我欲伴露卿
塔昆言出拒不成
武力摧卿床上疯
事后杀卿婢一名   *515*
我坏你身毁你名
我放他身卿怀中
杀他绝你拥抱情

（*505—518*）

75

'So thy surviving husband shall remain

The scornful mark of every open eye;   *520*

Thy kinsmen hang their heads at this disdain,

Thy issue blurr'd with nameless bastardy:

And thou, the author of their obloquy:

   Shalt have thy trespass cited up in rimes,

   And sung by children in succeeding times.   *525*

76

'But if thou yield, I rest thy secret friend:

The fault unknown is as a thought unacted;

A little harm done to a great good end

For lawful policy remains enacted.

The poisonous simple sometimes is compacted   *530*

   In a pure compound; being so applied,

   His venom in effect is purified.

(519—532)

75
520. scornful: 受嘲笑的
521. kinsmen: 族人
522. blurr'd: 更损
     bastardy: 奸情
523. obloquy: 耻辱

76
526. rest: 保持
     secret: 保密
527. unacted: 没有犯错
529. enacted: 通过
530. simple: 草药
     compacted: 混合

75

卿之夫君受讥讽
纵然活着羞辱名   520
族人低头受众轻
因此奸情后无荣
耻辱创始皆由卿
看人歌谣唱丑行
孩童成群作和声   525

76

倘若从我保卿名
过错不晓似无踪
小错做出比大功
可以宽恕法容情
毒物可掺可汁浓   530
纯洁化后物中成
毒素毒性消无踪

(519—532)

---

531. pure compound: 良药
532. venom: 毒液

77

'Then, for thy husband and thy children's sake,

Tender my suit: bequeath not to their lot

The shame that from them no device can take,   *535*

The blemish that will never be forgot;

Worse than a slavish wipe or birth-hour's blot:

    For marks descried in men's nativity

    Are nature's faults, not their own infamy.'

78

Here with a cockatrice' dead-killing eye   *540*

He rouseth up himself, and makes a pause;

While she, the picture of true piety,

Like a white hind under the gripe's sharp claws,

Pleads, in a wilderness where are no laws,

    To the rough beast that knows no gentle right,   *545*

    Nor aught obeys but his foul appetite.

(533—546)

77

534. Tender my suit: 答应我的恳求
    bequeath: 把……给予后代

535. device: 方法

536. blemish: 污点

537. a slavish wipe: 奴隶的烙印
    birth-hour's blot: 生来的缺陷

538. descried: 发现

78

540. cockatrice: 毒蛇

542. piety: 虔敬

543. hind: 母鹿
    gripe: 兀鹰

545. gentle right: 温情公理

77

为了夫君为稚童
受我请求莫慢轻
蒙受耻辱洗不清   535
污点永远记忆中
耻过为奴残障情
虽有缺陷归出生
全因自然非污名

78

妖蛇杀人冷眼睛   540
站起身来话语停
露卿纯洁似天生
白鹿被抓遭兀鹰
没有王法祷告空
野兽不知礼与情   545
满足食欲难逃生

（533—546）

79

But when a black-faced cloud the world doth threat,

In his dim mist the aspiring mountains hiding,

From earth's dark womb some gentle gust doth get,

Which blows these pitchy vapours from their biding,　　*550*

Hindering their present fall by this dividing;

 So his unhallow'd haste her words delays,

 And moody Pluto winks while Orpheus plays.

80

Yet, foul night-waking cat, he doth but dally,

While in his hold-fast foot the weak mouse panteth:　　*555*

Her sad behaviour feeds his vulture folly,

A swallowing gulf that even in plenty wanteth:

His ear her prayers admits, but his heart granteth

 No penetrable entrance to her plaining:

 Tears harden lust, though marble wear with raining.　　*560*

（547—560）

79

548. aspiring: 高耸入云的

549. gust: 一阵狂风

550. pitchy: 黑暗的
　　biding: 地点

551. Hindering: 阻止的

552. unhallow'd: 邪恶的

553. Pluto: 普路托，冥王

Orpheus: 俄耳浦斯，
歌手，诗人

80

554. dally: 嬉戏

555. panteth: 气喘

556. vulture folly: 贪馋的欲望

559. plaining: 抱怨

79

乌云一朵遮天空
阴雾掩蔽高山峰
地球子宫生轻风
漆黑水气吹散形　　　　　　　　　*550*
预防水气落高空
她用言语延暴行
诗人奏乐冥王听

80

坏猫夜醒瞎闹腾
老鼠被抓喘气中　　　　　　　　　*555*
女子肃容男贪情
欲壑难填永不平
心里不装耳白听
露卿哀诉一场空
滴水穿石泪煽情　　　　　　　　　*560*

(547—560)

81

Her pity-pleading eyes are sadly fixed

In the remorseless wrinkles of his face;

Her modest eloquence with sighs is mixed,

Which to her oratory adds more grace.

She puts the period often from his place;   565

    And midst the sentence so her accent breaks,

    That twice she doth begin ere once she speaks.

82

She conjures him by high almighty Jove,

By knighthood, gentry, and sweet friendship's oath,

By her untimely tears, her husband's love,   570

By holy human law, and common troth,

By heaven and earth, and all the power of both.

    That to his borrow'd bed he make retire,

    And stoop to honour, not to foul desire.

（561—574）

81

562. remorseless: 无情的

564. oratory: 谈吐

566. midst the sentence so her accent breaks: 她的话时断时续

82

568. conjures: 恳求

Jove: Jupiter, 朱庇特，罗马神话主神

570. untimely: 不合时宜的

572. all the power of both: 天地一切神

573. borrow'd bed: 当天晚上露克丽丝让他睡的床

574. stoop: 弯腰

81

露卿眼睛苦苦盯
塔昆皱面无表情
文雅谈吐长叹声
露卿雄辩人动情
句号随意全由情　　　　　　565
话语勿停句子中
开言两次话方成

82

我接塔昆有感情
你想害他来冒充
我有冤情告天庭　　　　　　570
你害清廉辱门风
表面像他非真形
像他天神有尊荣
天神行事凡俗惊

（561—574）

83

Quoth she, 'Reward not hospitality   *575*

With such black payment as thou hast pretended;

Mud not the fountain that gave drink to thee;

Mar not the thing that cannot be amended;

End thy ill aim before thy shoot be ended;

   He is no woodman that doth bend his bow   *580*

   To strike a poor unseasonable doe.

84

'My husband is thy friend, tarot his sake spare me;

Thyself art mighty,—for thine own sake leave me;

Myself a weakling,—do not, then, ensnare me;

Thou look'st not like deceit, —do not deceive me.   *585*

My sighs, like whirlwinds, labour hence to heave thee:

   If ever man were moved with woman's moans,

   Be moved with my tears, my sighs, my groans:

(*575—588*)

83
576. pretended: 假装
578. Mar: 损坏
579. thy shoot be ended: 你的发射完成
580. woodman: 猎人
581. doe: 母鹿

84
584. weakling: 弱者
     ensnare: 诱惑；陷害
585. deceit: 骗子
586. whirlwinds: 旋风
     hence: 从此地
     heave: 扔

83

凭着天神她求情　　　　　　　575
骑士绅士友谊风
无缘之泪丈夫情
神圣法律人道诚
凭天凭地凭神灵
回他床边速速行　　　　　　　580
不从邪欲从尊荣

84

露卿闻言塔昆听
恩将仇报无客情
污泥勿染泉水清
打破之物修不成　　　　　　　585
发射未去瞄准星
猎夫随意便弯弓
不到季节鹿不成

（575—588）

85

'All which together, like a troubled ocean,

Beat at thy rocky and wrack-threatening heart,   *590*

To soften it with their continual motion;

For stones dissolved to water do convert.

O, if no harder than a stone thou art,

   Melt at my tears, and be compassionate!

   Soft pity enters at an iron gate.   *595*

86

'In Tarquin's likeness I did entertain thee:

Hast thou put on his shape to do him shame?

To all the host of heaven I complain me,

Thou wrong'st his honour, wound'st his princely name.

Thou art not what thou seem'st; and if the same,   *600*

   Thou seem'st not what thou art, a god, a king;

   For kings like gods should govern every thing.

(589—602)

85

590. wrack-threatening: 威慑航船的
592. convert: 改变
594. compassionate: 有同情心的

86

598. To all the host of heaven I complain me:
     我要诉冤天神听
599. princely name: 帝王姓氏
600. if the same: 如果是这样
602. govern every thing: 做事有分寸

85

丈夫尔友尔念情

尔有身份放我行　　　　　590

我本弱者不需网

尔对我非骗人精

我欢赶尔像狂风

男若不忍女哀鸣

我哭我哀尔动情　　　　　595

86

眼泪悲欢海洋成

打击石心害人精

行动不断石软松

水常侵击石头溶

呜呼不比石头硬　　　　　600

随泪溶解怜娇容

慈心进入铁门中

(589—602)

87

'How will thy shame be seeded in thine age,

When thus thy vices bud before thy spring!

If in thy hope thou darest do such outrage,   605

What darest thou not when once thou art a king?

O, be remember'd, no outrageous thing

    From vassal actors can be wiped away;

    Then kings' misdeeds cannot be hid in clay.

88

'This deed will make thee only loved for fear;   610

But happy monarchs still are fear'd for love:

With foul offenders thou perforce must bear,

When they in thee the like offences prove:

If but for fear of this, thy will remove;

    For princes are the glass, the school, the book,   615

    Where subjects' eyes do learn, do read, do look.

(603—616)

87

603. be seeded: 成熟
604. vices: 罪恶
    bud: 萌芽
605. outrage: 蛮横行凶；凌辱
607. outrageous: 蛮横的；无耻的
608. vassal actors: 犯罪的普通人

88

611. monarchs: 君王
612. foul offenders: 罪大恶极的人
    perforce: 不得已地
613. When they in thee the like offenses
    prove: 恶徒责你有恶行

87

年纪虽轻罪不轻

罪恶萌芽已生成

身为王储敢横行　　　　　　　605

若为君主毁苍生

呜呼牢记莫凡庸

大错铸成难抹平

王罪岂能埋坟茔

88

此行使你爱为惊　　　　　　　610

贤明君主如履冰

万恶之徒要忍痛

恶徒责你有恶行

若要贤达戒淫情

君主师书明镜称　　　　　　　615

臣民学读常观形

（603—616）

89

'And with thou be the school where Lust shall learn?

Must he in thee read lectures of such shame?

Wilt thou be glass wherein it shall discern

Authority for sin, warrant for blame,   *620*

To privilege dishonour in thy name?

 Thou back'st reproach against long-living laud,

 And makest fair reputation but a bawd.

90

'Hast thou command? by him that gave it thee,

From a pure heart command thy rebel will: *625*

Draw not thy sword to guard iniquity,

For it was lent thee all that brood to kill.

Thy princely office how canst thou fulfil,

 When, pattern'd by thy fault, foul Sin may say,

 He learnt to sin, and thou didst teach the way?   *630*

(617—630)

89

619. discern: 看出

620. Authority for sin, warrant for blame: 犯罪的权柄，施暴的理由

621. privilege: 给予特权
  dishonour: 耻辱

622. reproach: 指责
  long-living laud: 流芳百世的赞誉

623. bawd: 鸨母

89

岂可为校淫为生

淫棍学习淫课程

你为荒淫做明镜

让他犯法又纵情　　　　　　　620

给他特权用你名

你纵诽谤毁美声

你使美誉老鸨行

90

你若有权赖苍穹

纯洁心灭欲火升　　　　　　　625

拔剑保卫邪恶行

反叛之罪洗不清

怎能有你君王行

你有前例罪有凭

学你犯罪胡乱行　　　　　　　630

（617—630）

90

624．him：　上帝

625．rebel will：　反叛的淫欲

626．iniquity：　罪恶

627．brood：　孵出

628．Thy princely office how canst thou fulfil：　你如何能善尽帝王的职责

629．pattern'd by thy fault：　你为犯罪首开先例

91

'Think but how vile a spectacle it were,

To view thy present trespass in another.

Men's faults do seldom to themselves appear;

Their own transgressions partially they smother:

This guilt would seem death-worthy in thy brother.　　635

　　O, how are they wrapped in with infamies

　　That from their own misdeeds askance their eyes!

92

'To thee, to thee, my heaved-up hands appeal,

Not to seducing lust, thy rash relier:

I sue for exiled majesty's repeal;　　　　　　640

Let him return, and flattering thoughts retire:

His true respect will prison false desire,

　　And wipe the dim mist from thy doting eyne,

　　That thou shalt see thy state, and pity mine.'

(631—644)

91

631. vile: 卑鄙的，可耻的
632. trespass: 罪过
634. transgressions: 犯罪
　　　smother: 覆盖
636. wrapped in with infamies: 犯下罪行，却不肯认账
637. askance: 斜眼看

91

想想何等尴尬容

别人学习你暴行

自己过错难看清

文过饰非掩真情

别人犯错判死刑　　　　　　　　　635

犯罪不认罪非轻

呜呼可耻可恨名

92

求你求你双手擎

莫让性欲莽撞行

尊严复辟我恳请　　　　　　　　　640

尊严正位邪无踪

阿谀奉承靠边行

清除阴翳眼睛明

你我身分要权衡

（631—644）

92

638. heaved-up hands:　举起的手

639. seducing:　诱惑
　　thy rash relier:　莽撞的依从性欲

640. sue:　向⋯⋯请求
　　exiled majesty's repeal:　退位的尊严
　　exiled:　放逐的
　　repeal:　撤销

642. His true respect will prison false desire:
　　他的认真考虑会把邪念拘管

643. thy doting eyne:　你痴迷的双眼

93

'Have done,' quoth he: 'my uncontrolled tide   *645*

Turns not, but swells the higher by this let.

Small lights are soon blown out, huge fires abide,

And with the wind in greater fury fret:

The petty streams that pay a daily debt

    To their salt sovereign, with their fresh falls' haste   *650*

    Add to his flow, but alter not his taste.'

94

'Thou art,' quoth she, 'a sea, a sovereign king;

And, lo, there falls into thy boundless flood

Black lust, dishonour, shame, misgoverning,

Who seek to stain the ocean of thy blood.   *655*

If all these petty ills shall change thy good,

    Thy sea within a puddle's womb is hearsed,

    And not the puddle in thy sea dispersed.

(645—658)

93

646. swells the higher by this let:　越阻挡
越是高涨
let:　阻挡
647. abide:　持续
648. fret:　愤怒
650. salt sovereign:　大海
falls' haste:　迅速倾注

94

652. sovereign king:　伟大的的君王
653. boundless flood:　汪洋
654. Black lust:　黑心的欲望
misgoverning:　管理不当
657. puddle's womb:　泥潭
hearsed:　埋葬
658. dispersed:　散开

93

塔昆厉言止露卿   645
劝阻难挡怒潮生
小火易减烈焰腾
风助火势鬼神惊
小溪昼夜流海中
咸味不改浪涛惊   650
淡水虽多无影踪

94

她说塔昆海洋形
君王之比不可轻
邪欲无耻荒唐行
玷污血统好名声   655
小恶如毁塔昆形
海洋囚入坏子宫
并非泥淖入海中

(645—658)

95

'So shall these slaves be king, and thou their slave;

Thou nobly base, they basely dignified;   *660*

Thou their fair life, and they thy fouler grave:

Thou loathed in their shame, they in thy pride:

The lesser thing should not the greater hide;

    The cedar stoops not to the base shrub's foot,

    But low shrubs wither at the cedar's root.   *665*

96

'So let thy thoughts, low vassals to thy state',

'No more,' quoth he; 'by heaven, I will not hear thee:

Yield to my love; if not, enforced hate,

Instead of love's coy touch, shall rudely tear thee;

That done, despitefully I mean to bear thee   *670*

    Unto the base bed of some rascal groom,

    To be thy partner in this shameful doom.'

（*659—672*）

95

660. nobly base: 君王变奴仆
    basely dignified: 奴才要称王
661. fouler grave: 坟墓
662. loathed: 不愿意的
663. The lesser thing should not the greater
    hide: 小物怎掩大物形
664. cedar: 雪松

96

666. low vassals: 贱奴
668. enforced hate: 激起的仇怨
669. coy touch: 温存的爱抚
670. despitefully: 恶意地；怀恨地
671. rascal groom: 贱奴伙伴

95

君臣颠倒奴才称

高贵卑贱贱尊荣   *660*

仆为你坟你赐生

你遭凌辱仆放纵

小物怎掩大物形

杉树岂让灌木荣

灌木凋枯杉树挺   *665*

96

由你支配邪念生

塔昆打断不愿听

从我不必强迫行

非是爱抚野兽情

事完看你更贱轻   *670*

抱你贱奴床上挺

贱奴伴你耻辱中

(*659—672*)

97

This said, he sets his foot upon the light,

For light and lust are deadly enemies:

Shame folded up in blind-concealing night,   *675*

When most unseen, then most doth tyrannize.

The wolf hath seized his prey, the poor lamb cries;

  Till with her own white fleece her voice controll'd

  Entombs her outcry in her lip's sweet fold:

98

For with the nightly linen that she wears   *680*

He pens her piteous clamours in her head;

Cooling his hot face in the chastest tears

That ever modest eyes with sorrow shed.

O, that prone lust should stain so pure a bed

  The spots whereof could weeping purify,   *685*

  Her tears should drop on them perpetually.

(673—686)

97

675. blind-concealing night: 隐蔽万物的
     茫茫黑夜
676. tyrannize: 肆无忌惮
678. fleece: 羊毛
679. Entombs her outcry in her lip's sweet fold: 呼喊声囚芳唇中

97

塔昆说完灭烛明

光明肉欲岂同生

羞耻躲藏夜幕中　　　　　　　　675

最黑暗时有暴行

狼抓到羊羊哀鸣

白色羊毛止哀声

呼喊声囚芳唇中

98

露卿睡衣塔昆用　　　　　　　　680

窒息露卿哀叫声

贞洁眼泪洗面孔

塔昆被洗面烫红

呜呼奸淫污女红

床上污能泪洗清　　　　　　　　685

露卿眼泪洒不停

（673—686）

98

680. linen: 衣
681. pens: 窒息
　　　piteous clamors: 哀声叫嚷
682. chastest tears: 最贞洁的眼泪
684. prone: 强烈的
685. The spots whereof, could weeping purify: 床上污能泪洗清
686. Her tears should drop on them perpetually: 露卿眼泪洒不停

99

But she hath lost a dearer thing than life,

And he hath won what he would lose again:

This forced league doth force a further strife;

This momentary joy breeds months of pain;   *690*

This hot desire converts to cold disdain:

    Pure Chastity is rifled of her store,

    And Lust, the thief, far poorer than before.

100

Look, as the full-fed hound or gorged hawk,

Unapt for tender smell or speedy flight,   *695*

Make slow pursuit, or altogether balk

The prey wherein by nature they delight;

So surfeit-taking Tarquin fares this night:

    His taste delicious, in digestion souring,

    Devours his will, that lived by foul devouring.   *700*

(687—700)

99

689. forced league: 强逼成奸

690. momentary joy: 短暂的快活

691. This hot desire converts to cold disdain:
欲火人鄙冷冰冰

692. Pure chastity is rifled of her store:
贞操失窃哀露卿

100

694. full-fed hound: 喂饱了的猎犬
gorged hawk: 喂饱的苍鹰

695. unapt: 不宜

696. balk: 怠工

698. surfeit-taking: 纵欲的
fares: 进餐

700. foul devouring: 狼吞虎咽

99

露卿所失贵于命
塔昆所获会无踪
强逼成奸多抗拒
顷刻之欢数月疼   690
欲火人逼冷冰冰
贞操失窃哀露卿
奸贼得逞欲更穷

100

看那饱餐犬与鹰
不追淡味不飞腾   695
行动迟缓又怠工
心喜猎物欲放生
纵欲塔昆今夜情
尝鲜反觉胃酸疼
色如饿狼反丧生   700

（687—700）

101

O, deeper sin than bottomless conceit

Can comprehend in still imagination!

Drunken Desire must vomit his receipt,

Ere he can see his own abomination.

While Lust is in his pride, no exclamation   705

    Can curb his heat, or rein his rash desire,

    Till, like a jade, Self-will himself doth tire.

102

And then with lank and lean discolour'd cheek,

With heavy eye, knit brow, and strengthless pace,

Feeble Desire, all recreant, poor, and meek,   710

Like to a bankrout beggar wails his case:

The flesh being proud, Desire doth fight with Grace,

    For there it revels; and when that decays,

    The guilty rebel for remission prays.

(701—714)

101

701. conceit: 沉思

703. Drunken Desire: 烂醉的欲望
    receipt: 收入

704. abomination: 厌恶，憎恨

705. pride: 高潮
    exclamation: 呼喊

706. curb: 控制

rein: 驾驭
rash desire: 欲火

707. jade: 劣马
Self-will: 逞能

101

呜呼深罪比幽冥
沉思罪孽千万重
烂醉欲望吐尽情
自己丑态看分明
大发淫威他纵情   *705*
淫欲太热呼不应
劣马累垮太逞能

102

瘦削苍白露面孔
皱眉垂眼步态松
欲望衰弱怜无形   *710*
破产乞丐悲苦境
狂傲肉欲天不容
贪欢一时影无踪
叛贼祈祷法无情

（701—714）

102
708. lank: 瘦的
  lean: 精瘦的
  discolour'd cheek: 苍白脸宠
710. recreant: 怯懦的
  meek: 缺乏勇气的
711. wails: 恸哭
713. revels: 狂欢

714. remission: 宽恕

103

So fares it with this fault-ful lord of Rome,   *715*

Who this accomplishment so hotly chased;

For now against himself he sounds this doom,—

That through the length of times he stands disgraced:

Besides, his soul's fair temple is defaced;

  To whose weak ruins muster troops of cares,   *720*

  To ask the spotted princess how she fares.

104

She says, her subjects with foul insurrection

Have battered down her consecrated wall,

And by their mortal fault brought in subjection

Her immortality, and made her thrall   *725*

To living death and pain perpetual:

  Which in her prescience she controlled still,

  But her foresight could not forestall their will.

(715—728)

103

715. fares: 进展
     fault-full: 犯罪的
719. defaced: 损伤外观
720. muster: 集合，聚集
721. spotted princess: 蒙污的公主，指塔昆的灵魂，用单词 she 表达

103

罗马王子犯罪行   *715*

热烈企求欲成功

自己宣告遭严惩

世世代代蒙恶名

灵魂圣殿毁圣容

废墟之上焦虑生   *720*

蒙污王子何魂灵

104

灵魂答曰乱臣横

圣殿神墙成虚空

罪孽深重情难容

迫使灵魂受苦刑   *725*

活地狱中苦无穷

劫难在其预料中

消除劫难却不能

（715—728）

104

722. her subjects: 她的感觉。欲望、激情
     insurrection: 暴动

723. battered: 打烂
     consecrated: 神圣的

724. subjection: 征服

725. thrall: 奴隶

727. prescience: 预知

728. foresight: 先见，预见
     forestall: 防止

105

Even in this thought through the dark night he stealeth,

A captive victor that hath lost in gain;   *730*

Bearing away the wound that nothing healeth,

The scar that will, despite of cure, remain;

Leaving his spoil perplext in greater pain.

    She bears the load of lust he left behind,

    And he the burthen of a guilty mind.   *735*

106

He like a thievish dog creeps sadly thence;

She like a wearied lamb lies panting there;

He scowls, and hates himself for his offence;

She desperate with her nails her flesh doth tear;

He faintly flies, sweating with guilty fear;   *740*

    She stays, exclaiming on the direful night;

    He runs, and chides his vanisht, loathed delight.

(729—742)

105

730. victor: 征服者
732. despite: 尽管
733. perplexed: 困惑的，纠缠不清的

106

736. thence: 从那里
737. wearied: 疲倦的

panting: 喘息
738. scowls: 皱眉
739. she desperate with her nails her flesh doth tear: 她抓伤痕怒火熊
741. direful: 可怕的，悲痛的
742. chides: 责骂
loathed: 厌恶的

105

塔昆夜想欲潜踪
被俘胜者兼输赢　　　　　　　730
创伤带走医不成
伤痛永留于心灵
痛不欲生害露卿
女身被污痛伤情
塔昆良心折磨中　　　　　　　735

106

男像癞狗溜回营
女像羔羊喘息声
他皱眉头恨丑行
她抓伤痕怒火熊
男慌潜逃无影踪　　　　　　　740
女留咒骂夜绝情
男跑诅咒欢不生

（729—742）

107

He thence departs a heavy convertite;

She there remains a hopeless castaway;

He in his speed looks for the morning light;   *745*

She prays she never may behold the day,

'For day,' quoth she, 'night's scapes doth open lay,

   And my true eyes have never practised how

   To cloak offences with a cunning brow.

108

'They think not but that every eye can see   *750*

The same disgrace which they themselves behold;

And therefore would they still in darkness be,

To have their unseen sin remain untold;

For they their guilt with weeping will unfold,

   And grave, like water that doth eat in steel,   *755*

   Upon my cheeks what helpless shame I feel.'

(743—756)

107

743. convertite: 悔改者

744. castaway: 被排斥的人

747. night's scapes doth open lay:
'scapes=escapades, 越轨行动。披露
夜间事端

749. cloak: 掩盖

108

750. not but: 仅仅

754. they their guilt with weeping will
unfold: 眼泪会泄罪真情

755. like water that doth eat in steel: 像镪
水腐蚀钢铁一般

107

他离沉重忏悔情
她遭抛弃不欲生
他盼东方快黎明　　　　　　　745
她想永在黑夜中
她言昼报夜中情
一双贞洁好眼睛
不会狡黠掩实情

108

我有双眼能看清　　　　　　　750
耻辱总留我眼中
我愿黑暗留眼睛
不见罪恶不言声
泪眼会泄罪真情
铜遇镪水则毁形　　　　　　　755
我面刻画羞耻容

　　　　　　　　　　　　　　（743—756）

109

Here she exclaims against repose and rest,

And bids her eyes hereafter still be blind.

She wakes her heart by beating on her breast,

And bids it leap from thence, where it may find   *760*

Some purer chest to close so pure a mind.

 Frantic with grief thus breathes she forth her spite

 Against the unseen secrecy of night:

110

'O comfort-killing Night, image of hell!

Dim register and notary of shame!   *765*

Black stage for tragedies and murders fell!

Vast sin-concealing chaos! nurse of blame!

Blind muffled bawd! dark harbour for defame!

 Grim cave of death! whispering conspirator

 With close-tongued treason and the ravisher!   *770*

(757—770)

109
757. repose: 安眠
758. bids: 命令，吩咐
  hereafter: 从此以后
762. Frantic: 狂暴的
  spite: 恶意，怨恨

110
764. comfort-killing: 屠杀欢乐
765. notary: 公证人
766. fell: 残忍的
767. nurse of blame: 罪恶的保姆
768. muffled: 包裹的
  defame: 诽谤
769. conspirator: 阴谋家

109

斥骂休眠与宁静
永远想要瞎眼睛
愤然捶胸心房惊
愿心跳走别处生　　　　　760
纯胸装下净心灵
悲恸欲绝发怨情
怨恨黑夜鬼精灵

110

黑夜地狱杀安宁
记录耻辱人证明　　　　　765
悲剧谋杀保护屏
罪恶保姆万恶生
蒙面老鸨隐罪名
狰狞洞府鬼路通
叛逆强奸密谋成　　　　　770

（757—770）

111

'O hateful, vaporous, and foggy Night!

Since thou art guilty of my cureless crime,

Muster thy mists to meet the eastern light,

Make war against proportion'd course of time;

Or if thou wilt permit the sun to climb   775

His wonted height, yet ere he go to bed,

Knit poisonous clouds about his golden head.

112

'With rotten damps ravish the morning air;

Let their exhaled unwholesome breaths make sick

The life of purity, the supreme fair,   780

Ere he arrive his weary noon-tide prick;

And let thy misty vapours march so thick,

That in their smoky ranks his smother'd light

May set at noon, and make perpetual night.

(771—784)

111
772. cureless: 无法治愈的
773. Muster: 聚集
774. proportion'd course of time:
　　按部就班的时间
776. wonted height: 通常高度

112
779. exhaled: 呼出的
　　unwholesome: 不卫生的
780. the supreme fair: 明艳的晨曦，太阳
781. his weary noon-tide prick: 他的疲倦
　　的正午时分
783. smoky ranks: 烟雾
784. set at noon: 午间日落

111

可恨长夜湿雾蒙
我有罪孽你造成
堵截东方之光明
抗击时间即定程
如果你许太阳升　　　　　　　　　775
趁他未回西天宫
金头顶上毒云升

112

腐败湿气染晨空
致病气息妄逞凶
毒害纯洁之生命　　　　　　　　780
太阳未登午时程
浓重湿雾已聚成
阳光埋于烟雾中
中午日落黑洞洞

（771—784）

113

'Were Tarquin Night, as he is but Night's child,   *785*

The silver-shining queen he would distain;

Her twinkling handmaids too, by him defiled,

Through Night's black bosom should not peep again:

So should I have co-partners in my pain;

　And fellowship in woe doth woe assuage,   *790*

　　As palmers' chat makes short their pilgrimage.

114

'Where now I have no one to blush with me,

To cross their arms, and hang their heads with mine,

To mask their brows, and hide their infamy;

But I alone alone must sit and pine,   *795*

Seasoning the earth with showers of silver brine,

　Mingling my talk with tears, my grief with groans,

　　Poor wasting monuments of lasting moans.

(785—798)

113

786. silver-shining queen: 银光四射的女王，月亮
　　　distain: 污染
787. handmaids: 侍女，星星
　　　defiled: 弄脏；玷污
789. co-partners: 伙伴
790. assuage: 缓和
791. palmers: 朝圣者

113

塔昆是夜之所生   785

污染中天银月明

污辱其婢多晶莹

不再窥望透夜胸

有人分担我心疼

苦痛有伴可减轻   790

香客闲聊缩路程

114

倘若无人陪羞容

双臂抱头泣无声

遮住眉眼盖丑行

惟我枯坐憔悴形   795

银雨落地咸味生

话中含泪悲欢同

可怜纪念长心疼

（785—798）

114

793．cross their arms and hang their heads with mine:　双臂抱头泣无声

794．mask their brows and hide their infamy:　遮住眉头盖丑行

795．sit and pine:　坐着发愁

796．Seasoning the earth:　给大地添些味道

　　　silver brine:　银色的咸水，眼泪

798．Poor wasting monuments of lasting moans:　可怜纪念长心疼

115

'O Night, thou furnace of foul-reeking smoke,

Let not the jealous Day behold that face   *800*

Which underneath thy black all-hiding cloak

Immodestly lies martyr'd with disgrace!

Keep still possession of thy gloomy place,

  That all the faults which in my reign are made

  May likewise be sepulchred in thy shade!   *805*

116

'Make me not object to the tell-tale Day!

The light will show, character'd in my brow,

The story of sweet chastity's decay,

The impious breach of holy wedlock vow:

Yea, the illiterate, that know not how   *810*

  To cipher what is writ in learned books,

  Will quote my loathsome trespass in my looks.

(799—812)

115
799. foul-reeking: 臭气蒸腾
801. all-hiding cloak: 遮没一切的斗篷
802. martyr'd: 遭苦难
804. reign: 统治，黑夜
805. sepulchred: 埋葬

116
806. tell-tale: 饶舌的，搬弄是非的

807. character'd: 写出来
808. sweet chastity's decay: 完美的贞操的凋枯
809. impious: 不虔诚的
     breach: 破坏
     wedlock: 婚姻
     vow: 盟誓
811. cipher: 阅读
812. Loathsome trespass: 丑陋的罪恶

115

呜呼夜炉臭烟生

别让白昼疑我容　　　　　　800

黑袍之下我藏形

忍辱含垢藏面孔

地盘漆黑我不行

藏你治下罪恶情

阴影长埋似无生　　　　　　805

116

饶舌白昼可消停

别在我脸写分明

贞洁破坏毁操行

说我背弃神圣盟

即使文盲也知情　　　　　　810

虽然不懂高深经

可于我面见丑行

（799—812）

117

'The nurse, to still her child, will tell my story,

And fright her crying babe with Tarquin's name;

The orator, to deck his oratory,   *815*

Will couple my reproach to Tarquin's shame;

Feast-finding minstrels, tuning my defame,

 Will tie the hearers to attend each line,

 How Tarquin wronged me, I Collatine.

118

'Let my good name, that senseless reputation,   *820*

For Collatine's dear love be kept unspotted:

If that be made a theme for disputation,

The branches of another root are rotted,

And undeserved reproach to him allotted

 That is as clear from this attaint of mine   *825*

 As I, ere this, was pure to Collatine.

(813—826)

117

815. deck: 加工润色

816. couple: 赶超

817. Feast-finding minstrels: 赶集的歌者，为饮宴助兴的乐师
tuning my defame: 唱我的受辱

118

820. senseless reputation: 纯洁的声誉

822. theme for disputation: 辩论的课题

823. The branches of another root are rotted: 另外一株树的枝子也要凋枯

824. undeserved reproach to him allotted: 他受到了耻辱

825. attaint: 耻辱

117

保姆哄孩讲我情
塔昆名字吓幼婴
雄辩家为言辞清　　　　　　　　　*815*
诅骂塔昆提我情
赶集歌者唱我名
观众歌词倾耳听
塔昆污我夫填膺

118

先前我有好名声　　　　　　　　*820*
不辱为夫科拉廷
倘若众口辩我情
它树枝干亦凋零
不该受辱科拉廷
夫与我辱不关情　　　　　　　　*825*
犹如我忠科拉廷

（*813—826*）

119

'O unseen shame! invisible disgrace!

O unfelt sore! crest-wounding, private scar!

Reproach is stampt in Collatinus' face,

And Tarquin's eye may read the mot afar,　　　　　*830*

How he in peace is wounded, not in war.

　　Alas, how many bear such shameful blows,

　　Which not themselves, but he that gives them knows!

120

'If, Collatine, thine honour lay in me,

From me by strong assault it is bereft.　　　　　*835*

My honey, lost, and I, a drone-like bee,

Have no perfection of my summer left,

But robb'd and ransacked by injurious theft:

　　In thy weak hive a wandering wasp hath crept,

　　And suckt the honey which thy chaste bee kept.　　*840*

(827—840)

119

828. unfelt sore: 未发现的耻辱
　　crest-wounding: 家族声誉的毁坏
830. afar: 从远处
832. Alas: 哎呀
833. but he that gives them knows: 打击者自己知道

119

羞颜未见惭无踪
隐私伤疤伤未疼
耻辱印面科拉廷
塔昆虽远能看清　　　　　　　　　　830
和平受伤非战争
呜呼众人挨打疼
挨者不如打者清

120

荣誉寄我科拉廷
暴力掠夺荣无踪　·　　　　　　　　835
蜂蜜失去像工蜂
夏天收获今成空
盗贼尽夺不留情
爬进蜂房一黄蜂
吸蜜岂管蜂王疼　　　　　　　　　　840

（827—840）

120
835．assault：　暴力，攻击
　　　bereft：　bereave 的过去分词。夺去
836．drone：　雄蜂
837．Have no perfection of my summer left：
　　　我的整个夏天已化为乌有
838．ransack'd：　抢劫
　　　injurious theft：　盗贼

839．hive：　蜂巢
　　　wasp：　黄蜂
840．chaste：　贞洁

121

'Yet am I guilty of thy honour's wrack,—

Yet for thy honour did I entertain him;

Coming from thee, I could not put him back,

For it had been dishonour to disdain him:

Besides, of weariness he did complain him,   *845*

    And talk'd of virtue:—O unlookt-for evil,

    When virtue is profaned in such a devil!

122

'Why should the worm intrude the maiden bud?

Or hateful cuckoos hatch in sparrow's nests?

Or toads infect fair founts with venom mud?   *850*

Or tyrant folly lurk in gentle breasts?

Or kings be breakers of their own behests?

    But no perfection is so absolute,

    That some impurity doth not pollute.

(841—854)

121
841. wrack: 损坏
845. of weariness he did complain him:
　　　他抱怨自己疲劳
846. talk'd of virtue: 满口仁义道德
847. profaned: 亵渎

122
848. intrude: 闯进
　　　maiden bud: 蓓蕾
849. cuckoos: 杜鹃
　　　hatch: 孵卵
　　　sparrow's nests: 麻雀巢
850. toads: 蛤蟆
　　　fair founts: 美好的泉水
　　　venom: 毒液

121

我也有错损你荣

招待塔昆是你朋

因你而来拒不成

慢待于他失体统

他言疲倦声连声　　　　　*845*

满口仁义恶妖精

亵渎仁义我不清

122

为何蓓蕾遭害虫

杜鹃孵卵雀巢中

蛤蟆毒泥污泉清　　　　　*850*

暴烈性欲藏心胸

王有王命王不听

十全十美贞洁清

虚伪罪恶污点生

（841—854）

---

851. folly: 淫念
　　　lurk: 潜藏
852. behests: 命令

123

'The aged man that coffers-up his gold   *855*

Is plagued with cramps and gouts and painful fits;

And scarce hath eyes his treasure to behold,

And like still-pining Tantalus he sits,

And useless barns the harvest of his wits;

   Having no other pleasure of his gain!   *860*

   But torment that it cannot cure his pain.

124

'So then he hath it when he cannot use it,

And leaves it to be master'd by his young;

Who in their pride do presently abuse it:

Their father was too weak, and they too strong,   *865*

To hold their cursed-blessed fortune long.

   The sweets we wish for turn to loathed sours

   Even in the moment that we call them ours.

(855—868)

123

855. coffers-up: 储存
856. cramps: 痉挛
    gouts: 痛风
    painful fits: 疼痛痉挛
858. still-pining: 永远挨饿
    Tantalus: a son of Zeus who was punished by perpetual hunger and thirst with unreachable food and drink always in sight, 坦塔罗斯，宙斯之子，被罚永远饿渴，眼前有食不能得，眼前有水不能饮
859. barns: 谷仓

123

老人存金贪心生　　　　　　　*855*

抽搐痉挛又痛风

看见宝藏不转睛

坦塔罗斯永受刑

永受饥渴无安宁

智慧财富不见功　　　　　　　*860*

只有折磨难疗疼

124

他有财富享不成

后人掌管他有情

挥霍殆尽一场空

父弱子强家难兴　　　　　　　*865*

财兼祸福运不通

心中甜食苦酸成

一朝欲食却无情

　　　　　　　　　　　　　　（855—868）

124

864. abuse: 挥霍，滥用

866. cursed-blessed: 造孽而得到的

867. The sweets we wish for turn to loathed
sours:心中甜食苦酸成

868. Even in the moment that we call them
ours: 一朝欲食却无情

125

'Unruly blasts wait on the tender spring;

Unwholesome weeds take root with precious flowers;   *870*

The adder hisses where the sweet birds sing;

What virtue breeds iniquity devours:

We have no good that we can say is ours,

But ill-annexed Opportunity

Or kills his life or else his quality.   *875*

126

'O Opportunity, thy guilt is great!

'Tis thou that executest the traitor's treason;

Thou sett'st the wolf where he the lamb may get;

Whoever plots the sin, thou point'st the season;

'Tis thou that spurn'st at right, at law, at reason;   *880*

And in thy shady cell, where none may spy him,

Sits Sin, to seize the souls that wander by him.

(869—882)

125
869. Unruly blasts: 狂风
870. Unwholesome weeds: 腐败的野草
871. adder: 毒蛇
     hisses: 嘶嘶作声
872. iniquity: 邪恶
     devours: 吞掉
873. We have no good that we can say is
     ours: 难言何宝存房中

874. ill-annexed: 引起恶果的

126
877. executest: 促成
878. sett'st: 放在，引向
880. spurn'st: 踢开
881. shady cell: 阴暗巢穴
882. the souls that wander: 过往的灵魂

125

嫩枝摧残怪狂风
好花根旁莠草生   *870*
毒蛇吐信好鸟鸣
罪恶吞噬好事情
难言何宝存房中
恶果机遇相互生
或毁或改不留情   *875*

126

呜呼机遇罪不轻
你助叛贼罪行成
狼捕羔羊你助行
恶行由你定日程
无道无法理不通   *880*
罪恶在你洞穴生
不见身影捕魂灵

（869—882）

127

'Thou makest the vestal violate her oath;

Thou blow'st the fire when temperance is thaw'd;

Thou smother'st honesty, thou murder'st troth;   885

Thou foul abettor! thou notorious bawd!

Thou plantest scandal, and displacest laud,

    Thou ravisher, thou traitor, thou false thief,

    Thy honey turns to gall, thy joy to grief!

128

'Thy secret pleasure turns to open shame,   890

Thy private feasting to a public fast,

Thy smoothing titles to a ragged name,

Thy sugar'd tongue to bitter wormwood taste:

Thy violent vanities can never last.

    How comes it, then, vile Opportunity,   895

    Being so bad, such numbers seek for thee?

(883—896)

127

883. vestal: 古罗马神话中灶神 Vesta 的
    信女，须起誓保持贞洁
    violate: 违反

884. temperance: 节制
    thaw'd: 融化

885. troth: 忠贞

886. abettor: 教唆犯

887. laud: 赞美

889. gall: 胆汁

128

891. a public fast: 大众持斋
892. smoothing titles: 炫赫的头衔
893. wormwood: 苦艾
895. vile Opportunity: 下贱的机会
896. such numbers: 这么多的人

127

你使圣女失贞行
你煽火焰欲念融
你毁贞操害忠诚 885
无耻诲淫诱后生
散布谣言毁尊荣
淫棍叛徒奸贼行
蜜变胆汁喜变疼

128

公开丑行缘私情 890
大众持斋小宴成
赫赫官衔变恶名
甜言苦艾分不清
狂热虚荣转眼空
可耻机遇实无行 895
众人苦追理难通

(883—896)

129

'When wilt thou be the humble suppliant's friends

And bring him where his suit may be obtained?

When wilt thou sort an hour great strifes to end?

Or free that soul which wretchedness hath chained?　　*900*

Give physic to the sick, ease to the pained?

　　The poor, lame, blind; halt, creep, cry oat for thee;

　　But they ne'er meet with Opportunity.

130

'The patient dies while the physician sleeps;

The orphan pines while the oppressor feeds;　　*905*

Justice is feasting while the widow weeps;

Advice is sporting while infection breeds.

Thou grant'st no time for charitable deeds:

　　Wrath, envy, treason, rape, and murder's rages,

　　Thy heinous hours wait on them as their pages.　　*910*

(897—910)

129
897. suppliant's friends: 恳求者的朋友
898. suit: 乞求
899. sort an hour: 安排一个时间
900. wretchedness: 可怜；悲惨
901. physic: 药品
902. halt: 蹒跚
　　creep: 爬行

130
905. oppressor: 压迫者
906. Justic is feasting: 法官在吃酒席
907. Advice is sporting: 当局在游戏
908. grant'st: 授予
　　charitable deeds: 慈善者
910. heinous: 极可恨的，极凶残的
　　pages: 小听差，小侍从

129

何时为友为贫穷
贫困朋友得欢情
选定时间止斗争
释放困苦之魂灵　　　　　　　　　　　900
病人得医痛者轻
穷盲跛者呼救声
蹒跚匍匐运不通

130

医生睡眠病人终
孤儿饿死主肥轻　　　　　　　　　　　905
寡妇哭向官宴中
当局游乐多疫情
无暇去做善事情
怒妒叛奸杀逞凶
无耻时刻都顺恭　　　　　　　　　　　910

（897—910）

131

'When Truth and Virtue have to do with thee,

A thousand crosses keep them from thy aid:

They buy thy help; but Sin ne'er gives a fee,

He gratis comes; and thou art well appaid

As well to hear as grant what he hath said.   *915*

My Collatine would else have come to me

When Tarquin did, but he was stay'd by thee.

132

'Guilty thou art of murder and of theft,

Guilty of perjury and subornation,

Guilty of treason, forgery, and shift,   *920*

Guilty of incest, that abomination;

An accessary by thine inclination

To all sins past, and all that are to come,

From the creation to the general doom.

(911—924)

131

912. crosses: 障碍

914. gratis: 免费地
     appaid: 满意

915. As well to hear as grant what he hath
     said: 听他一开口求助你立刻就允许

916. else: 要不然

132

919. perjury: 假誓，伪证
     subornation: 教唆；唆使发假誓

920. forgery: 伪造文书
     shift: 欺诈

921. incest: 乱伦
     abomination: 厌恶

922. accessary: 同谋，帮凶
     inclination: 随心所欲

131

求你美德与真诚
百般刁难道不行
美真出资罪凭空
罪得帮助你高兴
一张开口就应承　　　　　　　　*915*
塔昆欲携科拉廷
夫主被留你帮凶

132

杀人盗窃多罪行
伪誓教唆作伪证
叛逆欺诈伪文成　　　　　　　　*920*
乱伦伤天害理行
因你嗜好因你成
古往今来罪孽生
你逃干系万不能

（*911—924*）

133

'Misshapen Time, copesmate of ugly Night,   925

Swift subtle post, carrier of grisly care,

Eater of youth, false slave to false delight,

Base watch of woes, sin's pack-horse, virtue's snare;

Thou nursest all, and murder'st all that are:

    O, hear me, then, injurious, shifting Time!   930

    Be guilty of my death, since of my crime.

134

'Why hath thy servant Opportunity

Betray'd the hours thou gavest me to repose,

Cancell'd my fortunes, and enchained me

To endless date of never-ending woes?   935

Time's office is to fine the hate of foes;

    To eat up errors by opinion bred,

    Not spend the dowry of a lawful bed.

(925—938)

133

925. copesmate: 同谋
926. Swift subtle post: 迅速善变的使者
    grisly care: 凶事，恐怖的事
927. false delight: 虚荣
928. Base watch of woes: 悲哀的更夫
    sin's pack-horse: 罪恶的坐骑
    virtue's snare: 美德的囹圄

931. Be guilty of my death, since of my crime: 你既然害我犯了罪，就应该害我死去

133

丑时陪伴丑夜行 　　　　　925

使者善变善役凶

吞食青春奴虚荣

灾祸更夫罪孽牲

美德入网毁无形

呜呼时间骗人精 　　　　　930

教我犯罪地狱行

134

时间有奴机遇称

夺我休闲理不通

压我好运财无成

厄难困我何时穷 　　　　　935

时间使命仇恨清

成见谬误不得逞

岂能坏我鸳鸯情

(925—938)

134

934. Cancell'd my fortunes: 取消了我的幸运
　　　enchained: 束缚

935. To endless date of never-ending woes: 无穷无尽的悲哀

936. Time's office is to fine the hate of foes: 时间的职责是消除敌人的仇恨

937. To eat up errors by opinion bred: 消除成见产生的错误

938. Not spend the dowry of a lawful bed: dowry, 嫁妆。不是糟蹋合法婚姻的嫁妆

135

'Time's glory is to calm contending kings,

To unmask falsehood, and bring truth to light,   *940*

To stamp the seal of time in aged things,

To wake the morn, and sentinel the night,

To wrong the wronger till he render right,

  To ruinate proud buildings with thy hours,

  And smear with dust their glittering golden towers;   *945*

136

'To fill with worm-holes stately monuments,

To feed oblivion with decay of things,

To blot old books and alter their contents,

To pluck the quills from ancient ravens wings,

To dry the old oak's sap, and cherish springs,   *950*

  To spoil antiquities of hammer'd steel,

  And turn the giddy round of Fortune's wheel;

(939—952)

135

939. contending kings: 争战的帝王

940. unmask: 暴露

941. stamp the seal of time in aged things:
  给老朽事物打上岁月印痕

942. wake the morn: 唤醒黎明
  sentinel: 守卫

943. render right: 弃恶从善

944. ruinate: 毁灭

945. smear: 弄脏；玷污

135

解王纷争时光荣
揭穿谎言真理明　　　　　　　*940*
旧事旧物印暗红
唤醒黎明夜值更
打击恶者从善行
日月磨损宝殿崩
辉煌堡垒竟尘封　　　　　　　*945*

136

高大牌坊虫蛀空
衰朽归入遗忘经
涂改古籍换内容
拔掉老鸦身上翎
橡树液干新苗生　　　　　　　*950*
铁打古物毁无形
命运轮转何时停

（939—952）

136
946. worm-holes:　虫蛀的窟窿
947. oblivion:　健忘
948. blot:　污毁
949. quills:　翎毛
950. sap:　汁浆
　　 cherish springs:　滋养幼苗

952. turn the giddy round of Fortune's
　　 wheel:　推动命运女神的法轮

137

'To show the beldam daughters of her daughter,

To make the child a man, the man a child,

To slay the tiger that doth live by slaughter,   *955*

To tame the unicorn and lion wild,

To mock the subtle in themselves beguiled,

   To cheer the ploughman with increaseful crops,

   And waste huge stones with little water-drops.

138

'Why work'st thou mischief in thy pilgrimage,   *960*

Unless thou couldst return to make amends?

One poor retiring minute in an age

Would purchase thee a thousand thousand friends,

Lending him wit that to bad debtors lends:

   O, this dread night, wouldst thou one hour come back, *965*

   I could prevent this storm, and shun thy wrack!

(953—966)

137

953. beldame: 老太婆

956. unicorn: 独角兽

957. mock the subtle in themselves
    beguiled: beguiled, 欺诈的。嘲笑那
    些疑虑过多的聪明人士

959. waste huge stones with little water-
    drops: 磨穿巨石小水滴

138

960. mischief: 恶作剧

962. One poor retiring minute in an age:
    一辈子若能有一分钟退回去

963. purchase: 赢得

964. bad debtors: 赖账者

966. shun: 避开
    wrack: 打击

137

老太女儿女儿生
幼童成人老幼童
嗜血猛虎杀无生　　　　　　　955
独角兽驯狮不凶
优柔寡断受嘲讽
鼓舞农人庄稼丰
水穿巨石点滴功

138

你做坏事在行程　　　　　　　960
弥补过失莫再凶
一次回头路万通
朋友千万你必赢
赖账之人学聪明
可怜夜退几刻钟　　　　　　　965
我避风暴我避风

（953—966）

139

'Thou ceaseless lackey to eternity,

With some mischance cross Tarquin in his flight:

Devise extremes beyond extremity,

To make him curse this cursed crimeful night:　　　　　*970*

Let ghastly shadows his lewd eyes affright;

　　And the dire thought of his committed evil

　　Shape every bush a hideous shapeless devil.

140

'Disturb his hours of rest with restless trances,

Afflict him in his bed with bedrid groans;　　　　　*975*

Let there bechance him pitiful mischances,

To make him moan; but pity not his moans:

Stone him with harden'd hearts harder than stones;

　　And let mild women to him lose their mildness,

　　Wilder to him than tigers in their wildness.　　　　*980*

(967—980)

139

967. lackey: 仆人
968. mischance: 天幸，灾难
　　　cross: 反对
969. Devise extremes beyond extremity: 策划出比极端还要极端的东西
971. ghastly: 可怕的
972. dire: 可怕的
973. hideous: 丑陋的，可怕的

139

奔波童仆为永恒
别让塔昆得太平
造出超过极端行
塔昆诅咒一夜情 *970*
鬼影震骇色眼惊
想到罪恶难安宁
每棵树都化妖精

140

连做恶梦睡不成
床上呻吟不安宁 975
让他倒霉莫留情
让他呜咽让他疼
心比石硬让他挺
温存女子失温情
比之恶虎还要凶 *980*

（967—980）

140

974. trances: 恍惚；发呆
975. Afflict: 使苦恼，折磨
　　 bedrid: 卧床不起
976. bechance: 发生在
977. moans: 呻吟
978. Stone him with harden'd hearts harder than stones: 用硬过石头的硬心向他投射

141

'Let him have time to tear his curled hair,

Let him have time against himself to rave,

Let him have time of Time's help to despair,

Let him have time to live a loathed slave,

Let him have time a beggar's orts to crave,   *985*

　　And time to see one that by alms doth live

　　Disdain to him disdained scraps to give.

142

'Let him have time to see his friends his foes,

And merry fools to mock at him resort;

Let him have time to mark how slow time goes   *990*

In time of sorrow, and how swift and short

His time of folly and his time of sport;

　　And ever let his unrecalling crime

　　Have time to wail th' abusing of his time.

(981—994)

141

981. curled hair: 卷发
982. rave: 胡言乱语
984. loathed slave: 令人厌恶的贱奴
985. orts: 吃剩的食物
　　crave: 恳求
986. alms: 施舍物
987. Disdain to him disdained scraps to give: 不肯给他残羹剩饭

141

给他时间揪发疼

给他时间骂罪行

给他时间援无踪

给他时间做侍童

给他时间讨饭生　　　　　　　　　985

看到乞丐也无情

一勺羹也吃不成

142

看见敌人原友朋

得意蠢才笑他熊

悲伤时间缓慢行　　　　　　　　　990

嬉戏时间一刻钟

给他时间道理明

让他犯罪悔不成

光阴浪费痛伤情

（981—994）

142

989. merry fools: 小丑
　　resort: 采用
990. mark: 察觉
992. folly: 浪荡
　　sport: 嬉戏
993. unrecalling: 无法勾销
994. Have time to wail th' abusing of his time:
　　有时间痛悼他浪费的光阴

143

'O Time, thou tutor both to good and bad,   *995*

Teach me to curse him that thou taught'st this ill!

At his own shadow let the thief run mad,

Himself himself seek every hour to kill!

Such wretched hands such wretched blood should spill;

 For who so base would such an office have   *1000*

 As slanderous deathsman to so base a slave?

144

'The baser is he, coming from a king,

To shame his hope with deeds degenerate:

The mightier man, the mightier is the thing

That makes him honour'd, or begets him hate;   *1005*

For greatest scandal waits on greatest state.

 The moon being clouded presently is mist,

 But little stars may hide them when they list.

(995—1008)

143

998. Himself himself seek every hour to kill: 时刻想杀掉自己

999. wretched hands: 脏手
  wretched blood: 脏血

1000. For who so base would such an office have: 因为，谁如此卑鄙，竟然做这样的事情

1001. As slanderous deathsman to so base a slave: 当如此下贱的奴才的执行死刑者

143

为师好坏不分清　　　　　　　　995
时间教我骂奸凶
强盗见影跑似疯
时刻想毁自身形
脏手脏血正相称
谁能卑鄙做事情　　　　　　　　1000
去为贼奴行死刑

144

出身帝王卑鄙行
堕落行为毁前程
伟人要有伟人行
不管是恨还是荣　　　　　　　　1005
伟人之错举世惊
明月云遮人知情
随意隐身由小星

（995—1008）

144
1003. shame: 使丢脸；使痛感羞愧
　　　　degenerate: 堕落
1004. mightier man: 伟人
1005. begets: 带来
1006. greatest scandal waits on greatest state: 最大的丑闻跟着最高的地位
1008. list: 愿意

145

'The crow may bathe his coal-black wings in mire,

And unperceived fly with the filth away;   *1010*

But if the like the snow-white swan desire,

The stain upon his silver down will stay.

Poor grooms are sightless night, kings glorious day:

    Gnats are unnoted wheresoe'er they fly,

    But eagles gazed upon with every eye.   *1015*

146

'Out, idle words, servants to shallow fools!

Unprofitable sounds, weak arbitrators!

Busy yourselves in skill-contending schools;

Debate where leisure serves with dull debaters;

To trembling clients be you mediators: *1020*

    For me, I force not argument a straw,

    Since that my case is past the help of law.

(1009—1022)

145
1009. mire: 泥坑
1010. unperceived fly: 飞去没人看见
1012. silver down: 银白色的软毛
1013. grooms: 仆人
1014. Gnats: 蚊子
     unnoted: 没人理会
     wheresoe'er: 在任何地方

146
1016. idle words: 废话
1017. Unprofitable sounds: 无益的声音
     arbitrators: 裁判，仲裁人
1018. skill-contending schools: 竞技学校
1019. Debate where leisure serves with dull
     debaters: 与闲人为伍，和他们辩
     论

145

乌鸦洗翅污泥中

无人知晓飞天宫　　　　　　　　　*1010*

雪白天鹅有此行

泥染羽毛洗不清

平民如夜王天明

随意乱飞由蚊蝇

每双眼睛盯苍鹰　　　　　　　　　*1015*

146

废话浅薄蠢人童

无益声音仲裁庸

竞技学校可胡行

有闲为伍争辩雄

抖颤官司去调停　　　　　　　　　*1020*

露卿不会出一声

判我案子法无能

（*1009—1022*）

1020. To trembling clients be you mediators: 做颤抖的诉讼人的调停者

1021. I force not argument a straw: 对于词讼纷争，我不屑于辩说一句

1022. my case is past the help of law: 我的案子法律无法救援

679

147

'In vain I rail at Opportunity,

At Time, at Tarquin, and uncheerful Night;

In vain I cavil with mine infamy,   1025

In vain I spurn at my confirm'd despite:

This helpless smoke of words doth me no right.

　　The remedy indeed to do me good

　　Is to let forth my foul defiled blood.

148

'Poor hand, why quiver'st thou at this decree?   1030

Honour thyself to rid me of this shame;

For if I die, my honour lives in thee;

But if I live, thou livest in my defame:

Since thou couldst not defend thy loyal dame,

　　And wast afeard to scratch her wicked foe,   1035

　　Kill both thyself and her for yielding so.'

(1023—1036)

147

1023. rail at: 责骂
1025. cavil with: 挑剔
1026. spurn at : 蔑视
　　　confirm'd despite: 注定难逃的侮辱
1029. foul-defiled blood: 一腔已遭败坏的热血

148

1030. quiver'st: 战栗
　　　decree: 法令
1033. defame: 耻辱
1034. dame: 夫人，贵妇人
1035. afeard: afraid, 害怕
　　　scratch: 搔，抓
　　　wicked foe: 邪恶的仇家
1036. yielding: 屈从的；受辱的

147

骂运骂时骂夜空
诅咒塔昆皆无功
责骂无耻西北风　　　　　　　　*1025*
蔑视委屈无效能
空谈岂能裁决公
我有药方奇效生
污血放出神自清

148

为何手抖为指令　　　　　　　　*1030*
铲除我辱为你荣
我死你生有尊荣
我活你伴羞辱生
保卫贤妇你不能
杀死仇家你不行　　　　　　　　*1035*
你死妇亡钢刀横

（*1023—1036*）

149

This said, from her be-tumbled couch she starteth,

To find some desperate instrument of death:

But this no slaughter-house no tool imparteth

To make more vent for passage of her breath;   *1040*

Which, thronging through her lips, so vanisheth

   As smoke from Aetna, that in air consumes,

   Or that which from discharged cannon fumes.

150

'In vain,' quoth she, 'I live, and seek in vain

Some happy mean to end a hapless life.   *1045*

I fear'd by Tarquin's falchion to be slain,

Yet for the self-same purpose seek a knife:

But when I fear'd I was a loyal wife:

   So am I now: —O no, that cannot be;

   Of that true type hath Tarquin rifled me.   *1050*

(1037—1050)

149

1037. be-tumbled: 凌乱的
     couch: 床榻
1038. desperate instrument: 杀人的器具
1039. slaughter-house: 屠场
     imparteth: 提供
1040. vent: 出口；通风孔
1041. thronging: 拥挤

1042. Aetna: 意大利西西里岛东北部一火山名
     consumes: 消逝
1043. discharged cannon fumes: 火炮发射后的浓烟

149

说完床上跃露卿
自杀欲寻铁器凶
家非屠场不能成
只求唇间多窟窿　　　　　　　　　　　　　　*1040*
怒怨满腔火熊熊
火山喷烟空气中
大炮发射硝烟浓

150

又言难活悲露卿
欲寻短路无器皿　　　　　　　　　　　　　　*1045*
塔昆弯刀欲夺命
我寻利刃了此生
我有恐惧为妻忠
贤妻典型有始终
塔昆毁我不可能　　　　　　　　　　　　　　*1050*

（*1037—1050*）

150
1045. hapless: 不幸的
1046. falchion: 中世纪弯形的大刀；剑
1047. self-same: 同样的
1048. when I fear'd: 当我怕的时候
1050. rifled me: 抢夺

151

'O, that is gone for which I sought to live,

And therefore now I need not fear to die.

To clear this spot by death, at least I give

A badge of fame to slander's livery;

A dying life to living infamy: *1055*

  Poor helpless help, the treasure stol'n away,

  To burn the guiltless casket where it lay!

152

'Well, well, dear Collation, thou shalt not know

The stained taste of violated troth;

I will not wrong thy true affection so,   *1060*

To flatter thee with an infringed oath;

This bastard graff shall never come to growth:

  He shall not boast who did thy stock pollute

  That thou art doting father of his fruit.

(1051—1064)

151

1054. badge: 标记
       slander's livery: 耻辱的号衣
1055. A dying life to living infamy: 让生存的耻辱一死了之
1056. Poor helpless help: 可怜无补的补救
1057. guiltless casket: 无辜的珠宝匣子

151

呜呼无缘去求生

目标失去死路通

清洗污点再登程

丑闻制服有尊荣

刚烈一死胜辱生　　　　　　　　　　　*1055*

无奈珠宝被盗空

无奈宝盒烈火中

152

可爱吾夫科拉廷

勿尝婚姻受辱名

不愿如此负你情　　　　　　　　　　　*1060*

不媚我夫海誓空

杂种岂能延门庭

不让塔昆夸连声

他的儿子夫亲生

（*1051—1064*）

152

1059. stained taste:　受污的滋味
　　　violated troth:　受辱的婚姻
1060. true affection:　真情
1061. infringed oath:　已毁的誓约
1062. bastard graff:　杂种成胎
1063. He shall not boast who did thy stock pollute:　玷污你家族的恶人，休想有机会夸口
1064. That thou art doting father of his fruit:　你是塔昆的愚蠢的爱的儿子的父亲

153

'Nor shall he smile at thee in secret thought,　　　　*1065*

Nor laugh with his companions at thy state;

But thou shalt know thy interest was not bought

Basely with gold, but stol'n from forth thy gate.

For me, I am the mistress of my fate,

　And with my trespass never will dispense,　　　　*1070*

　Till life to death acquit my forced offence.

154

'I will not poison thee with my attaint,

Nor fold my fault in cleanly-coin'd excuses;

My sable ground of sin I will not paint,

To hide the truth of this false night's abuses:　　　　*1075*

My tongue shall utter all; mine eyes, like sluices,

　As from a mountain-spring that feeds a dale,

　Shall gush pure streams to purge my impure tale.'

(1065—1078)

153
1066. thy state: 你的境遇
1068. Basely: 卑鄙地
　　　from forth: from, 从……那里
1070. trespass: 罪行
　　　dispense: 宽赦
1071. Till life to death: 死亡
　　　acquit: 宣告无罪；了结

154
1072. attaint: 玷污
1073. cleanly-coin'd excuses: 巧言辩解
1074. sable: 黑色
　　　paint: 粉饰
1075. abuses: 弊病
1076. sluices: 水闸
1077. dale: 谷，溪谷
1078. gush: 涌出
　　　purge: 清洗

153

不让对你暗讥讽　　　　　　　　　　*1065*
当众耻笑夫困境
你知财富清白名
不是赎买被盗空
我有办法了残生
我决不饶我罪行　　　　　　　　　　*1070*
死亡方能罪账清

154

不以我错污你名
不愿推脱我罪名
不愿粉刷罪地明
不愿遮掩荒谬情　　　　　　　　　　*1075*
口要说完有眼睛
放水山谷泉流清
冲我污秽留清名

（1065—1078）

155

By this, lamenting Philomel had ended

The well-tuned warble of her nightly sorrow,　　　　*1080*

And solemn night with slow sad gait descended

To ugly hell; when, lo, the blushing morrow

Lends light to all fair eyes that light will borrow:

　　But cloudy Lucrece shames herself to see,

　　And therefore still in night would cloister'd be.　　*1085*

156

Revealing day through every cranny spies,

And seems to point her out where she sits weeping;

To whom she sobbing speaks: 'O eye of eyes,

Why pry'st thou through my window? leave thy peeping:

Mock with thy tickling beams eyes that are sleeping:　　*1090*

　　Brand not my forehead with thy piercing light,

　　For day hath nought to do what's done by night.'

(1079—1092)

155

1079. lamenting: 伤心的
　　　Philomel: 夜莺, 据希
　　腊神话, 由受辱的公主菲洛美化成
1080. warble: 歌
1081. gait: 步态
1082. the blushing morrow: 脸红的早晨
1085. cloister'd: 使与世隔绝

156

1086. cranny spies: 通用缝隙探望
1088. sobbing: 哭泣
　　　eye of eyes: 太阳
1089. leave thy peeping: 你不要窥视
1090. tickling beams: 使人兴奋的光线
1092. day hath nought to do what's done by night: 黑夜里的事与白昼没有关系

155

到此无言悲夜莺

夜间衰恸悠扬鸣　　　　　　　　　*1080*

庄严黑夜缓慢行

降入地狱晨光红

借给美目盼光明

耻于见己烈露卿

永驻黑夜隐身形　　　　　　　　　*1085*

156

白昼探望狭缝通

指示人哭名露卿

露卿望阳哭悲声

为何窥窗觑我情

光线戏人眼醒忪　　　　　　　　　*1090*

光芒烙额刺眼睛

白昼黑夜不关情

　　　　　　　　　　　　(1079—1092)

157

Thus cavils she with every thing she sees:

True grief is fond and testy as a child,

Who wayward once, his mood with nought agrees: *1095*

Old woes, not infant sorrows, bear them mild;

Continuance tames the one; the other wild.

    Like an unpractised swimmer plunging still,

    With too much labour drowns for want of skill.

158

So she, deepdrenched in a sea of care,   *1100*

Holds disputation with each thing she views,

And to herself all sorrow doth compare;

No object but her passion's strength renews;

And as one shifts, another straight ensues:

    Sometimes her grief is dumb, and hath no words   *1105*

    Sometimes 'tis mad, and too much talk affords.

(1093—1106)

157

1093. cavils: 挑剔

1094. fond: 天真的
     testy: 易怒的

1095. wayward: 任性的
     his mood with nought agrees:
     他对什么都不满意

1096. bear them mild: 绝不暴躁

1097. Continuance tames the one:
     长久的折磨把前者驯服了
     the other wild: 后者撒野

158

1100. drenched: 浸透的

1101. disputation: 争论

1103. passion's strength: 烦忧

1104. ensues: 接着发生

157

凡事挑剔有露卿
真切悲痛似顽童
别扭万事皆不通   1095
旧苦温和悲不同
旧事易驯新野性
初学游泳乱扑腾
有力无技溺水中

158

深陷苦恼海洋中   1100
看到事物便论争
人间忧患比己生
桩桩件件烦恼情
烦恼不断理不清
有时苦痛哑无声   1105
有时狂说像发疯

（1093—1106）

159

The little birds that tune their morning's joy

Make her moans mad with their sweet melody:

For mirth doth search the bottom of annoy;

Sad souls are slain in merry company;   *1110*

Grief best is pleased with grief's society:

   True sorrow then is feelingly sufficed

   When with like semblance it is sympathized.

160

'Tis double death to drown in ken of shore;

He ten times pines that pines beholding food;   *1115*

To see the salve doth make the wound ache more;

Great grief grieves most at that would do it good;

Deep woes roll forward like a gentle flood,

   Who, being stopt, the bounding banks o'erflows;

   Grief dallied with nor law nor limit knows.   *1120*

(1107—1120)

159

1109. mirth: 欢笑，高兴
    annoy: 恼火

1110. Sad souls are slain in merry company:
    愉快人群断肠疼

1111. Grief best is pleased with grief's
    society: 悲痛最喜悲陪同

1112. sufficed: 满足的

1113. semblance: 外表；相似

160

1114. in ken of shore: 陆地在望

1115. ten times pines that pines beholding
    food: 守食挨饿痛千重

1116. salve: 药膏

1119. bounding banks: 堤

1120. dallied: 嘲弄的

159

晨间小鸟唱歌声
甜曲使她更伤情
欢乐总纳苦恼生
愉快人群断肠疼　　　　　　　　　　*1110*
悲痛最喜悲陪同
同病相怜感涕零
相遇知音心平衡

160

见岸淹死双倍疼
守食挨饿痛千重　　　　　　　　　　*1115*
看见膏药伤更疼
悲哀万分遇救星
大悲如河流不停
遇阻堤溃泛滥生
悲受轻视胡乱行　　　　　　　　　　*1120*

　　　　　　　　　　　　　（1107—1120）

161

'You mocking birds,' quoth she, 'your tunes entomb

Within your hollow-swelling feather'd breasts,

And in my hearing be you mute and dumb:

My restless discord loves no stops nor rests;

A woeful hostess brooks not merry guests: 1125

　　Relish your nimble notes to pleasing ears;

　　Distress likes dumps when time is kept with tears.

162

'Come, Philomel, that sing'st of ravishment,

Make thy sad grove in my dishevell'd hair:

As the dank earth weeps at thy languishment,   1130

So I at each sad strain will strain a tear,

And with deep groans the diapason bear;

　　For burthen-wise I'll hum on Tarquin still,

　　While thou on Tereus descant'st better skill.

(1121—1134)

161
1121. entomb:　埋葬
1122. hollow-swelling:　虚空的
1124. discord:　不和
1125. brooks:　容忍
1126. Relish:　乐于
　　　nimble:　灵活的
1127. Distress:　悲痛

dumps:　忧郁的曲调

162
1129. grove:　鸟经常出入的小树林
　　　dishevell'd:　松散杂乱的
1130. dank:　阴湿的
　　　languishment:　悲伤

161

她言鸟儿别嘲讽
鸟胸收入呜啭声
别出声音让我听
心乱难辨节律清
哀妇不受欢客情　　　　　　　　*1125*
乐音送与喜人听
苦人泪眼听悲声

162

菲洛美来诉奸情
鸟来筑巢发蓬松
湿土听歌痛伤情　　　　　　　　*1130*
我听洒泪泪不停
沉痛呻吟伴哀声
忒柔斯事妙音清
我以伴唱塔昆哼

（*1121—1134*）

1131. I at each sad strain will strain a tear:
　　　我听悲歌感涕零
1132. diapason: 和谐
1133. burthen-wise: 帮腔
　　　hum: 哼
1134. Tereus: 蒂留斯，强暴妻
　　　妹菲洛美

695

163

'And whiles against a thorn thou hear'st thy part,   *1135*

To keep thy sharp woes waking, wretched I,

To imitate thee well, against my heart

Will fix a sharp knife, to affright mine eye;

Who, if it wink, shall thereon fall and die.

    These means, as frets upon an instrument,   *1140*

    Shall tune our heart-strings to true languishment.

164

'And for, poor bird, thou sing'st not in the day,

As shaming any eye should thee behold,

Some darkdeep desert, seated from the way,

That knows not parching heat nor freezing cold,   *1145*

Will we find out; and there we will unfold

    To creatures stem sad tunes, to change their kinds:

    Since men prove beasts, let beasts bear gentle minds.'

(1135—1148)

163

1136.　wretched I: 我触目惊心
1138.　affright: 恐吓
1139.　wink: 闭眼
　　　　thereon: 在其上
1140.　frets: 弦柱

164

1144.　dark deep desert: 僻远幽暗的荒漠
　　　　seated from the way: 偏僻的
1145.　parching: 烘烤；使焦干
1146.　unfold: 展开
1147.　sad tunes: 悲歌
1148.　men prove beasts: 人被证明变成兽

163

靠着尖刺你用胸　　　　　　　　*1135*
撕心巨痛头脑清
我用利刃对我胸
像你一样我心惊
一打瞌睡了此生
乐器弦柱同样功　　　　　　　　*1140*
调准心弦奏哀情

164

可怜鸟儿昼不鸣
羞于见人不吱声
荒漠偏僻少人行
没有酷暑与霜冰　　　　　　　　*1145*
我们唱出辛酸情
禽兽听到人性生
人变野兽兽温情

（1135—1148）

165

As the poor frighted deer, that stands at gaze,

Wildly determining which way to fly,   *1150*

Or one encompast with a winding maze,

That cannot tread the way out readily;

So with herself is she in mutiny,

　To live or die, which of the twain were better,

　When life is shamed, and death reproach's debtor.   *1155*

166

'To kill myself,' quoth she, 'alack, what were it,

But with my body my poor soul's pollution?

They that lose half with greater patience bear it

Than they whose whole is swallow'd in confusion.

That mother tries a merciless conclusion   *1160*

　Who, having two sweet babes, when death takes one,

　Will slay the other, and be nurse to none.

(1149—1162)

165

1149. stands at gaze: 站着呆望

1151. encompast: 环境
　　　winding maze: 迷宫

1152. tread the way readily:
　　　安然找到出路

1153. mutiny: 叛变

1154. twain: 两者

1155. death reproach's debtor:
　　　死亡也是指责的负债者

166

1156. alack: 呜呼！啊呀！

1159. in confusion: 在混乱中

1160. merciless conclusion: 残忍的办法

1162. be nurse to none: 一个也不哺乳

165

野鹿呆望因受惊
不知何方去逃生　　　　　　　　　*1150*
犹如行人入迷宫
难找出路安然行
犹豫烦恼有露卿
生死选择知何从
生已受辱死讥评　　　　　　　　　*1155*

166

她言自杀为何情
身体受辱污魂灵
损失其半防守精
不像全失痛伤情
如此母亲训不成　　　　　　　　　*1160*
两孩一个已丧生
再杀一个不心疼

（1149—1162）

167

'My body or my soul, which was the dearer,

When the one pure, the other made divine?

Whose love of either to myself was nearer,   *1165*

When both were kept for heaven and Collatine?

Ay me! the bark pill'd from the lofty pine,

His leaves will wither, and his sap decay;

So must my soul, her bark being pill'd away.

168

'Her house is sack'd, her quiet interrupted,   *1170*

Her mansion batter'd by the enemy;

Her sacred temple spotted, spoil'd, corrupted,

Grossly engirt with daring infamy:

Then let it not be call'd impiety,

If in this blemish'd fort I make some hole   *1175*

Through which I may convey this troubled soul.

(1163—1176)

167
1165. Whose love of either to myself was
nearer: 哪个最爱哪个轻
1167. the bark pill'd: 剥了皮的
lofty pine: 乔松
1168. sap decay: 汁液干涸

168
1170. sack'd: 劫掠

1171. mansion: 大厦；官邸
batter'd: 猛击
1172. sacred: 神圣的
1173. Grossly engirt: 粗暴地包围
daring infamy: 大胆的罪行
1174. impiety: 不虔敬
1175. blemish'd fort: 稀烂的堡垒
1176. convey: 运送

167

躯体灵魂孰重轻
一个神圣一纯清
皆许夫君与天庭　　　　　　　　　*1165*
哪个最爱哪个轻
乔松若剥外皮层
呜呼叶枯汁流馨
灵魂不存因销形

168

她家遭劫扰安宁　　　　　　　　　*1170*
敌毁大厦荡然平
庙宇被掠污损重
大胆罪恶围几层
不必认作不敬行
凿个小孔残堡中　　　　　　　　　*1175*
外送受困我魂灵

　　　　　　　　　　　　　　（1163—1176）

169

'Yet die I will not till my Collatine

Have heard the cause of my untimely death;

That he may vow, in that sad hour of mine,

Revenge on him that made me stop my breath.   *1180*

My stained blood to Tarquin I'll bequeath,

    Which by him tainted shall for him be spent,

    And as his due writ in my testament.

170

'My honour I'll bequeath unto the knife

That wounds my body, so dishonoured.   *1185*

'Tis honour to deprive dishonour'd life;

The one will live, the other being dead:

So of shame's ashes shall my fame be bred;

    For in my death I murder shameful scorn:

    My shame so dead, mine honour is new-born.   *1190*

(1177—1190)

169

1179. vow: 发誓

1181. stained blood: 污血

     bequeath: 保留；传下

1182. tainted: 腐坏的

1183. his due writ in my testament:
     他的欠债，在我遗嘱上写清

170

1186. deprive: 剥夺

1189. shameful scorn: 羞辱

1190. My shame so dead, mine honour is
     new-born: 羞辱一去得新荣

169

不死我等科拉廷
提前死亡诉冤情
在我死时誓言明
逼我死者账算清　　　　　　　　*1180*
留我污血塔昆送
他污我血他说清
报仇遗嘱写分明

170

我赠利刃我尊荣
伤我躯体耻辱清　　　　　　　　*1185*
羞辱结束荣誉生
生命虽死留威名
耻辱灰烬烈名生
一生羞辱账目清
羞辱一生得新荣　　　　　　　　*1190*

（*1177—1190*）

171

'Dear lord of that dear jewel I have lost,

What legacy shall I bequeath to thee?

My resolution, love, shall be thy boast,

By whose example thou revenged mayst be,

How Tarquin must be used, read it in me:　　　　　　*1195*

　　Myself, thy friend, will kill myself, thy foe,

　　And, for my sake, serve thou false Tarquin so.

172

'This brief abridgement of my will I make:—

My soul and body to the skies and ground;

My resolution, husband, do thou take;　　　　　　　*1200*

Mine honour be the knife's that makes my wound;

My shame be his that did my fame confound;

　　And all my fame that lives disbursed be

　　To those that live, and think no shame of me.

(1191—1204)

171
1191. Dear lord of that dear jewel I have lost:
　　最珍贵物已无踪
1194. By whose example thou revenged
　　mayst be: 按我榜样冤洗清
1196. Myself, thy friend, will kill myself,
　　thy foe: 我，你的朋友，杀了我自
　　己，你的敌人

172
1198. abridgment: 简单说明
1200. My resolution, husband, do thou take:
　　我之刚烈夫继承
1202. confound: 毁灭
1203. disbursed: 分配

171

最珍贵物已无踪
留与夫君何物行
夫得贞烈与爱情
按我榜样冤洗清
报仇雪恨法自明　　　　　　　　　1195
你友为敌毁我生
灭掉塔昆不留情

172

我之遗嘱甚简明
归还天地肉与灵
我之刚烈夫继承　　　　　　　　　1200
尖刀夺去我之荣
耻辱塔昆来继承
我之不朽之美名
送与宽容诸友朋

(1191—1204)

173

'Thou, Collatine, shalt oversee this will;　　　　　　*1205*

How was I overseen that thou shalt see it!

My blood shall wash the slander of mine ill;

My life's foul deed, my life's fair end shall free it.

Faint not, faint heart, but stoutly say "So be it."

　　Yield to my hand; my hand shall conquer thee:　　*1210*

　　Thou dead, both die and both shall victors be.'

174

This plot of death when sadly she had laid,

And wiped the brinish pearl from her bright eyes,

With untuned tongue she hoarsely calls her maid,

Whose swift obedience to her mistress hies;　　　　　*1215*

For fleet-wing'd duty with thought's feathers flies.

　　Poor Lucrece' cheeks unto her maid seem so

　　As winter meads when sun doth melt their snow.

(1205—1218)

173

1205. oversee: 监督

1207. the slander of mine ill: 我的罪过和丑名

1208. My life's fould deed my life's fair end shall free it: 我以洁白的一死，荡涤污黑的行径

1209. Faint not, faint heart: 脆弱的心，不必伤心

stoutly: 勇敢地

174

1213. brinish: 微咸的

1214. untuned tongue: 反常的音调
　　　 hoarsely: 嘶哑地

1215. hies: 赶往

1216. fleet-wing'd duty: 展翅疾飞尽义务

1218. meads: 草地

173

执行遗嘱科拉廷 *1205*
我真胡涂你看明
我之丑闻血洗清
一死消我此罪行
脆弱之心言遵命
手要克心贞烈行 *1210*
双双死去双双赢

174

决意自杀心伤疼
泪珠抹去亮眼睛
呼唤婢女沙哑声
急见夫人婢女忠 *1215*
忠顺之心插翅行
可怜面颊惨露卿
冬日草地雪消融

（1205—1218）

175

Her mistress she doth give demure good-morrow,

With soft-slow tongue, true mark of modesty,   *1220*

And sorts a sad look to her lady's sorrow,

For why her face wore sorrow's livery;

But durst not ask of her audaciously

    Why her two suns were cloud-eclipsed so,

    Nor why her fair cheeks overwasht with woe.   *1225*

176

But as the earth doth weep, the sun being set,

Each flower moisten'd like a melting eye,

Even so the maid with swelling drops 'gan wet

Her circled eyne, enforced by sympathy

Of those fair suns set in her mistress' sky,   *1230*

    Who in a salt-waved ocean quench their light,

    Which makes the maid weep like the dewy night.

(1219—1232)

175

1219. demure: 拘谨的，娴静的
1222. For why: Because, 因为
    livery: 号衣
1223. durst: dare 的过去式，
    敢
    audaciously: 大胆地
1224. cloud-eclipsed: 乌云遮蔽的

176

1226. the sun being set: 太阳尚未升起
1227. moisten'd: 湿的
    melting eye: 泪汪汪的眼睛
1229. enforced: 实施的
1231. quench: 熄灭
    （译注者按：该诗段婉约、凄楚、
    精细、柔美）

175

婢女问安语声轻
语调舒缓头顺从   *1220*
见主悲伤亦愁容
主妇面上悲云生
不敢斗胆问真情
乌云遮盖两眼睛
悲哀冲洗娇面容   *1225*

176

大地哭泣日未升
鲜花潮湿泪眼睛
婢女眼睛也发红
大颗泪珠圆眼生
同情主妇两颗星   *1230*
咸海水中验光明
哭如夜露婢女情

（1219—1232）

177

A pretty while these pretty creatures stand,

Like ivory conduits coral cisterns filling:

One justly weeps; the other takes in hand   *1235*

No cause, but company, of her drops spilling:

Their gentle sex to weep are often willing;

    Grieving themselves to guess at others' smarts,

    And then they drown their eyes, or break their hearts.

178

For men have marble, women waxen, minds,   *1240*

And therefore are they form'd as marble will;

The weak oppressed, the impression of strange kinds

Is formed in them by force, by fraud, or skill:

Then call them not the authors of their ill,

    No more than wax shall be accounted evil   *1245*

    Wherein is stamped the semblance of a devil.

                                  (1233—1246)

177

1234. conduits: 管道
coral cisterns filling: 珊瑚水池喷溅

1236. drops spilling: 泪流满面

1238. others' smarts: 别人的苦痛

178

1241. marble will: 大理石般的意图

1242. The weak oppressed, the impression of strange kinds: 弱者受压立显形

1243. Is formed in them by force, by fraud, or skill: 暴力欺诈陷阱成

1244. their ill: 他们罪孽

1245. No more than wax shall be accounted evil: 蜡上印有恶魔形

1246. Wherein is stamped the semblance of a devil: 不该怨蜡怨妖精

177

二美伫立俏身形
象牙雕刻水池中
珊瑚池里哭露卿　　　　　　　　　*1235*
婢女陪哭也动情
温柔女性泪晶莹
别人痛苦也心疼
伤心痛哭掩芳容

178

女心好似蜡做成　　　　　　　　*1240*
男心大理石头硬
弱者受压立显形
暴力诡诈陷井成
她们不该担罪名
蜡上印有恶魔形　　　　　　　　*1245*
不该怨蜡怨妖精

（*1233—1246*）

179

Their smoothness, like a goodly champaign plain,

Lays open all the little worms that creep;

In men, as in a rough-grown grove, remain

Cave-keeping evils that obscurely sleep: 1250

Through crystal walls each little mote will peep:

　　Though men can cover crimes with bold stern looks,

　　Poor women's faces are their own faults' books.

180

No man inveigh against the wither'd flower,

But chide rough winter that the flower hath kill'd: 1255

Not that devoured, but that which doth devour,

Is worthy blame. O, let it not be hild

Poor women's faults, that they are so fulfill'd

　　With men's abuses: those proud lords, to blame,

　　Make weak-made women tenants to their shame.   1260

(1247—1260)

179

1247. champaign: 平坦广阔
1249. In men: 对男人来说
　　　rough-grown grove: 桠杈横生的林木
1250. Cave-keeping evils: 穴居的罪恶
　　　obscurely: 黑暗中
1251. mote: 尘埃
1252. cover: 掩盖

180

1254. inveigh: 猛烈抨击
1256. Nor that devoured, but that which doth devour: 该骂吞食者,不是被吞者
1257. hild: held, 担承
1259. men's abuses: 男人的骄纵
1260. weak-made women: 弱女子
　　　tenants to their shame: 将他们的丑事出租

712

179

女子美好平原平
可见爬行小毛虫
男子森林桠杈生
邪恶穴居闷睡中　　　　　　　　　　*1250*
纤毫毕露墙水晶
男人掩罪装正经
弱女脸上记罪行

180

不可谴责花凋零
痛骂毁花有寒冬　　　　　　　　　　*1255*
应骂吞者被吞疼
呜呼女被男欺凌
过错非由女担承
错在老爷太骄横
蹂躏弱女罪不轻　　　　　　　　　　*1260*

（*1247—1260*）

181

The precedent whereof in Lucrece view,

Assail'd by night with circumstances strong

Of present death, and shame that might ensue

By that her death, to do her husband wrong:

Such danger to resistance did belong,   *1265*

   That dying fear through all her body spread;

   And who cannot abuse a body dead?

182

By this, mild patience bid fair Lucrece speak

To the poor counterfeit of her complaining:

'My girl,' quoth she, 'on what occasion break   *1270*

Those tears from thee, that down thy cheeks are raining?

If thou dust weep for grief of my sustaining,

   Know, gentle wench, it small avails my mood:

   If tears could help, mine own would do me good.

(1261—1274)

181

1261. precedent: 判例
1263. ensue: 接着发生
1266. dying fear through all her body
    spread: 死后的恐怖散到她全身去
1267. abuse: 糟蹋

182

1268. mild patience: 温和的耐心
    bid: 命令
1269. counterfeit: 肖像
1272. sustaining: 支撑
1273. wench: 少女
    small avails: 几乎无益于

181

今有例证看露卿
午夜遭袭不欲生
死后免辱也不能
死亡辱没科拉廷
挺身反抗危险生　　　　　　　　　1265
死后恐怖罩露卿
糟蹋尸体谁不行

182

此刻难忍美露卿
对己肖像怨连声
女儿为何泪晶莹　　　　　　　　　1270
顺着面颊流不停
哭我悲苦痛伤情
须知我痛难减轻
姑娘眼泪用不成

（1261—1274）

183

'But tell me, girl, when went' —and there she stay'd   1275

Till after a deep groan—'Tarquin from hence?'

'Madam, ere I was up,' replied the maid,

'The more to blame my sluggard negligence:

Yet with the fault I thus far can dispense,—

   Myself was stirring ere the break of day,   1280

   And ere I rose was Tarquin gone away.

184

'But, lady, if your maid may be so bold,

She would request to know your heaviness.'

'O, peace!' quoth Lucrece: 'if it should be told,

The repetition cannot make it less,   1285

For more it is than I can well express:

   And that deep torture may be call'd a hell

   When more is felt than one hath power to tell.

(1275—1288)

183

1276. hence: 从此地

1278. sluggard: 懒惰的

      negligence: 疏忽，粗心大意

1279. dispense: 免除

184

1283. heaviness: 烦恼

1285. it: 悲哀

1288. more is felt than one hath power to
      tell: 感受虽多，却没有力量说出

183

姑娘禀我塔昆情　　　　　　　　*1275*
询问深叹有露卿
那贼走时奴未醒
婢女责己睡失明
说我偷懒有冤情
破晓之前起床行　　　　　　　　*1280*
起床之前贼无踪

184

夫人饶婢问事情
斗胆问主何气生
莫问莫问言露卿
讲说我悲难减轻　　　　　　　　*1285*
那事现时难说清
苦像地狱十八层
言语无力说不成

　　　　　　　　　　　　　　　（*1275—1288*）

185

'Go, get me hither paper, ink, and pen,—

Yet save that labour, for I have them here.　　　　*1290*

What should I say?—One of my husband's men

Bid thou be ready, by and by, to bear

A letter to my lord, my love, my dear:

　Bid him with speed prepare to carry it;

　The cause craves haste, and it will soon be writ.　　*1295*

186

Her maid is gone, and she prepares to write,

First hovering o'er the paper with her quill:

Conceit and grief an eager combat fight;

What wit sets down is blotted straight with will;

This is too curious-good, this blunt and ill:　　　　*1300*

　Much like a press of people at a door,

　Throng her inventions, which shall go before.

(1289—1302)

185
1289. hither: 这里
1290. save that labour: 不必费事了
1292. by and by: 不久以后
1295. The cause craves haste: 事很紧急

186
1297. hovering: 翱翔，盘旋
　　　quill: 鹅毛笔

1298. Conceit: 想法；奇想
　　　an eager combat fight: 冲突激烈
1299. What wit sets down is blotted straight
　　　with will: 心智写下的东西立即被
　　　情感抹掉
1300. curious-good: 纤巧
　　　blunt: 生硬
1301. a press of people: 挤了很多人
1302. inventions: 太多的想法

185

拿纸墨笔我要用

不用去拿这儿行　　　　　　　　　　　*1290*

怎么告诉科拉廷

通知夫君一仆从

立即送信到军营

越快越好火急行

暂等片刻信写成　　　　　　　　　　　*1295*

186

婢女出去唤仆从

拿起翎管心翻腾

思想悲哀剧烈冲

理智情感不相容

太瘟太火都不行　　　　　　　　　　　*1300*

恰如人群门口涌

争着出门乱哄哄

　　　　　　　　　　　　　　　　　（1289—1302）

187

At last she thus begins: 'Thou worthy lord

Of that unworthy wife that greeteth thee,

Health to thy person! next vouchsafe t' afford—　　　　*1305*

If ever, love, thy Lucrece thou wilt see—

Some present speed to come and visit me.

　So, I commend me from our house in grief:

　My woes arc tedious, though my words are brief.'

188

Here folds she up the tenour of her woe,　　　　*1310*

Her certain sorrow writ uncertainly.

By this short schedule Collatine may know

Her grief, but not her grief's true quality:

She dares not thereof make discovery,

　Lest he should hold it her own gross abuse,　　　　*1315*

　Ere she with blood had stain'd her stain'd excuse.

(1303—1316)

187

1303. Thou worthy lord: 夫君大鉴

1304. unworthy wife: 拙妻
　　　greeteth: 致意

1305. Health to thy person: 祝你健康
　　　vouchsafe: 屈尊
　　　t': to

afford: 授予；准予

1306. If ever: 那么

1308. commend me: 我向你致敬

1309. My woes are tedious, though my
　　　words are brief: 我的话寥寥无几，
　　　我的苦绵绵不尽

187

终于动笔夫君称

向你致意有拙荆

祝你健康见露卿　　　　　　　　　　　　*1305*

如想团聚速登程

向你致意伴心疼

盼君立即离军营

书信虽短苦无穷

188

折起信纸含悲情　　　　　　　　　　　　*1310*

十分悲哀未写明

聪明清亮科拉廷

可知短信苦恼情

叙述未详悲露卿

她盼污辱血洗清　　　　　　　　　　　　*1315*

避免误会言不明

（*1303—1316*）

188

1310. tenour:　信笺

1311. Her certain sorrow writ uncertainly:
　　　 并未写明她悲哀的内容

1312. schedule:　笺

1314. thereof:　因此

1315. her own gross abuse:　她自己的过错

1316. Stain'd excuse:　被污的经过

189

Besides, the life and feeling of her passion

She hoards, to spend when he is by to hear her;

When sighs and groans and tears may grace the fashion

Of her disgrace, the better so to clear her   *1320*

From that suspicion which the world might bear her.

   To shun this blot, she would not blot the letter

   With words, tiff action might become them better.

190

To see sad sights moves more than hear them told;

For then the eye interprets to the ear   *1325*

The heavy motion that it doth behold,

When every part a part of woe doth bear.

'Tis but a part of sorrow that we hear:

   Deep sounds make lesser noise than shallow fords,

   And sorrow ebbs, being blown with wind of words.   *1330*

(*1317—1330*)

189

1317. passion: 激情；感情

1318. hoards: 贮藏

   by: 在她旁边

1319. grace the fashion: 点缀她的受辱

1322. shun: 回避

   shun this blot: 避免这种污辱

190

1326. heavy motion: 悲惨的动作

1327. every part a part of woe doth bear:

   每一个演员都有一段悲惨经过

1329. sounds: 港湾

   fords: 浅滩

1330. ebbs: 落潮

189

露卿积蓄悲愤情
细告夫君盼倾听
眼泪悲欢叙述中
受辱呻吟不成声　　　　　　　　　*1320*
世人猜疑可廓清
避免污辱信未明
行动响亮言语轻

190

眼见惨像胜耳听
目睹惨像有眼睛　　　　　　　　　*1325*
逐一解释耳朵听
身体各部负冤情
所听仅为痛表层
深海低于浅流声
悲哀落潮语言风　　　　　　　　　*1330*

（*1317—1330*）

191

Her letter now is seal'd, and on it writ,

'At Ardea to my lord with more than haste.'

The post attends, and she delivers it,

Charging the sour-faced groom to hie as fast

As lagging fowls before the northern blast: *1335*

Speed more than speed but dull and slow she deems:

Extremity still urgeth such extremes.

192

The homely villain court'sies to her low;

And, blushing on her, with a steadfast eye

Receives the scroll without or yea or no,   *1340*

And forth with bashful innocence doth hie.

But they whose guilt within their bosoms lie

Imagine every eye beholds their blame;

For Lucrece thought he blusht to see her shame:

(1331—1344)

191

1333. The post attends: 信差在一旁待命
1334. sour-faced groom: 板着面孔的仆
      人
      hie: 赶往
1335. lagging fowls: 迟飞的候鸟
      northern blast: 北风

192

1338. villain: 仆人
      court'sies: 行屈膝礼
1339. steadfast eye: 目不转睛
1340. scroll: 纸卷；函件
1341. bashful: 害羞的，忸怩的
      bashful innocence: 羞怯的窘态

191

露卿书信已漆封
烦寄夫君勿缓行
交与信差正色听
命令仆佣赴军营
落后飞禽借此风　　　　　　　　　　*1335*
再快不达火急情
人到紧急极端行

192

仆人向她深鞠躬
双目凝视频泛红
接过书信不言声　　　　　　　　　　*1340*
带着窘态急登程
人若亏心人心惊
感觉世人知隐情
仆人脸红惊露卿

（*1331—1344*）

193

When, silly groom! God wot, it was defect   *1345*

Of spirit, life, and bold audacity.

Such harmless creatures have a true respect

To talk in deeds, while others saucily

Promise more speed, but do it leisurely:

    Even so this pattern of the worn-out age   *1350*

    Pawn'd honest looks, but laid no words to gage.

194

His kindled duty kindled her mistrust,

That two red fires in both their faces blazed;

She thought he blusht, as knowing Tarquin's lust,

And, blushing with him, wistly on him gazed;   *1355*

Her earnest eye did make him more amazed:

    The more she saw the blood his cheeks replenish,

    The more she thought he spied in her some blemish.

(1345—1358)

193

1345. silly groom: 淳朴的仆人
      God wot: 天晓得
      defect: 缺乏
1346. audacity: 大胆
      true respect: 真诚的品性
1348. talk in deeds: 喜欢把事做
      saucily: 漂亮地

1350. worn-out age: 美好的往日
1351. Pawn'd: 保证；发誓
      gage: 保证

194

1352. kindled duty: 激发的敬意
1353. blazed: 燃起
1355. wistly: 目不转眼地

193

天真汉子神看清   *1345*

不敢冒险少激情

只是认真做事情

另一种人大不同

狡猾答应不执行

他是世人好仆从   *1350*

忠实做事不言声

194

露卿反疑仆忠诚

两人面颊泛赤红

她疑仆人知真情

脸红心跳对仆从   *1355*

她越凝视仆越惊

她见仆人面颊红

更疑仆人知奸情

（*1345—1358*）

1357. replenish: 充满

1358. spied: 察见，发现

     blemish: *污点*

195

But long she thinks till he return again,

And yet the duteous vassal scarce is gone.   *1360*

The weary time she cannot entertain,

For now 'tis stale to sigh, to weep, and groan,

So woe hath wearied woe, moan tired moan,

   That she her plaints a little while doth stay,

   Pausing for means to mourn some newer way.   *1365*

196

At last she calls to mind where hangs a piece

Of skilful painting, made for Priam's Troy;

Before the which is drawn the power of Greece,

For Helen's rape the city to destroy,

Threatening cloud-kissing Ilion with annoy;   *1370*

   Which the conceited painter drew so proud,

   As heaven, it seem'd, to kiss the turrets bow'd.

(1359—1372)

195

1360. duteous: 忠心的
    vassal: 仆人
    scarce: 刚刚
1362. stale: 枯燥乏味
1363. woe hath wearied woe: 悲哀累乏
    了悲哀
1364. plaints: 哀诉

196

1367. Priam: 普里阿摩斯,
    特洛伊国王
1370. Threatening: 威胁
    cloud-kissing: 高耸入云的
    Ilion: 伊利昂, 特洛伊别
    名
    annoy: 生气

195

她想很久仆回程
实则忠仆刚出行　　　　　　　　　　*1360*
时间漫长坏心情
悲泣呻吟付秋风
悲哀疲倦欢无声
露卿哀诉方暂停
寻找新路吐悲情　　　　　　　　　　*1365*

196

想到特洛伊战争
传说古老油画精
希腊军队围都城
海伦受辱城墙倾
参天楼台似无踪　　　　　　　　　　*1370*
灵慧画家才气横
欲吻塔尖笑苍穹

　　　　　　　　　　　　　　　（1359—1372）

1371. conceited: 有才华的
1372. turrets: 塔
　　　 bow'd: 俯身

197

A thousand lamentable objects there,

In scorn of nature, art gave lifeless life:

Many a dry drop seem'd a weeping tear,   *1375*

Shed for the slanghter'd husband by the wife:

The red blood reek'd, to show the painter's strife;

　　And dying eyes gleam'd forth their ashy lights,

　　Like dying coals burnt out in tedious nights.

198

There might you see the laboring pioneer   *1380*

Begrimed with sweat, and smeared all with dust;

And from the towers of Troy there would appear

The very eyes of men through loop-holes thrust,

Gazing upon the Greeks with little lust:

　　Such sweet observance in this work was had,   *1385*

　　That one might see those far-off eyes look sad.

(*1373—1386*)

197
1373. lamentable: 悲苦的
1374. In scorn of nature: 凌驾于自然
1376. slaughter'd husband: 被屠杀的丈夫
1377. reek'd: 冒烟；冒水蒸气
1378. gleam'd: 闪烁
　　ashy lights: 灰白的光
1379. tedious nights: 漫漫长液

198
1380. laboring pioneer: 操作的工兵
1381. Begrimed: 弄脏
　　smeared: 玷污
1383. loop-holes: 孔洞
　　thrust: 张望

197

形象上千可怜形
艺高生活形象生
无数干色淌眼泪　　　　　　　　　　　　　　*1375*
夫君被杀放悲声
赤血淋漓画艺精
灰色光留灰眼睛
渐熄炭火黑夜中

198

君见劳苦有工兵　　　　　　　　　　　　　　*1380*
汗水泥水劳作中
都城城墙有眼睛
男兵窥望希腊兵
满怀敌意不放松
油画细腻画军情　　　　　　　　　　　　　　*1385*
远方凄惨泪眼睛

（1373—1386）

1384. lust: 欢乐
1385. observance: 视察
Such sweet observance in this work
was had: 这幅奇妙的作品, 竟这样
精巧传神

1386. That one might see those far-off eyes
look sad: 从那些远处的眼睛里,
能看出悲痛之情

199

In great commanders grace and majesty

You might behold, triumphing in their faces;

In youth, quick bearing and dexterity;

And here and there the painter interlaces   *1390*

Pale cowards, marching on with trembling paces;

    Which heartless peasants did so well resemble

    That one would swear he saw them quake and tremble.

200

In Ajax and Ulysses, O, what art

Of physiognomy might one behold!   *1395*

The face of either ciphered either's heart;

Their face their manners most expressly told:

In Ajax' eyes blunt rage and rigour roll'd;

    But the mild glance that sly Ulysses lent

    Show'd deep regard and smiling government.   *1400*

(1387—1400)

199

1389. dexterity: 灵巧
1390. interlaces: 使交织
1391. Pale cowards: 脸色苍白的懦夫
    trembling paces: 战兢兢举步
1392. heartless peasants: 无勇的村夫
1393. quake: 战栗

200

1394. Ajax: 埃阿斯，特洛
    伊战争中的希腊英雄
    Ulysses: 尤利西斯，特
    洛伊战争中的希腊英雄
1395. physiognomy: 视相术
1396. ciphered: 计算

199

大将脸上见威风
得胜将军得胜容
青年活跃又机灵
画家又加人装熊 *1390*
苍白懦夫战兢兢
无勇之众可怜虫
乌合之众无队形

200

大埃阿斯有己容
尤利西斯有己风 *1395*
画家画人技术精
面部表情显心情
大埃阿斯怒气生
尤利西斯计谋成
柔和目光露雍容 *1400*

（1387—1400）

1397. told: 揭示
1398. blunt rage: 躁怒
　　　rigour: 残酷
1399. sly: 狡猾的
1400. smiling government: 从容含笑的自制

201

There pleading might you see grave Nestor stand,

As 'twere encouraging the Greeks to fight:

Making such sober action with his hand,

That it beguiled attention, charm'd the sight:

In speech, it seem'd, his beard, all silver white,　　　　*1405*

　　Wagg'd up and down, and from his tips did fly

　　Thin winding breath, which purl'd up to the sky.

202

About him were a press of gaping faces,

Which seem'd to swallow up his sound advice;

All jointly listening, but with several graces,　　　　*1410*

As if some mermaid did their ears entice,

Some high, some low, —the painter was so nice;

　　The scalps of many, almost hid behind,

　　To jump up higher seem'd, to mock the mind.

(*1401—1414*)

201

1401. pleading: 劝说的
　　　Nestor: 内斯特，特洛伊
　　　战争时希腊的贤明长者

1403. sober action: 庄严的挥动

1404. beguiled attention: 引人注意
　　　charm'd the sight: 逗人爱看

1406. Wagg'd up and down: 上下抖动

1407. Thin winding breath: 回旋的气息
　　　purl'd up: 袅袅飘向空中

202

1408. About him: 在他周围
　　　a press of gaping faces: 张着嘴的
　　　一大群人

1410. graces: 表情

201

奈斯特演讲从容

受鼓舞希腊士兵

庄严手挥动生风

逗人爱诱人心情

银白长髯说话声　　　　　　　　　*1405*

双唇上下动不停

圈圈呼气飞天空

202

听众张嘴侧耳听

想把忠告吞腹中

听者各有各神情　　　　　　　　　*1410*

好像妖女诱人声

高矮不同画艺精

多人被遮数无穷

想要蹦高认真听

（*1401—1414*）

1411. mermaid:　鲛人；美人鱼
　　　 entice:　诱使
1413. scalps:　被头发遮挡住的
1414. mock the mind:　嘲讽观众的想象力

203

Here one man's hand lean'd on another's head,   *1415*

His nose being shadow'd by his neighbour's ear;

Here one, being throng'd, bears back, all boll'n and red;

Another, smother'd, seems to pelt and swear;

And in their rage such signs of rage they bear,

    As, but for loss of Nestor's golden words,   *1420*

    It seem'd they would debate with angry swords.

204

For much imaginary work was there;

Conceit deceitful, so compact, so kind,

That for Achilles' image stood his spear,

Grip'd in an armed hand; himself, behind,   *1425*

Was left unseen, save to the eye of mind:

    A hand, a foot, a face, a leg, a head,

    Stood for the whole to be imagined.

                          (1415—1428)

203

1417. being throng'd, bears back: 被挤得后退

    all boll'n and red: 肿胀

1418. pelt: 咒骂

    swear: 发誓

1419. in their rage such signs of rage they bear: 他们以暴躁的心情，做着暴躁的姿势

1420. but for: 要不是

204

1423. compact: 紧凑的

1424. Achilles: 阿喀琉斯，特洛伊战争中希腊大英雄

1425. Grip'd: 握着

203

一人按住人头顶　　　　　　　　*1415*

人耳遮鼻看不清

被按红脸向后撑

一个窒息怒骂生

人人欲露相貌凶

若非怕误良言听　　　　　　　　*1420*

拔剑拼杀不留情

204

想象艺术称洞精

虚拟假托自然成

阿喀琉斯矛枪挺

披甲手执人无踪　　　　　　　　*1425*

英雄出现想象中

手足头腿或面孔

想象之力形象成

（*1415—1428*）

1426. save to the eye of mind:　除非用心
　　　智的眼光

205

And from the walls of strong-besieged Troy

When their brave hope, bold Hector, marcht to field,   *1430*

Stood many Trojan mothers, sharing joy

To see their youthful sons bright weapons wield;

And to their hope they such odd action yield,

    That through their light joy seemed to appear,

    Like bright things stain'd, a kind of heavy fear.   *1435*

206

And from the strond of Dardan, where they fought,

To Simois' reedy banks the red blood ran,

Whose waves to imitate the battle sought

With swelling ridges; and their ranks began

To break upon the galled shore, and than   *1440*

    Retire again, till meeting greater ranks,

    They join, and shoot their foam at Simois' banks.

(1429—1442)

205

1430. Hector: 赫克托耳，特洛伊战争中的特洛伊英雄

1432. wield: 挥动

1433. such odd action yield: 以罕见的举止

206

1436. strond: 海滨

Dardan: 达丹，特洛伊城所在地区名

1437. Simois: 西摩伊斯河，离特洛伊城不远

reedy banks: 芦苇纷披的河岸

1439. ridges: 脊

1440. galled: 损伤的

1441. ranks: 排，横列

205

都城被围万千重
主将赫克托出城　　　　　　　　　　　*1430*
城头母亲好心情
英雄儿男兵器精
举止罕见送英雄
君见轻松喜悦中
亮物污染尤重重　　　　　　　　　　　*1435*

206

达丹海滨血殷红
西摩伊岸苇悲声
河水也想学战争
河岸受损波浪凶
拍岸退潮待潮生　　　　　　　　　　　*1440*
更大波浪期待中
西摩伊岸浪拍声

（*1429—1442*）

207

To this well-painted piece is Lucrece come,

To find a face where all distress is stelled.

Many she sees where cares have carved some,   1445

But none where all distress and dolour dwelled,

Till she despairing Hecuba beheld,

 Staring on Priam's wounds with her old eyes,

 Which bleeding under Pyrrhus' proud foot ties.

208

In her the painter had anatomized   1450

Time's ruin, beauty's wrack, and grim care's reign:

Her cheeks with chops and wrinkles were disguised;

Of what she was no semblance did remain:

Her blue blood changed to black in every vein,

 Wanting the spring that those shrunk pipes had fed,   1455

 Show'd life imprison'd in a body dead.

(1443—1456)

207

1444. distress: 悲痛
  stelled: 绘满；汇聚
1445. Many she sees where cares have
  carved some: 她见到许多面孔，都
  有忧患的留痕
1446. dolour: 忧伤，悲哀
  dwelled: 存在

1447. despairing: 绝望的
  Hecuba: 赫卡柏，特
  洛伊亚 Priam 之妻
1448. Priam: 普里阿摩斯，特洛伊最后
  一位国王，Hector 和 Paris 之父
  old eyes: 老眼昏花
1449. Pyrrhus: 皮洛斯，Achilles
  之子，在特洛伊战争中杀死了 Priam

207

走过看画有露卿
想找一人惟愁容
不少面孔忧愁情　　　　　　　　*1445*
没有一面全悲生
赫卡拍后有愁容
惊望夫伤不转睛
仇敌足下热血红

208

此处画家显才能　　　　　　　　*1450*
红衰恨磨岁无情
裂纹皱褶频变形
当年风韵涉无踪
蓝色血管变黑红
血管源泉水已空　　　　　　　　*1455*
垂死躯体禁残生

（*1443—1456*）

208

1450. anatomized:　显示
1451. grim care's reign:　愁恨难免
1452. chops:　裂纹
　　　disguised:　毁损容貌
1453. semblance:　丰韵
1455. those shrunk pipes:　干瘪的血管

209

On this sad shadow Lucrece spends her eyes,

And shapes her sorrow to the beldam's woes,

Who nothing wants to answer her but cries,

And bitter words to ban her cruel foes: *1460*

The painter was no god to lend her those;

   And therefore Lucrece swears he did her wrong,

   To give her so much grief, and not a tongue.

210

'Poor instrument,' quoth she, 'without a sound,

I'll tune thy woes with my lamenting tongue;   *1465*

And drop sweet balm in Priam's painted wound,

And rail on Pyrrhus that hath done him wrong;

And with my tears quench Troy that burns so long;

   And with my knife scratch out the angry eyes

   Of all the Greeks that are thine enemies.   *1470*

(1457—1470)

209
1458. beldam's: 老太婆的
1460. ban her cruel foes: 诅咒她的残暴
      的敌人
1461. lend: 赋予

210
1466. balm: 止痛药膏
1467. rail on: 谴责
1468. quench: 扑灭
1469. scratch: 剜出

209

注视惨相悲露卿
美女老妪哀共鸣
老妪一切答露卿
惟欠痛骂仇敌声   *1460*
画家非神无此能
她怨画家真不公
只让受苦不喊疼

210

她言可怜不发声
我有喉舌歌悲情   *1465*
膏药为夫敷伤痛
责骂仇敌伤英雄
眼泪浇灭战火熊
刀子剜出敌眼睛
希腊残暴太无情   *1470*

（1457—1470）

211

'Show me the strumpet that began this stir,

That with my nails her beauty I may tear.

Thy heat of lust, fond Paris, did incur

This load of wrath that burning Troy doth bear:

Thy eye kindled the fire that burneth here;   *1475*

   And here in Troy, for trespass of thine eye,

   The sire, the son, the dame, and daughter die.

212

'Why should the private pleasure of some one

Become the public plague of many moe?

Let sin, alone committed, light alone   *1480*

Upon his head that hath transgressed so;

Let guiltless souls be freed from guilty woe:

   For one's offence why should so many fall,

   To plague a private sin in general?

(1471—1484)

211

1471. strumpet: 妓女
1473. fond Paris: 痴情的帕里斯
     incur: 招致
1474. load of wrath: 愤怒
1476. for frespass of thine eye: 为了你的
     眼睛的过失

212

1479. public plague: 共同的灾难
     moe: more 更多的
1480. light: 降临
1481. trangressed: 侵越
1483. why should so many fall: 为何让如
     此多的人受过
1484. plague: 惩罚

211

看到娼妇起战争
指甲抓破美娇容
王子与你滥用情
天公动怒焚都城
烧起大火你眼睛　　　　　　　　　　　1475
眼睛过错人无生
父子妻女地狱行

212

帕里斯偷海伦情
酿成灾难伤众生
谁有罪过谁担承　　　　　　　　　　　1480
罪由一人该受惩
无辜不该蒙冤情
一人有罪连众生
惩罚一人众逢凶

（1471—1484）

213

'Lo, here weeps Hecuba, here Priam dies,   *1485*

Here manly Hector faints, here Troilus swounds,

Here friend by friend in bloody channel lies,

And friend to friend gives unadvised wounds,

And one man's lust these many lives confounds:

   Had doting Priam checkt his son's desire,   *1490*

   Troy had been bright with fame, and not with fire.

214

Here feelingly she weeps Troy's painted woes:

For sorrow, like a heavy-hanging bell,

Once set on ringing, with his own weight goes;

Then little strength rings out the doleful knell: *1495*

So Lucrece, set a-work, sad tales doth tell

   To pencill'd pensiveness and colour'd sorrow;

   She lends them words, and she their looks doth borrow.

（1485—1498）

213

1486. Troilus: 特洛伊罗斯，
特洛伊国王 Priam 之子
swounds: 昏倒
1487. friend by friend: 朋友偎靠着朋友
1488. friend to friend: 朋友面对着朋友
unadvised wounds: 无意中伤害
1489. confounds: 挫败；遭殃

1490. doting Priam: 昏聩的特洛伊国王
普里阿摩斯

214

1492. feelingly: 动感情地
painted woes: 画中的惨祸

213

嗚呼妇哭夫无生   *1485*

英雄昏倒子伤疼

血泊沟渠躺亲朋

敌友不分杀无情

一人好色害众生

国王戒子荒唐行   *1490*

都城火灭光艳升

214

泪洒疆场她同情

悲哀沉重一口钟

遇到撞声摆不停

稍一用力奏哀声   *1495*

露克丽丝用此情

睹画悲哀诉苦衷

她借神形画借声

（*1485—1498*）

1493. heavy-hanging bell: 沉重悬垂的钟

1494. Once set on ringing, with his own weight goes: 只消撞那么一下，它自会摆动不停

1495. rings out: 发出
doleful knell: 凄楚的影响

1496. set a-work: 开始悲思触动

1497. pencill'd pensiveness: 图画中的忧郁

1498. She lends them words, and she their looks doth borrow: 她借给他们言语，借用他们的愁容

215

She throws her eyes about the painting round,

And who she finds forlorn she doth lament.   *1500*

At last she sees a wretched image bound,

That piteous looks to Phrygian shepherds lent:

His face, though full of cares, yet show'd content;

  Onward to Troy with the blunt swains he goes,

  So mild that Patience seem'd to scorn his woes.   *1505*

216

In him the painter labour'd with his skill

To hide deceit, and give the harmless show

An humble gait, calm looks, eyes wailing still,

A brow unbent, that seem'd to welcome woe;

Cheeks neither red nor pale, but mingled so   *1510*

  That blushing red no guilty instance gave,

  Nor ashy pale the fear that false hearts have.

(1499—1512)

215

1500. forlorn: 被遗弃的
     lament: 悲痛
1501. wretched image: 可怜的形象
     bound: 被缚的
1502. piteous looks: 可怜的表情
     Phrygian: 弗里吉亚的，弗里吉亚

为小亚细亚中西部古国。一说
Phrygian 为特洛伊别名
     lent: 给予
1504. blunt swains: 乡民

216

1507. deceit: 狡猾

215

放眼看画找悲情
每见悲者悲情生   *1500*
后见一人缚绑绳
一群牧人随同情
面带忧愁意纵容
乡民伴随都城行
忍辱负重耐心成   *1505*

216

精意刻画画家情
不露狡黠露善行
步安神静泪眼睛
眉头舒展对苦情
面色不白也不红   *1510*
红时亏心有错生
白时心虚畏惧成

（1499—1512）

1508. gait: 步态
   wailing: 悲恸的
1511. blushing red no guilty instance gave:
   红的时候不像是心中有愧
1512. ashy pale: 灰白

217

But, like a constant and confirmed devil,

He entertain'd a show so seeming just,

And therein so ensconced his secret evil,   *1515*

That jealousy itself could not mistrust

False-creeping craft and perjury should thrust

    Into so bright a day such black-faced storms,

    Or blot with hell-born sin such saint-like forms.

218

The well-skill'd workman this mild image drew   *1520*

For perjured Sinon, whose enchanting story

The credulous old Priam after slew;

Whose words, like wildfire, burnt the shining glory

Of rich-built Ilion, that the skies were sorry,

    And little stars shot from their fixed places,   *1525*

    When their glass fell wherein they view'd their faces.

(1513—1526)

217

1513. confirmed: 冥顽成性

1514. seeming just: 俨然正直真诚

1515. therein: 在那里
    ensconced: 隐藏

1517. False-creeping craft: 奸谋
    perjury: 伪证

1518. such black-faced storms: 这样的黑

风暴

218

1521. perjured: 发假誓的
    Sinon: 奸细
    enchanting story: 迷人的故事，
花言巧语

1522. credulous: 轻信的

217

作恶多端坏妖精

道貌岸然装真诚

包藏祸心善隐形　　　　　　　　　　*1515*

多疑善猜难知情

阴险欺诈奸谋成

青天白日黑浪生

圣徒蒙冤罪非轻

218

刻画西农画艺精　　　　　　　　　　*1520*

假誓惑人国王坑

国王轻言早丧生

话如火药烧都城

荣誉化灰天伤情

固定位置落小星　　　　　　　　　　*1525*

明镜破碎难照形

（1513—1526）

1523. shining glory: 赫赫威势
1525. fixed places: 固定位置
1526. When their glass fell: 它们的宝镜
迸落，"宝镜"指特洛伊
wherein: 在哪方面

219

This picture she advisedly perused,

And chid the painter for his wondrous skill,

Saying, some shape in Sinon's was abused;

So fair a form lodged not a mind so ill: *1530*

And still on him she gazed; and gazing still,

   Such signs of truth in his plain face she spied,

   That she concludes the picture was belied.

220

'It cannot be,' quoth she, 'that so much guile'——

She would have said 'can lurk in such a look';   *1535*

But Tarquin's shape came in her mind the while,

And from her tongue 'can lurk' from 'cannot' took:

'It cannot be' she in that sense forsook,

   And turn'd it thus, 'It cannot be, I find,

   But such a face should bear a wicked mind: *1540*

(1527—1540)

219

1527. advisedly: 煞费苦
心地
perused: 细阅

1528. chid: 责骂；责怪
wondrous: 惊人的

1529. some shape in Sinon's was abused:
画错了西农的神情

1530. So fair a form lodged not a mind so ill:
这样正派的外表,容不得那样的坏心

1532. Such signs of truth in his plain face
she spied: 在他朴实的相貌里，她
发现了真诚的明证

1533. the picture was belied: 这幅画画得
不像

219

煞费苦心观图形

画笔神妙怪画工

西农形象非真容

相貌堂堂非奸雄　　　　　　　　　　*1530*

留心细察察不停

画面西农惟真诚

露卿断言画走形

220

她言奸计不可能

想说不藏好外形　　　　　　　　　　*1535*

塔昆影子入脑中

难免代替不可能

她赋新义不可能

本来该事不可能

心恶面善变可能　　　　　　　　　　*1540*

（1527—1540）

220

1534. guile:　狡诈，诡计

1535. lurk:　潜伏

1538. forsook:　遗弃

1540. wicked mind:　邪恶的心机

221

'For even as subtile Sinon here is painted,

So sober-sad, so weary, and so mild,

As if with grief or travail he had fainted,

To me came Tarquin armed; so beguiled

With outward honesty, but yet defiled   *1545*

  With inward vice: as Priam him did Cherish,

  So did I Tarquin; so my Troy did perish.

222

'Look, look, how listening Priam wets his eyes,

To see those borrow'd tears that Sinon sheeds!

Priam, why art thou old, and yet not wise?   *1550*

For every tear he falls a Trojan bleeds:

His eye drops fire, no water thence proceeds;

  Those round clear pearls of his, that move thy pity,

  Are balls of quenchless fire to burn thy city.

(1541—1554)

221

1541. subtile: subtle, 狡诈的

1542. sober-sad: 庄重忧郁
      weary: 疲惫的

1543. travail: 痛苦

1544. beguiled: 欺诈的

1545. defiled: 玷污的

1546. vice: 罪恶

as Priam him did Cherish: 正像普
里阿摩斯接待了他（西农）那样

1547. perish: 覆亡

221

画中狡诈之西农
疲惫严肃又温情
哀伤劳苦发昏中
塔昆见我肖其形
心怀叵测貌真诚　　　　　　　　　　*1545*
模仿国王待西农
塔昆毁我好都城

222

国王倾听湿眼睛
只见假泪阴西农
为何老王事不明　　　　　　　　　　*1550*
每滴假泪兵血红
泪是战火非水清
溜圆珠泪骗同情
不灭火球烧都城

　　　　　　　　　　　　　　　　　　（*1541—1554*）

222

1548. listening: 倾听的

1549. sheeds: 流泪

1551. every tear he falls a Trojan bleeds:
他流的每一滴眼泪，叫一个特洛亚
人流血

1552. no water thence proceeds: 没有水
流出来

1553. round clear pearls: 滚圆清澈的珍珠

1554. balls of quenchless fire: 不灭的火球

223

'Such devils steal effects from lightless hell;   *1555*

For Sinon in his fire doth quake with cold,

And in that cold hot-burning fire doth dwell;

These contraries such unity do hold,

Only to flatter fools, and make them bold:

 So Priam's trust false Sinon's tears doth flatter,   *1560*

 That he finds means to burn his Troy with water.'

224

Here, all enrag'd, such passion her assails,

That patience is quite beaten from her breast.

She tears the senseless Sinon with her nails,

Comparing him to that unhappy guest   *1565*

Whose deed hath made herself herself detest:

 At last she smilingly with this gives o'er;

 'Fool, fool' quoth she, 'his wounds will not be sore.'

(1555—1568)

223

1556. quake: 颤抖

1557. cold hot-burning fire: 寓居在严寒里的烈焰

1558. These contraries such unity do hold: 这些相反的东西如此和谐如一

1559. Only to flatter fools and make them bold: 只能给愚人壮胆，令他们无

所顾忌

1560. Priam's trust false Sinon's tears doth flatter: 西农的泪水使普里阿莫斯深信不疑

224

1562. enrag'd: enraged, 怒火如焚

such passion her assails: 她这样愤

223

魔鬼盗宝于幽冥　　　　　　　　　　*1555*
火烧冷战有西农
熊熊烈焰严寒中
和谐事物不相容
蠢人壮胆敢胡行
国王因泪信西农　　　　　　　　　　*1560*
西农泪水烧都城

224

言讲到此动感情
原有耐心不在胸
抓破画中西农形
西农犹如卿灾星　　　　　　　　　　*1565*
厌恨之火心中生
随后微笑停愚行
傻子撕他他不疼

（*1555—1568*）

激的情绪涌起
1564. the senseless Sinon: 这个无知觉的西农
1566. made herself detest: 使他厌恶自己
1567. give o'er: 结束
1568. sore: 痛

225

Thus ebbs and flows the current of her sorrow,

And time doth weary time with her complaining   *1570*

She looks for night, and then she longs for morrow,

And both she thinks too long with her remaining;

Short time seems long in sorrow's sharp sustaining:

   Though woe be heavy, yet it seldom sleeps;

   And they that watch see time how slow it creeps.   *1575*

226

Which all this time hath overslipp'd her thought.

That she with painted images hath spent;

Being from the feeling of her own grief brought

By deep surmise of others' detriment;

Losing her woes in shows of discontent.   *1580*

   It easeth some, though none it ever cured,

   To think their dolour others have endured.

(1569—1582)

225

1570. time doth weary time: 时间使时间感到厌倦

1571. morrow: 明天

1572. remaining: 作伴

1573. sorrow s sharp sustaining: 痛苦煎熬

1574. Though woe be heavy, yet it seldom sleeps: 悲哀虽然沉重，他却不肯睡眠

1575. they that watch see time how slow it creeps: 不眠的人们知晓时间爬得多慢

226

1576. overslipp'd: 溜走

225

潮涨潮落比悲情

时间听悲露倦容　　　　　　　　　　　*1570*

盼来黑夜盼天明

二者长伴都不行

短时显长极痛生

悲哀沉重睡不成

失眠观时蜗牛行　　　　　　　　　　　*1575*

226

时间溜去无影踪

她观油画痛伤情

揣测他人痛苦中

忘掉自己苦难情

画内画外分不清　　　　　　　　　　　*1580*

不能根除痛减轻

自己苦痛他人经

（1569—1582）

1578. from…brought:　brought away, 忘掉
1579. surmise:　揣测，想象
　　　detriment:　伤害，不幸
1580. discontent:　悲苦
1581. easeth some:　有些缓解

227

But now the mindful messenger, come hack,

Brings home his lord and other company:

Who finds his Lucrece clad in mourning black;   *1585*

And round about her tear-distained eye

Blue circles streamed, like rainbows in the sky:

    These water-galls in her dim element

    Foretell new storms to those already spent.

228

Which when her sad-beholding husband saw,   *1590*

Amazedly in her sad face he stares:

Her eyes, though sod in tears, lookt red and raw,

Her lively colour kill'd with deadly cares.

He hath no power to ask her how she fares;

    Both stood, like old acquaintance in a trance,   *1595*

    Met far from home, wondering each other's chance.

(1583—1596)

227
1583. the mindful messenger: 谨慎的信差
1585. clad: 穿衣
    mourning black: 黑色丧服
1586. tear-distained eye: 泪汪汪的眼睛
1587. streamed: 展开
1588. water-galls: 虹彩
    dim element: 阴暗的天空; 露克丽

丝的面孔
1589. those already spent: 那些已消歇的

228
1590. her sad-beholding husband 她面色
    严肃的丈夫
1592. sod in tears: 被泪水浸着
    red and raw: 红肿

227

小心信差回家中

几位贵客陪主公

发现穿黑悲露卿 　　　　　　*1585*

蓝圈圈绕泪眼睛

好像彩虹架天空

预报不祥两道虹

新的风暴要发生

228

严肃丈夫见此情 　　　　　　*1590*

惊恐注视悲惨形

眼眶泪烫肿又红

绝望褪尽粉面容

无力询问妻近情

故旧伫立迷惘中 　　　　　　*1595*

异地不知彼影踪

（1583—1596）

1593. deadly cares: 极度哀伤

1594. fares: 过活

1595. in a trance: 恍惚地；昏睡状态

1596. wondering each others chance: 不知
　　　彼此的去迹来踪

229

At last he takes her by the bloodless hand,

And thus begins: 'What uncouth ill event

Hath thee befall'n, that thou dost trembling stand?

Sweet love, what spite hath thy fair colour spent?   *1600*

Why art thou thus attired in discontent?

　　Unmask, dear dear, this moody heaviness,

　　And tell thy grief, that we may give redress.'

230

Three times with sighs she gives her sorrow fire,

Ere once she can discharge one word of woe: *1605*

At length address'd to answer his desire,

She modestly prepares to let them know

Her honour is ta'en prisoner by the foe;

　　While Collatine and his consorted lords

　　With sad attention long to hear her words.   *1610*

(1597—1610)

229
1598. uncouth:　不知道的
1599. befall'n:　降临
1600. spite:　伤害
　　　fair colour:　妍丽血色
1601. attired:　穿
1602. Unmask:　揭开
　　　moody heaviness:　愁云惨雾

1603. redress:　治疗

230
1605. discharge:　喷吐
1606. address'd:　诉说
1609. his consorted lords:　同来的贵族
1610. sad attention:　沉重的关注心情

229

拉住纤手问真情
手无血色何苦衷
站着发抖何灾星
为何褪尽娇丽容　　　　　　　　　　　1600
身穿丧服为何情
亲人诉冤我倾听
我们救你出火坑

230

未诉悲哀叹三声
欲诉悲哀说不成　　　　　　　　　　　1605
最后听从科拉廷
含羞让人知真情
强敌毁她名节清
夫君会同众友朋
心情沉重要听明　　　　　　　　　　　1610

（1597—1610）

231

And now this pale swan in her watery nest

Begins the sad dirge of her certain ending:

'Few words,' quoth she, 'shall fit the trespass best,

Where no excuse can give the fault amending:

In me moe woes than words are now depending;　　　　*1615*

　　And my laments would be drawn out too long,

　　To tell them all with one poor tired tongue.

232

'Then be this all the task it hath to say:

Dear husband, in the interest of thy bed

A stranger came, and on that pillow lay　　　　*1620*

Where thou wast wont to rest thy weary head;

And what wrong else may be imagined

　　By foul enforcement might he done to me,

　　From that, alas, thy Lucrece is not free.

(1611—1624)

231

1611. pale swan:　惨白的天鹅
1612. dirge:　哀歌，挽歌
1613. trespass:　罪行
1615. moe:　more, 更多的
　　　depending:　pending, 迫近的
1617. poor tired tongue:　疲惫的舌头

232

1618. be this all the task it hath to say:　这些话就是我必须说出的全部
1619. in the interest of thy bed:　你的床位
1621. wont:　惯常于
1623. foul enforcement:　卑污的胁迫
1624. alas:　哎呀

231

惨白天鹅水巢中
临近死亡哀歌声
勿需多言讲罪行
没有借口能宽容
话短悲长痛心中　　　　　　　　*1615*
疲惫舌头讲冤情
我要哭诉长时听

232

话要简练夫君听
你有卧榻本干净
生人来睡歇身形　　　　　　　　*1620*
你有枕头本清静
生人强暴我伤情
灾祸临头躲不成
露克丽丝弱身形

（*1611—1624*）

233

'For in the dreadful dead of dark midnight,   *1625*

With shining falchion in my chamber came

A creeping creature, with a flaming light,

And softly cried, "Awake, thou Roman dame,

And entertain my love; else lasting shame

　　On thee and thine this night I will inflict,   *1630*

　　If thou my love's desire do contradict.

234

' "For some hard-favour'd groom of thine," quoth he,

"Unless thou yoke thy liking to my will,

I'll murder straight, and then I'll slaughter thee,

And swear I found you where you did fulfil   *1635*

The loathsome act of lust, and so did kill

　　The lechers in their deed: this act will he

　　My fame, and thy perpetual infamy."

(1625—1638)

233

1625. dreadful dead: 阴森可怖静悄悄

1626. falchion: 刀，剑

1629. entertain my love: 接受我的爱

1630. inflict: 使承受

1631. contradict: 反抗

234

1632. hard-favour'd groom: 丑陋的奴才

1633. yoke: 使听命

1635. swear: 宣称

1636. loathsome: 讨厌的

1637. lechers: 好色的人

233

| 可怕子夜黑暗中 | *1625* |

一人举烛而潜行

侵我寝处短剑明

低唤罗马贵妇名

快来接受他爱情

若要违抗辱门庭　　　　　　*1630*

家族长蒙坏名声

234

先杀小厮手无情

不遂他愿万不能

再夺妻命辱妻名

主仆幽会辱门庭　　　　　　*1635*

被人撞见刀无情

杀死二人得美名

妻得坏名洗不清

（*1625—1638*）

235

'With this, I did begin to start and cry;

And then against my heart he set his sword,   *1640*

Swearing, unless I took all patiently,

I should not live to speak another word;

So should my shame still rest upon record,

    And never be forgot in mighty Rome

      Th' adulterate death of Lucrece and her groom.   *1645*

236

'Mine enemy was strong, my poor self weak,

And far the weaker with so strong a fear:

My bloody judge forbade my tongue to speak;

No rightful plea might plead for justice there:

His scarlet lust came evidence to swear   *1650*

    That my poor beauty had purloin'd his eyes;

    And when the judge is robb'd, the prisoner dies.

(1639—1652)

235

1640. against my heart he set his sword: 他用刀直抵我的心窝

1641. I took all patiently: 除非我一切依了他

1644. mighty Rome: 伟大的罗马

1645. adulterate death: 私通而亡

236

1647. so strong a fear: 如此害怕

1648. bloody judge: 凶蛮残忍的法官
    forbade: 禁止

1649. rightful plea: 公正的辩士
    plead: 据理力争

1650. scarlet lust: 猩红的肉欲
    came evidence: 当证人

1651. purloin'd: 偷窃

235

听言欲发呼叫声
他以尖刀抵妻胸   *1640*
声言倘若不顺从
立夺妻命冤不鸣
罗马史上留坏名
露克丽丝有奸情
勾引仆人淫荡行   *1645*

236

贱荆懦弱敌强横
强横恐怖妻无能
法官不容妻辩明
律师不辩心不公
猩红肉欲诱眼睛   *1650*
发誓妻美灾祸生
法官被骗囚死刑

（1639—1652）

237

'O, teach me how to make mine own excuse!

Or, at the least, this refuge let me find,—

Though my gross blood be stain'd with this abuse,　　　*1655*

Immaculate and spotless is my mind;

That was not forced; that never was inclined

　　To accessary yieldings, but still pure

　　Doth in her poison'd closet yet endure.'

238

Lo, here, the hopeless merchant of this loss,　　　*1660*

With head declined, and voice damm'd up with woe,

With sad-set eyes, and wretched arms across,

From lips dew-waxen pale begins to blow

The grief away that stops his answer so:

　　But, wretched as he is, he strives in vain;　　　*1665*

　　What he breathes out his breath drinks up again.

（*1653—1666*）

237

1653. make mine own excuse: 为我自己辩护

1654. refuge:　避难；权益之计

1655. gross blood:　血肉之躯
　　　abuse：罪行，虐待

1656. Immaculate：纯洁的

1658. accessary yieldings：倾向于做帮凶

1659. Doth in her poison'd closet yet endure：在已遭败坏的胸膛里，它依然不屈如故

238

1661. damm'd up：哽塞

1662. sad-set eyes：眼神凄恻而凝固

237

呜呼教妻申冤情

至少妻想痛减轻

污染妻身此罪行　　　　　　　　　　　*1655*

心地纯洁似水晶

不受强暴不帮凶

身躯受辱心灵清

永葆清纯重操行

238

请看商人亏营生　　　　　　　　　　　*1660*

垂头哽咽不作声

眼睛凄惨手抚胸

嘴唇如蜡褪鲜红

吹气哀痛不言中

终日徒劳苦苦撑　　　　　　　　　　　*1665*

呼气吸气煎熬中

　　　　　　　　　　　　　　　　　(1653—1666)

---

wretched arms across:　不幸的双 　　　　　重新吸回
臂抱起

1663. dew-waxen pale:　苍白如蜡

1666. what he breathes out his breath drinks
up again:　刚叹一口气，吸气时又

239

As through an arch the violent roaring tide

Outruns the eye that doth behold his haste,

Yet in the eddy boundeth in his pride

Back to the strait that forc'd him on so fast;   *1670*

In rage sent out, recalled in rage being past:

    Even so his sighs, his sorrows, make a saw,

    To push grief on, and hack the same grief draw.

240

Which speechless woe of his poor she attendeth,

And his untimely frenzy thus awaketh: *1675*

'dear lord, thy sorrow to my sorrow lendeth

Another power; no flood by raining slaketh.

My woe too sensible thy passion maketh

    More feeling-painful: let it, then, suffice

    To drown one woe, one pair of weeping eyes.   *1680*

(1667—1680)

239
1667. arch: 拱门
1668. Outruns: 超过
1669. eddy: 漩涡
      boundeth: 跳动
1670. strait: 狭窄的通道
1671. recalled in rage being past: 又怒气
    冲冲的退转

1672. make a saw: 有如拉锯
1673. To push grief on，and back the same
    grief draw: 驱使悲痛出动，又引这
    悲痛回还

240
1674. poor she: 可怜的露克丽丝
1675. frenzy: 狂乱

239

波浪呼啸过桥孔
水流太速耀眼睛
水成漩涡又升腾
水面狭窄急急冲   *1670*
急出急收急流程
哀叹拉锯前后倾
怨气进出不吱声

240

可怜女子痛无声
唤醒昏迷科拉廷   *1675*
夫君愁苦我新生
大雨激清势不轻
我有悲哀夫同情
格外难堪格外疼
淹没悲苦双眼睛   *1680*

（1667—1680）

1677. no flood by raining slaketh：激流不
　　因雨而把速度降低
1679. suffice：满足

241

'And for my sake, when I might charm thee so,

For she that was thy Lucrece,——now attend me:

Be suddenly revenged on my foe,

Thine, mine, his own: suppose thou dost defend me

From what is past: the help that thou shalt lend me   *1685*

   Comes all too late, yet let the traitor die;

   For sparing justice feeds iniquity.

242

'But ere I name him, you fair lords,' quoth she,

Speaking to those that came with Collatine,

'Shall plight your honourable faiths to me,   *1690*

With swift pursuit to venge this wrong of mine;

For 'tis a meritorious fair design

   To chase injustice with revengeful arms:

   Knights, by their oaths, should right poor ladies' harms.'

(1681—1694)

241

1681. charm: 对……有魅力

1682. now attend me: 现在请你注意听
我说

1684. his own: 他自身的仇敌

1687. For sparing justice feeds iniquity:
太仁慈只能助长邪恶

242

1688. fair lords: 诸位大人

1690. plight: 保证

1691. swift: 迅速

1692. meritorious: 有功的

1693. chase injustice with revengeful arms:
用复仇的武器除奸

1694. Knights, by their oaths, should right
poor ladies, harms: 骑士们们凭
着誓言应该救助柔弱夫人的不幸

241

为我魅力为我情
请你注意你露卿
报仇雪恨如雷霆
我俩仇敌毁前程
护我免辱科拉廷   *1685*
来迟灭敌不留情
助长不义滥宽容

242

我要指出仇敌名
我求大人保真诚
帮助朋友科拉廷   *1690*
迅速报仇洗冤情
我力除奸道义明
众人称赞侠义行
骑士护女铲不平

（1681—1694）

243

At this request, with noble disposition   *1695*

Each present lord began to promise aid,

As bound in knighthood to her imposition,

Longing to hear the hateful foe bewrayed.

But she, that yet her sad task hath not said,

   The protestation stops. 'O, speak,' quoth she,   *1700*

   'How may this forced stain be wiped from me?'

244

'What is the quality of mine offence,

Being constrained with dreadful circumstance?

May my pure mind with the foul act dispense,

My low-declined honour to advance?   *1705*

May any terms acquit me from this chance?

   The poison'd fountain clears itself again;

   And why not I from this compelled stain?'

(1695—1708)

243
1695. noble disposition: 慷慨的气质
1697. As bound in knighthood to her
     imposition: 对于她这项吩咐，
     骑士们义不容辞
1698. bewrayed: 泄露，暴露
1700. protestation: 主张
1701. forced stain: 强加的耻辱

244
1702. quality: 类型
1703. constrained: 强逼
1704. dispense: 赦免
1705. low-declined honor: 低落的名声
1706. terms: 申辩
     acquit: 宣判无罪
1708. compelled stain: 强加的污浊

243

各位大人慷慨情　　　　　　　　　　1695
答应助女铲不平
骑士行侠大道成
盼她快说仇敌名
悲惨任务来说明
止住誓言智露卿　　　　　　　　　　1700
被逼蒙羞如何平

244

我有罪过威逼成
罪过属于何类型
心纯能免我罪名
重振低落之名声　　　　　　　　　　1705
申辨可免我罪刑
泉源污染可澄清
为何难说受辱名

（1695—1708）

245

With this, they all at once began to say,

Her body's stain her mind untainted clears;　　　　　*1710*

While with a joyless smile she turns away

The face, that map which deep impression bears

Of hard misfortune, carved in it with tears.

　　'No, no,' quoth she, 'no dame, hereafter living,

　　By my excuse shall claim excuse's giving.'　　　*1715*

246

Here with a sigh, as if her heart would break,

She throws forth Tarquin's name: 'He, he,' she says,

But more than 'he' her poor tongue could not speak;

Till after many accents and delays,

Untimely breathings, sick and short assays,　　　　*1720*

　　She utters this, 'He, he, fair lords, 'tis he

　　That guides this hand to give this wound to me.

(1709—1722)

245
1710. untainted: 清洁
1712. deep impression: 深深的印痕
1714. no dame，hereafter living: 决不让以后的贵妇
1715. By my excuse shall claim excuse's giving: 以我的失足为借口，要求宽恕其失误

246
1719. many accents and delays: 经过多少次迟延，声调的多少次变化
1720. Untimely breathings, sick and short assays: 多少次非时的喘息。衰惫而短促的挣扎
1722. wound: 自杀

245

听此大家语同声
心纯体污可洗清　　　　　　　　*1710*
苦笑转脸有露卿
苦难皱纹折磨成
恶运眼泪雕刻功
以后妇女有冤情
别以我例求宽容　　　　　　　　*1715*

246

心要爆炸长叹声
说出塔昆恶姓名
舌头疲弱难说清
多次延搁变调声
急促喘息无力挣　　　　　　　　*1720*
诸位大人要听清
他手逼我了残生

　　　　　　　　　　　　　（1709—1722）

247

Even here she sheathed in her harmless breast
A harmful knife, that thence her soul unsheathed:
That blow did bail it from the deep unrest   *1725*
Of that polluted prison where it breathed:
Her contrite sighs unto the clouds bequeathed
  Her winged sprite, and through her wounds doth fly
  Life's lasting date from cancell'd destiny.

248

Stone-still, astonisht with this deadly deed,   *1730*
Stood Collatine and all his lordly crew;
Till Lucrece' father, that beholds her bleed,
Himself on her self-slaughter'd body threw;
And from the purple fountain Brutus drew
  The murderous knife, and, as it left the place,   *1735*
  Her blood, in poor revenge, held it in chase.

(1723—1736)

247
1723. sheathed: 入鞘
1724. thence: 从那里起
    unsheathed: 出鞘
1725. bail: 保释
1726. polluted prison: 受辱的躯体
1727. contrite: 悔悟的
    bequeathed: 遗赠

1728. sprite: 精神; 灵魂
1729. destiny: 命运

248
1730. deadly deed: 惨变
1731. lordly crew: 那一些贵人
1732. her bleed: 他鲜血涌溢

247

有害刀插无辜胸
灵魂出鞘出牢笼
一刀灵魂不安宁　　　　　　　　　　*1725*
脏污监牢逃魂灵
愧恨悲欢魂灵升
摒弃毁废我一生
直上云霄享永恒

248

如石呆立因震惊　　　　　　　　　　*1730*
诸位大人科拉廷
父亲看见鲜血红
扑向女儿老泪横
布鲁特斯拔刀锋
刀离源泉血殷红　　　　　　　　　　*1735*
刀拔血追报仇情

（*1723—1736*）

1733. threw:　扑
1734. purple fountain:　殷红泉源
　　　Brutus:　布鲁特斯，露克丽丝之父
1736. poor revenge:　可怜的复仇
　　　held it in chase:　奔出来向他追击

781

249

And bubbling from her breast, it doth divide

In two slow rivers, that the crimson blood

Circles her body in on every side,

Who, like a late-sacked island, vastly stood   *1740*

Bare and unpeopled in this fearful flood.

   Some of her blood still pure and red remain'd,

   And some lookt black, and that false Tarquin stain'd,

250

About the mourning and congealed face

Of that black blood a watery rigol goes,   *1745*

Which seems to weep upon the tainted place:

And ever since, as pitying Lucrece' woes,

Corrupted blood some watery token shows;

   And blood untainted still doth red abide,

   Blushing at that which is so putrefied.   *1750*

(1737—1750)

249
1737. bubbling: 冒泡的；滔滔不绝的
1738. crimson: 殷红，深红
1740. late-sacked island: 刚遭洗劫的岛
1741. bare: 裸体的。据文艺复兴肖像
    画，露克丽丝裸体自尽
    fearful flood: 可怕的洪水

250

1744. congealed face: 凝结的表面
1745. rigol: 圈
1746. tainted place: 污秽的地方
1747. pitying Luerece: 怜悯露克丽丝
1748. Corrupted blood: 污血
    watery token: 水的特征
1749. blood untainted: 纯洁的血
    abide: 坚持
1750. putrefied: 污秽的

249

殷红血液流出胸

缓缓流动两股成

环绕周身血泊红

她像荒岛洗劫空　　　　　　　　　*1740*

岛上居民已无踪

部分血液纯净红

部分污黑罪犯形

250

黑血不流已固凝

周边一圈血水清　　　　　　　　　*1745*

眼泪奔涌污染生

污血渗水怜露卿

从此水浆渗永恒

未遭污染血鲜红

如见污染难为情　　　　　　　　　*1750*

　　　　　　　　　　　　　　　（*1737—1750*）

251

'Daughter, dear daughter,' old Lucretius cries,
'That life was mine which thou hast here deprived.
If in the child the father's image lies,
Where shall I live now Lucrece is unlived?
Thou wast not to this end from me derived.   *1755*

    If children pre-decease progenitors,
    We are their offspring, and they none of ours.

252

'Poor broken glass, I often did behold
In thy sweet semblance my old age new born;
But now that fair fresh mirror, dim and old,   *1760*
Shows me a bare-boned death by time outworn:
O, from thy cheeks my image thou hast torn,
    And shiver'd all the beauty of my glass,
    That I no more can see what once I was.

(1751—1764)

251
1752. deprived: 夺去
1755. derived: 派生
1756. predecease: 比……先死
    progenitors: 祖先

252
1760. fair fresh mirror: 美好光洁的明镜
    dim and old: 晦暗无光
1761. bare-bond death: 骷髅
1763. shiver'd: 打碎

251

父亲呼女不欲生
生命被夺属老翁
孩子身上父身形
女儿已死我何生
如此结局生露卿   *1755*
孩子先死父母生
孩子先辈父继承

252

姣好影像破镜中
常见女儿青春生
光洁明镜灰朦胧   *1760*
照出骷髅衰年翁
女儿面颊毁我容
迷人宝镜碎片成
年轻风采付西风

(*1751—1764*)

253

'O time, cease thou thy course, and last no longer,   *1765*

If they surcease to be that should survive.

Shall rotten death make conquest of the stronger,

And leave the faltering feeble souls alive?

The old bees die, the young possess their hive:

    Then live, sweet Lucrece, live again, and see   *1770*

    Thy father die, and not thy father thee.'

254

By this, starts Collatine as from a dream,

And bids Lucretius give his sorrow place;

And then in key-cold Lucrece' bleeding stream

He falls, and bathes the pale fear in his face,   *1775*

And counterfeits to die with her a space;

    Till manly shame bids him possess his breath,

    And live to be revenged on her death.

(1765—1778)

253

1766. surcease: 让死亡

    that: who

1767. rotten death: 腐恶的死亡

    make conquest of: 征服

1768. faltering feeble souls: 摇摇欲坠的，孱弱的生命

254

1773. bids: 请求

    Lucretius: 露克瑞修斯，露克丽丝之父

1774. key-cold: 冰冷的

1775. bathes: 洗

1776. counterfeits: 肖像

    a space: 一阵子

253

鸣呼时间脚步停   *1765*

死者原来该长生

死神夺走强壮命

任由衰弱延残生

蜂死蜂房让年轻

应该你活乖露卿   *1770*

不该你死为父生

254

如梦方醒科拉廷

求妻允他放悲声

倒于冰冷血泊中

洗他惊恐灰面容   *1775*

痛不欲生陪露卿

男子廉耻脑子清

报仇雪恨活今生

         （1765—1778）

1777. manly shame bids him possess his
  breath: 男人的羞恶心，促使他恢
  复镇静

255

The deep vexation of his inward soul

Hath served a dumb arrest upon his tongue;   *1780*

Who, mad that sorrow should his use control,

Or keep him from heart-easing words so long,

Begins to talk; but through his lips do throng

    Weak words, so thick come in his poor heart's aid,

    That no man could distinguish what he said.   *1785*

256

Yet sometimes 'Tarquin' was pronounced plain,

But through his teeth, as if the name he tore.

This windy tempest, till it blow up rain,

Held back his sorrow's tide, to make it more;

At last it rains, and busy winds give o'er: *1790*

    The son and father weep with equal strife

    Who should weep most, for daughter or for wife.

(1779—1792)

255
1779. vexation: 苦恼，悲愤
1781. mad that sorrow should his use
    control: 愤恨悲哀控制了他们的
    活动
1782. heart-easing: 和缓心情
1783. throng: 密集
1784. thick: 口齿不清的

256
1786. plain: 清楚
1788. windy tempest: 狂暴的悲风
1790. busy winds give o'er: 风势减去
1791. equal strife: 同样的努力

255

深深痛苦刺心灵
舌头僵硬不成声　　　　　　　　*1780*
控制活动恨发疯
不能说话缓心情
微弱语言双唇中
想宽他心太匆匆
模糊咕哝难听清　　　　　　　　*1785*

256

偶有塔昆二字清
齿间迸出撕裂声
风暴欲来大雨倾
悲哀如潮奋力冲
风势减去大雨停　　　　　　　　*1790*
父亲女婿放悲声
哭女哭妻痛伤情

　　　　　　　　　　　　　　（*1779—1792*）

257

The one doth call her his, the other his,

Yet neither may possess the claim they lay.

The father says 'she's mine.' 'O, mine she is,'   *1795*

Replies her husband: 'do not take away

My sorrow's interest; let no mourner say

    He weeps for her, for she was only mine,

    And only must be wail'd by Collatine.'

258

'O,' quoth Lucretius, 'I did give that life   *1800*

Which she too early and too late hath spill'd.'

'Woe, woe,' quoth Collatine, 'she was my wife,

I owed her, and 'tis mine that she hath kill'd.'

'My daughter' and 'my wife' with clamours fill'd

    The dispersed air, who, holding Lucrece' life,   *1805*

    Answer'd their cries, 'my daughter' and 'my wife'.

(1793—1806)

257

1794. neither may possess the claim they lay: 两个都无法享有他们自许的权益

1797. My sorrow's interest: 我悲恸的专利

1799. wailed: 哀悼，悲痛

258

1801. too early and too late: 太早又太迟
    spilled: 抛洒

1803. 'tis mine that she hath kill'd: 她毁的是我的财产

1804. clamours: 喧嚷

1805. dispersed air: 震破了天
    who: which

257

两个都说拥露卿

无人独享亲爱情

父说我有女露卿　　　　　　　　　　*1795*

夫说露卿我心疼

各位悲哀是真情

露卿属我科拉廷

我该为她痛失声

258

父哭生下女露卿　　　　　　　　　　*1800*

太早太迟女丧生

夫哭我娶妻露卿

我拥烈妻竟轻生

我女我妻凄然声

露卿魂灵天收容　　　　　　　　　　*1805*

我女我妻震长空

（*1793—1806*）

259

Brutus, who pluckt the knife from Lucrece' side,

Seeing such emulation in their woe,

Began to clothe his wit in state and pride,

Burying in Lucrece' wound his folly's show.　　　　*1810*

He with the Romans was esteemed so

　　As silly-jeering idiots are with kings,

　　For sportive words and uttering foolish things:

260

But now he throws that shallow habit by,

Wherein deep policy did him disguise;　　　　*1815*

And arm'd his long-hid wits advisedly,

To check the tears in Collatinus' eyes.

' Thou wronged lord of Rome,' quoth he, 'arise:

　　Let my unsounded self, supposed a fool,

　　Now set thy long-experienced wit to school. '　　　　*1820*

（1807—1820）

259

1808. emulation: 竞赛; 争执

1809. clothe his wit in state and pride:
　　　 给滑稽谈吐穿上华丽的衣服

1810. folly's show: 傻相

1811. esteemed: 评价

1812. silly: 愚蠢的
　　　 jeering: 嘲弄

1813. sportive: 嬉戏的

260

1814. by: away, 去掉

1815. Wherein: 在哪方面
　　　 deep policy: 深谋远虑
　　　 disguise: 做出

1816. long-hid: 深藏已久的

259

布鲁特斯拔刀锋
二人悲痛伤露卿
他从愚钝变英明
露卿伤处傻隐形   *1810*
罗马人中蠢才形
酷似弄巨王官中
信口开河小聪明

260

放弃轻薄之作风
深谋远虑露真形   *1815*
拿出深藏真聪明
止住哭泣科拉廷
罗马大将身要挺
我非蠢才露真容
我对群贤话言明   *1820*

（*1807—1820*）

1817. check: 制止
1818. wronged lord of Rome: 受害的罗
     马武将
1819. unsounded self: 高深莫测
1820. set thy long-experienced wit to
     school: 教训你这阅历深的聪明人

261

'Why, Collatine, is woe the cure for woe?

Do wounds help wounds, or grief help grievous deeds?

Is it revenge to give thyself a blow

For his foul act by whom thy fair wife bleeds?

Such childish humour from weak minds proceeds:　　*1825*

　Thy wretched wife mistook the matter so,

　To slay herself, that should have slain her foe.

262

'Courageous Roman, do not steep thy heart

In such relenting dew of lamentations;

But kneel with me, and help to bear thy part,　　*1830*

To rouse our Roman gods with invocations,

That they will suffer these abominations,

　Since Rome herself in them doth stand disgraced,

　By our strong arms from forth her fair streets chased.

(*1821—1834*)

161

1822. grievous deeds: 痛心的事迹

1824. foul act: 卑污罪咎

1825. weak minds: 软弱的心头
　　proceeds: 发出

1827. slay herself that should have slain her
　　foe: 竟然自杀了，她本应该杀她
　　的敌人

262

1828. steep: 浸泡

1829. relenting: 缓和的
　　dew: 露水；泪水
　　lamentations: 悲伤；恸哭

1830. bear thy part: 尽你一份责任

1831. rouse our Roman gods with
　　invocations: 用祈祷惊起罗马天神

261

难道苦能救苦情

伤不治伤愁不轻

恶人害妻大罪行

尖刀岂能对己胸

懦弱行为像顽童　　　　　　　　*1825*

你妻薄命有错行

刚刀杀敌莫轻生

262

奉劝罗马众将听

伤心切莫太痴情

和我同跪洗冤情　　　　　　　　*1830*

祈祷罗马天神惊

恶人污辱失尊荣

天神俯允动刀兵

罗马大街灭奸雄

（1821—1834）

1832. abominations: 憎恨
1833. stand disgraced: 失掉光辉
1834. By our strong arms from forth her fair
　　　streets chased: 从罗马干净的街衢
　　　上，把恶人驱除干净

263

'Now, by the Capitol that we adore,   *1835*

And by this chaste blood so unjustly stained,

By heaven's fair sun that breeds the fat earth's store,

By all our country rights in Rome maintained,

And by chaste Lucrece' soul that late complained

    Her wrongs to us, and by this bloody knife,   *1840*

    We will revenge the death of this true wife.'

264

This said, he struck his hand upon his breast,

And kist the fatal knife, to end his vow;

And to his protestation urged the rest,

Who, wondering at him, did his words allow: *1845*

Then jointly to the ground their knees they bow;

    And that deep vow, which Brutus made before,

    He doth again repeat, and that they swore.

(1835—1848)

263

1835. Capitol: 罗马小山上的朱庇特神殿
     adore: 崇拜；敬慕

1836. chaste blood: 贞洁的血迹

1837. the fat earth's store: 丰腴大地孕育
     了五谷

1838. all our country rights in Rome
     maintained: 罗马国土固有的权益
     和法制

1839. late complained: 刚才声冤的

264

1843. fatal knife: 致命的尖刀

1844. protestation: 声明；断言

1845. wondering at: 对……惊异
     did his words allow: 赞成他的
     意见

1846. bow: 鞠躬

263

指着神庙誓愿同　　　　　　　*1835*
贞洁受辱血迹腥
哺育万物太阳红
罗马权利国和平
露克丽丝新冤情
血染尖刀血迹红　　　　　　　*1840*
报仇雪恨告露卿

264

英雄说完手捶胸
亲吻尖刀誓词终
敦促他人步调同
众人大惊齐赞成　　　　　　　*1845*
同跪在地表志诚
布鲁特斯言众声
重复誓愿洗冤情

（*1835—1848*）

265

When they had sworn to this advised doom,

They did conclude to bear dead Lucrece thence,   *1850*

To show her bleeding body thorough Rome,

And so to publish Tarquin's foul offence:

Which being done with speedy diligence,

   The Romans plausibly did give consent

   To Tarquin's everlasting banishment.   *1855*

(1849—1855)

265

1849. advised doom:　深思熟虑的主张
1850. thence:　从那里起
1851. thorough:　throughout, 贯穿
1852. publish:　宣布
1853. speedy diligence:　雷厉风行的义举
1854. plausibly:　欢呼地
    consent:　赞成

265

誓愿共图大业成
露卿遗体罗马行   *1850*
鲜血淋漓诉冤情
宣布塔昆万恶行
干脆利索民赞同
罗马公众恨同声
永赶全家离京城   *1855*

（1849—1855）

IV A LOVER'S COMPLAINT

Ⅳ 情女怨

题解

    原文为 A Lover's Complaint，梁实秋译为《情人怨》，孙法理译为《情女怨》，黄雨石译为《情女怨》。该诗为一遗弃女子的哀怨，故从孙、黄二先生，译为《情女怨》。

1

From off a hill whose concave womb reworded

A plaintful story from a sistering vale,

My spirits t' attend this double voice accorded,

And down I laid to list the sad-tuned tale;

Ere long espied a fickle maid full pale，   5

Tearing of papers, breaking rings a-twain,

Storming her world with sorrow's wind and rain.

2

Upon her head a platted hive of straw，

Which fortified her visage from the sun，

Whereon the thought might think sometime it saw   10

The carcass of a beauty spent and done：

Time had not scythed all that youth begun,

Nor youth all quit；but, spite of heaven's fell rage,

Some beauty peept through lattice of sear'd age．

1

1. concave: 凹的
   womb: 山谷
   reworded: 回响
2. sistering: 相怜的
3. attend: 倾听
   double voice: 回响

accorded: 和谐
4. list: 倾听
5. espied: 看见
   fickle: 感情方面易变的；激动的
6. papers: 情书
   a-twain: 分为二

1

邻山空谷悲歌声
凄惨故事深溪中
反复吟唱吾关注
身卧静听悲苦情
激动姑娘苍白容　　　　　　　5
指环揪掉信撕碎
风雨悲痛风暴中

2

宽边草帽遮面容
挡住骄阳护女红
细察面上透娇媚　　　　　　　10
今日憔悴昔倾城
岁月未销女娉婷
对此娇女天公怒
衰年囚栅窥画屏

2
8. platted: 以辫状编成
　　hive: 蜂巢式帽子
9. fortified: 设防
　　visage: 脸
10. whereon: 在她脸上
　　the thought: 有心人
　　it: the thought, 引申为有心人

11. carcass: 尸体
　　spent and done: 磨损毁灭
12. scythed: 刈倒
13. quit: 消逝
　　spite of: 尽管
　　fell: 凶恶的
14. lattice: 格子窗，喻皱纹
　　sear'd: 凋谢干枯

3

Oft did she heave her napkin to her eyne,　　　　　*15*

Which on it had conceited characters,

Laundering the silken figures in the brine

That season'd woe had pelleted in tears，

And often reading what contents it bears;

As often shrieking undistinguisht woe，　　　　　*20*

In clamours of all size, both high and low.

4

Sometimes her levell'd eyes their carriage ride,

As they did battery to the spheres intend;

Sometimes diverted their poor balls are tied

To th' orbed earth; sometimes they do extend　　　*25*

Their view right on; anon their gazes lend

To every place at once, and, nowhere fixt,

The mind and sight distractedly commixt.

3

15. heave: 举起
    napkin: 手绢
    eyne: 眼睛（复数）
16. conceited: 精妙离奇的
17. Laundering: 冲洗
    brine: 海水
18. season'd: 调味

pelleted: 形成小球
20. shrieking: 尖声叫喊
21. clamours: 喧嚷

4

22. levell'd: 瞄准
    carriage: 炮架
    ride: 移动

3

女捧手绢细端详　　　　　　　　*15*

绢上深情写文章

泪洗丝绣旧图案

悲伤郁结泪闪光

有时细读苦情长

有时呜咽不尽意　　　　　　　　*20*

低泣嚎啕柔情伤

4

有时秀目像炮筒

两弹欲发射苍穹

有时转头向地面

可怜眼球诉苦衷　　　　　　　　*25*

有时直盯不转睛

凝视对象为万物

心眼茫然难寻踪

---

23. battery:　battery, 炮的待发射状态
24. diverted:　转向
　　balls:　眼球
25. orbed earth:　环球，地球
26. anon:　立刻
28. distractedly:　发狂地，精神错乱地
　　commixed:　混合

5

Her hair, nor loose nor tied in formal plat,

Proclaim'd in her a careless hand of pride;   30

For some, untucked, descended her sheaved hat,

Hanging her pale and pined cheek beside;

Some in her threaden fillet still did bide,

And, true to bondage, would not break from thence,

Though slackly braided in loose negligence.   35

6

A thousand favours from a maund she drew

Of amber, crystal, and of beaded jet,

Which one by one she in a river threw,

Upon whose weeping margent she was set;

Like usury, applying wet to wet,   40

Or monarch's hands that lets not bounty fall

Where want cries some, but where excess begs all.

5

29. plat: 辫状物

30. Proclaim'd: 表明
    a careless hand of pride: 骄傲的手懒
    于梳妆

31. untucked: 散开
    sheaved: 打辫编成

32. pined: 憔悴, 消瘦

33. threaden fillet: 纺织的束发带
    bide: 持续

34. true to bondage: 牢牢缚住, 影射信
    守贞操

35. slackly: 懒散地
    braided: 把头发编成辫子地
    loose negligence: 漫不经心, 粗心大
    意, 不修边幅

5

秀发未经精意梳
自持靓丽天然图   *30*
帽边垂下一缕发
遮住面颊苍白枯
缎带挡住发一绺
扎时随意松不了
疏而不漏美人头   *35*

6

篮中珍宝随意扔
玛瑙墨玉紫水晶
一件一件河心落
人呆河泣似无声
洒泪滚利湿万重   *40*
又如昏王赐财物
富者愈富穷愈穷

6

36. maund: 篮子
37. amber: 琥珀
　　beaded jet: 黑玉串珠
39. weeping margent: 潮湿的河岸边
　　set: 坐着

40. usury: 高利贷
　　wet: 眼泪，河流
41. monarch: 帝王
　　bounty: 赐物
42. excess: 富人
　　begs: 贪婪地要求

7

Of folded schedules had she many a one,

Which she perused, sigh'd, tore, and gave the flood;

Crackt many a ring of posied gold and bone,   *45*

Bidding them find their sepulchres in mud;

Found yet moe letters sadly penn'd in blood,

With sleided silk feat and affectedly

Enswathed, and seal'd to curious secrecy.

8

These often bathed she in her fluxive eyes,   *50*

And often kist, and often gan to tear;

Cried, 'O false blood, thou register of lies,

What unapproved witness dost thou bear!

Ink would have seem'd more black and damned here!'

This said, in top of rage the lines she rents,   *55*

Big discontent so breaking their contents.

7
43. schedules: 信件
44. perused: 阅读
45. posied: 刻有诗句的
46. sepulchres: 坟墓
47. moe: more, 更多
48. sleided: 用丝线捆着分开
　　feat: 整洁
49. Enswathed: 捆住, 系住

8
50. fluxive: 流动的
　　fluxive eyes: 两眼的泪水
52. register: 登记注册
53. unapproved: 假的
54. damned: 可恶
55. rents: 撕开

7

书信若干甚整齐
读撕投水伴叹息
铭文指环质金骨　　　　　　　　　45
全被掰碎葬污泥
血书更多写惨凄
缎带捆扎妙精致
漆封牢固保玄机

8

如同眼泪洗情书　　　　　　　　　50
不时亲吻想毁除
呜呼谎言虚伪血
谈何证据无用处
墨水书写更黑污
极度愤怒来读信　　　　　　　　　55
极度不满撕情书

9

A reverend man that grazed his cattle nigh—
Sometime a blusterer, that the ruffle knew
Of court, of city, and had let go by
The swiftest hours, observed as they flew,   *60*
Towards this afflicted fancy fastly drew,
And, privileged by age, desires, to know
In brief the grounds and motives of her woe.

10

So slides he down upon his grained bat,
And comely-distant sits he by her aide;   *65*
When he again desires her, being sat,
Her grievance with his hearing to divide:
If that from him there may be aught applied
Which may her suffering ecstasy assuage,
'Tis promised in the charity of age.   *70*

9
57. reverend: 年老的
    grazed: 放牧
    nigh: 附近
58. blusterer: 好说大话的人
    ruffle: 狂徒
61. afflicted: 折磨，苦恼
    fancy: 女子

    afflicted fancy: 害相思病的泪人儿
63. motives: 原因

10
64. slides: 缓缓坐下
    grained: 磨光的
    bat: 拐杖
65. comely-distant: 恰当的距离

9

附近古稀牧羊人
爱说大话阅历深
宫廷城市大场面
肯学不废好光阴　　　　　　　　　　　*60*
慢步走向断肠人
年迈想知年少女
如此悲伤何起因

10

拐杖上头坐老人
靠近姑娘不靠身
坐稳又将姑娘问　　　　　　　　　　　*65*
愿听根由把忧分
老者尽力又尽心
愿为姑娘减苦痛
年老之人凭善真　　　　　　　　　　　*70*

---

67. divide: 分担
68. aught: 任何事情
 applied: 可用来治疗
 If that from him there may be aught
 applied: 他是否能有什么帮助

69. ecstasy: 出神，销魂，入迷
 assuage: 缓和，减轻
70. charity of age: 老年人的同情心

11

'Father,' she says, 'though in me you behold

The injury of many a blasting hour,

Let it not tell your judgement I am old;

Not age, but sorrow, over me hath power:

I might as yet have been a spreading flower,   *75*

Fresh to myself, if I had self-applied

Love to myself, and to no love beside.

12

'But, woe is me! too early I attended

A youthful suit—it was to gain my grace—

Of one by nature's outwards so commended,   *80*

That maidens' eyes stuck over all his face:

Love lackt a dwelling, and made him her place;

And when in his fair parts she did abide,

She was new lodged, and newly deified.

11
72. blasting: 伤害
75. spreading: opening, 绽放的
76. Fresh to myself: 我无比鲜艳
76—77. if I had self-applied
      Love to myself: 如果我孤芳自赏

12
78. woe: 不幸

attended: 注意
79. suit: 求爱
    grace: 爱情
80. commended: 称赞
81. stuck: 盯着看, 目不转睛地看
82. dwelling: 住所
83. abide: 逗留, 住
84. deified: deify, 把……神化, 崇拜

11

叫声老伯她开言
见我伤痛受熬煎
虽经岁月莫谓老
年龄不比悲凶残
我如吐蕊花苞鲜 75
鲜活自赏慎自爱
岂管他人表爱怜

12

不幸年少不知情
为一青年托终生
惊慕青年好容貌 80
无数姑娘失灵魂
爱无寄托想小生
要趁年轻得真爱
姑娘心安青云行

13

'His browny locks did hang in crooked curls;   *85*

And every light occasion of the wind

Upon his lips their silken parcels hurls.

What's sweet to do, to do will aptly find:

Each eye that saw him did enchant the mind;

For on his visage was in little drawn   *90*

What largeness thinks in Paradise was sawn.

14

'Small show of man was yet upon his chin;

His phoenix down began but to appear,

Like unshorn velvet, on that termless skin,

Whose bare out-bragg'd the web it seem'd to wear: *95*

Yet show'd his visage by that cost more dear,

And nice affections wavering stood in doubt

If best were it as was, or best without.

13

85. locks: 一绺头发

86. occasion: 吹拂

87. parcels: 一绺绺发丝
    hurls: 猛投
    silken parcels: 柔丝般的一绺绺头发

88. What's sweet to do, to do will aptly find:
    aptly, 恰当地。该行诗句意为:要寻开

心,随处都有开心事

89. enchant: 用魔法迷惑;使喜悦

90. visage: 脸,面容
    in little: 细微的小画家

91. largeness: 宏大
    thinks: 设想
    sawn: 看见

13

浅褐发鬓曲低垂   *85*

时有轻风款款吹

发如柔丝唇前偎

要想开心心愿遂

姑娘见他都痴迷

幻想天堂描脸上   *90*

美妙具体又细微

14

男子下巴痕迹新

恰好凤毛细软匀

丝绒覆盖肤细嫩

皮肤夸口原貌真   *95*

脸色因此更显尊

温柔爱情难确定

有须无须孰风神

14

92. small show of man: 青年人刚出现的
　　一点胡须

93. phoenix down: 凤凰的茸毛

94. unshorn: 未修剪的
　　velvet: 天鹅绒
　　termless: 年轻的

95. bare: 光滑柔软

out-bragg'd: 超过
web: 覆盖
wear: 显出

96. that cost more dear: 更显得英俊高贵

97. wavering: 犹豫不决

98. If best were as it was, or best without:
　　是最好有胡须，还是最好没有胡须

15

'His qualities were beauteous as his form,

For maiden-tongued he was, and thereof free;   *100*

Yet, if men moved him, was he such a storm

As oft' twixt May and April is to see,

When winds breathe sweet, unruly though they be.

His rudeness so with his authorized youth

Did livery falseness in a pride of truth.   *105*

16

'Well could he ride, and often men would say,

"That horse his mettle from his rider takes:

Proud of subjection, noble by the sway,

What rounds, what bounds, what course, what stop he makes!"

And controversy hence a question takes,   *110*

Whether the horse by him became his deed,

Or he his manage by the well-doing steed.

15

100. maiden-tongued: 娘娘腔
     thereof: 因此
     free: 讨人喜欢
103. unruly though they be: 狂暴无比
104. authorized: 特许的
105. livery: 穿衣服, 装饰
     falseness: 虚假

16

107. mettle: 气概；精神
     That horse his mettle from his rider
     takes: That horse takes his mettle
     from his rider, 那匹马因骑手而神骏
108. subjection: 驾驭
     sway: 控制
109. course: 马跑
110. controversy: 争论
     hence: 因此

15

性格体格皆诱人

娘娘腔也悦人心 　　　　　　　　*100*

如被惹怒雷霆震

四月五月多风云

柔风狂暴吓煞人

年纪轻轻他粗暴

装扮诚实得众心 　　　　　　　　*105*

16

他善骑马人称奇

骏马健走因他骑

他善驱策善控制

绕跳奔走忽停蹄

众人纷纷提问题 　　　　　　　　*110*

骏马因他露绝技

他因骏马称善骑

17

'But quickly on this side the verdict went:

His real habitude gave life and grace

To appertainings and to ornament,   *115*

Accomplisht in himself, not in his case:

All aids, themselves made fairer by their place,

Came for additions; yet their purposed trim

Pieced not his grace, but were all graced by him.

18

'So on the tip of his subduing tongue   *120*

All kind of arguments and question deep,

All replication prompt, and reason strong,

For his advantage still did wake and sleep:

To make the weeper laugh, the laugher weep,

He had the dialect and different skill,   *125*

Catching all passions in his craft of will:

17
113. verdict: 定论；裁决
114. habitude: 仪态举止
115. appertainings: 所属
     ornament: 服装
116. case: 环境
117. aids: 额外的装饰
118. for: 作为
     trim: 美化装饰

119. Pieced: 增光
     graced: 美化，使优美

18
120. subduing: 征服的
122. All replication prompt: 一切随机应答
123. For: To, 对于
     wake and sleep: 说话或保持沉默
125. dialect: 雄辩技巧
126. craft of will: 说服人的技巧

17

很快决定不迟疑
真才带来真生机
十分优雅多光彩   115
全靠自身无他期
一切随属沾便宜
格外美妙多光彩
原为增奇实益奇

18

能言善辩好口才   120
问题深奥侃侃来
敏捷回答求论证
随时由他来安排
能使悲者笑口开
笑者哭泣他善辩   125
众人同情众开怀

819

19

'That he did in the general bosom reign

Of young, of old; and sexes both enchanted,

To dwell with him in thoughts, or to remain

In personal duty, following where he haunted: *130*

Consents bewitched, ere he desire, have granted;

And dialogued for him what he would say,

Asked their own wills, and made their wills obey.

20

'Many there were that did his picture get,

To serve their eyes, and in it put their mind;   *135*

Like fools that in th' imagination set

The goodly objects which abroad they find

Of lands and mansions, theirs in thought assigned;

And labouring in moe pleasures to bestow them

Than the true gouty landlord which doth owe them.   *140*

19

127. general bosom:　每个人的心
　　reign:　王国

128. enchanted:　迷住

129. dwell:　保持

130. In personal duty:　作他的仆人
　　haunted:　常去

131. Consents:　同意的人

bewitched:　着魔

133. Asked:　要求

20

134. that:　who
　　picture:　画像

136. set:　set forth, 宣布；认为

137. goodly:　吸引人的

19

众人口中地位高
老少男女乐陶陶
着魔粉丝随身侧
时时为他把心操　　　　　　　　　*130*
唯命是听应他招
他未开言已知意
随声附和不用教

20

他之画像属众人
放上眼皮迷在心　　　　　　　　　*135*
傻妞沉醉傻幻想
贪得沃野第连云
富有财产感天神
放在心里找乐趣
真正主人不欢欣　　　　　　　　　*140*

---

objects: 情景，录像　　　　　　bestow: 把……赠与；应用
abroad: 远离家乡的　　　　140. gouty: 痛风的；患风湿病的
138. mansions: 官邸
　　theirs in thought assigned: 想象中属
　　他们所有
139. laboring in moe pleasures: 努力感到
　　更多的欢欣

21

'So many have, that never toucht his hand,

Sweetly supposed them mistress of his heart.

My woeful self, that did in freedom stand,

And was my own fee-simple, not in part,

What with his art in youth, and youth in art,   *145*

Threw my affections in his charmed power,

Reserved the stalk, and gave him all my flower.

22

'Yet did I not, as some my equals did,

Demand of him, nor being desired yielded;

Finding myself in honour so forbid,   *150*

With safest distance I mine honour shielded:

Experience for me many bulwarks builded

Of proofs new-bleeding, which remain'd the foil

Of this false jewel, and his amorous spoil.

21

142. Sweetly supposed: 甜蜜地设想

143. that did in freedom stand: 我完全自由

144. fee-simple: 英国法律上"处置权不受
限制的，绝对所有的不动产"
not in part: 不是部分地

145. What with his art in youth and youth in
art: 由于他青春的风华和美妙的青春

146. charmed power: 魅力

147. Reserved the stalk: 保存了根蒂

21

未摸他手大姑娘

已经献上真心肠

我亦可悲自由女

别人难分一寸香

半由年轻半专长　　　　　　　　*145*

委身与他享魅力

送花留根入梦乡

22

我不去学众姑娘

有求于他欲望强

我守贞操保荣誉　　　　　　　　*150*

保持距离图安详

经验集起铁围墙

鲜血淋漓出证据

假人假义假心肠

22

148. equals:　和我同龄和同等地位的姑娘们

149. yielded:　屈从

152. bulwarks:　堡垒

153. new-bleeding:　血淋淋的
proofs new-bleeding:　最近被毁的姑娘们

foil:　黑暗的

154. false jewel:　假珠宝; 珠宝失色
amorous spoil:　爱情被毁

23

'But, ah, who ever shunn'd by precedent   *155*

The destined ill she must herself assay?

Or forced examples, 'gainst her own content,

To put the by-past perils in her way?

Counsel may stop awhile what will not stay;

For when we rage, advice is often seen   *160*

By blunting us to make our wits more keen.

24

'Nor gives it satisfaction to our blood,

That we must curb it upon others' proof;

To be forbod the sweets that seem so good:

For fear of harms that preach in our behoof.   *165*

O appetite, from judgement stand aloof!

The one a palate hath that needs will taste,

Though Reason weep, and cry, "It is thy last."

23

155. shunn'd: 躲避
    precedent: 先例
156. destined: 注定
    assay: 尝试
157. content: 满足
158. by-past perils: 前人的覆辙
159. cousel: 劝告

awhile: 暂时
161. blunting: 弄钝
    keen: 锋利的

24

163. curb: 控制，约束
    proof: 经验，经历
164. forbod: 禁止

23

谁听劝告去躲灾   *155*
灾祸注定躲不开
勉强警觉讨没趣
前人覆辙后人来
听言偶人暂徘徊
一旦发疯耍蛮横   *160*
忠言逆耳随性来

24

他人虽有痛苦经
不强阻我好心情
诱人禁果难躲避
人们警告不愿听   *165*
欲念理性怎相容
最后一回尝一口
理性哭喊欲不惊

---

    sweets: 美味
165. preach: 讲道，训诫
    behoof: 利益
166. judgement: 原因，理由，理性
    aloof: 避开，远离
167. palate: 味觉，嗜好
    needs: 必须

25

'For further I could say, "This man's untrue,"

And knew the patterns of his foul beguiling;   170

Heard where his plants in others' orchards grew,

Saw how deceits were gilded in his smiling;

Knew vows were ever brokers to defiling;

Thought characters and words merely but art,

And bastards of his foul adulterate heart.   175

26

'And long upon these terms I held my city,

Till thus he 'gan besiege me: "Gentle maid,

Have of my suffering youth some feeling pity,

And be not of my holy vows afraid:

That's to ye sworn to none was ever said;   180

For feasts of love I have been call'd unto,

Till now did ne'er invite, nor never woo.

25

170. patterns: 方法；诡计
     foul: 罪恶的
     beguiling: 消遣性的
171. plants: 孽种
172. deceits: 欺骗

gilded: 镀金
173. brokers: 淫媒
     defiling: 玷污
175. bastards: 私生子；杂种
     adulterate: 通奸的
     foul adulterate heart: 肮脏淫邪心肠

25

我道此人骗人精
手段下流把女坑　　　　　　　　*170*
别人果园孽种养
笑里藏刀装正经
明知誓言老鸹声
情书甜言加蜜语
荒谣无耻孽障生　　　　　　　　*175*

26

由此我意坚守城
终有一天他进攻
姑娘怜我青年苦
静听我誓缘真情
惟对姑娘言心灵　　　　　　　　*180*
我曾赴过婚禧筵
别人未请请爱卿

26
176. city:　贞洁的堡垒
177. besiege:　围攻
178. some feeling pity:　一些怜悯
179. holy vows:　神圣誓言
180. That's:　what is

181. feasts of love:　爱情宴席
182. did ne'er invite, nor never woo:　从来没有请过人，也没有求过婚

27

"'Ail my offences that abroad you see
Are errors of the blood, none of the mind;
Love made them not; with acture they may be,   *185*
Where neither party is nor true nor kind:
They sought their shame that so their shame did find;
And so much less of shame in me remains,
But how much of me their reproach contains.

28

"'Among the many that mine eyes have seen,   *190*
Not one whose flame my heart so much as warm'd,
Or my affection put to the smallest teen,
Or any of my leisures ever charm'd:
Harm have I done to them, but ne'er was harmed;
Kept hearts in liveries, but mine own was free,   *195*
And reign'd, commanding in his monarchy.

27
183. offences: 罪行；过失
     abroad: 公开
184. blood: 欲念
185. acture: 身体行为
186. true: 真情
     kind: 挚爱

187. They: 那些女子
188. so much less of shame in me remains:
     我心中的耻辱感越少
189. reproach: 责备

27

君见公然我罪行
根在欲念非心灵
爱不造孽色造孽　　　　　　　　　　*185*
双方皆无真感情
自找耻辱耻辱生
我之耻辱本有限
他们痛骂他们疯

28

我之所见多女人　　　　　　　　　　*190*
没有热情暖我心
我之感情未伤害
无人搅乱我心神
我害她们我免侵
其心为奴我心避　　　　　　　　　　*195*
高高在上人称君

28
190. the many:　许多姑娘
191. flame:　火焰
　　　warm'd:　温暖
192. teen:　折磨
193. leisures:　休闲
　　　charm'd:　迷惑

194. Harm have I done to them, but ne'er
　　　was harmed:　我害得她们心碎,自
　　　己从未伤感心碎
195. liveries:　仆人衣服
196. reign'd:　称王
　　　commanding:　居高临下的
　　　his monarchy:　国王陛下

29

'"Look here, what tributes wounded fancies sent me,

Of paled pearls and rubies red as blood;

Figuring that they their passions likewise lent me

Of grief and blushes, aptly understood   *200*

In bloodless white and the encrimson'd mood;

Effects of terror and dear modesty,

Encamped in hearts, but fighting outwardly.

30

'"And, lo, behold these talents of their hair,

With twisted metal amorously impleach'd,   *205*

I have received from many a several fair—,

Their kind acceptance weepingly beseech'd,—

With the annexions of fair gems enricht,

And deep-brain'd sonnets that did amplify

Each stone's dear nature, worth, and quality.   *210*

29
197. tributes: 礼物
     wounded facies: 因爱情而心碎的姑
     娘们
198. rubies: 宝石
199. Figuring: 象征
200. aptly understood: 贴切的表露

201. encrimson'd: 深红色的
202. terror: 畏惧
     dear: 充满深情的
     modesty: 害羞
203. Encamped: 扎营
     fighting outwardly: 外表上战斗

29

伤心礼物伤心情

珍珠灰白宝石红

苦痛羞耻作礼物

激情尽在不言中　　　　　　　　　*200*

不见血色脸臊红

惶恐羞惭情难禁

深植内心露峥嵘

30

君看金发结同心

全属丝缠献情真　　　　　　　　　*205*

各位美女赠所爱

哭求赠我我珍存

镶嵌宝石美在心

商籁情诗说成色

宝石天价觅知音　　　　　　　　　*210*

30

204. talents: 宝贝

205. twisted metal: 缠绕的金属丝

　　amorously: 多情地

　　impleach'd: 交织

206. many a several fair: 许多美人

207. beseech'd: 恳求

208. annexions: additions, 添加

209. deep-brain'd: 巧妙的

　　amplify: 放大

31

'"The diamond,—why, 'twas beautiful and hard

Whereto his invised properties did tend;

The deep-green em'rald, in whose fresh regard

Weak sights their sickly radiance do amend;

The heaven-hued sapphire, and the opal blend   *215*

With objects manifold: each several stone,

With wit well blazon'd, smiled or made some moan.

32

'"Lo, all these trophies of affections hot,

Of pensived and subdued desires the tender,

Nature hath charged me that I hoard them not,   *220*

But yield them up where I myself must render,

That is, to you, my origin and ender;

For these, of force, must your oblations be,

Since I their altar, you enpatron me.

31

212. whereto: 向那里；对那个
     invised: 看不见的
     tend: 注意
213. em'rald: 祖母绿；绿宝石
214. Weak sights: 减弱的视力
     amend: 改正

215. heaven-hued: 蓝色
     sapphire: 蓝宝石
     opal: 蛋白石
     blend: 混杂
216. manifold: 多样的
     each several stone: 每块宝石
217. well blazoned: 精心题辞

31

美丽坚硬有钻石

含而不露太坚实

看到深色祖母绿

盲人可得复明时

天蓝青玉白玉持　　　　　　　　　215

各种感情各种玉

懊恼微笑两交集

32

纪念品乃缴获成

强压爱恋灭热情

内心不敢私藏有　　　　　　　　　220

赐与他人献我情

管我始终君神明

只作贡品来献祭

我为祭坛君神灵

32

218. Lo: 看，瞧
　　trophies: 纪念品
　　affections hot: 热情
219. pensived: 忧郁的
　　subdued desires the tender: 强压下的
　　爱欲

220. charged: 下命令
　　hoard: 珍藏
221. render: 给予
222. ender: 结束
223. oblations: 奉献
224. altar: 祭坛
　　empatron: 庇护

33

"'O, then, advance of yours that phraseless hand,   *225*

Whose white weighs down the airy scale of praise;

Take all these similes to your own command,

Hallow'd with sighs that burning lungs did raise;

What me your minister, for you obeys,

Works under you; and to your audit comes   *230*

Their distract parcels in combined-sums.

34

"'Lo, this device was sent me from a nun,

A sister sanctified, of holiest note;

Which late her noble suit in court did shun,

Whose rarest havings made the blossoms dote;   *235*

For she was sought by spirits of richest coat,

But kept cold distance, and did thence remove,

To spend her living in eternal love.

33

225. advance: 举起

　　phraseless: 无法形容的

226. white: 白皙

　　the airy scale of praise: 空洞的赞美

227. similes: 爱的标记

228. Hollow'd: 化为神圣

　　burning lungs: 烧灼肺腑的

　　raise: 引起

229. minister: 仆从

230. audit: 账册

231. distract parcels: 零星的东西

33

举起玉手难形容　　　　　　　　　*225*

白皙赞誉份量轻

伤心标记全拿去

烧灼肺腑哀叹声

我为奴仆本服从

听从命令来记账　　　　　　　　　*230*

她们奉献总数清

34

这件刺绣出尼姑

圣洁修女拔头筹

近日拒绝显贵点

显贵财富惊登徒　　　　　　　　　*235*

群豪殷实猛追求

态度冷淡距离远

永恒爱河一生谋

34

232. device: 表记；刺绣

233. sister sanctified: 圣洁的修女

234. her noble suit in court: 一位显贵对她的追求

shun: 拒绝

235. rarest havings: 罕见的人品

blossoms: 朝臣

dote: 倾心

238. living: 生活

eternal love: 神圣的爱

35

"'But, O my sweet, what labour is't to leave

The thing we have not, mastering what not strives,— *240*

Paling the place which did no form receive,

Playing patient sports in unconstrained gyves?

She that her fame so to herself contrives,

The scars of battle 'scapeth by the flight,

And makes her absence valiant, not her might. *245*

36

"'O, pardon me, in that my boast is true:

The accident which brought me to her eye

Upon the moment did her force subdue,

And now she would the caged cloister fly:

Religious love put out religion's eye: *250*

Not to be tempted, would she be immured,

And now, to tempt all, liberty procured.

35

239. labour: 困难的任务
      leave: 放弃
240. strives: 反对
241. Paling: 筑栅防护
      the place which did no form receive:
      人迹不至的修道院
242. patient sports: 忍耐的技艺

unconstrained: 非强迫的
gyves: 手铐，脚镣
243. she that her fame so to herself
      contrives: 她如此精心维护自己的名
      声
244. The scars of battle scapeth by the
      flight: 落荒而逃，哪来的战争创伤

35

叫声我爱我难丢

无法控制无法留　　　　　　　　　240

圈起未留爱痕地

无拘无束无忧愁

孤芳自赏奇女流

战斗伤痕她逃避

全因勇敢非力优　　　　　　　　　245

36

我之夸口非无由

与她碰面非我谋

我有魅力服美女

修道院中不苦修

真修眼让真爱优　　　　　　　　　250

出家苦修躲诱惑

男欢女爱岂能丢

---

245. absence:　隐逸
　　　valiant:　勇敢的
　　　might:　力量过人

36

246. in that:　既然
　　　boast:　夸口

248. Upon the moment:　立即
　　　subdue:　制服

249. caged:　笼子似的
　　　cloister:　修道院

250. Religious love put out religion's eye:
　　　虔诚的爱使得虔诚的眼睛痴迷

251. Not to be tempted, would she be
　　　immured:　为不受诱惑，她出家苦修

252. tempt:　冒险
　　　procured:　充分享受

37

'"How mighty, then, you are, O, hear me tell!

The broken bosoms that to me belong

Have emptied all their fountains in my well,   255

And mine I pour your ocean all among:

I strong o'er them, and you o'er me being strong,

Must for your victory us all congest,

As compound love to physic your cold breast.

38

'"My parts had power to charm a sacred nun,   260

Who, disciplined, ay, dieted in grace,

Believed her eyes when they t' assail begun,

All vows and consecrations giving place:

O most potential love! vow, bond, nor space,

In thee hath neither sting, knot, nor confine,   265

For thou art all, and all things else are thine.

37

253. mighty: 强大

254. bosoms: 心

255. fountains: 泉水，喻所有姑娘的心
　　 well: 水井，喻讲话男子之心

256. ocean: 海洋，喻诗中女主人公之心

257. strong o'er them: 比她们强

258. congest: 聚集起来

259. compound love: 复合的爱
　　 physic: 医治

38

260. parts: 品质

261. dieted in grace: 上帝佑护

37

你太强大听我言
痴女心碎为爱怜
众心如泉注我井   255
井水归你海洋宽
我狠你强你冠冕
一切胜利我汇聚
讨你欢心绽笑颜

38

我之才情迷尼姑   260
虔诚对天苦自修
不能不服眼中色
神圣誓约付东流
大爱誓律道院书
牵缠约束皆无用   265
你即一切一切奴

---

262. assail: 进攻
263. consecrations: 奉献
264. most potential love: 最强有力的爱
　　 bond: 戒条
　　 space: 修道院清静

265. sting: 伤害
　　 knot: 缠结
　　 confine: 限制
266. all things else are thine: 一切都属于你

39

'"When thou impressest, what are precepts worth

Of stale example? When thou wilt inflame,

How coldly those impediments stand forth

Of wealth, of filial fear, law, kindred, fame!　　　　*270*

Love's arms are peace, 'gainst rule, 'gainst sense, 'gainst shame:

And sweetens, in the suff'ring pangs it bears,

The aloes of all forces, shocks, and fears.

40

'"Now all these hearts that do on mine depend,

Feeling it break, with bleeding groans they pine;　　　　*275*

And supplicant their sighs to you extend,

To leave the battery that you make 'gainst mine,

Lending soft audience to my sweet design,

And oredent soul to that strong-bonded oath

That shall prefer and undertake my troth."　　　　*280*

39
267. impressest:　下命令
268. stale:　陈腐的
　　　inflame:　燃烧
269. impediments:　障碍物
270. filial fear:　孝道
　　　kindred:　亲情
271. arms:　武器

272. sweetens:　甜蜜
　　　stuff'ring:　承受的
　　　pangs:　剧痛
273. aloes:　芦荟

40
275. with bleeding groans they pine:　她们
　　　憔悴不堪，哭泣，流血

39

你占我心万言空
你燃我心财无踪
孝心法律成障碍
亲族荣誉冷冰冰　　　　　　　　*270*
爱之武器胜律荣
爱之理智苦带蜜
芦荟可医暴与惊

40

依赖我心有众心
泣血哀我碎心人　　　　　　　　*275*
哀叹求你憔悴泣
莫再伤我血淋淋
聆听我爱柔情真
灵魂接受我信誓
有我真情言我心　　　　　　　　*280*

---

276. supplicant: 哀求
277. battery: 攻击
278. Lending: 借给
　　soft audience: 温和的听取
　　sweet design: 殷勤好意
279. oredent: 信任
　　strong-bonded oath: 坚决的誓言
280. undertake: 实现
　　troth: 真正的爱

41

'This said, his watery, eyes he did dismount,

Whose sights till then were levell'd on my face;

Each cheek a river running from a fount

With brinish current downward flow'd apace:

O, how the channel to the stream gave grace!   *285*

Who glazed with crystal gate the glowing roses

That flame through water which their hue encloses.

42

'O father, what a hell of witchcraft lies

In the small orb of one particular tear!

But with the inundation of the eyes   *290*

What rocky heart to water will not wear?

What breast so cold that is not warmed here?

O cleft effect! cold modesty, hot wrath,

Both fire from hence and chill extincture hath.

41
281. dismount: 垂下
282. levell'd: 对准
283. fount: 泉源，喻眼睛
284. brinish: 咸的
     apace: 飞快地，迅速地
285. grace: 辉煌
286. glazed: 灼灼燃烧

glowing roses: 盛开的玫瑰
287. their hue encloses: 玫瑰的颜色被罩上

42
288. what a hell: 加强语气
     witchcraft: 魔力
289. orb: 滴
290. inundation: 泛滥

41

青年说完泪眼垂
盯着我看情痴迷
双颊流下泉两股
咸水奔流势湍急
美哉河流两岸奇　　　　　　　　*285*
玫瑰盛开水晶罩
玫瑰隔水色芳菲

42

我谓老伯魔力藏
小小泪珠将我诓
两眼一起发洪水　　　　　　　　*290*
泪水磨穿石心肠
冰冷心胸暖洋洋
贞操冷竣情炽烈
泪水面前均投降

291. rocky heart: 石头心肠；铁石心肠
293. cleft effect: 双重效果
　　　cold modesty: 冷峻的贞操
　　　hot wrath: 火热的怒气
294. from hence: 来自眼泪
　　　extincture: 熄灭

43

'For, lo, his passion, but an art of craft,   *295*

Even there resolved my reason into tears;

There my white stole of chastity I daffed,

Shook off my sober guards and civil fears;

Appear to him, as he to me appears,

All melting; though our drops this difference bore,   *300*

His poison'd me, and mine did him restore.

44

'In him a plenitude of subtle matter,

Applied to cautels, all strange forms receives,

Of burning blushes, or of weeping water,

Or sounding paleness; and he takes and leaves,   *305*

In either's aptness, as it best deceives,

To blush at speeches rank, to weep at woes,

Or to turn white and swoon at tragic shows:

43
295. art of craft: 狡诈
296. resolved: 溶化
297. white stole: 白袍
      daffed: 脱掉
298. sober guards: 理智的防卫

civil fears: 对礼仪的恐惧
300. melting: 融化
      bore: bear 的过去时，意为怀有
301. poison'd me: 毒害了我
      mine did him restore: 我给他治了病

43

可见狡猾为他情　　　　　　295
理智化泪我动容
脱下贞洁白铠甲
放弃自卫行不经
我也学他泪交融
两人洒泪不相同　　　　　　300
他毒我慈治病行

44

痛恨此人计多端
骗起人来不一般
时而洒泪是红脸
时而苍白想机关　　　　　　305
斟酌恰好骗闺媛
闻淫脸红闻苦泣
面白昏厥见景惨

44

302. plenitude: 许多
　　subtle matter: 花样
303. cautels: 诡计
305. swounding paleness: 惨白
306. aptness: 聪明，灵巧
　　as it best deceives: 最能骗人的

307. speeches rank: 粗话
　　weep at woes: 见苦难哭泣
308. turn white and swoon at tragic shows:
　　看见悲惨景象就立即脸色苍白昏厥过
　　去

45

'That not a heart which in his level came

Could scape the hail of his all-hurting aim,   *310*

Showing fair nature is both kind and tame;

And, veil'd in them, did win whom he would maim:

Against the thing he sought he would exclaim;

When he most burnt in heart-wished luxury,

He preached pure maid, and praised cold chastity.   *315*

46

'Thus merely with the garment of a Grace

The naked and concealed fiend he cover'd;

That th' unexperient gave the tempter place,

Which, like a cherubin, above them hover'd.

Who, young and simple, would not be so lover'd?   *320*

Ay me! I fell; and yet do question make

What I should do again for such a sake.

45

309. level:　射程; 注意

310. hail:　弹药
　　　all-hurting aim:　每发必中

312. veil'd:　戴着面具的
　　　maim:　残害

313. sought:　追求

exclaim:　谴责

314. heart-wished luxury:　心中欲火如焚

315. preached:　宣扬

46

316. the garment of a Grace:　风度翩翩的
　　　外衣

45

一旦女人入射程
必被击中难逃生　　　　　　310
温良雅驯装表面
戴着面具猎花容
本想得到先装凶
胸中怒火腾腾起
口赞处女贞操情　　　　　　315

46

披着外衣装亲仁
遮掩隐藏恶魔心
无经验者受诱惑
诱者天使驾祥云
爱河坠入少年人　　　　　　320
坠爱河兮我迷惑
再遭此难何计寻

---

317. naked and concealed fiend:　赤裸隐藏
　　的魔鬼
　　cover'd:　掩藏
318. unexperient:　天真
　　tempter:　诱惑

319. cherubin:　小天使
321. fell:　失足
　　question make:　询问
322. such a sake:　这样的事

47

'O, that infected moisture of his eye,

O, that false fire which in his cheek so glow'd,

O, that forced thunder from his heart did fly,   *325*

O, that sad breath his spongy lungs bestow'd,

O, all that borrow'd motion sceming ow'd,

Would yet again betray the fore-betray'd,

And new pervert a reconciled maid!'

47
323. infected moisture: 有害的眼泪
325. forced thunder: 勉强的雷
     fly: 爆出
326. spongy lungs: 海绵般的肺
     bestow'd: 挤出
327. borrow'd motion: 假装的表现
     seeming ow'd: 好像是真的

328. the fore-betray'd: 受过欺骗的
329. new-pervert: 再次堕落
     reconciled: 悔过的

47

眼湿润兮含假情
脸燃烧兮假火腾
胸有雷兮勉强炸   325
肺有哀兮虚软声
固有物兮借来风
被骗之人再受骗
悔过修女诱惑中

V THE PASSIONATE PILGRIM

V　激情朝圣者

题解

　　原文为 The Passionate Pilgrim, 黄雨石译为《爱情的礼赞》，梁实秋译为《热烈的情人》，孙法理译为《激情飘泊者》。此编译作《激情朝圣者》。

1

When my love swears that she is made of truth,

I do believe her, though I know she lies,

That she might think me some untutor'd youth,

Unskilful in the world's false forgeries.

Thus vainly thinking that she thinks me young,   *5*

Although I know my years be past the best,

I smiling credit her false-speaking tongue,

Outfacing faults in love with love's ill rest.

But wherefore says my love that she is young?

And wherefore say not I that I am old?   *10*

O, love's best habit is a soothing tongue,

And age, in love, loves not to have years told.

  Therefore I'll lie with love, and love with me,

  Since that our faults in love thus smother'd be.

1

3. untutor'd youth: 没有经验的青年

4. forgeries: 诡计

5. vainly thinking: 错误地认为

7. smiling credit: 微笑着信任
   false-speaking tongue: 说谎的嘴

8. Outfacing faults in love: 爱情外部之错
   love's ill rest: 爱情之不安

9. wherefore: 为什么

11. soothing tongue: 讨好的话

12. age, in love, loves not to have years told:
    迟暮的爱不喜欢谈年龄

13. lie with love: 因爱欺骗

14. smother'd: 掩盖
    该诗与莎士比亚第 138 首十四行诗大
    同小异。

1

吾爱有海誓　　言她情真纯
吾笃信吾爱　　知谎不认真
好使她认为　　无知青年人
不知虚伪世　　不知奸谋深
妄想她认为　　吾年正青春　　　　　　　　*5*
她心如明镜　　盛年吾无存
明知她撒谎　　吾信非真心
双方打交道　　不以诚为邻
为何吾不言　　她心非忠贞
为何她不语　　吾乃衰年人　　　　　　　　*10*
呜呼最佳爱　　外表忠诚寻
老者谈恋爱　　不喜谈青春
吾对她撒谎　　她言非认真
双方皆有短　　假话保自身

2

Two loves I have, of comfort and despair,

That like two spirits do suggest me still;

My better angel is a man right fair,

My worser spirit a woman colour'd ill.

To win me soon to hell, my female evil   *5*

Tempteth my better angel from my side,

And would corrupt my saint to be a devil,

Wooing his purity with her fair pride.

And whether that my angel be turn'd fiend,

Suspect I may, yet not directly tell: *10*

For being both to me, both to each friend,

I guess one angel in another's hell:

    The truth I shall not know, but live in doubt,

    Till my bad angel fire my good one out.

2
2. still: 持续地
3. right fair: 非常漂亮
4. color'd ill: 脸色黑
5. To win me: 引导我
   female evil: 恶劣女性

8. Wooing his purity with her fair pride:
    她卖弄风情向他的纯洁求爱
11. both to each friend: 二者成为朋友
12. hell: 地狱
    该诗与莎士比亚第144首十四行诗大致相同。

2

舒心与绝望　充吾二爱人
总在驱使吾　两个守护神
美者为天使　貌徒大街寻
恶者似精怪　黑面一妇人
那位母夜叉　骗吾地狱寻　　　　　　　5
善良美天使　被诱离吾身
蛊惑善天使　恶魔堕其心
邪恶加纵欲　破坏其纯真
是否变魔鬼　天使已沉沦
仅管有疑窦　结论何处寻　　　　　　　10
二者均难吾　结成朋友亲
吾猜一天使　随入地狱门
真情吾难探　永远疑心存
直到那恶魔　释放天使身

3

Did not the heavenly rhetoric of thine eye,

'Gainst whom the world could not hold argument,

Persuade my heart to this false perjury?

Vows for thee broke deserve not punishment.

A woman I forswore; but I will prove,   5

Thou being a goddess, I forswore not thee:

My vow was earthly, thou a heavenly love;

Thy grace being gain'd cures all disgrace in me.

My vow was breath, and breath a vapour is;

Then, thou fair sun, that on this earth doth shine,   10

Exhale this vapour vow; in thee it is:

If broken, then it is no fault of mine.

If by me broke, what fool is not so wise

To break an oath, to win a paradise?

3

1. heavenly rhetoric: 天堂般雄辩
2. argument: 争论
3. perjury: 假誓
4. broke: 破誓
   deserve: 该，值得
5. forswore: 发誓抛弃
6. Thou being a goddess, I forswore not thee:

你是女神，我没有发誓拒绝你
8. Thy grace being gain'd cures all disgrace
   in me: 你的垂青可治愈我的耻辱
11. Exhale: 蒸发
14. To break an oath, to win a paradise:
    放弃一个誓言，赢得一个天堂
    该诗酷似《爱的徒劳》第 4 幕第 3 场
朗格维（Longaville）所咏之十四行诗。

3

能说会道俊眼睛
举世想驳一场空
欲劝我改先前誓
纵改誓言不受惩
不近女色我誓明　　　　　　　　5
君为天仙我动情
君为仙女我尘世
可雪我耻君垂青
誓为言兮话气蒸
照我泥土日当空　　　　　　　　10
我誓蒸发入君体
誓破非我错中行
我因破誓笑笨虫
天堂难换誓言空

4

Sweet Cytherea, sitting by a brook

With young Adonis, lovely, fresh and green,

Did court the lad with many a lovely look,

Such looks as none could look but beauty's queen.

She told him stories to delight his ear,   5

She show'd him favours to allure his eye;

To win his heart, she toucht him here and there;

Touches so soft still conquer chastity.

But whether unripe years did want conceit,

Or he refused to take her figured proffer,   10

The tender nibbler would not touch the bait,

But smile and jest at every gentle offer:

   Then fell she on her back, fair queen, and toward:

   He rose and ran away; ah, fool too froward.

4

1. Cytherea: 西塞利亚，即维纳斯
   brook: 小河，溪
2. Adonis: 阿多尼斯，阿童尼
3. court: 向……求爱
   lad: 男孩，少年
4. Such looks as none could look but
   beauty's queen: 只有美的女神才能
   有如此美色

6. allure: 引诱，吸引
8. conquer chastity: 征服童贞
9. conceit: 理解
10. figured proffer: 她的明显的挑逗
11. tender nibbler: 娇嫩的小鱼
12. jest: 玩笑
14. fool too forward: 太难控制的傻瓜，不
    可理喻的蠢货

4

西塞利亚坐河边
阿多尼斯美容颜
女神甜美抛媚眼
美后自胜众天仙
女神故事动心颜　　　　　　　　　　5
女神弄姿入眼帘
挨挨抚抚讨人爱
柔情似水君子怜
不解风情美少年
女神求爱虚无言　　　　　　　　　　10
小鱼不肯吞鱼饵
一笑置之不缠绵
女神仰卧对青天
美男逃走愚难言

5

If love make me forsworn, how shall I swear to love?

O never faith could hold, if not to beauty vowed:

Though to myself forsworn, to thee I'll constant prove;

Those thoughts, to me like oaks, to thee like osiers bowed.

Study his bias leaves, and makes his book thine eyes,   *5*

Where all those pleasures live that art can comprehend.

If knowledge be the mark, to know thee shall suffice;

Well learned is that tongue that well can thee commend:

All ignorant that soul that sees thee without wonder;

Which is to me some praise, that I thy parts admire: *10*

Thine eye Jove's lightning seems, thy voice his dreadful thunder,

Which, not to anger bent, is music and sweet fire.

   Celestial as thou art, O do not Jove that wrong,

   To sing heaven's praise with such an earthly tongue.

5

3. constant prove: 忠贞不变
4. oaks: 橡树
   osiers: 柳树
   bowed: 鞠躬
5. Study: 学生
   bias: 俯身学习
   leaves: 荒废

make his book thine eyes: 把你的眼睛当书读
6. art: 学问
   comprehend: 拥抱
   Where all those pleasures live that art can comprehend: 你的眼中含有一切学问所能包含的乐趣
7. suffice: 满足

860

5

为爱背誓缘真情

誓为美女爱永恒

我虽背誓为美女

橡树化柳爱忠诚

荒废学业读君容　　　　　　　　　　　　5

一切学问君眼中

世上知识全占有

赞美君容得深功

不称赞君人不灵

我赏君才我享荣　　　　　　　　　　　　10

声如雷鸣目如电

非是震怒广乐声

天仙恕我真多情

尘世语赞仙姝容

---

8. commend: 推荐，表扬

11. Jove: 宙斯

13. Celestial: 天的

该诗出自《爱的徒劳》第 4 幕第 2 场，教区牧师纳森聂尔（Sir Nathaniel）所咏之十四行诗，内容基本上相同。

6

Scarce had the sun dried up the dewy morn,

And scarce the herd gone to the hedge for shade,

When Cytherea, all in love forlorn,

A longing tarriance for Adonis made

Under an osier growing by a brook,   *5*

A brook where Adon used to cool his spleen:

Hot was the day; she hotter that did look

For his approach, that often there had been.

Anon he comes, and throws his mantle by,

And stood stark naked on the brook's green brim: *10*

The sun lookt on the world with glorious eye,

Yet not so wistly as this queen on him.

He, spying her, bounced in, whereas he stood:

'O Jove,' quoth she, 'why was not I a flood!'

6

1. dewy morn: 晨露
2. hedge: 篱笆边
3. forlorn: 悲伤
4. tarriance: 逗留
6. Adon: 阿多尼斯
   spleen: 脾脏
7. that: who

9. Anon: 立刻
   mantle: 衣服
10. stark: 赤裸裸的
    brim: 岸
12. wistly: 欲望得不到满足的
13. spying: 发现
    bounced in: 跳进

6

太阳未干湿清晨
羊未靠篱寻凉荫
西塞利亚相思苦
阿多尼斯伤女心
溪边柳下走女神　　　　　　　　　　*5*
阿多尼斯常光临
女神急遇天气热
盼望美男来柳林
美男来后敞衣襟
赤身露体绿河滨　　　　　　　　　　*10*
太阳灼灼尘世照
怎比凝视痴女神
美男跳溪隐其身
女叹非溪暗伤心

7

Fair is my love, but not so fair as fickle,

Mild as a dove, but neither true nor trusty,

Brighter than glass and yet, as glass is, brittle,

Softer than wax and yet as iron rusty:

    A lily pale, with damask dye to grace her,   *5*

    None fairer, nor none falser to deface her.

Her lips to mine how often hath she joined,

Between each kiss her oaths of true love swearing!

How many tales to please me hath she coined,

Dreading my love, the loss thereof still fearing!   *10*

    Yet in the midst of all her pure protestings,

    Her faith, her oaths, her tears, and all were jestings.

7
1. fickle: 感情易变的，感情无常的
3. brittle: 脆弱的
4. wax: 蜡
5. damask: 大马士革染色，灰红色
6. deface: 使失面子

9. coined: 捏造
10. Dreading: 担心
    thereof: 因此
11. protestings: 爱情表白
12. jestings: 笑话

7

吾爱虽美举止轻
柔如斑鸠不信诚
明如玻璃容易碎
软如蜡兮铁锈生
白百合加玫瑰色　　　　　　　　5
美轮美奂又虚空

我俩接过多少吻
她逢亲吻明誓真
满口谎言取悦我
怕失我爱失我心　　　　　　　　10
近乎纯洁表白语
真誓眼泪为骗人

She burnt with love, as straw with fire flameth;

She burnt out love, as soon as straw out-burneth;

She framed the love, and yet she foil'd the framing;   *15*

She bade love last, and yet she fell a-turning.

　　Was this a lover, or a lecher whether?

　　Bad in the best, though excellent in neither.

---

13. burnt with love:　爱情燃烧
14. burnt out love:　爱情烧完
15. framed the love:　制造爱情
　　foil'd:　毁掉
16. bade love last:　bade, bid 的过去时，吩
　　咐。该短语意为：想让爱情永久
　　a-turning:　反复无常

17. lecher:　纵欲的人
　　whether:　哪一个
18. Bad in the best:　佳品中的次品；纵然
　　高明也是坏；想做得最好实则糟糕
　　though excellent in neither:　即非最坏，
　　亦非最好

她心有爱草火熊
她爱烧完草灰生
她造爱情又撕破　　　　　　　　　　*15*
她爱久远又返程
难辨情人与荡妇
糟透谁也不高明

8

If music and sweet poetry agree,

As they must needs, the sister and the brother,

Then must the love be great 'twixt thee and me:

Because thou lovest the one and I the other.

Dowland to thee is dear, whose heavenly touch   *5*

Upon the lute doth ravish human sense;

Spenser to me, whose deep conceit is such

As passing all conceit needs no defence.

Thou lovest to hear the sweet melodious sound

That Phoebus' lutes the queen of music, makes;   *10*

And I in deep delight am chiefly drown'd

Whenas himself to singing he betakes.

　One god is god of both, as poets feign;

　One knight loves both, and both in thee remain.

8

2. needs:　need
　the sister and the brother:　兄妹
5. Dowland:　(1563—1625?) 当时最著名之
　作曲家兼琴师
6. lute:　琴
　ravish:　使出神
7. spenser:　斯宾塞

deep conceit:　深沉妙笔
8. passing all conceit needs no defence:
　不同凡响，不用我夸饰
10. Phoebus:　福玻斯，太阳神
11. drown'd:　乐在其中
12. Whenas:　when
　betakes:　开始歌唱
13. feign:　捏造

8

倘若乐诗可协调
兄弟姐妹乐逍遥
你我之爱天堂美
各有所喜乐陶陶
道兰德琴仙乐飘　　　　　　　　　　5
听者出神上九霄
斯宾塞诗称沉郁
想象神奇立高标
福玻斯琴神韵高
音乐女王弹拨娇　　　　　　　　　　10
女神诗句我陶醉
浅吟低唱魂魄销
乐神诗神诗人谣
骑士双美把你挑

9

Fair was the morn when the fair queen of love,

*   *   *   *   *   *   *   *   *

Paler for sorrow than her milk-white dove,

For Adon's sake, a youngster proud and wild;

Her stand she takes upon a steep-up hill: *5*

Anon Adonis comes with horn and hounds;

She, silly queen, with more than love's good will,

Forbade the boy he should not pass those grounds:

'Once,' quoth she, 'did I see a fair sweet youth

Here in these brakes deep-wounded with a boar,   *10*

Deep in the thigh, a spectacle of ruth!

See, in my thigh,' quoth she, 'here was the sore.'

　　She showed hers: he saw more wounds than one,

　　And blushing fled, and left her all alone.

9
　该诗原文缺第二行。
1. the fair queen of love: 美貌的爱之女
　王，维纳斯
3. milk-white dove: 乳白色的鸽子
5. steep-up: 陡峭的
6. hounds: 猎犬

8. Forbade: 禁止
9. fair sweet youth: 甜美的少年
10. brakes: 丛林
11. thigh: 大腿
　a spectacle of ruth: 可人可怜的场景
12. sore: 伤
14. blushing fled: 脸红逃走

9

美爱神于美清晨

* * * * * * * *

脸色惨白斑鸠过
狂傲阿多尼斯亲
陡峭山坡站女神　　　　　　5
童男号角猎犬跟
痴情爱情心良善
勿过险地少年人
她言一人正青春
野猪重伤在丛林　　　　　　10
可怜在腿深伤口
又言自伤求怜悯
展示大腿多伤痕
童男吓跑留女神

10

Sweet rose, fair flower, untimely pluckt, soon vaded,

Pluckt in the bud and vaded in the spring!

Bright orient pearl, alack, too timely shaded!

Fair creature, kill'd too soon by death's sharp sting!

    Like a green plum that hangs upon a tree,   *5*

    And falls through wind before the fall should be.

I weep for thee and yet no cause I have;

For why thou left'st me nothing in thy will:

And yet thou left'st me more than I did crave;

For why I craved nothing of thee still: *10*

    O yes, dear friends I pardon crave of thee,

    Thy discontent thou didst bequeath to me.

10

1. vaded: 枯萎

3. orient pearl: 东方明珠
   alack: 呜呼！啊呀！
   too timely shaded: 过早埋没

5. plum: 梅子

8. left'st me nothing in thy will: 你的遗嘱里什么也没有留给我

9. crave: 恳求

11. I pardon crave of thee: 我恳求你的宽恕

12. bequeath: 遗赠

10

早摘玫瑰美无踪
青春枯萎蓓蕾形
东方明珠早失色
美人早摧死无情
青梅掛树遇大风　　　　　　　　　　　*5*
不该落时尘埃中

我为你哭无理由
你有遗憾我何图
你留遗产超我想
我本对你无所求　　　　　　　　　　　*10*
好友宽恕连声呼
你留给我惟哀愁

873

11

Venus, with young Adonis sitting by her

Under a myrtle shade, began to woo him:

She told the youngling how god Mars did try her,

And as he fell to her so fell she to him.

'Even thus,' quoth she, 'the warlike god embraced me,' *5*

And then she clipp'd Adonis in her arms;

'Even thus,' quoth she, 'the warlike god unlac'd me,'

As if the boy should use like loving charms;

'Even thus' quoth she, 'he seized on my lips,'

And with her lips on his did act the seizure: *10*

And as she fetched breath, away he skips,

And would not take her meaning nor her pleasure.

    Ah, that I had my lady at this bay,

    To kiss and clip me till I run away!

11

2. myrtle: 桃金娘树

3. youngling: 年轻人
   Mars: 战神玛尔斯
   try: 挑逗

6. clipp'd: 搂抱

7. unlac'd: 宽衣解带

8. like: 同样的

9. seized: 亲吻

10. seizure: 亲吻

11. fetched breath: 喘气
    skips: 逃, 匆匆离开

12. take: 接受

13. that: 但愿
    bay: 山脉中的凹处

11

维纳斯与阿童尼

山桃树下意痴迷

女告童男战神事

女神心中童男奇

战神拥抱求爱急 5

她搂童男情依依

战神脱我女神服

童男应学莫迟疑

战神吻我猛吮吸

女吻童男黏兮兮 10

女神喘息男逃走

不解风情不足奇

愿我姑娘也情迷

拥我吻我我逃离

12

Crabbed age and youth cannot live together:

Youth is full of pleasance, age is full of care;

Youth like summer morn, age like winter weather;

Youth like summer brave, age like winter bare.

Youth is full of sport, age's breath is short;   5

　　Youth is nimble, age is lame;

Youth is hot and bold, age is weak and cold;

　　Youth is wild, and age is tame.

Age, I do abhor thee; youths I do adore thee;

　　O, my love, my love is young!   10

Age, I do defy thee: O, sweet shepherd, hie thee,

　　For methinks thou stay'st too long.

12
1. Crabbed: 脾气乖戾的
4. brave: 辉煌
5. sport: 嬉戏欢乐
6. nimble: 敏捷
9. abhor: 厌恶
　adore: 爱慕

11. defy: 蔑视
　　hie: 赶往

12

衰老青年难共存
青年欢快老伤心
青年夏晨老冬日
青年绿夏老岁昏
青年嬉戏老喘息   *5*
青年敏捷老迟疑
青年果敢老冷酷
青年痴狂老屏息
我怕老年敬青春
我爱青春年少人   *10*
我拒老年牧人好
莫呆太久应抽身

13

Beauty is but a vain and doubtful good;

A shining gloss that vadeth suddenly;

A flower that dies when first it 'gins to bud;

A brittle glass that's broken presently:

   A doubtful good, a gloss, a glass, a flower,   *5*

   Lost, vaded, broken, dead within an hour.

And as goods lost are seld or never found,

As vaded gloss no rubbing will refresh,

As flowers dead lie wither'd on the ground,

As broken glass no cement can redress,   *10*

   So beauty blemished once forever lost,

   In spite of physic, painting, pain and cost.

13

2. gloss: 光泽
4. presently: 立刻
7. goods lost are seld or never found:
  seld=seldom, 很少。失去的货物很难复
  得或永难找回
8. rubbing: 擦
  refresh: 闪亮

10. cement: 水泥；胶泥
  redress: 修补
11. blemished: 污损
12. physic: 药物
  painting: 脂粉
  pain and cost: 痛苦和金钱

13

美之为善疑而空
辉煌光泽一闪中
鲜花吐蕊先枯萎
玻璃破碎脆弱形
伪善玻璃失光明　　　　　　　　　5
速去枯萎花儿红

宝物失去寻无踪
褪色物件擦不明
花儿死去躺在地
玻璃破碎粘不成　　　　　　　　　10
美遭玷污治疗空
钱苦脂粉皆无能

14

Good night, good rest. Ah, neither be my share:

She bade good night that kept my rest away;

And daffed me to a cabin hang'd with care,

To descant on the doubts of my decay.

   'Farewell,' quoth she, 'and come again tomorrow:'   *5*

   Fare well I could not, for I supped with sorrow.

Yet at my parting sweetly did she smile,

In scorn or friendship, nill I conster whether:

'T may be, she joy'd to jest at my exile,

'T may be, again to make me wander thither: *10*

   'Wanders' a word for shadows like myself,

   As take the pain, but cannot pluck the pelf.

14
1. neither be my share: 两者都与我无关
2. bade: 祝
   kept my rest away: 使我无法入睡
3. daffed: 送
   a cabin hang'd with care: 充满忧愁的
   斗室
4. descant: 悲痛
   the doublts of my decay: 惟恐失恋

6. supped with: 啜饮
8. nill: will not
   conster: 考虑
9. jest at: 开玩笑
   exile: 流放
10. thither: 那儿
11. shadows: 幽灵
12. pelf: 不义之财；钱财

14

晚安安睡我无福
她道晚安我心忧
她让我睡我愁困
品尝失恋有疑窦
她道晚安明朝候   5
一夜难眠多苦愁

我苦离别她开颜
讥讽好意我猜难
或为高兴赶我走
或为有意让我选   10
行尸走肉我无颜
苦头吃尽求报难

15

Lord, how mine eyes throw gazes to the east!

My heart doth charge the watch; the morning rise

Doth cite each moving sense from idle rest.

Not daring trust the office of mine eyes,

    While Philomela sits and sings, I sit and mark,   *5*

    And wish her lays were tuned like the lark;

For she doth welcome daylight with her ditty,

And drives away dark dreaming night:

The night so packed, I post unto my pretty;

Heart hath his hope and eyes their wished sight;   *10*

    Sorrow changed to solace and solace mixt with sorrow;

    For why she sigh'd, and bade me come tomorrow.

15
1. gazes: 凝视
2. charge the watch: 催促钟表
   the morning rise: 清晨
3. cite: 呼唤
   moving sense: 感官
4. daring: 敢
   office: 功能
5. Philomela: 菲罗墨拉（菲洛美），
   雅典公主；夜莺
   mark: 倾听
6. lays: 歌曲
7. ditty: 小调，小曲
9. packed: 打发走
   post: 赶紧走
   pretty: 爱人
11. solace: 安慰

15

苍天看我望东方
怨钟太慢我心慌
晨曦之中感官紧
不敢太信我目光
我闻夜莺我恐惶　　　　　　　　　　*5*
但愿云雀鸣寒窗

云雀鸣唱迎清晨
驱赶黑夜梦阴沉
送走黑夜寻我爱
心怀希望眼见真　　　　　　　　　　*10*
悲哀安慰相杂混
叹气邀我明朝临

Were I with her, the night would post too soon;

But now are minutes added to the hours;

To spite me now, each minute seems a moon;   *15*

Yet not for me, shine sun to succour flowers!

 Pack night, peep day; good day, of night now borrow:

 Short night, to-night, and length thyself tomorrow.

---

14. minutes added to the hours: 一分钟一
分钟才积成小时，时间过得太慢，度
日如年
15. spite: 刁难
16. shine sun: 让太阳照耀
 succour: 援助

17. Pack night: 黑夜赶紧去
 peep day: 白昼快快来
 of night now borrow: 从夜里借来
18. Short night: 短一点吧，黑夜

和她同坐夜不长
无她分钟长难量
气闷一刻一个月　　　　　　　　　　　*15*
且让花儿晒太阳
夜去昼来借夜光
缩短今夜昼吉祥

VI SONNETS TO SUNDRY NOTES OF
MUSIC

VI 情歌拾贝

题解

　　原文为 *Sonnets to Sundry Notes of Music,* 黄雨石译为《乐曲杂咏》，梁实秋译为《杂调情歌》，孙法理译为《配乐小诗》。Sonnets 释为"十四行诗"不严谨，因集中多为歌谣小调。Sundry 意为"各种各样的"，Notes 意为"音调"、"音符"。篇名直译为《各种音调之歌谣》，似嫌直露，故译作《情歌拾贝》，拟为《激情朝圣者》之续。

1

It was a lording's daughter, the fairest one of three,

That liked of her master as well as weft might be

Till looking on an Englishman, the fair'st that eye could see,

Her fancy fell a-turning.

Long was the combat doubtful that love with love did fight,   5

To leave the master loveless, or kill the gallant knight:

To put in practice either, alas, it was a spite

Unto the silly damsel!

But one must be refused; more mickle was the pain

That nothing could be used to turn them both to gain,   10

For of the two the trusty knight was wounded with disdain:

Alas, she could not help it!

Thus art with arms contending was victor of the day,

Which by a gift of learning did bear the maid away:

Then, lullaby, the learned man hath got the lady gay;   15

For now my song is ended.

1

1. lording's: 贵族的

2. liked of her master: 爱上了她自己教师

4. fell a-turning: 芳心转向

5. doubtful: 不可预见的

6. kill: 使心碎

  gallant: 豪侠的

7. spite: 怨恨

8. damsel: 年轻女人，闺女

9. mickle: 多

11. distain: 鄙弃

13. art: 学问

  arms: 武器

  contending: 战斗

  victor: 胜利者

15. lullaby: 唱催眠曲，唱摇篮曲

1

贵胄三女她娉婷
爱上教师动感情
看见英国人英俊
芳心正斗争

两种爱情斗不清　　　　　　　　　5
教师武士都心疼
抛弃杀戮皆不可
姑娘真痴情

拒绝一位痛难生
两位满意怎可能　　　　　　　　　10
武士伤心遭冷遇
无助她心疼

文与武斗前者赢
才学获得姑娘情
最终学者得佳丽　　　　　　　　　15
我歌到尾声

2

On a day, alack the day!

Love, whose month was ever May,

Spied a blossom passing fair,

Playing in the wanton air:

Through the velvet leaves the wind   5

All unseen gan passage find;

That the lover, sick to death,

Wisht himself the heaven's breath,

'Air,' quoth he, 'thy cheeks may blow;

Air, would I might triumph so!   10

But, alas! my hand hath sworn

Ne'er to pluck thee from thy thorn:

Vow, alack! for youth unmeet:

Youth, so apt to pluck a sweet.

Thou for whom Jove would swear   15

Juno but an Ethiope were;

And deny himself for Jove,

Turning mortal for thy love.'

2

　　该诗可参见《爱的徒劳》第 4 幕第 3
场杜曼（Dumaine）所咏之诗。
2. whose month: 爱的月份
3. spied: 看到
　　blossom: 花（尤指果树之花）
　　passing fair: 娇艳无比
4. wanton: 爱玩的

5. velvet: 天鹅绒
6. gan: began
9. thy cheeks may blow: 可能吹拂你面
　　庞，小仙鼓起两腮吹气
10. would I might triumph so: 但愿我如此
　　得意
12. thy thorn: 你的刺丛

2

有一天兮有一天

爱情总在五月间

看见鲜花艳无比

嬉戏风中乐疯癫

风在茸茸绿叶间   *5*

无影无踪胡乱钻

情人即将憔悴死

愿化阵风上九天

风儿吹颊他开颜

我学风儿胜利观   *10*

呜呼举手我有誓

不向尖刺摘花鲜

勿再发誓小青年

青春折花自在观

天神见你也发誓   *15*

天后丑陋实不堪

放弃天神之尊严

与你相恋要下凡

---

13. for youth unmeet: 不应该发誓的
    年轻人
14. apt: 喜爱
    sweet: 香花
15. Jove: 乔武，罗马神话主神

16. Juno: 朱诺，罗马神话中之天后
    Ethiope: 黑人
17. deny himself for Jove: 乔武否认
18. Turning mortal for thy love: 为了爱你
    而变成凡人

3

My flocks feed not,

My ewes breed not,

My rams speed not;

All is amiss:

Love's denying,　　　　　　　　　　　　5

Faith's defying,

Heart's renying,

Causer of this.

All my merry jigs are quite forgot,

All my lady's love is lost, God wot:　　　　10

Where her faith was firmly fixt in love,

There a nay is placed without remove.

One silly cross

Wrought all my loss;

O frowning Fortune, cursed, fickle dame!　　15

For now I see

Inconstancy

More in women than in men remain.

---

1. flocks: 羊
2. ewes: 母羊
3. rams: 公羊
   speed: 发情
4. amiss: 不顺当
5. denying: 否认
6. defying: 蔑视
7. renying: 废弃

8. Causer: 因为
9. jigs: 英国乡间的一种跳跃式三步舞
10. wot: 知道
12. nay: 拒绝
   remove: 不动摇
13. cross: 不幸
15. fickle dame: 变化无常的女神
17. Inconstancy: 轻浮，善变

3

羊群不食

母不孕兮

公不情兮

全不顺兮

正灭爱情   *5*

正改忠诚

虚伪心中

全由此生

我之欢歌忘无存

我之情人太狠心   *10*

深植忠心于挚爱

无情不字太伤人

失恋无缘

造成难堪

女神善变恨难安   *15*

我心已明

杨花爱情

女子比男更无行

In black mourn I,

All fears scorn I,   *20*

Love hath forlorn me,

    Living in thrall:

Heart is bleeding,

All help needing,

O cruel speeding,   *25*

    Fraughted with gall.

My shepherd's pipe can sound no deal:

My wether's bell rings doleful knell;

My curtal dog, that wont to have play'd,

Plays not at all, but seems afraid;   *30*

    My sighs so deep

    Procure to weep,

In howling wise, to see my doleful plight.

    How sighs resound

    Through heartless ground,   *35*

Like a thousand vanquisht men in bloody fight!

---

19. In black mourn I:　我穿着黑色的丧服
20. All fears scorn I:　我藐视一切恐惧
21. Love hath forlorn me: 爱情已经抛弃我
22. thrall:　束缚
24. needing:　需要
25. speeding:　命运
26. Fraughted with gall:　负载着痛苦
27. no deal:　一点也不
28. wether's bell:　风铃

doleful knell:　哀悼的丧钟
29. curtal dog:　短尾牧羊犬
　　wont to have play'd:　过去常常欢腾
32. Procure:　因为，由于
33. howling wise:　号啕痛哭
　　doleful plight:　悲哀的苦境
34. resound:　荡漾
36. vanquisht:　伤残的；击败的

我穿丧服

恐惧全无　　　　　　　　20

爱弃我苦

我忍孤独

心血奔流

求救急呼

在劫何图　　　　　　　　25

苦胆汁流

我有牧笛吹不成

我有手铃赛丧钟

短尾爱犬兴冲冲

不再玩耍恐惧生　　　　　30

我叹深深

我泪淋淋

见命悲惨痛哭人

回乡叹声

荒原无情　　　　　　　　35

血战痛呼千百兵

Clear wells spring not,

Sweet birds sing not,

Green plants bring not

Forth their dye;   40

Herds stand weeping,

Flocks all sleeping,

Nymphs back peeping

Fearfully:

All our pleasure known to us poor swains,   45

All our merry meetings on the plains,

All our evening sport from us is fled,

All our love is lost, for Love is dead.

Farewell, sweet lass,

Thy like ne'er was   50

For a sweet content, the cause of all my moan:

Poor Corydon

Must live alone;

Other help for him I see that there is none.

39—40. bring not / Forth: 不展现

40. dye: 染色

43. Nymphs: 宁芙，希腊罗马神话中居于
   山林水泽中的仙女；美女
   peeping: 偷瞧

45. swains: 牧人

49. lass: 姑娘

52. Corydon: 科里东，古罗马诗弗吉尔
   （Virgil, 公元前 79—19）《田园诗》
   第二部里的牧羊人名字

清泉不喷

小鸟无音

草木无荫

五色不真　　　　　　　　　　　　40

痛哭牛群

沉睡羊群

宁芙窥人

惊慌失神

一切农人有穷欢　　　　　　　　45

一切欢聚原野观

一切游戏夜间逝

一切爱情誓不还

再会姑娘

娇媚无双　　　　　　　　　　　　50

给我甜蜜痛苦长

可怜牧人

独自生存

一旦求人何处寻

4

Whenas thine eye hath chose the dame,

And stall'd the deer that thou shouldst strike,

Let reason rule things worthy blame,

As well as fancy partial like:

  Take counsel of some wiser head,   *5*

  Neither too young nor yet unwed.

And when thou comest thy tale to tell,

Smooth not thy tongue with filed talk,

Lest she some subtle practice smell,—

A cripple soon can find a halt;—   *10*

  But plainly say thou lovest her well,

  And set thy person forth to sale.

4

1. Whenas:　When
2. stall'd:　套住
 strike:　动手
3. worthy blame:　该受斥责
4. fancy:　用情
 partial like:　偏见

8. filed talk:　做作的谈话
9. subtle practice:　诡计
 smell:　察觉
10. halt:　瘸子
12. set thy person forth to sell:　对你自己开个价

4

你选中意中姑娘
套住鹿要有主张
如何行动靠理智
切莫让偏见张狂
聪明人可以帮忙　　　　　　　　　*5*
不年轻入过洞房

向她表明真爱情
不装斯文去奉承
怕她疑你有诡计
跛子最知瘸子情　　　　　　　　　*10*
如何爱她说分明
自标身价权衡中

What though her frowning brows be bent,

Her cloudy looks will calm ere night:

And then too late she will repent   *15*

That thus dissembled her delight,

    And twice desire, ere it be day,

    That which with scorn she put away.

What though she strive to try her strength,

And ban and brawl, and say thee nay,   *20*

Her feeble force will yield at length,

When craft hath taught her thus to say:

    'Had women been so strong as men,

    In faith, you had not had it then.'

---

13. What though:　尽管
16. dissembled her delight:　掩饰她的高兴
20. ban and brawl:　咒骂喧嚷

不要管她皱眉头
天黑之前怒气无
良机错过她懊悔　　　　　　　　　*15*
心中高兴莫怕羞
天亮之前她多愁
轻蔑拒绝情郎丢

她苦用力和你拼
咒骂叫喊伤你心　　　　　　　　　*20*
终究投降缘力弱
狡黠教她语出唇
女有力量像男人
休想得到女钗裙

And to her will frame all thy ways;   *25*

Spare not to spend, and chiefly there

Where thy desert may merit praise,

By ringing in thy lady's ear:

 The strongest castle, tower and town,

 The golden bullet beats it down.   *30*

Serve always with assured trust,

And in thy suit be humble true;

Unless thy lady prove unjust,

Press never thou to choose anew:

 When time shall serve, be thou not slack   *35*

 To proffer, though she put thee back.

---

25. to her will frame all thy ways: 想尽办
法适合她的意愿
26. Spare not to spend: 该花钱时就花
27. merit praise: 优点受到赞美
28. ringing in thy lady's ear: 在你的女郎
耳边吹风
32. assured: 可靠的

33. in thy suit be humble true: 你求爱时要
低声下气而真诚
34. Press: 急于寻找
35. When time shall serve, be thou not slack:
时机成熟了，你不要迟疑
36. proffer: 贡献

一切举措随她心　　　　　　25
舍得花钱为美人
你有优点得赞赏
姑娘耳边闻佳音
城中堡垒最坚贞
黄金炮弹轰作尘　　　　　　30

永远服务献殷勤
求爱时节常屈身
姑娘若无他人念
不可厌旧而喜新
切莫松懈机会临　　　　　　35
她虽拒绝莫灰心

The wiles and guiles that women work,

Dissembled with an outward show,

The tricks and toys that in them lurk,

The cock that treads them shall not know.   *40*

  Have you not heard it said full oft,

  A woman's nay doth stand for nought?

Think women still to strive with men,

To sin and never for to saint:

There is no heaven, by holy then,   *45*

When time with age shall them attaint.

  Were kisses all the joys in bed,

  One woman would another wed.

---

37. wiles and guiles: 诡计，骗术

39. toys: 狂想，怪想

 lurk: 潜藏

43. strive: 争强斗胜

46. attaint: 玷污

女人常玩鬼花头
迷你外表有他图
隐藏伎俩小诡计
踩蹬雄鸡不知由　　　　　　40
不闻人言常常留
女人说不君莫愁

试想女子欲嫁男
不愿生活像圣贤
生活原非天堂景　　　　　　45
老来才有圣洁观
接吻全为床第欢
女去找女结良缘

But, soft! enough—too much, I fear—

Lest that my mistress hear my song: *50*

She will not stick to round me on the ear,

To teach my tongue to be so long:

  Yet will she blush, here be it said,

  To hear her secrets so bewray'd.

---

51. will not stick to round me on the ear:
 毫不留情地打我耳光
54. bewray'd: 泄露

我要小声莫再言
怕她听到怒火添
夫人听唱我挨骂
长舌男人够可怜
她已脸红听我言
夫人秘密我说穿

5

Live with me, and be my love,
And we will all the pleasures prove
That hills and valleys, dales and fields,
And all the craggy mountains yields.

There will we sit upon the rocks,   5
And see the shepherds feed their flocks,
By shallow rivers, by whose falls
Melodious birds sing madrigals.

There will I make thee a bed of roses,
With a thousand fragrant posies,   10
A cap of flowers, and a kirtle
Embroider'd all with leaves of myrtle.

5
3. dales: 谷，溪谷
4. craggy: 峻峭的
7. falls: 瀑布
8. madrigals: 牧歌
10. posies: 花束
11. kirtle: 外裙
12. Embroider'd: 绣

5

呼君前来做爱人
共度时光共欢欣
心谷沟壑田野上
崇峦叠峰快活神

我俩同坐岩石边　　　　　　　　5
牧羊人挥牧羊鞭
溪水清浅瀑布落
好鸟鸣唱情歌闲

我为君铺玫瑰床
千万花束吐芳香　　　　　　　　10
花冠一顶长裙舞
饰满花纹桃金娘

A belt of straw and ivy buds,

With coral clasps and amber studs;

And if these pleasures may thee move,   *15*

Then live with me and be my love.

LOVE'S ANSWER

If that the world and love were young,

And truth in every shepherd's tongue,

These pretty pleasures might me move

To live with thee and be thy love.   *20*

---

13. ivy buds: 常春藤花苞
14. coral: 珊瑚
    clasps: 扣子，钩子
    amber studs: 琥珀胸饰

草带一根长春藤
珊瑚扣环琥珀钉
倘若芳心能打动　　　　　　　15
与我生活爱无穷

情人答言

倘若世间爱情真
每个牧人言内心
美妙欢乐打动我　　　　　　　20
与君生活恩爱深

6

As it fell upon a day

In the merry month of May,

Sitting in a pleasant shade

Which a grove of myrtles made,

Beasts did leap and birds did sing,   *5*

Trees did grow and plants did spring;

Every thing did banish moan,

Save the nightingale alone:

She, poor bird, as all forlorn,

Lean'd her breast up-till a thorn,   *10*

And there sung the dolefull'st ditty,

That to hear it was great pity:

'Fie, fie, fie,' now would she cry;

'Tereu, Tereu!' by and by;

That to hear her so complain,   *15*

Scarce I could from tears refrain;

6
1. fell upon:　碰巧
7. banish moan:　消除悲伤
9. as all forlorn:　好不心酸，好不凄惨
10. up-till:　朝向
11. dolefull'st ditty:　最悲哀的歌儿
13. fie:　呸

14. Tereu:　特鲁（拟声词）
　　by and by:　不久以后
16. refrain:　忍住

6

生平碰巧有一天
正是欢乐五月间
坐在惬意绿荫下
山桃树丛皆欢颜
野兽跳跃百鸟鸣　　　　　　　*5*
树木丰茂瑞草生
一切一切免不快
除了天公有夜莺
可怜鸟儿剩孤独
胸脯荆刺血模糊　　　　　　　*10*
唱出歌儿最愁苦
听者不堪心更忧
呸呸呸呸叫连声
特鲁特鲁又连呼
听她哀怨听她诉　　　　　　　*15*
眼泪汪汪几时休

For her griefs so lively shown

Made me think upon mine own.

Ah, thought I, thou mourn'st in vain!

None takes pity on thy pain: *20*

Senseless trees they cannot hear thee;

Ruthless beasts they will not cheer thee:

King Pandion he is dead;

All thy friends are lapp'd in lead;

All thy fellow birds do sing,   *25*

Careless of thy sorrowing.

Even so, poor bird, like thee,

None alive will pity me.

Whilst as fickle Fortune smiled,

Thou and I were both beguil'd.   *30*

---

23. King Pandion: 潘狄翁国王，生公主菲
勒米拉（菲洛美，菲罗墨拉）
（Philomela）。公主死后化夜莺
24. lapp'd in lead: 用铅棺材盛殓

30. beguil'd: 受骗

如此哀恸之悲鸣
勾起我思我心疼
我想你悲兮无用
苦痛难惹人动情　　　　　　　　　*20*
无知树木不会听
残暴野兽怎共鸣
潘狄翁王已死去
所有亲朋铅棺中
其他鸟儿正争鸣　　　　　　　　　*25*
不会理睬你哀情
同病相怜见此鸟
同样悲伤无人疼
命运善变露笑容
你我受骗不知情　　　　　　　　　*30*

Every one that flatters thee

Is no friend in misery.

Words are easy, like the wind;

Faithful friends are hard to find:

Every man will be thy friend   *35*

Whilst thou hast wherewith to spend;

But if store of crowns be scant,

No man will supply thy want.

If that one be prodigal,

Bountiful they will him call,   *40*

And with such-like flattering,

'Pity but he were a king;'

If he be addict to vice,

Quickly him they will entice;

---

36. wherewith: 用以
37. crowns: 硬币
    scant: 不够，不足
    if store of crowns be scant: 如果存钱
    不够
39. prodigal: 挥霍的
40. Bountiful: 慷慨豪放

41. such-like: 这样的
42. Pity but he were a king: 遗憾的是他
    不是国王
43. be addict to vice: 沉溺于罪恶
44. entice: 诱惑

人人口头恭维你
皆非知己患难中
话易出唇像刮风
忠诚朋友难寻踪
人人皆可为你友　　　　　　　　35
因你有钱设宴中
手头拮据物不丰
无人接济示友情
一人挥霍又放荡
众人送他慷慨名　　　　　　　　40
说出话来去奉承
他非国王不合情
如果他意在作恶
即刻他堕地狱中

If to women he be bent,   *45*

They have at commandement:

But if Fortune once do frown,

Then farewell his great renown;

They that fawn'd on him before

Use his company no more.   *50*

He that is thy friend indeed,

He will help thee in thy need:

If thou sorrow, he will weep;

If thou wake, he cannot sleep;

Thus of every grief in heart   *55*

He with thee doth bear a part.

These are certain signs to know

Faithful friend from flattering foe.

---

45. be bent: 喜爱
46. commandement: 戒律
48. his great renown: 他的盛名
49. fawn'd: 巴结
57. certain signs: 确切标准
58. flattering foe: 溜须的敌人

如果他意在美人　　　　　　45
立刻堕入女掌心
命运之神眉头皱
他之声名无处寻
从前巴结之众人
如今再不和他亲　　　　　　50
如果作为真朋友
患难相帮全身心
你若悲伤友泪流
你醒友醒挂心头
无论心中有何苦　　　　　　55
他总为你分忧愁
一切标准说与人
假敌真友泾渭分

VII THE PHOENIX AND TURTLE

VII　凤凰与斑鸠

1

Let the bird of loudest lay,

On the sole Arabian tree,

Herald sad and trumpet be,

To whose sound chaste wings obey.

2

But thou shrieking harbinger,   5

Foul precurrer of the fiend,

Augur of the fever's end,

To this troop come thou not near!

3

From this session interdict

Every fowl of tyrant wing,   10

Save the eagle, feather'd king:

Keep the obsequy so strict.

题目
Turtle: turtledove, 斑鸠

1
1. lay: 歌唱
2. Arabian tree: 阿拉伯凤树
3. Herald: 宣布
   sad: 讣告

trumpet: 哀乐
4. chaste wings: 贞纯的众鸟

2
5. shrieking: 尖叫
   harbinger: 先行官
6. Foul precurrer: 邪恶的执事
   fiend: 恶魔

1

好鸟鸣啭展歌喉
飞上凤树最上头
讣告宣布奏哀乐
百鸟遵命舞哀愁

2

叫声刺耳猫头鹰   *5*
魔鬼之徒鬼神惊
忠于死神称信士
梦想入围万不能

3

飞扬跋扈霸道称
想入葬礼路不通   *10*
瑞禽严格遵礼法
羽族之王有雄鹰

---

7. Augur: 预言者
  fever's end: 死亡

11. feather'd king: 羽族之王
12. obsequy: 葬礼

3
9. session: 会场
  interdict: 禁止

4

Let the priest in surplice white.

That defunctive music can,

Be the death-divining swan,   15

Lest the requiem lack his right.

5

And thou treble-dated crow,

That thy sable gender makest

With the breath thou givest and takest,

'Mongst our mourners shalt thou go.   20

6

Here the anthem doth commence:

Love and constancy is dead;

Phoenix and the turtle fled

In a mutual flame from hence.

4
13. surplice: 白色法衣
14. defunctive: 死亡的
15. death-divining swan: 对死亡有预感的
    天鹅
16. requiem: 挽歌

5
17. treble-dated: 三倍长寿的

18. sable gender makest: 生出黑色的后代
20. 'Mongst our mourners shalt thou go:
    你务必参加哀悼的队伍

6
22. constancy: 忠贞
24. mutual flame: 彼此的火焰

4

祭司执礼着白袍
天鹅临死叫声高
深知乐理露灵性   15
领作弥撒有绝招

5

乌鸦寿命显超长
凭着气息生育强
幼雏天生成黑羽
参加赞礼不用忙   20

6

随之送葬唱哀辞
爱情忠贞化尘泥
凤凰斑鸠皆飞走
烈焰腾腾无消息

7

So they loved, as love in twain   *25*
Had the essence but in one;
Two distincts, division none:
Number there in love was slain.

8

Hearts remote, yet not asunder;
Distance, and no space was seen   *30*
'Twixt the turtle and his queen:
But in them it were a wonder.

9

So between them love did shine,
That the turtle saw his right
Flaming in the phoenix' sight;   *35*
Either was the other's mine.

7
26. essence:　精髓

8
29. remote:　遥远
　　asunder:　分开
32. wonder:　奇迹

9
33. shine:　电光闪灼
34. right:　清楚的
36. mine:　自我

7

如此深爱相偎依　　　　　　　25

心心相印不分离

爱之精灵成一体

数字被杀热恋期

8

两心相隔又相依

虽有距离空间迷　　　　　　　30

斑鸠已经到皇后

赤心相爱称奇迹

9

爱火燃烧两者间

斑鸠可见其有权

凤凰眼中爱火现　　　　　　　35

不分彼此心相连

10

Property was thus appalled,

That the self was not the same;

Single nature's double name

Neither two nor one was called.   *40*

11

Reason, in itself confounded,

Saw division grow together,

To themselves yet either neither,

Simple were so well compounded;

12

That it cried, "How true a twain   *45*

Seemeth this concordant one!

Love hath reason, reason none,

If what parts can so remain."

10

37. Property: 物性
    appalled: 使丧胆
38. self: 自我
39. single nature's double name: 同一本质的两个名称
40. neither two nor one was called: 既不叫做二，也不叫做一

11

41. confounded: 惶惑
43. to themsehes yet either neither: 二者全不知谁是自己
44. Simple were so well compounded: 这单一体又是复合体

10

本性由此其震惊

自我失去原面容

两个称谓一本质

称一称二理不通　　　　　　　　　　　　*40*

11

理智自身也恐慌

合二为一由双方

双方均不明身份

单一复合变无常

12

理智高叫叹双方　　　　　　　　　　　　*45*

二者忠诚一何强

爱情为主智为仆

分离双方和谐章

12

46. concordant:　一致的

47. reason none:　理智便无理

48. If what parts can so remain:　如果分离
的两部分总是如此

13

Whereupon it made this threne

To the phoenix and the dove,   *50*

Co-supremes and stars of love,

As chorus to their tragic scene.

THRENOS

1

Beauty, truth, and rarity,

Grace in all simplicity,

Here enclosed in cinders lie.   *55*

2

Death is now the phoenix' nest;

And the turtle's loyal breast

To eternity doth rest,

13
49. whereupon: 因此
      threne: 哀歌
51. Co-supremes: 并列的君王
52. chorus: 合唱

小题目
THRENOS: 哀歌，挽歌

1
53. rarity: 至上的感情
54. Grace in all simplicity: 最质朴处见风
      流
55. cinders: 灰烬

2
57. loyal breast: 忠贞的情怀
58. To eternity doth rest: 与不朽长相偎依

13

理智有感唱哀歌
凤凰斑鸠爱情多　　　　　　　50
堪称明星与旗手
悲哀场景悲音合

哀歌

1

稀有感情美与真
优雅高贵出真纯
化作灰烬聊藏身　　　　　　　55

2

凤巢凤巢今何存
斑鸠忠贞胸无尘
双双安息永存真

3

Leaving no posterity:

'Twas not their infirmity,   *60*

It was married chastity.

4

Truth may seem, but cannot be;

Beauty brag, but 'tis not she;

Truth and beauty buried be.

5

To this urn let those repair   *65*

That are either true or fair;

For these dead birds sigh a prayer.

3
59. posterity: 后代
60. infirmity: 体弱
61. married chastity: 婚后仍童身

4
62. Truth may seem, but cannot be: 似真
    者，真不见
63. brag: 吹嘘

5
65. urn: 瓮；缸
    repair: 经常去
67. sigh: 叹气
    prayer: 祈祷

3

永远安息无子孙
不为体魄不顶真　　　　　　60
只缘婚后保童身

4

好像是真却非真
自称为美美何寻
美真葬礼泪沾襟

5

常来看顾真美人　　　　　　65
骨灰瓮中逝鸟存
逝鸟默祷美与真

APPENDIX

1   The Origin of Shakespeare's Sonnets

The prime period of Shakespeare's artistic creations was under the reign of Queen Elizebath I, when the Renaissance was at its summit in England. The flourishing of literature was first revealed in the writing of poetry. In the sky of English poetry, there were many shining stars, among which Shakespeare was a very bright one, because his 154 sonnets reflect a bright colour in the artistic creations of sonnets in England. Driven by the curiosity of getting to the bottom of things and tracing to the source, it is necessary for people to know the origin and development of sonnet in order to fully appreciate Shakespeare's achievement in his writing of sonnets. This section is intended to track down the origin of Shakespeare's sonnets from two countries: Italy and Britain.

1.1 The birth place of sonnets in Italy

When we talk about the origin of Italian sonnets, it can be divided into two parts or two periods: the first period before Dante and the second period after Dante. The first period was one when sonnet was born and grew in Italy while the second period was the period of great prosperity.

The reason why Dante is chosen as the dividing line is Dante is regarded as the last man of the old period and the first one in the new period. The old period

refers to the Middle ages or medieval ages; the new period is the Renaissance. In Italy, in the later period of medieval ages, i.e. 13th century and 14th century, folk literature was springing up. Sonnet emerged as the times required. The term sonnet in Italian is "sonetto", meaning "little sound" or "song".

The begetter of the Italian sonnet is Giacomo da Lentini(1200?—1250), who has written 22 sonnets, one of which is as the following in Italian (or Sicilian dialect):

Io m'aggio posto in core a Dio servire,	*a*
Com'io potesse gire in paradise,	*b*
Al santo loco ch'aggio audito dire	*a*
U'si mantien sollazzo, gioco e riso.	*b*
Sanza mia donna non li voria gire,	*a*
Quella c'ha blonda testa e claro viso,	*b*
Ch'e sana lei non poteria gaudier,	*a*
Estando da la mia donna diviso.	*b*
Ma non lo dico a tale intendimento,	*c*
Perch'io peccato ci volesse fare,	*d*
Se non veder lo sno bel portamento,	*c*
E lo bel viso e'l morbido a sguardare:	*d*
Chè lo mi teria in gran consolamento,	*c*
Veggendo la mia donna in ghioria stare.	*d*

The rhyme scheme of his sonnet is *abab abab cdc dcd*, 11 syllables each line.

There is another claim that the first begetter of Italian sonnet is Gittone d'Arrezzo (?—1294). There were many sonneteers at that period: Rinaldo d'Aquino (1240?—1250), Guido Guinizelli (1235?—1276), Guido Cavalcanti (1255?—1300). Cavalcanti and Dante often wrote sonnets to one another using the same rhyme sequence. Cino do Pistoia (1270?—1336) was also a friend of Dante as Cavalcanti. Cecco Angiolieri (1260?—1313) wrote 128 sonnets, and Folgore da San Gimignano (?—?) created 32 sonnets and was very active in 1309—1317. The masterpiece of Angiolieri is *S'I' fossi foco*, unconventional and unrestrained, audacious and pungent. Many critics hold it is his excellent sonnet.

Dante Alighieri (1265—1321), famous for his long poem *Ladivina commedia*, *Devine Comedy*, also wrote 25 sonnets in his collection of poems *La vita nouva*, *The New Life*, the following of which is showing his deep love for Beatrice who died young but lived much longer in Dante's heart:

A ciascun' alma presa

A ciascun' alma presa e gentil core	*a*
nel cui cospetto ven lo dir presente,	*b*
in ciò che mi rescrivan suo parvente,	*b*
salute in lor segnor, cioè Amore.	*a*
Già eran quasi che atterzate l'ore	*a*
del tempo che onne stella n'è lucente	*b*
quando m'apparve Amor s ubitamente,	*b*
cui essenza membrar mi dà orrore.	*a*
Allegro mi sembrava Amor tenendo	*c*
meo core in mano, e ne le braccia avea	*d*
Madonna involta in un drappo dormendo.	*c*

Poi la svegliava, e d'esto core ardendo	*d*
lei paventosa umilmente pascea.	*c*
appresso gir lo ne vedea piangendo.	*d*

The rhyme scheme of this sonnet is *abba abba cdcdcd*, 11 syllables each line.

The great representative of Italian sonnet is Francesco Petrarca (1304—1374) because his main literary contribution is his writing of *Il canzoniere, The songs,* of 366 sonnets to express his profound love for a young fair lady Laura. One of the sonnets is as follows:

Solo e pensoso

Solo e pensoso i più deserti campi	*a*
Vo mesurando a passi tardi e lenti	*b*
e gli occhi porto per fuggire intenti	*b*
ove vestigio uman l'arena stampi.	*a*
Altro schermo non trovo che mi scampi	*a*
dal mani festo accorger de le genti;	*b*
perchè ne gli atti d'allegrezza spenti	*b*
di fuor si legge com'io dentro avampi:	*a*
si ch'io credo omai che monti e piagge,	*c*
e fiumi e selve sappian di che temper	*d*
sia la mia vita, ch'è celata altrui.	*e*
Ma pur si aspre vie nè si selvage	*c*
cercar no so ch'Amor non venga sempre	*d*
ragionando con meco, ed io con lui.	*e*

The Italian sonnet is divided into 2 parts, like the ancient Chinese poem, *ci*.

The first part is an octave, two quatrains, by which a problem is described. The second part is a sestet, two tercets, by which a solution is given. As a rule, the ninth line is a volta, a turn, which is a signal to indicate the transition from the problem to a solution. The three sonnets mentioned above are good illustrations.

In the sonnet written by Lentini, the rhyme scheme of the octave is *abab abab*, while in the sonnet by Dante, the rhyme scheme is *abba abba*. As for the sestet, the rhyme schemes of both Lentini and Dante are all the same: *cdcdcd*.

The Petrachan sonnet, as we can see from the poem above, is the standard Italian sonnet which is a very influential pattern in the history of sonnet writing. The rhyme scheme of the octave is *abba abba*, while the rhyme scheme of the sestet is *cde cde*. The Petrachan sonnet is very fine, smooth, careful, and exquisite, and the rhyme scheme of the octave is a good example, because the rhymed words *campi, lenti, intenti, stampi, scampi, genti, spenti,* and *avampi* are almost the same in rhyme. The rhyming scheme of the sestet *cde cde* is very popular in Europe.

Giovanni Boccaccio (1313—1375), an author of the famous work *Decameron,* wrote some sonnets, one of which is as follows:

Vetro son fatti I fiumi

Vetro son fatti I fiumi, ed I ruscelli	*a*
gli serra di fuor ora la freddura;	*b*
vestiti son i monti e la pianura	*b*
di bianca neve e nudi gli arbuscelli	*a*
l'erbette morte, e non cantan gli uccelli	*a*
per la stagion contraria a lor natura;	*b*
borea soffia, ed ogni creatura	*b*
sta chiusa per lo freddo ne'sua ostelli.	*a*

938

Ed io, dolente, solo ardo ed incendo	*c*
in tanto foco, che quell di Vulcano	*c*
a rispetto non è una favilla;	*d*
e giorno e notte chiero, ʻa giunto mano,	*c*
alquanto d'acqua il mio signor, piangendo,	*c*
nè posso impetrar sol una stilla.	*d*

The rhyme scheme of this sonnet is *abba abba ccdccd*, 11 syllables each line. The rhyme scheme of the octave is the same as that of Dante, while the rhyme scheme of the sestet is *ccd ccd*, which is a variety. In the standard Italian sonnets, the rhyme schemes of the second part, the sestet, are usually *cdcdcd, cddcdc, cdecde, cdeced, cdcedc*, and *ccdccd*, the sixth of which belongs to Boccaccio. By the way, there are 4 rhyme schemes in the Petrarchan form: *abba abba cde cde, abba abba cdcdcd, abba abba cce dde,* and *abba abba cde cde.*

1.2 The sonneteers before Shakespeare in England

Affter some 200 years of the Petrarcan sonnets, there was a golden period of sonnet writing in England as well as in France where there were two famous sonneteers: Pierre de Ronsard (1524—1585) and Joachim Du Bellay (1522—1560), both of whom wrote sonnets with the French pattern, i.e. the rhyming scheme is *abba abba cc deed*, or *abba abba cdc dcd*, 12 syllables each line. Whereas in England, there were 4 important sonneteers before Shakespeare:

Sir Thomas Wyatt (1503?—1542) was famous for his imitation of Petrarch's *Sonnets to Laura*. The main contribution of Wyatt is his own form of the sonnet, three quatrains, and one couplet, and the rhyming scheme is *abab abab abab cc*. Wyatt's sonnets are full of passion, rich in images, and very vigorous.

Henry Howard, Earl of Surrey (1517?—1547) was, like Wyatt, famous for naturalizing Renaissance poetic modes in English by cultivating the sonnet.

Surrey's rhyme scheme of sonnet is *abab cdcd efef gg*. Surrey translated Virgil's *Aeneid* into English in the form of blank verse, iambic pentameter. The English version of Petrarch's sonnet *Love, That Doth Reign and Live Within My Thought* is a good model of the English pattern sonnet which Shakespeare used in nearly all of his 154 famous sonnets.

Edmund Spenser (1552?—1599), *poet's poet*, finished his first important poem *The Shepherd's Calendar* in 1579, and began his masterpiece *Faerie Queene* in the same year. Spenser's love sonnets *Amoretti* (1591—1595) was published in 1595. There are 89 sonnets in *Amoretti*, the rhyme scheme of which is *abab bcbc cdcd ee*, known as the Spenserian sonnet. The 8th sonnet is the English pattern, or the Shakesperean pattern. The whole collection *Amoretti* including *Sonnet 15* is in honor of Spenser's bride Elizabeth Boyle:

Sonnet 15

Ye tradefull merchants, that with weary toile	a
Do seeke most pretious things to make your gain,	b
And both the Indias of their treasures spoile,	a
What needeth you to seeke so farre in vaine?	b
For loe my love doth in her selfe containe	b
All this world's riches that may farre be found.	c
If saphyres, loe her eyes be saphyres plaine;	b
If rubies, loe her lips be rubies sound;	c
If pearls, her teeth be pearls both pure and round	c
If yvorie, her forhead yvory weene;	d
If gold, her locks are finest gold on ground;	c
If silver, her faire hands are silver sheene	d
But that which fairest is, but few behold:	e

Her mind, adornd with vertues manifold.   *e*

Spenserian sonnet is famous for its own unique rhyme scheme, i.e. 5 pairs of rhymed words, meaning that the rhyme has changed 5 times. Nevertheless, the Shakespearean sonnet or the English sonnet is popular because its rhyme has changed 7 times and people find it is easy to imitate it. Although people praise the Spenserian sonnet because of its unity, strictness, clearity, elegance, and exquisiteness, there are not so many people who are eager to imitate it. The poems written by Spenser are both beautiful and full of true feelings, thus all of them can be ranked among the best poems in the history of world literature. In England, Spenser is Li Bai, a very famous poet in the Tang Dynasty 1500 years ago in China, in England. The 75th sonnet in his *Amoretti* has been popular in China for about 100 years, especially the two lines: "*My verse your Vertues rare shall eternize, / And in the heavens wryte your glorious name*". The beauty and the emotion of these two lines are the same as that of the last two lines in Shakespeare's Sonnet 18. But the 15th sonnet in *Amoretti* is so exellent that Shakespeare cannot be compared with it in poem writing.

Philip Sidney (1554—1586), famous both for his noble character and prose romance, *The Arcadia*, wrote *Astrophil and Stella*, Starlover and Star, a collection of 108 sonnets and 11 songs. The sonnets were intended to record the Sidney's reflection of his love affairs with Penelope Devereux who was not Sidney's devoted lover because she was not a woman of icy virtue. The 37th sonnet is worth reading and appreciating:

My mouth doth water, and my breast doth swell,   *a*
　　My tongne doth itch, my thoughts in labour be;   *b*
　　Listen then, lordlings, with good ear to me,   *b*
For of my life I must a riddle tell.   *a*
Towards Aurora's court, a nymph doth dwell,   ˎ   *a*

Rich in all beauties which man's eye can see,   b

Beauties so far from reach of words, that we   b

Abase her praise, saying she doth excel: a

Rich in the treasure of deserved renown,   c

Rich in the riches of a royal heart,   d

Rich in those gifts which give the eternal crown;   c

Who though most rich in these and every part,   d

Which make the patents of true wordly bliss,   e

Hath no misfortune, but that Rich she is.   e

The arrangement of the lines in this sonnet is at random but the sonnet has its own pattern or genre from which the readers can feel the passion of a young poet. The rhyming scheme is *abba abba cdcd ee*, iambic pentameter, which is the same as that of Spenser. As to the content, the sonnet can be divided into 4 sections. The first section is line 1 to line 4, which tells the young poet is crazy in his love affairs and wants to reveal his inward feeling to people. The second section is line 5 to line 8, the young poet compares his lover with a fairy in paradise. The third section is line 9 to line 12, from which both the physical value and the spiritual value of his lover are beyond one's dream. The fourth section is line 13 to line 14, which holds beauty is universal, beauty is everything.

Beauty is here; beauly is there; beauty is universal; beauty is everywhere. In the garden of sonnets, a hundred flowers are in blossom, which is a spectacular scenary. When flowers of all sorts are blooming in a riot of colour, a most beautiful one is showing itself. Introduced by Wyatt and Surrey, the sonnet writing standardized by Petrarch was at the apex in England when Sparser wrote his *Amoretti* and Sidney wrote his *Astrophil and Stella*. Shakespeare, inspired by Euterpe for lyrics, Thalia for pastoral, and Erato for love poetry, created 154 greatest sonnets. Thus Shakespeare has laid a solid foundation for the further

development of sonnet writing in England. By the early period in the 17th century, John Donne wrote 19 very fine sonnets under the tile of *Holy Sonnets*. Milton wrote political sonnets such as *On the late Massacre in Piedmont*, and *When the Assault Was Intended to the City*. On September 3, 1802, Wordsworth wrote his famous sonnet *Composed upon Westminster Bridge*. Keats wrote his wellknown sonnet *On First Looking into Chapman's Homer*. In 1819 Shelley wrote his romantic sonnet *Ozymandias*. Between 1847 and 1850, Elizabeth Barrett Browning compesed her collection *Sonnets from the Portuguese*.

2   The Contents of Shakespeare's Sonnets

From the year 1591 to the year 1597, about 6 or 7 years, Shakespeare wrote 154 sonnets in all, which were published in the year 1609 by Thomas Thorpe, a publisher. There is a famous "dedication" form which readers can see the poems dedicated to the "begetter". The begetter, Mr.W.H. can be regarded as Henry Wriothesley, the third Earl of Southampton (1557—1624), or William Herbert, the third Earl of Pembroke (1580—1630). The 154 sonnets are composed of 2155 (154×14+1−2) lines, the reason of which is that the 99th sonnet is composed of 15 lines, while the 126th sonnet is composed of 12 lines. By the way, the 145th sonnet is tetrametre in form, not the usual pentameter.

2.1 The Arrangements of the Poems

There are several different types of the arrangements of Shakespeare's 154 sonnets.

(1) According to Qian Zhaoming, Shakespeare's sonnets are divided into 8 parts: ① 1—14, 16, 17, are Shakespeare's persuasion of his handsome young friend to get married; by the way, Sonnet 15 is about the relation between the poet and time; ② 15, contends with time; ③ 18—58, although the contents are complex, there is a clear description of his friend's mistake which tells the adultery between his friend and his mistress; ④ 59—75, are about time, poets, friends and the real world; ⑤ 76—96, are about the art of poetry; ⑥ 97—108, are describing Shakespeare and his friend, departing and meeting again; ⑦ 109 —126, express Shakespeare's thoughts of destiny and fortune, and show his loyalty to friendship; ⑧ 127—152, are all about a dark lady; ⑨ 153—154, explore the well-known Greek and Roman myth to praise the eternity of love.

(2) Liang Shiqiu, a famous scholar and Shakespearean expert, prefers an arrangement among 20 different arrangements, which can be found in the work *The Sonnets Songs & Poems of Shakespeare* compelled by Oscar James Campbell. There are 154 sonnets written by Shakespeare, however, Compbell's arrangement covers 152 sonnets, 9 parts: ① 1—17, persuade his friend to get married and have children, 17 sonnets in all; ② 18—26, express the friendship between the poet and his friend, 9 sonnets in all; ③ 127—132, tell the early relationship between the poet and the dark lady, 6 sonnets in all; ④ 27—47, are about the poet's travelling, his friend and his dark lady committing adultery, 21 sonnets in all; ⑤ 133—142, tell the dark lady's infidelity for the second time, 10 sonnets in all; ⑥ 48—66, are about his friend's disloyalty, and the unsteadibility of human life, 19 sonnets in all; ⑦ 67—108, reveal the difficulty in the friendship between the poet and his friend, 42 sonnets in all; ⑧ 143—152, tell the awareness of the poets resulting in the departure from the dark lady, 18 sonnets in all; ⑨ 109—126, describe the compromise between the poet and his friend, 28 sonnets in all. It is a pity that the last 2 sonnets (153—154) are excluded, which are generally considered as the summery of the whole creation of all the sonnets, especially sonnet 154. The arrangement of the order of the whole sonnets is puzzling, because it is not easy to remember, although it is easy to understand.

(3) Zhan Siyang, the author of the book *A Survey of Shakespeare*, has divided the whole sonnets into 15 parts: ① 1—7, persuading his friend to have a family; ② 18—19, poems giving people eternity; ③ 20—32, praising friendship and love; ④ 33—52, the pains caused by the pertruder; ⑤ 53—65, the beauty of his friend; ⑥ 66—72, the twists and turns of his love affairs and the social environment; ⑦ 73—87, the worry of the coming of becoming old; ⑧ 88—89, the worry of being forsaken by his friend; ⑨ 100—120, the relapses of his friendship and the consolidation of it, which can be further divided into 4 parts: a. 100—103, the breaking off of the friendship, his regret, and their reconciliation of their friendship; b. 104—108, praising his lovely friend; c.

109—113, giving the reason of leaving his lovely friend; d. 114—120, from romance to reality and solidarity; ⑩121—126, the description of the inwardness, the personality, and the character of the poet. Remember, sonnets 1—126 are divided into 10 parts; ⑪ 127—130, the original beauty, the ordinary beauty and the melancholy beauty of the dark lady, and the analytic and critic viewpoint of desire, passion and lust; ⑫ 131—136, the dark lady having another lover; ⑬ 137—145, because of his mistress's infidelity, the poet being nearly in despair, struggling in disappointment in his love affair; ⑭ 146—152, making love with his dark lady and leaving her; ⑮ 153—154, by means of two Greek poems to cure Shakespeare's love sickness.

(4) In *The Globe Illustrated Shakespeare* by Howard Staunton, there is an arrangement by Mr. Brown which I prefer. Mr. Brown holds that 152 of the 154 sonnets should be divided into 6 poems, or 6 parts: ① stanzas (sonnets) 1—26, to his friend, persuading him to marry; ② stanzas (sonnets) 27—55, to his friend, who had robbed the poet of his mistress, forgiving him; ③ stanzas (sonnets) 56—77, to his friend, complaining of his coldness, and warning him of life's decay; ④ stanzas (sonnets) 78—101, to his friend, complaining that she prefers another poet's friend, and reproving him for faults that may injure his character; ⑤ stanzas (sonnets) 102—126, to his friend, excusing himself for having been some time silent, and disclaiming the charge of inconstancy; ⑥ stanzas (sonnets) 127—152, to his mistress, on her infidelity. However, sonnets 153—154 should be included as the 7th poem and as the stanzas 153—154, because these two sonnets, or stanzas, are the summary of the whole collection.

Although Mr. Brown's arrangement is concise and precise which is easy to understand and remember, it can't reveal the rich content of the whole collection. Readers can not be clear about the very famous sonnets and lines written by Shakespeare.

2.2 Three Famous Sonnets

The first one is Sonnet 18, which is well known both at home and abroad.

> *Shall I compare thee to a summer's day?*
> *Thou art more lovely and more temperate:*
> *Rough winds do shake the darling buds of May,*
> *And summer's lease hath all too short a date:*
> *Sometime too hot the eye of heaven shines,*
> *And often is his gold complexion dimm'd;*
> *And every fair from fair sometime declines,*
> *By chance, or nature's changing course, untrimm'd;*
> *But thy eternal summer shall not fade,*
> *Nor lose possession of that fair thou ow'st;*
> *Nor shall Death brag thou wander'st in his shade,*
> *When in eternal lines to time thou grow'st:*
> > *So long as men can breathe, or eyes can see,*
> > *So long lives this, and this gives life to thee.*

You are so beautiful that I can't compare you with the lovely summer's day, because you are more beautiful and gentler than the good and fine summer's day. In summer, there will be occasionally the heavy and violent wind which would shake off the tender and lovely buds of the lovely summer's day. The duration of summer's allotted time is extremely short. Sometimes the sun is too hot because of its bright sunshine. Very often the sun's beautiful, gold coloured appearance is clouded. Every beautiful thing sometimes declines, and every beautiful face sometimes declines, both of which are stripped of beauty by fortune, good or ill, or by the changeable order or process of nature. Nevertheless, your beautiful eternal summer will never fade. You will never lose your beauty that you owe. The god of death will never boast that you are walking in the shadow of death.

Your life will never be controlled by the god of death, if you grow and live and exist in my immortal poem as long as time lasts. If human beings exist in this world and their eyes can see everything clearly, and my eternal poem lives in the human society, my eternal poem will give you immortality definitely.

Summer is very beautiful because of its beautiful colour, its beautiful shape, its beautiful odour, its beautiful plants and flowers, its tender and suitable weather, it is a shame that summer is not eternal, it is just a short span of time. Summer has several weak points: short, changeable, violent wind and terrible heat. By my speculation of the aspects of summer, it seems that the eternity of beauty is somewhat dull, tedious and monotonous. Difference is beauty. Change is beauty. Something new is beauty. Something surprising is beauty. Something moving is beauty. That's the aesthetic experience of human being for maybe millions of years.

The second one is Sonnet 66, which is often selected by the Chinese scholars as the mirror of the real sociely.

Tired with all these, for restful death I cry, —
As, to behold Desert a beggar born,
And needy Nothing trimm'd in jollity,
And purest Faith unhappily forsworn,
And gilded Honour shamefully misplaced,
And maiden Virtue rudely strumpeted.
And fight Perfection wrongfully disgraced,
And Strength by limping Sway disabled,
And Art made tongue-tied by Authority,
And Folly, doctor-like, controlling Skill,
And simple Truth miscall'd Simplicity,
And captive Good attending captain Ill;

Tired with all these, from these would I be gone,
Save that, to die, I leave my love alone.

I feel very disgusted about all the unfair and ugly social phenomona. I am determined and I am crying and shouting that I am longing for a peaceful death to rest. I see very often that a deserving person is born a beggar. A noentity who lacks all merit is dressed up in finery. The purest and the best faith and loyalty is unfortunately and mischievously forsaken and abandoned. The high ranks, the golden, glorious honours are given to wrong persons, i.e, unworthy people. A pure maiden of good virtue is forced rudely and shamelessly to turn into a prostitute. A true person of real perfection is wrongfully treated as a disgraced one. A very strong healthy person is regarded as a very weak disabled one as incompetent and crippling. Learning and art are ordered to be quiet and silent. A fool is acting like a doctor and is controlling and ordering and oppressing those who have good judgement and those who are able to do a good job. The clear and useful and plain truth is slandered as silliness or folly. The people who are good and helpless have to obey the vicious amy officer. Tired of all these ugly social phenomena, I am determined to leave this society. As if I should die, I would leave my beloved forever.

The third one is Sonnet 116, which is held high as the best one in the expression of feeling and emotion of love.

Let me not to the marriage of true minds
Admit impediments. Love is not love
Which alters when it alteration finds,
Or bends with the remover to remove:
O, no! it is an ever-fixed mark.
That looks on tempests, and is never shaken,

949

It is the star to every wandering bark,

Whose worth's unknown, although his height be taken.

Love's not Time's fool, though rosy lips and cheeks

Within his bending sickle's compass come;

Love alters not with his brief hours and weeks,

But bears it out even to the edge of doom.

If this be error, and upon me proved,

I never writ, nor no man ever loved.

As to the marriage of true lovers, I can't allow the existence of the obstacles between them. When you find that a lover changes his or her mind, then love is not love. Love is not love when love turns in a new direction along with one who takes things away as time takes away beauty. Oh, it can't be love. Love is like a very solid seamark, i.e. a beacon or lighthouse which steadily watches the violent storm. The beacon can't be broken by the waves or storm. The beacon is the North Star to the boat which is not clear about its way. The North Star's influence is incalculable, though its altitude can be estimated. Love is not a plaything or mockery to a time, although rose-coloured or rose-like lips and cheeks are seasonal and vulnerable in the encircling reach or range of bending sickle of time. Love is not as changeable as the brief hours, days or weeks. Love sticks it out till the end of life, till doomsday. If this is a mistake which proves against me, I have written nothing, and I have loved no man.

2.3 Sonnets 38, 40, 41, 42, 50, 51, 80, 36and 96

(1) Sonnet 38

This sonnet is very knowledgeable, especially the first line "How can my Muse want subject to invent", which includes two issues: ①Muse   There are 9 muses in Greek mythology: 1st, (Clio, Klio), history; 2nd, Calliope (Kalliope),

epic, historic poems, 3rd, Euterpe, music and poetry; 4th, Thalia, comedy; 5th Melpomene, tragedy, 6th Terpsichore, dancing; 7th, Erato, lyric, love and marriage, 8th, Polyhymnia, song and oratory, and 9th, Urania, astronomy. Shakespeare holds that his friend is *"the tenth muse, ten times more in worth / Than those old nine which rhymes invocate"* ② Rhetoric　There are five elements in the classic rhetoric: inventio, dispositio, elocutio, memoria and pronunciatio. In the first line, the last word "invent" has its original Latin form: inventio.

(2) Sonnets 40, 41, 42

All these three sonnets are about the adultery committed by his friend with Shakespeare's or (the poet's) mistress. *I cannot blame thee for my love thou usest; / But yet be blamed, if thou this self deceivest / By wilful taste of what thyself refusest* (40). Shakespeares says to his friend: *Those pretty wrongs that liberty commits, / When I am sometime absent from thy heart* (41). In Sonnet 42, Shakespeare says *That thou hast her, it is not all my grief, / And yet it may be said I loved her dearly*. The order of the first part in Sonnet 42 should be *It is not all my grief that thou hast her*.

(3) Sonnet 45

This sonnet is also knowledgeble for its 8th line *Sinks down to death, opprest with melancholy*. There are four humours in the human body, according to the provential medical science in the middle ages, i.e. blood, phlegm, choler and melancholy. The term melancholy refers to black bile.

(4) Sonnets 50, 51

The descriptions of the poet's ill treating his horse are profoundly impressive. *The beast that bears me, tired with my woe, / Plods dully on, to bear that weight in me. His rider loved not speed, The bloody spur cannot provoke him on, / That sometimes anger thrusts into his hide* (Sonnet 50), *Then should I spur, though mounted on the wind. Then can no horse with my desire keep pace* (Sonnet 51).

The terrible bloody spur is not only the terror to a beast, but also a terror to human body and human mentality.

(5) Sonnet 80

This sonnet reveals how Shakespeare competes with his rival poet, George Chapman or Christopher Marlowe. *Or, being wrackt, I am worthless boat, / He of tall building and of goodly pride.* (Sonnet 80). Shakespeare feels *now my gracious numbers are decayed, / And my sick Muse doth give another place* (Sonnet 79). Shakespeare tells his friend *I grant thou wert not married to my Muse*, because other poets *have devised / What strained touches rhetoric can lend, / Thou truly fair wert truly sympathized / In true plain words by thy true-telling friend* (Sonnet 82). Shakespeare considers himself as a poet who tells his friend truth whenever and wherever.

(6) Sonnet 36, 96

Sonnet 36 is to Shakespeare's friend which reveals that there is separable spite between them. Sonnet 96 is also written to his friend and expresses his faith and loyalty in their friendship. These two sonnets are noticed for the repetation of the last two lines, line 13 and line 14, in both of them: *But do not so; I love thee in such sort, / As, thou being mine, mine is thy good report.* These same two lines are said to be the same couplets.

From the above analysis, it is obvious that when he was still young, Shakespeare created 154 sonnets as a dedication to a noble handsome young man. All the sonnets are the descriptions and speculations of the three aspects: truth, kindness, and beauty. The three aspects can be summed up with one word: Love. We can say the theme of the 154 sonnets is the love of his friend, the love of his arts, the love of the dark haired lady, and the love of nature. It is love that makes the world move. It is love that makes Shakespeare create his sonnets. It is Shakespeare's love that makes the eternity of his artistic creation.

3   The Versification of Shakespeare's Sonnets

In order to be a man of letters, Shakespeare in his literary career created 154 sonnets, 2 long narrative poems and various other poems. It is well-known that Shakespeare's sonnets have a great literary appeal to both the men of letters and the majority of readers all over the world. People are not only entertained and amused by his contents, emotion and genre, but also by his good skill or versification in the creation of his poems. The versification of Shakespeare's sonnets can be divided into 4 parts: lines, rhymes, rhythms and rhetoric.

3.1 The Lines

The line arrangement is one of the characterizations of poetry. Shakespeare's sonnets are composed of 2155 (154×14+1−2) lines. There are usually 14 lines in each sonnet, but in the 99th sonnet, there are 15 lines:

99

The forward violet thus did I chide:

Sweet thief, whence didst thou steal thy sweet that smells,

If not from my love's breath? The purple pride

Which on thy soft cheek for complexion dwells

In my love's veins thou hast too grossly dyed.

The lily I condemned for thy hand;

And buds of majoram had stoln thy hair:

The roses fearfully on thorns did stand,

On blushing same, another white despair;

A third, nor red nor white, had stoln of both,

And to his robbery had annext thy breath;

But, for his theft, in pride of all his growth

A vengeful canker eat him up to death.

    More flowers I noted, yet I none could see

    But sweet or colour it had stoln from thee.

The first line is considered as an extra, introductory line, the last word *chide* of which is rhymed with the last word *pride* in the third line. The rhyme scheme of the rest 14 lines is *abab cdcd efef gg*, the rhythm of which is iambic pentameter.

Sonnet 126 is held as the thesis of the whole collection of the 154 sonnets, however, it is the shortest one, 12 lines in all, with the striking different rhyme scheme: *aa bb cc dd ee ff*, which may be regarded as a set of six heroic couplets:

126

O thou, my lovely boy, who in thy power

Dost hold time's fickle glass, his sickle-hour;

Who hast by waning grown, and therein show'st

Thy lovers withering, as thy sweet self grow'st;

If Nature, sovereign mistress over wrack,

As thou goest onwards, still will pluck thee back,

She keeps thee to this purpose, that her skill

May Time disgrace, and wretched minutes kill.

Yet fear her, O thou minion of her pleasure!

She may detain, but not still keep, her treasure:

    Her audit, though delay'd, answer'd must be,

And her quietus is to render thee.

Strictly speaking, according to the lines, Sonnet 99 and Sonnet 126 can not be considered as two sonnets. However, since the time of the collection is long, about 7 years, and the generosity and the open-mindedness of the collectors and publishers and the readers as well, these two poems are compiled into the collection of the 154 sonnets written by Shakespeare.

3.2 Rhymes

In poem, rhyme is the similarity or sameness of the accented vowel sound of the end of words or lines, which has the aesthetic functions. It is well-known that Shakespearean sonnet or English sonnet is one of the two famous types of sonnets in the history of world literature. The other type is the Italian or Petrarchan sonnet. The rhyme scheme of Shakespearean sonnet is *abab cdcd efef gg* with the exceptions of sonnet 99 and sonnet 126. It is believed that when he wrote his sonnets, Shakespeare was very careful in his rhyme scheme and very strict with his poetic creation. However, when readers read all the 154 sonnets carefully, there are many places which show clearly that Shakespeare did not write his sonnets in an extremely careful way. There are some 19 pairs of unrhymed words which should be rhymed:

1st, Sonnet 1, line 2 and line 4, *die* and *memory*;

2nd, Sonnet 13, line 6 and line 8, *were* and *bear*;

3rd, Sonnet 16, line 6 and line 8, *unset*, and *counterfeit*;

4th, Sonnet 17, line 2 and line 4, *deserts* and *parts*;

5th, Sonnet 25, line 5 and line 7, *spread* and *buried*; perhaps the specific pronunciation of the word *buried*;

6th, Sonnet 30, line 2 and line 4, *past* and *waste*;

7th, Sonnet 31, line 2 and line 4, *dead* and *buried*; perhaps the specific

pronunciation of the word *buried*;

8th, Sonnet 33, line 2 and line 4, *eye* and *alchemy*;

9th, Sonnet 35, line 6 and line 8, *compare* and *are*; perhaps eye rhyme is used here;

10th, Sonnet 42, line 6 and line 8, *her* and *her*, just a repetition of the same word;

11th, Sonnet 52, line 5 and line 7, *rare* and *are*, perhaps eye rhyme;

12th, Sonnet 54, line 5 and line7, *dye* and *wantonly*;

13th, Sonnet 62, line 1 and line 3, *eye* and *remedy*;

14th, sonnet 105, line 1 and line 3, *idolatry* and *be*;

15th, Sonnet 109, line 10 and line 12, *blood* and *good*, perhaps eye rhyme;

16th, Sonnet 112, line 9 and line 11, *care* and *are*, maybe eye rhyme;

17th, Sonnet 116, line 10 and line 12, *come* and *doom*;

18th, Sonnet 138, line 2 and line 4, *lies* and *subtleties*;

19th, Sonnet 140, line 5 and line 7, *were* and *near*.

From the above examples, it is obvious that there is no rhyme issue from Sonnet 63 to Sonnet 104. It is true that there is a structure issue in sonnet 99. The reason is well-known that at this time of poetic creation, Shakespeare was morose and cautious since his poetic rivals were too honorable and too influential. The technique of writing sonnet should be put at the first place. While in the other sonnets, Shakespeare's intention is to express his strong feeling of friendship, youth, love, and sex, therefore the subtlety of his poetry is somewhat neglected.

3.3 Rhythms

Rhythm is in poetry the regular arrangement of repeated stressed and unstressed syllables, which depends on the metrical pattern. Shakespeare tries his best in his employment of the poetic technique of rhythm while writing his

famous sonnets.

It is obvious that Sonnet 18 is his cautious artistic creation using the iambic pentameter:

18

Shall I | compare | thee to | a sum | mer's day?

Thou art | more love | ly and more tem | perate:

Rough winds | do shake | the dar | ling buds | of May,

And sum | mer's lease | hath all | too short | a date:

Sometime | too hot | the eye | of heav | en shines,

And of | ten is | his gold | complex | ion dimm'd;

And ev | ery fair | from fair | sometime declines,

By chance | , or na | ture's chang | ing course | , untrimm'd;

But thy | eter | nal sum | mer shall | not fade,

Nor lose | posses | sion of | that fair | thou ow'st;

Nor shall | Death brag | thou wan | der'st in | his shade,

When in | eter | nal lines | to time | thou grow'st:

So long | as men | can breathe | , or eyes| can see,

So long | as lives | this, and this | gives life | to thee.

Readers can see clearly that there are some variations in the iambic pentameter: 1st, in line 2, the third foot, *ly and*, is the pyrrhic pattern, 2nd, in line 14, the last line, the third foot *this, and this*, is the anapest pattern.

116

Let me | not to | the mar | riage of | true minds

Admit | imped | iments.| Love is | not love

Which al | ters when | it al | tera | tion finds,

Or bends | with the | remove | er to | remove:

O, no! | it is | an ev | er-fix | ed mark。

That looks | on tem | pests, and | is nev | er shaken,

It is | the star | to ev | ery wan | dering bark,

Whose worth's | unknown, | although | his height | be taken.

Love's not | Time's fool, | though ros | y lips | and cheeks

Within | his bend | ing sick | le's com | pass come;

Love al | ters not | with his | brief hours | and weeks,

But bears | it out | even | to the | edge of doom.

　　If this | be er | ror, and | upon | me proved,

　　I nev | er writ, | nor no | man ev | er loved.

In Sonnet 116, although it is the best one of all the 154, there are more exceptions in its metrical pattern. 1st, in line 1, the forth foot, *riage of*, is in the pyrrhic pattern. 2nd, in line 2, the fourth foot, *Love is*, is the trochee pattern. 3rd, in line 4, the second foot, *with the*, is in the pyrrhic pattern. 4th, in line 5, the first foot, *O, no*, is the spondee pattern. 5th, in line 6, the third foot, *pests, and*, is the pyrrhic pattern. 6th, in line 7, the fifth foot, *dering bark*, is the anapest pattern. 7th, in line 9, the first foot, *Love's not*, is the trochee pattern, while the second foot, *Time's fool*, is the spondee pattern. 8th, in line 11, the first foot, *Love al*, is the spondee pattern. 9th, in line 12, the third foot, *even*, is the trochee pattern; the forth foot, *to the*, is the pyrrhic pattern; the fifth or the last foot, *edge of doom*, is the amphimacer pattern. 10th, in line 13, the third foot, *ror, and*, is the pyrrhic pattern.

Sonnet 145 is not iambic pentameter, but in the pattern of iambic tetrameter. The 12th line consists of 9 syllables, which is between tetrameter and pentameter.

145

Those lips | that Love's | own hand | did make

Breathed forth | the sound | that said | 'I hate'

To me | that lan | guisht for | her sake:

But when | she saw | my woe | ful state.

Straight in | her heart | did mer | cy come,

Chiding | that tongue | that ev | er sweet

Was used | in gi | ving gen | tle doom;

And taught | it thus | anew | to greet;

'I hate' | she al | ter'd with | an end,

That fol | low'd it | as gen | tle day

Doth fol | low night, | who like | a fiend

From heav | en to | hell is | flown a | way;

'I hate' | from hate | away | she threw.

And saved | my life, | saying— | 'Not you.'

There are also some 7 variations in its metrical pattern: 1st, in line 2, the first foot, *Breathed forth*, is the trochee pattern; 2nd, in line 3, the third foot, *guisht for*, is the trochee pattern. 3rd, in line 5, the first foot, *Straight in*, is the trochee pattern. 4th, in line 6, the first foot, *Chiding*, is the trochee pattern. 5th, in line 9, the third foot, *ter'd with*, is the pyrrhic pattern. 6th, in line 12, the second foot, *en to*, is the pyrrhic pattern; while the third foot, *hell is*, is the trochee pattern, and the forth foot, *flown a*, is also a trochee pattern. 7th, in line 14, the third foot, *saying*, is the trochee pattern. The 6th one can be regarded as 3 minor variations.

3.4 Rhetoric

Shakespeare is very skillful in his use of rhetorical devices since he knows clearly that rhetoric is the art of using language effectively in his poetic creation.

Many figures of speech could be easily observed in his sonnets. In this section only 3 of them are discussed, i. e. parallelism, repetition, and punning.

66

Tired with all these, for restful death I cry, —

As, to behold *Desert a beggar born,*

And *needy Nothing trimm'd in jollity,*

And *purest Faith unhappily forsworn,*

And *gilded Honour shamefully misplaced,*

And *maiden Virtue ruddy strumpeted.*

And *fight Perfection wrongfully disgraced,*

And *Strength by limping Sway disabled,*

And *Art made tongue-tied by Authority,*

And *Folly, doctor-like, controlling Skill,*

And *simple Truth miscall'd Simplicity,*

And *captive Good attending captain Ill;*

Tired with all these, from these would I be gone,

Save that, to die, I leave my love alone.

The origin of parallelism in Greek is *parallelismos*, meaning *alongside one another*. In Sonnet 66, from the second line *Desert beggar born*, to the twelfth line *And captive Good attending captain Ill*, there are 11 lines in all to create the beauty of aesthetics of unity. In this sonnet, the rhetorical technique repetition is also employed in its very effective way: a. *Tired with all these* appears in the first line and the thirteenth line as well; b. *And* is at the beginning of the line repeatedly 10 times. By the way, this rhetorical or literary tradition is greatly inherited by Walt Whitman (1819—0892) in his *Song of Myself* and several other poems.

135

Whoever hath her wish, thou hast thy *Will*,

And *Will* to boot, and *Will* in overplus;

More than enough and I that vex thee still,

To thy sweet <u>will</u> making addition thus.

Wilt thou, whose <u>will</u> is large and spacious,

Not once vouchsafe to hide my <u>will</u> in thine?

Shall <u>will</u> in others seem right gracious,

And in my <u>will</u> no fair acceptance shine?

The sea, all water, yet receives rain still.

And in abundance addeth to his store;

So thou, being rich in *Will*, add to thy *Will*

One <u>will</u> of mine, to make thy large *Will* more.

  Let no unkind, no fair beseechers kill;

  Think all but one, and me in that one *Will*.

Punning, or to pun, is to play on words which have different meanings and senses, or connotations. In his sonnet 135, Shakespeare has punned the word *will* since it is a polysemic. The word *will*, in the poem, has 7 different meanings: William Shakespeare, wishes, sexual desire, passion, temper, sexual organs (male and female), and the friend's name. The three *Will*'s in line 1 and line 2 may imply the poet's name, wishes, sexual desire, and male or female genitals. The *will* in line 4 means vagina and penis. In line 5, *will* indicates vagina, while in line 6 *will* refers to penis. The word *will* in line 7 means wishes and sexual desire, and *will* in line 8 has the same meaning. *Will* in the midde of line 11 means sexual desire, while the second *Will* in this line refers to another man named *Will* or sexual desires, or vagina. The first *will* in line 12 refers to sexual desire or penis,

while the second *Will* may refer to vaginal capacity, sexual desire or another lover *Will*'s penis. The last *Will*, or the 13th *Will*, implies William Shakespeare, desire, or penis. The punning of the word *will* can also be found in sonnet 136 and Sonnet 143. The word *will* is a polysemy, which has its primary meaning as a strong mental power as its central signification. When using this word, pay attention to its generalization and its specialization. Take care of its elevation or amelioration and its degradation or degeneration. Its antonornasia can be observed as two persons, one is William Shakespeare, the other is another lover of the dark skined lady who is very fickle with strong sensual desire.

When poetry is considered, discussed and studied, the poetic techniques can not be ignored or waved aside like cobweb since poetry is an art which has its longest history in the origin and development of human literature for its good genre and great beauty both on the surface structure and in the deep structure. The poetic techniques are to reveal the beauty in form and in structure. Therefore the very important skills of the arrangement of the poetic lines and the rhymes, rhythms and rhetoric will definitely arouse sense of beauty among the majority of readers. When creating a poem, or sonnet, poets as well as laymen should persist in writing in accordance with the versification, i.e. the poetic principles or the aesthetic laws and try their best to avoid vialations. Poem is poem, poet is poet. Sonnet is sonnet. It is necessary to lay a firm and solid foundation of poetic writing. Shakespeare has set up a good example for the men of letters although occasionally he has somewhat minnor errors in his sonnet writing technically.

4   The Exploration of *Venus and Adonis*

The period of Renaissance in England lasted some 100 years since the early 16 century to the end of the century during which the reign of Queen Elizebath I lasted 45 years (1558—1603). Shakespeare (1564—1616) knew clearly that poetic creation was the literary vogue at that time and wrote his famous long narrative poem *Venus and Adonis* which was very popular at that time after its printing. The young people read Shakespeare's *Venus and Adonis* and took much delight or pleasure in it. One of the reasons why people enjoyed Shakespeare's poetic work is the popularity of Venus and Adonis. It is no doubt that Venus and Adonis are the 2 protagonists in the poem, but it is out of question that Venus and Adonis are the 2 topics in West Asia mythology, Greek mythology and Roman mythology. Based on the study of mythology, it is entertaining to explore the origin and development of Venus, the goddess of beauty in the three great myths, and the high place as a super nature of Adonis, the young rosy Shepherd, in West Asian mythology. The mythical love story has been given a humanist explanation.

4.1 The Influence of West Asian Methology

On the earth, or in the universe, the birth of human race is a mystery, while the birth of myth is a wonder. Myth is a great creation during the childhood of human race, which is so beautiful, fantastic, fascinate, and amusing that it has exterted a great wonderful influence and impact on the human race from his or her childhood to his or her adulthood. It is difficult to go back to the exact date of the origin of the world myth, but the world myth could be further divided into 5

hierarchies: Asian myth, European myth, American myth, African myth, and Oceanian myth. The 5 hierarchies could be further divided into subhierarchies: Egypt, Babylon, Persia, Arabia; Sri Lanka, India, Tibet; Siberia, Mongolia, China, Japan, Kerea; Greece, Rome, German; North America, Central America, South America; Sahara, The West Coast, East and South Africa, Madagascar; Polynesia, Melanesia, Micronesia, Australia. Among all the subhierarchies of the world myths, Greek and Roman myths are the most influencial myths in the world. It is no doubt that Greek myth is the origin of Roman myth though the latter is very, very influential during and after the great period of Renaissance and the reign of Elizabeth I.

4.2 Venus (Aphrodite) in Greek and Roman Methology

The legend of the birth of Aphrodite is that when Kronos or Cronos cut off Uranus's phallus with a sharp sickle, he flung the immortal member into the sea, where it floated amid white foam. Inside the divine flesh a goddess was nurtured, whom the Greeks called Aphrodite, *She who came from the foam*. Aphrodite was and is worshipped in Cyprus, Cytherea, Corinth, Carthage, and Sicily.

Aphrodite or Venus was born in the foam of the sea, or broadly speaking, the Mediterranean Sea. The exact location of the goddess's birth place is Cythera or Kithira, in Italian, Cerigo, an island to the south of Greece, or the Peloponnesos peninsula. Aphrodite first arrived in Cyprus, an island near Asia Minor, Syria and Lebanon. Then she came to Corinth, the northeast part of Poloponnesos peninsula, wellknown city-state for its luxury in ancient Greece. Aphrodite was then worshipped in Carthage, a famous ancient slavery state, now located in Tunis. Finally the goddess Aphrodite, Venus, was worshipped in Sicily, the big Italian island to the south of Italy.

Aphrodite, as a goddess of love, has special epithets, like Kallipygos, Greek word, kálos, beauty + pygē buttocks, *She of the beautiful buttocks*; Morpho,

Greek word, morphē, form, the shapely; and Ambologera, *She who postpones old age*. At Corinth, a place name in Greece, in the ancient times, there were even temple prostitutes.

Aphrodite has several other meanings or senses: Apostrophia, she who turns herself away; Androphonos, man killer; Tymborychos, gravedigger; Anosia, the unholy; Epitymbidia, she who is upon the tombs; and the most striking significance, Pasiphaessa, the far shining queen of the underworld. Aphrodite was also regarded by the Athenians as the oldest Moirai, the singular form of which is Moira, meaning the goddess of fate.

Being an unfaithful wife of Hephaistos, in Roman mythology, Volcan, which is more popular, the crippled ugly smith god, Aphrodite (Venus in Roman mythdogy) loved the war god Ares, or Mars in Roman mythology. Aphrodite had several children: Eros or Amor a god of love, Anteros, Hymen, a god of marriage, and Hermaphroditus, son of Hermes, a god of husbandary, who was a rosy young boy. Hephaistos was outraged and then devised a trap of subtle chains and caught Aphrodite and Ares together in bed, calling the Olympian gods to witness his shame, but all the gods laughed except Poseidon, in Roman mythology, Neptune, who promised a suitable atonement on behalf of the gods.

Aphrodite had strong antipathies, fixed unconquerable dislikes or hatreds for others. Thus she slew Hippolytos, a chaste and upright son of King Theseus; she changed Polyphontē, who murdered the former king, killing his sons then marrying the queen Merope, into an owl; and she transformed Myrrha, a beauty and mother of Adonis, into a myrtle tree.

The following may be taken as having been the most usual to be 12 in number composed of the same gods in both Greek and Roman mythology: Zeus (Jupiter), Hera (Juno), Poseidon (Neptune), Demeter (Ceres), Zeus's elder sister, the goddess of fruits, grain and vegetation; Artemis (Diana), the goddess of the moon, Hephaestos (Vulcan), the god of fire, Athene (Minerva), the goddess of

wisdom, Ares (Mars), the god of war, Aphrodite (Venus), the goddess of love and beauty, Hades (Pluto), the god of the underworld, Hermes (Mercury), the messenger, and Hestia (Vesta) the goddess of the home-fire.

Aphrodite (Venus) has 4 lovers, one is Ares (Mars), and their children are Harmonia, daughter; Eros, in Roman mythology Cupid, love god; Anteros, god of mutual love; Phobos, in Roman mythology, Pavor, God of the anxities of love; and Deimos, the threatening spirit. The second lover is Hermes, in Roman mythology, Mercury, messenger, their child is Hermaphroditus, rosy handsome young boy. The third one is Archises, a grandson of Troyan king Ilus, their child is Aeneas, a hero in Troyan war. The fourth one is Adonis, the young rosy shepherd.

There are many symbols for Aphrodite (Venus) which can be slassified as two categories: the 1st category includes cockle, dove, sparrow, ram, hare, dolphin, swan, and tortoise; the 2nd category includes apple, rose, poppy, and myrtle. Aphrodite (Venus) also has a mysterous charming girdle on her waist.

Aphrodite (Venus), although usually regarded as the godders of love in a common sense, was also worshiped as the goddess of productiveness, of poetry and art in the best times of Greece, but in the times of luxury, she was considered the goddess of many kinds. Influenced by the oriental culture and the Mediteranean culture, Aphrodite (Venus) was the goddess of pretecting commerce. Under the title of Urania Aphrodite was the goddess of the power of love; while under the title of Aphrodite Pandemos, Aphrodite was the goddess of love among men. The fishermen and sailors held Aphrodite as the goddess of the smiling sea, the peaceful sea, and the prosperous vayages. With the change of seasons, Aphrodite was also the goddess of gardens and flowers. Aphrodite was viewed as a goddess of married life and marriage ceremonies, in brief, a goddess of marriage. On a beautiful day, Aphrodite got the reputation of the most beautiful by Paris, or Alexandros, for her promising of the loveliest wife on earth to Paris, despite of the promisings of the throne of Asia by Hera, and the immortal fame as a hero by Athene. To sum up, Aphrodite (Venus) is the goddess of love,

beauty, marriage, sea, commerce, productiveness, poetry, art, gardens, and flowers, 10 functions in all. Compared with Guanyin, a Bodhissattva, in Buddhism, Guanyin is more divine, while Aphrodite (Venus) is more human.

In astronomy, the Roman way of the names of the gods to name the planets in the solar system is very popular internationally: the 1st planet, Mercury (Hermes), then Venus (Aphrodite), Mars (Vulcan), Jupiter (Zeus), Saturn (Cronos), Uranus, the ancient god of heaven in Greek mythology, Neptune (Poseidon), and Pluto (Hades) god of the underworld and the god of wealth. From the above examples, it can be seen clearly that except Uranus, all the other 7 gods are from Roman mythology, and the second planet Venus is the most beautiful star in the heaven at night. In Homer's epic, Pluto was the king of the underworld.

4.3   Adonis in Greek and Roman Mythology

Adonis, although regarded as the young rosy shepherd in Greek and Roman mythology, was originally the god of nature and the incarnation of the withered plants in Semitic mythology. Adonis was worshipped by the Phoenicians in Syria, Asia Minor. In Semitic, the first four letters of Adonis, Adon, has the meaning of *lord*. In Phoenicia and Syria, Adonis was worshipped in Byblos, while in Cyprus Adonis was worshipped in Paphos. The death and resurrection of Adonis were widely celebrated in Asia Minor by people especially women in mid-summer and the women both in Greece and Italy as well.

Adonis' birth place and the myth of the love affair between him and Aphrodite (Venus) has been the household word in the world. According to Greek mythology, Myrrha or Smyrna had an unnatural love for her father Cinyras, king of Cyprus, the earliest singer and musician. Myrrha refused to honour Aphrodite and Aphrodite smoted her. When Cinyras knew the truth and wanted to kill her with his sword, Myrrha was changed by gods into a myrtle and gave birth to Adonis. The birth place of Adonis was the island Cyprus, situated to the west of

Syria, with his Syrian equivalent, Thamuz the god of reproduction. Adonis, the young rosy shepherd, was Aphrodite's (Venus's) special favourite and was killed by wild boar, which was said to be the incarnation of Hephaestos (Vulcan) who envied the love affair.

Hades, brother of Zeus, king of the underworld, or Zeus of the lover world, had his queen Persephone, daughter of Dementer, goddess of the earth and agriculture. Persephone was once asked to take care of Adonis by Aphrodite. Therefore, after the death of Adonis, Aphrodite and Persephone quarreled over his possession. In accordance with the decision of Zeus, a third part of the year was with Persephone, the queen of the dead, a third part of the year was with Aphrodite, the goddess of beauty, and another third part of the year was for Adonis to dwell by himself. Adonis was worshipped in Syria and Greece.

4.4 The Love Affair between Venus and Adonis

The custom and the behaviour of the southern European people decide the behaviour of the gods both in Greek mythology and Roman mythology. It is said that the people in south Europe, influenced by the climate of Mediterranean Sea, lived freely and romantically. It is also said that the Greek and Roman mythology can be considered as the story of common people. Therefore, Zeus or Jupiter, although the supreme deity, was not faithful to his queen Hora or Juno, and consorted with other goddesses, nymphs, and women, under the disguise, of various forms and shapes. Leda, queen of Sparta, was approached by Zeus in the form of a swan, and Helen was their offspring. Zeus, in a form of a shower of gold, penetrated to Danae, daughter of king Acrisius, and their child Perseus was born and became the great hero in Greek and Roman mythology, and in astronomy a constellation was named in honour of him, Perseus. Aphrodite, the most beautiful goddess of heaven, sea and earth, also has many romances, one of which is the love story between her and Adonis.

According to Canaanite or Semitic mythology in west Asia, Aphrodite was the goddess of the Phoenicians, originally the goddess of the East, named Astarte, the goddess of reproduction and love. Adonis was also originally the rosy young shepherd in Canaanite mythology. Both Aphrodite and Adonis were worshipped in Byblos and Paphos, the former is in Syria, while the latter is in Cyprus. Canaan is really a great mysterious place because it has produced the great religion and the great goddess of beauty and the world famous handsome young shepherd. Both Aphrodite and Adonis were borrowed into Greek mythology and Roman mythology.

During the Renaissance period in England, the appearance of Shakespeare's *Venus and Adonis* was the eulogy of passionate love from woman as the healthy antidote of the asceticism of the Medieval Ages. Can we say that Aphrodite (Venus) gave way to her carnal desires and the goddess of beauty was indulged in sensual pleasures? Love is people's instinct. Love is people's needs. Love is people's desire. Love is people's life. Love is blind. Love is purposeful. Love is ideal. Love is romantic. Venus (Aprodite) fell in love with Adonis because the goddess of beauty appreciated the beauty of the young rosy shepherd Adonis wholeheartedly and wanted very much to combine with him. Venus wanted to be a happy goddess since she did not get pleause from Vulcan (Hephaistos), an ugly old cripple smith. Owing to no love between Venus and Volcan the so called couple had no offspring. What a tragic married life! Venus is not an ascetic. Venus is vigorous and passionate to persue an ideal, genuine, authentic, and earthly love like all women who dream their sweet dream to obtain.

4.5 Aphrodite (Venus) and Adonis in Literature and Fine Arts

Aphrodite (Venus) and the love affair between the goddess and Adonis are the favourite of great poets, playwrights, sculptors, and painters. Homer (800?—700? B.C.) described the topic in both his *Iliad* and *Odyssey*. Publius Ovidius

Naso (43—? B.C.) in his *Metamorphoses* spent 237 lines in Chapter 10 to depict in detail the love affair between Venus (Aphrodite) and Adonis. Euripides (480—460 B.C.) in his play (tragedy) *Hippolytus* reveals the character of Aphrodite (Venus), the protagonist, through the soliloquy of the goddess: *Great is my power and wide my fame among mortals and also in heaven; / I bless those that respect my power, and disappoint these who are not humble toward me.*

There are 6 famous sculptures about Venus: *Venus Accroupie, Venus Genetrix* by Kallinachos, *Venus Kallipygod, Venus of Medici, Venus of Milo* (*Melos*) which is the most famous one, and *Venus of Savignaro.* In the history of European painting, many painters created great paintings of Venus and Adonis, e.g. Annibale Carracci (1560—1609) and his *Venus and Anchises*; Francois Boucher (1703—1770) and his *Mars and Venus Caught by Vulcan*; and Jean Auguste Dominique Ingres (1780—1867) and his *La Source.* Other painters such as Tiziano Vecelli (1477—1576?), Nicolos Poussin (1594—1665), and Peter Paul Rubens (1577—1640) created great and glorious works to be the eulogy on Venus and Adonis.

The legend or myth of Venus and Adonis can be traced to remote antiquity. The romantic story took place mainly in and around the Mediterranean Sea. Love is the human nature. Love story is people's favourite even though the story is the love affair between goddess and a young rosy shepherd. It is necessary for people to study in detail myths or mythology, which can not be simply and arbitrarily judged as ignorance or superstation. The Greek and Roman mythology should be considered as the great valuable literary heritage and cultural legacy greatly influenced by the ancient West Asian mythology. The mythical romantic love stories belong to good world literature which is very helpful to the readers and scholars to have a profound understanding of Shakespeare's original work. The rich imagination during the childhood of human race has painted many beautiful

pictures in front of people which are very helpful to people's aesthetic imagmation, aesthetic judgment, aesthetic idea, and aesthetic enjoyment.

5   Love and Nature in *Venus and Adonis*

The origin of *Venus and Adonis* is Ovid's *Metamorphoses*, although Shakespeare has created a Renaissance Venus who is very passionate with true earthly love. The whole poem is composed of 1194 lines, 199 staves of sesta rima, iambic pentameter, i.e. six-lined decasyllabic stanza, rhymed *ababcc*. Venus is the Roman goddess of beauty, love and marriage in Roman mythology, the equivalent of Aphrodite in Greek mythology. Adonis is the young rosy shepherd in Greek and Roman mythology as well as in West Asian mythology, beloved by Aphrodite or Venus. In the poem, Venus, a beautiful, passionate lady, detains the shepherd boy Adonis, hugging him, kissing him, and crying in order to win his love. Nevertheless, Adonis, unripe of love, leaves Venus for hunting and is killed by a wild boar, which is said to be the incarnation of Vulcan, the husband of Venus, whereas, in west Asian mythology, boar is held as a sacred animal. The blood of Adonis changes into a flower, Anemone, which Venus mourningly brings and returns to Pathos, Cyprus. This section discusses the earthly goddess Venus, the shepherd boy Adonis, and the descriptions of the tears of the goddess, the horses, the birds, the plants, and the natural setting in general.

5.1 The Earthly Goddess Venus

In Shakespeare's long narrative poem *Venus and Adonis*, Venus has separated herself from her dual personalities: *Aphrodite Uranos* and *Aprodite Pandemos*, and has completely been a humane *Aprodite Pandemos*, goddess Venus, full of earthly love. Venus reminds readers of many female protagnists in the literary works or folklore, such as the female protagonist in *Eugene Onegin* by Aleksander Sergeyevich Pushkin (1799—1837), Anna in *Anna Karenina* by

Count Lev Nikolayevich Tolstoy (1828—1910), Fairy VII in Chinese folklore, a popular legend, *The Fairy Marriage*, Helena in Shakespeare's comedy *Midsummer Night's Dream*, another Helena in Shakespeare's another comedy *All's Well that Ends Well*, Jailer's Daughter in Shakespeare's romance *The Two Noble Kinsmen*, all of them are brave and passionate to woo another half, althongh with different personalities and various methods.

The whole poem is wholly about how Venus, the goddess of beauty, woos Adonis, the young rosy sheherd. The whole process of wooing is very difficult because Adonis is as callous as cold-blooded animal. The value of this long poem just lies in its difficulty. Eating and love are the two elements which are the human nature. Every people have the desire to appreciate beauty. Although Venus bravely and passionately pursues earthly love, it is beyond reproach. It is rational for Adonis who loves hunting and is indulged in it, being ignorant of love. Venus in Roman mythology has an equivalent Aphrodite in Greek mythology. It is a common knowledge that myth is the reflection of the aspects of the society and the culture in the childhood of human race. It was not a shame in ancient Greece and Rome for woman to woo a handsome young man or a handsome juvenile. Contrarily, it is the topic people take delight in talking about. Epikouros (341—270 B.C.), a philosopher in ancient Greece, advocated hedonism when he held that the wise conduct of life is attained by reliance on the evidence of senses. Epikouros had a famous saying: *Nothing to feel in death. Good can be attained. Evil can be endured.* The image of Venus created by Shakespeare is the embodiment of sensualism and hedonism by Epikouros, and is the bursting of humanism in the Renaissance in Enland, and is the devastive denial of the Platonian spiritual love or platonic love initiated by Plato (427—347 B.C.) in his *Philebus*. However, human race with both biological attribute and social property is the mixture of animal, humanity and divinity. Human race or people need both earthly love and spiritual love. To deny or ignore either of them is to deny or

ignore the natural instincts of human race. God is created by human race. The common or the earthly people have created human race, philosophers, and spiritual love. Spiritual love also offers people maximum spiritual satisfaction and enjoyment and treat. Both Shakespeare's goddess of beauty and Plato have something to recommend. Although human race has his divinity, asceticism is not acceptable; although human race has desire, it is not acceptable to indulge in sensual pleasures. Venus keeps telling Adonis a carpe diem philosophy. Since it is philosophy, it must be valuable to human life. This philosophy is one which Shakespeare tells human race by way of the goddess of beauty, Venus, who keeps wooing Adonis, the young rosy shepherd. Venus is young, vigorous, shining, fresh and beautiful: *pleasand fountains* (234)*, sweet bottom grass* (236)*, and round rising hillocks* (240). The above description of the body of Venus, the most beautiful goddess, is like an amazing and sensuous oil painting, and here Shakespeare compares the body of Venus to a garden where a lovely deer plays in.

In Shakespeare's long narrative poem the descriptions of human desire or lust are bold and free. To be bold is to be brave. To be brave is not barefaced. People need to pay attention to the occasion when mentioning love desire, sexual desire, carnal desire, or lust. These desires, however, are not shameful, not wicked, not vicious, not something evil. When he was 29, as a young poet, Shakespeare dedicated this long narrative poem to an aristocrat, who was only 20. Both of them were young, full of sap, courageous and upright. It could be imagined that Shakespeare and the aristocrat were on friendly term in thinking. It is no wonder that at that time the poem was very popular among the young readers and was printed 15 times. In the formal occasion, people should be serious, straightening clothes and sitting properly; in daily life, however, people should enjoy family happiness. It is not suitable to be pedantic. Enjoy daily life, enjoy nature, enjoy one's whole life, enjoy one's youth. Enjoy Shakespeare's poetic art.

Love is kind of illness or sickness or disease. Love is labour. Love is courage, love is bravery. Love is energy, love is vigour, love is physical power, love is motive power. Love is idea, love is hope. Love is living, Love is life. Love is palpitation, love is vitality. Love is taste, love is interest. Love is youth, love is human life. Love is intelligence and wisdom, love is art. Love is devotion and contribution, love is dedication. Love is benevolence, love is friendship. Love is goodness, love is beauty. Love is charm, love is Helen. Love is clear spring or fountain, love is fresh flower, love is fine rain, love is rainbow. Love is infatuation, love is insanity. Love is loss, love is devastation. Love is everything. Love is difficult. That's why Venus, the goddess of love, is so popular all over the world.

The love of Venus, the goddess of love and beauty, is selfish, authentic, great and holy. In the poem, the description of Venus can be summed up in three words: desire, missing, and commemoration, As for desire, Shakespeare spends a great part of the space, which may be said in gaudy colours, or as magnificent as a cadenza. The whole poem is coming straight to the point: Venus wooing Adonis at the very first stanza. The desire that Verus wooes Adonis is expressed by both the language and the action of the goddess. The language is used by Venus to show her extreme beauty, to show how Venus was loved deeply by Mars, the war god, to tell Adonis the philosophy of hedonism, and to tell Adonis that he needs to get married and beget his children. Adonis, unremoved by the goddess, left the goddess mercilessly. Venus, being worried about the security of Adonis, the young rosy sheherd, missed her sweetheart the whole night. Their actions and behaviours are expressed in language. After Adonis changed into a flower, Anemone, Venus, the goddess, shew her deep grief with language. The actions and behaviour Venus employed to express or show her desire or love are embrace, hug, and kisses, which are the intimate behaviours of the touching and combination of skins, fleshes, and bodies. To express the missing of Adonis by

the goddess, the crying and tears of the goddess, and her rushing on the wild field and in the bushes are fully described. It is better to say that it was the behaviour of a country girl than that it was the action of a goddess. The commemorating action of the goddess towards Adonis who was dead because of the serious wound by a wild boar, was holding Anomene, and on her light chariot driven by her silver doves, flying back to Paphos, a holy place in Cyprus, where Venus, the goddess of love and beauty is worshiped, and where Adonis is piously worshipped by women, both from Asia and Europe.

Shakespeare, by way of the words of Venus, the goddess of beauty, describes her extreme beauty in a moving and stirring way:

> *Thou canst no see one wrinkle in my brow,*
> *Mine eyes are grey, and bright, and quick in turning;*
> *My beauty as the spring doth yearly grow,*
> *My flesh is soft and plum, my marrow burning,*
> > *My smooth moist hand, were it with thy hand felt,*
> > *Woud in thy palm dissolve, or seem to melt.*
> > > *(139—144)*

Influenced by *Book 10* in Ovid's *Metamorphoses*, Shakespeare depicts Venus' rushing:

> *And as she runs, the bushes in the way,*
> *Some catch her by the neck, some kiss her face,*
> *Some twin'd about her thigh to make her stay,*
> *She wildly breaketh from their strict embrace,*
> > *Like a milch doe, whose swelling dugs do ache,*
> > *Hasting to feed her fawn hid in some brake.*
> > > *(871—876)*

To the tears of the goddess, lines 191—192 are the side description; lines 95—96 and lines 833—834 are the implied deseription; lines 949—950 are the introductory description and the questions for the god of death by Venus, the goddess of beauty, immediately after which are the two stanzas (955—966) to describe the pouring tears in a meticulous way and in an exquisite way:

> *Here overcome, as one full of despair,*
> *She vail'd her eylids, who like sluice stopp'd*
> *The crystal tide that from her two cheeks fair*
> *In the sweet channel of her bosom dropp'd;*
>> *But through the fold-gates breaks the silver rain,*
>> *And with his strong course opens them again.*
>
> *O how her eyes and tears did lend and borrow!*
> *Her eyes seen in the tears, tears in her eye,*
> *Both crystals, where they view'd each other's sorrow,*
> *Sorrow that friendly sighs sought still to dry;*
>> *But like a stormy day, now wind, now rain,*
>> *Sighs dry her cheeks, tears make them wet again.*
>>
>> *(955—966)*

This kind of description of tears can also be found in Shakespeare's *A Lover's Complaint* (281—287). At the very beginning of this long narrative poem *Venus and Adonis*:

> *Even as the sun with purple-color'd face*
> *Had ta'en his last leave of the weeping morn,*
> *Rose-cheek'd Adonis hied him to the chase;*
> *Hunting he lov'd, but love he laugh'd to scorn.*

(1—4)

Although these four lines depict the tears of mother nature, which in fact are the tears of the goddess of the dawn, Aurora, weeping to be left by the sun god, as a matter of fact this description serves as a foil to the description of the tears of Venus, the goddess of beauty. If it is said that the description in several different stanzas are used to give vent to the strong emotion to love by a woman or young lady, then, various kinds of descriptive techniques allow the image of tears reappear in front of the readers in a very vivid artistic genre.

The origin of the tears of goddess Verus is indeed her true feeling. The goddess is sweet and charming, soft and tender. Her beauty also lies in her pure whiteness and her crystal like brightness. A gentleman or a handsome prince should have tender affection for her. Don't be headstrong to her. It is because of Adonis' coldness that the good chance is lost forever.

5.2 The Young Rosy Shepherd Adonis

Concerning Adonis, a young rosy shepherd in Shakespeare's poem, love is not his luck, love is not his happiness, although he is loved and wooed by the extreme beauty, Venus. At the very beginning of the poem, Shakespeare tells the readers: *Rose-cheeked Adonis hied him to the chase / Hunting he loved, but love he laughed to scorn (3—4)*. Being seized by Venus, Adonis was *red for shame, but frosty in desire (36)*. Being kissed by Venus, Adonis *saith she is immodest, blames her miss (53)*. Although Venus was tortured to woo Adonis by every means with her great burning passion, the result was in vain and Venus was only a lovesick goddess. The pursuit of happiness and love vanished like soap bubbles. The young rosy shepherd Adonis even told the difference between love and lust. In love affairs, Adonis was unripe and acted as a green hand and did not appreciate Venus' true love. Adonis was totally in rage when he saw his horse

run a way with a Spanish mare as he was wooed by Venus. After ruthlessly leaving Venus who wooed him bitterly and wholeheartedly, Adonis was killed bya wild boar in his night hunting. Adonis was lucky: the extremely beautiful goddess Venus approaching him, loving him, missing him. When he was dead and changed into Anemone, Adonis was still deeply loved by the goddess and became the god worshiped by women. Adonis was a brilliant and immortal figure in Greek and Roman mythology and an artistic model winning universal praise. Adonis was unlucky: being too young to enjoy beauty, nor being able to grasp the chance to enjoy love offered by Venus. Adonis was very young but became a martyr who sacrificed his life for asceticism. Adodis clung obstinately to his own way or hunting and finally met with his death. It was a tragedy that Adonis even gave an account of the so called Platonic love which he was not quite sure. Both the physical Adonis and the spiritual Adonis were the victim or prey of the true love.

5.3 The Descriptions of the Aninals

The description of an eagle is the simile of Venus:

> *Even as an empty eagle, sharp by fast,*
> *Tires with her beak on feathers, flesh, and bone,*
> *Shaking her wings, devouring all haste,*
> *Till either gorge be stuff'd, or prey be gone;*
> $\qquad$ *(55—58)*

The description of the boar is impressing:

> *But this foul, grim, and urchin-snouted boar,*
> *Whose downward eye still looketh a for a grave*
> *Ne'er saw the beauteous livery that he wore—*

Witness the entertainment that he gave.

(1105—1110)

Shakespeare describes a dive-dapper:

Like a dive-dapper peering through a wave,

Who being look'd on, ducks as quickly in;

(85—86)

A dive-dapper is the simile of Adonis. Shakespeare has a peaceful description of a deer:

I'll be a park, and thou shalt be my deer:

Feed where thou with, on mountain, or in dale;

(231—232)

The image *deer* is a metaphor of Adonis.

Shakespeare uses 4 stanzas to describe the hare, the first of which is as follows:

And when thou hast on foot the purblind hare,

Mark the poor wretch, to overshut his troubles,

How he outruns the wind, and with what care

He cranks and crosses with a thousand doubles:

The many musits through the which he goes

Are like a labyrinth to amaze his foes.

(679—684)

Shakespeare emplores 11 stanzas (259—234) to describe Adonis' trampling, a strong horse, and a breeding jennet, a small Spanish nare, although the latter is given merely a few lines. The descriptive techniques are mainly two categories: the descriptions of the movement, *breaketh, goes, rushes, snorts, neighs, leaps, bounds, crusheth, glisters, trots, told, scuds, fanning, answers, knew, spurns, scorns, beating, vails, stamps, bites, perceiving, left, and outstripping,* and the static description (295—300):

> *Round-hoof'd, short-jointed, fetlocks shag and long,*
> *Broad breast, full eye, small head, and nostril wide,*
> *High crest, short ears, straight legs and passing strong,*
> *Thin mane, thick tail, broad buttlck, tender hide,*
> > *Look what a horse should have he did not lack,*
> > *Save a proud rider on so proud a back.*
> > > *(295—300)*

Although it is not a battle steed, it is a fine horse. Shakespeare, a young poet, praises it highly. This fine horse is waiting for a handsome prince, and is keeping silent, without showing its intentions. This description of Adonis' horse is a very good observation in every detail.

The description of the snail is also a simile of Venus:

> *Or as the snail, whose tender*
> *Shrinks backward in his shelly cave with pain,*
> *And there, all smoth'red up, in shade doth sit,*
> *Long after fearing to creep forth again;*
> > *(1033—1038)*

Several other animals and birds are also described or mentioned by

Shakespeare in his long narrative poem, such as *dove, crows, vulture, hounds, caterpillars, lark, doe, fawn, adder, lion, dogs, and fishes,* which could be considered as his description of the part of mother nature.

5.4 The Descriptions of the Plants

Shakespeare also describes or mentions some plants: *The field's chief flower, sweet above compare* (8); *roses* (10); *blue-vein'd violets* (125); *sturdy trees* (152); *herbs; sappy plants* (165); *seeds* (167); *shadow* (176); *grass* (236); *brakes obscure and rough* (237); *wood* (323); *bud* (416); *leaf* (416); *the mellow plum* (528); *grapes* (601); *thorny trembles* (629); *embracing bushes* (629); *tender spring* (656); *brier* (705); *myrtle grove* (865); *violet* (936); *weed* (1055); *mulberries* (1103); *ripe-red cherries* (1103); and *berries* (1104). Among all the plants and flowers, Venus, the goddess of beauty, loves the purple flower best:

> *By this the boy that by her side lay kill'd*
> *Was melted like a vapor from her sight,*
> *And in his blood that on the ground lay spill'd,*
> *A purple flow'r sprung up, check'red with white*
> *(1165—1168)*

This purple flower is also named Anemone which is held as the incarnation of Adonis, the young rosy shepherd.

5.5 The Descriptions of the Nature in General

From the very beginning through to the end of the long narrative poem *Venus and Adonis*, Shakespeare's description of the natural settling is impressing. *Even as the sun with purple-color'd face / Had ta'en his last leave of the weeping morn* (1—2). In the midday, *And Titan, tired in the midday heat / With burning*

eye did holy overlook them (177—178). Shakespeare mentions *a copse* (259) and then describes the night: *The night of sorrow now is turn'd to day* (481). Through the words by Adonis, Shakespeare writes: *Look the world's comforter with weary gait / His day's hot task hath ended in the west; / The owl night's herald shrieks, 'tis very late; / The sheep are gone to fold, birds to their nest* (529—532). Venus runs *through the dark laund* (813), lying *in the dark* (827) *in some mistrustful wood* (826). *The sun ariseth in his majesty, / who doth the world so gloriously behold / That cedar tops and hills seem burnish'd gold* (856—858). In line 865, *a myrtle grove* is mentioned and in line 871 *the bushes* are mentioned as well. In the 1191 and 1193 are two brief descriptions: *the empty skies* and *Paphos*.

In his long narrative poem, Shakespeare's descriptions of the animals, plants, and the natural scenery have provided readers more spots to appreciate, which the artistic works should do with the characteristics of education with pleasure. In the scenic spots, reader feel as if they went back to the 16th century England, in Shakespeare's native place Stratford-upon-Avon, Warwickshire, appreciating and enjoying fully and happily the legendary pastoral scenary there at the bank of Avon. On the wild field, in the forest, accompanied by animals and birds, readers could enjoy the offer and bless of mother nature, feeling relaxed and happy, carefree and joyous. The lively atmosphere bestowed by mother nature reappear in Shakespeare's comedies: *A Midsummer Night's Dream, Twelfth Night, As You Like It*, and *The Merry Wives of Windsor*, and it is said that the origin of Windsor in the comedy is Stratford-upon-Avon.

It is held by scholars that the creation of the long narrative poem *Venus and Adonis* is in accordance with Shakespeare's personal experience of love, because in 1582, at the age of 18, Shakespeare got married with maiden Anne Hathaway of Stratford, who was 26, 8 years older than Shakespeare. Anne Hathaway was only a yeoman's daughter, then how could young Shakespeare fall in love with

her? One answer is that Anne kept wooing Shakespeare like Venus does to Adonis in Shakespeare's poem. *Venus and Adonis* is a long love poem, in which the female protagnist is successfully created because her passion and love are charming, attractive, authentic, genune, and humane. The decriptions of both the two protagnists and the setting are worth reading for their natural beauty. To praise and enjoy the natural beauty is people's passion and needs. To describe and praise the great combination of male and female and the great love is the holy task or mission of a great poet, because human race need passion, love, even lust. Both the deities Venus and Adonis' and the poem are immortal.

6   The Two Protagonists in *Lucrece*

The Rape of Lucrece is one of the two long narrative poems written by William Shakespeare which tells an age-old lengemdary historical story of the tragedy of Lucrece who was a chaste and undefined noble lady raped by Tarquin, a prince of Roman sovereign before the year 510 B.C. The poem was very popular among both the poets and readers, because in Shakespeare's time, it was published 6 times. The first edition was in the year 1594, 22 years before Shakespeare passed away in 1616. In the 22 years, it was published once about 5 years because of its genre and the vogue at that time. The success of the long narrative poem lies mainly on its glorious tradition and the two protagonists: Tarquin and Lucrece.

6.1 The Origin of the Poem

The lengendary story of Lucrece was very famous in the Roman history, therefore many writers or poets created their literary works in honour of Lucrece, the noble Roman lady, the saint.

Ovid (43 B.C.—18 A.D.) wrote his *Fasti* describing the event of Lucrece based on *History of Rome Book I* written by Livy (284—204 B.C.) about the crime of Tarquinius. In the years between 1566—1575, William Painter also translated Livy's history entitled *The Palace of Pleasure*. Samuel Daniel (1562—1619) created his complaint poem *Complaint of Rosamond*.

Geoffrey Chaucer (1340?—1400) wrote his *The Legend of Good Women* perhaps in the year 1385 in the 10-syllable rhymed couplets or heroic couplets. In this poem, Chaucer has praised poetically 10 famous women: ①Cleopatra, ②

Thisbe, ③Dido, ④Hypsipyle and Medea, ⑤Lucretia, ⑥Ariadne, ⑦Philomela, ⑧Phyllis, and ⑨Hypermnestra. Cleopatra was the queen of Egypt. Thisbe was a devoted lover of Pyramus in an Asian legend. Dido was a queen in Roman mythology. Both Hypsipyle and Medea were noble ladies in Greek mythology. Ariadne was a clever lady in Greek mythology. Philomela was an Athenian princess who changed into a nightingale. Phyllis was a princess in Greek mythology. Hypermnestra was a princess in Greek mythology who shew mercy on her husband. Here comes Lucrece. Chaucer, father of English literature, the founder of 10-syllable line poetry, uses 205 lines, line 1680—line 1885, to describe the lengendary story of Lucrece. In the section, the fifth one, Chaucer highly praises the extraordinary beauty of Lucrece and severly condemns the shamelessness of Tarquin. When Ardea, an important ancient city, 24 miles from the south of Rome city, was besieged by the powerful Roman troop for a long time, one evening, after supper, Collatine, one of the Roman generals, praised his wife Lucrece with his peers. Then Tarquin, prince of the Roman king, went with Collatin to his home in Rome in the evening to see his wife Lucrece, where he was shocked by her beauty. Tarquin, after returning to the military tent, kept thinking of Lucrece, and also in the evening, he went to Lucrece's chamber secretly and stealthly and raped Lucrece who had no way out but told her husband Collatine the event. Collatine and his friends as well as his relatives rebelled against the Roman sovereign and overthrew it immediately after the crime. Thus the event of Lucrece is traditionally considered as the foundation of the founding of Roman Republic. Consequently, Lucrece was admitted posthumously Saint Lucrece like Saint Joan of Arc.

In the Proloque, Chaucer was rebuked by the god of love for he only wrote the shame and crime of women in his creative work *Troilus and Criseyde* and his translation of *The Romance of the Rose (Roman de la Rose)*. Abiding by the instruction of the God of love, Chaucer created *The Legend of Good Women*,

which has laid a solid foundation of Shakespeare's creation of *The Rape of Lucrece*.

6.2 Tarquin

In Shakespeare's long narrative poem *The Rape of Lucrece*, there are two ways of spelling of this main male charater, one is Tarquin, the other is Tarquinius, whose whole name is Sextus Tarquinius. Tarquin's father was the king of Rome, who is named Lucius Tarquinius, but people would call him Superbus for he was excessively proud of himself.

(1) Psychological Analysis of Tarquin's Crimes

According to Sigmund Freud (1856 — 1939), the structure of one's personality can be devided into 3 parts: id, ego, and superego. The term id can be defined as the part of one's unconscious mind where many personal basic needs, feelings and desires are supposed to exist, which wants instant gratification and pleasure. The term id can be considered as the synonym of instincts and impulses. The definition of ego is the part of mind which tries to experience and react to the outside world in a logical, practical and rational way in order to get what id wants, and its synonym is humanity. *Superego* is the part of mind that monitors the id and the ego to make a person be aware of his or her conscience and feel guilty if she does something wrong. The synonym of superego is divinity.

(2) The biological reasons for Tarquin's crime

It is supposed to be two biological reasons for Tarquin's crime: the first is his criminal private desire, the second is his distinct of animal. Beauty is a kind of property which is very attractive and amusing. Tarquin, a young prince, admires the beauty of Lucrece and wants to possess or plunder it out of his ambition and greediness. Tarquin is lascivious and licentious: "*Sextus Tarquinius being inflamed with Lucrece's beauty*" (*THE AUGUMENT*);

> *Borne by the trustless wings of false desire*
> *Lust-breathed Tarquin leaves the Roman host*
>
> *(2—3)*

With his Roman blade (505), Tarquin went into Lucrece's chamber stealthily and raped Lucrece shamelessly and ruthlessly. One's lust is gratified, nevertheless, the other's beauty is almost completely destroyed.

(3) The intrigue and manoeuvre of Tarquin's crime

To attain his evil aim, Tarquin mainly employs two intriques or manoeuvres.

The first one is his cunningness. Tarquin, as a monster like robber of beauty and chasteness, knows clearly how to across the sea by a trick, i.e., to practice deception. When Tarquin came to Lucrece's house, Shakespeare writes "*O! rash false heat, wrapp'd in repentant cold*"(48). Tauquin knows how to conceal his true characteristic, "*Whose inward ill no outward harm express'd*"(91).

> "*For that he colour'd with his high estate,*
> *Hiding base sin in plaits of majesty;*
> *That nothing in him seem'd inordinate,*
> *Save sometime too much wonder of his eye*
>
> *(92—98)*

Tarquin is "*Far from the purpose of his coming thither*"(106) Lucrece could see "*No cloudy show of stormy blustering weather / Doth yet in this fair welkin once appear* "(108—109). All the lines reveal the appearance of Tarquin at that time, which is somewhat like Macbeth *recept* Duncan at his house. Tarquin's moving towards Lucrece's chamber at night is just like Macbeth wants to murder Duncan at dark night, which reveals that Tarquin's cunningness also lies in his action. "*Away he steals with open listening ear*"(283). "*Into the chamber wickedly he stalks / And gazed on her yet unstained bed*"(365—366).

The second manoeuvre is Tarquin's quibble or indulgence in sophistry with

horrible threat. When readers read Stanzas 74, 75, 76 and 77 (512—539), one can't help feeling extremely angry with Tarquin with deep hatred.

> *'Lucrece,' quoth he, 'this night I must enjoy thee:*
>
> *If thou deny, then force must work my way,*
>
> *For in thy bed I purpose to destroy thee:*
>
> *That done, some worthless slave of thine I'll slay,*
>
> *To kill thine honour with thy life's decay;*
>
> > *And in thy dead arms do I mean to place him,*
> >
> > *Swearing I slew him, seeing thee embrace him.*
>
> > > *(512—518)*

Tarquin then tells Lucrece her husband, her kinsmen and "*Thy issue blurr'd with nameless bastardy*"(522). Tarquin, like Richard III, forces Lucrece to give up and permit him to enjoy her.

(4) Tarquin's Losses after the Crime

After his vicious crime, Tarquin suffers from at least 4 losses. The first one is that Tarquin betrays his friendship with Collatine, a Roman general, husband of Lucrece. Tarquin and Collatine are together in the war of the besieged Ardea. They two and the other principal men of the army meet at the tent of Tarquin one evening chatting in the harmonious atmosphere. How could Tarquin intend to enjoy the beauty of Lucrece, his close friend's wife? Therefore Tarquin has lost his friendship with Collatine. The second loss is that Tarquin neglects his official affairs and fogets his position as the prince of Rome. The war is going on, but Tarquin just wants to seek pleasure and intends to rape a noble lady. How can people say Tarquin is a qualified general in the war and a worthy successor of the Roman king, Lucius Tarquinius? It's a shame that Tarquin has lost his high position. Shakespeare says Tarquin "*His honour, his affairs, his friends, his state,*

/ *Neglected all*' (45—46). The third loss is that Tarquin tramples on his ethics or moral principles. To be a good prince, Tarquin is not allowed to be lascivious and loose in morals. Inflamed by Lucrece's extreme beauty, Tarquin dare risk universal condemnation. People can see clearly in reality Tarquin risks both universal and historical condemnation. The fourth loss is Tarquin's fame and reputation. Before the crime, no one knows the real character and personality of the prince, so Lucrece gives a welcome to him for he is a noble prince. Then "*is Tarquin brought unto his bed*" (120). How could Tarquin cheat and destroy such a good noble lady, with his high prestige swept away?

(5) The Foolishness of Tarquin

It is without question that Tarquin is a criminal, but it is without the question that Tarquin is a politician or tyrant because of his foolishness or ignorance of political or ruling strategies or skills. When you want to save people, try your best to help him or her. When you want to kill people, try by every means to destroy him or her completely. In the human history, a ruler, usually a double dealer, is very savage and fierce. He or she is stone-hearted and kills people like flies as Richard III does, or kills people without spilling blood as Claudius does to his brother, or destroys root and branch as Macbeth does. Tarquin, however, doesn't know how to obtain his aim and protect himself and his royal family as well. He does everything at night secretly. He doesn't know how to deal with Collatine and his relatives and his close friends in his own savage way. Tarquin, in the long narrative poem, is low in intelligence quotient in his political career, and his emotion quotient is completely a mess.

6.3 Lucrece

If we say Tarquin is a character described and portrayed in various sections, then Lucrece is a full grown image true to life. Lucrece has 6 strong points or virtues in the long narrative poem.

(1) Beauty.   The beauty of Lucrece is the principle charm of the whole poem which attracts so many readers and critics for so many years in the human history. Lucrece's beauty first appears in *THE ARGUMENT*: "*At that time Sextus Tarquinius being inflamed with Lucrece's beauty*". Then in Stanza 2, lines 11—14, "*To praise the clear unmatched red and white / Which triumpht in that sky of his delight, / Where mortal stars, as bright as heaven's beauties, / With pure aspects did him peculiar dutie*", the celestial beauty of Lucrece could be read and appreciated. Shakespeare employs Stanza 54, lines372—378 and Stanzas 56—60, lines 386—420, 6 stanzas, 42 lines in all, to depict in detail the beauty of a sleeping lady, Lucrece:

> *Look, as the fair and fiery-pointed sun,*
> *Rushing from forth a cloud, bereaves our sight;*
> *Even so, the curtain drawn, his eyes begun*
> *To wink, being blinded with a greater light:*
> *Whether it is that she reflects so bright,*
> > *That dazzleth them, or else some shame supposed;*
> > *But blind they are, and keep themselves enclosed.*
> > > *(Stanza 54, lines 372—378)*

Lines 386—387 are the beautiful description of Lucrece's hand and cheek: "*Her lily hand her rosy cheek lies under, / Cozening the pillow of a lawful kiss*". Lines 396—397 are the praise of Lucrece's sweat and eyes: "*With pearly sweat, resembling dew of night. / Her eyes, like marigolds, had sheathed their light*". Lucrece's hair is depicted together with her breath: "*Her hair, like golden threads, play'd with her breath; / O modest wantons! wanton modesty!*" Lucrece's breasts are very amazing and charming: "*Her breasts, like ivory globes circled with blue, / A pair of maiden worlds unconquered*". Here is the detailed obsertation and portraying of the captivating beauty: "*Her azure veins, her alablaster skin, / Her*

coral lips, her snow-white dimpled chin." (419—420) Here is the extreme beauty in the world. This is the beauty people should admire and praise. This is the beauty people should cherish and protect without any question. This beauty should be as long as the human history. This beauty is definitely eternal.

(2) Hospitality.　As a noble Roman lady, Lucrece is very hospitable to Tarquin. "*When at Collatium this false lord arrived, / Well was he welcomed by the Roman dame.*" (50—51) Lucrece also provides accommodation for Tarquin: "*For then is Tarquin brought unto his bed, / Intending weariness with heavy sprite*" (120—121) "*For, after supper, long he questioned / With modest Lucrece, and wore out the night*" (122—123).

(3) Kindness.　As a gentle noble lady as in the Argument, "*Collatinus finds his wife, though it were late in the night, spinning amongst her maids*", it is obvious that Lucrece is very kind to her maid. Her maid gives "*Whose swift obedience to her mistress hies*" (1215). "'*But tell me girl, when went'* — *and there she stay'd / Till after a deep groan—'Tarquin from hence?'*—*"* (1275—1276) Lucrece is panting because of Tarquins crime. Here is her maid's question and Lucrece's reply: "'*But, lady, if your maid may be so bold, / She would request to know your heaviness.' / 'O, peace!' quoth Lucrece: 'if it should be told, / The repetition cannot make it less*'" (1282—1285). The four lines reveal a harmonious relationship between Lucrece and her maid. Her maid obeys Lucrece order and asks a servant to send a letter for Lucrece: "*The homely villain court'sies to her low; / And, blushing on her, with a steadfast eye*"(1338—1339); "*For Lucrece thought he blusht to see her shame*"(1344) Lucrece is not only kind to her maid and servant, but also honest to both of them, which shows she has such a high morality and virtue.

(4) Fidelity.　Lucrece loves her husband Collatine and expresses her fidelity to him when she hears Tarquin tells her "*her husband's fame, / Won in the fields*

of fruitful Italy ”(*106—107*) On hearing *"decks with praises Collatine's high name, / Made glorious by his manly chivalry / With bruised arms and wreaths of victory"* (*108—110*) Lucrece shows *"Her joy with heaved-up hand she doth express, / And, wordless, so greets heaven for his success"*? (*111—112*) with her whole-hearted fidelity. When Tarquin dreams that Lucrece's hand is held by Tarquin, Shakespeare tells us *"Forced it to tremble with her loyal fear!"*(*261*)   In her soliloquy, Lucrece says, *"Yet am I guilty of thy honour's wrack, — / Yet for thy honour did I entertain him; / Coming from thee, I could not put him back, / For it had been dishonour to disdain him"* (*841—844*). Lucrece holds *"I will not poison thee with my attaint"*(*1071*). In the whole narrative poem, there are many lines to reveal Lucrece's fidelity, devotion or loyalty to Collatine. All of what she thinks, what she says, and what she acts is just one theme: Lucrece is devoted to Collatine's cause and is brave to protect his cause.

(5) Chastity.   Chastity is defined as decent and modest and not having sexual intercourse except with the person to whom one is married. Lucrece has her own valuable chastity, though stained by Tarquin, later purified by her husband Collatine who takes revenge on Tarquin. Lucrece's chastity results in her virtue. Lucrece is *"Cooling his hot face in the chastest tears / That ever modest eyes with sorrow shed"*(*682—683*). It is a pity and shame that *"Pure Chastity is rifled of her store"* (*692*). However, Lucrece's pure mind is left and she intends to find *"Some purer chest to close so pure a mind"* (*761*). Although her sweet chastity is destroyed, Lucrece is said to possess her sweet chastity in her mind. Flower is still flower in spite of the intruding of worm. Shakespeare says, *"O! let it not be hild / Poor women's faults, that they are so fulfill'd / With men's abuses: those proud lords, to blame"*(*1257—1259*). Lucrece is confident that *"Immaculate and spotless is my mind"* (*1656*).

(6) Unyieldingness.   It is obvious that Lucrece is upright in her personality

and unyielding when facing threat and violence although she is destroyed by a licentious prince. When Tarquin wants to enjoy her, Lucrece "*With vehement prayers urgeth still*" (*475*). How can Lucrece bear the humiliation upon her by licentious Tarquin? Lucrece thinks her husband Collatine would "*Kill both thyself and her for yielding so*"(*1036*). Then "*from her betumbled couch she starteth, / To find some desperate instrument of death*" (*1037—1038*). To express her loyalty to her husband, Lucrece says, "*I will not poison thee with my attaint, / Nor fold my fault in cleanly-coin'd excuses; / My sable ground of sin I will not paint, / To hide the truth of this false night's abuses*" (*1072—1075*). After the humiliation Lucrece does not want to commit suicide at once because she is waiting for Collatine to tell him the truth. When Collatine with his company comes home, Lucrece is in black. Immediately after telling them the crime committed by Tarquim, Lucrece "*Even here she sheathed in her harmless breast / A harmful knife, that thence her soul unsheathed*" (*1723—1724*). The unyielding noble lady has defended her virtue and reputation by her brave death.

Lucrece also has 4 weakpoints:

(1) Naiveness: In the evening, a strange young man, although a prince, comes to her house. As a hostess and a beautiful young lady, Lucrece will naturally and certainly make an appraisal of the intention and purpose of Tarquin's coming. Being an honest and kind hearted young lady, Lucrece doesn't know enough about the evil nature of people. Therefore licentious Tarquin is welcomed warmly and politely by the hostess (50—51).

(2) Negligence: After dinner, Tarquin is sent to bed in her house by Lucrece. Although it is not Lucrece's mistake to be hospitable to her guest, precautions should be taken to be prepared for any contingency. No trace of precautions can be found in the long narrative poem. It is contrary to reason. A young lady should be always on guard when something odd has happened in the evening when her husband isn't at home.

(3) Infantilism.   How to deal with a robber is something like how to deal

with a venomous snake or a beast of prey. As stern law, a bayonet, a sword, and a brave counter attack are waiting for a robber. A soldier's sword and broadsword are waiting for a venomous snake. A hunting rifle is waiting for a beast of prey. However it is infantile or naive for Lucrece to offer a piece of advice to a licentious prince like a robber, a venomous snake, or a beast of prey. The demon like Tarquin can not be persuaded out of the idea of raping Lucrece, since he is inflamed by the extreme beauty of Lucrece. In the narrative poem, Shakespeare spends 13 stanzas (stanzas 84—96), 91 lines (582—672) to tell readers how Lucrece tries by every means to discourage the licentious devil like Tarquin from committing a crime. It is no wonder that Lucrece's infantilism is completely a vain attempt.

(4) Low IQ.   If she is Lady Macbeth, Lucrece would persuade her husband Collatine to lead his army to rebel against Tarquin royal family and overthrow them. If she is Portia, Lucrece could win over Tarquin by her wisdom then his conspiracy would meet with failure. If she is Katherina, the shrew, Lucrece would fight bravely against Tarquin regardless of her life or death, not to mention her reputation or fame. If she is King Lear's eldest daughter Goneril, or his second daughter Regan, Lucrece would be adept at scheming and Tarquin would be taken in by her and be controlled at her own will. Nevertheless, Lucrece is like Gertrude, the queen, Hamlet's mother, nearly meekly submitting to oppression and maltreatment, enduring humiliation and swallowing an insult without making it public courageously and boldly. Lucrece is like Ophelia who becomes insane because of the strong stimulus after her father Polonius is killed by Hamlet's mistake. Lucrece is like Desdemona, without her preparation for all contingencies, falling into a trap by Iago, scoundrel and an evildoer. Lucrece is also like Constance, mother to Arthur who is the nephew to King John. When Arthur is dead by scheme, Constance has no way out but feels lamentable and cries piteously. If Lucrece is Joan of Arc, Tarquin would be utterly routed. However,

Lucrece is Lucrece, who has no ability to win over the evil violence, but has her own instinct of subsisting and her own vanity of pratecting her own reputation. The strategy she would adopt is merely waiting: waiting for the opportunity of taking revenge. How could Lucrece endure her galling shame and humiliation? What Lucrece could do is ordering her servant to ask her husband to come back home and condemning Tarquin's crime, then committing suide. Later Lucrece is admitted posthumously saint for her uprightness and unyieldingness.

Both Tarquin and Lucrece are tragic protagonists. Tarquin, the prince, is not notorious originally, while Lucrece, the noble lady, has her beauty and chastity. Inflamed by beauty, the former has lost his way. Because of hospitality, the later's chastity doesn't stay. *Id*, *ego* and *superego* should be clearly distinguished; kindness, beauty and virture are accumulated. The licentious prince is for thousands of years condemned; the unyielding lady is eternally commended.

7   The Creative Technique of *Lucrece*

Samuel Johnson (1709—1784) says in his *Preface to Shakespeare*, "The end of writing is to instruct; the end of poetry is to instruct by pleasing." Shakespeare's *Lucrece* is a poem coincided with Johnson's literary proposition. Lucrece is like Peter Ilyich Tchaikovsky's (1840—1893) *The Sixth (Pathetique) Symphony*. Lucrece is like Ludwig van Beethoven's (1770—1827) *The Fifth Symphony*, or *The Eroica*. *Lucrece* is just like a Chinese meticulous brushwork, realistic painting with fine brushwork and close attention to details and in deep and bright colours. The structure, the rhetoric, the contrast of the descriptions, and the usage of symbolism are the 4 striking characteristics of the genre of the whole narrative poem.

7.1 Structure

The synonym of the term structure is form, which could be divided into two parts: one is its metrical pattern, the other is its arrangement of the stanzas and the lines.

(1) Metrical pattern.   The metrical pattern of the whole narrative poem refers to its rhyme scheme, which is the rhyme royal, 7 lines for each stanza, rhymed as *ababbcc*. The rhythm of each line is generally iambic pentameter. Stanza 62 (428—434) is a very good example of Shakespeare's cautious use of the rhyme scheme: *fighting, effecting, delighting, respecting, expecting, striking,* and *liking,* the end rhyme of each is *ing,* which looks like the uniform of rhymed words. However, when readers read them carefully, it is found that the rhyme scheme is still *ababbcc*. The 2 words *fighting* and *delighting* are rhymed in the last but one syllable of each. The other 3 words *effecting, respecting* and *expecting* are rhymed in accordance with the same law. Still the other 2 words

striking and *liking* are rhymed as *fighting* and *delighting* but not the same pattern. The pronunciation of *striking* and *liking* is sonorous and forceful.

(2) The arrangement of the stanzas and the lines. There are 265 stanzas in all which are composed of 1855 lines. The whole narrative poem is divided into 7 sections in accordance with its content: ①boasting, which can be found both in *the Argument* and Stanzas 2, 3, 4, 5, and 6, 5 stanzas, 35 lines in all; ②sneak, stanzas 1 and 7, 2 stanzas, only 14 lines in all; ③ravishment, Stanzas 8—105, 98 stanzas, 686 lines, as the longest section; ④lamentation, stanzas 106—190, 85 stanzas, 595 lines, the second longest one; ⑤informing, Stanzas 191—195, 5 stanzas, 35 lines; ⑥looking at the oil painting, Stanzas 196—226, 31 stanzas, 217 lines; and ⑦revenge, Stanzas 227—265, 39 stanzas, 273 lines.

7.2 Rhetoric

A narrative poem, or narrative verse, has been classified into 3 main categories: epic, metrical romance and ballad. If we say Shakespeare's *Venus and Adonis* is a long narrative poem of romance, then *Lucrece* is the narrative verse of legend. To reveal successfully the ancient Roman legend of Lucrece *(509 B.C.)*, strong and powerful rhetoric is used here and there by Shakespeare. Parallelism, as a very common device or technique in poetry, is frequently employed in *Lucrece*. In employing the device of parallelism, or repetition, the repetition of prepositional phrases is the most common phenomena in *Lucrece*. In Stanza 82, lines 568-572, when Lucrece tries to persuade Tarquin out of his criminal behaviour, 5 "*by*" or "*By*" phrases are paralled in order to strengthen the power of her speech. Near the end of the poem, when Brutus, the Roman general, one of Collatines' close friends gives his speech to moblize the Roman citizen to fight against the Tarquim royal family, 4 "*by*" phrases and 2 "*By*" phrases are used by him (Stanza 263, lines 1835—1839). More "*to*" and "*To*" phrases can be read when Lucrece complains after the devastative humiliation, about 3 stanzas, 18

lines (Stanzas 135—137, lines 939—958), which has the function of citing numerous facts of the real world. The verbal phrases also appear in Stanza 141 when *Lucrece* complains and curses time, 5 "*Let*" phrases being paralled (981—985). The suitable use of rhetoric is the help to enforce the artistic effect of the narrative verse and reach the artistic aim of variation.

7.3 Description

In the aesthetic case, the end, or the aim, of a poem is the enjoyment. In order to convey this enjoyment, to reach the narcissus of people's mind, good and decent descriptions in *Lucrece* can be divided into 8 parts: ①cenery, ②action, ③psychology, ④portrait, ⑤language, ⑥spectacle ⑦detail, and ⑧morality.

(1) Scenery

It is obvious that the scenery in the long narrative poem is the *night* which is described by Shakespeare as a terrible death like hell:

> *Now stole upon the time the dead of night,*
> *When heavy sleep had closed up mortal eyes:*
> *No comfortable star did lend his light,*
> *No noise but owls' and wolves' death-boding cries;*
> *Now serves the season that they may surprise*
>   *The silly lambs: pure thoughts are dead and still,*
>   *While lust and murder wakes to stain and kill.*
>
>   *（162—168）*

This famous description finds its way in *Macbeth* about 12 years after its creation: "*With Tarquin's ravishing strides, towards his design / moves like a ghost*"(*Macbeth*, II. i. lines 55—56). Charles Dickens (1812—1870) is also influenced by Shakespeare in his novel *Oliver Twist* when describing the night

"*the somber shadows thrown by the trees upon the ground, looked sepulchral and deathlike, from being still*". According to his philosophy of composition, Edgar Allan Poe (1809—1849) emphasizes the beauty of melancholy by creating the terrible night atmosphere in his famous poem *The Raven*. Here, John Keats (1795—1821) is requested to change his famous line "*tender is the night*" in his famous *Ode to a Nightingale* into "*terror is the night*". Night, in Shakespeare's tragic works, often symbolizes the time when something evil takes place like Macbeth wants to murder Ducan and Hamlet sees the ghost of his father at the very beginning of the tragedy *Hamlet*.

(2) Action.   Although there are not so many actions in the narrative poem, the description of the actions of the two protagonists can not be ignored. To describe Tarquin's actions, the words *inflamed, smothering, departed, withdrew, stealeth, violently ravished*, and *speedeth* are used in *THE ARGUMENT*, from which the process of committing a vicious crime can be felt. In the narrative verse, there are still some lines to describe his actions: "*Pawning his honor to obtain his lust*"(156), "*And now this lustful lord leapt from his bed / Throwing his mantle rudely o'er his arm*"(169—170), "*His falchion on a flint he softly smiteth*"(176). Then "*his guilty hand pluckt up the latch / And with his knee the door he opens wide*"(358—359). "*His hand, that yet remains upon her breast / Rude ram, to hatter such an ivory wall*" (463—464). "*So surfeit-taking Tarquin fares this night*" (698). Tarquin "*like a thievish dog creeps sadly thence*"(736). The expression "*a thievish dog*" is a suitable simile for Tarquin's image.

As for Lucrece, in *THE ARGUMENT, spinning, hastily dispatcheth, attired in mourning habit, taking an oath of them for her revenge, reveal'd the actor, and whole manner of his dealing, and withal suddenly stabb'd herself* are all the expressions to describe the actions of another protagonist. In the long narrative poem, Lucrece, as hostess, a Roman dame, "*welcomed*" (51) Tarquin at Collatium without doubting the character or personality of the stranger, and, after

dinner, "*brought*"(120) Tarquin "*unto his bed*"(120). When Tarquin wants to ravish her while she is sleeping, Lucrece "*dares not look; yet, winking, there appears / Quick-shifting antics, ugly in her eyes* (458—459). "*So his unhallow'd haste her words delays*" (552), "*Which to her oratory adds more grace*" (564). However, her oratory is in vain since Lucrece is violently ravished by Tarquin. Lucrece is panting (737), Lucrece is cursing and complaining. At dawn, Lucrece writes a letter and asks her servant to send it to her husband Collatine. Then Lucrece looks at a piece of oil painting, complaining and tearing the beauty of Helen with her nails and *the senseless Sinon* (1564) as well. When her husband comes home, Lucrece is found *clad in mourning black* (1585). After telling him her tragic story, our beautiful and chaste Lucrece *sheathed in her harmless breast / A harmful knife, that thence her soul unsheathed* (1723—1724).

(3) Psychology.   The description of Tarquin's psychological condition is found in the 3rd part of the narrative verse, ravishment, Stanzas 8—105, 686 lines, while the descriptions of Lucrece's psychological mind are in two parts, the 4th part, lamentation, and the 6th part, looking at the oil painting.

① Tarquin's psychological reality. In the 3rd part, there are descriptions of the reality of the process of Tarquin's psychological activities. First, Tarquin disguises his desire or lust: *For that he colour'd with his high estate, / Hiding base sin in plaits of majesty* (92—93). Second, a robber knows how to obtain other's property: *As one of which doth Tarquin lie revolving / The sundry dangers of his will's obtaining* (127—128). Third, Tarquin is in the contradictory condition when he wants to realize his desire: *And in his inward mind he doth debate / What following sorrow may on this arise* (185—186). *Yea, though I die, the scandal will survive* (204), *That my posterity, shamed with the note* (208). Fourth, his lust gives Tarquin an illusion: *And bow her hand, in my hand being lockt / Forced it to tremble with her loyal fear* (260—261). At last, lust wins over reason, when Tarquin says, "*Then, childish fear avaunt! debating die*"(274).

"*Desire my pilot is, beauty my prize*"(279).

② Lucrece's psychological emotion. In the first 3 parts including *THE ARGUMENT*, Lucrece's psychological emotion can be regarded as normal: She is spinning with her maids deep in the night; she gives Tarquin a reverend welcome. When Tarquin intends to ravish her, Lucrece even tries to persuade him out of the depravity of his course but in vain. Nevertheless, in the fourth part, immediately after the ravishment, Lucrece's emotion is very changeable. She rails at night, time, opportunity, and Tarquin. Lines 764—770 are famous in Luerece's complaint or soliloquy: *O comfort-killing Night, image of hell! / Dim register and notary of shame! / Black stage for tragedies and murders fell! / Vast sin-concealing chaos! nurse of blame! / Blind muffled bawd! dark harbour for defame! / Grim cave of death! whispering conspirator / With close-tongued treason and the ravisher!* Tarquin is Night's child since he has a black heart with his black hands. When she wants to find some desperate instrument of death (1038), Lucrece changes her mind: *Yet die I will not till my Collatine / Have heard the cause of my untimely death* (1177—1178). After her servant leaving to inform Collatine, Lucrece is looking at an oil painting full of hatred: she wants to tear the beauty of Helen for she thinks Helen is a strumpet; she also tears the senseless Sinon with her nails (1564) since she regards Sinon as a hypocrite and the disaster of Troy. Lucrece is full of mourning, full of despair, and full of hope but in black when Collatine comes home, which is the signal that Lucrece will commit suicide.

(4) Portrait.   From *THE ARGUMENT* one cannot find how beautiful Lucrece is, but in the second stanza of the narrative verse, Shakespeare describes the extraordinary beauty of the Roman dame: *To praise the clear unmatched red and white / Which triumpht in that sky of his delight, / Where mortal stars, as bright as heaven's beauties, / With pure aspects did him peculiar duties* (11—14). This kind of beauty is amusing, and Tarquin is amazed by such a beauty. After 53 stanzas, 372 lines, the sleeping beauty appears in 7 stanzas, 49 lines (372—420). The first description of the sleeping beauty is people's general impression *as the*

fair and fiery-pointed sun (372). The next stanza (381—385) is the description of the feeling of Tarquin's eyes. Then in lines 386—392, one can see Lucrece's lily hand and rosy cheek. Lucrece's fair hand is like an April daisy, her sweat is pearl like and her eyes are like marigolds (393—399). Tarquin sees the hair of Lucrece, like golden threads (400), play with her breath. Lucrece's breasts look like ivory globes circled with blue (407), as if a pair of secret, unknown world. There are also two lines of the detailed escription of *"Her azure veins, her alabaster skin, / Her coral lips, her snow-while dimpled chin"* (419—420). In Europe, this is a piece of oil painting of Lucrece's portrait, meticulous and attractive. If it is in China, it is a piece of traditional Chinese painting of the portrait of Lucrece, which is realistic with fine brush work and close attention to details. After reading so many lines, in fact 371 lines, readers see the celestial sleeping beauty in the dark evil night. When they see Helen, the world famous beauty, the Greek soldiers come to understand why they spend 10 years in the Troyan War and it is a worthy fighting for them. Lucrece also has her celestial beauty like Helen. No wonder Tarquin risks his Roman royal family to ravish Lucrece.

(5) Language.   Here the definition of the term language is discourse or logue. The term logue refers to dialogue and monologue or soliloquy. In this narrative verse the loques of the two protagonists occupy a great or large space like the singing and reciting in Chinese opera.

① Tarquin's logue.   There 153 lines for Tarquin's monologue or soliloquy and dialogue with Lucrece. In lines 181—182, Tarquin gives his speech for the first time: *As from this cold flint I enforced this fire, / So Lucrece must I force to my desire.* Then Shakespeare spends 8 stanzas, 56 lines, to reveal that Tarquin is full of worries or misgivings or hesitancies. *"Shameful it is; —ay, if the fact be known: / Hateful it is; —there is no hate in loving"* (239—240). Tarquin has an illusion when he says, *"she took me kindly by the hand, / And gazed for tidings in my eager eyes"* (253—254). The illusion tempts him to make an evil decision, *"who fears sinking where such treasure lies?"* （280）. The treasure refers to,

according to Tarquin, desire and beauty. In his dialogue with Lucrece, Tarquin intimidates her and says "*some worthless slave of thine I'll slay, / To kill thine honour with thy life's decay; / And in thy dead arms do I mean to place him, / Swearing I slew him, seeing thee embrace him.*" (515—518). Ignoring Lucrece's advice, Tarquin says "*No more*"(667) and commits a crime and goes back to his tent stealthily. From his logue, his sophistry, it is obvious that Tarquin's conscience is gradually lost owing to his desire and lust.

②Lucrece's logue.   There are 642 lines of Lucrece's logue in the whole narrative verse. It is a striking phenomenon that in the 3rd part, ravishment, Shakeseare gives Lucrece 13 stanzas, 91 lines (575—644)(652—672) for her advice. After Tarquin has left her chamber, Lucrece's complaint is the longest one, from Stanza 107 to Stanza 148, except stanza 109, more than 40 stanzas in all, 283 lines. If we say the action and the logue of Tarquin are something like Beethoven's *The Fifth Symphony*, then Lucrece's complaint is something like Peter Ilyich Tchaikovsky's *The Sixth (Pathetique) Symphony*. The whole complaint can be considered as Shakespeare's deep thinking philosophically about night, time, opportunity, and Tarquin, to say briefly, about human life, society and the universe. The space of Lucrece's last speech to her father, her husband and the Roman generals is not so large, but it is something like Beethoven's *The Eroica*. It cannot be imagined that Lucrece dare give Tarquin the prince a moral and political lesson: *How will thy shame be seeded in thine age, / When thus thy vices bud before thy spring! / If in thy hope thou darest do such outrage, / What darest thou not when once thou art a king?*(603—606). When she is in deep grief, Lucrece in vain rails *at Opportunity, / At Time, at Tarquin, and uncheerful Night* (1023—1024). Looking at an oil painting while waiting for her husband Collatine, Lucrece wonders *Why should the private pleasure of some one / Become the public plague of many moe?*(1478—1479). Lucrece is really upright and unyielding when she says "*plight your honourable faiths to me, / With swift*

pursuit to venge this wrong of mine;"(1690—1691).

(6) Spectacle.   Spectacle, or scene, has its literary function of depicting or portraying characters, heightening the atmosphere and deepening the leitmotiv or motif, then helping the development of the plot. In the 41th stanza, lines 283—284, *"Away he steals with open listening ear, / Full of foul hope and full of fond mistrust"*and lines in the 44th stanza (302—305) *"The locks between her chamber and his will, / Each one by him enforced, retires his ward; / But, as they open, they all rate his ill, / Which drives the creeping thief to some regard"* are examples to portray the thief like Tarquin, the Roman prince. Thought it is not a large spectacle, it is poisonous and full of terror. While near the end of the narrative verse, there is a large spectacle depicting the tragic atmosphere and pushing the plot going forward quickly and dramatically. When Lucrece commits suicide, *"Stone-still, astonisht with this deadly deed, / Stood Collatine and all his lordly crew"*(1730 — 1731), Lucrece's father throws himself to her self-slaughtered daughter, and Brutus, a famous Roman general, draws the knife from the purple blood, *"And bubbling from her breast, it doth divide / In two slow rivers, that the crimson blood / Circles her body in on every side, /Who, like a late-sackt island, vastly stood / Bare and unpeopled in this fearful flood. / Some of her blood still pure and red remain'd, / And some lookt black, and that false Tarquin stain'd."*(1737—1743) This spectacle is heralding and harbingering the birth of Shakespeare's great tragedies. Although she cannot clutch at the throat of her fate, Lucrece's spirit of unyieldingness reveals she is a real chaste heroine in human history.

(7) Detail.   To describe the character or the scene in detail is to reflect the nature and the characteristic of the object in the literary work in order to deepen the theme of a poem or a novel. In the 3rd part, ravishment, Shakespeare depicts Tarquinin in detail to reflect this thief like villain: *As each unwilling portal yields him way, / Through little vents and crannies of the place / The wind wars with his*

torch to make him stay, / And blows the smoke of it into his face, / Extinguishing his conduct in this case; / But his hot heart, which fond desire doth scorch, / Puffs forth another wind that fires the torch(309—315). Now Tarquin is just like a ghost with jack-o'-lantern or will-o'-the-wisp entering the gate of hell despite the fact that his weak conscience tries to provent him from committing a vicious sin. The horrible detailed spectacle of Lucrece committing suicide results from Tarquin's evil doing: "*About the mourning and congealed face / Of that black blood a watery rigol goes, / Which seems to weep upon the tainted place: / And ever since, as pitying Lucrece' woes, / Corrupted blood some watery token shows; / And blood untainted still doth red abide, / Blushing at that which is so putrefied.*" (1744—1750) How carefully does Shakespeare observe the blood shed by Lucrece when she is lying dead by stabbing her breast with a harmful knife! The blood is classified into 3 categories: black blood, red blood and the watery rigol. The red blood is the red flower; the red blood is the chaste noble dame.

(8) Morality.   There are two definitions about this long poem, one is a long narrative verse, and another is a long philosophical lyrical poem. From these two definitions we know Shakespeare expresses his philosophical contemplation by way of telling an age-old legend and there are many philosophical issues, including morality, being pondered through the 2 protagonists and others. The morality of Lucrece is expressed many times and many places in the long poem which should be paid great attention to, but here we mainly discuss the morality of Tauquin, especially his shamelessness.

Lucrece, a chaste noble Roman dame, upright and unyielding, is violently ravished out of the shamelessness of Tarquin who knows clearly it is shameful to rape Lucrece but does not feel ashamed. Tarquin is flamed by Lucrece's beauty, giving way to his carnal desires and deliberately breaking a rule. At first his weak conscience and intuitive knowledge try to prevent him from violating the rule but in vain owing to his powerful uncontrolled lust. Tarquin has an illusion that the

dark night can conceal his evil doing, but he doesn't know God knows dearly and evidently if one does something wrong in a cabinet. The impulse is like a devil, and the flame of lust will burn oneself up. The evil doer will definitely be punished by God. Human being cannot accept asceticism as their discipline. However, indulging in sensual pleasures will meet with shame and punishment. Tarquin with his falchion and violence has obtained his aim, his sensual pleasure, and, at the same time, destroyed himself completely. One who is so obssesed with the desire will be extremely vicious and shameless. The extreme shamelessness can be read in Stanzas 74, 75, lines 512—525. It is naïve for Tarquin to think "*The fault unknown is as a thought unacted*" (527). It is well known that the mills of God grind slowly, but they grind exceeding small and that justice has a long arm.

7.4 Symbols

The etymology of the term symbol is the Greek word *symbolon*, meaning *mark, token, ticket, watchword, outward sign, covenant, emblem or sign*. Now the definition of the term symbol is an image that represents a person, idea, etc. The symbols in Shakespeare's long narrative verse can be divided into 3 categories:

1st, the minor ones. There are many examples of such symbols: At the beginningof the poem, the color white symbolizes virtue; red, beauty; lilies, virtue; roses, beauty; and in the middle of the poem, the word dove symbolizes a beautiful lady, while hawk symbolizes a villain.

2nd, the big one, the night. In the poem the word night symbolizes many evil things: the hell, the lust, the black heart, the black hand, the thief, or the black blood.

3rd, the curious one, the oil painting. In lines 1366—1568, 202 lines, Lucrece is looking at an oil painting of the fall of Troy which may be said as a digression, but it is really a very good symbol which symbolizes the real society at Lucrece's time or the whole world in the human history. The rape of Helen is

the reason of the fall of Troy. The rape of Lucrece is the reason of the fall or banishment of the Tarquin royal family. Helen may symbolize Lucrece although Lucrece hates her deeply and regards her as a strumpet and tears Henlen's beauty with her nails (1471—1472). Sinon, a hero, is held as the enemy of Troy by Lucrece and is also torn by Lucrece's nails. Although she is in deep mourning and deep hatred, Lucrece becomes mature and gets to look at the real society into its deep structure.

In the oil painting there are still many important characters, such as Priam, Ajax, Ulysses, Nestor, Achilles, Hector, Paris, and Hecuba, who may symbolize the VIP at the early time of Rome, in the Elizabethan society, or in the modern society.

At the age of 30, Shakespeare wrote his long narrative verse *Lucrece* after writing *Venus and Adonis* and other 7 plays: the 3 parts of *Henry VI*, *Richard III*, *The Comedy of Errors*, *Titus Andronicus*, and *The Taming of the Shrewl*. From *Lucrece*, Shakespeare's literary creative technique becomes mature and profound philosophically, sociologically, ethically and psychologically in its structure, rhetoric, description, and symbol. The long narrative poem is undoubtedly the prelude of the birth of the great tragedies from the year 1601 to the year 1606.

8   The Rhetorical Devices in *A Lover's Complaint*

In the year 1609, *A lover's Complaint* was printed and published together with the 154 sonnets written by William Shakespeare. This complaint poem is in rhyme royal, a stanza form of seven decasyllabic lines rhyming *ababbcc*. The form of the stanza is known as the Chaucerrian Stanza, because Chaucer created his poems *Troilus and Criseyde*, and *The Parlement of Foules* employing it. There is a pastoral setting, a deep valley, for the poem. The poet heard a forsaken maiden telling an old shepherd her tragic love story. When she was young, innocent, and proud of her beauty, the maiden was infatuated with a handsome young man and showed her blind passion. Because of his honey words and tears, she trusted him and gave out her chastity. When she was forsaken, she wanted to destroy the whole world. She threw all her treasure: amber, crystal and beaded jet, into a river. She kissed and tore the love letters written in blood into pieces. The long poem is composed of 47 stanzas, 329 lines in all, the rhythm of which is iambic pentameter. There is a dispute that whether Shakespeare is the author or not. Reading through the poem, readers can easily feel the artistic genre is the same as that of his other works. Although it is uncertain whether Shakespeare wrote the poem, scholars cannot find other poet who is certainly the author. The forsaken lady in the poem reminds readers of the lovers in classic Chinese literature such as Du Shiniang in Feng Menglong's *Stories to Warn the World*, and *The Birds of Jiao Zhongqing* or *Peacocks Southeast Traveling*, and Tang Wan in *To the Tone Phoenix Hairpin*, and the heroine in Pushkin's (1799—1834) masterpiece *Eugene Onegin*. Now this chapter focuses its attention on the rhetorical devices in this famous complaint poem.

8.1 Comparison

The Greek for rhetoric is rhētōr, meaning "speaker in the assembly".

The definition of the term rhetoric is commonly the art of using language impressively, persuasively and skillfully in speech or writing. It is obvious that Shakespeare knows clearly how to use the rhetoric device in his artistic creation. Reading the long complaint verse *A lover's Complaint*, the rhetoric devices or the figures of speech Shakespeare employed in his writing could be classified into 4 categories: comparison, antithesis, alliteration and parallelism.

When the term rhetoric is mentioned, the other term comparison immediately comes to people's mind. There are 6 rhetoric concepts belonging to comparison: simile, metaphor, personification, zoosemy, euphemism, and metonymy.

Simile.   In Latin, *simile* is the neuter form of *similis*, meaning *like*. It is an explicit comparison with the clear recognizable words *like* or *as*. In the 6th stanza, the poet, Shakespeare, finds a maiden throwing her amber, crystal and beaded jet into a river *Like usury* (40): The expression *Like usury* is the first usage of the figure of speech or rhetoric device *simile*. Then in the 11th stanza, when the maiden tells her story to the old shepherd who wants to accompany her when she is in deep grief, *I might as yet have been a spreading flower* (75), the second *simile* is employed here. To describe the handsome young man the maiden says his skin is *Like unshown velvet, on that termless skin* (94), which is the last simile in the long verse.

Metaphor.   The term metaphor comes from Greek *metaphora*, meaning "carrying from one place to another". Now the definition of it is a word or phrase indicating something different from the literal meaning. Linguistically, metaphor is focus of cognitive linguistics. Obviously, the 7th line of the 1st stanza *"storming her world with sorrow's wind and rain"* is a metaphor. The second

metaphor is the description of the young man's evil character *"Heard where his plants in other's orchards grew" (171)*. When depicting the young man's tears, the 5 lines can be regarded as one metaphor:

> *Each cheek a river running from a fount*
> *With brinish current downward flow'd apace;*
> *O, how the channel to the stream gave grace!*
> *Who glazed with crystal gate the glowing roses*
> *That flame through water which their hue encloses.*
>
> *(283—287)*

It could also be said that there are 9 minor metaphors in this description, such as *river*, *fount*, *brinish current*, *channel*, *stream*, *crystal gate*, *glowing roses*, *flame* and *hue*. This is an amusing picture of the young man's tears, although he is villain for he has cheated so many innocent girls. This description of tears can also be easily found in Shakespeare's long narrative verse of romance *Venus and Adonis* when he spends two stanzas, 12 lines, depicting the tears of the goddess Venus and Adonis (955—966). In line 310, the word *hail* is also a metaphor, indicating the power and cunningness of the hypocritical young man. In line 93, the expression *His phoenix down* is also a metaphor, which is a beautiful description of the young man's moustache or beard.

Personification.   This figure of speech refers to the attribution of human qualities to something that is without life. Looking at the love letters written in blood, the forsaken girl cries, *"O false blood, thou register of lies, / What unapproved witness dost thou bear!"* (52—53). The word blood is an object, but here it acts as a person, a liar, a hypocrite. The 168th line *Though Reason weep, and cry, "It is thy last"* is another personification.

Zoosemy.   Contrary to personification, the definition of zoosemy is that the

figure of speech zoosemy is the comparison of human being to an object without life. In lines 101—102 in the 15th stanza, there are two lines describing the temper of the young man: *Yet, if men mov'd him, was he such a storm. / As oft 'twixt May and April is to see.*

Euphemism. The origin of the word in Greek is *euphēmismós*, meaning *fair speech*. In modern English, euphemism refers to the use of mild, indirect, or vague words or phrases in place of something thought to be unpleasant. When the girl is seduced by the hypocritic young man, Shakespeare writes these lines: *There my white stole of chastity I deft, / Shook off my sober guards and civil fears; / Appear to him, as he to me appears, / All melting* (297—300). The girl has eaten the forbidden fruit. Lines 309—310 could be another euphemism: *That not a heart which in his level came / could escape the hail of his all-hurting aim.* Many a girl has been seduced by the villain like the young guy. In line 92, the expression *Small show of man* is also euphemism, meaning the moustache and the beard of a young man.

Metonymy.   The etymology of metonymy is a Greek word *metōnumíā*, meaning *name change*. The modern definition of the word metonymy is the name of one part of a object is the substitution of the object itself. The 11th line "*The carcass of a beauty spent and done*" is a metonymy. The word *carcass* is the substitution of a human being. In line 89 "*Each eye that saw him did enchant the mind*", *Each eye* is the substitution of each young girl. In line 309, the word *heart* refers to emotion, feeling, love, and a young girl.

8.2 Antithesis

The origin of the word antithesis is a Greek word *antíthesis*, meaning *opposition*. In modern English, fundamentally, the term antithesis indicates contrasting ideas marked by the choice and arrangement of word. When describing the moustache and the beard of the handsome young man, Shakespeare

writes a line: "*If best, were it as was, or best without*" (98), which is a good example of his use of antithesis. The 124th line *To make the weeper laugh, the laugher weep* is also antithesis. The other example is the 145th line: *What with his art in youth, and youth in art*.

8.3 Alliteration

The etymology of the term *alliteration* is the Latin word *alliteration*, meaning the repetition of the consonants or the first letter at the beginning of words. There are striking examples of this figure of speech in the poem. "*Upon her head a platted hive of straw*" (8) is the first one. The second one is "*Oft did she heave her napkin to her eyne*" (15). Then the line "*If best, were it as was, or best without*" (98), though it is regarded as the antithesis, it is also held as an example of alliteration. There are still 9 lines which can be considered as the examples of Shakespeare's use of the figure of speech, alliteration: ①*Whether the horse by him because his deed* (111); ②*So many have, that never toucht his hand* (141); ③*To put the by-past perils in her way* (158); ④*To be forbad the sweets that seem so good* (164); ⑤*Till now did ne'er invite, nor never woo* (182); ⑥*Harm have I done to them, but ne'er was harmed* (194); ⑦*With wit well blazon'd, smiled or made some mean* (217); ⑧*The broken besoms that to me belong* (254); and ⑨*What rocky heart to water will not wear* (291).

8.4 Parallelism

The etymology of the term *parallelism* is the Greek word *paralogismós*, meaning "*alongside one another*". The modern definition of it is that two or more words or expressions, clauses or sentences, whether metrical, lexical, figurative, or grammatical, are of similar construction and meaning placed together in balance. The term parallelism may include both parallelism and repetition.

Parallelism.   Although this figure of speech is very commonly used in

poetry, the use of it is not frequent in *A Lover's Complaint*. There are still some examples of the usage of parallelism in this narrative poem. First, the 109th line *What rounds, what bounds, what course, what stop he makes* is the parallelism of the objects in a clause describing the young man's horse. By the way, the four *whats* in this line could also be considered as the example of the use of alliteration. Second, the 270th line: *Of wealth, of filial fear, law, kindred, fame*, is the parallelism of prepositional phrases. From the 3 words *filial, fear*, and *fame*, it is obvious another example of alliteration. The parallelism of phrase can easily be found in the 271th line: *Love's arms are peace, 'gainst rule, 'gainst sense, 'gainst shame*. Now, let's look at the first 5 lines of the last stanza:

> 'O, that infected moisture of his eye
> O, that false fire which in his cheek so glow'd,
> O, that forced thunder from his heart did fly,
> O, that sad breath his spongy lungs bestow'd,
> O, all that borrow'd motion seeming ow'd,
>   (323—327)

These 5 lines could be definitely regarded as a typical example of the usage of parallelism. It is obvious that 5 *that phrases* are placed side by side, nearly balancing each other. Other rhetoric devices could be found in these 5 lines.

Repetition.   The definition of the literary or rhetorical term repetition is repeating the same sound, the same word, the same phrase, the same clause, or the same sentence. In our daily life or social life repetition is very common, while in poetry repetition is the essential element. In line 257: *I strong o'er them, and you o'er me being strong*, the repetition of the same adjective *strong* appears. The repetition of the same preposition *of* is in line 270: *Of wealth, of filial fear, law, kindred, fame*. In lines 323—327, the repetition of the interjection *O* can be seem at the very beginning of each of the 5 lines which is classified as the repetition of

beginning words. The relative pronoun *that* is also repeated 5 times in order to strengthen the aesthetic beauty of unity.

8.5 The Synthetic Usage of the Rhetoric Devices

When it comes to the artistic features of *A Fair Maiden* in the *Classic of Poetry* in Chinese literature, the methods like *fu* (exposition), *bi* (comparison), and *xing* (stimulus or analogy) are like the methods of narration, comparison, and analogy in the long poem written by Shakespeare.

> *By riverside are cooing*
> *A pair of turtledoves;*
> *A good young man is wooing*
> *A maiden fair he loves.*
>
> (*Translated by Xu Yuan Zhong*)

The birds in the poem are the metaphors of the two lovers: the handsome young man and an attractive fair lady. A blending of exposition or narration, comparison, and stimulus is the characteristic of this famous classic Chinese poem *A Fair Maiden* which is a love song depicting the lovesickness handsome young man suffering in courting a fair maiden. Shakespeare also employs the 3 techniques in the first stanza, 7 lines, in his *A lover's Complaint*:

> *From off a hill whose concave womb re-worded*
> *A plainful story from a sistering vale,*
> *My spirits t'attend this double voice accorded,*
> *And down I laid to list the sad-tun'd tale;*
> *Ere long espied a fickle maid full pale,*
> *Tearing of papers, breaking rings a-twain,*

Storming her world with sorrow's wind and rain.

(1—7)

The metaphor *womb* symbolizes the warmth of our mother earth. In the phrase *a sistering vale*, people can see a connected vale or valley with an adjective *sistering* as a metaphor *sister like*. If the word *sistering* cannot be held as a metaphor concerning rhetoric, we can say that the English language has such a function because the word *sistering* is a very vivid impression or image. The 7th line *Storming her world with sorrow's wind and rain* is also a metaphor because the 3 images *storming*, *wind* and *rain* symbolizes the maiden's extreme anger.

In the history of Chinese literature, in the poetry of the Wei, Jin and Six Dynasties, the very beginning of the famous narrative poem *Peacocks Southeast Traveling*: *A pair of peacocks a-flight to the southeast traveling. At every couple of leagues they look back faltering,* is a beautiful metaphor as the image peacocks symbolize the two heartbroken lovers, to say exactly, a couple, Jiao Zhongqing, and Liu Lanzhi. Liu Lanzhi, a bride of Jiao Zhongqing, would rather commit suicide by jumping into a river than remarry another guy after Jiao Zhongqing's death. In the Southern Song Lyrics, there are two famous poems written by Lu You and Tang Wan who were a good couple but they were compelled to divorce owing to the oppression of Lu You's mother. At the very beginning of Lu You's poem *To the Tune Phoenix Hairpin*, it reads: *Pink tender hand, / yellow-corded wine, / city crammed with spring hues, willow by garden wall; / east winds hateful, / the one loved, cold— / a heart all sadness, / parted how many years?* Here the images *hand, wine, city, spring hues, willow by garden wall* and *east winds* are all metaphors of the great poet Lu You's extreme sadness when he saw Tang Wan again after their divorce. Tang Wan also wrote a poem to the same tune to reveal her heartbroken emotion in a drizzle *What plight for flowers rashly dropped and dampened, / My ailing soul will break 'neath strain one day, / As*

ropes on a swing, through wearing, give away. The metaphors of the dropped *flowers* and *ropes on a swing* are the sad and lamentable image of a divorced lady in very poor health.

200 years later, William Wordsworth imitated Shakespeare's poetic technique in his famous short poem:

> *I wondered lonely as a cloud*
> *That floats on high o'er vales and hills,*
> *When all at once I saw a crowd,*
> *A host of golden daffodils;*
> *Beside the lake, beneath the trees,*
> *Fluttering and dancing in the breeze.*

The phrase *as a cloud* is simile, while the present participle *dancing* is personification. The beginning of the poem is the imitation of *A lover's Complaint*: first the setting, second the wandering of the poet, then the beautiful scenery: the daffodils.

It has been a topic that a forsaken lady complains about her sadness and tragedy for thousands of years in the history of literature. Shakespeare, thanks to his passionate and talented creative poetic capacity, has written this long narrative poem *A Lover's Complaint*, in which an impressive image of a hypocritic, young man is successfully created. It is no doubt that Shakespeare's success depends largely on his suitable use of rhetoric devices. Both the first stanza and the last stanza are beautifully written. It is interesting, entertaining and amusing that the figure of speech in the first stanza makes the stanza even more attractive, while the usage of the rhetoric devices enforces the strength of the poem and the passion of the forsaken lady, therefore the last stanza is the most beautiful one on the

sense of sadness and the sense of beauty, although it seems that the last stanza is not the ending of the poem but the climax of it.

9   The Origin and the Themes of *The Passionate Pilgrim*

It is a collection of Shakespeare's love poems or songs, in which Shakespeare's meditation of love, friendship, youth and age can be felt. The first two poems are just like sonnet 138 and sonnet 144 in the 154 sonnets. Poems 3 and 5 are taken from *Loves Labour's Lost* (Ⅳ.iii.56—59, Ⅳ.ii. 100—113). Poems 4, 6, 9 are Shakespeare's prewritings of *Venus and Adonis*, although the first two are in the sonnet forms, the third one is composed of 18 lines, 9 couplets, rhymed *aabb ccdd eeff gghh ii*. There are 15 poems, 217 lines in all, in this collection, including sonnets, couplets and sestets. There are several authors of *The Passionate Pilgrim*. It is certain that Shakespeare wrote 4 poems in the collection. Although scholars are not sure about the authority of the other poems, readers can still enjoy the true feeling and beauty of them. The line "*sweet Cytherea, sitting by a brook*" and the whole poem will give young readers much more entertainment for its romance, its genuine love, and its natural or spontaneous passion. This chapter is going to discuss the authorship and the theme of each poem in this whole collection.

9.1 Shakespeare's Sonnets and *The Passionate Pilgrim*

Shakespeare's sonnets 138 and 144 appear in his collection of poems *The Passionate Pilgrim*:

138

When my love swears that she is made of truth,	1
I do believe her, though I know she lies,	2
That she might think me some untutor'd youth,	3

Unlearned in the world's false subtleties.   4

Thus vainly thinking that she thinks me young,   5

Although she knows my days are past the best,   6

Simply I credit her false-speaking tongue: 7

On both sides thus is simple truth supprest.   8

But wherefore says she not she is unjust?   9

And wherefore say not I that I am old?   10

O, love's best habit is in seeming trust,   11

And age in love loves not to have years told: 12

    Therefore I lie with her and she with me,   13

    And in our faults by lies we flatter'd be.   14

The Passionate Pilgrim

1

When my love swears that she is made of truth,   1

I do believe her, though I know she lies,   2

That she might think me some untutor'd youth,   3

Unskilful in the world's false forgeries.   4

Thus vainly thinking that she thinks me young,   5

Although I know my years be past the best,   6

I Similing credit her false-speaking tongue: 7

Outfacing faults in love with love's ill rest.   8

But wherefore says my love that she is young   9

And wherefore say not I that I am old?   10

O, love's best habit is a soothing tongue,   11

And age, in love loves not to have years told.   12

    Therefore, I'll lie with love, and love with me,   13

    Since that our faults in love thus smother'd be.   14

Generally speaking, *Sonnets 138* and the lst poem in *The Passionate Pilgrim* are almost the same, but when we compare the two editions carefully here are at least 6 striking differences between them as the differences are clearly recognizable. The 6th line of each should be distinguished: in Sonnet 138, it reads *Although she knows my days are past the best*, while in *The Passionate Pilgrim Although I know my years be past the best*. Grammatically, the third person singular and the first person singular belong to the basic issure which cannot be ignored. Then comes the 8th line: in *Sonnets 138, On both sides thus is simple truth suppressed*, while in *The Passionate Pilgrim, Outfacing faults in love with love's ill rest*. Two different expressions and ideas can be read and felt. It is difficult to decide which line is better. Therefore it is better for readers to choose in accordance with their own favour.

Here are *Sonnet 144* and the 2nd poem in *The Passianate Pilgrim*:

144

Two loves I have of comfort and despair,	1
Which like two spirits do suggest me still:	2
The better angel is a man right fair,	3
The worser spirit a woman colour'd ill.	4
To win me soon to hell, my female evil	5
Tempteth my better angel from my side,	6
And would corrupt my saint to be a devil,	7
Wooing his purity with her foul pride.	8
And whether that my angel be turn'd fiend	9
Suspect I may, yet not directly tell;	10
But being both from me, both to each friend,	11
I guess one angel in another's hell:	12
Yet this shall I ne'er know, but live in doubt,	13

Till my bad angel fire my good one out.   14

The Passionate Pilgrim

2

Two loves I have, of comfort and despair,   1

That like two spirits do suggest me still: 2

My better angel is a man right fair,   3

My worser spirit a woman colour'd ill.   4

To win me soon to hell, my female evil   5

Tempteth my better angel from my side,   6

And would corrupt my saint to be a devil,   7

Wooing his purity with her fair pride.   8

And whether that my angel be turn'd fiend   9

Suspect I may, yet not directly tell: 10

For being both to me, both to each friend,   11

I guess one angel in another's hell: 12

The truth I shall not know, but live in doubt,   13

Till my bad angel fire my good one out.   14

However, there are only 4 slight differences between *Sonnets 144* and the 2nd poem in *The Passionate Pilgrim*: the 4th line, *The* and *My*; the 8th line, *foul* and *fair*; the 11th line, *from* and *to*; and the 13th line, *Yet this shall I ne'er know, but live in doubt* and *The truth I shall not know, but live in doubt*. Though the differences are not as many as those in *Sonnet 138* and the 1st poem in *The Passianate Pilgrim*, readers cannot make their choice easily without careful meditation. It is amusing that there are 5 angels in this poem which have different meanings. It has been more than 400 years since the printing and publication of the 2 collections of Shakespeare's poems. Facing these 2 valuable historical documents, people is required to cherish them and study them and make a good use of them.

9.2 *The Passionate Pilgrim* and *Love's Labor's Lost*

The 3rd poem in *The Passionate Pilgrim* is similar to Longaville's poem or sonnet in *Love's Labor's Lost, IV,iii,58—71*:

Did not the heavenly rhetoric of thine eye,	1
'Gainst whom the world could not hold argument,	2
Persuade my heart to this false perjury?	3
Vows for thee broke deserve not punishment.	4
A woman I forswore; but I will prove,	5
Thou being a goddess, I forswore not thee:	6
My vow was earthly, thou a heavenly love;	7
Thy grace being gain'd cures all disgrace in me.	8
My vow was breath, and breath a vapour is;	9
Then, thou fair sun, that on this earth doth shine,	10
Exhale this vapour vow; in thee it is:	11
If broken, then it is no fault of mine.	12
If by me broke, what fool is not so wise	13
To break an oath, to win a paradise?	14

Longaville

Did not the heavenly rhetoric of thine eye,	1
'Gainst whom the world can not hold argument,	2
Persuade my heart to this false perjury?	3
Vows for thee broke deserve not punishment.	4
A woman I forswore; but I will prove,	5
Thou being a goddess, I forswore not thee:	6
My vow was earthly, thou a heavenly love;	7

Thy grace being gain'd cures all disgrace in me.   8

Vows are but breath, and breath a vapour is: 9

Then, thou fair sun, which on my earth dost shine,   10

Exhalest this vapour-vow; in thee it is: 11

If broken then, it is no fault of mine.   12

If by me broke, what fool is not so wise   13

To lose an oath, to win a paradise?   14

Longaville, as Dumain in the same play, is also a lord with the king of Navarre, and falls in love with Maria, an attendant lady to a princess of France, but in vain. Beauty is a significant form. Poem is a significant form. It can be easily seen that the arrangement of the lines of the 2 editions are different, especially the last 2 lines. The former one is gentle while the latter one is lively. The differences in words are: in the 9th line, *My vow was breath* and *Vows are but breath*; in the 10th line, *that* and *which*, *this* and *my*; and in the 11th line, *Exhale* and *Exhalest*. It seems that the diction in *Love's Labor's Lost* is more helpful to reveal the inner world of a character, Longaville. The 3rd poem *in The Passionate Pilgrim* is more like a love song in a general sense.

There are a few differences between the 5th poem in *The Passionate Pigrilm* and sir Nathaniel's poem in *Love's Labor's Lost, IV. ii.105—18*:

5

If love make me forsworn, how shall I swear to love?   1

O never faith could hold, if not to beauty vowed: 2

Though to myself forsworn, to thee I'll constant prove;   3

Those thoughts, to me like oaks, to thee like osiers bowed.   4

Study his bias leaves, and makes his book thine eyes,   5

Where all those pleasures live that art can comprehend.   6

If knowledge be the mark, to know thee shall suffice;   7

Well learned is that tongue that well can thee commend: 8

All ignorant that soul that sees thee without wonder;   9

Which is to me some praise, that I thy parts admire: 10

Thine eye Jove's lightning seems, thy voice his dreadful thunder, 11

Which, not to anger bent, is music and sweet fire.   12

  Celestial as thou art, O do not Jove that wrong: 13

  To sing heaven's praise with such an earthly tongue.   14

Sir Nathaniel

If love make me forsworn, how shall I swear to love?   1

  Ah, never faith could hold, if not to beauty vow'd!   2

Though to myself forsworn, to thee I'll faithful prove;   3

  Those thoughts, to me were oaks, to thee like osiers bow'd.   4

Study his bias leaves, and makes his book thine eyes,   5

  Where all those pleasures live that art would comprehend.   6

If knowledge be the mark, to know thee shall suffice;   7

  Well learned is that tongue that well can thee commend: 8

All ignorant that soul that sees thee without wonder;   9

  Which is to me some praise, that I thy parts admire: 10

Thy eye Jove's lightning bears, thy voice his dreadful thunder,   11

  Which, not to anger bent, is music and sweet fire.   12

Celestial as thou art, O pardon Jove this wrong,   13

That sings heaven's praise with such an earthly tongue.   14

9.3 The Themes of other Poems

In *The Passionate Pilgrim*, there are 4 poems, poems 4, 6, 9, and 11, describing the love affairs between Venus and Adonis. In poems 4 and 6, the

goddess is Cytherea. Cytherea is the goddess in Greek mythology, who has another name Cerigo in Italian. In Greek, it is called Kithira, the lsland of Kithira, which is situated to the south of Greece. Cytherea is also another name of Venus, while the original one is Aphrodite, the goddess of productiveness side by side with beauty and love.

Poem 4 depicts the first stage of the love affairs between Venus and Adonis: *Sweet Cytherea, sitting by a brook / with yong Adonis, lovely, fresh and green(1 —2)*. Poem 6 tells readers how Venus under the osier by a brook catches sight of Adonis beathing in the brook: *Anon he comes, and throws his mantle by, / And stood stark naked on the brook's green brim (9—10)*. Poem 9 describes how Venus entices Adonis, which is very erotic. In Poem 11 Venus embraces Adonis and kisses him: *And then she clipt Adonis in her arms (6)*; *And with her lips on his did cat the seizure (10)*. There is a Chinese saying: if a lady wooes a gentleman, it is a piece of paper; if a gentleman wooes a lady, it is a high mountain. The meaning is that is easy for a lady to woo a gentleman. In the poem, Venus is very passionate and active to woo Adonis, but the handsome young lad cannot appreciate her love, maybe he is too young to know a lady's love. If fish is not hungry, how can it be eager to swallow fish bait? It is true that Venus is beautiful, passionate and authentic, but all her labour is lost.

Poem 7 depicts a fickle woman *Mild as a dove, but neither true nor trusty (2)*. The poet sighes with feeling *How many tales to please me hath she coined (9)* and wonders *Was this a lover, or a lecher whether (17)*.

Poem 8 draws a beautiful picture to reveal the relationship between art and love: *If music and sweet poetry agree, / As they must needs the sister and the brother, / Then must the love be great 'twixt thee and me (1—3)*. Poetry and music are so closely related that they two cannot be devided easily. It is a great pleasure to be good at both poetry and music. If you are not good at both of them, you cannot repel either of them. It will be very amazing to be good at one of them.

At the Yangtze River, there is a Pipa lady with the Duputy Chief of Jiujiang Prefecture, Bai Juyi. The beautiful music of Pipa, the musical instrument, is no longer heard, but Bai's poem has been reading more than 1000 years. If there is no Pipa girl, there will be no Pipa song, i.e. Bai's poem. If there is no Pipa song, who knows the Pipa girl? I wish poetry, music and love be combined to be a harmonious lively oil painting.

Poem 14 tells a lover, a lady, is cold to the poet and it is hard and difficult for the poet to guess what she really thinks. *Yet at my parting sweetly did she smile (7). 'T may be, she joy'd to jest at my exile (9).* It is true that love is torture.

Poem 15 relates a universal truth, to stay with one's sweet heart is so happy that it seems time goes too fast. When the poet is waiting for his lover, *My heart doth charge the watch; the morning rise / Doth cite each moving sense from idle rest (2—3).*

To sum up, all the poems mentioned above, poems 4, 6, 7, 8, 9, 11, 14 and 15, including poems 1, 2, 3, and 5, 12 poems in all, are the poems about love and love affairs.

The other 3 poems have different themes which are related to love and love affairs. Poem 10 expresses the poet's mourning for his dead friend: *Sweet rose, fair flower, untimely pluckt, soon vaded (1).* When readers read the words *rose, fair flower*, it is hard for them to decide whether the dead is a young man or young lady. Therefore the first line of the poem is melancholy and it is beautifully written. Poem 12 sings the praises of the young and bewails the old: *Crabbed age and youth cannot live together / Youth is full of pleasance, age is full of care (1—2). Youth is nimble, age is lame (6).* Poem 13 is the philosophical thinking of the term beauty. Beauty is short, beauty is fragile, beauty is nihilistic. *Beauty is but a vain and doubtful good (1). So beauty blemisht once for ever lost (11).*

To people all over the world, love is a honey word which is pleasing and

lively. Thanks to William Jaggard who printed *The Passionate Pilgrim in* 1599, readers can appreciate the collection of love poems except a few poems concerning friendship, the aged and the youth. It is said love is the motivation of the world. Reading the love poems in the collection, readers will feel that love is romantic, love is sweet, love is bitter, love is difficult, and love is the instinct of the human being. Love is an unalterable principle. *The Passionate Pilgrim* has remained and will remain lively on people's lips, although there are some debates about the authorship of some poems in the whole collection.

10   The Analysis of *Sonnets to Sundry Notes of Music*

There are 6 poems in this collection. The first poem is about a fickle woman. The second one is nearly the same as a poem by Dumain, a lord attending on the King of France in *Love's Labor's Lost VI.iii.97—116*, persuading a young man to pluck fresh flowers. The third expresses the sad feeling of a forsaken young shepherd. The fourth tells how to win a girl's love. The fifth is about the love affairs between a good boy and a fair girl. The sixth poem teaches how to tell a true friend from a false one.

The whole collection is composed of 220 lines: Poem1, 16 lines, 4 stanzas, the first 3 lines of each stanza are rhymed *aaa bbb ccc ddd*, while the last line of each stanza is not rhymed; Poem 2, 18 lines, 9 couplets; Poem 3, 54 lines, 3 stanzas, 18 lines for each stanza, not strictly rhymed; Poem4, 54 lines, 9 staves of sesta rima, iambic pentameter, rhymed *ababcc*; Poem5, 20 lines, 5 stanzas, rhymed *aabb*; and Poem 6, 58 lines, 29 couplets.

10.1 The Origin and Content of Poem 2

Sonnets to Sundry Notes of Music

2

On a day, alack the day!	1
Love, whose month was ever May,	2
Spied a blossom passing fair,	3
Playing in the wanton air:	4
Through the velvet leaves the wind	5

All unseen gan passage find;   6

That the lover, sick to death,   7

Wisht himself the heaven's breath,   8

'Air,' quoth he, 'thy cheeks may blow;   9

Air, would I might triumph so!   10

But, alas! my hand hath sworn   11

Ne'er to pluck thee from thy thorn: 12

Vow, alack! for youth unmeet: 13

Youth, so apt to pluck a sweet.   14

Thou for whom Jove would swear   15

Juno but an Ethiope were;   16

And deny himself for Jove,   17

Turning mortal for thy love.'   18

Love's Labor's Lost

Dumaine

On a day—alack the day!—   1

Love, whose month was ever May,   2

Spied a blossom passing fair,   3

Playing in the wanton air: 4

Through the velvet leaves the wind   5

All unseen, can passage find;   6

That the lover, sick to death,   7

Wisht himself the heaven's breath,   8

<u>Air</u>, quoth he, thy cheeks may blow;   9

Air, would I might triumph so!   10

But, <u>alack</u>, my hand is sworn   11

Ne'er to pluck thee from thy thorn;—   12

Vow, alack, for youth unmeet,   13

Youth so apt to pluck a sweet!   14

Do not call it sin in me,	15
That I am forsworn for thee;	16
Thou for whom Jove would swear	17
Juno but an Ethiop were;	18
And deny himself for Jove,	19
Turning mortal for thy love.'	20

(99—118)

There are 2 lines more (Line 15 Line 16) than in *Sonnets to Sundry Notes of Music*. In *Love's Labour's Lost* there are 20 lines, while in *Sonnets to Sundry Notes of Music*, there are 18 lines. It is rashional, logical and metrical that the 2nd poem is composed of 20 lines, because 5 stanzas, each stanza 4 lines, do have a beauty of unity. To write a poem which is supposed to have 5 quatrains seems a better choice for an adult poet like Shakespeare and for a gentle man Dumain in the play who tries by every means to woo Katharine, an attendant lady to a princess of France.

Poem 2 expresses the emotion of a young man in love similar to the poem by Dumain, a handsome and optimistic young lord. Love is sweet. The colour of love is captivating. When people view, admire and enjoy the sight of flowers, people also love and protect them wholeheartedly with deep feeling. Do be careful! Don't eat the forbidden fruit. When Jove carries on a clandestine love affair, Juno turns into an ugly black woman. The writing technique of this poem is that of narration, comparison and analogy as can be seen from the 18 or 20 lines of the poem. The first 8 lines are the usage of narration and comparison: one day in May, a very beautiful flower was in full bloom dancing in the gentle wind with the beautiful setting of the green leaves, and then a lovesick young man expresses his true emotion or lamentation of love. In the poem the expression *a blossom*

passing fair (3) is a comparison or metaphor of a beautiful attractive charming lovely young girl. The word *May* symbolizes the very opportunity of love. The wanton air, the wind and the velvet leaves are all the beautiful things in the emusing environment for young lovers. Therefore the rest of the poem (6 or 8 lines) is analogy of the young man who cries *Vow, alack! for youth unmeet: / Youth, so apt to pluck a sweet* (13—14). This poem is well-knit, pure and fresh, revealing one's deep true feeling, and spreads far and wide among the readers, becoming an oft-quoted and widely loved love poem.

10.2 The Origin and Content of Poem 5

Poem 5 is a very popular poem which is very romantic and is considered as a beautiful lyric. It is said the origin of the poem is by two poets: one is Christopher Marlow (1564—1593), who wrote the famous pastoral lyric *The Passionate Shepherd to His Love*, the other is Sir Walter Raleigh (1552—1618), who wrote *The Nymph's Reply to the Shepherd*. Nymph refers to in mythology a young graceful beauty.

The origin of the first part of poem 5 is composed of 6 stanzas, in which the 4th stanza and the last stanza are excluded in poem 5 in *Sonnets to Sundry Notes of Music*:

Come live with me, and be my love;
And we will all the pleasures prove
That hills and valleys, dales and fields,
Woods or steepy mountain yields.

And we will sit upon the rocks,
Seeing the shepherds feed their flocks
By shallow rivers, to whose falls

Melodious birds sing madrigals.

And I will make thee beds of roses,
And a thousand fragrant posies;
A cap of flowers, and a kirtle
Embroider'd all with leaves of myrtle;

A gown made of the finest wool
Which from our pretty lambs we pull;
Fair-lined slippers for the cold,
With buckles of the purest gold;

A belt of straw and ivy-buds,
With coral clasps and amber studs:
An if these pleasures may thee move,
Come live with me, and be my love.

The shephered-swains shall dance and sing
For they delight each May morning:
If these delights thy mind may move,
Then live with me, and be my love.

Green mountain, blue water, fresh flowers, singing birds, pearls, treasure, beautiful colthes, singing and dancing, are all ideal elements in this poetic and picturesque scenery of romantic love affairs. Pleasure, peace, youth, love are spring sunshine, the universal life, the motive of life, and the passion of art. It is the eternal topic and eternal spirit. The resources of all emotions come from the great interaction of *yin* and *yang*. It is also very dramatic since it seems a dialogue between a shepherd and his lover. The testameter enables the poem to be nimble, light and lovely, representing the heartfelt wishes of every pair of young lovers.

10.3 The Contents of Poems 1, 3, 4, and 6

Poem 1 tells a love story of a young girl who was the most beautiful one of the 3 daughters of a lord. The girl first fell in love with her schoolmaster, then met with another brave knight. It was very difficult for the girl to make a choice: she could not forsake her teacher, nor could she kill the knight. One must be forsaken and the knight was seriously wounded. In the competition between polite letters and martial arts, the former wan, and the teacher married the beautiful young girl. The poem can be regarded as a folk song, although it seems like a lullaby. In form, it is a brief one but ingenuous. In structure, it is carefully designed, the conflict is mainly in the 2nd stanza. In flavour, it is meaningful and thought-provoking. The theme of the poem is how a girl chose her husband which is a very common topic in daily life for all the people. *Then, lullaby, the learned man had got the lady gay; / For now my song is ended* (15—16). It is a love story that people love to see and hear.

Poem 3 is the second longest one, from line 1—54, 54 lines in all. The form or the structure of this poem is nimble, lovely and subtle, which coincides with the wave like the development of the psychological activity of the young man, a shepherd, the lover and the protagonist of the poem. The poetic technique of narration, comparison and analogy is also employed as readers can read in lines 1 —3, and lines 37—40: *My flocks feed not, / My ewes breed not, / My rams speed not* (1—3)*Clear wells spring not, / Sweet birds sing not, / Green plants bring not / Forth their dye.* These 2 narration like poetic sections could be considered as one comparison or metaphor, which is the fact that the young shepherd has lost his lovely girl. The rhetoric device is also very suitable, gentle and powerful, which is parallelism that can also be seen in the first 3 lines of this poem (1—3), and lines 37—40. Lines 45—48 *All our pleasures known to us poor swains, / All our merry meetings on the plains, / All our evening sport from us is fled, / All our love is lost,*

for Love is dead, although a very good example of parallelism, can be regarded as another comparison or metaphor: the young shepherd was forsaken forever.

It is a love song, it is a folk song, it is a complaint song, it is a pastoral song. Shakespeare has drawn an amusing and entertaining picture and has composed a melodious and lovely music with his lyric tone, his fresh colour, and his nimble rhythm. Although it is laden with grief, it is not downhearted. It is pure and fresh, it is meaningful and thought-provoking. The young people will be intoxicated with it for its sincerity and purity, for its tortuosity and winding. In this melancholy, beautiful scenery, readers will linger on and on, forgetting to return.

Poem 4 is also a long one, from line 1 to line 54, 54 lines in all, and it seems rational to tell the truth of love and the idea of how to win a girl's or a lady's love. This poem is composed of 9 stanzas of sesta rima, like that of *Venus and Adonis*, but in the form of iambic tetrameter, rhymed *ababcc*. The theme as well as the form of this poem makes the readers return to the real life from the romantic love affairs. The first stanza says *Let reason rule things worthy blame* (3), which can be held as the general idea of the whole poem. The second stanza gives a suggestion: *when thou comest thy tale to tell, / Smooth not thy tongue with filed talk* (7—8). The third stanza says that if she is angry, don't be afraid of it, because she will be kind and gentle again. The fourth stanza tells a truth that if a girl says no to you and curses you, in fact *Her feeble force will yield at length* (21). The fifth stanza suggests a young guy should try to do everything for his lover, *Spare not to spend* (26). The sixth stanza advices that the young man should always serve the girl whole-heartedly and be unyielding. The seventh stanza says the girl's tricks are not so serious and are easy to deal with. The eighth stanza tells that a girl wants to live a real life with her lover or husband. *Were kisses all the joys in bed, / One woman would another wed* (47—48). The last stanza is a humorous conclusion: *But, soft! enough—too much, I fear—Lest that my mistress hear my song* (49—50).

Poem 6 is the longest one, 58 lines in all, among the 6 poems, and can be divided into 3 sections. The first section, from line 1—line 20, describes a beautiful scenery in May: *Sitting in a pleasant shade / Which a grove of myrtles made, / Beasts did leap and birds did sing, / Trees did grow and plants did spring* (3—6). Then the nightingale appears. The second section, from line 21—line 44, tells the nightingale: *Senseless trees they cannot hear thee; / Ruthless beasts they will not cheer thee* (21—22). The third section (45—56) tells, as mentioned above, how to tell a true friend from a false one: *Faithful friends are hard to find* (56). *He that is thy friend indeed, / He will help thee in thy need* (49—50). Perhaps these two lines are the origin of the famous proverb: a friend in need is a friend indeed.

In *Sonnets to Sundry Notes of Music*, both the contents and genre are various and entertaining: Poem 2 is full of gentility; Poem 6 is a lyric with the beautiful scenery; Poem 1 is a folk song like a mini drama; Poem 3 is nimble and light hearted; Poem 4 is cunning and humorous; and Poem 5 is world famous for its beauty and romance. To know the origin of all the 6 poems is the academic affair of Shakespeare studies, while to read the poems and enjoy the beauty is the aesthetic needs for the readers. People will treasure and cherish this collection of lyrics.

11   The Cross-culture Contemplation of

The Phoenix and Turtle

According to a legend, phoenix is an Arabian bird, living in the nest of spices and perfumes. Phoenix is a symbol of beauty, rarity and immortality. Turtle is turtledove, symbolizing the constancy in love. The whole poem *The Phoenix and Turtle* is composed of 67 lines, 2 sections. The lst section has 52 lines, 13 quatrains, trochaic tetrameter, rhymed *abba*. The 2nd section *THRENOS* has 15 lines, 5 tercets or triplets, trochaic tetrameter, rhymed *aaa bbb* .... This chapter is gong to discuss the images of the phoenix and turtle and other birds, the idea of the poets, the philosophical implication, and the aesthetic assessment, in accordance with both the background of Chinese culture and the setting of western or foreign culture.

11.1 The Image of the Phoenix

In western culture, the word phoenix has at least 3 definitions. The lst one, in Greek mythology, is that Phoenix is one of the 3 sons of king Agenor who is the son of Poseidon and Libya. Phoenix has a sister Europa who is carried away by Zeus disguised as a bull. The 2nd one is that Phoenix is the tutor of the great hero Achilles in Trojan War. The 3rd is the most famous and popular one that phoenix, in Arabian mythology, is a mythical bird in the desert, living lonely for 500 or 600 years before burning itself to death atop a pyre of aromatic twigs of spices and perfumes, and keeping beating the phoenix's wings. After the burning, out of the ashes, there is the resurrection of a new phoenix, self-generated.

In Shakespeare plays, the word phoenix has 3 different definitions. lst, the definition of phoenix is the mythical bird, e.g. in his romance *The Tempest, III. iii, 21—24*: when Sebastian says to Prospero, *Now I will believe / That there are unicorns; that in Arabia / There is one tree, the phoenix throne, one phoenix / At this hour reigning there.* In his history *Henry VIII, V. iv. 39—40*, Cranmer says to the king, *but as when / The bird of wonder dies, the maiden phoenix, / Her ashes new create another heir / As great in admiration as herself.* The 2nd definition of phoenix is the name of an inn as in his comedy *The Comedy of Errors I. ii 74—76,* when Dromio of Ephesus says to Antipholus of of Syracuse, *My charge was but to fetch you from the mart / Home to your house, the Phoenix, sir, to dinner; / My mistress and her sister stays for you.* The first letter of the word is capitalized because it is a proper name. The 3rd definition of the word is the proper name of a ship, as can be read from his comedy *Twelfth Night V. i .60—61* when the lst officer says to Orsino, Duke of Illyria, *this is that Antonio / That took the Phoenix.*

In China, phoenix is a lengendarily lucky divine bird, and is the king of birds. Its head looks like the sky; the eyes, the sun; the back, the moon; the wings, the wind; the claws, the earth; and the tail, the latitude.

According to descriptions by the ancient Chinese people, phoenix has a snake's head, a swallow's chin, a tortoise's back, a turtle's waist, a crane's crown (a crown is comb like, in the shape of glossy ganoderma, in Latin, *Ganoderma lucidum*), a chicken's beak, a swan goose's front part, a fishtail, an egret's claws, and a mandarin duck's cheeks. Phoenix features colorful feathers with various textures. The feather texture over the head represents virtue; that on the wings, rites; that on the back, righteousness; that over the breast, benevolence; and that over the belly, faith. So the phoenix is a propitious bird incorporating benevolence, righteousness, rites, virtue, and faith. It flies beyond the four seas. Peace will prevail in the world whenever the bird appears. The image of phoenix

implies auspiciousness, peace, serenity, and a happy life. There are many famous saying concerning phoenix: numerous rare birds dancing around a phoenix; precious and rare as phoenix feathers and unicorn horns; dragons flying and phoenixes dancing, a phoenix turning to the sun; a phoenix flying around a peony blossom and dragon and phoenix bringing prosperity, to name only a few.

In his famous poem *The sorrow of Separation*, Qu Yuan (340—278 BC), the great Chinese romantic poet, mentions phoenix many a time: *I rode in a phoenix carriage driven by four Jade-decorated dragons; A phoenix acted as vanguard, I ordered the phoenix to fly fast day and night; The phoenix spread its wings to bear the cloud. It flew high and rhythmically* (Zhang Bingxiang), and *On phoenix Wings the Dragon Pennons lay / With Plumage bright they flew to lead the way* (Yang Xianyi and Gladys Yang).

In accordance with the western culture, the image phoenix is heroic and brave, and seems more philosophical; while concerning Chinese culture, that of phoenix is auspicious and happy and seems more harmonious. Phoenix, though legendary, is an auspicious bird that people love to see and hear in China. In Qu Yuan's poem, it seems the image phoenix is more practical, while in Shakespeare's plays phoenix seems both heroic and practical.

Kuo Mo-jo (1892—1978) published *The Nirvana of the Feng and Huang* on January 30 and 31, 1920. As a great modern romantic poet, Kuo Mo-jo praises highly the resurrection of the Feng and Huang, i.e. the phoenix. *Is it he who sings for joy, or is it fire? / It is joy itself that sings for joy! / It is joy itself that sings for joy! / Only joyfully singing, / Only joyfully singing! / Singing! / Singing! / Singing!* (*Chinese Literature, No.10, 1978*. Foreign Languages Press, Beijing, 1978)

11.2 The Images of Turtle, Eagle, Swan, and Crow

Compared with phoenix, turtle is common. In Shakespeare's *The Phoenix and Turtle*, turtle refers to turtle-dove which is like a dove but with a long tail,

though common, and has a pleasing soft cooing to the ears. Turtle-dove also shows its affectionate behaviour towards its mate and young. So in Shakespeare's poem, turtle-dove is the symbol of the constancy in love. There is a Chinese saying that the crying of the turtle-dove is touching people's heart. In Chinese history, during the *The Five Dynasties* (907—960), there was an emperor Liu Zhiyuan (895—948) of the State of Han, who was called Turtle-dove when becoming a son-in-law though he was still a poor soldier. Thus it can be seen that in China turtle-dove has the meaning of son-in-law, or one's husband.

There are 3 kinds of birds which are permitted to attend the ceremony of the Nirvana of the phoenix and the turtle. The first one is eagle which is held as the large strong meat-eating bird of prey with hooked beaks and sharp claws and very good eyesight as the *fowl of tyrant wing* (Shakespeare), and as the king of birds. Eagle is regarded as the symbol of hero as readers can read from Maxim Gorky's (1868—1936) prose poem *Ode to Eagle: Eagle sometimes flies lower than chicken, but chicken can never fly as high as eagle.* In Chinese culture, eagle is also a symbol of hero, and in the traditional Chinese painting, eagle is often drawn together with the pine tree to symbolize the brilliant hero. The second bird is *the death-divining* (Shakespeare) swan, meaning the swan can foresee its own death and sings a dirge when it is about to die. The swan reminds readers of the famous ballet *The Swan Lake* and the 4 lovely cygnets and the music by Peter Ilyich Tchaikovsky (1840—1893), the great Russian musician. Swan symbolizes purity and nobility and the unsullied. There is also a very famous Chinese saying: a toad lusting after a swan's flesh, meaning, aspiring after something one is not worthy of. The third is the crow, living thrice as long as the normal span of life, which is biologically a large shiny black bird with strong bill found nearly worldwide with a low, loud sharp cry which may be considered as the cry of people at a funeral ceremony. In western culture, the bird crow symbolizes longevity because it is regarded as a *treble-dated crow* (Shakespeare). In China,

crow is considered as the bad omen because there is an old saying, people will die as soon as the crow cries. However there is a very famous line in the Chinese poetry: *Moon goes down, frost is on and crows cry on* (Wang Fanglu), *or When the moon is down, the raven crows with sky frostbite* (Liu Junping) or *At moonset cry the crows, streaking the frosty sky* (Xu Yuan Zhong) in the poem entitled *Mooring by the Maple Bridge at Night* by poet Zhang Ji in the Tang dynasty.

11.3 The Poet's Contemplation

Universally, the great poets in the world express their profound religious and philosophical pondering and contemplation in their great works: e.g.Homer (800?—700? B.C.) and his *Iliad* and *Odyssey*; Dante (1265—1321) and his *Divine Comedy*; Goethe (1749—1783) and his *Faust*; Aleksandr Sergeyevich Pushkin (1799—1837) and his *Eugene Onegin*; Walt Whitman (1819—1892) and his *Leaves of Grass*. The great Chinese poet Qu Yuan has 6 famous lines in his *The Sorrow of Separation: Nine Fields of Orchids, at one Time I grew, / For Melilot a hundred Acres too* (Yang Xianyi and Gladys Yang); *The way was long, and wrapped in Gloom did seem / As I urged on to seek my vanished Dream.*(Yang Xianyi and Gladys Yang); *But since my Heart did love such Purity, / I'd not regret a thousand Deaths to die* (Yang Xianyi and Gladys Yang). Shakespeare in his play *Hamlet*, his masterpiece, writes his philosophical contemplation through his protagomist Hamlet: *To be, or not to be —— that is the question: / Whether 'tis nobler in the mind to suffer / The slings and arrows of outrageous fortune / Or to take arms against a sea of troubles, / And by opposing end them.* (*Hamlet III. i .55—59*)

In form the poem *The Phoenix and Turtle* is composed of 2 sections: the first 13 stanzas and the *THRENOS*. In meaning the first section can be further divided into 2 parts: the 1st part has 5 stanzas introducing the mourning ceremony; the 2nd part is the next 8 stanzas depicting the nirvana of the phoenix and turtle; the

3rd part is the threnos of the 2 holy birds. Shakespeare, in his poignant brevity of the poetic language, describing the funeral ceremony: *Here the anthem doth commence: / Love and Constancy is dead, / Phoenix and the Turtle fled / In a mutual flame from hence* (the 6th stanza).The nirvana of the phoenix in the conflagration becomes the immortality. Love and constancy will be more beautiful. God will bless human ever more. *So between them love did shine, / That the Turtle saw his right / Flaming in the Phoenix sight, / Either was the other's mine*（the 9th stanza）. So magnificent! So passionate! So illusory! So happy! The first 2 stanzas in *THRENOS* are 6 lines: *Beauty, Truth, and Rarity, / Grace in all simplicity, / Here enclos'd, in cinders lie* (the 1st stanza); *Death is now the Phoenix' nest, / And the Turtle's loyal breast / To eternity doth rest* (the 2nd stanza). The three treasures: beauty, truth and rarity, though destroyed, will revive in the future. Don't burst into tears, restrain your grief. The real world is dynamic and vigorous.

The flame of *The phoenix and Turtle* reminds readers of the funeral fire of Beowulf: *Upon the hill the men-at-arms lit a gigantic funeral fire. Black wood-smoke whirled over the conflagration. Heaven swallowed up the smoke.*

The funeral ceremony varies from country to country, and from culture to culture, therefore there are several forms of it: burial of the dead in the ground, water-burial, sea-burial, boat coffin burial, celestial burial by which bodies are exposed to birds of prey, cremation, and cliff coffin burial. There is an old Chinese saying, it is peaceful to be buried in the ground. But nowadays as the population explosion becomes serious, cremation becomes more prevailing.

Li Bai (701—762), a great Chinese romantic poet, wrote 2 famous lines: *I follow that crazy person, who lives in ancient Chu State, / And chant the Phoenix Song to laugh at the sacred Kong Qiu*, in his poem *Lushan Mountain Ballad to Lu Xuzhou*. Kong Qiu is the name of Confucious. Actually Confucious is a respectful form of address.

Du Fu (712—770), a great Chinese realistic poet, wrote a poem *To Minister Wei*, in which there are 4 famous lines: *I want to stand out firmly / And be an high official bravely / To advice His Majesty / To build a pure and honest society.*

11.4 Death, Life, Truth, Love and Beauty in the Poem

There are several profound philosophical issues in Shakespeare's *The Phoenix and Turtle*: death and life, truth, love, and beauty. It is said that because of the puzzle or the riddle of death and life, there appear the famous religions: Christianity, Islamism, Buddhism, Taoism, and Confucianism. Both paradise and hell are created for human race. Shakespeare in *The phoenix and Turtle* praises highly the resurrection after death. Rabindranath Tagore (1861—1941), a famous Indian poet, wrote in his *Stray Bird*: *Let life be beautiful like spring flowers and death like autumn leaves.* There are two well-known Chinese proverbs: 1st, *rather be a shuttered vessel of jade than an unbroken piece of pottery,* meaning, *to die in glory than live in dishonour*; 2nd, *rather die than submit.* There is also a common Chinese saying: *It is better to live bitterly than to die bravely* or *rather live bitterly than die bravely.* There is a common sense both in western culture and Chinese culture that death is the stop of living, which signifies coldness and detachedness, one's body being destroyed, being thrown away, being burnt, being eaten, and being rotten in the darkness or in the flame, where it is called hell. Life, however, signifies clothing, eating, accommodation and transportation, one's talking and laughing, one's seven emotions, namely, joy, anger, sorrow, fear, love, hate and desire. Life also signifies living, working and playing. The symbol of life is warmth, tender feeling, attentiveness, gentility and softness. As a common sense, therefore, life symbolizes spring. Life is paradise. People sing dirge or thrones to death; people sing anthem to life. The other philosophical issue is love. It is a legend that human was originally a round flesh ball. God cut it into two parts or two spheres, one is man, and another is woman. These two parts want to

be a united one. The desire of the combination between man and woman is called love. In Shakespeare's *The Phoenix and Turtle*, there are 4 lines: *That it cried, How true a twain / Seemeth this concordant one! / Love hath reason, reason none, / If that parts can so remain* (the 12th stanza). *Single nature's double name / Neither two nor one was called* (the 10th stanza). *Saw division grow together* (the 11th stanza).

The terminology truth is a very difficult philosophical issue. It may be seen that truth, as an entrance in a dictionary, may have at least 4 definitions: 1st, that which is true; 2nd, the state or quality of being true; 3rd, sincerity and honesty; and the 4th, a fact or principle proven to be valid. Truth, in the 4th sense, usually is hard to explain, whether it is relative or absolute, or what value the truth has, or how to examine truth. This philosophical issue is always profound and heavy and complex and complicated. What does Shakespeare mean when he mentions *truth* in his *The phoenix and Turtle*? Sincerity, honesty, or the ovalid principle? The definition of truth can be both concrete and abstract: truth here refers to the loyalty to love from the phoenix and turtle, and to the valid principle of love. The 14th and the 15th stanzas are Shakespeare's imaginary and poignant philosophical contemplation.

Beauty, as an entrance in a dictionary, has at least 3 definitions: 1st, a person, usually female, beautiful; 2nd, something beautiful; 3rd, combination of qualities that give pleasure to the senses, eye or ear, or to the mind. The 3rd definition belongs to the category of philosophy, to be more exactly, a branch of philosophy or a new discipline, aesthetics, which deals with the nature of art and beauty. Shakespeare's *The Phoenix and Turtle* expresses his pondering of the terminology of beauty especially in the part of *THRENOS*. *Truth may seem, but cannot be; / Beauty brag, but 'tis not she; / Truth and beauty buried be* (the 17th stanza). Here the term beauty is both philosophical and realistic. Beauty refers both the phoenix and the turtle and their sincere love and the nature of beauty. The nirvana of the

phoenix and the turtle is a beauty of brilliance, The brilliance may be in the twinkling of an eye, but the twinkling is eternalty. The nirvana of the phoenix and the turtle is heroic and brave. To be heroic and brave is the persuit of life for human race. It is the people's desire to be dynamic and vigorous since people are reluctant to be insipid and mediocre.

Shakespeare's famous poem *The phoenix and Turtle*, though in a poignant brevity, has created the immortal images of the phoenix and turtle. The philosophical and aesthetic issues in the poem are still under discussion and many different theories come into being. The issues of death, life, truth, love and beauty will continue to be the focus of the attention both of the common people and the scholars and experts. The brilliant image of phoenix is the hope or paradise of human race.

12   The Relationship between Shakespeare's

Poems and Plays

While creating his plays, comedy, history, tragedy, and romance, Shakespeare wrote many poems: *Venus and Adonis (1593), Lucrece (1594), The Phoenix and Turtle (1601), 154 Sonnets (1609), A Lover's Complaint (1609), The Passionate Pilgrim (1609),* and *Sonnets to Sundry Notes of Music (1609).* The miniature of Shakespeare's comedy and legend can be seen in *Venus and Adonis,* although it has a metencholy and tragic end. The succinct summary of Shakespeare's tragedy and history can be found and felt in *Lucrece.* It is obvious that Shakespeare's main contribution lies in his play, especially his 4 great tragedies, however, his contribution to the creation of poems can not be ignored. Scholars are attracted by his sonnets and have made contributions to the study and research of all his sonnets, because his sonnets are the real process or reality of Shakespeare's meditation or contemplation of humans and the world. However, the other poems written by Shakespeare should also be held as the organic components of Shakespeare's artistic creation and the good cultural setting of Shakespeare's plays. The relationship between Shakespeare's poems and plays is the main theme of this chapter, in which the poems and plays in ancient Greece and Rome, in the Medieval Ages, and in Renaissance are discussed in detail, and the reason why Shakespeare is a great poetic playwright has been explored.

12.1 Poems and Plays in Ancient Greece and Rome

There were three great Greek tragic poets: Aschylus (525—456 B.C.), author of *Prometheus Vinstus,* Sophrocles (496—406 B.C.), autor of *Oedipus Tyranus,*

1046

and Euripides (480—406 B.C.), author of *Medea*. Their plays can be called both poetic plays and dramatic poems. In *Medea* by Euripides, there is a chorus composed of Corinthian women. At the beginning of the tragedy, a nurse tells Medea that her husband Jason sleeps beside a royal bride, Medea cries, *Oh! My grief! the misery of it all! Why can I not die? Oh misery, the things I have suffered, cause enough for deep lamentation! O you cursed sons of a hateful mother, a plague on you! And on your father! Ruin seize the whole household!* It is said poets grow out of melancholy tone and out of indignation. Though being a witch, Medea is very devoted to Jason and makes a great contribution to him. How could Jason betray his dear wife, Medea, upright and fierce? The reflection of Medea to Jason's betrayal is very emotional and violent. The soliloquy of Medea here is not a poem, but it is as same as a poem, and it is stronger than a poem. Another playwright Aristophanes (448—380 *B.C.*), author of *Acharnians*, *Knights*, and *Birds*, is held as a great comic poet.

In ancient Greece, poem was considered as the same as play, therefore, Aristotle (384—322 B.C.), the great philosopher and artistic critic and aesthetician, wrote his famous theoretical work *Poetics*, in which he traced the special origins and development of tragedy and comedy. Aristotle's theory of imitation oppears in the second section of the first chapter: *Epic poetry and tragedy, comedy also and dithyrambic poetry, and the music of the flute and of the lyre in most of their forms, are all in their general conception modes of imitation.* Concerning tragedy, Aristotle says in Chapter 6, *Tragedy, then, is an imitation of an action that is serious, complete, and of a certain magnitude; in language embellished with each kind of artistic ornament, the several kinds being found in separate parts of the play; in the form of action, not of narrative; through pity and fear affecting the proper purgation of these emotions.* The original word of *purgation* is *katharsis* which is a religious term, meaning the act or result of being made pure and free from evil.

Although there was no obvious trace between poem and play in ancient

Roman literature, there were a number of well-known poets, playwrights and artistic critics as well. The ancient Roman playwright Plautus (254?—184 B.C.) wrote his two famous comedies: *Menaechmi* and *Miles Gloriosus*. Terence (190—159? B.C.) also wrote his famous comedies *Hecyra* and *Adelphone*.The tragedy playwright Seneca (4?—65 A.D.) was well-known for his *Medea* and *Trojan Woman*. There were two famous and influential poets in ancient Rome: Virgil (70—19 B.C.), the author of *Aeneid*, the guide of Danti who wrote *The Divine Comedy*, and Ovid (43 B.C.—18 A.D.), the author of *Metamorphoses*, who had a significant influence on Shakespeare. Horace (65—8 B.C.), a great poet and literary critic and aesthetician in ancient Rome, was highly appreciated by Virgil, and wrote in verse a famous work *Ars Poetica*, *Art of Poetry*, in which there is a well-known statement of the art of play: *A play which after representation would be called for and put again on the stage should be neither shorter than five acts nor lengthened beyond them.*

12.2 Poems and Plays in the Medieval Ages

After the down fall or the decline of the Roman Empire, then the Middle Ages began from the year 476 A.D. to the year 1500 A.D. for more than 1000 years, during and after which was the great Renaissance period between the 14th and 17th centuries. It could be assumed that the most part of the Middle Ages was the brewing period or the ferment period or the dormancy and hibertation period, or the gestation, of the very great flourishing period, Renaissame. In the most part of the Middle Ages and before the great period of Renaissance, the brilliant creations of literary works, poems and plays, were in the dark in Europe. Despite the decline of literature, the influential dramatic works were still created anonymously. Christianity was the dominant theme of almost all the plays such as Creation Plays, Miracle Plays, Mystery Plays, *The Second Shepherd's Play*, Morality Plays and *Everyman*. In *Everyman*, the character Good Deeds' soliloquy

is oft-quoted and widely loved: *All earthly things are but vanity; / Beauty, Strength, and Wisdom do man forsake, / Foolish friends, and Kinsmen, that fair spoke— / All flee except Good Deeds, and that am I.* The soliloquy tells what Everyman could be accompanied after his death.

12.3 Poems and Plays in Renaissance

It is a common knowledge in the domain of literature that the earliest literary form in the development of human race is poetry. Human race needs history, story, performance, and singing, therefore, epic appeared, such as *Gilgamesh, Iliad, Odyssey, Edda,* and *Beowulf.* Because of the needs of the performance, drama or play appeared. To express the pleasure, and jubilation, *comedy* was created. To reveal the human life, lot, and destiny, *tragedy* was performed. To tell the human history, *history* was very popular. To tell an entertaining story, *legend (romance)* was on the stage. To express and reflect the various needs of human race, many different kinds of dramas or plays were invented. Both poetry and plays have artistic epithets respectively. Both poetry and plays can develop either independently or jointly. A poet could be a playwright and a playwright could be a poet as well. It is a new and dynamic atmosphere if poet and playwright are as well blended as milk and water or in complete harmony, interacting on each other, complementing each other, supplementing each other, each shining more brilliantly in other's company. Ancient Greek tragedy and comedy are rich in poetic flavour; while ancient Roman tragedy and comedy form ties with the 9 Muses. Christopher Marlowe (1564—1593), was both a poet and a playwright. William Shakespeare (1564—1616) was both a playwright and a poet. The poems written by both of them have won universal praise and enjoyed great popularity, and the plays created by both of them are always performed on the stage. It is out of question that poem and play are in the harmonious relation and they help each other forward.

12.4 Poems in Shakespare's Plays

In *Hamlet II. ii. 284—287*, the protagonist Hamlet's soliloquy is a piece of beautiful poem or hymn eulogizing human race: *What a piece of work of a man! How noble in reason! / How infinite in faculty! In form, in moving, / How express and admirable! In action how like / An angel! In apprehension how like a god! The / Beauty of the world! The paragon of animals!* What is mankind? This is a riddle through out the ages. Animal or human? Humanity or divinity? Id or ego, or superego? Domestic animal bred in a pen, a fold, a sty, or in a suitable place to breed, or just wild animal? All of the answers are beautiful. All of the thoughts are romantic. All of the answers reveal a healthy mentality. What has been said above can be acclaimed as the acme of perfection. A folk song could be heard in *Troilus and Cressida III. i .116—125:*

> *Pandarus*
>> *Love, love, nothing but love, still more!*
>> *For, oh! love's bow*
>> *Shoots buck and doe:*
>> *The shaft confounds,*
>> *Not that it wounds,*
>> *But tickles still the sore.*
>> *These lovers cry o! o! they die!*
>> *Yet that which seems the wound to kill,*
>> *Doth turn o! o! to ha! ha! he!*
>> *So dying love lives still:*
>> *O! O! a while, but ha! ha! ha!*
>> *O! O! groans out for ha! ha! ha!*
> *Heigh-ho!*

After Lord Chamberlain Polonius' death, Ophelia, his daughter, becomes crazy and sings many a time in Scene 5, Act 4, from *How should I your true love know* (23) to *God'a' mercy on his soul* (197), 8 times in all, (4+4+1+3+8+8+3+10)

totally 41 lines, the 8 lines (47—54) among which are frequently cited by researchers and scholars:

> *Ophelia*
>
> *(Sings)*
>
>> *Tomorrow is Saint Valentine's day,*
>>
>> *All in the morning betime,*
>>
>> *And I a maid at your window*
>>
>> *To be your Valentine.*
>
>> *Then up he rose, and donned his clothes,*
>>
>> *And dupped the chamber door;*
>>
>> *Let in the maid, that out a maid*
>>
>> *Never departed more.*
>>
>>> *(47—54)*

12.5 Shakespeare's Theory of Poetry in his Sonnets

When Shakespeare was in his prime in both writing poems and plays, how to be a great poet was a great issue since there was another poet, perhaps Christopher Marlowe (1564—1593) or Edmund Spenser (1552—1599), whose poems were in various forms and quick in change. In Sonnet 76, there are two lines which may be held as the poetic style Shakespeare was pursuing: *So all my best is dressing old words new, / Spending again what is already spent.* Shakespeare was confident that his poem: *And found such fair assistance in my verse (Sonnet 78); In true plain words by thy true-telling friend (Sonnet 82); My tongue-tied Muse in manners holds her still (Sonnet 85); Me for my dumb thoughts, speaking in effect (Sonnet 85).* People would not say Shakespeare's poems are full of power and grandeur, flowery and magnificent, however,

Shakespeare's literary works, both his poems and his plays, are actually plain and thoughtful, genuine and vigorous, since he was full of passion and very cautious in his diction. Therefore Shakespeare is worthy of the name of a great poetic playwright.

12.6 Shakespeare's Theory of Play

Concerning the forms of the plays, by way of Polonius, Lord Chamberlain, Ophelia's father, Shakespeare mentions in lines 351—355, Scence ii, Act II, *Hamlet*, tragedy, comedy, history, pastoral, pastoral-comical, historical-pastoral, tragical-historical, tragical-comical-historical-pastoral, 8 forms in all of the plays at his time. He also says, *Seneca cannot be too heavy, / Nor Plautus too light*. No matter what genre the play has, it is good and charming to be just right as luck would have it. This kind of genre of art is like delicious wine for many, many years, and like bitter taste good medicine, for both of them are either good for taste and stomach or good for curing long time disease. A good play genre can be both spiritual food and spiritual medicine. From the speech, the great influence of the ancient Roman plays by Seneca and Plautus on Shakespeare could not be ignored.

Hamlet (Shakespeare) tells the actors: *Speak the speech, I pray you, as I pronoun'd to you, trippingly on the tongue, but if you mouth it, as many of our plays do, I had as live the town-crier spoke my lines. Nor do not saw the air too much with your hand, thus, but use all gently, for in the very torrent, tempest, as I may say, whirlwind of your passion, you must acquire and beget a temperance that may give it soothness.(III. ii.1—5).* When speaking the speech, it is very important to focus on the unspoken words in a play left to the understanding of the audience or readers. The speech can't be too straightforward or outspoken. The acts of the actors and actresses also should be carefully designed. It is just like that in the Chinese opera, the actions of hands, eyes, bodies, hair, and steps

are all conventionized, practiced, and performed, and have the strong artistic appeal.

Shakespeare says in *Hamlet, the purpose of playing, whose end, both at the first and now, was and is, to hold as 'twere the mirror up to nature* (*III. ii.21—24*) The famous saying that play is the mirror up to nature is a well-known viewpoint by Shakespeare. If the performance is overdone, the actors and actresses are mad and crazy. If the performance comes tardy off, the actors and actresses are like fools and idiots. If the language of the play is vulgar, the play is in poor taste. Be considerate to your audience, and protect the environment of the dramatic ecology.

How to act as clowns? Shakespeare points out: *let those that play your clowns speak no more than is set down for them* (*Hamlet III. ii. 26—27*). The clown is not foolish or ugly. The clown is clever, lively and lovely. The characteristic of the clown is that he is quick in mind and has many ways to deal with the difficult situation. The action of the clown is nimble, and his performance is very expressive. The rule of the clown is to make the whole play lively and to lead the development of the play. The clown often says something philosophical, gladdening the heart and refreshing the mind. It is incompetent for the clown who only intends to make people laugh. The neutral and mild beauty is the soul of all kinds of arts.

As for stylistics, Shakespeare points out by way of Polonius in *Hamlet II. ii. 95—96, brevity is the soul of wit / And tediousness the limbs and outward flourishes.* Less is more. Things are valued in proportion to its rarity. A few words are valued because they are concise and comprehensive. Those who talk on and on in a flow of eloquence are often simple-minded.

In *As You Like It II. vii. 139—142*, Jaques, Lord attending Duke Senior, living in banishment, says, *All the world's a stage, / And all the men and women merely players: / They have their exists and their entrances; / And one man in his time*

plays many parts. Shakespeare compares the human society to a stage since he is a playwright. If the entire world is a stage, then the life of people is also a stage. All the men and women are players who want to give out a good performance. It will be a great pleasure for people to be free from the stage. This metaphor reveals Shakespeare's philosophical meditation of the common people in general.

Generally speaking, a poet is a poet, a playwright is a playwright. It is not rational to require a poet to be a playwright. It is unnecessary to ask a playwright to be a poet. Actually, it is a good phenomenon that a poet is also good at his creation of plays, while a playwright also writes poems to add the literary flavour to his plays. A poem which is play like could avoid the utter lack of substance, or the devoid of content. A play which is poem like could avoid the three forms of vulgarity: philistine, unrefinedness, and flattery. Homer's *Iliad* and *Odyssey* are play like, while the tragedies and comedies in ancient Greece and Rome were even considered as poems by the great literary critics. In the medieval ages, the plays *The Second Shepherd's Play* and *Everyman* were written entirely in the form of two long poems. Just like Christopher Marlowe, Shakespeare was a poet and a playwright as well. Shakespeare's *Venus and Adonis* is the herald of his comedies, while *Lucrece* is the forerunner of his tragedies. From *A Lover's Complaint* the melancholy fate of the women could be felt; from *The Passionate Pilgrim* the romantic pastoral love could be touched; from *Sonnets to Sumdry Notes of Music* the excellent tradition of songs and folk songs could be discovered; and from *The Phoenix and Turtle*, the philosophical meditation of death, life, and love could be found. ·

It is well-known that in Chinese traditional opera, both singing and reciting play a very important role, and the audience of the play and the readers of the scripts could sing, recite, and appreciate the poetic words and lines of the singing and reciting. Two of the reasons why the Chinese traditional opera is so popular

all over the country are the poetic singing and reciting. From Hamlet's soliloquy *"To be, or not to be, — that is the question"*, a blank verse, a serious philosophical play appears. From Ophelia's singinging of a love song, *Hamlet* looks like a romance. From the singing of Pandarus, Uncle to Cressida, in *Troilus and Cressida, III. i . 116—120*, it seems that a local play is performed in English, or a local Chinese opera is on the stage, both with a large audience.

A great poet was produced in Warwickshire, a great playwright was born at the bank of Avon. Shakespeare, a king of all playwrights, has also written many excellent poems. Both his poems and his plays are genuine and amazing classical works which should be read and appreciated wholeheartedly in order to dig out the profound philosophical meaning and significance. The artistic works created by Shakespeare are the valuable treasures which attract thousands of visitors and scholars from all over the world. People will enjoy the valuable works and obtain the sense of beauty from them after reading them carefully and cautiously. People will feel blessed after reading his works or watching the performances of his plays.

WORKS CITED

[1] Aldington, Richard. *The Viking Book of Poetry of the English-Speaking World*. New York, 1958.

[2] Assimov. *Assimov's Guide to Shakespeare*. New York, 2003.

[3] Bate, Jonathan. *William Shakespeare Complete Works*. London, 2008.

[4] Bevington, David. *Shakespeare, The Poems*. USA: Bantam Books, 1988.

[5] Bullen, Arthur Henry. *The Complete Works of William Shakespeare*. London, 2005.

[6] *Chinese Literature*. 1978(10). Beijing: Foreign Languages Press, 1978.

[7] Collerell, Arthur. *A Dictionary of World Mythology*. Oxford: Oxford Press, 1986.

[8] Evans, G. Blakemore. *The Riverside Shakespeare*. Boston, 1974.

[9] Gollancz, Isreal. *The Temple Shakespeare*. Now York, 1911.

[10] Harvey, Sir Paul. *The Oxford Companion to Classical Literature*. Oxford: Oxford University Press, 1984.

[11] Kittrege, George Lyman. *The Portable Shakespeare, Seven Plays, The Sonnets, Selections from other Plays*. Penguin Books, 1977.

[12] Liu Junping. *New Version of Old Gems*. Beijing: Zhonghua Book Company, 2002.

[13] Murray, Alexander S. *Manual of Mythology*. New Delhi: Carol Publishers, 1986.

[14] Stauton, Howard. *The Globe Illustrated Shakespeare*. New York, 1979.

[15] Trayler, Michael. *The Complete Works of William Shakespeare (Wordsworth Editions)*. London, 1996.

[16] Wang Fanglu. *An Exploration of Translation of 300 Poems in Tang Dynasty into Baihua and English Versions*. Shanghai: Fudan University Press, 2010.

[17] Wells, Stanley. *The Oxford Shakespeare(2nd edn)*. Oxford, 2006.

[18] Yang Xianyi, Gladys Yang. *Selected Elegies of the State of Chu*. Beijing: Foreign Languages Press, 2001.

[19] Yuan Xingpei. *Gem of Classical Chinese Poetry* Creative Translation by Xu Yuan Zhong. Beijing: Zhonghua Book Company, 2000.

[20] Zhang Bingxing. *100 Best Chinese Classical Poems*. Beijing: Zhonghua Book Company, 2001.

[21] Zhu Chengyao. *Auspicions Designs of China*. China Travel & Tourism Press, 2002.

AFTERWORD

It has been more than 30 years since I began to read Shakespeare's *Macbeth*, one of the four great trgedies advised by my beloved teacher Shen Wenlin. In 1980, Guided by a British teacher Julian, I first met Sonnet 18 and had a blurry impression on the poetic writing, and I knew that *King Lear* is very difficulty to understand and appreciate, because Julian said his teacher spent his whole life studying *King Lear*, but he could not fully comprehend it. It was the year 1979, when I read Shakespeare's comedy. *The Mid-Summer Night's Dream* and cautiously read *Titus Adonicus*, the bloody and horrible tragedy, which is not so popular, and I gave a brief speech on it in a literary solon hosted by my dear English teacher Shang Quanrong.

In 1984, I wrote an essay on Henry V in English, after which I asked for guidance from my dear teacher Shang Quanrong and Professor Li Funing, and had my ambition to have a fully understanding of Henry V, the ideal king both in English history and English literature.

In 1987—1988, When I further studied in Peking University, I finished reading the whole volumn of the *Temple Shakespeare* and put *Venus and Adonis* into Chinese version and wrote a paper *The Tears of the Goddess* in order to get help from Professor Li Funing and Dr. Gu Zheng kun, who then had given very sincere and valuable guidance and anthentic suggestions.

To have had solid theoretical foundation of Shakespearan study, I spent a long time reading and translating the works of aesthetics and watching both the foreign plays and Chinese traditional operas. Then in 2003, at first I wanted to go to Beijing Normal University to have a profound understanding of linguistics,

there a foreign teacher Michael gave lectures on Shakespeare for a semester, and asked his post graduates to have group discussions and write papers on Shakespeare. At that time I was deeply impressed by has gentle and attractive teaching and encouragement, and wrote several pieces of paper on Shakespeare after reading 20 plays from *Oxford Shakespeare*.

In 2009 when attending a meeting in Jinan, Shandong province, I was told by Professor Lu Gusun that when he was young, *Hamlet* was his favourite, but now *King Lear* is his favourite.

I have been dreaming to visit Stratford-upon-Avon, Warwickshare in UK all my life. However, I went to visit the Folger Shakespeare Library in Washington in the year 2009, where the acdamic atmosphere had very strong and profound appeal to me and I was determined to devote the rest of my life, maybe 20 or 30 years, to the study and translation of Shakespeare, despite the saying that I am too ambitious.

With the help of my teachers and friends I have finished this work *Shakespeare's Poems*, in which there are 3 longer ones and 4 shorter ones, with 12 articles in English except the *Preface* and the *Introduction*. The whole 6129 lines of the poems have been put into Chinese verson in new classical Chinese poetic style with detailed notes. It's a pleasure that I dare to deal with this age old issue entirely on my lunatic wild effort.

Zhu Tingbo

April 29, 2011